NOTHING BUT!

NOTHING BUT!

BOOK FIVE:
ALL IS FAIR IN LOVE AND WAR

Brigadier Samir Bhattacharya

PARTRIDGE
A Penguin Random House Company

To order additional copies of this book, contact
Partridge India
000 800 10062 62
www.partridgepublishing.com/india
orders.india@partridgepublishing.com

CONTENTS

DEDICATION

This Book is dedicated to my two very talented daughters-in-law Shonali and Malvika and also to my three daughters Hitu—Shalu and Seema because without their encouragement and support this book would have never have been written.

Family Trees of the Eight Families
(Principal Characters Only)

1 Sikandar Khan—Muslim Family from Kashmir
   First Generation—Sikandar Khan—Wife Zainab Khan—Brother Sarfaraz
   Khan
   Second Generation—Curzon Sikandar Khan—Wife Nusrat Shezadi
   Third Generation—Ismail Sikandar Khan
   Fourth Generation—Shiraz Ismail Khan(Adopted Son of Ismail Sikandar
   Khan)
   Fifth Generation—Paramveer Singh Bajwa (Peevee for short) son of Shiraz
   Ismail Khan and Shupriya Sen—adopted by Monty and Reeta Bajwa

2 Harbhajan Singh Bajwa—Sikh Family from Kashmir
   First Generation—Harbhajan Singh
   Second Generation—Gurcharan Singh Bajwa—Wife Harbir Kaur
   Third Generation—Daler Singh Bajwa—wife Simran Kaur
   Fourth Generation—Montek Singh Bajwa—wife Reeta—sister Loveleen
   Fifth Generation—Rohini Bajwa (Dimple—nickname—Husband
   Bharat Padmanaban

3 Sonjoy Sen—Bengali Hindu Family from Calcutta
   First Generation—Sonjoy Sen
   Second Generation—Naren Sen—Wife Shobha Sen
   Third Generation—Samir Sen—Ronen Sen—wife Mona Sen—Purnima Sen
   Fourth Generation—Shupriya Sen
   Fifth Generation—Paramveer Singh Bajwa (Son of Shiraz Ismail Khan
   and Shupriya Sen)

4 Apurva Ghosh—Bengali Hindu Family from Chittagong
   First Generation—Apurva Ghosh
   Second Generation—Debu Ghosh—Wife Hena Ghosh
   Third Generation—Arup Ghosh—Swarup Ghosh—Anup Ghosh—Mona
   Ghosh
   Fourth Generation—Lalima Ghosh daughter of Arup and Galina Ghosh
   and Shupriya Sen (daughter of Ronen Sen and Mona Ghosh)

Fifth Generation—Paramveer Bajwa (son of Shiraz Ismail Khan and Shupriya Sen—adopted by Montek and Reeta Bajwa)

5 Haji Abdul Rehman—Afridi Pathan Muslim Family from Peshawar
First Generation—Haji Abdul Rehman
Second Generation—Attiqur Rehman—Wife Nafisa Rehman
Third Generation—Gul Rehman—Wife Zubeida—Aftab Rehman—
Arif Rehman—wife Ruksana—Shenaz Rehman(wife of Nawaz Hussein)
Fourth Generation—Aslam Rehman—Wife Farzana—Fazal Rehman—
wife Samina—Mehmooda—Husband Karim Malik—Saira Rehman
wife of Riaz Mohammed Khan(Shiraz Ismail Khan)—`Salim
Rehman—wife Aasma
Imran Hussein(son of Shenaz and Nawaz Hussein—adopted as
Shiraz Ismail Khan by Colonel Ismail Sikandar Khan
Fifth Generation—Samir Rehman(son of Aslam and Mehmuda)
Nasreen Rehman(Daughter of Aslam amd Mehmuda—Shezadi
Rehman(Sherry—Gammy daughter of Saira and Shiraz(Riaz
Mohammed Khan)Tojo(son of Saira and Shiraz)
Samira Rehman(daughter of Fazal and Samina)—Shafiq Rehman
(son of Fazal and Samina Rehman—)

6 Shaukat Hussein—Muslim Family from Calcutta
First Generation—Shaukat Hussein
Second Generation—Dr Ghulam Hussein—Wife Suraiya Hussein
Third generation—Nawaz Hussein—wife Shenaz Hussein
Fourth Generation—Imran Hussein(Shiraz Ismail Khan) later found and
adopted by Colonel Ismail Sikandar Khan
Fifth Generation—Paramveer Singh Bajwa (son of Shiraz Ismail Khan
and Supriya Sen adopted by Monty and Reeta Bajwa)

7 Edwin Pugsley—Anglo Indian Family from Calcutta
First Generation—Richard Pugsley
Second Generation—Edwin Pugsley—wife Laila Pugsley
Third Generation—Shaun Pugsley—Debra Pugsley—Sandra Pugsley—
Richard Pugsley—Veronica Pugsley

8 Colonel Ronald Edwards—Only son of Roland and Gloria Edwards—
British Family from England—First Generation

CHAPTER-1

The World Order Changeth

On 17th November, 1984 a fortnight after Mrs Gandhi's cremation, when Delhi was back to normal, Monty threw a farewell party for his dear friend Lt Colonel Pushpinder Singh. Those present that evening were mostly Monty and Pushy's common old school and college pals, some of whom were now in senior and responsible government jobs. The only topic under discussion that evening was whether the killing of the Sikhs was an organized planned affair to teach them a lesson, or was it a spontanoeus reaction by the people of their grief and anger that went out of control. When one of the guests a Hindu businessman remarked that it was spontaneous and rather unfortunate, Monty who was an eye witness to some of those killings, looting and arson gave it back to him in good measure.

"Oh come on yaar, the systematic manner and the cruel and inhuman way in which those killings were carried out on innocent Sikhs is something that we all should be ashamed about. And it was far from an expression of grief and spontaneous anger if you ask me. And if you so desire, I can with logic and facts prove it to you,"added Monty as he gave his friend Deepak Mehra the well to do old jeweller friend of his from Karol Bagh a dirty look.

"But you being a Sardar without a turban though will naturally take that point of view and I don't blame you for it either. But whatever has happened is bloody shameful and I wonder if the same logic and actions would have prevailed if a Hindu had killed the Prime Minister. And what is still worse is that this sought of free for all hooliganism and murder took place in the very heart of the capital city and under the very noses of our many top political masters. And the pity was that even Doordarshan closed all its eyes and ears and only focused its cameras on a dead Mrs Gandhi. I am sure they could have atleast shown pictures of the vandalism and atrocities that were committed so brazenly and so very openly by those beastly gangs that were

1

hired by the Congress bosses of Delhi," said Mukesh Agarwal as he raised a toast to the host

"Yes and I fully agree with Mukesh. Those senseless killings were indeed reprehensible and we who proudly profess to be the world's largest democracy should bury our heads in the sand. The fact is that we are bloody utterly hypocritical when it comes to admitting the bloody truth. And this is all a political gimmick that is pepperd with catchy slogans like 'Garibi Hatao', which to me frankly is nothing but eyewash. And this was truly reflected during the emergency, when the poor 'garib' people of this city were forcibly 'Hataod'(evicted) and thrown out mercilessly from their homes and shops at Turkman Gate and from other such places by the ambitious and young Sanjay Gandhi. And now it has happened again in the Trans-Jamuna slums of Trilokpuri and Mongolpuri where according to a modest estimate over a thousand 'Garib', poor Sikhs were killed and 'hataod' for good from their homes and in a manner that is simply unthinkable in a civilized world and society. Imagine putting tyres on young teenage boys and roasting them alive, or gang raping young girls and then slicing their throats for gold and silver. And I am not exaggerating one bit. These are all facts because I too as a volunteer member of the fact finding team that was organized by the Peoples Union for Democratic Rights and Peoples Union for Civil Liberties had seen it with my own eyes, and I also heard about it from those who were victims of such inhuman atrocities. And I am therefore fully convinced that these barbarian acts were part of the well organized plan that were marked by acts of both deliberate commissions and omissions by important political leaders of the Congress (I) and without whose concurrence, directions and active connivance these merciless killings could never have taken place. And ironically Trilokpuri was the dumping ground for the poor people of Turkman Gate and the juggi jopri wallas (slum dwellers) who had been forcibly evicted on orders of the then crown prince of India Sanjay Gandhi during the emergency of 1975," added Monty as he played them a recorded tape and showed them a few photographs of the roasted bodies of men, women and children lying in heaps of filth and the hacked limbs and torsos of human beings rotting away in the dirty gutters. As the voices on that tape of the wailing mothers, widows and daughters whose near and dear ones had died in that terrible massacre narrated their heart rendering stories, some of the ladies in the party began to sob and cry. These were only some of the interviews that Monty had conducted live in the infamous Block Number 32 of Trilokpuri and at the Farsh Bazaar relief camp.

"Yes and I think Monty is damn well right and had not the army reached there on 3rd November, it would have been still worse. Therefore, I think ours is a damn sham democracy and with our politicians being compulsive liars who only talk big, give lectures and make money. And I think that the time has come when they should be told where to get off or else we will be inviting more trouble for the poor people of this country who at election time are always taken for a bloody ride. And all this bloody hoo-ha about appointing a high level commission by the government to find out the truth and bring the culprits to book is nothing else but to gain time, prepare the required alibis for those involved and consequently prove their innocence. And like in most such cases where the government is directly involved, this will carry on and on and on till kingdom come. With their expertise in such kind of cover up operations, this will also be one of those massive volumes which I am afraid will never see the light of the day and if people think that the guilty will be punished then I am afraid they are living in a fool's paradise, because in this country, politicians who are the biggest crooks are never punished, they are only rewarded,"said Lt Colonel Pushpinder Singh as he smiled sarcastically and thanked the host and the hostess for the fabulous meal.

As Pushy was about to leave, Monty presented him with a Gita, a Koran and a Guru Granth Sahib in a silver case that had the letters MMG neatly engraved on it. Monty had been told by his late father that in the Indian Army where every religion was equally respected, the most effective weapon for forging unity amongst the troops and winning a war was not the M.M.G. the Medium Machine Gun or the rocket launcher and the 81 mm mortar, but the respect by all and irrespective of their religion, caste or creed of the regiment's Mandir, Masjid and the Gururdwara. The respect for a brother soldier's religion in the army was a very big morale booster and a winning factor in war, but for the politicians the soldier it seems was now becoming a pawn in their hands and that I am afraid is not at all a healthy sign thought Monty, as Pushy raised the old school toast of 'Never Give In.'

As a return gift, Pushy gave Reeta Bhabhi a beautiful Bonzai Banyan tree and a card that read, 'When a giant tree falls, the earth shakes.' These were the exact words the young Indian Prime Minister Rajiv Gandhi had used when he defended the violence in Delhi. But Pushy had also added to it the words,'But when a Gandhi falls only the cronies of the Congress party and their goons shake.' This was typically Pushy's way of showing his utter displeasure of being born a Sikh in India. During partition they had lost not only their property, but a large number of their near and dear ones too and Pushy was then only five years old, when he with his parents came as penniless refugees from across the border. But both his mother and father had worked very hard to bring him up. An ordinary overseer by profession, his father to begin with had set up a small lathe machine in a garage in old Delhi, but later he branched off into real estate and the booming construction business. Pushy had been given the best of education and felt sad leaving his father behind. Though the house in Friend's Colony had been burnt down, but that did no unduly worry him. What really worried him now was whether the riots in Delhi will have its fallout in Punjab and elsewhere in the world, and whether his father would be safe to stay on in Delhi. He had the money alright but no security.

As the year 1984, which was disastrous for the country was about to come to an end, on the night of 3rd and 4th December another ghastly tragedy of gigantic proportions took away thousands of lives of innocent poor men, women and children while they were fast asleep. This happened in the city of Bhopal that was once a noble and princely Muslim State in the heart of India and which was now the capital of the large Indian state of Madhya Pradesh.

A week earlier Monty, Reeta, Dimpy and Peevee had all gone to attend the 5th Jammu and Kashmir Rifles Reunion at the Regimental Centre at Jabalpur. The regimental reunion held every four to five years was an occassion where retired officers, JCO's, NCO's, Jawans and war widwos are honoured and felicitated by the regiment. This was therefore an event that was filled with nostalgia and the Bajwa family by virtue of their late father Lt Colonel Daler Singh Bajwa and foster brother Major Shiraz Ismail Khan, both being highly decorated soldiers of that regiment were special invitees to all the functions. The Reunion at Jabalpur with his father Lt Colonel Bajwa's old colleagues and with those others who had served with Shiraz was full of both happy and sad memories for Monty who as a young boy had learnt a lot from the regiment, when the Regimental Centre was part of the Maharaja of Jammu and Kashmir's State Force and was located at Satwari near Jammu. It was now a full fledged regiment of the Indian Army with twenty regular battalions and was considered to be one of the very best. During the solemn wreath laying ceremony at the Regimental War Memorial, when the Roll of Honour Book was trooped in by the honour guard, it was a touching scene. As the smart JAK Jawans{soldiers) in their colourful ceremonial uniforms while doing the slow march to the haunting music of the regimental brass band playing the dirge approached the war memorial, there was pin drop silence. And as they with precision timing of their well rehearsed rifle drill took their position around the war memorial it was indeed a proud moment for the Centre Adjutant. When this was followed by a general salute and the buglers sounded the haunting notes of the rouse, Monty and Reeta just could not hide away their tears. It brought back to them all the old and happy memories of their late father, mother and brother Shiraz.

After the long four day Regimental Reunion get together, Monty and family left for Bombay. There were going on a holiday first to the financial capital of India and from there to Goa. Thanks to his builder friend, Monty's investment for a penthouse flat at Cuffe Parade had paid off handsomely and a contract with new tenant through the broker had to be signed. It was on the 2nd of December evening, that they caught the Howrah-Bombay Mail from Jabalpur and they were all extremely lucky to cross Bhopal before midnight. Had there been even a few hours of delay that was quite normal with such long distance trains then they too would have probably become victims of that terrible gas tragedy that unfolded itself early next morning in that old and historical city.

In 1969, the giant United States chemical company Union Carbide had set up a plant in Bhopal for the manufacture of pesticides which during that period was in great demand. But the demand had now fallen drastically and the American business giant was making recurring losses. They were over producing the MIC, the methyl isocynate gas and it was not selling. In the early morning hours of 3rd December 1984, a holding tank of 43 tonnes capacity got over heated and it released a toxic gas that was heavier than air. With the plant located close to the already over populated city, the deadly MIC gas mixture rolled along the streets, the side streets and the lanes and bylanes and into the populated areas of the old city. Coughing and rubbing their eyes the people just did not know what had hit them till the alarm was raised. But by then the damage had been done. As the people started fleeing from the city there was panic all around. Though an alarm system to warn the people and the factory workers of such an eventuality existed inside the plant, but fearing that it would only cause more fright and panic, it had been switched off. As people kept sleeping death stalked them from every nook and corner as the gas kept on polluting the morning air. By around midday, when the authorities realized the damage caused by the deadly MIC gas and started taking proper relief measures, the gas had already taken a massive toll. Within twenty four hours, the killer gas had taken away more than 3000 lives and the possibility of another couple of thousands losing their lives or being incapacitated forever loomed large. It was one of the worst man made tragedies that could have been avoided had the management of that Union Carbide factory at Bhopal and their big bosses in India and in the United States maintained the safety checks and balances, and did not go in for the cost cutting measures to make more profits.

Meanwhile in Moscow with General Zia's latest decision to call for a people's referendum on the 19th of December had angered Ruksana. She with her husband Arif Rehman was visiting Shiraz and his family. As it is the loss of so many lives in Bhopal had mentally disturbed her. It was a city of her maternal grandmother that she with her parents prior to partition visited every winter and she had very happy childhood memories of that city with its many lakes and palaces. To let of her steam, she accused the Mulla General and President of Pakistan of being a first class hypocrite. In order to keep himself in power, Zia very cleverly wanted to test the will of the people of Pakistan on an issue that was totally religious in nature and that had been very cleverly initiated by him. He wanted the people to give their verdict and endorse the process that was started by him to bring all laws in conformity with the injunctions of Islam, as laid down in the Holy Koran and the Sunnah. He therefore wanted the people's verdict whether they supported the continuation of that process for the smooth and orderly transfer of power to the elected representatives of the people? And if the people said yes, then the Mulla General would automatically get an extension and remain as President for another five years.

"What bloody bullshit and I think this Mulla President of ours in uniform with his stupid policies of rapid Islamization will ruin this country. The man is only playing to the tune of the damn half educated clerics and taking the illiterate people for a bloody ride simply because he does not want to leave both his powerful chairs. This is damn ridiculous and it will further anger the MRD, while the Jamaat-e-Islami will be only too glad to implement it. This would lead not only to more tensions and strife, but it may also well start breeding Khomeinis and Saddams from among the Shias and Sunnis in this already divided land. And I regret to say that thanks to this big religious divide amongst the Muslims where the two sects cannot even see eye to eye with one another, this kind of religious referendum will make matters worse. As it is the 'Zakat' for the Shias to contribute their share towards the poor and the needy has been put on hold and this kind of exemption to them is nothing but a religious gimmick," said an angry Ruksana who had become a Zia hater from the day Zia usurped power. Zia had kept promising the people the return to civilian rule from the day he took over in July 1977, and it was now nearly eight years since then that he has been harping on it.

"My God you are always dead right Ammijaan," said Shiraz as he read out the result of the referendum that was received by the embassy over the telex machine on 20th December. As per the authorities, 62.12 percent had voted in the referendum and 97.71 percent had said yes to Zia's proposals. That meant that Zia would remain President for another five years till 1990.

"That is really a pity. The man who has no sense of punctuality and who is always late for his appointments, the same man has given himself another five years extension to further ruin this country. "Allah Bhala karre is muluk ka" (May Allah look after the country) said a disgusted Ruksana as all of them with the two grandchildren, the five year old Gammy and two year old Tojo went to the nearby park for some fresh air. As Gammy on her ice skates with her father went round and round the skating rink, Arif confided to his wife Ruksana that he too was fed up in the manner in which the Afghan rebels were being handled by the ISI and he was therefore seriously thinking of quitting.

"With General Mulla Zia's policy of Islamization now reaching well across the Durand Line and American arms flooding the countryside, Afghanistan I am afraid may also follow Iran's footsteps. However, the only difference will be that whereas Iran is being ruled by a fanatic Shia cleric, Afghanistan will probably one day in the near future be ruled by some mad Sunni Mulla and that I pray should never ever happen,"added Arif Rehman as Ruksana softly held her husband's hand and that tender signal was enough for Arif to make up his mind and to put in his papers. He was soon going to be sixty five and though he was sure that his tenure would be extended by atleast a year if not more, he was just not interested. From 31st December, 1984 afternoon Arif Rehman was a fully retired man.

Having secured his place as President of Pakistan for another five years with a fake referendum, President Zia very confidently announced on 12th January, 1985 that elections would soon be held, but it would only be on a non party basis. This not only had a negative impact on all the major political parties in the country, but it also angered the Pakistan intelligentsia. And the MRD meeting at Abbotabad to restore democracy not only castigated the referendum as a big political fraud and a subterfuge, but they also decided to boycott the elections that were to be held in the last week of February.

Commenting on the MRD's decision to boycott the elections and ZIA's new formula of holding elections on a non party basis, Gul Rehman quipped."I wonder if a simple question such as, do you elect General Zia ul Haq as President of Pakistan for another five years had been put to the people without colouring it with religion, and if the people had been told that they were only required to answer by saying yes or no, then Zia I am afraid would have never got the referendum that he now claims to be the voice of the people."

Meanwhile in India with the Congress (I) under Prime Minister Rajiv Gandhi having secured a thumping majority in the Indian parliament, there was at least now a hope that life would change for the better. The Congress Party cashing in on the sympathy wave had totally routed the opposition and the people of India had given Rajiv much more than the required two third majority in the Lok Sabha. They were sincerely hoping that the young Prime Minister with his many election promises would herald in a new era of good and honest governance. He was already being referred to as 'Mr Clean' and expectations were naturally running very high. This was also the centenary year of the Congress Party and it was the best gift that the party could have given itself. The election tornado that had swept the country had given the party an unprecedented 444 seats in parliament and it had left all the opposition parties combined together licking their wounds. They had been so badly beaten and battered that there was hardly any opposition left quipped the handsome Prime Minister very modestly, when asked by the press for his comments on his party's massive election victory

"But Papa without a strong opposition in a large democracy like India this could be rather dangerous. Don't you think so? I mean it could lead to a complete one party rule and the Congress may well bulldoze their way through all important issues and legislations which may in the long run prove counter productive,"said Dimpy as she read aloud a recent quote from the author and journalist Shashi Tharoor to her father. The quote 'India is not a developing country. It is a highly developed nation in an advanced state of decay'was published in the 'India Today', a widely read newsmagazine that was founded an edited by an enterprising young businessman by the name of Aroon Purie and who in ten years time since the magazine came on to the news stands, had brought in a new wave of journalism that was not only informative and investigative, but it also brought home the naked truth to the people of India. It not only covered national and state politics in detail, but also every other discipline with subjects ranging from sports to fashion, to cinema and people who mattered in the country and in the whole wide world.

Like Rajiv Gandhi, Aroon Purie too was a Doon School product with a degree from the London School of Economics. With Suman Dubey and Inderjit Badhwar as his editors and both of whom were also Doscos, Aroon Purie a chartered accountant as the Editor-in-Chief was determined to make the Indian politicians and others accountable to the people of the vast diversified country. Heretofore, thanks to the government controlled media like the All India Radio and Doordarshan the people of India it seems were always being taken for a jolly ride. The people were only being shown or told of what the government wanted them to see or hear. But with the television now about to become a mass media under Rajiv's plan to reach out to the people and with VCR's and VCP's now freely available in the open market, Aroon Purie had other ideas. His teams with video cameras would now break the monopoly of Doordarshan by reaching out to the people and cover events that would bring home the hard facts of what was happening where and why. 'India Today' besides publishing the magazine, would also now periodically present in visual form video cassettes on the happenings and events that mattered to the people of India. These could either be bought, subscribed to and were also available on hire through the many video parlours and libraries that had started mushrooming in towns and cities throughout the country.

On hearing that Shashi Taroor quote from her intelligent daughter, Monty said. "But that is not being fair my child and I for one am quite sure that the new young Prime Minister if given the opportunity will definitely stop the rotten decay that has set in and take India into the 21st Century, but provided ofcourse he gets rid off all the deadwood in the Congress party and brings in new young fresh blood who are not only progressive in their outlook, but who are also genuinely honest and who want to come into public life with a true sense of purpose and a strong desire to eradicate poverty and corruption, and which unfortunately like cancer has spread into all walks of life in this country," said Monty while presenting his daughter with a book on Golda Meir's life.

"Yes and we hope that someday you too will make us proud by emulating some of the great qualities of that great Israeli woman," said Reeta as she too presented her daughter with a autographed photo of Mother Teresa standing amidst the ruins of Trilokpuri. During the terrible killings of the Sikhs in Delhi, the good Mother Teresa was there in person at various relief camps consoling those who had suffered so miserably and Reeta too as a volunteer was there helping out the poor in whatever little manner that she could.

'Well now that you have quoted Sashi Tharoor, let me tell you something more about this handsome young intellectual who is not only a a prolific writer, but also a great thinker. Incidently the Keralite is a Stephanian like me and he once played the role of Anthony in a Mira Nair's college production of 'Anthony and Cleopatra.'. Besides being an outstanding actor, he was also a very good debater, a fond cricket lover and above all a brilliant scholar. He was also the President of the college student's union and the founder of the Quiz Club. With a doctorate from the Fletcher School of Law and Diplomacy, Tufts University, Massasuchettes, he was ideal material for the the Indian Foreign Service, but he chose to work in the United Nations to help refugees worldwide and believe you me with his dedication and commitment to the cause, he will one day make a name for himself and for India too," added Monty while showing his daughter two old paper cuttings that he had preserved. The first one had a ten year old Shashi Tharoor receiving a prize for his first story that was published by the newspaper Bharat Jyoti way back in 1966, and the second was an occasion in 1976, when Shashi Tharoor at the age of twenty received the award for the best Indian journalist under thirty.

"My God what a good looking man and I believe he will be only thirty next March,'said an excited Dimpy as she had a closer look at the two photographs and then added. "'But, by the way Papa is he married ?"

"Why are you interested? But I am afraid in case you are, then it is already a bit too late. I believe he got married to an Indian girl named Tillotamma as soon as he crossed twentyone and they have more or less now settled in the United States," said Monty with a mischievous smile on his face.

On 26th January, 1985 a day that happened to be Shupriya's 35th birthday and India's 35th Republic Day, Shupriya was pleasantly surprised, when Monty landed up early morning at her apartment near St John's Wood. He was on his way back to India from New York where he had signed another big lucrative contract for the export of Kashmiri carpets and shawls and since he was passng throgh London, he decided to break journey for a day and wish Shupriya in person. That afternoon having wished her many many happy returns of the day, Monty presented her with a huge bouquet of 35 giant red roses. After that he opened his Samsonite briefcase and one by one took out four neatly packed small gifts. The first one was a miniature silver photoframe with a photograph of Peevee in his school uniform and a

greeting card from him that read. "Hi Mom Number two, I love you too."
The second one was a small velvet box that contained a set of two dozen
coloured sequences. These small roundels that were commonly known
as 'Bindies or Bindiyas' were extensively used by the Indian ladies to add
to their beauty. It signified the mystic third eye and was considered to be
a symbol of good fortune and wisdom. Placed between the eyebrows and
on the forehead it was now fashionable to match it with the colour of the
saree or the salwar kameez that one wore for the day. In her card Dimpy
wrote. "Dear Aunty I know for sure that your beautiful face needs no
lighting up, but for my sake wear a red saree with a red bindi today."Dimpy
was only trying to convey to her that she should never consider herself to
be a widow and that the family would always be with her and by her side
whenever it was needed. The third gift was from Monty and Reeta. It was
a solid gold key studded with rubies and with the words. "May it open all
your doors to your future happiness, prosperity and success in your career."
And finally when Monty took out the fourth gift from the brief case and
Shupriya inquisitively asked "And pray tell me from whom is this last from
?" Monty though feeling a little embarrassed said. "This is from somebody
very very special to you and to all of us and only once when you open it
you will find out for yourself." And having given that awkward reply to her,
Monty handed over the last gift to her and quietly excused himself and went
to the bathroom. But by the time Monty returned, the tears in Shupriya's
eyes said it all. The beautiful carved big ivory box contained sets of medals
and ribbons that included the gold Victorian guinea that was given by Lord
Curzon to Curzon Sikandar Khan, the Victoria Cross that was won by that
gallant soldier at Flanders in 1915, the Military Cross and the Mahavir
Chakra that were awarded to Colonel Ismail Sikandar Khan, and the Veer
Chakra and the Param Veer Chakra that had made her late husband Major
Shiraz Ismail Khan a national hero. And right at the bottom of that box was
a forces letter with a small cut out of Shiraz's handsome face pasted on it.
The two line letter was the last one that Shiraz had written hurriedly to her
on the day he crossed into enemy territory for carrying out the two deadly
missions in December 1971. It was all in block capital letters and the last
line read. "PLEASE DO NOT FORSAKE ME OH MY DARLING. I AM
OUT ON A VERY IMPORTANT MISSION, BUT DO NOT WORRY, I
WILL BE BACK SOON. WITH ALL MY LOVE, DABLO."

Unfortunately the letter that was written by Shiraz on 9th December,
1971 never got to Shupriya, because by then she was already in Bangalore
with Monty, and Monty only got it when he went to Delhi for the

investiture ceremony on 26th January 1972. That was also the day when Shupriya had turned twenty two and on his return to Bangalore Monty simply did not have the heart to give it to Shupriya who was then carrying Shiraz's child. That afternoon of 26th January, 1985, while consoling Shupriya, Monty said.

"Be very careful with all these memorabilia and specially the letter with the photograph. Do keep them safely in a bank vault till Peevee grows up, because one day when he becomes a young man we may have to perforce tell him the truth."

That evening Monty took Shupriya out for dinner to 'Maharani'. It was a very popular Indian restaurant in Soho that served delicious Indian cuisine and that to at very reasonable rates. At a nearby table were a group of Pakistani and Indian students. They were discussing the current political situation in their respective countries. While the Indians were confident that their new young Prime Minister Rajiv Gandhi would look forward to improve bilateral relations with Pakistan, the Pakistani students were however a little skeptical. Not that they liked Zia, but they were all of the view that unless the Kashmir problem was solved, the relations between the two countries would never improve. Hearing their animated conversation and arguments becoming louder and louder by the minute, Monty very diplomatically requested for a corner table that was far away from the vociferous debaters.

"I hope it does not end up with fisticuffs," whispered Monty very softly to Shupriya while he escorted her to the new table.

In the meantime, with Ronald Reagan having been sworn in for a second term of office as President of the United States, General Zia's mood was once again upbeat. With the Soviet troops still in Afghanistan, Zia could keep banking on American support both economically and militarily and thereby further consolidate his position in the country. Having won the referendum, Zia however now started distancing himself from his erstwhile colleagues in uniform. Except for a handful of Generals like Rahimuddin Khan and General Akhtar who were now either related or were going to be related to him in the near future, most of the others were slowly and quietly being sidelined or retired. Both the Generals were holding very important high offices. General Rahimuddin Khan was Chairman Joint Chief's of Staff Committee, while General Akhtar was the Director General ISI, and both of them Zia trusted implicitly. However, there were others too who could be said to be close to Zia also. And one of them was Lt General KM Arif who was now tipped to take over as the Vice Chief of Army Staff in March, though he was far too junior in the ladder.

Despite the boycott by the MRD, the elections on a no party basis in Pakistan were generally peaceful and on 20th March, 1985 President Zia decided to follow a unique method of selecting and nominating the Prime Minister. A day earlier he gave out his mind to his Chief of Staff, Major General Waheed and told him that he would instead of nominating one candidate for the post of PM would recommend three names to all the members of the National Assembly informally and then let them through a secret ballot choose the best man. To get the drill going the next day, the Chief of Staff was directed to print the ballot papers with special envelopes and also have the procedure and drill for voting placed inside it. And all this was done overnight by the Printing Corporation of Pakistan at Islamabad. On the next day and before the voting was to finally take place, a happy Zia with his trade mark toothy smile decided to meet all the elected members in a group from their respective provinces. The first group consisted those who were from Baluchistan, followed by those from the NWFP, Punjab and finally Sind. To help in the balloting, Zia nominated the Chief of Staff and his own Military Secretary, Brigadier Mahmud Ali Durrani. Then suddenly after having met all the National Assembly members, Zia changed his mind and he unilaterally nominated Mr Mohammed Khan Junejo as the new Prime Minister of the country. And as a result of which the hard work that was put in by his Chief of Staff simply became redundant.

Later that evening Zia was however in for a rude shock, when the Prime Minister asked him point blank as to when the Martial Law would be lifted in the country. Taken aback by that question, Zia parried it off by telling the PM that he would lift it once he was confident that Mr Junejo was in full control of the situation in Pakistan. But Zia was smart too. He therefore on the very first sitting of the National Assembly had the crucial Eighth Amendment duly passed and under this amendment, all Presidential orders, ordinances, martial Law regulations, martial law orders were affirmed, adopted and declared, notwithstanding judgement of any court or on any other ground. In other words, under this amendment, Zia could at anytime dismiss the Prime Minister and his government as also dissolve both the National and Provincial Assemblies.

Born on 18th August, 1932, Mohammed Khan Junejo hailing from the Tharparkar Region of Sind Province with a diploma in Agriculture from England had got into politics at a very early age. In 1963, at the age of 31, he was appointed a Minister in the West Pakistan Government, but thereafter had faded into relative obscurity after Bhutto was ousted by the military. He was known to be strong in his convictions and was keen for the return of the country to democratic civilian rule.

While Pakistan with Zia in the hot seat and a relatively unknown Mohammed Khan Junejo as Prime Minister got busy guiding the destiny of their people, in India, Rajiv Gandhi with Narasimha Rao as his Home Minister and a few other of his trusted aides, most of whom were Doscos were racking their brains on how to bring back normalcy to Punjab. This was the most important task on his agenda and it had to be achieved through secret parleys and talks with the Akali leaders and their emissaries. Being a very sensitive issue it had to be handled not only very diplomatically, but firmly too.

But the appalling revelations a month after Mrs Gandhi's assassination by the top boss of the DIB, Director Intelligence Bureau to the Prime Minister's Principal Secretary that there were moles inside the PMO, (Prime Minister's Office) and that they had been passing highly classified formation that were very sensitive in nature to enemy agents had sent shock waves through the corridors of power. The man most shaken was none other than Mr PC Alexander. He was the man who was directly in charge of the PMO and he had no clue that such scandalous things were happening under his very nose. He had been retained by Rajiv Gandhi as his Principal Secretary and felt ashamed about it. On 18th January, the day the spy scandal inside the PMO surfaced, Dr Alexander immediately put in his papers and for the next couple of weeks the scandal became the talk of the town as all leading newspapers and magazines played it up to the hilt. A week or so later, when Justice C K Thakkar, the man who was heading the commission of enquiry into the assassination of Mrs Gandhi confided to the powers that be that the needle of suspicion also pointed to RK Dhawan, Mr Alexander was even more disturbed. And when the old loyal retainer was given his marching orders by no less a man than the Prime Minister himself, and was told to proceed on long leave and that his services were no longer required at the PMH, the Prime Minister's House, Dhawan did not know what had hit him. He had very loyally served the Nehru-Gandhi family morning, noon amd night, for seven days a week and three sixty five days year after year and was given no reason as to why he was being chucked out so very unceremoniously. This was the last thing that Dhawan expected as a New Year's gift from the Gandhi family.

'But do you think Dhawan is involved in any way, because frankly speaking I don't think so ? Yes the very fact that not a single bullet hit him looks to be rather intriguing though. But then miracles do happen at times I guess and it is one's luck and destiny that counts. Either the two assassins were crack shots or Dhawan was well away from their line of fire. But to give him the boot in this manner and even before the enquiry is finally over that I don't think was in good taste. And if he was really involved, why would he have risked his life that day. He could have easily reported sick and stayed away from duty that morning and I therefore think that Justice Thakkar is barking up the wrong tree," added Monty as he ordered another gin and bitters for Unni his journalist friend, while they sat in the cozy comfort of the twenty four hour coffee shop on the ground floor of the yet to be fully completed Le Meridien Hotel at the junction of Number 1 Windsor Place and Janpath.

"And what about this recent spy scandal right in the heart of the PMO? Do you think anything will ever come out of it and frankly speaking with you journalists always looking for such juicy scoops, I think you all should know a lot better?" said Monty somewhat sarcastically as Unni helped himself to another cocktail sausage and said.

"Maybe we do, but do you think the government is a bloody fool. With their huge mandate in parliament, they will disclose nothing and I won't be surprised if it dies its natural death. Well if it was a defence secret that had leaked out from Army Headquarters, I am sure the poor guy in uniform would have probably faced a court martial and would have been crucified by now. But believe you me these civilians working in the PMO's office will probably get away with it very lightly. After all no less a person than the Principal Secretary to the Prime Minister is equally responsible for this shameful episode, but he has very conveniently put in his papers and which I am sure will not be accepted and that will be the end of the matter," added Unni as he ordered for a plate of finger chips and another glass of chilled beer for Monty.

"Yes, I guess you are right because till now I have only seen and heard of senior military officers even in the rank of senior Generals like Kler, Shahbeg Singh and a few others being thrown out on charges of making some ill gotten money, and of other junior officers in the famous Samba Spy Case being sent to jail, but have you ever heard of a senior bureaucrat ever being given the boot, or a politician being sent behind bars. At the most all that they are asked to do is to resign and in some cases these blue eyed boys thanks to their political contacts even get suitably rewarded by being given some plum postings abroad," added Monty in disgust as he gave a few more examples of the Jeep scandal during Krishna Menon's time, the Jayanti

Shipping scandal, the Mundra case during TT Krishnamachari's tenure as Finance Minister, the Maruti Deal during Mrs Gandhi's reign and the recent Antulay episode of collecting funds in the so called name of charity. All these cases had rocked the Nehru and the Indira governments in the past, but did any of the politicians and bureaucrats ever go to jail. The jails I am afraid with free boarding and lodging is only reserved for thieves, murderers, swindlers and such like others who have no political Godfathers. But some of them who are still inside like Charles Shobraj the serial killer, or Sunil Batra, Vipin Jaggi, Rakesh Kaushik of the famous Vidya Jain murder case, they are all I believe having a whale of a time inside thanks to the corrupt jail staff. All of them so I have been told are living like kings and they are the ones who are actually running the jail. The place for reform today in direct connivance with the jail superintendent and staff I am told has become a den for smugglers, dope peddlers and those who have the right contacts and the money. They are in fact living in luxury inside the prison," said Monty as he showed his journalist friend a newspaper article that had appeared in the Indian Express in the early 1980's and that had led to the removal of BL Vig, the corrupt Superintendent of the Tihar Jail, a jail that was now the most notorious jail in the country. "And the saddest part was that no action whatsoever was taken against Vij and he was simply transferred back to his home state of Haryana. And the best part was that Zail Singh who was then the Home Minister, when he visited the jail to check on the veracity of the Indian Express report, the Minister was himself horrified, when he was presented with a bottle of booze by one of the inmates who was totally drunk," added Monty. And in order to prove that he was not bluffing Monty gave his journalist friend a copy of the case study that had been conducted by Sudip Majumdar on the prison conditions inside the Tihar Jail.

Corruption in the capital too by the politicians and their henchmen had also by now taken centre stage and tongues in Delhi were wagging as to how government land at such prime locations and of very high value near Connaught Place was given away at practically throwaway prices to Mr Charanjit Singh of Campa Cola and Pure Drinks, and to Mr Lalit Suri, a Delhi businessman to build their hotels that were supposed to be ready before the Asiad, but were still not fully completed. There were also strong rumours of a big politico-business nexus in such like deals and the involvement of petty clerks and assistants working with high profile ministers were being bandied about quite openly, but without mentioning any specific names. Besides money changing hands, the hoteliers were also believed to be entertaining these intermediaries with free rooms and meals from time to time with a view to generate goodwill and increase their prospects of generating more business in future. After all Delhi was the capital of India and there were no dearth of official foreign delegations, business delegations, businessmen seeking favours and such like others who were regular visitors to the capital.

It was Charanjit Singh's father Sardar Mohan Singh who had introduced Coca Cola to India after independence and their Pure Drinks Group, a private limited company practically had the monopoly of the soft drink business in India till Coke in the 1970's was asked to pack up and leave. Thereafter, the company started manufacturing Campa Cola as a substitute and that wasn't doing too badly either. Though during the 1984 riots in Delhi, the Pure Drinks factory had been targeted, but by then Pure Drinks as a business group had made good political contacts and in roads into in the right echelons of the ruling Congress party and the government at the centre. This was considered a must if one had to make any headway in the 'License Raj' and probably as a result of this Mr Charanjit Singh's and his company had been allotted prime land for the construction of Hotel Le Meridien that was required to be completed prior to the opening of the 1983 Asian Games, but even by early 1985 it was not yet fully ready. Lalit Suri too was not a professional hotelier, but he with his good contacts had ventured into it by promising to construct a five star or a four star hotel prior to the Asian Games on the land that was allotted to him near Connaught Place. Though the construction work of The Holiday Inn Crowne Plaza Hotel had started, but it also was much behind schedule. An alumunus of St Columbus High School and Sri Ram College of Commerce, Delhi, Lalit Suri was born in Rawalpindi on 15th April, 1947. In 1971 he had joined 'Delhi Automobiles Limited'. It was the family business, but he always kept his eyes and ears open. With the License Raj in India providing the real key to business opportunities for those who had the right political contacts, the young and enterprising Lalit Suri, an automobile engineer who manufactured vehicle bodies decided to venture out into the hotel business for the rich and the famous.

Later that evening when Monty returned home and told Dimpy that the new young Indian Prime Minister Rajiv Gandhi's attitude towards the technological advancement of the country was soon to be put on the fast track and which would definitely open India to the world, Dimpy said.

"Well Papa, looking at the way Delhi is growing and being the capital city I am sure it will now even grow faster under the new dynamic Prime Minister, therefore, instead of running around and doing all this export-import business where there are so many hassles, why don't you simply get into the lucrative real estate business instead?"'

"That indeed is a splendid idea, and to tell you the truth my good friend Mukesh Agarwal and I are already into it in a small way. In fact we have jointly bought 10 acres of land, 5 acres each and that too side by side just outside the city limits and on the way to Gurgaon. And according to an insider in the Government of Haryana who is also very close to the Chief Minister's son, a master plan has already been prepared for Gurgaon and that place being close to the Indian capital therefore has all the potential of becoming a goldmine, and I wont be surprised if that once small sleepy town becomes a veritable money spinner in the coming decade. And with the DLF Group now concentrating in building a mega township there, that place is bound to one day become as they say in English a neighbours envy and the owners pride. However, for the time being Mukesh Uncle and I intend building our small little farm houses there and register ourselves as farmers to save on taxes," said Monty as he showed his daughter the exact location of the land on a tourist map of Haryana State.

"And while we are at it let me also tell you something about DLF, the Delhi Land and Finance. It was a company that was once considered the major builder and developer of South Delhi till 1957, and thereafter when the Delhi Development Act came into force and the state assumed control of the real estate development in the capital city, the DLF very wisely shifted their focus to the periphery of the capital," said Monty to his daughter while explaining to her why it was not possible any longer to buy and develop land for housing and for commercial use in Delhi. "And it all started with an enterprising family of lawyers and landowners from the nearby town of Bulandshahar who in 1946 even before partition knew the value of land in and around Delhi and had built the first residential colony at Krishna Nagar in East Delhi. Then in 1960 a young, enterprising and dashing cavalry officer from the famed Deccan Horse Regiment of the Indian Army took over the reins of the family business. Born on 15th August, 1931, Major Kushal Pal Singh after serving for nine years in the Indian Army was now guiding the fortunes of his father-in-law, Chaudhary Ragvendra Singh's reality business. In fact I believe quite a few years ago while he with his team was scouting for more land in that area around Gurgaon, he by chance bumped into Rajiv Gandhi and his school friend Arun Singh. They were returning to Delhi from somewhere and their car had developed some mechanical trouble. While the car was being repaired, when KP Singh told them about DLF's mega project and how he planned to develop it by stages, both were highly impressed. And frankly speaking Mukesh Uncle and I also did our little homework too and we also came to the conclusion that one day and that too in the not too distant future, Gurgaon will be a real goldmine," added Monty while Reeta cautioned him to be doubly careful before signing any papers. According to her there have been quite a few cases of some unscrupulous clerks and officers from the Haryana State government department of land revenue acting as touts and agents and who have been taking people for a ride on such dubious land deals.

While Indians looked forward to a a better future under their young Prime Minister, there was more trouble for General Zia in Pakistan. Eversince the hanging of Nasir Baluch and the sentencing of Ayaz Samoo to the gallows in early March, life in Karachi, the financial capital of Pakistan had become very tense. The two PPP activists who had been charged with the murder of political opponents were ardent followers of the late Zulfiqar Ali Bhutto and General Zia therefore with his military courts were only too keen to get rid of them. The situation got further aggravated, when on 15th April, Bushra Zaidi a student of Sir Syed Girls School and College was overrun by a speeding public transport bus at Nazimabad, a suburb of Karachi. That day evening after the poor girl had died in hospital and while Aslam Rehman Khan with his wife Farzana and their three year old daughter Nasreen were doing their weekly vegetable shopping at the Sadar Bazaar market, a flare up between the Pathans and the Punjabis on one side and the Mohajirs on the other seemed imminent. Heeding the advice of the kind old Pathan fruit vendor to stop shopping and to return home immediately, Farzana with Nasreen in her arms went back to the car. Normally Aslam Rehman while his wife did the shopping he kept sitting in the car and kept himself occupied either by reading a book or a magazine. He hated vegetable shopping because Farzana had the habit of bargaining for every little thing and Aslam Rehman just could not stand it. But that day when Farzana and Nasreen came back, Aslam was not in the car and the car was locked. There were already rumors that clashes between rival groups had broken out inside the old city and Farzana was now very nervous. It was also getting dark and there was no sign of her husband. Then suddenly there was an explosion. Somebody it seems had thrown a hand made bomb into a tailor's shop that belonged to a Mohajir. The shop was only a hundred yards away from where the car was parked and Aslam Rehman luckily was inside the bookshop next door, when the bomb went off. Hearing the blast, Aslam Rehman immediately ran outside and was fortunate enough to receive only a minor wound on his forearm, when a shard of flying glass got embedded inside. As

19

Aslam Rehman quickly bundled the family into the car and sped away with his hand bleeding, another loud explosion was heard. And by the time they reached home the battle lines it seems had already been drawn up. While Farzana very carefully removed the glass piece from her husband's forearm and applied some antiseptic to the wound, Aslam Rehman said.

"I wonder when this country will ever be united. I agree that the death of the young girl was indeed rather unfortunate and irrespective of the fact whether she was a Pathan, a Punjabi, a Baluchi, a Sindhi or a Mohajir is not important. And no matter to which caste, creed, or community she belonged to, what is far more important is that she was a Mussalman and a Pakistani first. And even if the driver was at fault, then the law should take its own course and people should not take law into their own hands. There should be some sense of discipline in this country or else such like incidents could flare up into an ethnic conflict that will be very difficult to control,'"added Aslam Rehman as he put a few drops of brandy to act as an antiseptic on the wound and requested his wife to apply a bandage to it.

Aslam Rehman was dead right when on the very next day an ethnic violence rocked Karachi. It was even worse than the Hindu-Muslim riots of August 1947 as Pathans, Sindhis and Punjabis got together to teach the Mohajirs a lesson of their lives. By evening the death toll had risen so very high that both the civil police and the army had to be called out and a strict curfew imposed on the city. While the military and the civil police patrolled the streets of Karachi that night, Aslam Rehman with an army escort from his Embarkation Headquarters made a quick tour of the city to assess the damage done. It seemed that though the Mohajir community had a sizable population in Karachi and most of whom were originally from Delhi, Agra and from other towns of erstwhile United Provinces, but they were the ones who were always at the receiving end of the ethnic strife. Such kind of flare ups of Muslims versus Muslims or Shias versus the Sunnis had now become a common feature of life in the city, but it had got even more pronounced on 18th March, when the APMSO, the All Pakistan Mohajir Student's Organization was restructured as the MQM, the Mohajir Quami Movement under their fiery leader Altaf Hussain. What started as a student movement was now becoming more and more political in nature and with Karachi being the commercial capital, every political party wanted a piece of that cake too.As Aslam Rehman drove past the English Boot House on Elphinstone Street, the famous shop that was owned by the well to do Mian family who had migrated from Delhi during partition, he remembered the first pair of patent black leather shoes that his father Gul Rehman had presented to him on his 17th birthday and just before he joined the PMA at Kakul. Aslam Rehman's father Gul Rehman had been patronizing this shop from the early 1940's when it was very much a part of old Delhi and Aslam Rehman now wondered whether the enterprising Mian family would have been much better off had they opted to stay back in India. Later that night as he cruised along Burns Road with its famous food and sweet shops that were all closed thanks to the curfew, Aslam Rehman wished that Abdul Khaliq's sweet shop was open. His Shahi Halwa was simply out of this world and once upon a time this too was a famous landmark of Chandni Chowk, Delhi. As it is the ethnic problem in Karachi was posing more than a headache for President Zia, and when the exiled PPP leaders like Abdul Hafeez Pirzada and Mumtaz Bhutto sitting in England formed the SBPF, the Sind, Baloch, Pashtun Front and in their manifesto of 18th April demanded a confederation of all the Provinces and with each being given the right to secede if required, it now looked as if Pakistan was on the verge of another kind of political upheaval.

"But this is simply ridiculous and I wonder what are our politicians in exile are upto. First it was the great womanizer and cradle snatcher Mustafa Khar who wanted to stage a coup, and now there is this trio of jokers consisting of Pirzada, Mumtaz and Afzal Bangash who simply want to Balkanise Pakistan further and I wonder what Miss Benazir Bhutto and her mother Nusratji are doing sitting in London?" said Ruksana Begum as her five year old grand daughter, Nadia Rehman escorted by her parents Salim Rehman and Aasma with three month old son Shabir Rehman in a pram walked in with a big chocolate cake and a big bunch of red roses.

"My God, from where the hell did you all arrive suddenly and that too without any prior notice. And why the cake and the flowers,"added Ruksana looking rather surprised.

"Well I guess age is fast catching up with both of you it seems because Ammijaan it is your 60th birthday today and had it not been for us, you would have probably kept sitting the whole day at home and doing nothing. We could have wished you over the telephone Grandma, but today being a special day we therefore thought that we will give you a pleasant surprise with 60 red roses, a cake, and a huge hug, "said little Nadia as she lovingly kissed her grandmother.

"Ya Allah, that is really a shame and at least I should have remembered, but then she doesn't look more than thirty even now and therefore it is not my fault," said a beaming Arif Rehman as he ran to the bar and put a bottle of champagne for cooling inside the fridge. Meanwhile Salim Rehman rang up Uncle Gul Rehman and Aunty Zubeida and invited them for dinner. And few minutes later there was a call from Washington. It was Shiraz and Saira and their children on the line and all of them were wishing Ruksana a very happy sixtieth birthday.

On that 21st of April, while the Rehmans were celebrating Ruksana's 60th birthday at Peshawar, in London, Shupriya was busying finalizing two important confidential reports. The first one dealt with the activities of those Pakistani politicians who were in exile in England and the second one dealt with Dr Chauhan and his organization who were trying to whip up support for a separate Khalistan. And though Mustafa Khar was now considered a spent force by the PPP and had been sidelined by the Bhutto family completely, the person to watch was the 32 year old daughter of the late founder of the party. On 5th January, her father's birthday as Benazir presided over a meeting of the PPP in London, the news arrived that her sister Sanam had been blessed with a daughter and the girl had been named Azadeh which in Persian meant freedom. A true fighter to the core, Benazir was now operating from her 10th floor apartment at 111, Lauderdale Towers, Barbican, London, EC2. The flat on a high rise building was close to the St Paul's Cathedral and provided good security too. It was also a home and an office to Dr Niazi and a few other PPP leaders. The PPP was now very much a part of the MRD and they too had boycotted the recent elections in the country. In order to generate an awareness that the PPP was still very much active and alive; the party had launched a monthly magazine called 'Amal'. It was basically a propaganda publication to keep the exile community up to date on events in Pakistan. Copies were also smuggled periodically into Pakistan to keep the PPP in contention as a viable political force for the future

Though the activities of the PPP in England was not a cause of great worry to the Indian High Commission in England, but the activities of Dr Jagjit Singh Chauhan and his bunch of cronies had become a very serious and disturbing factor. The self styled President of Khalistan had not only been expressing his views openly in the British press, but was also expressing his pro-Khalistani views over the Independent Television network. Certain groups of militant Sikhs in the United Kingdom were not only indulging in virulent anti-India propaganda, but they were also advocating sabotage and the elimination of those Sikhs who were not willing to tow their line. Shupriya therefore in her report stressed the urgent need to seek the goodwill and assistance of the British Prime Minister. She wanted Mrs Thatcher's government to caution the Sikh community in her country and warn them not to get involved in India's internal problems.

Meanwhile faraway In Washington, Shiraz as Counselor Political was however not happy in the manner in which Pakistan was being used by the Reagan Administration and the CIA to fight their proxy war against the Soviets in Afghanistan. In order to keep Zia happy and to keep him in the chair, the White House had decided to turn a blind eye to Pakistan's renewed efforts to build the nuclear bomb. No economic sanctions under the Pressler amendment could now be brought about against Pakistan if the White House certified that Pakistan had not embarked on a nuclear weapons programme and the Reagan Admimistration now it seems was only too willing to certify it. With Islamisation in Pakistan going on in full swing and with the strong possibility of the Pakistani scientists and government passing on the nuclear secrets to Libya's Gaddafi and other such like Muslim nations, there could now be a real danger of an Islamic Nuclear Bomb that could destroy the world thought Shiraz as he noted it in his little red diary under the caption. 'Dr Qadeer Khan vindicated by Supreme Court, Holland.' This was the title of an article that had appeared in one of the Pakistani newspapers on the 28th of March, 1985.

While the Reagan administration with the help of the CIA and the ISI were busy in their effort to unite all the major Afghan guerilla groups to step up their activities against the Russians in Afghanistan, there was once again a change of guard at Kremlin. With the ailing Konstantine Chernenko having died on 10th March, the Communist Party of the Soviet Union had lost three of their top leaders in a span of less than three years. With the old guard of Brezhnev, Andropov and now Chernenko in their graves, the party elected the comparatively young fifty four year old Mikhail Sergeivich Gorbachov as the new General Secretary of the Communist Party.Born on 2nd March, 1931, at Stavropol, Gorbachov was only eleven years old, when the Germans in August 1942 occupied the city. As a young boy he had seen the hardships of life, but he was intelligent, hardworking and good in his studies. Coming from a peasant family and having finished school he had once helped his father harvest a record crop on their collective farm and was awarded at the age of 16 the Red Banner of Labour. Thereafter having studied Law at the Moscow University, he became an active party member. On 25th September, 1953, while completing his law, he at the young age of 22 married his sweetheart Raisa Maksimovna whom he had met in Moscow. On return to Stavropol, Gorbachov immersed himself in party work and by 1970 became the First Party Secretary of the Stavropol Region. His consistent efforts to improve and reorganize the working of the collective farms in his region and the living condition of the workers soon paid him handsome dividends, and at the age of forty he was made a member of the powerful CPSU Central Committee, and in 1979 was elevated to the Politburo as a candidate member, and a year later to that of a full member. Now at the age of 54 he had became the first Russian leader who was born after the Revolution to lead the country, and thus the new younger generation of the Russians were now looking forward to a more progressive and dynamic leadership.

CHAPTER-2

Terror Incorporated

Meanwhile at Islamabad, Salim Rehman Khan having served in Afghanistan was now actively involved in coordinating the activities of the seven major rebel organizations of the Afghan Mujaheedins who had shown their willingness to form an alliance. In May, the seven Peshawar based guerrilla organizations was formed and the military operations against the Soviets were stepped up as more sophisticated weapons like rocket launchers and the highly effective Stringer anti aircraft missiles kept arriving from the various CIA sources. With active assistance in terms of weapons, equipment and money power pouring in from countries like China and Saudi Arabia, the fight against the Soviets in Afghanistan got a further boost. Soon the emergence of freedom fighters from various Muslim countries and specially those from the Arab world fighting shoulder to shoulder with the Afghan Mujaheedeen brothers added a complete new dimension to the war. Notable amongst them was the young Osama Bin Laden from Saudi Arabia whose fanatical attitude towards the western world and the Russians gave a new twist to terrorism.

As the Mujahideens stepped up their guerrilla warfare, the Russian army and especially those newly inducted recruits from the Central Asian Soviet Republics started losing their morale and the will to fight. On being constantly engaged and targeted by the Afghan and Arab Mujaheedins in the vast countryside, quite a few of them had also now started deserting, while others got addicted to drugs. Simultaneously in the Middle East, Arab terrorist organizations like the Hezbollah, Abu Nidal, and others had also stepped up their activities against the Americans by resorting to kidnappings, assassinations and hijacking of aircrafts. Not to be left behind, and as a sequel to 'Operation Blue Star,' the Sikh militants both abroad and in India were also gearing up to take their revenge in a similar fashion against the people of India and and against those Sikhs who were now trying to patch up with the Rajiv government. As word about a likely 'Punjab Accord' between the government and Longowal, the leader of the Akali Dal leaked out, the militancy in Punjab also gained momentum. Moreover, the Supreme Court judgment that was delivered by the Chief Justice of India, VV Chandrachud and his five member bench on the Shah Bano case on 23rd April also sparked off a controversy that would soon have a devastating effect not only on the minority Muslim community in the country, but also on the politics of religion that was waiting to be exploited by those who advocated a Hindu Raj. The Muslim lady in question by the name of Shah Bano had filed a case for maintenance under Section 125 against her husband who was a lawyer. Mohammed Ahmed Khan had married Shah Bano, his first cousin from his mother's side in 1932, while he was still a student and the couple also produced three sons and two daughters. But in 1946, her husband married again Halima Begum, who was also his first cousin and thereafter it seems Shah Bano had been neglected. Having gone old, she had filed a case asking for maintenance and it was granted by the lower courts. But since her husband was a lawyer and had the right to appeal to the Supreme Court, he had been granted that privilege. Unfortunately when the Chief Justice gave the Bench's verdict in Shah Bano's favour, the learned judge inadvertently also made a critical remark about Islam and their personal laws, which to the Muslims of India seemed offensive in nature. According to them it was not only an attack on their religion, but also on their rights to their own religious personal laws and as a consequence of which not only the Muslims had taken to the streets, but many of the Congress MP's in the Indian parliament fearing that the Supreme Court judgment would have a negative impact on their vote banks started to convince Rajiv Gandhi to enact a law in Parliament that would overturn the Supreme Court's judgment and Rajiv unfortunately it seems fell for it.

"By God, I think politics and so called democracy in this country is another name for hypocrisy," said Reeta to her husband as she read in the papers about the nation wide protests that were being propagated and organized by the political leaders from all communities against the poor old lady who as a Muslim had only asked for maintenance in her old age and had been granted the same by the highest court in the country.

"Well I guess in politics the political leaders are like chameleons. They keep changing their colours and their spots as per their own convenience and who cares what happens to this damn country as long as they can retain their powerful chair and rake in the millions for posterity," said Monty as he helped himself to one more chilled beer and switched on Radio Pakistan to listen to the latest news about the communal disturbances in Karachi that had been sparked off by Bushra Zaidi's death.

"Thank God it is now peaceful there and the Pakistanis have not made an issue of the Shah Bano case either," added Monty as Dimpy added some more soda into her father's beer mug and said.

"Pappa if you ask me frankly, I think politicians whether here or across the border in Pakistan or even for that matter anywhere in the world today are nothing but parasites. For most of them it is like a family heirloom and a stepping stone to power and money, but without any accountability whatsoever. And who cares what happens to the poor. In any case they can always be lured and bought during election time and it is always their vote that counts and we as middle class citizens of this country will be the one who will always suffer and yet keep the government coffers full by paying our taxes honestly," said Dimpy as she showed her father the report on the number of actors and actresses in Bollywood and other political leaders of national stature who had not paid their taxes for years together and all that they received was just a notice from the income tax authorities.

"But sweetheart these people are a privileged class by themselves, and these reports are only for public consumption to keep the masses happy and to tell them that nobody is above the law, and that's about it. And if you think that anyone of them will ever be convicted for tax evasion then it will not be in our life time that much I can assure you," said Monty with a sly smile as Reeta asked for the soup to be served.

On the 17th of May 1985 and on the following day, many places in India and particularly the capital Delhi were rocked by a spate of terrorist bomb attacks. The attacks were all in public places like the bus stand, railway stations, busy shopping areas, trains and even cycle and auto-rickshaws were not spared. By that weekend the death toll was 80 and with another 50 or so injured and some of them critically. The militant Sikhs had struck with vengeance and there was now once again the fear of a backlash against the community not only in the capital, but at othet places too and they were all mortally scared to death.

It was a Friday that day and Monty was also lucky to escape death by a whisker when on that evening he went to drop a businessman friend of his at the busy Inter State bus stand near Kashmiri Gate in Old Delhi. And as soon the gentleman who was Monty's main supplier of export brassware from Moradabad taken his seat in the long distance Uttar Pradesh Roadways bus, Monty seeing the huge weekend crowd decided to get away quickly from the scorching heat and the stink of that public place. As he got into his car and checked the time it was nearing 7 pm. That evening he had another appointment with his buyer from the United States at the Delhi Gymkhana and he could not afford to be late. No sooner had he cranked the engine, when huge explosions rocked the area. The time bombs hidden in transistor radios had ripped through the public buses causing a big fire and panic all around. Though Monty very much wanted to get back and check whether his friend was safe or not, but it was impossible as a near stampede had broken out. Soon the stench of burning bodies with acrid smoke engulfed the entire area as people ran for safety.

Early next morning as reports about similar blasts having taken place in other states of India started coming in and when there was no word from his business friend from Moradabad, Monty knew that he was probably no more. That black Friday was the worst terrorist onslaught ever since India became independent and it gave a clear signal to the young Indian Prime Minister Rajiv Gandhi that the Punjab problem must be tackled politically and expeditiously. And while Rajiv Gandhi's think tank got busy in finding a viable and honourable solution to the Punjab imbroglio, in the Middle East the ugly head of terrorism again raised its head. The disgruntled Muslim terrorist outfits in the Middle East and particularly those based in Lebanon were gearing up for revenge. The Israeli attack on Lebanon had not been forgotten and the Abu Nidal Organization was only looking for an opportunity and it came on 14th June. On 14th June, 1985 which also happened to be a Friday, the TWA flight 847 from Athens to Rome was hijacked by a group of Lebanese terrorists soon after it took off at 10.10 AM, and the pilot Captain John Testrake was forced at gun point to fly to Beirut. After the Boeing 727 with 153 passengers and crew landed at Beirut, a strange game of shuttle service to Algiers and back began with passengers being released at intervals and as and when the various demands of the hijackers were being met progressively. In response to the hijackers demand to have the aircraft fully refueled which was complied with, 19 passengers who were not Jews or Americans were released. The aircraft then was taken to Algiers where after a five hour stopover and having released 20 more passengers the aircraft returned back to Beirut. With the demands of the hijackers that included among others the release of all Lebanese prisoners held by Israel still not being met, the hijackers who had by now been identified as those belonging to the Hezbollah shot dead Robert Stehem, an American Navy Diver and by next morning with additional armed men on board, it flew back to Algiers where another 65 passengers were released.

By now it was nearly twenty four hours since the drama began and the pilot and his dedicated crew members were dead tired. None the less all of them showed tremendous patience and tenacity to keep the tempers of the hijackers cool. On Sunday, 16th June the aircraft once again returned to Beirut and this time they released eight Greek citizens including Demis Roussos a popular Greek pop singer in exchange for one of their accomplice who was in jail in Greece. On Monday 17th June, the remaining 40 hostages were offloaded and were taken to some secret location while the negotiations continued. All this while flight attendant Uli Derickson showed remarkable sense of duty and courage while acting as an interpreter and calming the nerves of the hijackers that had nearly reached a breaking point. When the Algiers airport authorities refused to refuel the aircraft unless it was paid for, it was Uli who came to the rescue when she paid 5,500 US Dollars for 6000 gallons of aviation fuel through her own Shell Oil credit card. Uli was also instrumental in saving the lives of many American and Jew passengers by hiding their passports so that they could not be singled out.

While the hijack drama was still being played out in Beirut, a place that was once known as the Paris of the East, Monty on 21st June received an urgent trunk call from his friend Lt Colonel Pushpinder Singh from Vancouver, Canada informing him that he would be arriving by the Air India flight 182 from Toronto by the late evening of the 23rd and had requested if he could be picked up from Palam airport. Pushy had lost his father recently and he was coming to attend the three day 'Akhand Path,' a religious ceremony that entails the complete non stop recitation of the holy Guru Granth and which was scheduled to begin on the 24th morning. But unfortunately Pushy couldn't make it as he with all the 329 other passengers and crew on board the Air India Boeing 747 'Kanishka' met their watery grave in the Atlantic Ocean. A bomb that was placed by some militant Sikhs from the Babbar Khalsa organization in Canada inside a checked in suitcase had blown the aircraft into smithereens while it was cruising at 31,000 feet south of Ireland. It was 0715 hrs GMT, when the aircraft suddenly vanished from the radar screen. That was the scheduled time for the Air India flight to land at the Heathrow airport in London for refuelling, but the aircraft had been delayed by over an hour and a half at Montreal itself. The air traffic controllers at the Shannon International Airport in Ireland who were till then tracking the flight successfully did hear a crackling sound on the radio, but after that there was no contact whatsoever. The blip on their radar screen of flight 182 had disappeared. By the time the ocean going container vessel

'Laurential Forest' arrived at the aircraft's last known position, the debris from the aircraft were floating on the sea and there were no survivors.

"My God what a terrible double tragedy for the family," said Reeta when on the last day of the 'Akhand Path' the confirmed news arrived that there were no survivors at all The mystery of what actually happened during the flight of AI 182 became clear when it was reported that another suitcase bomb had exploded at the International Airport in Tokyo when the luggage was being off loaded from a Canadian Pacific flight that had landed at a little after 6 AM on that very morning itself. The suitcase containing the deadly bomb was to be transferred to the Air India flight 301 that was scheduled to take off from Tokyo for Delhi via Bangkok a few minutes later. The suitcase bomb that was meant to blow up the Air India aircraft at the Tokyo airport itself it seems had gone of slightly prematurely. When the intelligence sleuths in Canada and Tokyo started sniffing around, they found some very incriminating clues that clearly pointed towards the fact that both the Air India flights had been targeted by the Sikh extremists who were based in Canada. According to the investigations that were carried out by the Canadian authorities a certain gentleman by the name of Mr Singh on the evening of 16th June using the telephone number of the Sikh Gurdwara at Ross Street, Vancouver had booked one ticket in the name of Mr A Singh on the Canadian Pacific Airlines Flight 003 to Tokyo on 22nd June and he was scheduled to catch the connecting Air India flight 301 from Tokyo to Delhi from there. But this particular ticket was never picked up. On 20th June, another telephone caller made another two airline reservations. The first one was in the name of Jaswant Singh from Vancouver to Montreal on the Canadian Pacific Airlines flight CP 086 and the other in the name of Mohinderbal Singh from Vancouver to Tokyo on Canadian Pacific Flight CP 003 and thereafter from Tokyo to Bangkok on the connecting Air India flight 301. However, an hour or two later a change in the bookings was requested for, when the caller cancelled flight 086 to Montreal from Vancouver for Mr Jaswant Singh and did a fresh booking in the same name from Vancouver to Toronto on flight CP 060 on the same very day and with an additional request to have the passenger wait listed on the connecting Air India flight 181/182 from Toronto to Delhi. A while later a man wearing a saffron coloured turban paid 3005 Dollars in cash at the Canadian Pacific ticketing office in Vancouver, but had the names changed to that of M Singh on flight CP 060 to Toronto and L Singh to Tokyo on CP 003. On 22nd June, 1985 at around 1330 GMT, a gentleman who identified himself as Manjit Singh called up to confirm his reservation on Air India flight

181/182 and was told that he was wait listed. At 1550 GMT, a certain 'Mr Singh' checked in at the Vancouver Airport for the CP 060 flight to Toronto and requested that his dark brown Samsonite suitcase be transferred directly to the Air India Flight 182 from Toronto to Delhi. And though Jeannie Adams at the Canadian Pacific Airlines counter initially refused since the passenger was wait listed on the Air India flight, but she later relented. At 1618 GMT the CP Flight 060 departed for Toronto, but without Mr Singh on board. At 2022 hrs, the CP flight 060 landed at Toronto 12 minutes behind schedule. At Toronto 'Mr Singh's Samsonite suitcase was transferred to Air India flight 181, which was flying first to Montreal to pick up a spare engine and from there to London, Delhi and Bombay. The stop over at Montreal was therefore the cause for the delay and from Montreal it became flight 182 and at 0715 on the morning of 23rd June, the aircraft vanished from the radar screen. The brown Samsonite suitcase that had been loaded in the forward cargo hold of the ill fated aircraft at Toronto had exploded over the Atlantic in the general area south of Ireland killing all 329 people on board. The terrorist had presumably timed the bomb to explode on arrival at Heathrow, but because of that delay at Montreal, it had exploded over the Atlantic prematurely.

What happened at Tokyo luckily was not very damaging and according to the initial investigations that were carried out by the RCMP, the Royal Canadian Mounted Police in Canada the sequence of events leading to the bombings were as follows. Three hours after Mr Manjit Singh's baggage on CP flight from Vancouver to Toronto had left, 'Mr L Singh' checked in with his luggage to catch the Canadian Pacific flight 003 from Vancouver to Tokyo. This aircraft also took off minus the passenger, but with his suitcase intact on board. Having landed safely at around a little after 6 O'clock in the morning at Tokyo, and while the luggage was being taken to the waiting Air India aircraft, there was big explosion and as a result of which two Japanese baggage handlers died and four others were severely injured. The perpetrators of both these dastardly acts in which so many innocent lives of men, women and children from different nationalities including Sikhs had lost their lives had a profound negative effect on the so called Babbar Khalsa led Khalistan movement, and as a result of which a solution to the Punjab problem that Rajiv Gandhi and the Akalis were seeking and without losing face on either side was now very much on the cards.

Moreover, the two explosions that took place within a span of one hour and that were primed to target two international flights of India's national carrier Air India also gave a clear signal to the world that terrorism in the sky was not the prerogative only of those living in the Arab world. And as a consequence of which though the Air India's mascot the 'Maharaja' as usual kept smiling but the bookings on Air India flights plummeted drastically. The fact that terrorism had now become an international phenomenon and a bargaining counter was also very much evident to the whole wide world, when on 30th June; the 39 remaining hostages from the TWA hijack drama that had started on 14th June were finally released. But it wasn't for free as the Abu Nidal Organization in a secret agreement with the Israelis had negotiated successfully for the subsequent release of some 735 Lebanese Shiite prisoners that were being held by Israel. And a week later, when Frank Camper a former United States Marine Commando and a Viet Nam veteran who was also known as the Guru of the mercenaries worldwide and who ran private training courses in guerrilla warfare at his 77 acre heavily wooded site along the Worrier River in Birmingham, Alabama revealed that he had trained Lal Singh and Ammand Singh two Canadian Sikhs in the art of bomb making, the cat was now it seemed out of the bag as a hunt for the Sikh killers for the bombing of the Kanishka and the explosion at Tokyo airport further intensified.

Meanwhile in Pakistan, the General Court Martial of all those officers who had been charged for the conspiracy to overthrow General Zia that was codenamed 'Operation Galaxy' was also now coming to an end. And on 14th July, 1985 when Major General Mohammed Hussein Awan, the Presiding officer awarded all the accused jail sentences ranging from 10 to 25 years it was now a closed chapter. But four days later on the morning of 18th July, when the youngest in the Bhutto family, Shah Nawaz Bhutto was found dead in his apartment at Cannes in the beautiful French Riviera, tongues in Pakistan also started wagging.

'But Abbu do you think that the ISI had a hand in the young Bhutto's murder," asked Salim Rehman's wife Aasma as she helped her father-in-law Arif Rehman Khan to tidy up the library that also had a number of rare English books of the 18th and 19th Centuries. This was from the collection of late Doctor Colonel Attiqur Rehman's palatial house at Peshawar and the books had been gifted to his youngest grandson as per the old man's will. Taking out the old classic titled 'Gone With The Wind' from the bookshelf, Arif Rehman having read a small passage from it said.

'You know Aasma dear falling in love first with someone and then marrying somebody else because the first one had broken the engagement may be the cause for the young man's death. Because according to a reliable source, the young Bhutto it seems had fallen in love with Nasrulli, a

Turkish girl who had also become his fiancée. But when Shah Nawaz got involved with the Al-Zulfiqer and related terrorist activities, Nasrulli had broken off the engagement. And now it seems that the junior Bhutto was also not pulling on well at all with his Afghan wife Rehana and therefore had committed suicide by taking some poison. According to the grapevine the couple had separated twice, but because of their only young three year old daughter Sassi they had reconciled. But something terrible must have happened that day or else why should the young man whose very name Shah Nawaz in Urdu means 'The King of Kindness' take his own life," added Arif Rehman.

'Yes, but you may be a bit wrong about the suicide angle my dear brother,' said Gul Rehman as he walked in with a copy of a local French paper published from Cannes and which reported that the French police were investigating the case and that the possibility of murder could not be ruled out either.

"But all the same it must be really terrible for the poor mother, Nusrat Bhutto and who I believe was also there in Cannes when it all happened that morning," said Ruksana Begum as she wheeled in her six month old grandson Shabir, while her six year old grand daughter Nadia kept playing away with her new Barbie doll that her grand father had presented her with.

"But then if you say that this was not the handy job of Zia and his ISI, then who do you think is behind this alleged murder," asked Aasma.

"Well for the moment the French police are not ruling out his wife's involvement directly or indirectly either," said Gul Rehman as he handed over a box of Black Magic chocolates to Nadia who immediately forgot her Barbie doll and clutching the box to her chest ran inside the kitchen to have it opened by the cook.

While the Bhutto's were mourning the death of their dearest Gogi, a condolence message from Zia to Mrs Nusrat Bhutto arrived. This raised hopes that the body which was still in the custody of the Cannes Police on release may be allowed to be taken back to Larkhana for a proper burial in a grave next to his father. While the Bhutto family friends and retainers at Larkhana were preparing for the funeral, hectic secret talks to bury the Punjab problem in India once and for all between the Akalis and the Rajiv Gandhi government was also in progress. Monty however got wind off it over a drink at the Press Club with his old correspondent friend Unni. According to Unni's information, it was Mr RD Pradhan an IAS officer from the Maharashtra cadre who was now the Union Home Secretary and it was he who was delicately dealing with the Punjab problem, and the chances of an honourable settlement being worked out in the near future looked bright indeed. It was however to be kept top secret till both the sides had signed on the dotted line and that came about on 24th July 1985, when no less a person than the Prime Minister of India Rajiv Gandhi and Sant Longowal the leader of the Akali Dal put their signatures to it,

To celebrate the historic declaration that marked young Rajiv Gandhi's debut as a political leader with vision, Monty on that very weekend itself held an impromptu party in his house at Defence Colony. Among the few invitees that evening was his friend Unni who seemed very optimistic about the Punjab Accord, and Charu Brar his classmate from Sanawar who was of the view that this would not be acceptable to the hardliners within the Akali Dal, and definitely not to the militant Sikhs who were still dreaming about an Independent State of Khalistan.

"Yes there is no doubt that the accord includes compensation to those innocent persons killed, fair recruitment into the army, an enquiry into the riots in Delhi, Kanpur and Bokaro, rehabilitation of those discharged from the army, a review of the Gurdwara Act, Chandigarh to be given to Punjab, fair distribution of the river waters to the farmers of Punjab etc etc, but nothing will be achieved till we win the hearts and minds of the people. First the attack on the Golden Temple and then the wholesale massacre of Sikhs in Delhi that unfortunately was carried out as a well coordinated and pre-planned pogrom, that was reminiscent of Nazi Germany has not yet been forgotten, and these two deadly wounds I am afraid will not heal so very easily till the culprits like HKL Bhagat, Sajjan Kumar and others who are still roaming free and ruling as Congress overlords are brought to book," said Charu Brar who had come all the way from Ludhiana for the party. And having realised that the debate could spark of a serious argument between friends, Dimpy who was listening in very tactfully decided to change the topic with an impromptu party game.Having improvised a loud hailer with the day's edition of the 'Hindustan Times', Dimpy said rather loudly

"Well dear uncles and aunties no more politics please for we are going to play Queen of Sheba, but with a slight difference. The two teams will not be a mixed one but it is going to be a competition exclusively between the gentlemen on one side and the ladies on the other and in which both my parents will also participate and therefore please listen carefully because I as the Queen of Sheba would like all my demands to be met as fast as possible. Therefore my first demand to begin is for a fresh bouquet of roses and that too with not less than five roses if you please, and the team that gets it first and within the specified time limit of three minutes will open its account."

When Dimpy blew the whistle to begin the game, and as all of them ran down the staircase, screaming and shouting, Monty's new tenant from the Italian Embassy who had recently arrived from Rome was not in the least amused. In fact he was horrified, when some of the more enthusiastic players ran across the flower beds and plucked away the beautiful roses from the garden. However to keep the Italian happy, Monty immediately after the game was over sent him a bottle of red wine together with a letter of apology. When the party ended that evening on a happy note for everybody, Charu Brar invited Monty and his family for his 20th wedding anniversary that he was planning to celebrate at his father-in-law's big farm house near his wife's ancestral village of Sherpur in the Sangrur District of Punjab.

"It is going to be one real big two day picnic that will include a visit to the local Gurdwara in the morning, followed by breakfast, lunch and of course the anniversary dinner and dance and which could well carry on till next morning and therefore do please come well prepared to stay with us from the morning of 20th August till the evening of the 21st or it could be extended till the evening of the 22nd also incase the hangover still lingers on,"said Charu as he handed over the special invitation card to Reeta Bhabhi. And while Charu Brar got busy making arrangements for his 20th wedding anniversary, both India and Pakistan were also getting ready to celebrate their 38th Independence Day. The Independence Day celebrations both in Pakistan and India seemed to be one of joy that year, when the Prime Minister of Pakistan, Mr Junejo in his 14th August address told his people that martial law in the country would be lifted before the end of the year, and on the very next day Rajiv Gandhi in his first address from the Red Fort in Delhi made the announcement that the Assam Accord between the government and the AASU, the All Assam Student's Union early that morning had also been signed by both sides. The AASU had been agitating against the influx of Bangladeshis and Nepalese into the state of Assam for a very long time, but the Centre it seems were not in the least bothered till it took a communal turn. The accord therefore was another feather in the cap for the young Indian Prime Minister and also for Prafulla Kumar Mahanta, the young President of the AASU who promptly formed Asom Gana Parishad, the political wing of the party.

It was early on that Tuesday morning of 20th August, 1985 when Monty with a saffron coloured turban on his head and with Reeta and Dimpy for company drove down in his Maruti car to the Kamowal Sahib Gurdwara that was located near the village of Sherpur. On arrival they found that preparations were being made to welcome the Akali Dal President, Sant

Longowal who was scheduled to address the local people later in the day about the recently concluded Punjab Accord, and for the dire need for peace to return to the State. Once the prayers for Charu Brar and his family were over at the Gurdwara,and the delicious 'Khada Prashad 'had been served to all, the Brar's with their guests returned for a fabulous breakfast of the various types of stuffed 'Parathas' that only the Punjabis could make.

"But tell me frankly what your gut feeling Puthar is. Do you think that Sant Longowal will be able to carry the people with him and restore total peace in Punjab?" askedCharu's father-in-law in his usual soft tone as Monty helped himself to another big Gobiwale Parathe.

"Yes sir, I do hope so, but right now it is too early to say. There is no doubt that the soft spoken Longwal has made an impressive beginning by getting the other two main Akali leaders Tohra and Badal to give their blessings to the award, but the point at issue now is whether the militants who are angry with the deal will give him a chance to carry it forward," said Monty as Dimpy reminded her father to go slow on the parathas since lunch and dinner were also a part of the celebrations.

"And now that the Sant has also announced that the Akali Dal would contest all the seats both in the State Assembly and in the Lok Sabha for the coming elections to be held on the 22nd of September, and that is also are a good sign," added Reeta as she poured some more ice cold butter milk into the oldman's big silver glass.

At around 3 PM, when Longowal's arrival at the rally near the Gurdwara was heralded with loud renderings of 'Bole Sonehal, Sat Sri Akal,' Charu with Monty in his jeep also raced to the Gurdwara to welcome the Akali leader. Both of them were very keen not only to hear the Akali Dal President's address, but also to assess the general feeling of the public who they knew would definitely ask him some difficult and searching questions. There was pin drop silence as the Akali Dal leader in measured words laced with the need to maintain peace in the land of the five rivers made an impassioned plea to the large congregation. But no sooner had he finished speaking, when two young Sikhs who were sitting a few paces in front of him got up and fired at the old man who was seated on the dais. They seemed to be poor shots though as they both missed the target completely. And what was still more surprising to Monty was that there was not a single bodyguard around the Sikh leader as he tried to regain his composure and breath. And a minute or so later, when Longowal said,' Please let me breathe properly, I am quite safe' and the cordon that had been created around him moved away, a third assassin, Harinder Singh sitting also in the first row pounced forward and fired at point blank range. This time however Longowal's bodyguards retaliated and fired back, but by then it was already a bit too late. As Charu and Monty watched the bloody cold blooded murder of the man who was only trying to bring peace in the strife torn state, it was now evident that the militant faction in Punjab was once again back into action. Out of the three killers, Harinder Singh Billa had been shot dead by the Sant's bodyguard, another named Gian Singh had been captured, but Jarnail Singh Halwara the third assassin had managed to escape in that melee.

Though Longowal was immediately rushed to the hospital, but by evening he was no more and had died without even regaining consciousness. Not only was the 20th wedding anniversary party of Charu and Bawa Brar at the farm cancelled that evening, but even Rajiv Gandhi's forty first birthday celebrations that day became a day of mourning for him and his family. He called the dastardly act as not only a tragedy for Punjab, but for the whole country too.

Surprisingly on 21st August, 1985 while India was mourning the death of Harchand Singh Longowal, in Pakistan, Shah Nawaz Bhutto was being laid to rest near his father Zulfiqar Ali Bhutto's grave at the family's graveyard in Larkana. Colonel Aslam Rehman Khan who had been specially deputed to oversee that there were no political overtones to the burial ceremony watched in total silence as Benazir Bhutto the eldest in the Bhutto family in that awful summer heat with tears dripping down her beautiful face saw her dearest brother's body being bathed tenderly by the Maulvis and the Al Murtaza household staff. It was indeed a very poignant scene and more so because Benazir loved her brother Gogi more than anybody else in this world. Finally when the body was covered with the 'Kaffan,' the unstitched Muslim burial shroud, she broke down completely.

I guess some day we will all have to die thought Aslam Rehman as he read the short bio-data of the young man while his body was being placed in the waiting ambulance car. He was the only Bhutto who had not gone to Harward and as a young boy had been sent to the Military Cadet School at Hassan Abdal by his father. But that kind of strict discipline it seems was not for him as he later came back and was put into the International School in Islamabad. From there he went to the American College at Leysin, Switzerland and it was there that he met his Turkish girlfriend Nasrulli. The so called young Chief of Staff of the AZO, who with his brother Murtaza wanted to take revenge on Zia for murdering his father and someday hoped to become the country's Minister for Tourism was now nothing but a family name that would be written in the history of the Bhutto's, and for whose burial people in thousands from the Bhutto fiefdom at Larkhana had gathered that day to give him a final send off.

"Allahu Akbar, God is Great," shouted the waiting crowd as the ambulance with Shah Nawaz's body slowly made its way to the family graveyard. "Inna li Allah, wa inna ilahi rayun" (To God we belong and to him we must all return) chanted the people holding their arms out and their palms in the air while reciting that Muslim prayer for the dead. As Shah Nawaz's body was put in the grave, Colonel Aslam who had come incognito and as an ordinary citizen in a Pathani suit joined the others in the 'Fateha,' the hand raising act of prayer and submission. That evening soon after the burial was over, a meeting was held by the PPP leaders at Al Murtaza to formulate their political strategy once the martial law was to be lifted as promised by end December. After the traditional 'Soyem' ceremony on the third day, when Benazir returned to 70, Clifton in Karachi, she was accorded a warm welcome by her well wishers who had gathered in very large numbers to pay their condolences, but on 27th August her family home once again became a ninety day detention centre for her with the usual twenty four hour armed police guards surrounding the place and others in civil dress snooping around as before.

In early September, 1985 while Benazir was under detention in Karachi, Shupriya heard the news about the 'Titanic' having been found at the bottom of the Atlantic Ocean and some 400 miles off the coast of Newfoundland. On hearing that story over the BBC, she was both happy and sad. According to her mother who came from the old stevedore family of Chittagong, the eldest brother of her mother's grandfather had also died in that terrible tragedy. He it seems had gone to London on some work, but without telling anybody at home he had bought the cheapest third class passage for the ship's maiden voyage to New York. He had boarded the ship at Southampton at noon on 10th April, 1912 and never returned. The largest passenger ship of the White Star Line with well over 2000 passengers and crew had met its watery grave on the night of 14/15th April when at about 1140 on that Sunday evening it collided with a massive iceberg and sank within two hours and forty minutes and before any help could arrive. The Titanic did send SOS messages, but by the time the ships in the near vicinity arrived on the scene, it was all over. Though a few did survive the disaster, but Shupriya's great grand maternal grandfather like most of the others on board met a watery grave.

A few days later while browsing through a magazine, when Shupriya read about how the wreckage of the Titanic was found and that there was also now a possibility of salvaging it, she felt even happier. Maybe they will find a lot of treasure and hopefully return the same to the rightful owners, thought Shupriya. But she also wondered if the skeletons of those who were still trapped inside the holds of the ship would ever be returned to their next of kin. While browsing through the magazine Shupriya also found an interesting advertisement about an eleven day pleasure cruise that was being offered by an Italian travel agency. It was a cruise that was scheduled to commence from Genoa to Naples, Alexandria, Port Said, Ashdod and return via Limassol, Rhodes, Piraeus, Capri, and back to Genoa. Since the travel company concerned were giving a very good deal and that too at a reasonable price, Shupriya who was very keen to see all these interesting and famous historical tourist spots of the world rang up Reeta in Delhi and gave her the offer to join her for the cruise.

Three weeks later on 25th September, Reeta met up with Shupriya at Zurich. They had decided to spend a few days sightseeing in Switzerland before leaving for the cruise. Late on the evening of 1st October, while they were on their way to Genoa they heard over the BBC radio that Israeli aircrafts had successfully attacked the PLO headquarters in Tunis, and on the next day morning as they were getting ready to board the cruise liner for the grand cruise, the full story of why and how the Israelis carried it out was splashed in all the leading newspapers.

It seems that on 25th September morning on Yom Kippur day, while Reeta was on her way to Zurich by the Air India flight, 'Force 17,' an elite commando force of the PLO had killed three innocent Israelis who were cruising on their yacht off the coast of Larnaca in Cyprus. After being routed by the Israelis from Lebanon in 1982, the PLO had moved its base to Hammam-al-Shatt, a seaside village that was 12 miles from the capital Tunis. In retaliation for the killing of the three Israelis, the Israeli cabinet had given the go ahead for 'Operation Wooden Leg'. This was the codename for the dare devil Israeli Air force to carry out a surprise raid on a target that was 1500 miles from home and this was indicative enough that the Israelis were determined to cripple the fighting capabilities of the PLO and it was irrespective of where they were based. The codename 'Wooden Leg' for the air operation was therefore very apt. On that 1st October, 1985 at 10 AM on a clear Tuesday morning, eight F-16 Fighting Falcons with eight F-15 Eagles as backup with their guns blazing swooped down and bombed the PLO Headquarters with complete impunity and total surprise. It was once again a dare devil operation that involved flying undetected low over the Mediterranean Sea and also included refueling in mid air. The devastating attack was to be followed by a quick getaway, and involved another refueling drill in the air and then return to the base, and all this the Israeli Air force had achieved with total perfection. Within six to seven minutes the PLO headquarters in a cluster of sand coloured buildings were devastated rubble. The surprise raid had also killed more than 60 Palestinians and Tunisians and had injured scores of others. Their leader Yassar Arafat however was indeed lucky to have escaped the bombing since he was not present there at that time. Though the raid was condemned and provoked a huge outcry even in the United States, but it seems that the Israelis simply couldn't careless. Hemmed in by the Arab countries from three sides it was for them the Israelis a question of their very own survival.

"I must say that the Israelis know how to deal with their enemies, but I hope this will not mar the peace process that the Americans are trying to broker in the Middle East," said Shupriya to Reeta as they drove down from their hotel in a cab to the port of Genoa. While boarding the beautiful and imposing passenger liner 'Achille Lauro', Shupriya noticed that most of the 600 passengers were Europeans and Americans, while the members of the crew were either Italians or Portuguese. The ship was formerly known as 'Whilliam Ruys' and whose keel was laid way back in 1938 in the Netherlands, but it came into service only after the war with its first maiden voyage in early December, 1947. In 1964, the ship was sold to the Italian Lauro Line and was renamed the 'Achille Lauro' after the former Mayor of Naples. With extensive modifications and modernization it was now a pleasure boat that had been in service since 1966.

Delighted with the well furnished independent cabin to themselves on the upper deck, Shupriya and Reeta enjoyed every moment of the well conducted cruise. It was full of merry making with parties and games and with delightful food and wine thrown in as part of the package, as the nearly 200 meters long ship made its way through the beautiful blue waters of the Mediterranean Sea to Alexandria on the northern most tip of Egypt. On Sunday and the night before the big boat reached Alexandria, Mr Leon Klinghoffer an elderly American Jew from Manhattan, New York on a wheel chair celebrated his wife Marilyn's 59th birthday. Seeing the elderly couple enjoying themselves, while looking after their many guests, Shupriya couldn't help but remark that life is what one makes of it and no physical handicap or age should mar one's style. Next day, when the ship berthed at Alexandria, and while most of the others went on a conducted sight seeing tour of Alexandria and Cairo, Shupriya and Reeta decided to stay back as both of them with three nights of non stop partying were dead tired, and moreover they were not interested in visiting big cities since all of them were practically the same everywhere. Besides them there were a few others also including the elderly Mr and Mrs Klinghoffer who decided to skip the whirlwind sightseeing tour of the two cities.

On that Monday 7th October, as the Captain of the ship, Gerardo De Rosa set sail for the next leg of the cruise to Port Said, and from where on that very evening he was supposed to pick up the 600 odd passengers who had been taken for the sight seeing tour of Alexandria and Cairo, four armed Palestinians gunmen with semi automatic weapons, hand grenades and explosives seized and hijacked the ship. Firing their weapons wildly like mad men, when the leader announced over the ship's loud speaker system for all passengers to quietly assemble in the ship's main dining room, everybody was taken by complete surprise. They also threatened to kill any passenger who dared to disobey their orders. Shupriya and Reeta who were already in the dining room enjoying their dessert just could not believe when they recognized the four men. They had also boarded the ship at Genoa with them and nobody ever thought that they were terrorists from the PLF, the Palestinian Liberation Front that they claimed to be now. They were armed to the teeth and Shupriya who had kept her cool wondered how they had managed to get all those weapons, ammunition and explosives on board the big liner. Reeta however became very nervous, when one of the hijackers kept pointing the gun at her and kept fiddling with a grenade in his hand.

While all the passengers on board were herded into the dining room, the Captain was ordered to sail to the Port of Tartus in Syria. As the ship made its way to Tartus, the Captain through a radio message contacted the Egyptian Port Authorities and informed them of what had happened. The hijackers too now opened their mouths and demanded the release of 50 Palestinians including Sami Qantar who in 1979 had killed three Israelis. All of them were now inside Israeli jails and the hijackers also gave an ultimatum that if their demands were not met within the next twenty four hours, they would blow up the ship and all on board on the high seas.

By Tuesday afternoon with the Syrians refusing permission for the ship to dock at Tartus, and the Israelis refusing to meet with the hijackers demand, the situation had reached a crisis point. Having given a warning and an ultimatum that they will not hesitate to kill the first passenger if their demands were not complied with by 1 PM, the terrorist selected their first target. God knows whether it was through pity, anger or otherwise, the target was non other than the old American Jew on the wheelchair. The terrorists not only shot Klinghoffer in cold blood, but they also dumped him with his wheelchair into the sea.

"My God these people mean business it seems, thought Shupriya as she tried to calm a near hysterical Reeta as news about the cold killing was made known to them. Mrs Klinghoffer who had initially gone into a state of shock was now wailing and nobody knew who would be next on the list. As time passed by, the terror among the passengers also steadily kept increasing. At 7 PM, with the Syrian and the Cyprus governments unwilling to entertain the request of the hijackers to dock, the ship once again set sail. It seems that by now the terrorists, the passengers and the crew were apprehensive that some sought of a rescue mission may be in the offing, but that could be even more dangerous thought Shupriya as she tried to figure out the various possibilities open to all the players in this terrifying drama on the high seas. With an American having been killed and with the threat from the terrorists that more Americans and Jews would be targeted, the possibility of a rescue mission by the Americans and the Israeli Special Forces could not be ruled out either. But a rescue operation could be dangerous too and could result in more deaths of the crew and the passengers, and since it was an Italian liner, the Italian government too must be making their own plans contemplated Shupriya as she in order to calm her own nerves started playing a game of patience with the deck of playing cards that she found lying on the table nearby.

Early next morning, when the ship anchored 15 miles off Port Said, it seemed that the worst was over. There was no rescue mission during the hours of the darkness and word had also come through that the negotiations between the Egyptians and Abul Abbas the Secretary General of the PLF who had arrived from Tunis was also in progress. For Shupriya and Reeta that Wednesday the 9th of October was the longest day ever as they kept praying for the safety of all on board. Their prayers were answered when at dusk the four terrorist boarded an old tug boat of the Suez Canal Authority and were taken ashore. The traumatic 50 odd hours with the four terrorists on board threatening to blow up the ship on the high seas had taken its toll as Shupriya and Reeta caught the next available flight back from Cairo to London. While they were still in transit, another high drama for the capture of the four hijackers was being planned by the United States of America and for which the American President Ronald Reagan had already given his blessings. And he had also in his stern message that was loud and clear warned the terrorists around the world that they could run but they could not hide. This act of getting the four terrorists was now to take place in the skies above the Mediterranean Sea.

Less than thirty hours after the hijack on the high seas had ended, and as per the understanding between the Egyptian authorities and the PLF, a special Egyptian Boeing 737 with the four hijackers and the two PLF negotiators, together with a few Egyptian diplomats and security officials on board took off from Cairo's Al Maza Military airport for Tunis. A little while later as it flew south over the island of Crete, the aircraft had more company as four F-14 Tomcat fighter interceptors of the US Navy from the aircraft carrier 'Saratoga' flew in and dipped their wings thus giving the international signal to the Egyptian pilot to follow instructions and land, or else be ready to be shot down. The Egyptian pilot fearing the worst complied immediately. An hour and fifteen minutes later on that evening of 10th October, the Egyptian Boeing 737 landed at the Sigonella Air Base in Sicily and was surrounded by US soldiers and Italian Carabinier. Soon the four hijackers were taken into custody by the Italians. But even before this hijack drama began on the Mediterranean Sea, there was already bad news for the Americans, when the Islamic Jihad from Lebanon announced that it had executed William Buckley who had been kidnapped a year and a half earlier on 16th March, 1984 by the Islamist Group Hezbullah. Born on 30th May, 1928, the 57 year old United States Ex Army Officer had seen action and had been awarded a Silver Star in Korea. He had also while in the CIA served as a senior adviser to the Vietnamese Army and thereafter was posted to the United States Embassies in Zaire, Cambodia, Egypt and Pakistan. He was a very high level CIA operative in Beirut and it was widely believed that he too with his boss William Casey had held secret negotiations with Iran for the release of the American hostages in Teheran during Ronald Reagan's run up to the Presidency in 1980. In 1983, Buckley had succeeded Ken Haas as the CIA's Beirut Station Chief with the cover appointment of a Political Officer. The loss of the man who loved collecting toy soldiers and antiques and who himself was an amateur artist was according to CIA's information killed by his captors on or about the 3rd of June, 1985 and Shiraz who had known him casually though while Buckley was posted in Pakistan in 1978-1979 was wondering why Islamic Jihad had announced it so late and that too without returning the body. To Shiraz this looked somewhat fishy since according to his own sources in the Middle East, soon after Buckley's abduction Ronald Reagan had signed the National Security Decision Directive 138. This had been drafted by Lt Colonel Oliver North with the proviso for secret arms for hostages deal with Iran of which Hezbollah was very much a part and parcel. Shiraz had also heard some rumours about a covert arms deal with Iran that the Americans were working on, and which concerned the arming of the US backed Contra rebels in neighbouring Nicaragua.

During that month of October 1985, while Reeta was away in London, Dimpy with her father decided to attend the Founder's Day celebrations at Sanawar. On the way as they stopped by for lunch with Charu Brar's family at Ludhiana, they were witness to a very interesting program of ballad singing that was being held at the Kalgidhar Gurdwara in the heart of the city. The two leading performers on the stage were the two sisters Surjit Kaur and Jaspal Kaur. The duo had by now become household names in Punjab as they with their ballad singing castigated Mrs Gandhi and her Generals, while at the same time kept singing the praises of Bhindranwale, Bhai Amrik Singh and others for their valiant stand during the storming of the Golden Temple. The two sisters who were also known as 'Bibian Nabhewalian' with their ballad singing had inducted new blood into the Khalistani movement. There ballads to uphold the honour of the Khalsa and their religion had undoubtedly raised the morale of the militants because just a few weeks ago their gun toting cadres had eliminated Lalit Maken and Arjan Dass, two prominent Congress workers who it seems had taken an active part in the slaughter of the Sikhs in Delhi and were on their hit list. And it all happened in the heart of the national capital New Delhi.

Lalit Maken and his wife Geetanjali were killed on 31ˢᵗ July, 1985 in front of their own house at Kirti Nagar by Ranjit Singh Gill whose father was the Vice Chancellor of the Punjab Agricultural University and Ranjit had come there with two other accomplices and all of them in broad daylight escaped on a scooter. Two weeks later three young men at around 9.20 AM before the shops had opened drove into the Laxmi Market on a scooter where Arjan Dass had his office and shot him dead. The place was barely 50 meters from the main road and the assailants got lost in the busy morning traffic. The cold killings had other heavy weights in the Congress like HKL, Bhagat, Sajjan Kumar, Dharam Dass Shashtri, and Jagdish Tytler now running for cover. According to various eyewitnesses all of them like Lalit Maken and Arjan Dass were the ones who had reportedly master minded the slaughter of the Sikhs after the assassination of Mrs Gandhi in Delhi, and even after FIR's were launched against them, the Delhi Police had very conveniently not recorded them in the diary.

Meanwhile in Punjab the two singing duo of 'Bibian Nabhawalian' who had earlier been arrested under the 'Unlawful Activities Act' had become a very contentious issue. And once the number of protests by the people including the one that was led bythe SGPC president Tohra reached the Government House, Shri Arjun Singh the new Governor who had been specially appointed to bring about peace in Punjab it seems relented. Freedom of speech after all was a constitutional right.

"But Pappa just tell me where will all this anger, killings and hatred for one another take us. The militants among the Sikhs it seems are not going to be cowed down so very easily and frankly speaking the so called Punjab Accord seems to have achieved nothing, at least not as yet," said Dimpy as they hit the road to Sanawar via Chandigarh next morning.

"Yes in a way you a right, but these things take time my dear and time as you know is always a great healer. And now with Surjit Singh Barnala as Chief Minister and the Akali Dal back in power in the State with a good majority, let us hope for the best," said Monty as he handed over the wheels to his daughter.

Rohini Bajwa alias Dimpy was now a little over twenty years old and since she had not made it to the IFS cadre in her first attempt, she was now studying hard to give it another try in the coming year. She had been selected for the IAS, but was not interested in becoming another pen pushing run of the mill bureaucrat. Like her aunt Shupriya, she too wanted to become a career diplomat that would enable her to see the world. That day while on their way to Sanawar they halted for a while at 'Flanders', the old beautiful bungalow with a garden that was built by Colonel Reggie at Kasauli and which was gifted by him to the late Colonel Ismail Sikandar Khan and who in turn as per his will had bequeathed it to his adopted son Shiraz Ismail Khan. But now the property legally belonged to Param Veer Singh Bajwa and though Monty was taking care of it, he had not told Dimpy or Peevee about it as yet.

After the grand Founder's Day celebration at Sanawar was over, Monty, Dimpy and Peewee returned to 'Flanders' for a short holiday. The idea was to use the place and to ensure that it was being well looked after and maintained by the new caretaker, a retired Havildar from Colonel Daler Singh's old regiment, the 4th Battalion of the Jammu and Kashmir Rifles and who was a local and whom Monty had appointed only recently.

During those three days stay at 'Flanders' and before Peevee returned back to school, Monty told him many stories about his own father the late Colonel Bajwa's childhood and his many friends like Colonel Ismail Sikandar Khan and Gul Rehman Khan who were known as the three musketeers in the IMA and he also talked about Colonel Reginald Edwards, the good

British army officer who had built Flanders and who was like a father figure to the three musketeers. These were the same stories that Monty had heard when he was young and he now felt very proud telling them to Peevee. But when Peewee was told that the good Colonel Reggie who was also a good Shikari had died on the 6th September, 1965 at the ripe old age of 90 when the Indian troops crossed the international border to attack Lahore, and that the two double barrelled guns that was on display over the mantelpeice would be his on his 18th birthday, he was simply thrilled.

Having celebrated his thirteenth birthday in June, Peevee was now in senior school. Though he was fairly tall for his age and good looking like his father Shiraz, but he had little or no interest in his studies. He was an average student who was fond of the stage and his greatest ambition was to become a great film director like Satyajit Ray or at best a good stage and screen hero like Sanjay Dutt, who was also from his own school. Peevee was also a good mimic and he was also very fond of music be it of any kind, filmy, pop, classical, western or instrumental. He was also gifted with a good voice and had therefore decided that after finishing school he would ofcourse attend college and after his graduation if possible join the National School of Drama, or else try his luck either in acting or cinematography or direction at the Film and Televisin Institute at Pune. Among the Indian actors, he was very fond of Amitabh Bachchan, Sanjeev Kumar and Nasiruddin Shah, but he did not care much for the oldies like Devanand, Rajesh Khanna and Jitendra who according to him had become very stereotyped. Among the singers, Kishore Kumar and Mohammed Rafi were his faourites, but as far as direction was concerned it was Satyajit Ray who topped his list with BR Chopra coming in as a close second. Strangely enough it was his best friend and classmate Sujoy Majumdar who had given him the bug to become an actor. Sujoy was from a rich Bengali family of Calcutta. Hise father was a film distributor and the family also owned a couple of cinema halls in the city. Sujoy himself was movie bug and it was during the last summer vacations, when Peevee spent a fortnight with him in his palatial house in North Calcutta that he too got the bug. For those fourteen days it was only movies, movies and more movies, as they visited cinema halls, the film studios at Tollygunge and saw scores of Satyajit Ray's classics that were dubbed in English on the video. On one occasion he was also introduced to the great movie director and even shook hands with him. This was during the release of his new film 'Ghare-Baire' which was another masterpiece of flawless direction by Satyajit Ray.

Satyajit Ray more popularly known to his young admirers as Manikda was born on 2nd May, 1921 in a fairly well to do learned and talented family of North Calcutta. His grandfather, Upendrakishore who was also a close friend of Rabindranath Tagore was himself a writer, painter, a violin player and a composer. Satyajit's father, Sukumar Ray whom he unfortunately lost very early in life was also a very accomplished poet and writer. The family's main business was printing and publishing, and young Manick from childhood was fascinated with printing blocks and processes. Manick was only three years old, when his father died and with the printing business faltering badly he with his mother moved to his maternal uncle's house in Bhowanipur, South Calcutta. It was here that he met his cousin Bijoya for the first time and they got married later. Right from his school days at Ballygunge Government School, the young Satyajit was fascinated with movies and the movie world. In 1936, he joined Presidency College where amongst his books one could always find popular Hollywood film magazines like Photoplay, cinema posters and such like trivia. At the age of 19 and having graduated succesfully he gave up further studies and went to Shantiniketan. With his natural flair for drawing and painting he learnt art under the great Nandlal Bose, but returned to Calcutta in 1942 to pursue his one and only hobby of seeing movies. It was wartime and Calcutta was teeming with American GI's and British Tommies and as a result of which there were no dearth of good English films. All the latest movies from Hollywood and from the Pinewood and RKO Studios in UK were hitting the screens every week and Satyajit could pick and choose the best. In 1943, he got his first job as an assistant visualizer at DJ Keymers, an advertising agency. Simultaneously he also designed cover pages for the Signet Press that promoted and published books in the Bengali language. It was for this very printing press that Satyajit Ray had designed the cover of Bibhutibhushan Banerjee's Bengali novel about rural Bengal that Ray later in 1955 made it into his classic film 'Pather Panchali', (The Song of the Little Road.) It was the great master's debut film that got him world wide recognition and thereafter there was no looking back for the genius from Bengal.

"Don't worry Dad, one day I too will become like Manickda or if not like him than like Amitabh Bacchan maybe', said Peevee very proudly as he showed Monty and Dimpy his many scrap books on films, film songs and music.

"Arre hamare chhote filmy hero, pehle aapne padahi pur tho dhyan deo, nahi tho tu zaroor fail hojayega.' (Well my dear little film hero, you first better concentrate on your studies or else you will definitely fail) said Dimpy in a teasing manner as she proudly showed her father a few pencil sketches of Peevee's favourite actors like Amitabh, Zanjeev and, Hema whicht the young boy had drawn and which were also now part of the scrap book.

"Arre Beta tu tho Bada Chuppe Rustam Nikla. Aab tu acting wakting ka sapna chod aur Piccasso, wikasso ka sapna dekh. Aajkaal art mein bhi bahut paisa hai." (Well I must admit that your talent in art has come as quite a surprise to me and therefore instead of aspiring to become a film star you should dream about becoming a a Picasso instead. And that is because art today also fetches good money too." said a beaming Monty as he hugged Peevee and then with his permission very carefully tore off all the pencil sketches that were in Peevee's scrap book.

"Don't worry I am going to send all these to both your Mammas, one and two who are now in London and I am sure they will be simply delighted to see your work," added Monty as he neatly put all of them them inside a newspaper.

"But Papa our young Picasso must also authenticate his work by signing all of them because you never know someday these very sketches may fetch us a fortune," said Dimpy rather seriously as she handed over her pen to Peevee to do the needful.

As compared to other girls of her age, Dimpy was far more mature, sedate and a down to earth person. Though she like other girls did mix with boys in the university and went out with all of them for movies, theatres and jam sessions, but she did not have a steady boy friend. Her priorities in life were very clear. She was not only a brilliant student, but also a good debater and the ladies tennis champion in the university. And as far as her looks and figure were concerned she was much above the average. Standing at five feet and seven and a half inches without shoes, she was the tallest girl in the university and had therefore been nicknamed as 'Lambi Dimpy' meaning the tall Dimpy. On their way back to Delhi after dropping Peevee back to school, Dimpy having read about a man by the name of Dhirubhai Ambani and who had lately been making waves in the Indian Press and in Bombay's financial market very seriously asked her father.

"But Dad how is it possible that the man whose is a real rag to riches story and who I believe now rakes in millions every year for his Reliance Textiles does not pay any taxes at all?

"Well all I can say is that the man must be some sought of a financial genius," said Monty as they stopped by at Ambala Cantonment for some delicious 'Dhaba'(Roadside eatery) food. The Deluxe Dhaba near the main interstate bus stand off the main GT Road that was run by an enterprising

Sardar was still very much in business, despite the fact that the militancy in Punjab and neighbouring Haryana had not died down.

"I guess when it comes to good Punjabi food everything is fair in love and war," said the burly Sardar owner of the 'Dhaba' in his broken English as he took down the order and then having switched on to his colloquial Punjabi very apologetically and softly added."Lekin Sahibjii, Police walenu khilate pilate saada dhanda ka tho kunda hogaya Aab aap hi batao ke is desh mein Shanti aur Imandari kub aaeghi. Mere Pita aur Mata 1947 mein jub mein 10 baras ka tha woh bichare subh kuch Pakistan mein chod kar ek chule ke saath issi jagah chhole bathure bechne ka business shuru kiya tha, aur mein roj daudthe daudthe sawari walon ko aapne Ma ki banayi hui woh shaandar tasty chane-bature sirf char anna ke hisaab se bechtha tha. Us time bhi police wale yahaan the, lekin who kabhi muft mein nahin khaya karte the. Aab tho sub Khilao-Pilao ka zamana hai Sahib aur jahan Dhirubhai Ambani ka sawal hai woh bhi zaroor khilata pilata hi hoga nahin tho woh bhi bichara mere pita jaiise channa—bature ke badle petrol pump mein khade khade aaj bhi sabke gadi mein petrol hi bharta hota hoga."

("Sahib by feeding the policemen on duty and that to on demand and not being paid for is costing me very dearly these days. Even at partition there were policemen on duty too but they never ate free. These days unfortunately we have to live in a country of such freebooters, and as far as Mr Ambani is concerned I am sure that he to must be freebooting the babus, the bureaucrats and the ministers that matter, or else he too would have remained a petrol pump attendant all his life. In 1947 as a ten year old boy when we came as refugees from Pakistan I used to sell those delicious eats that my mother used to make for four annas a plate at this very bus stand," added the well informed Sardar while ordering two cold Campa Colas on the house for Monty and Dimpy.

"Sardar Sahib ye baat toh aapne khoob kaha, lekin dekh lena wohi Dhirubhai Sahib ek din phir Petrol hi bechega lekin Aden mein nahin balki sare Hindustan mein. ((Yes what you said is quite true but believe you me that one day the same Dhirubhai will be selling oil not at some petrol pump in what is now called Saana and not Aden, but in the whole of India too,') said Monty as he gave a short resume about the hard working and enterprising business man from Chorwad in Gujrat whose mantra had become 'If the public believes and trusts in me, I will never let them down.'

Born on 28th December, 1932, at Chorwad in the Junagadh District of Gujrat, the third son of a local village school teacher, Dhirajlal Hirachand Ambani popularly known as Dhirubhai in just thirty years had become a tycoon whose very name spelt money for all those who invested in his ever expanding business ventures. The boy of 16 who had gone to Aden to seek his future had returned to Bombay in the early fifties and with just Rupees 500 in his pocket had started his amazing rags to riches story. But he had a vision and a dream and it all started when he with his cousin Champaklal Damani established their first office 'Reliance Commercial Corporation' at Masjid Bunder in Bombay. That small room of 350 square feet with one table, three chairs and a telephone soon became a hub of activity as Dhirubhai studied the market very carefully and soon got himself established. The 10th Class pass Dhirubhai who started life working in Aden as an attendant in a gas station was no doubt an intelligent manipulator, but he also had the business brain that others didn't. The young man who while in Aden which was then still a part of the British Empire had kept buying the Yemeni Rial which was of pure silver and then made a small profit by melting it and selling it as sterling silver through the London Bullion exchange had learned the value of money the hard way. According to the man himself it was no doubt money for jam, but money was money and thereafter he took every opportunity and ensured that the money stayed and was not wasted away frivolously. Living in a one bedroom room chawl at the crowded Jaihind Estate in Bhuleshwar he taught his two young toddler sons, Mukesh and Anil Ambani the same values. In 1966 the Ambanis had established their first textile plant at Naroda near Ahmedabad and by their innovative methods of marketing soon made their 'Vimal' brand a household name in India. Vimal was the name of the son of Dhirubhai's elder brother Ramniklal, the man who had brought him to Aden. 'Only Vimal' and 'Only Reliance' now became the by word for those who had full trust in the man and his products and they happily bought Reliance shares and debentures whenever it was offered. The man had no egos at all and in the age of the license Raj in India he knew whose palms had to be greased when and how. In 1980, when Mrs Gandhi came back to power, the 48 year old Dhirubhai shared the platform with her at her victory rally. Although he was now in 1985 involved in a bitter turf battle with Nusli Wadia of Bombay Dyeing since they were both producing competing products, and Ram Nath Goenka of the Indian Express while using his chartered accountant Gurumurthy and others to write articles that would tarnish Dhirubhai's image, but the man from Chorwad now was like a lion from Junagadh and he took all of them on single handedly. The man who had started the equity cult in India and who had only recently been crowned as the king of the stock market, when he made the bear cartel from Calcutta who were trying to short sell the Reliance shares in the market look like bloody fools was now all set with his long term ideas to take Reliance into the twenty first century. Not only did he dream big, but he also translated that into reality," added Monty while explaining to his daughter Dimpy as to how without breaking the tax laws, Dhirubhai's Reliance paid zero tax to the country's exchequer.

It was early during that month of November 1985 and while Monty got busy with his export business of sending more Kashmiri shawls and carpets to the United States for the on coming Christmas season, Benazir Bhutto was released from detention in Pakistan. And though she went back into exile in London but she also hoped to come back once the martial law as promised by Zia was lifted by the end of the year. Meanwhile on the 6th of November, the Royal Canadian Military Police in Canada raided the homes of Talwinder Singh Parmar, Inderjit Singh Reyat, Surjan Singh Gill, Hardial Singh Johal, Manmohan Singh and Ripudman Singh Malik for their alleged involvement in the bombing of the two Air India Boeings. All of them were Sikhs and members of the Babbar Khalsa and they were now living in British Columbia, Canada. While the majority of the Sikhs in Canada were taken aback by the raids that were carried out by the RCMP the Royal Canadian Mounted Police, but for young Peevee the 6th of November too was a sad day, when he learnt that one of his favourite actors, Sanjeev Kumar had passed away so very suddenly. He had died of a severe heart attack and was only 47 years old.

Born on 9th July, 1938, Harihar Jariwala a Gujrathi whose screen name was Sanjeev Kumar had made his debut in the 1960 film 'Hum Hindustani', but it was only in 1970 that he achieved full stardom with his memorable performance in the film 'Khilona'. Later his portrayal as 'Thakur' in the blockbuster film 'Sholay' had also made him a superstar. The winner of the 1971 Best Actor National Award for his role in the film 'Dastak' and the man who was once supposed to have beeen madly in love with Hema Malini had died a bachelor.

Meanwhile in Moscow, Shiraz on learning about the proposed Reagan-Gorbochev meeting in Geneva on the 19th of November felt very happy. It brought a ray of hope that the Cold War and the nuclear arms race that had been threatening the world would soon be over. And a day later on 20th November, when the first version of Windows 1.0 that would soon revolutionize the world and bring people closer together was released by the young founder of Microsoft Corporation, Bill Gates, Shiraz felt even happier. Bill Gates was born on 28th October, 1955 in Seattle, Washington.

He came from a well to do rich family and graduated from Lakeside School in 1973. At 17, Gates formed a venture with his friend Paul Allen to make traffic computers based on the Intel 8008 processor. While at Harward University he met his future business partner, Steve Ballmer and on 26th November, 1976 the trade name of his company 'Microsoft' was registered. A mathamateical whiz kid he launched his first retail version of Microsoft Windows on 20th November, 1985 and before he even reached 30, and was now already a multi-millionaire. Though he had made tons of money, Bill Gates at heart was a philanthropist who always liked to help the poor and the needy.

And while the computer age was bringing the world a little closer, and the signs of the thawing of the 'Cold War' kept reducing the likelihood of a future nuclear war, there was however no let up in the terrorist activities in the Middle East and in India's Punjab. On 23rd November, three gunmen hijacked the Egypt Air Flight 648 that was enroute from Athens to Cairo and the aircraft was made to force land at Malta. A day after the landing, the Egyptian Commandos made a bloody hash of the rescue operation that left behind 58 people dead and amongst them were Karim Malik's aged parent's who were returning from a sight seeing tour of Greece.The Egypt Air Boeing 737 was hijacked soon after it took off from Athens at 9 PM by three Palestinians from the dreaded Abu Nidal Organization. It was a Saturday and Karim Malik who had come on some official work to the Pakistan Embassy in Cairo from Islamabad was waiting at the Cairo airport to receive his parents, when the public address system announced that the flight had been hijacked. Since Karim was going to be busy for a week in Cairo, he had sent his aged parents on a three day sightseeing tour of Athens and other tourist spots nearby. When he got the news that the hijackers about whom at that moment of time he knew nothing about except that they had commandeered the pilot to fly to Malta, he was slightly confused. If the hijackers were Arabs then the likely destination should have been either Tunis or Tripoli or Benghazi or even Beirut and some other city in the Middle East, but why Valetta in Malta thought Karim while praying for the safety of his parents. And the real story came to light only when the pilot Hani Galal despite being refused permission to land at Valetta and with the runaway lights deliberately switched off by the Maltese airport authorities safely brought his damaged aircraft down at Luqa Airport. The hijacking had started shortly after the aircraft was airborne fro Athens when the leader of the hijackers Omar Resaq started checking all passports of the passengers in order to identify their nationalities. And while he was doing that he was fired upon by the Egyptian Security Service Agent on board. During that firefight one of the hijackers and the agent both died, while the aircraft's fuselage was punctured. As per the orders of the hijackers, the aircraft was bound for Libya, but because of pressurization problems, the aircraft was forced to descend down to 10,000 feet. Moreover some of the passengers were injured during the shoot out on board and the aircraft did not have sufficient fuel either. So the only viable alternative left was to land at Malta. On landing at Valetta, the 11 passengers and the two flight attendants who were also injured were released. Soon the aircraft was cordoned off by armed personnel from the Maltese Army and the negotiations began. On learning about the crises, the Maltese Prime Minister Dr Bonnici had rushed to the control tower. He refused to withdraw the Maltese armed guard and have the aircraft refueled unless all the remaining passengers were released. Finding themselves in a corner and with the Maltese authorities refusing to play up to their demands, the hijackers with vengeance shot dead Tamar Artzi, an Israeli women and then gave an ultimatum that they would shoot one every fifteen minutes till all their demands were met. And as time elapsed more fatal shooting of the passengers also started as another Israeli woman Nitzan Mendelson became the second victim. And a little while later when three Americans, Patrick Scott Baker. Scarlett Marie Rogenkamp and Jackie Pflug were killed by the hijackers all the other passengers were simply petrified. As a consequence of this senseless slaughter of innocent people the Egyptians with the blessings of the Maltese government decided to act. The Egyptian Al-Saiqa 777, a special forces counter terrorism combat unit that had been trained by officers from the elite US Delta Force were now given the task and they flew in with their commander, Major General Kamal Attia and the four American officer advisors for the daring rescue operation. In order to ensure that the remaining two hijackers on board were fully exhausted and tired, and also to gain time to prepare a plan for the assault, it was decided that the negotiations should carry on throughout the night and the Egyptian Commandos dressed as waiters and caterers with breakfast would then make an entry early morning and finish them off before the terrorists had time to react. But the plan badly misfired when probably in their enthusiasm to finish of the task early, the Egyptians commandos well before the planned time for the raid attacked the passenger and the luggage compartment doors with explosives. This once again led to another shoot out both inside and outside the aircraft as the hijackers now also started lobbying grenades on the Egyptian forces. The raid unfortunately soon turned into a bloody fiasco. And when the total count was taken 56 out of the remaining 88 passengers had been killed, while two members of the crew and many others were injured. In that melee and unaware to the authorities the hijack leader, Omar Rezaq gave them the slip. Having got rid of his weapon and hood and pretending to be an injured passenger, the injured Omar was also taken with the others to the St Luke's General Hospital in Valleta. But luck soon ran out on Rezaq, when some of the other injured passengers recognized him and he was promptly arrested. It was undoubtedly a bloody Sunday at Malta and one of the deadliest in the history of hijacking. Late that evening, when Karim Malik arrived from Cairo to claim the bodies of his loving parents, he was simply shocked. The holiday trip to Athens had ended in a tragedy that Karim had never imagined.

Meanwhile in the Indian State of Punjab, the Sikh militants too had intensified their operations by killing innocent Hindus and all those who were trying to bring about peace in the land. And to top it all, the gang wars in Bombay's underworld also took a vicious turn when rival groups belonging to Haji Mastan, Karim Lala, Varadharajan Mudaliar and other such big Dons of Bombay and their many henchmen went on a killing and extortion spree in the financial capital of India. The 'Supari' or the contract killings had become the order of the day, and one could even get his rival bumped off even for a song. The underworlds of Bombay with their clout were also now getting ready to enter the tinsel world of Bollywood.

While the crime situation in Bombay was bad it was even worse in New York, when Monty with his export consignment of Kashmiri shawls, carpets and Moradabad brassware landed there on the 11th of December, 1985 at the JFK airport. The gang wars in the financial capital of America had also taken a deadly turn as rival groups gunned down one another in broad daylight and Monty on 16th December was witness to one such gory killing when two Mafia bosses, Paul Castellano and Thomas Bilotti were shot dead in front of Spark's Steak House on New York's East 46th Street adjoining the 2nd Avenue. It was around 6 o'clock in the evening and already quite dark, when Monty while doing window shopping at the 46th East and Second Avenue crossing noticed four men identically dressed in long light trench coats and black Cossack style fur caps walk past him. Must be all brothers thought Monty, when suddenly a minute or two later the rat-a—tat of machine gun fire shook the busy neighbourhood. The streets were full of people doing their Christmas shopping and soon everybody including Monty ran for cover. As the big Black Lincoln car driven by Bilotti stopped near the Steak House and 'Big Paulie" the name that was given to Paul Castellano, the New York Mafia boss got out of the car, he was shot six times on the head and died instantly. An unarmed Bilotti who also had stuck his head out from the side window of his car to see what was happening was also taken care off. The assassins having completed the job now ran hell for leather to the Second Avenue crossing where the getaway car was still idling. And as soon as they got inside, it sped away through the ever busy Manhattan traffic.

"My God I thought the Al Capone days were over and this kind of killing in the heart of New York really takes the cake," remarked Monty to a passerby as the NYPD police cars and ambulances with their lights flashing and sirens blaring descended on the ghastly scene. Not wishing to get involved, Monty quietly walked across to Third Avenue. That very evening John Gotti who had masterminded the killing had become the new Don of the powerful Gambino family in New York. Organized crime it seems was in their blood.

A few days later and with time in his hands, Monty who had heard about Bhagwan Rajneesh decided to visit his controversial township called Rajneeshpuran that had sprung up near the small town of Oregon in the State of North Carolina. The so called spiritual leader from India it seems had got into trouble with the American Immigration Authorities and Monty was keen to see as to what really went on inside that big ashram that had off late become rather controversial. Monty had heard that the so called Bhagwan or the revered one who espoused free love and good life had been put under arrest. And since he was suffering from many serious ailments, he was therefore now undergoing treatment in the medical cell of some jail near the town of Charlotte in North Carolina. Rajneesh Chandramohan Jain was born on 11 December, 1931 in Kuchawada, a small village in the Narsinghpur District of Madhya Pradesh that was not very far from Jabalpur. He was a good student and a gifted speaker. After completing his Master of Arts in Philosophy, he started teaching the subject in a college as a lecturer and in 1966 became a Professor at Jabalpur University. But with his non traditional views on sex and values of life, he soon gave up his teaching job and started holding meditation camps to propagate his own teachings and philosophy.By 1971 he became known as Bhagwan Rajneesh and started preaching his ideas about God, man and life to disciples from an apartment in Bombay. With his art of convincing others and non traditional meditating techniques, his discourses started growing in popularity and funds for an exclusive Ashram also started pouring in. In 1974, he with his many followers, men and women moved to Poona where he opened the 'Rajneesh Ashram' in the city's posh locality called Koregaon Park. As his fame and name as a modern spiritual icon spread far and wide, a very large number of people from the moneyed western world started arriving in droves to seek solace at his ashram in Pune. By the time the 1970's had ended, the man who was now known literally as 'Bhagwan' (God) to his disciples had become a phenomenon and a cult that openly preached free love, meditation and laughter to his many devotees. With funds in the Rajneesh coffers bursting at the seams, he left Pune and went to the United States to open his international commune there. Entering on a visa for medical treatment, he opened his famous commune at Wasco County, Oregon and thus Rajneeshpuram was born. But soon thereafter there was trouble both within the commune and outside it too as stories about criminal misconduct and financial irregularities started making the rounds. Suffering from acute diabetes and other diseases, Osho it seems had lost his control over the immense wealth that he had accumulated. And he had now been arrested for trying to flee from the United States.

When Monty visited the commune he was no doubt highly impressed with the large number of Rolls Royce cars that were parked there, but that man who was now known as Osho and whom he wanted to meet was not available. He was still languishing in the jail near Charlotte and was waiting to face charges for immigration violations. According to those in the commune who were very close to him, the professor from Jabalpur who had started his public discourses and meditation camps sitting on a wooden platform from Bombay's Palm Beach School in 1968, and who now at 54 years of age sported a diamond studded Swiss watch and Gucci goggles was indeed very sick and was keen to go back to Pune.

It was 27th December, 1985 in the early hours of the morning that Monty having celebrated Christmas with his American importers who were mostly Gujrathi and Sindhi immigrants, he took the Air India flight from New York to Delhi via London. However, late that afternoon on arrival at Heathrow for a three hour stop over and refuelling, when he found that very strict security measures had been imposed at the airport he rightly sensed that something was wrong. Since transit passengers were not even allowed to disembark, Monty got busy with his accounting till such time the passengers from London started boarding. And it was only then that he came to know the truth. Early on that morning and just a few hours earlier at 0815 hrs GMT, the Rome and Vienna International Airports had been attacked by groups of terrorists simultaneously and the targets were passengers who were queuing up for the El Al flights to Tel Aviv. At Rome's Leonardo Da Vinci airport, four Palestinian gunmen had walked up to the El Al check-in counter and had opened fire with assault rifles and grenades that resulted in the death of 16 people and wounded many more. Likewise few minutes later three Palestinian terrorists had carried out a similar attack at the Schwechat Airport at Vienna resulting in the death of two and wounding 39 others. The targets were obviously Israelis and the likely motive was revenge and retaliation against the bombing of the PLO headquarters at Tunis that was carried out by the dare devil Israeli pilots during Operation Wooden Leg.

"My God I wonder when all this terrible hatred and enmity between the Israelis and the Arabs who are sons of the same soil ever end," thought Monty as he opened another Leon Uris latest best seller that was titled 'The Haj.' Leon Uris was Monty's favourite author and there was not single book of his starting from the first 'Battle Cry' that was published in 1953 that Monty had not read. Leon Uris was born on 3rd August, 1924 in Baltimore, Maryland and was the son of a Polish born Jew immigrant. The family after having spent a year in Palestine after World War 1 had immigrated to the United States. Leon who never even graduated from high school joined the US Marine Corps and had served during the Second World War in the Pacific and at Guadalcanal as a radioman. After the war, Leon who had failed in English three times while in school now started his life writing about his war experiences in various magazines. And when in 1950, Esquire published the first one; he was on the road to fame. His first book 'Battle Cry' showed the toughness and the courage of the US Marines and who like him had fought the Japs. The Exodus his most famous novel about the history of the Jews from the late 19th century to the founding of Israel was an outright worldwide best seller and his latest 'The Haj' was ironically a book on the secret machinations of foreigners that kept the pot boiling in the Middle East. And while Monty during that long flight was totally engrossed with the latest Leon Uris best seller, he had no idea that General Zia-ul-Haq of Pakistan and the Indian Prime Minister Rajiv Gandhi had held talks on ushering in lasting peace in the subcontinent.

CHAPTER-3

1986-The So Called Year of International Peace!

By the time Monty returned home from the United States there was good news both for India and Pakistan. Zia-ul-Haq's visit to Delhi and his talks with Rajiv Gandhi on 26th of December to bring about peace in the troubled subcontinent had been greeted with optimism by the people of both the countries. Particularly happy was Shiraz in Moscow, when it was officially made known that the leaders of both the nations had pledged to make a step by step approach to improve relations and had also committed their firm resolve not to attack each other's nuclear installations. Earlier, when the two leaders had met at the United Nations meeting of the heads of states in October, Rajiv had even invited Zia to the opening of one of India's own nuclear installations and that indeed was a good gesture thought Shiraz. That was the second time that these two leaders had met. The first time was of course in Moscow during Chernenko's funeral, and it was on that sad occasion that Shiraz came face to face with the young Indian Prime Minister. But at that United Nations meeting of the heads of states in New York the fact that the Indian Prime Minister had also met the Swedish Prime Minister Mr Olaf Palme and that the Bofors gun was also discussed was only known to a few.

On the 31st of December, 1985 Monty, Reeta and Dimpy while celebrating the New Year's Eve Ball at the Delhi Gymkhana prayed and hoped that the coming year should be a lot more peaceful not only for India and Pakistan, but also for the the whole wide world. On that very day late in the evening, the Rehman family too had gathered at their old ancestral 'Haveli' at Peshawar. They too were ushering in the New Year with their kith and kin and close friends. For them it was a double celebration. Not only had Martial Law been lifted, but Colonel Aslam Rehman Khan had been promoted to the rank of a Brigadier and was now on his way to command an active Brigade in the vital Uri Sector of Azad Kashmir.

To begin with, the two Rehman brothers, Gul and Arif in order to celebrate the revoking of the emergency in Pakistan and for the lifting of the martial law by Zia opened the two bottles of the rare French champagne that Shiraz had sent to them from Moscow. Though the emergency that had been in force for 20 long years since the 1965 war with India had also been revoked and the martial law as promised had been lifted by Zia, but the very fact that the Eighth Amendement to the Constitution had been passed by the National Assembly recently was severely criticized by Ruksana when she said somewhat sarcastically and loudly.

"Well having had the Eighth Amendment now approved by the National Assembly, the Mulla General I am afraid will never retire or ever hang up his boots. And most likely he may even go to his grave with his boots on," added the lady while proposing a toast in absentia to her son-in-law Shiraz and his family in Moscow.

While the common people of India and Pakistan felt that the year 1985 had been good for both the countries and they hoped that 1986 would be even better, but it was not to be so as America intensified their efforts to have the Pakistanis fight their dirty war against the Soviets in Afghanistan. The year 1986 also started disastrously for the Americans, when on 28th January, the Space Shuttle Challenger exploded seconds after it took off from Cape Canaveral. Salim Rehman Khan who was on an official visit to the Pakistan Embassy in Washington was shocked when he saw it live on television. The shuttle crew of seven that was led by Commander Dick Scobee had also on board Christa McAuliffe, a lady school teacher by profession. The mother of two would have become the first school teacher in space and Salim Rehman wondered how the family would now cope with this terrible tragedy. There were other family members of the crew at the site of the launch and who just minutes ago were smiling and laughing, but now they were all in tears. The disaster was a severe blow to the American space program. In the last 25 years they had lost only seven lives and in just one day that figure had been doubled. The Space Shuttle challenger was named after the 'HMS Challenger', a British Corvette which in the 1870's had carried out pioneering global marine expeditions, and its NASA designation was OV, Orbiter Vehicle-099. This was America's second space shuttle orbiter that had been in service since 4th April, 1983 when it carried out its first maiden flight. It had already completed nine missions successfully, but the 10th one lasted for only 73 seconds. The flight as per the original program was to have taken off on 22nd January, but due to bad weather, high wind and extreme cold temperatures it had been postponed only to disintegrate in flight it seems. The cause according to NASA was a faulty seal or O-ring in one of the solid rocket boosters.

Salim Rehman was visiting Washington on a secret mission. He was required to ensure that the consignment of the new weapon, the Stinger Missile that had been promised by the Americans to Pakistan was expedited. These were to be given to the Afghan Mujahideen fighters to knock off the Soviet menace of helicopter gun ships and aircrafts that were now being extensively used by the Russian troops in Afghanistan. The Stinger was a man portable infra-red homing short range surface to air missile that could be shoulder fired with a single operator. In 1982, during the Falklands War, the British SAS had been equipped with a small quantity of this sophisticated weapon clandestinely, and subsequent tests had proved that it was very effective against low flying helicopters, gun ships and even aircrafts. The mountainous terrain of Afghanistan was ideally suited for its role and it was through Charlie Wilson's effort that the deal it was believed had been finalised between the CIA and the Pakistan government.

One day while visiting the Zoo in Washington, Salim Rehman bumped into someone who once upon a time knew the Rehman family well but had now settled in Washington DC for good. Major General Mian Ghulam Jilani, whose army number was PA 42 had been a Japanese prisoner of war and at partition had opted for the Pakistan Army,. Born in 1914, the retired Major General was Gul Rehman Khan's contemporary in the Indian Military Academy at Dehradun but was a year junior to him in service. During the 1947-48 Kashmir Operations, Jilani had commanded the erstwhile and famous 4th Frontier Force Rifles and was later appointed as Commander of the Gilgit Force. He was also GOC East Pakistan and Commandant of the Quetta Staff College and on his retirement had entered politics. Being a staunch Pathan, he had joined the National Awami Party and had won his seat during the 1970 elections to the National Assembly from Mardan. Being an outspoken critic of Mr Bhutto he was arrested on trumped up charges by the Bhutto government in February 1973 and was sent to prison. During a visit to the hospital in 1975, the General managed to give the guards who were escorting him the slip and escaped. Later he and his wife Nancy Habiba Jilani were given political asylum in the United States. That day while exchanging notes with young Salim Rehman, the General who was Pakistan's first Military Attache to Washington recalled those lovely days, when he with just 11 years of service enjoyed the many diplomatic privileges that were accorded to the diplomatic corps and that too without any distinction of colour creed or nationality. Going down memory lane, the General was nostalgic about the war and his many colleagues who too irrespective of their colour, creed or religion came back as heroes. While the General talked about his old associations with the Piffers, he fondly remembered Major General Hayauddin. "Though my friend Mian Hayauddin was senior to me, but he was a very good man, an excellent officer and above all a gentleman to the core. Though his nickname was 'Gunga' and his father addressed him as 'Chocha' which meant red pepper in Pushto, Mian was truly a man of honour and one who generally kept his cool. And the only time I saw him really angry was in mid October 1947, when he had just taken over the command of the Bannu Brigade from his British counterpart. He was livid when he was told that Major Onkar Singh Kalkat, the previous Brigade Major of the Brigade who had opted for the Indian Army had left without his permission. Major Kalkat it seems was privy to the plans for 'Operation Gulmarg", the clandestine operation with the tribals that we were planning to launch in Kashmir and the Indian Sikh Major's sudden disappearance with his wife and family from Bannu had created a stir. But luckily for us the Indian High Command at that time did not bite his story. Though frankly speaking I now wish that they had and we would not have had this Kashmir problem perennially sitting over our heads. In fact that misguided adventure with the Pathan tribals literally gave Kashmir on a platter to India. Had the Indians been alerted in time, we would have probably not launched that disastrous operation. Consequently talks would have been held between Mr Jinnah and Mr Nehru and with Sardar Patel not being averse to the idea, Kashmir today with its majority Muslim population and without any bloodshed would have probably been an integral part of Pakistan," added the elderly General while inviting Salim Rehman home for some typical Frontier food.

Major General Mian Hayauddin was born on 2nd July. 1910 and was the son of Khan Bahadur Mian Wasiuddin who had served in the Archaeological Survey of India with distinction. The family was from Peshawar and it was the Khan Bahadur who with Sir Aurel Stein and Sir John Marshall was responsible in excavating and cataloging the Gandhara and Ashoka archaeological sites at Swat, Taxila and other places. Gunga was commissioned from Sandhurst into the 4/12 Frontier Force Regiment and commanded Sikh troops. Though a Pathan, he was not only fluent in speaking Punjabi, but he could also read and write in the Gurmukhi script. While commanding the 9/12 FF in Burma he was awarded the Military

Cross and was mentioned in dispatches for a record number of four times. During the 1948 operations in Kashmir, he commanded a Brigade in Poonch and later the 7th Infantry Division at Rawalpindi. In May 1955, he was posted to Washington DC as Chief of the Pakistan Military Mission. Unfortunately age was against him and he retired in 1960. But he did not sit at home. General Ayub Khan first appointed him as the Director General Mineral Resources and later he became the founder Managing Director of the Oil and Gas Development Corporation of Pakistan where he continued till he was appointed on 1st May 1965 as Chairman of the National Press Trust in the rank of a Cabinet Minister. But luck was not on his side. On 20th May, 1965 while leading a delegation of Pakistani journalists and high executives from the travels and tourism department of Pakistan, the flight PK 705 that they all were traveling in crashed. It was the inaugural flight of the newly formed PIA and it crashed while landing at Cairo during the early hours of the morning. Of the 119 passengers and crew, only 6 survived, but General Hayauddin unfortunately was not one of them and the irony of the whole thing was that some monkeys who were part of the shipment in the cargo hold of that Boeing 707 miraculously also survived," added retired General Jilani with moistness in his eyes as he with nostalgia showed Salim Rehman some old photographs of his soldiering days.

"That was indeed rather sad Sir," but I believe that Omar Qureshi the famous cricket commentator and journalist who was then the newly appointed head of the PIA's Public Relations Department did a very good job in informing and helping out the families of those who had been killed," said Salim Rehman as he read through the paper cutting about the crash that had been preserved in the photo album.

"Yes undoubtedly so and after all Omar was the son of an Army Doctor from the IMS and he too retired as a full Colonel like your grand father Colonel Attiqur," said the old man very proudly while showing Salim Rehman a photograph of the big Qureshi family that was a cricket team by itself.

"My God I can count eleven siblings and it is no wonder that Omar became a writer and a commentator on cricket," said Salim Rehman in good humour as he wished Uncle Jilani a very good evening and took his leave. And as he was leaving, when the old retired soldier said rather sadly that the present day Pakistam army under the Mulla General Zia was becoming a bit too Islamized and which was not good for the country, Salim Rehman agreed with him whole heartedly.

While Salim Rehman was busy in working out the arms deal with the Americans, there was a change of guard at the topmost level of the Indian Army in Delhi. On the 1st of February, 1986 General Sundarjee took over as the new Chief from General Arun Vaidya. The man who commanded the Western Army Command during Operation Bluestar was a thinking General and since 1982 he had been working on the modernization and mechanization of the Indian Army. He had taken over at a time when Rajiv Gandhi was the Prime Minister and his schoolmate Arun Singh was waiting in the wings to take over as the Minister of State for Defence. No sooner had Sundarji put on his new pips; he decided to set his ideas on paper. In order to convince the young Prime Minster and Arun Singh that there was a dire need for the country to get integrated fully in all defence matters, he gave a presentation with the other two service chiefs about the requirement for the Armed Forces of India to work in tandem and in close cooperation with the other ministries during any future war and thus he set the ball rolling for an high level military exercise and which he aptly named as 'Operation Brasstacks.' Operation Brasstacks would be a massive tri-service exercise that would be conducted initially as a war game in Delhi during the coming Monsoon season and would culminate in an unprecedented large scale two sided military exercise with troops during winter in the deserts of Rajasthan to test India's defence and offensive capabilities at the highest level. Having seen the merits of the New Chief's plans for the future and his desire to keep the Armed Forces well equipped with modern weapons, the Rajiv-Arun Singh duo from Dosco immediately gave their full support and approval.

While the Indian Army Headquarters in Delhi got busy in working out the modalities of conducting the war game, and in evaluating India's future requirements of sophisticated arms and equipment and especially that of the much delayed long range artillery gun that the Indian army had been long pressing for, and of which one of the main contenders was the Swedish arm's firm Bofors, the news arrived that Olaf Palme who was a good friend of India and of the new IndianPrime Minister had been assassinated. He had been shot by some unknown gunman at about 2330 hrs Swedish time on 28th February, when he with his wife Lisabeth were walking back home after a late night movie show in the heart of the Swedish capital of Stockholm. The Prime Minister was rushed to the hospital but was declared dead on arrival. He was shot twice in the stomach, while his wife who was shot in the back was lucky to survive. Olaf Palme had only a month ago visited India and the two Prime Ministers it seems had hit it off very well.

According to one of Monty's close friends in the IAS who was now a Senior Joint Secretary in the Ministry of Defence, the Bofors gun contract after the Swedish Prime Minister's visit to India it seems was on the fast track. However, in order to get a little more educated on how such huge defence contracts were evaluated and finalized, Monty decide to call on his old friend Unni from the Press Trust of India so that if need be Monty too could become an arms dealer in future. Off late, Monty had been hearing from very reliable sources that some big foreign arms producers from abroad in order to gauge the defence requirements of the Indian Armed Forces, were maintaining their liaison offices in the capital city and that they were hiring middlemen from India with good contacts in the concerned ministry who could broker the deals for them. It was big money and once the deal was finalized, the broker cum arms dealer could make a real killing. "So why the hell should I not try my luck" thought Monty as he drove to the Press Club of India to meet his friend Unni who was a regular at the bar in the evenings. In fact some of Unni's close friends including Monty referred to it as Unni's grand drawing room. Having been a bachelor for 60 long years, Unni's only interest in life now was to find out how much truth was there in every story that was connected with murky Indian politics and their leaders and most of whom without fail always had a holier than thou attitude, a pseudo moralistic approach to preach patriotism, maintained double standards and who always claimed that they were always above board. Unni's late father was a staunch leftist and a freedom fighter who died during the 1942 Quit India Movement, when Unni was only 16 years old. Ever since that day, Unni whose favourite author was Sir Arthur Conan Doyle decided that he too would one day become another Sherlock Holmes. After graduation he tried for the IPS so that he could become a CID or an officer of the IB, but was medically rejected. With his penchant for investigative journalism he did work for some 15 years with some leading newspapers and magazines, but when he found that the rich owners of these papers had become stooges and pawns of the politicians and they would not let him write the truth and the facts, he quit in disgust and later joined the PTI. He had only just retired a month ago from the Press Trust of india but he always kept his eyes and ears open.

"Don't be a bloody fool and a mutt and never for heaven's sake get into this shit of a business of so called arms deals.Yes, you might become a bloody millionaire overnight but you will not get any peaceful sleep thereafter, unless of course you have a big political Godfather to look after you and your family. But then that too I am afraid will not be guaranteed, because they will through their henchmen only use you, get their hefty cuts and then dump you on the road. But if you can become someone like Adnan Kashoggi, then it may be worth it," added Unni with a sarcastic smile as he lit his new Dunhill pipe and ordered a chilled beer for Monty and another large Rum and hot water for himself.

That cold winter evening after a few more large Old Monk Rums, Unni finally came out with his story on the Bofors gun. According to him the Indian Army since 1980 was on the look out for a good 155 millimetre medium range artillery gun of high caliber that would suit their requirements both in the mountains and in the plains. Being the ultimate users, Indian Army a few years ago had initially short listed four such reputed arms manufacturers, which included the Bofors of Swedish origin, the Sofna of France, the IMS gun from the UK and the Voest Alpine of Austria. All the four manufacturers were then required to submit the tenders and put in their bids and these bids were finally closed in September, 1985. Thereafter the evaluation process started and when both the Bofors and the Sofna guns had further been short listed both the mahufacturers and their agents to procure the massive deal went into top gear. This was nothing unusual and middlemen were always there fixing such deals, but this was not a small contract but the biggest that India would sign depending on who would finally emerge as the eventual winner. "It was however in October 1985, when Rajiv Gandhi met Olaf Palme at the United Nations meet in New York, that the Swedish Prime Minister it seems started lobbying actively for the contract. According to reliable reports, the Bofors firm was in deep financial trouble and with no big orders coming, there was even a talk that the Swedish arm's giant at Karlskoga with its 30,000 workers in their Bofors factory may soon go out of business. There were also strong rumours that the plant might even be closed down and that would mean making so many more Swedes jobless, and which Mr Palme's government did not want. Therefore to Unni it seemed very logical that the Swedish Prime Minister was very right in trying to convince the Indian Prime Minister that the Bofors besides being a very reliable weapon system, it was also willing to offer other terms like its manufacture in India and probably give a few guns gratis provided Bofors was given the contract. It is also believed that at that meeting in New York it was decided verbally and mutually between the two heads of states that incase Bofors was given the final contract then it should be a straight one to one clean cut deal between the two sides and no middlemen should be involved," added Unni as he topped up his Rum with some more hot water.

"But why did we not approach the Soviets for a similar gun, after all they are even today our biggest suppliers for tanks, aircrafts etc and now recently the MIG-27 too has been inducted into the Indian Air Force also," said Monty as Unni cleverly avoided the question with his usual "Arre how should I know yaar" reply and then carried on talking about his last visit to Sweden.

"It may also be interesting to learn a few more things about Bofors that I inadvertently came to know through an American deserter from Vietnam who had married and settled in the University town of Uppsala near Stockholm and where I had gone to deliver a lecture on Indo-Swedish Friendship program. According to the American, some disgruntled Engineer from Bofors having quit his job had spilled the beans. According to him, it seems that the Swedish Arms Company despite the Swedish Gvernment's stand on neutrality and to make the world safer had been regularly and illegally exporting lethal weapons, arms and ammunition to countries in West Asia including Iran and that these were being clandestinely routed through agents using the free ports like Singapore and others in that region. This was contrary to the Swedish Government's policy and the revelation naturally caused a sensation in Sweden because it was virtually a question of smuggling arms for business gains and it became very difficult for Bofors to explain how and why they were doing it," said Unni rather confidently.

"But then do you think that the murder of the Swedish Prime Minister has something to do with all this?" asked Monty as he quietly added some ice cubes into his big ceramic beer mug. Monty was a casual beer drinker and the second large strong bottle of 'Golden Eagle' it seems was a bit too much for him.

"Well not so far as India is concerned because the deal if at all it comes through has still to be formally signed by the two sides, but one thing is definitely clear after the Rajiv and Palme meeting in Delhi last month that there will be no middle men whatsoever," added Unni as another correspondent friend of Unni's who too was a regular at the bar joined them.

"Well in that case and since there will be no middleman I don't think I have a chance in hell and I might as well stick to my good old garment and carpet export business," said Monty as he checked his watch. It was nearing midnight and it was time for him to go home.

During that month of March 1986, while the dynamic new Indian army chief, General Sundarjee in India got busy in planning 'Operation

Brasstacks', in Bangladesh, General Ershad was trying to consolidate his hold on his countrymen. Fazal Rehman in Dhaka however felt happy that President Ershad had removed a large number of his senior military commanders from key civilian posts and had abolished the many military courts that had been set up in the country. Like General Zia in Pakistan, General Ershad in Bangladeh was also now aspiring to remain as President, but not in uniform. However, unlike General Zia of Pakistan who loved his armoured corps uniform, Ershad had greater political ambitions and was toying with the idea of forming his own 'Jatiyo Party', that he hoped would politically keep him on the hot seat as President. Very cleverly, Ershad therefore eased martial law in the country and announced parliamentary elections in May.

The Bangladesh Foreign Service being comparatively young, the promotions were therefore pretty fast. On 1st March, Fazal Rehman for his good work in Iran and at home had been seconded as a Senior Director to oversee the interests of Bangladesh in the recently founded South East Asian Regional Cooperation, designated in short as SAARC. SAARC was the brainchild of the late President of Bangladesh, General Ziaur Rehman who had initially mooted the concept for a regional economic trade bloc that would not only be of mutual benefit to all countries of the subcontinent, but would also promote the much needed goodwill and friendship amongst them. The idea was formally accepted by India, Pakistan and Bangladesh at a meeting in Colombo in 1981 and was formally established, when the first inaugural meeting of the entire member states that now also included Sri Lanka, Nepal, Maldives, and Bhutan was held in Dhaka on 7-8 December 1985. Though it was only the seven countries of the Indian Subcontinent that were involved, but it had a population of over a billion people who were economically very poor. The main thrust for cooperation was therefore to be laid on Agriculture, Rural Development, Telecommuniications, Transport and Human Resources Develpement. It was indeed a noble idea thought Fazal Rehman as he seriously took up his new assignment. The next SAARC summit was scheduled to be held at Bangalore in India in November 1986 and he and his wife Samina and their two children were eagerly looking forward to it. Daughter Sameera was now 11 years old and she was studying at the International School at Kodailkanal, while their four year old son Shafiq went to a crèche in Dhaka.

Meanwhile at the Minstry of Defence in Delhi, in the second week of March, after the Indian Prime Minisiter's return from the Olaf Palme funeral at Stockholm on 16th March, the long pending requirement of the Indian

Army for a good medium range artillery gun was given a sudden boost as the files for the approved weapon system started moving rather feverisly from one government office to another. According to Monty, when Unni conveyed to him the sequence of events of the secret file approving the Bofors gun as the first choice having been given the final go ahead on 24th March with the Prime Minister Rajiv Gandhi's signature on it, Monty just could not believe it.

"Well tell me how come suddenly the 'Babus' and the Officers of the concerned Ministry in South Block and in the PMO's secretariat have become so damn efficient. Because according to you my dear Unni Sir, General Sundarji had only just taken over as Chief on 1st February, and just 17 days later the Bofors gun has became the number one favourite. Then soon after Rajiv Gandhi's return from the Swedish Prime Minister's funeral on 16th March, the file it seems went into a fast gallop. And on 21st March to be precise, Arun Singh, the Minister of State for Defence gave his verbal clearance and that as you say has been recorded on the file, and by the 24th the file with the Prime Minister's signature was back in the Defence Ministry ! This must be some sort of a record in the Ministry, where files normally concerning defence deals moved only at a snail's pace, "added Monty as he ordered another large gin, lime and soda with a dash of bitters for his friend and confidante Unni. That afternoon of 26th March, 1986 for their usual weekly Saturday afternoon meetings and with Monty playing host, the venue was none other than the Embassy Bar and Restaurant at Connaught Place. It was one of Monty's favourite joints ever since his return to Delhi from Bangalore for good. The ambience was good, the drinks comparatively much cheaper and the snacks were simply delicious. Since the place was unusually crowded that afternoon with businessmen of a all shades entertaining their friends from the various ministries and government offices in Delhi, and some of whom Unni knew fairly well, Unni very diplomatically switched on to another hot subject that on that very day had made headlines in the United States. An article published by the New York Times had charged Kurt Waldhiem, the former Secretary General of the United Nations, and who was now running for the post of the President of Austria in being involved with Nazi war crimes. Born in a village near Vienna on 21 December, 1918, Kurt Waldhiem in 1941 had been drafted into the German Werchmacht and had served as a squad leader on the Russian Front and on being wounded in battle returned to Vienna and was posted at Thessaloniki, the headquarters of the infamous Austrian General Lohr and from where counter insurgency operations against Tito's partisan groups were being mounted rather ruthlessly. It had been alleged by the New York Times that Waldhiem in the summer of 1942 had played a major role in 'Operation Kozara' and in which thousands of partisans, civilians in a mass scale cleansing operation were brutally killed, while the Jews amongst them were also sent to the concentration camps. In 1945, Waldheim had surrendered to the British Forces in Carinthia and was later also wanted for war crimes by the War Crimes Commission of the United Nations, the very organization that he headed for two full terms till 1981. After the war, his boss General Lohr was executed, but Waldheim had managed to join the Austrian Foreign Service. The career diplomat who had served as his country's permanent representative at the UN headquarters in 1970 having lost in the Austrian Presidential elections in 1971 was however elected to head the United Nations as its Secretary General and he took over after U Thant retired in 1972.

"'Well crime I guess it seems at times does pay, and in this case it did and in a big way too as far as Mr Waldhiem is concerned. And though I have personally nothing against Mr Waldhiem who as the Secretary General had performed reasonably well and might have even got a third term had China not vetoed the proposal, but what is bugging me now is the pace at which criminalization in Indian politics and business is gathering momentum. And I hope that our Mr Clean, Rajiv Gandhi whose young political career has taken off with a bang does not get involved in what is now being termed as the strong politico-criminal-business nexus," said Unni as the waiter brought another plate of his favourite fried tiger prawns.

A week later, Monty found himself in West Berlin. He was there on a business cum pleasure trip at the invitation of his main German importer from Munich who was opening a new outlet in a posh area of the historic German city and not very far from the ugly Berlin Wall that separated the two nations of East and West. On 5th April, after the grand opening of the new store and to celebrate the occasion they all descended at the ever popular La Belle Discotheque. It was one of the popular joints in the city and being a Saturday it was as usual full of American GI's dancing away some with but most without their female partners. Having had a long tiring day, Monty with his hosts and friends enjoyed the evening thoroughly, and at around 0100 hours local time they called it a day. Monty went back to his hotel room, which was only a stones throw away from the discotheque and was soon fast a sleep. But a little later there was a shattering explosion that rocked the building and he immediately woke up with a start. Minutes later on hearing the cries of help, he quickly changed into his track suit and ran down the two floors to find out what the commotion on the street was all about. In fact had Monty with his host stayed back for another hour or so inside the disco, they too might have become casualties of that terrible terrorist bomb attack. The carnage was really terrible as Monty gave a helping hand to evacuate those who had been trapped inside. It seems that the bomb that had been placed under a table near the DJ's booth had exploded at 0150 hrs local time which corresponded to 2350 GMT and the impact was so great that the outside wall that was surrounded by a scaffolding for renovation work on the building had been blown off and this resulted in the collapse of the floor and the ceiling. This incidentally was the second explosion in West Berlin in a week. Only last Saturday, a bomb had wrecked the German-Arab Club in the city and seven Arabs were injured. Luckily the casualties at La Belle as far as deaths were concerned were only two and both were American soldiers. Private Nermin Hanway and Sergeant Kenneth Ford had died instantaneously, but the overall casualties among the American servicemen that night was very high indeed and for quite a few of them the injuries suffered would now be in the nature of a permanent disability thought Monty as he made it back to his hotel room at sunrise.

The next day, when Monty returned to Delhi and told his family about his narrow brush with death, his wife Reeta immediately decided to hold a three day 'Akhand Path' in the house. This was not the first time that Monty had a narrow escape, it had happened with him twice before too and with so much of traveling around that her husband had to do, and together with terrorism constantly on the increase both at home and abroad, Reeta was naturally worried. She therefore on that day tried to convince Monty to switch over to some other business that could be done even while sitting at home.

"Don't be crazy my darling. Only a coward businessman will think of sitting at home. After all one has to live and living is about meeting people, interacting with them on a one to one basis and these things just cannot be done over the telephone. It also involves entertaining the right people at the right time, showering them with gifts on birthdays, wedding anniversaries and of course also fulfilling their expectations during Diwali. And these things I am afraid just cannot be done from home, because if I start entertaining these characters here in our drawing room, then I am afraid it is you who will soon get fed up trying to look after them and get bored listening to all our shop talk. And in any case life has to be lived only once, so might as well make the best of it. And as they say in the army that if your name is written on the bullet then it is just bad luck, or if rape is inevitable then one might as well relax and enjoy it. So just forget about it and so let us keep singing Que SeraSera, whatever will be will be. "And no sooner had Monty uttered those words, when a smiling Dimpy walked in to give the good news that she had once again received the call to appear for her viva that was to be conducted by the UPSC next month. Dimpy was very confident that she would make it to the IFS this time and noticing the worried look on her mother's face told her to read Dale Carnegie's famous book. 'How to stop worrying and start living.'

"Yes that indeed is a very good book no doubt my love, but wait till you get married and have children, then as a mother you too will know what real worries are all about. However, under the present circumstances let me tell you that Mr Carnegie's other best seller that is titled 'How too win friends and influence people' is of no consequence to us Indians, because under the present circumstances if businessman like your father has to exist and make money honestly then I am afraid we are all living in a fool's paradise. Today unfortunately it is only those who follow the dictum of how to win over Politicians and influence their chamchas (lackeys) is what matters and counts. Because it is they and they alone who make it big and that too without any accountability whatsoever," added Reeta sarcastically while congratulating her daughter for the excellent marks that she had secured in the UPSC written examination.

On Monday morning, the 7th of April, 1986 while Reeta and Dimpy got busy in organizing the three day 'Akhand Path', and while the Granthis from the nearby Gurdwara arrived to make all the necessary arrangements that was scheduled to begin early next morning, Monty while having his first cup of tea was delighted to read the headlines in a newspaper that the dreaded criminal Charles Sobhraj had been arrested in Goa. It was in the morning edition of English daily and as Monty read in full details about the man who was also now known as 'the serpent' and 'the bikini killer,' he was surprised that the dreaded killer was still in India. Born on 6th April, 1944, in Saigon to an unwed Vietnamese mother and a Sindhi father, Charles Sobhraj found himself once again in handcuffs on his forty second birthday. The credit for his arrest on 6th April, 1986 went once more to Inspector Madhukar Zende of the Bombay Police who had earlier also in 1971 arrested the same man from Ashoka Hotel, New Delhi for robbery. The hardened criminal just three weeks ago on 16th March had caused a sensation, when while serving a 10 year jail sentence at the Tihar Jail he cooly walked out a freeman after he had used his usual modus operandi of drugging his victims. That night on the pretext of celebrating his birthday he had very cleverly drugged the jail staff and had escaped. And by next morning the massive manhunt had begun. Soon after Charles was born, his Indian father deserted the family and his mother after having an affair with a French Lieutenant in Indo China and producing more children kept shuttling between Saigon and Paris. This resulted in complete neglect of young Sobhraj who took to crime and he saw jail for the first time in 1963, when he was sentenced for robbery and sent to the Poissy prison near Paris. On release from prison, Sobhraj married his French sweetheart Chantal and the couple after having committed a spate of robberies on unsuspecting people whom they first befriended, they landed in Bombay. In 1971, a botched robbery at a jewelry shop inside Hotel Ashoka at Delhi led to his first arrest in India. Within 14 days the clever Sobhraj feigning serious illness was admitted to a hospital. At that time the Bangladesh war was on and one fine night during the blackout in the capital, he escaped to Afghanistan and got into the lucrative drug and arms business. From there he got on to the 'Hippie trail' that took him to the popular tourist spots in Thailand and Nepal. At these places he not only robbed his victims, but he also killed them. As the hunt for the physcopath killer intensified, he once again escaped and resurfaced back in India in 1976. But this time, when he with his two other foreign girl accomplices Barbara Smith and Mary Ellen while posing as tourist guides to a group of French post graduate students tried to drug them with pills that they said were for anti dysentery, it back fired on them. The high potency drug reacted faster than usual and when some of the students fell unconscious, the game was up. All three of them were arrested and during the interrogation, when the two girls confessed to the crime all of them were convicted and sent to the Tihar Jail. Sobhraj was about to complete his ten year sentence and the Thai warrant for his extradition was still hanging over his head. He was wanted by the Thailand Police for various murders that he had committed in that country and knew very well that if he was sent back he would surely be executed. He therefore on the eve of his likely extradition from India very conveniently escaped from Tihar with the hope that he would be caught and sent back to Tihar again. There he would once again have another prolonged stay of luxury and comfort with a coloured TV in his cell and gourmet food that he had been so used to earlier thanks to the corrupt jail authorities. And by the time his second term in the Indian prison would be over, the 20 year Thai arrest warrant for him would have expired and he would once again be a free bird. To cater for his old age needs, he had already started giving interviews to western authors and journalists with the hope that his life story that Richard Neville was proposing to write would someday become a best seller. On the day Sobhraj was re-arrested by Inspector Zende, he was enjoying himself at his favourite restaurant the O'Coqueiro in Goa. Located at Alto Porvorim and on the main road in Bardez, he was sitting as usual on the last table in the far corner and was waiting for a phone call. This was the only restaurant in that area that had a STD booth and Sobhraj had just made a call and he was waiting for a return call, when Inspector Zende pounced on him. As he was being taken away handcuffed he knew he would miss the delightful Goan and Portuguese cuisine that only cook Peter Fernandes could produce. That restaurant in north Goa was also Monty's favourite. He with his family and friends would always stop by to have the delicious baked crabs and the batter fried prawns that only O'Coqueiro's could produce.

On the evening of 9th April, 1986 while the three day Akhand Part entered its thirty sixth hour at Monty's Defence Colony residence, there was a call from London and Shupriya was on the line. She had heard about Monty's narrow escape in West Berlin and had called to wish him well. While she was on the phone, she also gave Monty the news that Benazir Bhutto and a few others from the PPP who were in exile in London were most probably on their way back to Pakistan. Benazir with a large number of some of her party people had been seen boarding a flight to Dhahran a few hours ago and the rumours were that they would take a connecting PIA flight from there direct to Lahore and where her Party workers were eagerly waiting to give her a resounding welcome the next morning.

"I hope General Zia has given his nod for her home coming and I hope the young ambitious lady who like Dimpy once also wanted to join the Foreign Service takes it easy or else the Pakistani President to keep himself in the hot seat may once again declare martial law," said Monty somewhat casually as he gave the telephone receiver to his daughter Dimpy who was eagerly waiting to give her favourite aunt the good news of her having made it to the interview stage for the second time and with much better marks in the written examination.

With the martial law having been lifted in Pakistan, and the promises of an election to be held in the near future having been made by President Zia, Benazir had decided that come what may she would go back to Pakistan and revive the PPP from its very grass roots. Encouraged by the recent happenings in the Phillipines, wherein President Marcos with his wife Imelda was forced to leave the country and seek asylum in the United States and the people having welcomed Corazino Aquino, the widow of the slain Nonoy Aquino as the country's new president, Benazir was confident that with some of the influential US Congressmen encouraging her to return, President Zia would not dare to touch her. The Russians were still in Afghanistan and with three million Afghan refugees inside the Pakistan, Zia badly needed the 4.2 Billion dollar military and economic aid that was pending approval from the US Congress. She knew that both she and her party, the PPP were anathema to the man who unfortunately thanks to her father had been made the army chief.

As soon as Benazir boarded the PIA flight to Lahore, Salim Rehman who had been sent especially to Dhahran to covertly watch the activities of the young lady and the 30 others from the PPP who were accompanying her was pleasantly surprised in the warm manner in which the Captain and the crew of the flight greeted her. She was not only being treated as a VIP, but her supporters had already started decorating the aircraft from inside with their party flags and stickers. Salim Rehman was even more shocked, when the pilot's voice over the intercom announced the aircraft's descent to Lahore and expressed his hearty welcome to the new PPP leader. As the approach for the landing was about to be made, the flight attendant even invited her to the cockpit to see for herself the massive crowds who were waiting to welcome her. Not only was she, but even Salim Rehman had never expected such a huge turnout as the aircraft taxied to a final halt and the doors were opened for the young lady to step out.

"I only hope they won't do a repeat of Nino Aquino here," thought Salim Rehman to himself when he saw the massive security arrangements that the government had made at the airport. Luckily everything went of well as Bhutto's daughter stepped on the very soil of the city that had condemned her father to death. On that morning of 10th April, as the decorated truck carrying the triumphant Benazir Bhutto literally inched its way slowly from the Lahore airport to the Minar-i-Pakistan and Iqbal Park, the sea of humanity that greeted her along the route with flowers, garlands and spontaneous applause was something that even the young lady had never expected.

"With the PPP banners of black, red and green colours flying everywhere and with the crowd shouting Zia must quit, Zia must go at the top of the voices, it must be giving the Mulla General the jitters," said Salim Rehman to his wife Aasma who had come to receive him at the airport but were now badly caught in a massive traffic jam.

"Maybe this is all staged managed to ensure that no harm comes to her and it could also be a sort of a warning to the military that she has the peoples power behind her," said Aasma as she filled a tall glass of the cold fresh nimboo-pani (fresh lime and soda) from the thermos flask that she had so very thoughtfully brought for her husband on that very warm April day.

While some of the American Senators welcomed the return of Benazir Bhutto to Pakistan, but the majority of them were upset about the terrorist attacks on the US troops in West Berlin that took place on the 5th of April at the La Bella Discothique and the bombing of the TWA flight 840 that took place a few days earlier while the aircraft was in the airspace above Greece. The needle of suspicion for both these dastardly attacks was now on Colonel Gaddafi of Libya who was a friend of Pakistan, and some of the Senators were now demanding a retaliatory action against him. 'Yes enough is enough,' said an angry President Reagan while authorizing his Joint Chiefs of Staff to plan a surgical strike at the very heart of Libya. The well planned air attack would now become the longest fighter combat mission in history. To the American President there was no doubt that the Libyan hand was very much behind the two cowardly bombings and he was bent upon teaching Gaddaffi a lesson of his life. Code named 'Operation El Dorado Canyon', the eighteen F-111's from the 48th Tactical Fighter Wing that was based in Britain in conjunction with 27 aircrafts from the aircraft carriers of the US Sixth Fleet in the Mediterranean Sea were battle ready on 14th April for their long range bombing missions. For the F-111's that were required to fly 1300 miles one way over the Atlantic, and then over the Straights of Gibralter and along the Mediterranean Sea to get to their designated targets it was no doubt a challenging task. While for the Naval fighter aircrafts operating from the aircraft carriers, 'Saratoga', 'Coral Sea' and 'America', it was all the more risky because the Libyan air defenses were on high alert. And this was due to the fact that the American 6th Fleet in order to keep pressure on the Libyans was already carrying out a series of maneuvers near the Gulf of Sidra. On 24th March, the Libyan air defense forces had fired SA-5 missiles at two F-14. Tomcats when they intercepted a Libyan Mig-25 that had flown fairly close to the American battle group. On the very next day, aircrafts from the US aircraft carriers struck in retaliation at the Libyan SAM site. There was also tension all around as the Soviet warships in the Mediterranean kept monitoring the movement of the American ships and aircrafts in that region. Therefore, in order to minimize their own losses, it was not only imperative for the American strike force to maintain total surprise and destroy the five designated targets with a lightening strike, but to also return back to base safely and preferably before first light the next day.

This kind of a joint and complex US Air Force, Navy and Marine Corps operation under the command of Vice Admiral Frank. B. Kelso II, the Commander of the Sixth Fleet was being undertaken for the first time and it was not at all going to be easy. Such military joint operations required a very high degree of cooperation and coordination between the three services and it also involved refueling in the air for at least a dozen times and that to while observing total radio silence. Though the strike force did have a few experienced pilots who had seen action in Vietnam, but most of the crew had never seen live combat and nor had they carried out refueling operations from the KC10's at night while maintaining radio silence. This operation therefore would not only blood them, but it would also prove to the world that the long arm of the American armed forces against terrorists and terrorism could reach out to any part of the globe if need be.

At around 17.30 hours GMT, the F-111's from England took off for their mission, and at around 2 AM GMT on the 15th of April, 1986 when they swooped down on their targets, the Libayans were taken completely by surprise. As the first three attack elements code named Remit, Elton and Karma dropped their bombs at the Azziziyah Barracks, the headquarters of the Libyan leader, which was also the command and control centre and reduced it to rubble, Gaddafi did not know what had hit him. He was however lucky to escape unharmed, but he had lost his adopted daughter Hannah and two of his sons were wounded. Overall the operation was a success. The Americans had not only succeeded in accurately targeting the terrorist naval base, the Azziziyah barracks and the military airfield at Tripoli, but also the Sidi Ballal Terrorist Camp and the military airfield at Bengazi. During the conduct of Operation El Dorado Canyon, the Americans only lost one F-111, which also resulted in the death of the two pilots Captain L.Ribas Dominicci and Captain Paul.F. Lawrence, but the experience gained by Colonel Sam, W. Westbrook III and his dare devil pilots of the 48th Tactical Fighter Wing was tremendous. Early on that morning of 15th April, 1986 when Shiraz and Saira in Moscow heard over the BBC about the daring American ten minute air raid on Libya that had resulted in the death of 37 Libyans and had also badly wounded around another 130, Saira said very sceptically.

"But tell me frankly. Do you think that such kind of retaliatory attacks by the Americans as a tit for tat will cow down Gaddafi and the other terrorist groups that have off late mushroomed in the Middle East? Because knowing the psyche of the Muslims and especially those of the poor Palestinians who have been crying themselves hoarse for a land of their own even before the State of Israel was born, and who today are still being kicked around like a football from pillar to post and from one country to another, they are not going to sit idle. Goaded by the fanatic Mullas from all sects who are always calling for a damn Jehad and especially so against the Americans and the Jews, this kind of war I am afraid will never ever end. An eye for an eye I am afraid is not the answer and it is high time that both the super powers stopped interfering in the affairs of other countries. By selling arms to their respective allies in the Middle East and elsewhere this has now become big business for them it seems. But what surprises me is that arms manufacturers in countries like Sweden who have been constantly propagating peace in this world, they too I believe are clandestinely exporting lethal arms and weapons to the Middle Eastern countries who seem to be perpetually getting at each others throats," added Saira as she laid breakfast for her husband and her seven year old daughter Gammy who was getting ready to go to her new Anglo-American International School. Founded in 1949, it was a coed school that was run by the members from primarily the US, British and Canadian Embassies for the children of the diplomatic community in the Soviet capital and Gammy whose registered school name was Shehzadi Rehman Khan had now become Sherry to her school friends. Since the name Shehzadi in Persian also meant 'Princess', some of her classmates also affectionately addressed her as 'Princy'.

While the Americans were still rejoicing over the air riads on Libya, the entire Rehman family on the 18th of April in Peshawar was glued to the television. They were all watching the finals of the Australasia Cup that was being played at Sharjah between India and Pakistan. After India had scored a respectable 245 runs for the loss of seven wickets in their allotted fifty overs, Salim Rehman in order to make the game a bit more interesting decided to become a bookie. With Pakistan now waiting to to give their reply Salim Rehman Khan was now offering two is to one for a Pakistan win, five to one for a tie and four to one for an Indian win. However, there was one condition and that was no adult would be allowed to bet more than a hundred rupees, while all children above the age of ten as a special case would be allowed to bet a maximum of rupees ten and the only exception being made was for Mehmuda's daughter Tarannum who was now nineteen and she could if she so desired bet up to rupees fifty.

"Agreed Chacha Jaan," said all the children in loud chorus as Aslam Rehman's son Vovka who was soon going to be fourteen ran to his grandfather and having come back with a crisp ten rupee note said 'Two to one on a win for Pakistan please'. Taking the cue from his cousin Vovka, young Javed also ran to his dad Karim Malik and he also wagered 10 rupees on a Pakistan win. But for Tarannum whose favourite was Roger Binny the good looking Indian medium pace bowler, she diplomatically put rupees twenty on a tie, and it was only Gul Rehman who put a hundred rupees for an Indian win.

As the two Pakistani opening batsmen Mudassar Nazar and Mohsin Khan walked in to open Pakistan's innings, all the children loudly clapped and shouted 'Pakistan Paindabad.' Then as the game progressed it simply became nerve wracking for everybody as fortunes kept fluctuating with every ball and over. Then as Pakistani wickets kept falling at one end, Javed Miandad who was batting like a champion held on doggedly at the other. At the close of the 49th over, with the score reading 235 for seven wickets and 11 more runs needed for victory, Zubeida and Ruksana could not take the excitement any more and both the ladies retired to the kitchen to make arrangements for the supper that evening. When the Indian captain gave Chetan Sharma the Indian medium pace bowler the ball to bowl the last over, Pakistan still needed 11 runs from six balls to win. On Chetan Sharma's very first delivery while trying to take a second run Wasim Akram was run out the match it seemed would go India's way. But on the second ball when Miandad with a beautiful on drive dispatched it to the fence, the smile was back on everybody's face. The third ball was swept by Miandad to long leg, but brilliant fielding by Roger Binny restricted it to only one run only. And while everybody else in the room was all tensed up it was only Tarannum who kept on clapping. There were now only three balls to go and six more runs were needed for a win. But when Chetan Sharma's fourth delivery had Zulqarnain clean bowled for nought, the match now really became a cliff hanger. With the Pakistan score card reading 241 for 9 as the last man Tauseef Ahmed walked in to face the fifth ball and four runs were still needed for a tie and five for a win, Vovka closed his eyes and invoked the spirit of Allah. Like spectators everywhere, the entire Rehman family too was on tenterhooks. It was a nail biting finish as Tauseef took his stance. Luckily he managed to just touch the ball and as advised by Miandad ran hell for leather to give his partner the final strike. And though on that ball Azaharuddin who was fielding at short cover had a shy at the stumps, but he missed it by inches, while Tauseef was still making his ground. A direct hit would have given India victory. Now there was only one ball to go and four runs to win for Pakistan as Miandad batting on a brilliant 110 not out surveyed the field, said a prayer and took his stance well forward of the popping crease. He was expecting a yorker and was determined to send it to the fence to tie the match, but when an equally nervous Chetan Sharma offered him a full toss and Miandad swung his bat with gusto all eyes were now on that ball. And as the ball sailed over and went clean out of the ground, there was pandemonium all around. Pakistan had won with a last ball six and the hero was none other than Javed Miandad of course. To celebrate that historic win, Salim Rehman took everybody out to dinner that evening and called up Shiraz in Moscow to give him the good news. Shiraz had placed both his hundred and that of Saira's too on a win by India and was disappointed when India after having made a solid start of 117 runs for the first wicket went on to lose the match by a whisker. "'With the two opening batsman Sunil Gavaskar the Indian run machine having contributed 92 runs and Shrikant with a blazing 75 there was no question of losing, but the Indians it seems do not have the killer instinct in them,"said Shiraz diplomatically as he opened a bottle of champagne to celebrate Pakistan's victory, while Gammy held on to the telephone receiver for uncle Salim Rehman at the other end to hear the loud bang from the bottle.

And while that fantastic last ball win by Pakistan over their arch rivals India was being celebrated by the Rehman family in Islamabad with champagne, in the USSR, the Vodka loving Russians were cursing the steep hike in alchohol prices. With the young Russian leader Mikhail Gorbachev now trying his very best to guide the country towards reforms that looked progressive and challenging, Shiraz was happy that the Russian economy that had stagnated during the Brezhnev era was now being given a fillip by promoting growth through partnerships with Western companies. Though Gorbachev's alchohol reform to fight the menace of the wide-spread alcoholism in the country did have its hiccups and was not a great success, but the sudden short supply of hard liquor together with the steep increase in the prices of vodka, wine and beer had not only led to a big drop in sales, but it also resulted in the product being sold in the black market for those diehards who just couldn't do without it. Both at the recent plenum of the Central Committee and at the XXVIIth Party Congress in February1986, when the dynamic young Secretary General had talked about 'Perestroika', restructuring, 'Glasnost' openness and the need for 'Uskoreniye' the acceleration of the economic development of the USSR things were looking fairly bright indeed. But on 26th of April, 1986 after a disaster that was unprecedented in the history of the Soviet Union and in the world struck the nation, the whole country went into mourning, At that unearthly hour of that 26th of April morning at 01.23 am, while the people in European Russia were fast asleep, a major explosion at the Chernobyl Nuclear Power

Plant near Kiev in the Ukraine became the worst ever nuclear accident in history. And Shiraz and his family were indeed very lucky not to have got contaminated by the widespread radioactive fall out that soon followed thereafter. They were on their way by car to Budapest in Hungary and had halted for the night at Kiev, the capital of Ukraine. The Chernobyl plant was near the town of Pripat which was 110 kilometres north—east of Kiev and close to the Ukrainian-Belarus border. Though the plume of the radioactive fallout drifted over the Western part of the Soviet Union and along the Eastern, Western and Northern parts of Europe, Shiraz and his family were lucky that it did not move southwards, Though the Russians initially tried to keep the disaster under wraps, but it was soon out in the open.

The plant with its four nuclear reactors was capable of producing 1 Gigawatt of electric power and it was the fourth reactor that had been scheduled for a shutdown for maintenance during the daylight hours of the 25th that had exploded and which resulted in a nuclear meltdown. The accident had occurred while an experiment was being carried out to test the ability of the reactor's turbine generator to generate the required quantity of electricity that could power the reactors safety systems and particularly the water pumps. It not only resulted in the deaths of many, but also in a massive evacuation program to rehabilitate and resettle over 330000 people from the affected area.

It was a Saturday morning and with spring season having set in Shiraz and family were looking forward to the picturesque long drive through Lvov and across the Russo-Hungarian border at Uzgorod into Hungary and where they would be the guests of the Pakistani Embassy. But unfortunately it all ended up with all of them being quarantined for the next four days inside their rooms at the Government's Intourist Hotel for foreigners in Kiev. Most disappointed was three year old Tojo who was not even allowed to step out into the hotel garden that had a playpen with a large number of gadgets and toys for children of his age to play with.

While Shiraz with his family kept cooling their heels at the Intourist Hotel in Kiev, a BBC report over the radio on the disturbing situation in the Indian state of Punjab on their programme 'Asia Today' got him worried. With the promises that were made to implement the Punjab accord between Rajiv Gandhi and Sant Longowal showing no signs of any tangible progress, the Sikh militants in the State had once again raised the cry for Khalistan. And when they on 29th April, 1986 assembled in thousands at the Akal Takht inside the Golden Temple and unfurled the Khalistani flag there was more trouble for the government. Once again the ugly head of terrorism had surfaced in the state and once again the Hindus and the Nirankaris were being targeted without pity or remorse. In quite a few incidents the Hindus who were traveling in public transport were pulled out of buses and trains and were shot dead mercilessly. There were problems in the neighbouring state of Jammu and Kashmir too where Hindu-Muslim riots had erupted following the unlocking of the Ram Janmabhoomi Temple at Ajodya, and which was followed by the corrupt and communal minded Chief Minister Ghulam Mohammed Shah's resolve to construct a mosque inside the state secretariat at Jammu. The ruthless killings of innocent people in Punjab and the Hindu-Muslim riots in Jammu and Kashmir was also being debated by the Bajwa family who as Sikhs had once again started feeling the heat in the capital city.

"But Pappa, both these subjects of whether it is a mosque or a temple are highly volatile, emotive and very sensitive issues and I wonder why Rajiv Gandhi and Ghulam Mohammed Shah had to rake them up now and at a time when Punjab is still passing through another bad phase of militancy," said Dimpy as she made the usual evening tea for her parents. Dimpy was shortly to appear in her viva and such discussions with her father on current affairs helped her in preparing for the interview.

"Well, before I give my frank opinion, let me first tell you a little more about the Ram Janmabhoomi and the Babri Masjid which are unfortunately very closely linked to one another and thereafter we will try and assess as to why is the Chief Minister of Jammu and Kashmir so keen to have a mosque inside the Jammu Secretariat," said Monty as he pointed out the town of Faizabad in the State of Uttar Pradesh on the atlas to his daughter. "Ram Janmabhoomi as the name suggests is the birth place of Lord Ram and according to the Ramayana, Ram was the seventh avatar and incarnation of Lord Vishnu. Situated on the banks of the River Sarayu it was part of the Kingdom of his father Raja Dashrath, the great Koshala King of Ajodya and according to the Hindus a Ram Temple was constructed at his birth place and it existed there on Ramkot Hill till the Moguls invaded India and demolished it. The place now is an important landmark of Faizabad and both Muslims and Hindus were now laying claims to it. In 1528, the temple was razed to the ground on the orders of the Moghul King Babar and a big mosque was built at the same very site by Mir Baki, Babar's Commander-in-Chief and who promptly named it as the "Babri Masjid" in honour of the Emperor. According to British historians even till the 19th Century, both Hindus and Muslims both peacefully worshipped together at this site and it thus came to be also known as 'Masjid-i-Janmasthan', the

Mosque of the Birthplace. To prevent disputes, the British had even put up a railing to separate the devotees during the hours of worship. While the Muslims prayed inside the mosque, the Hindus had a platform made outside that was known as the 'Ram Chabutara' and they made their offerings at that holy place. This arrangement was working very well till someone after India gained her independence in 1949 discovered an idol of Ram inside the mosque. And whether someone had very cleverly placed it inside, or it came by some miracle it is difficult to say. But all the same from that very day the dispute took a communal overtone with the Hindus and Muslims both claiming it as their own exclusive place of worship. The matter was then taken to court and the government on the contention that since it was a disputed case, a lock was put on it. In 1984, both the Vishwa Hindu Parishad and the Bharatiya Janata Party started a movement for the creation of the Ram Janmabhoomi temple at the disputed site and this gave the issue a new political twist and colour. And it got further politicized recently, when Rajiv Gandhi and his Congress Government at the Centre and in the State of Uttar Pradesh backed the judicial verdict of a district judge who ordered the sealed locks at the disputed structure to be opened to the Hindus. This not only opened the floodgates of political opportunism, but it also reopened the highly contentious issue of the Masjid versus Mandir claim to the site. Taking advantage of that judicial verdict, Rajiv Gandhi who only last year gave in to Muslim pressure in the Shah Bano case, now in order to restore the balance and keep the Hindu voters happy welcomed the opening of the locks," added Monty as he further explained to his daughter on where, how and why the Vishwa Hindu Parishad had now become a force to reckon with.

"The VHP as it was now popularly known was first mooted at a conference of Hindus in Bombay on 29th August, 1964 by MS Golwalkar who was then the supreme head of the RSS, the Rashtriya Sewak Sangh. It was Janamashtami Day, the day of Lord Krishna's birth and Golwalkar's aim was to unite all the Hindus of the world to maintain their identity and work for the cause of 'Hinduvta' and the Hindu religion. In 1966, the VHP was formally launched with Swami Chinmayananda as its first president and the former RSS member SS Apte as general secretary. With its slogan 'Dharma protects those who protect Dharma' and with the banyan tree as its symbol, the basic aim of the organization was to consolidate and strengthen the Hindu society, protect, promote and propagate Hindu values and to keep their Hindu identity intact.In 1984 the Youth Wing of the VHP was founded and it was called 'Bajrang Dal'. It was named after Lord Hanuman the most loyal disciple and follower of Lord Ram. But like in all other religions, the VHP too got gradually politicized when they joined hands with the BJP, the Bhartiya Janata Party and they too had now started making the temple a big issue. And if you personally ask me I think all these are nothing but political gimmicks by the political parties to keep their voters happy and therefore when it comes to buttering their bread they want it buttered on both the sides.On one side by the Muslims and on the other side by the Hindus depending upon the population mix of the various Indian states in general and the districts in particular,"added Monty while cautioning his daughter not to air such views on the subject during her interview by the UPSC board, and to talk about it only in general terms and that to only if asked.

It was on the 15th of May, 1986 when the final results were declared and Dimpy had made it this time with flying colours. She was third on the merit list and now nobody could stop her from becoming a career diplomat. On that same very day Benazir Bhutto who too once aspired to join the Pakistan Foreign Service returned home to her grandfather's house in Karachi. With her now being the sole occupant, 70, Clifton was no longer the same as it was during her father's time, when he was the Prime Minister. But with the tremendous response that she had received on returning to Pakistan, she now had high hopes of stepping into her late father's shoes. There was no doubt that the country was clamouring for a change back to civilian rule and she was confident that given a bit of luck she as the enigmatic leader of the PPP like her dear father would also lead the party to a resounding electoral victory.

But unfortunately Benazir had arrived at a time when Pakistan with three million Afghan refugees on its porous borders was going through the Kalashnikov culture as both lethal weapons and drugs fell into the wrong hands and found its way into the heart of the country and into Pakistan's financial capital and into the hands of hoodlums of the country's largest city Karachi. Moreover, with Zia still at the helm of affairs in Pakistan, the chances of the PPP coming back to power and that to with Bhutto's daughter as the Prime Minister in the new future seemed to be rather far fetched also. But Benazir was confident that with the current mood in Pakistan, the day was not far when the military will be forced to go back to the barracks.

Elsewhere in the Asian subcontinent while the two oil rich nations of Iraq and Iran were still slugging it out, the Russians were also now losing heart fighting the seven party Afghan alliances of the Mujahideen freedom fighters. And though the long drawn out Iran-Iraq war was slowly coming to a stalemate, but America's interest in that strategic oil rich area had also started growing. In 1984 after the US and Iraq officially restored diplomatic relations between the two countries, the CIA had secretly begun to supply Iraq with satellite intelligence and photograps that assisted Saddam's Air Force to conduct bombing raids into Iran. In a highly classified program that had the blessings of President Reagan and his top aides including the Vice President George W Bush, more than 60 officers from the US Defense Intelligence Agency were now also secretly providing detailed information to Iraq on Iran's troop deployment and their likely tactical battle plans with the result that the Iraqi air strikes against Khomeini's forces were proving to be rather effective. Simultaneously by now more sophisticated American arms and equipment had also started pouring into Saddam's army. Thus with covert assistance from the Americans, Saddam Hussein had embarked on a massive militarization drive. With the Reagan's administration policy to assist Saddam, Iraq was now getting whatever military hardware that she wanted and there were also reliable reports that some of the NATO countries like West Germany, Britain, France and Italy were also not only helping Iraq in setting up mass poison gas factories, but they were also providing components for missile development and the funds for the purchase of these deadly weapons was being made through funds that had been freed by the US Agricultural Department's Commodity Credit Corporation. During the early days of the war, with the hard currency being used for the purchase of arms and ammunition by Saddam, there were massive food shortages in Iraq. And in order to prevent Saddam's overthrow and to tide over the food problem, the Americans had given Iraq a loan to buy US grown commodities such as wheat and rice that had been very conveniently under written by the US Commodity Credit Corporation in case Iraq failed to repay it within the stipulated period of three years. That these massive loans were guaranteed by the USCCC was proof enough of America's deep interest in this oil rich region and the fact that by 1986 the loan amount had reached the staggering figure of 600 million US dollars, which would eventually turn bad it seems was not an issue at all. For the US in the war between Saddam's Iraq and Khomeni's Iran, oil rich Iraq had to be sustained at all costs.

"In 1984, the US Vice President George Bush through his personal intervention had got a loan of 500 million U S dollars sanctioned by the federal Export-Import Bank for Iraq to build an oil pipe line and that black gold was now of primary interest to the Americans and the western powers,"concluded Shiraz while completing his brief on the current political scenario in the strategic Gulf region of Asia. "The major worry for the Americans was that Iran should not be allowed to break through the strategic Fao Peninsula because in that case the Islamic revolution would spread to Kuwait and Saudi Arabia and that being also an oil rich area it would spell disaster for the Americans," added Shiraz as a footnote to the well made brief.

By the middle of 1986, as more sophisticated weapons from Charlie Wilson's Israeli connection started arriving for the Afghan Mujahideens through Pakistan, the casualty rate of Russia's 40th Army in Afghanistan also started mounting rapidly. To maintain secrecy, these weapons were given strange and unusual names like the 'Spanish Mortar', and 'Charlie's Horse' etc etc., The Spanish mortar that was fabricated by the Israelis was designed for the Mujahideens to communicate directly with American navigation satellites and bring down very accurate fire within inches of the designated targets. And Charlie's Horse that was named after Charlie Wilson was a mule portable, multi—rocketed device that was capable of playing hell with the Soviet armour and their troops in the open. The American hand held Stinger Missiles were also now in operation and the Soviet Hind helicopters were now feeling the heat too. To keep Zia happy, the Reagan Administration in Washington conveniently turned a blind eye to Pakistan's nuclear program. And with the recent Hindu-Muslim riots in Jammu and Kashmir, and the resurgence of militancy in Punjab, the Pakistani President was now also thinking of exploiting it to his own advantage.

Meanwhile in Bangladesh and following the footsteps of President Zia of Pakistan to remain in power, General Ershad the Chief Martial Law Administrator went one step further by holding parliamentary elections in his country not on a non party basis as President Zia-ul-Haq had done, but by allowing all political parties to contest for it. Though the eight party alliance of the Awami League with some other small parties agreed to participate, the seven party alliance led by the Bangladesh Nationalist Party decided to boycott it. When the results of the election that was held in that month of May gave Ershad's Jatiyo Party an absolute majority with 153 seats, the other parties now started crying foul and accused the Jatiyo Party and Ershad's men in uniform for having rigged the elections. But General Ershad was not the least bothered. He wanted it that way and he got it so that in the forthcoming Presidential election that was due in the month of October-November 1986 there would be no stopping him from being legitimately elected as the President of the country. And all that was required by him was to simply put in his papers as army chief in August and thereafter formally join the Jatiyo Party and be appointed as its chairman and then stand as a civilian candidate and be legally and democratically elected. Fazal Rehman's father-in-law Shamshul Haq who had been closely following the decline in the democratic values of his country and the lust for power by those in uniform eversince the country became independent was horrified, when the results of the parliamentary elections were declared.

"I think we will always remain a banana republic and holding elections in this manner is nothing but a farce and it will get us nowhere. With the martial law still very much in force these elections are a sham and I won't be surprised if the same conditions also prevail during the presidential elections later this year. I am afraid that simply by shedding his uniform, General Ershad will not be doing anybody a favour, because he as President will still be the Commander-in-Chief and the CMLA. And whom are we fooling anyway,' said the retired diplomat with a look of disgust in his face as he discussed the bleak future of Bangladesh with his son-in-law and advised Fazal Rehman to be very careful while signing all papers that may have a direct financial bearing on SAARC matters.

"Yes and this is a very wicked world my son and nobody should be trusted. Do remember that we all are from the same subcontinent and were once from the same stock too, but we are now from different countries and therefore when it comes to making easy money we are all in the same category to",' added Fazal Rehman's mother-in-law Abida Begum as she lovingly fed her grand-daughter Sameera with her favourite prawn curry and rice. Sameera was now eleven years old and had come on her first summer vacation from the International School at Kodaikanal in South India where the food in the hostel was tolerably good, but it was not as tasty like that of her grandmother's fabulous cooking. Opening her mouth wide for another big helping of that delicious and aromatic prawn curry rice, Sameera said.

"Baba you must bring both my grandparents along with you. And when all of come to Bangalore for the SAARC conference then all of you must also promise to visit me in school or else I will not speak to you.' And having given that ultimatum to her father, when Sameera lovingly kissed her grandma on her cheek, and took a promise from her too that she with her grandfather would come to visit her in school there was a big smile on Begum Abida's face.

In the following month of June 1986 and in that scorching heat of summer there were two surprise visitors to the Khyber Pass and to some of the Afghan refugee camps near the Afghan-Pakistan border. The first visitor was the tall and handsome Arab, Osama Bin Laden who had established a guest house in Peshawar for his Arab Mujahideen fighters that was named 'Baitul Ansar'. To this was also linked the Jihad Service Bureau which through its many publications motivated more Saudis and Arabs to voluntarily contribute and take an active part in the fight against the Soviets. Osama had now started his own camps inside Afghanistan that comprised of ex—servicemen from the Egyptian and Syrian armies as also volunteers from the Arab and Muslim World and the forces under his command had also carried out independent operations against the Russians in the general area of Khost. As a Mujahideen leader, Osama with his Jehadi fighters had acquitted himself well and was confident that with the common people's support, the Afghans who loved their freedom would soon have more Russians licking their wounds. As it is the Soviet troops in Afghanistan had suffered very heavy casualties and with rumours that Gorbachev was striving to mend fences with the Americans and bring an end to the cold war, the chances of the Russians withdrawing from Afghanistan in the near future also looked fairly bright. With his big monetary contribution to the Afghan cause and excellent motivational powers and administrative skills, Osama always kept a proper record of all those who had been enlisted, trained, and had seen action. A record of those who excelled and those who died for the cause were also registered. Thus the Al Qaeda which in English meant 'The Base' was now about to be born. The second important visitor to that war torn zone was Charlie Wilson. He was the influential Congressman from the United States who was primarily responsible for the arms supplies to the Mujahideen fighters. He was also the one who was responsible to covertly and through the ISI channels supply the sophisticated Stinger missiles to them. Thanks to Charlie Wilson, Pakistan was not only getting military and economic aid from America, but the Reagan Administration to keep Zia happy had also now chosen to turn a blind eye to Pakistan's nuclear program.

That very day somewhere near the Pakistan-Afghanistan border, Charlie Wilson accompanied by Bearden, the CIA chief in Islamabad was a special guest of the Mujahideen fighters and the ISI. And there was joy written all over Charlie boy's' face when he was presented with the spent grip-stock of the Stinger missile that had shot down the first Russian Hind helicopter inside Afghanistan. As Engineer Ghaffar the man who had fired that missile to knock off the Soviet helicopter gunship narrated his experience and one that had even brought the Commander of the Soviet 40th Army rushing to the scene, Salim Rehman who had accompanied the dignitary was now confident that under the new leadership of a liberal Gorbachev the long drawn out war in Afghanistan may probably soon be over. According to some of the senior commanders of the Mujahideen forces operating deep inside Afghanistan, the Soviet troops were now a demoralized lot. Moreover, with the factional split in the ruling PDPA, President Karmal had been recently deposed and Mohammed Najibullah the former chief of KHAD, the Afghan Secret Police had taken his place.

On 22nd June, 1986 while the Mujaheedins were once again getting ready to take on the Soviets, Shiraz was keenly watching the progress of the 1986 Football World Cup that was being played in Mexico. Too make the event a little livelier he threw a party for a few of his close Pakistani colleagues in Moscow and invited them them to watch the quarter final match between the hosts Argentina and England. With both sides evenly matched it was bound to be very well contested. And to make the party even merrier, Shiraz as usual became a bookie and gave odds at three to one for an England win. However, the condition was that the betting would only be in kind and not in cash and that it would be restricted to a maximum of four bottles of Black Label Skotch skotch whisky per individual. Though Argentina with their prolific striker Diego Maradona was being considered as the strong favourite to reach the next stage, Shiraz however was still banking for a surprise English win. With the in form Gary Linekar heading the goal tally, Shiraz was confident that England would humble the Argentineans this time. Though both the teams had ace players like Maradona and Linekar leading the attack, but this match he knew would be dictated by accurate passing and a solid finish by both the sides.

Both Maradona and Lineker were practically of the same age. Diego Maradona was born on 30th October, 1960 in a shantytown on the southern outskirts of Buenos Aries and had started his professional career with the Argentine Juniors, when he was not even 16 years old. Gary Winston Lineker was born a month later on 30th November at Leicester in England and he too started his football career with the Leicester City at practically the same very age. Both of them had played their first World Cup in 1982, and were now considered as the best strikers in the world. They were both also vying for the Golden Boot and Lineker had already scored five while Maradona had by now only two in his kitty. The last time England won the World Cup was in 1966, while Argentina had already won it twice and the last time was in 1978. The Argentineans were thus going to go all out to get to the finals and win the trophy for a record third time if possible. The match started on a very fast pace, but by half time the score still read England zero and Argentina zero. During lemon time while Shiraz topped up the whisky glasses of his guests, Saira walked in with the other ladies from the kitchen with a massive tray full of chicken lollipops that was beautifully garnished with a big Mexican jalapeno pepper complete with a moustache and a sombrero hat.

"That's little Pique the official mascot for the cup and do enjoy the match," said Saira as another lady guest got the Mahjong table ready in the other room for the ladies to begin their session. The real football action began in the fifty first minute when the mercurial Maradona scored the first goal for Argentina.

"But damn it all that was a clean bloody foul and he used his bloody hands too," shouted Shiraz in sheer disgust as the referee pointed to the centre line for the game to resume.

"Yes I think the referee and the two linesmen were sleeping because the television clearly showed that while trying to head the ball, Maradona very cleverly and deftly had also used his hands," said the First Secretary who too like Shiraz was backing the English team.

"None the less the whistle has been blown and a goal given and it cannot be disputed now," said the others who had wagered their bottles on Argentina. But three minutes later Maradona came up with a real beauty. The five feet five inch Argentinean using his strong legs and low centre of gravity with a complete solo effort had weaved through six English players and having covered an incredible 60 yards had banged the ball into the net.

"Well now there is no dispute at all. It was a golden goal through Maradona's magic and no matter who wins this particular goal is the goal of the century," said Shiraz as he passed the big two litre Black Label bottle around. Though England managed to score one in the eighty first minute through their own hero Lineker, but it was undoubtedly Argentina's day as they moved into the semi finals.

On 29th June for the World Cup Finals between Argentina and West Germany, Monty too hosted a party on the big the terrace of his Defense Colony house in New Delhi. In order to avoid people crowding around the television in his drawing room, Monty for that evening had set up four TV's in the four corners of his big terrace for the grand finals. The invitees that day included besides his own close friends and their families, a few senior bureaucrats from the Defense and Commerce ministries, a couple of serving army officers who were now full Colonels and Brigadiers and who as young officers had served under Monty's late father, and a Deputy Inspector General of Police who was an ex Sanawarian but was a few years junior to Monty in school. The DIG was now on deputation to RAW and was posted in the Cabinet Secretariat. Also invited to the grand party were Monty's Italian tenant and his family from the Italian Embassy.

Though 1986 was declared as the International Year of Peace by the United Nations, but there was hardly any peace neither in India nor in the world. Nonetheless in order to bring in the right atmosphere of friendship at the party, Reeta and Dimpy had hung a giant balloon in the shape of a football with the words 'Football for Peace' boldly written across it. As the giant balloon kept swinging in the gentle summer breeze from atop the Bajwa bungalow, Monty in order to add a little more colour to the party also had a full size 'Pique'made in the style of the Air India Maharajah. This innovative mascot with his hands folded in traditional namaste was kept at the entrance to the terrace for welcoming his guests.

As the two teams took the field, all the guests recharged their glasses and took their seats. One TV corner was exclusively for the children and the teenagers, while the other three were for the adults only. There was no betting generally, but those interested were taking private bets with their friends. Peevee was made in charge of the kiddie's corner and he like Monty was rooting for Argentina. In the first half it was a lackluster performance by the Germans as the Argentineans through a Jose Broun header took the lead. During the interval with Argentina one goal up, when Charu Brar who had especially come all the way from Ludhiana helped himself to another drink at the bar, he got into a business conversation with Monty's Italian tenant. Charu was keen to diversify into the two wheeler market whose sales in India as compared to the sluggish car makers of the Fiat Padmimi and the Ambassador models that were being produced in the country was simply galloping away. Though Charu in partnership with his cousin still had the dealership for the Premier Padmini at Ludhiana, but with the advent of the Maruti car, it was not doing as well as expected. Both the Italian Vespa and the Lambretta scooters when it was first introduced in India in the late fifties and early sixties was a runaway success and Charu was confident that if the Munjal's of Ludhiana could do it, then why couldn't he.

The success story of Mr Brij Mohan Munjal had always fasciniated Charu. In 1944 as a 20 year old, Brij Mohan with his three brothers had come to Amritsar from there village which was now in Pakistan and they had set up a small bicycle component unit. Three years later at partition they moved to Ludhiana which was a major hub of India's bicycle industry and the Munjals soon became one of the country's largest suppliers of cycle parts. In 1952 they went into manufacturing handlebars, front forks and cycle chains and by 1956 with financial help from the Punjab government they had set up their own Hero Cycle factory which was now a household name in India. In 1984, when they tied up with the famous Japanese Honda Company to manufacture and sell their new product which was named as the Hero Honda motorcycle and the first bike rolled out on Baisakhi day 1985, there was no looking back for them thereafter. When Charu narrated the Munjal success story to the Italian, he seemed impressed no doubt and advised Charu that in case he was really keen and serious to do business with the Italians then he should drop in for a drink at his residence the next evening and he would then advise him on how to go about it.

That evening, when the party ended with the Argentina team lifting the cup with a thrilling 3-2 finish against the West Germans and Maradona was declared as the best player of the tournament and the winner of the Golden Ball, Peevee was simply delighted. And to celebrate the event, when Peevee suddenly appeared with a guitar in hand to entertain the guests, everybody was taken by surprise. As he sang some old popular Hindi and English numbers like the way and manner in which Shiraz also often used to, there were tears in Monty and Reeta's eyes. Not only did he have his father's good looks, but the tremendous resemblance of his mannerisims and style of singing too was evident in the 14 year old lad's melodious voice.

On the next evening and with Monty for good company, when Charu Brar at the dot of seven rang the doorbell of the Italian downstairs, both of them were warmly greeted by the host and the hostess who very rightly were expecting them. After a brief discussion as to why the West Germans lost and why the Italians who were the defending world champions made an early exit from the world cup had been taken care off, the host having poured some more red wine into their glasses said.

'Well gentlemen if you want to seriously do business with the Italians then the best and the only away that I can suggest is that you first got to get to know Mr Octavio Quattrochhi. He is a good contact man who knows all the ropes and for he and his family India is now like a second home. He has been here since the mid sixties and I believe knows the Gandhi family well too. But since he is not on the Embassy staff and I hardly know him personally, therefore I am afraid you will have to find somebody else who will be able to introduce the two of you to him,' added the Italian as he called out to his wife to send another chilled bottle of the Italian Chianti Red wine. And as Monty kept enjoying the fruity scent and the dry taste of that 1970 vintage wine, Charu said in all seriousness

"Senor but before we start looking for the right man who will introduce us to Mr Quattrochhi, could you kindly tell us something more about him and the kind of a clout that you say he has with the mandarins in both the North and South Blocks, so that I come fully prepared for the introduction."

"Oh he is now much above all that and he with his clout now only talks to the concerned Ministers and to your young Prime Minister and his Italian wife, and maybe to a few secretaries in the government if need be. In fact the Quattrocchis I am told are now in and out of the Prime Minister's house most of the time, but I am afraid for a proper introduction to that man, you will have to look for someone very influential who is either close to those working inside the PM's house or is a part of the PMO's Secretariat in South Block. And even if you do manage to meet the Qattarocchis casually and get introduced to them in one of the many big social events in the capital where they are now regular as special invitees, that too I am afraid may not be the right place or the right time to do any business talk. But after the introduction if you do get a chance and can take him aside and impress upon him the need to do business with Italy, maybe that would do the trick," said the Italian with a mischievous smile on his face as Reeta walked in with the hot sizzling chicken tikkas and mutton sheek kebabs. Though they were all leftovers from the previous day's party, but these were the Italian's favourite Indian snacks and he made no bones about it.

Later on that very evening itself Monty and Charu drove down to the Press Club on Raisina Road. They were very keen to get some more inputs on the suave Italian businessman from Sicily, and were sure that if anybody knew anything more about Mr Qattarocchi, then it could be only Unni and they were damn well right.

"Don't be bloody crazy, that man is too big for both your damn boots and he does not talk to riff raffs like us. But one thing is for sure and that is if you can get close to him and if he likes you, then you are made boy. But if he does not like you then God help you. Needless to say that he and his wife Maria are very much a part of Delhi's elite creamy layer society and they have the right contacts too. Because in today's world of doing business in India one must first have the right contacts, and the higher the contact the better the business,"said Unni somewhat sarcastically and with a sly wicked smile on his face as he ordered two glasses of the Goan red wine that hardly anybody drank, but that was the only brand of wine that was available in that bar.

"Octavio Quatrocchi was born in Mascali, Catania, Sicily and he had first come to India in the mid 60's as a representative of the Italian Oil and Gas Firm Ente Nazional Indrocarburi, ENI for short. The company was into exploration of oil and gas, but Octavio soon became part of Snamprogetti which was a Milan based multinational company that was involved in engineering and construction of gas supply pipe lines and projects in India. 'It was during Mrs Gandhi's Prime Ministership and particularly so after Menaka was thrown out from Number I, Safdarjung Road and after the Italian 'Bahu' became her favourite, that Octavio and his wife Maria became regulars to the Gandhi household. But now with Rajiv Gandhi as the Prime Minister and Sonia as the first lady, Quttarocchis clout had increased manifold. He could now drop names shamelessly, walk into the offices of Minister's and Secretaries at will and without any prior appointment and also be received like a VVIP. The Italian by now it seems had also made deep inroads into India's lethargic and red tape ridden bureaucratic system. According to some senior bureaucrats in the Indian government who would not even care to even see the man's face if they could help it, the crafty Italian probably now also had his own moles inside the government too and these were basically from among the clerks, personal assistants and section officers working in the various ministries and with the concerned ministers and who for some small personal benefits would keep him informed about the various decisions and notings that were made at the top level and which personally concerned Snamprogettis and Quattrocchis business interests in India. And as a result of which the clever Sicilian was always one step ahead. In fact in one interesting incident, when a senior bureaucrat who had raised certain queries on a project where Quattrocchis and his company Snamprogetti was involved, and the file had been sent to the Minister concerned only a day before, the concerned secretary was himself surprised when the Italian on the very next day dropped in at his office to answer all those queries point wise. This could not have happened unless somebody had leaked it out to him, could it," added Unni as he ordered another large Rum for himself.

The first Indian fertilizer project that was given on a turn key contract to Quatrocchi's Snamprogetti was the IFFCO, the Indian Farmers and Fertilizers Cooperative at Phulpur, and between the period 1975 and now, the man had already bagged six more including the prestigious Rashtriya Chemicals and Fertilizers factory at Trombay. With his incredible success rate in getting contracts in India and that too at such a fast pace, it had people wondering as to who was this man with the Midas touch. There was no doubt that the lavish parties that he and his wife had been throwing for the men and women who mattered in India were now paying him and his company handsome dividends and he was always on the ball. In another interesting case when Haldor—Topsoe, a Danish firm was originally selected to set up the plant at Hazira that was being financed by the World Bank and it ultimately went to Snamprogetti, more eyes were raised. Sighting irregularities in giving the contract to the Italians, the World Bank withdrew its support, but nevertheless the government of India found other sources to finance the project. The name Snamprogetti and Quattarocchi with their Italian and Indian connection had now started making the rounds of the high flying Delhi social circles and as far as contracts were concerned, the Quattarocchi's could do no wrong. And while the Quattarocchi's Gandhi connection became the talk in South Block, the Indin Army Chief was busy in conducting 'Operation Brasstacks.'

While Rajiv Gandhi was happy with the selection of the Swedish Bofors Gun by the Indian Army and was impressed by General Sundarjee's spectacular conduct of 'Operation Brasstacks" that was being conducted as a war game by the Army Chief personally at the highest possible level for the first time in history an in New Delhi's beautifully laid and well maintained Army Cantonment, in Pakistan the rumblings between the Prime Minister and the President of that country had already started being talked about in the open. The Prime Minister of Pakistan, Mohammed Khan Junejo had hardly completed a year plus in office, when the rift between him and President Zia started blowing hot and cold. The unassuming leader from Sind was basically a down to earth man and had his own ideas on how to run the country. He did not want to remain just a puppet and was keen that all those senior military officers who had completed three years or more in the civil departments should now revert back to their service appointments and their places be filled by competent bureaucrats. The Governors of all the four Pakistani provinces were also senior army generals but they had all retired. However, Lt General Akhtar Abdur Rehman the DG ISI was on extension and Junejo was keen to have him replaced. But on this sensitive issue and appointment, Zia put his foot down because the Afghan situation demanded continuity. With Benazir back in Pakistan and the PPP once more regrouping fast as a viable political force under her, Zia needed the Generals to hold his hand. He was after all not only the President of the country but also the Commander-in-Chief and under the eighth amendment he could dismiss the Prime Minister and also abrogate both the National and the Provincial Assemblies at will.

During the first week of August 1986, while the President of Pakistan and his Prime Minister were busy haggling about the correct protocol to be followed during the forthcoming Independence Day celebrations at Islamabad, a group of diehard Sikh militants were planning to take revenge on the man who had ordered 'Operation Blue Star'. On his retirement, General Arun Vaidya had decided to settle down in Pune and he and his wife had just moved in to their new house on 26th May. They were looking forward to a nice peaceful retired life, when disaster struck. On the 10th of August, 1986 at about 10 o'clock in the morning, when the 60 year old ex Army Chief got into his private car and took the wheels with his dear wife beside him, he did not know that he would not return home alive. The couple had gone shopping and the General never realized that he was been tailed and stalked. The lone armed Head Constable from the Pune Police that was provided to him for his personal security was sitting comfortably in the rear seat with his weapon by his side as the car made its way to the Pune Cantonment bazaar. At around 11.30 a.m. while they were on their way back home after shopping and the General slowed down to negotiate a turn at a lonely crossing on the Rajendrasinghji Road that was not very far from the Headquarters of the Indian Army's Southern Command, a red coloured motor cycle came alongside and the man sitting on the pillion seat fired three shots from close range at the General's head and sped away. By the time his wife and the Head Constable realized what had happened, the General's bleeding head had slumped on his wife's shoulder. Having lost control of the vehicle, the car banged against a cyclist who luckily had jumped out at the nick of time and the car came to a halt in front of a compound wall of a nearby bungalow. The man who was responsible for the General's security stopped a matador van that was passing by and rushed him to the Command Military Hospital. Though it was only four kilometers away, but by the time they got to the hospital it was all over. The Sikh militants had taken their revenge.

While the nation wide hunt for the General Vaidya's killers was still on, in Karachi, Pakistan on the evening of 5th of September, 1986 a group of terrorists waited anxiously for the Pan-American flight from Bombay to land. It was Teacher's Day in India that day, when the Pan Am Clipper-73 with the twenty three year old attractive and charming Neerja Bhanot as the chief purser and her all Indian cabin crew of 12 flight attendants and 379 passengers took of from Neerja's home town of Bombay. This was the first time that the Pan Am flight on its Bombay-Karachi-Frankfurt-New York route was utilizing their newly trained Indian cabin crew, and Neerja the girl from Scottish Orphanage High School and St Xavier's College Bombay and a former model was in charge of all of them. She was hoping to be back by 7th September so that she could celebrate her 24th birthday with her dear parents and friends, but that was not to be.

It was very early in the morning, when the Pan Am 747 Jumbo landed at Karachi and it was at around 6 am local time that the passengers from Karachi started boarding the aircraft. Suddenly a van that had been modified to look like an airport security vehicle pulled up near the boarding ramp and four terrorists dressed as Karachi airport security guards stomped up the stairway and into the aircraft. All of them were heavily armed with assault rifles, pistols, hand grenades and belts that were filled with plastic explosives. Seeing them rushing up the stairs and with weapons at the ready, an alert Neeja Bhanot standing at the front doorway immediately over the intercom rattled off the special code to the pilot and his crew who were already inside the cockpit. Before the hijackers could enter the cockpit, thanks to Neerja initiative and presence of mind, the pilot and his flying crew escaped through the emergency hatch inside the cockpit. And it was only minutes ago that Karim Malik with his wife Mehmuda and their son Javed had just seen off their pretty nineteen year old daughter Tarannum. She had boarded the same flight and was on her way to Radcliffe. She had been given admission for the under graduates course and was looking forward to it. Luckily her parents were still at the airport and they were waiting for the flight to take off, when the alarm was sounded. The four hijackers had seized the aircraft alright but there was no crew to fly them to their destination which was Cyprus. The hijackers led by Zayed Hasan Safarini were all from the dreaded Abu Nidal outfit and they really meant business. They wanted to go to Cyprus to seek the release of some of their Palestinian comrades who were being held there and they made their demand in a very aggressive manner by threatening to shoot the passengers if the pilot and his crew did not return or a new crew sent at the earliest. The passengers were a mixed group of mostly Indians, Pakistanis and a few Europeans and Americans. A terrified Tarannum who was sitting near the window seat on the wing tip of the wide bodied aircraft was in tears, when one of the hijackers who was holding Neerja by her hair ordered her and her crew to collect all the passports from the passengers. Neerja Bhanot who was now the senior most crew member showed tremendous fortitude, presence of mind and courage as she told the passengers not to panic and do whatever the hijackers demanded. She knew fully well that it would be the Americans and the Jews who probably would be the first ones to be targeted and she therefore very cleverly while in the process of collecting the 400 odd passports from the passengers, managed to conceal more than 40 American passports by hiding them under a seat. After the passports had been collected, the leader Safarani with gun in hand walked through the aisle, while he kept asking passengers about their nationalities. Meanwhile sitting in the airport lounge while the negotiations with the hijackers and the Pakistan government were in progress, Karim Malik wondered how the four outsiders who were not even Pakistani citizens managed to get through the security gate and on to the aircraft with all their arms and ammunition and that to without being challenged.

"There has to be some collusion with the airport security staff or else how could they just walk in like that. I am sure big money must have changed hands and I hope and pray that no harm will come to the innocent passengers and to my daughter all of whom have been trapped inside and are now being held as hostages," said a visibly shaken Mehmuda as her son Javed brought her a cup of coffee.

"Yes, collusion cannot be ruled, but I think that once the passengers were inside the air craft, the pilot and the crew should not have escaped because they have now left them at the mercy of the hijackers. And I am afraid that under such a situation if the hijackers demands are not met, they may even go on a killing spree," said Karim Malik as he tried to reassure his wife that Muslims in the aircraft were probably safe.

As the hours passed by and with the demands of the hijackers still not being fulfilled, Safarini decided to act. At around 10 am next morning, Safarini pointing his gun at the passengers ordered Rajesh Kumar a 29 year old Indian to come up and stand near the front exit door which was open. Rajesh Kumar who was a naturalized American from California promptly obeyed. When he was told to kneel and keep both his hands behind his head, a shot rang out and his body was kicked out of the aircraft. As the body fell with a big thud on the tarmac, an ambulance was rushed to the scene. But by the time he was taken to the hospital, Rajesh was already dead. By late afternoon, while the negotiations were still on, the airport was packed with the relatives of passengers, the press, the TV and hundreds of onlookers. To Karim Malik it seemed that the authorities were purposely dragging the issue in order to create fatigue and despair among the hijackers who may for their own safety agree to free the passengers and ask for a getaway aircraft to fly them to a safe destination of their own choosing. Or else, there was also a possibility that the aircraft may be stormed by the crack Pakistani commandos during the hours of darkness, but that could prove to be dangerous for the passengers like it did in the case of his dear parents at Malta when the Egyptian commandos thoroughly messed up the operation.

Soon after sunset because of a mechanical failure, when the lights inside the aircraft began to dim and flicker, the hijackers fearing that a commando raid could be very much a possibility, their leader Safarini ordered all the passengers to move to the centre of the aircraft. Luckily for Tarannum who was already in the centre, the crowding around her from all sides and on the two aisles proved to be a blessing in disguise for her. At around 9.30 pm, when the lights went out completely and the aircraft was plunged into total darkness, Safarini gave his signal to the other highjackers to begin the bloody murderous carnage. While he with his buddy stood with guns at the ready facing the passengers from the front and the other two hijackers positioned themselves behind the crowd to the rear, it seemed that the hijackers were determined to carry out a premeditated massacre of the innocent passengers. Soon thereafter the four hijackers said a prayer in Arabic in the praise of Allah and the firing began. As the rat a tat of the automatic gun fire and the bursting of grenades rattled the aircraft from the inside, Neerja Bhanot very courageously opened the emergency exit. The brave young lady could have easily escaped the slaughter, but she stood there like a Joan of Arc to help the passengers get away first. Seeing her defiant attitude, one of the hijackers riddled her with bullets. Clutching her bleeding abdomen, Neerja then went to open the second exit door. Thanks to Neerja's exemplary courage and devotion to duty, only 20 passengers and crew had died. And even though quite a few had been injured, but the majority had lived to see another day and Tarannum Malik was one amongst them too. Though she had escaped unscathed, but she still was in a state of shock as she fell into her mother's arms.

It was on 7th September and on Neerja's 24th birthday that her heartbroken parents together with those of the 12 other Indian crew members who were on that ill fated flight received the coffins of their near and dear ones. Before Neerja's coffin was to be put inside the aircraft at Karachi, a weeping Tarannum with her parents by her side placed a bouquet of flowers on it. She now gave up the idea of going to Radcliffe and wanted to become an air hostess like Neerja. On the 6th of September, when two terrorists from the same Abu Nidal Organization killed 22 and wounded six other Jews inside the Neve Shalom synagogue in Istanbul, it seemed that the United Nation's call to make 1986 a year of peace was a far cry from reality.

While Neerja's body was being readied for cremation in Bombay, a freak accident on that 7th of September, 1986 between a Red Ind-Suzuki motorcycle and a civil truck near Pimpri on the Bombay-Pune highway came as a God sent gift to the Pune police. The two motor cyclists had been thrown off and had received injuries, but the bag that they were carrying had given them away. It contained the arms and ammunition that had killed

General Vaidya. While they were being taken in the police jeep to the Pimpri Police station, the two of them even started shouting slogans of 'Khalistan Zindabad', and kept proudly proclaiming that they were ones who had killed General Vaidya. It was entirely by a stroke of luck that the two killers, Harjindar Singh Jinda and Sukhdev Singh Sukka had been caught, but the militant problem in Punjab was far from over. Both were educated Sikhs and were sill in College, when they teamed up to take revenge on those who had dared to desecrate their holy shrine at Amritsar. With the capture of the two dreaded young Sikh militants, the top sleuths from the Indian Intelligence Bureau now got busy in thoroughly interrogating them. But it was not an easy task. Meanwhile the preparations for the forthcoming SAARC conference at Bangalore with added security were also given top priority.

The SAARC conference at Bangalore was to be held from 15ᵗʰ to !7ᵗʰ November,1986 and with India playing the host, it had to be doubly ensured that security for all the heads of state and for Rajiv Gandhi in particular was full proof. Luckily the three day conference passed of peacefully and to honour his promise to his daughter Sameera, Fazal Rehman with his parents after the conference visited the KIS, the Kodaikanal International School, where Sameera now 12 years old was studying as a boarder in class VII.

The coed school founded by American missionaries in 1901 was now a very prestigious institution for those who could afford it. Situated in the picturesque Palani Hills of the Indian State of Tamil Nadu, the school facing the lake basically catered for wards of very well to do people both from India and from abroad. And as a result of which it had a large number of foreign students from different countries and of different nationalities on its roll. Kodaikanal was also a very popular hill station, where Sheikh Abdullah had once been interned for a while.

Though Sameera was only 12 years old, but her favourites in the school campus was a tall handsome young lad in the senior section by the name of Arjun Rampal and his mother Gwen who was a teacher there. One day, while they were out on a family picnic and Fazal Rehman presented Sameera with a dozen cans of her favourite drink Pepsi Cola that he had brought specially for her all the way from Dhaka because they were not available in India, she was so thrilled and possessive about them that she carefully had them wrapped up in old newspapers and hid them inside her cupboard in the girls dormitory. There were still another ten days for the school to close for the winter vacations and since it was not feasible to share the whole lot with the 500 boys and girls in the school, she had therefore rationed it at the rate of one per day for herself. However, on the day the school finally closed,

Sameera sent the remaining two of them gift wrapped to the Principal with a card that read. 'In honour of Mr Christopher Sinclair, the bright old boy of our school and without whose contribution to Pepsico, life would have been such a big bore.'

Christopher Sinclair an American whizkid who though he was born in Hong Kong on 5th September, 1950, had spent his childhood in Bombay and was educated at KIS. Off late as a head honcho of Pepsi Foods and Beverages he was in the thick of battle with his ace rival Coca Cola. The Cola War in America was at its height, but under Sinclair, and the Pepsi campaign that it was the drink of the new generation, Coke it seems had lost out temporarily. No wonder Sameera and others like her from the KIS were indeed very proud of this particular ex-student's achievements.

Though Fazal Rehman's in-laws and the children were very keen to visit other cities and tourist spots in South India before returning back to Dhaka from Bangalore, but because of the ethnic conflict in Sri Lanka that had now rolled over into Tamil Nadu, Fazal Rehman for the sake of their own safery had to put his foot down.

"The influx of Tamil refugees by the thousands from the Northern and Eastern parts of Sri Lanka into southern India, and with some of them being heavily armed, the law and order situation had deteriorated considerably and it was therefore not worth taking any chances," said Fazal Rehman as he narrated to his in—laws certain confidential facts that were discussed during the SAARC conference on this very issue by Rajiv Gandhi and JR Jayawardhene, the heads of the two countries who were directly affected by it. Fearing that the Sri Lankan President could well be targeted by the militant Tamil groups who had been given asylum in India, the security during the SAARC meeting at Bangalore had been boosted up considerably. According to Indian intelligence agencies after the failure of the Thimpu talks between India and the rebel Tamil leaders of Sri Lanka in September 1985, the variousTamil militant groups like the LTTE, TELO,EROS, EPRLF and PLOTE had started functioning independently and they had now become a law unto themselves in the state.

On 1st November, 1986 Diwali Day and a fortnight prior to the opening of the SAARC conference at Bangalore, the EPRLF militants clashed with the local public in Madras and which resulted in the death of one civilian and injury to others. On that same very day there was another shoot out in a village in the Thanjavur District of the state, and this time the militants were from PLOTE. Therefore as a sequel to these incidents there were orders from the PMO directly to M.G.Ramachandran, popularly known as MGR, the

Chief Minster of the state that in view of the SAARC meeting at Bangalore, the militants in the state must be disarmed immediately. Though this was a tall and difficult order, but it was carried out diplomatically and successfully by the DGP of the State Police K. Mohandas on the 8th of November. It was a topsecret operation code named 'Operation Tiger' and was known only known to the Chief Minister of the state and his DGP.

"In order to work out a fair deal between the two warring sides that would be acceptable to both the sides, the two LTTE leaders at the behest of Rajiv Gandhi were summoned to Bangalore from Madras. Both Prabhakaran and his advisor Balasingham arrived by a special Indian Air Force aircraft and secret talks were held. When the talks failed and Prabhakaran returned to Madras, the Chief Minister of the State, MGR was lived and he in no uncertain terms told the LTTE supremo that he either played according to his, MGR's rules since it was his government that had permitted him to operate from Tamil Nadu, or else he should go back and fight for Tamil Eelam from his own country. The proud LTTE leader it is rumoured is therefore now planning to go back to Jaffna," added Fazal Rehman while deciding to spend two more days in Mysore in order to see the famous Brindawan Gardens and the Mysore Palace before flying back to Dhaka.

"Baba, this place is really like a fairyland," said a delighted Sameera as she watched with awe the burst of dazzling colours from the many dancing fountains as they in rthymic waves twirled and twisted to the delight of the huge weekend crowd. A little while later on hearing that age old song 'Jawan Hai Mohabat' from the vintage 1946 hit film 'Anmol Ghadi', that was being played by a picnic party on a cassette deck, an excited Samina immediately joined them. The picnic party was celebrating their grandparents' fiftieth wedding anniversary. This particular song was also her parent's favourite in the good old days, when they got married and which was only a few days before the country was partitioned in 1947. While Shamshul Haq and Abida Begum stood there silently listening to that haunting number of yesteryears, they sincerely felt that India instead of being divided should have remained as one homogenous entity.

But as the year 1986 which the United Nations had declared as the'International Year of Peace,' came to a close, the chances of peace and universal love that was so badly required in the troubled subcontinent was still nowhere in sight. Though there was a slight thaw in the Cold War posture of the two super powers when in order to stop the nuclear arms race, the two world leaders met in mid October at Reyjavik, the capital of Iceland and generally agreed that parity and equality in the deployment of strategic long range ballistic missiles must be maintained by both sides meticulously, but the tentacles of terrorism in the world had also started spreading its wings. There was no doubt that the agreement between the Soviets and the Americans on the arms issue had definitely ignited a ray of hope to make the world a safer place and eliminate each other's devastating first strike capability, but the proliferation and the use of the weapons of mass destruction falling into the hands of some unscrupulous and mad fanatical elements could not be totally ruled out.

CHAPTER-4

Tremors in the Subcontinent

While President Reagan and his Secretary of State for Defense, George Schultz on their return from Reykjavik were lauding over their success at the Iceland summit, another bombshell of an arms for hostage scandal shook the Reagan administration. On the 3rd of November, when Shiraz in Moscow read an article in the Lebanese newspaper Ash-Shhira that the United States had been selling weapons to Iran in order to secure the release of several American hostages who were being held by the pro-Iranian Hezbollah group in Lebanon, he simply did not believe it.

"I think this is all bloody bullshit because till now it was Saddam Hussein's Iraqis who were and still are I guess the main beneficiaries of American arms and ammunition in their fight against Iran. And now according to this Lebanese reporter it is the turn of the Iranians to be at the receiving end of this lethal largesse, but I just do not understand why ?" said Shiraz as he helped Saira to clean up the dishes.

"But this is nothing unusual as far as America is concerned. Please do not forget that a similar deal was struck by the same American President, when on the day of his inauguration in January 1980, all the staff members from the American Embassy in Teheran who were for months together being held as hostages in Iran were released by Khomeini in return for all the Iranian assets that had been frozen by the earlier Carter administration and that amount must have been in billions of dollars I am sure. And that sudden windfall and at that critical juncture also helped the Iranians in a big way to keep the war going against the Iraqis," replied Saira as she called out to her daughter Gammy to switch off the TV and to go to bed. Gammy thanks to the part time Russian maid who worked in the house was now quite fluent in the Russian language and she enjoyed the evening finale of the popular nightly children's program that was titled "Spakoinie Nochi'. The special programme of fables titled 'Good Night Children' was telecast

103

at 8 PM Moscow time everyday and it invariably had a good moral story to convey to all the children who loved watching it.

That Lebanese magazine was not very wrong, when on 25th November, 1986 President Reagan probably feeling guilty, admitted at a packed White House news conference that the funds derived from covert arms deals with the Islamic Republic of Iran had been diverted to buy weapons for the United States backed Contra rebels in Nicaragua. That statement by the American President now led to a bigger political and constitutional scandal than the Nixon Watergate affair. Hearing about the scandal that had exploded in the face of the Americans on TV that evening, Shiraz too was shocked.

"I think the Americans should never be trusted. With their money power and clandestine arms deals, they have I think gone a bit too far in implementing the Reagan Doctrine, which provides both overt and covert aid to anti—communist resistance movements not only in Nicaragua, but also in all Soviet backed governments in Asia, Africa and also in Latin America. And if Reagan thinks that his roll back policy will diminish the Soviet influence in these regions and open the door for democracy, then I am afraid he is sadly mistaken. He could not do it as yet in Vietnam, Libya, Iran or even for that matter in our own neighbourhood of Afghanistan and if he thinks that as and when the Soviets finally quit from Kabul; that nation will embrace democracy then he is being utterly stupid. I think this big brother attitude of the Americans to interfere and dictate what is good for which country must stop or else one day they will themselves have to face the music of terrorism and guerilla war at their own very doorstep, and Nicaragua is not very far from the the United States of America either,"said Shiraz as he helped Gammy with her homework.

On the next day, when Shiraz gave out his own assessment and appreciation of the fallout that this shameful Iran-Contra affair may have internally on the Reagan administration to his own Ambassador, His Excellency was highly impressed. According to Shiraz, the two masterminds behind the deal, Lt Colonel Oliver North, an NSC staffer and his boss John M Poindexter the National Security Advisor it seems were now in real big shit and the possibility of both of them being asked to quit by the President was now very much on he cards. This would undoubtedly save the President's own skin provided both of them did not in any way drag the President's consent into it. However, the two of them may be indicted if they were found guilty for the cover up was now also being hotly debated. But as far as Manuchehr Ghorbanifar was concerned, the middleman who brokered the arms deal to bring about the release of the American hostages that were being held by the Iranians in Lebanon, he will probably get away scot-free, while others like the Attorney General Edwin Meese, Richard Cheney, Robert Gates who instead of getting to the truth were it seems now more interested in protecting their own President. And all of them for their so called loyalty and if luck holds out they will probably be rewarded at some later opportune moment, 'added Shiraz as His Excellency invited him and Saira for cocktails the next day at his residence.

On returning home that evening and to satisfy himself that his own assessment on the Iran-Contra affair was factually correct, Shiraz while sitting late that night jotted down date wise whatever little he knew from his own sources about that murky deal that had put even the all powerful American President on a tailspin. It all began on 1st December, 1981, when President Reagan put his signature to the CIA sponsored paramilitary operations against Nicaragua and his government's support to the Contra rebels to overthrow the communist oriented Sandinista government. With the ever increasing Congressional opposition to the plan, both President Reagan and his Vice President, George Bush on 25th June 1985 with their close aides discussed a method on how to sustain the Contra war by circumventing Congressional power to curtail the CIA's paramilitary operations. They then came to the conclusion that it could be done by funding the operation with money coming through some of those countries that were friendly to the U.S. In spite of the fact that getting money from third countries for such a covert operation would be an impeachable offence and as was argued by the Secretary of State George Shultz, the Vice President Geeorge Bush intervened to say that it would be impeachable only if the US promises to give these third parties something in return for the money and not otherwise. And thus the green signal to the deal was given. On 16th March, 1985, Lt Colonel Oliver North in a comprehensive memo to Robert Macfarlane, the National Security Advisor had proposed a plan for approaching key donor nations like Saudi Arabia, Brunei and others for more funds to sustain the Contras who were operating against the Sandinista regime in Nicaragua from bases inside neigbouring Honduras. Then came into the picture Ghorbanifar the weapons broker and he managed to persuade the senior officials of US, Iran and Israel to utilize his expertise as a middleman in the arms for hostage deal. Thereafter, there were six covert arms transactions with Iran and the most controversial of these was the November 1985 shipment of 18 HAWK anti aircraft missiles, which was done without the required written Presidential sanction that was mandatory. In order to cover the lapse, the President signed it retrospectively on 5th December, 1985, but during the cover up and just before the scandal erupted, Poindexter in order to spare any further political embarrassment to the President had torn that crucial evidence up. Two days later on 7th December, 1985 President Reagan convened an extraordinary meeting of his top aides and advisors at the White House family quarters. When the question of shipping arms to Iran came up for discussion, both Casper Weinberger the Secretary of State for Defense and the Secretary of State, George Schultz were against the idea, but it went through because President decided that he could answer charges of illegality to his own people, but he could not forsake the chance of freeing the American hostages that were being held by the Hezbollah in Lebanon. The US now took direct control of the arms deals with Iran. Heretofore Israel was being used as the conduit for the delivery on the understanding that their stocks of American weapons and ammunition would be replenished. And finally when the lid was blown by the Lebanese newspaper, it not only tarnished the image of the American President who all this time had been advocating his long standing policy against dealing strongly with terrorists, but it also became very clear to Shiraz and others that the Americans to safeguard their own interests were capable of doing anything and everything possible. But the deal only paid of partly, when only three out of the 30 hostages were released.

Lt Colonel Oliver Laurence North popularly known as 'Ollie' who was the key figure in the Iran-Contra scandal was born on 7th October, 1943. He grew up in Philmont, New York and was commissioned as a Second Lieutenant from the United States Naval Academy in 1968. He was a career officer in the US Marine Corps and had served in Viet Nam where for his gallantry he was awarded the Silver Star, Bronze Star and two Purple Heart Medals. An alumnus of the Naval War College in Newport, Rhode Island, he attended the Cammand and Staff Course and graduated from there in 1981. Immediately thereafter on promotion to Lt Colonel, he was posted to the National Security Council. His troubles began when an over enthusiastic 'Ollie' overstepped his authority and started showing undue haste in finalizing the Iran-Contra deal. With the sale being made public now, he was fired by the President and was now waiting to testify before the Joint Congressional Committee on the Contra-Iran Deal that was soon to begin its hearings.

"I think some of them including poor Ollie are being made scapegoats, because such major decisions involving nations like the US and Iran who are supposed to be at logger heads with each other cannot be taken by such low ranking junior officers. I therefore feel that there is much more to it than what meets the eye and both President Reagan and Ayatollah Khomeini must be deeply involved in this so called murky affair," said Shiraz while enjoying his favourite 'Gaajar Ka Halwa" that was tasty no doubt, but not as tasty as Bibiji's.

"Yes and while Iran needs the weapons to fight Iraq, the Americans want to contain Communism by arming the Contras in Latin America, the UNITA rebels in Africa and the Mujahideens in Afghanistan and elsewhere, but they themselves do not want to go and fight," remarked Saira while feeling happy for her husband's promotion. Shiraz was now being posted as Minister and the Number 2 man in the Pakistani Embassy in Stockholm, Sweden and he was required to take up the new assignment by the first week of January, 1987.

While Shiraz and Saira were looking forward to their new posting that both of them knew would be far less stressful, the sectarian violence in Karachi had taken a very ugly turn. With drugs and weapons freely available in plenty it was like a daily mini civil war as the Pakhtuns and the Mohajirs with vengeance got at each other's throats. But that was not all and there were now reports that even women were not being spared. The news that women at the Karachi University Campus were being attacked by unknown assailants with lethal acid sprays was even more alarming. Dr Jameel Jalibi, the Vice Chancellor of the University who had earlier tried to suppress the news was also in a quandary. The assailants were using syringes and were spraying the deadly acid on the backs of innocent victims. This kind of a thing had never happened before.

"My God I wonder where will all these lead to," said a worked up Saira as she read about the bloody violence in the latest issue of the Pakistan Times in which it was reported that 70 people had been killed in the sectarian brutality in Karachi alone on the 15th of December. But as the year 1986 came to a close, what was now of even greater worry to Zia and Pakistan was the unusual massing of Indian troops along the Indo-Pakistan border and especially so in the desert region of Rajasthan. Though the Indian Government had notified Pakistan well in advance about the major military exercise that was being conducted by the Indian Army as a sequel to Brasstacks-1, Zia and his Generals were worried that with the continuing unrest in Sind, this could well be a pretext for India to cut Pakistan to size further. Therefore as a precautionary measure, he as the Commander-in-Chief issued orders to all his Corps Commanders and also to the Naval and Air Force Chiefs to be on full alert. As a consequent of which Pakistani units and formations had now come in eye ball to eye ball contact with the Indian forces deployed all along the Indo-Pak border, and the chances of another round between the two adversaries therefore could not be ruled out.

On the 31ˢᵗ of December 1986, while the Indian and Pakistani troops were ready to trigger off another war, Monty gave his wife a very unusual New Year's gift. On the advice of his builder friend from Bombay, he had very wisely purchased Rupees Ten thousand worth of Convertible Debentures in the recently floated Reliance issue in her name and was confident that with Mr Dhirubhai Ambani's business brain that amount would multiply at a very fast pace. The people's confidence in the man and his company was so very high that when the issue closed, the Indian public had contributed Rupees seven hundred crores though Dhirubhai's requirement was only Rupees one hundred and thirty two crores. The mega response by the public was a clear referendum to the man who always believed in sharing his profits with his share holders and who made them also proudly feel that they too were a part of his ever expanding business empire. Monty however felt sad that the financial genius from Gujrat who had suffered a paralytic stroke in February was also now being attacked and hounded by Mr Ram Nath Goenka and his newspaper 'The Indian Express'. According to insiders this had now become a dirty battle between Nusli Wadia and Dhirubhai because both were in the same business of manufacturing the raw material that was required for making the polyester yarn and fibre.

And while the Ambanis and the Wadias were getting into a legal battle, there was good news for the general public of India. In a historic move in that very year, the Chief Justice of India, PN Bhagwati and Justice VR Krishna Iyer of the Supreme Court had ruled that any Indian citizen, big or small, rich or poor, or for that matter any social action and consumer group could now file a PIL, a Public Interest Litigation in the Supreme Court of India and seek legal remedies in all cases where the interests of the general public or a section of the public were at stake. This was undoubtedly a landmark ruling and Monty felt happy that henceforth at least people who were not accountanble for their actions in the past would think twice before acting in an arbitrary manner.

With the advent of another year that signaled 40 years of independence for both India and Pakistan, it now seemed that the two countries were getting ready for the fourth round and that to in real earnest. As India with the deployment of two armoured divisions supported by infantry and air power continued with Operation Brasstacks-2 to test her offensive capabilities, alarm bells in Pakistan had started ringing. Therefore in response to India's aggressive posture, Zia too ordered his two armoured divisions to move close to the Indo-Pak border in the Punjab and along the neigbouring frontier with Jammu and Kashmir.

It was mid January, 1987 while tempers on the Indo-Pak borders were still high that Monty with Reeta and Peevee decided to make it by road to Sanawar, and while they were on their way they got caught in a massive traffic jam on the busy Grand Trunk Road near Ambala. The army it seems was carrying out their military manouevres and they obviously had first priority to that strategic and important road link. So when they were stopped and they saw the huge convoys of armoured tanks and armoured carriers on trailers moving at a fairly good speed and overtaking them, they did not mind it at all. But when an excited Peevee waved out to the jawans and said rather loudly 'Agar Mauka Mile is baar tho Salon Pakistan walon ko mere naam se khub acchi dhulai karna, ta ki unko unka Nani yaad ajaye.', (If you get the opportunity this time, then give those bloody Pakistanis such a bloody nose that they will remember their grandmothers). On hearing that coming from the 15 year old, an angry Reeta said. "Come on Param Veer that is not the way one should talk to people. I can understand your feelings of patriotism, but you could have used better polite and parliamentary language in expressing your thoughts, and this certainly is not the way a Sanawarian behaves!" Seeing Reeta so very upset, Peevee immediately apologized and said "I am very sorry Mom." And once the road was again re-opened to the general public and Monty turned towards the link road to Chandigarh, Reeta said to Monty.

"With the bulk of the army now deployed on our borders, and with train services being disrupted for the induction of more troops to the already volatile Punjab, do you really think that there will be another war?'"

"Well atleast not to my knowledge or else by now both the Americans and the Russians would have been breathing down our necks, and by now they would have definitely intervened diplomatically. But since that hasn't happened, I think this is only saber rattling by both the sides. Though Gorbachev did visit India recently, but that was only a courtesy call and was basically to cement the already existing close friendship ties between the two nations. However he did also give India a 1.2 Billion Dollar loan on generous terms and also agreed to sell the latest and sophisticated MIG-29 fighter bombers to us, but that was probably to withhold our government's criticism of the Soviet intervention in Afghanistam. Moreover, neither India nor Paksitan with all their internal problems, both domestic and economic can really afford to take on one another at this juncture, and it would be rather stupid of them if they do so. As it is Rajiv Gandhi's charisma as a political leader and a man in a hurry to change the face of India is slowly evaporating thanks to people like his cousin Arun Nehru and such like others who unfortunately it seems were giving him wrong advice and that indeed is another sad story And though the Prime Minister has now dropped this cousin of his from his cabinet and has realized that he cannot afford to alienate the old guard in the party and has therefore reconciled with Mr Sharad Pawar and Farouk Abdullah, but he also knows fully well that if he has to survive, then a policy of co-existence with the old party potentates is the only answer for him. In fact his popularity today is no longer what it was two years ago. It has taken a big nose dive and people are also losing confidence in him. With the accord in Punjab having failed miserably and his much touted economic reform programme being sabotaged by the bureaucrats and the 'Babus' who are simply delaying the regulations by adding more red tape to the already cumbersome method of getting licenses so that their earning from bribes do not dry up, I really feel pity for the poor chap. His intentions and ideas are no doubt very good and noble, but he must also deliver," added Monty as they stopped for lunch at a roadside 'Dhaba' near the foot hills.

On their return journey from Sanawar, Monty and Reeta decided to stay a few days with Charu Brar and his family at Ludhiana. While they were the there for those three days, Punjab it seems was back to square one. With the rift in the ruling Akali Dal, the five high priests of the Golden Temple with the support of the SGPC President G.S. Tohra and backed by the separatists and secessionist elements from within the party were now demanding the resignation of the Chief Minister Surjit Singh Barnala. The local villagers close to the border were also cursing the Indian Army for ruining their fields. Fearing that there could be another war; quite a few had also vacated their homes near the border and had sought refuge in the interior. Analysing the current situation in Punjab, Charu's father, retired Brigadier Brar who was aware that the presence of the army in the state was only part of the large scale 'Operation BrasssStacks-2" exercise that was being conducted by the Indian Army and that it had nothing to do with hunting for Sikh militants said.

"You know it is indeed rather unfortunate and sad that our so called political leaders of today both at the centre and in the states have a one track mind and that unfortunately if I may add very candidly only spells out the fact that this bloody country can go to hell, but the the politicians must remain on their bloody chairs and go on forever. In fact politics or 'Rajnithi' as they say in Hindi has today become a family profession of corruption and of corrupting people at all levels of society. It is now a lucrative business where scruples, integrity, honesty and loyalty are not only a thing of the past, but the less one has of these qualities, the more are the chances of getting to the top. Because with money, family ties and in the name of religion, most of them are only exploiting the poor and the illiterate for there own personal gains. Because in this country and even after forty years of so called freedom, it is the poor and the illiterate who still constitute the majority and they are therefore the real vote bank for these blood suckers. And as far as you and I are concerned we form the minority middle class and our votes hardly count. Therefore and unless we give priority to education and literacy in this country, and rope in good and honest leaders, this sad situation I am afraid will continue and I wont be the least surprised if tomorrow you find goondas and history sheeters ruling over us. By dragging in religion into politics, introducing caste factors wherever and whenever it suits their needs, these so called 'Netas' are actually making a mockery of democracy. The need today is to eradicate poverty, eliminate caste politics and make people aware that first and foremost they are Indians with equal rights and privileges and that they cannot simply be taken for a ride with catchy slogans and false promises at election time. I am not saying that the average Indian voter is stupid or totally ignorant of what is happening around him, but he is today being exploited by all and sundry. Look at our so called city corporators for example. Most of them are school dropouts who as sychophants hang on to the tail of their political masters as slaves, and then gradually graduate as MLA's, MP's and Ministers to fill their own pockets, while all the time shouting corruption hatao and garibi hatao. In fact some of them for their gross misdeeds and misdemeanors in public life should be lined up and shot if you ask me and then only probably the system may change for the better or else we will have to keep on suffering and live through it as muted spectators. It should be realized that no matter how powerful one may be militarily, but it is the economic power of a nation that dictates who is strong and who is weak. Had that not been the case, then Mr Gorbachev today would not be talking about restructuring, openness and corruption in what was once the powerful Soviet Union," added Brigadier Brar the veteran Second World War hero while cautioning his son Charu to keep away from Punjab politics.

In the last week of January, as tensions along the long Indo-Pak border kept mounting, in a rather surprise move the Prime Minister Rajiv Gandhi shifted VP Singh who was his Minister of Finance to the Defense Ministry. Defense was till then being looked after by the Prime Minister and his old buddy from Doon School Arun Singh, and this sudden changeover in the midst of a serious border crisis that could have led to a war with Pakistan surprised all political Pundits in the country. Therefore in order to find out why and what was the reason for this untimely shift, Monty as usual called on his old trusted friend Unnikrishnan at the Press Club.

"Well according to what I have heard my friend is that the two of them, that is the the Prime Minister and the erstwhile Finance Minister who is now the country's new Defense Minister have off late not been pulling on very well with each other. And the reasons are manifold, but the main one being that VP Singh as the Finance Minister had started probing deep into some of the fertilser contracts that had off late been given to that slimy Italian Qattarochhi and his company Snapprogetti. In fact in one of his notings I believe VP had even asked for an explanation from the secretary concerned as to why Snamprogetti which had over quoted was still being considered for a particular contract and Rajiv I am told had overruled it. Then there was this question of acquiring the Westland helicopters from the United Kingdom and on that too I am told VP had some serious objections, but Rajiv Gandhi as PM decided to exercise his final authority over it. V.P. Sngh had also started confronting the big business houses and some top industrialists with raids and tax evasion charges by the income tax and revenue authorities and these were powerful people who funded the party. When they complained to Rajiv of harassment, Rajiv then decided to shift him to Defense. But knowing Mr VP Singh's character and his nature of probing into high profile deals while he was in the Finance Ministry, I don't think he will last very long in Defense either. Because now that he is incharge of Defense where military arms deal runs into millions, and which the country can ill afford, he will be yet another spoke in the wheel. And knowing fully well that the man with royal blood who is believed to be straight forward and honest, I don't think he will survive in that chair either," added Unni as he give a short brief on the man whom he perceived to be an exception to the rule.

"Born on 25th June 1931, Viswanath Pratap Singh is the adopted son of Raja Bahadur Ram Gopal Singh of Manda. He was educated at Allahabad and Poona Uniiversities and he came into politics as a young student leader soon after India got her independence. In 1957, he actively participated in the Bhoodan Movement of Acharya Vinobha Bhave and had even donated a well established farm in village Pasna, in Allahabad District to the noble cause of land to the landless. He was an experienced politician with a clean image and had served creditably under Mrs Gandhi as a junior minister in her cabinet. In June1982, he was appointed the Chief Minister of India's largest state, Uttar Pradesh but resigned two years later on moral grounds for not being able to eradicate the dacoit menace in his state. In January 1983, he became the Union Minister for Commerce and after Mrs Gandhi's death, Rajiv on 31st December 1984 appointed him as the country's finance minister. Though a Rathore Rajput from a large Zamindari family of Manda in Uttar Pradesh, VP as he was commonly known is basically a man of principles and one who is not afraid of calling a spade a spade if need be. But then these qualities of morality, rectitude, decency and integrity etc etc or whatever one may call them will one day lead to his own downfall, because such men are misfits in the murky world of Indian politics today,' added Unni as he snapped his fingers at the barman and with his usual broad smile ordered another round of drinks for Monty and himself. This was Unni's fourth large gin with bitters and Monty being aware that the man's habit of talking more and more with every additional peg would soon turn into a monologue, he therefore very cleverly on the pretext that there were visitors waiting for him at home, excused himself and left.

During that winter of 1987, while Indian and Pakistani troops sat facing each other eyeball to eyeball on the border, the Pakistani cricket team touring India kept tensions low as the five match test series between the two rival sides got under way. And it got a further boost when President Zia expressed his desire to watch the first day's play during the third test match that was to begin at the Sawai Mansingh Stadium in Jaipur from the 21st of February. Responding positively to Zia's request and to allay all fears and doubts that 'Exercise Brasstacks 'was only a high level training event and that India had no intentions whatsoever of starting a war, the Indian Prime Minister Rajiv Gandhi too decided to give the President of Pakistan good company during the match.

"That is what I call good cricket diplomacy," said Monty as he with all his Sanawarian friends decided to drive down to Jaipur for the first day's play. All of them were very keen to see what Zia-ul-Haq looked like in real life and Peevee who was on his winter vacations from Sanawar also expressed his desire to tag along with them

"Sure and may be he will give you his autograph too, but you will have to be really clever to get close to him because the security undoubtedly will be very tight and though our seats are right next to the pavilion, but you will have to use all your ingenuity to get in there," said Charu Brar somewhat jokingly as a delighted Peevee hugged his father and said.

"Don't worry Dad, you just wait and watch, and I will not only get General Zia's autograph, but that of our own handsome Prime Minister too."

With security being very tight and despite the fact that they all had reserved seats in the first enclosure next to the members stand and the pavilion, Monty with his friends and Peevee reached the stadium an hour and a half in advance. Though Peevee was only 15 years old, but he with his good height, strong built and handsome features looked every inch like a young college going student. Before entering the stadium Peevee bought himself a souvenir book that had all the photograps of the two teams together with their cricket statistics and a scorecard. He had also brought along with him from home two small newspaper cut-outs of the Pakistani President and the Indian Prime Minister, a bottle of gum, two minature flags of both the nations that he had made himself and a green ball point pen. Having neatly pasted the photographs of the two VIP's on the scorecard, he fixed the Pakistani flag in Rajiv's hand and the Indian tricolour in President Zia's hand and then wrote below it boldly in green colour and in block capital letters 'Cricket for Peace and May Both Sides Win'.

And in order to try and somehow get an entry into the pavilion, Peevee had therefore come prepared to look like a budding state level cricketer. Dressed in white flannels and with proper cricket boots and a blue blazer to go with it, he decided to take a chance and to somehow get inside the VIP enclosure. Normally on such big matches a few of the promising cricketers at state level were detailed for VIP duties inside the main pavilion, but for that a proper volunteers badge, a security cleared identity card and a rosette was required and this was only possible if he could find someone who would be willing to part with it for a premium and for which was Peevee was prepared to shell out a maximum of a hundred rupees that was inside his purse. The second alternative was to get in as a press correspondent or a press photographer, but for that he still required a proper press accredition card. Finding no luck with the a few state level cricketers that he had approached, Peevee now waited for the press party that was scehduled to arrive from Delhi by a special bus anytime. And as soon as it arrived, Peevee posing as if he was part of the reception committee for the press welcomed all of them and then offering his services as a helper to carry the heavy video camera equipment of one of the cameramen from Doordarshan, he very confidently and boldly walked inside with him. Soon he found himself on the open ground and in the company of the policemen who had been put on duty near the VIP enclosure. A few minutes later and just before the VVIP's were about to arrive, and while all the press people with their cameras got ready to shoot the event, Peevee quietly took a seat in the press enclosure inside the main pavilion.Once the formal introductions to the two teams were over, and the VVIP's were back in their seats, Peevee felt a lot more relieved. The match started disastrously for India, when their star player Sunil Gavaskar was caught by Javed Miandad to the bowling of Imran Khan for a duck. But thereafter with some sensible batting by Srikanth and Mohinder Amarnath with the score reading at the first drinks break at 45 for one, Peevee with full confidence walked up to the Pakistan President's ADC and requested him if he could help in getting him an autograph on the special scorecard that was made by him and at anytime that was convenient to the visiting VIP. Then realizing that his movements were being tracked by the many security men in their typical safari suits who were hovering around the place, Peevee made a quick exit and returned back to his original seat next to his father in the neigbouring enclosure. His gallant effort however it seems had failed, when he saw the Pakistan President with a broad grin on his face and with his entire entourage making an exit from the ground.

While on the return journey, when Peevee talked about his failed attempt in getting the Pakistani President's autograph, Monty was very upset. "But you must never do such foolish things. It is very dangerous. Even letters carry bombs these days and I must say you have been very lucky to get away, or else you could have have been hauled up for breach of security and there would have been hell to pay. By your folly, not only you, but all of us would have been in deep trouble explaining to the police, but thank God the ADC was a decent guy and he did not report the matter," said Monty as Charu Brar in order to diffuse the tension very aptly started to sing loudly one of his old favourite songs "Mera Prem Patra Padh Kar, Tum Naraz Nahona' ("Please don't be upset by reading my love letter). It was from the famous 1965 Raj Kapoor film 'Sangam'and Charu was indirectly referring to Peevee's bright idea of promoting Indo-Pakistani friendship through cricket.

Though the short Zia-Rajiv cricket diplomacy did diffuse the tension on the Indo-Pak border, but in the Ministry of Defence in New Delhi's South Block tensions were running high. Unni's prediction was damn well right, when a couple of weeks later, the Defense Minister ordered a probe into a big defense deal. It all began, when VP Singh received a telegram from the Indian Embassy in Bonn which stated that the firm HDW, the well known ship builders at Kiel from whom India had ordered a few submarines were unwilling to bring down their prices on the plea that they were required to pay a 7% commission to an Indian agent on the deal. According to Unni, VP Singh was called by the Prime Minister to his office and when Rajiv showed his displeasure for holding an enquiry into that matter, VP Singh on 12th April decided that enough was enough and he put in his papers and decided to resign from the cabinet. The rift got further aggravated, when VP Singh further ordered an inquiry into Ajitabh Bachchan's business dealings. The Bachchans and the Gandhis were very close family friends and Ajitabh's elder brother the more famous Amitabh who at the behest of Rajiv had joined politics and had become a Member of Parliament from Allahabad I believe also felt rather embarrassed. VP Singh was therefore politely told to reconcile to the issue and an offer I believe was also made to him to rejoin and get back to the Finance Minister's chair if he so desired, but VP Singh on principle declined.

And while Rajiv Gandhi in India was busy coping with the serious internal crisis in his cabinet, Shupriya in London received her new posting order. She was now going on promotion as Counselor Political to trouble torn Sri Lanka and her reporting date was on 17th April, which happened to be Good Friday of the Easter holiday week. She seemed very happy with a posting near home and looked forward to it. Meanwhile Shiraz too had reported to the Pakistan Embassy at Stockholm. His move had been delayed by two months firstly because his replacement in Moscow had not arrived, and secondly because after Gorbachev's visit to India, the Pakistan Government was very keen to find out what specific military hardware and economic assistance were now being provided by the Russkies to the Indians.

For Saira and Shiraz, the delay in moving to Stockholm proved to be a blessing in disguise since it gave them an opportunity to rub shoulders with the high and mighty from the United States and other leading developed nations who had come as special invitees to Moscow to listen to the Soviet Leader Mikhail Gorbachev's concept of 'Glasnost' and his vision to make the world a safer place to live in. It was literally a gathering of world celebrities that day as Saira and Shiraz took their seats inside the beautiful ornate hall of Moscow's famous Kremlin Palace.

"Look, Look there is the handsome Hollywood hearthrob Gregory Peck standing there next to the writer Norman Mailer," said an excited Saira as Shiraz also pointed out to her his favourite author Graham Greene who was seen chatting with Gore Vidal.

"My God isn't that Yoko Ono, the wife of the late John Lennon talking to Pierre Cardin!' exclaimed Saira as the announcement was made for everyone to take their seats. As Gorbachev spoke with a free and open mind on that inauguration day of the three day conference that was billed as 'The Conference for a Nuclear Free World and the Survival for Mankind,' it became quite evident to Shiraz and other well wishers that the Soviet leader was waging an almost desperate struggle to shake the Soviet society out of its stupor and modernize its crumbling economy through a process of quick restructuring programme. Mr Gorbachev was not only willing to open out to the western world, but he even went to the extent of saying that history must be seen for what it is factually and not otherwise. To put a brake on the rampant corruption that had spread like cancer during the Brezhnev era, he had even arrested Yuri Charbanov, the departed leader's son-in-law and had him put in prison. Yuri Charbanov was not an ordinary Soviet Citizen; he was also once the Deputy Minister for Interior during his father-in laws long reign and that was not so very long ago. Listening to the new Soviet leader who meant every word of what he said were Andrei Sakharov and a few other Soviet dissidents who had been recently released from detention. That day while talking to one of them, Shiraz who till then had only heard about Stalin's Gulag, became a little more wiser about that dreaded God forsaken place where thousands of Russians had been excommunicated since the Stalin era and from where only a few were lucky to have returned back alive.

"What a shame. You mean to say that you have never heard of Magadan before?"said one of the recently released dissidents as he went on to explain as to how one could get there, and at the same time also added that God forbid nobody henceforth should ever be sent there. "Well the Gulag is a notorious place far away in Siberia and a port on the Sea of Okhotsk in the Magadan Oblast of Russia. It is also the administrative region that bears the same name and where I as a young man of twenty was a guest of Comrade Stalin for a good fifteen years," said the elderly man while punctuating his story with good humour. "'The prison camps in the dreaded Gulag were of course well away from the city and they were deep in the interior of that far eastern and godforsaken area of Mother Russia,. But it had solid gold reserves and we the young prisoners in that freezing icy weather were used as labourers to dig for it. The labour camp was situated in the Kolyma River Basin and was not far from the Bilibino Nuclear Power Station. But now of course it is a completely different place than what it used to be in the late forties, when I was a prisoner there," said the man while explaining to Shiraz the daily routine that they as prisoners had to follow at the Gulag. "At 5 a.m.in that biting Siberian cold weather, the guard would bang on the iron doors and my partner and I would get up from our miserable ten feet by five feet den that only had two wooden beds. And then after a hurried breakfast of some measly stale bread with kasha, which was nothing but plain watery vegetable soup and hot water, we were all taken under a heavily armed escort to the mining area. Day in and and day out it was the same old damn routine, but if you like monotony young man then it is the ideal place to be in," added the grey haired man with a crafty smile on his shrunken face. He was a Russian Jew and a renowned academician and his second confinement in the Gulag was thanks to Brezhnev, when he strongly condemned the Communist Government's effort to stifle the voices of Jews who wanted to migrate to Israel and he happened to be one of them. That was his only crime.

It was on first death anniversary of Olaf Palme, when Shiraz with his family landed at the Arlanda International Airport in Stockholm. In spite of their sincere efforts to trace the ex Prime Minister's killer, the Swedish police were still groping in the dark. There were now strong rumours that Palme might have been bumped off because of his efforts to stop the sale of illegal Swedish arms to Iran and had therefore provoked Khomeini's wrath. Or it could also be a personal vendetta by someone who may have paid off the assassin to settle old personal scores with the victim. But whatever be the case it was a black mark on the police force of the country that preached neutrality and it still had no clue as to the motive of the crime, thought Shiraz as the polite Swedish custom officer seeing the red diplomatic passports saluted cleared the baggage promptly.

Meanwhile in and around the middle of March 1987, when the Time Magazine's Bureau Chief in New Delhi Ross H Munro published an exclusive interview with President Zia of Pakistan and Zia categorically confrmed to him that Pakistan was capable of building a nuclear bomb whenever it desired, Shiraz having read about it while he was still in Moscow was simply taken aback. This disclosure coming staright from the horse's mouth further confirmed what Mr Kuldip Nayyar a respected veteran Indian journalist and his Pakistani friend Mushahid Hussein who was also a respected newspaper editor in Pakistan of the paper 'The Muslim' had only a month or so ago written about and according to them Pakistan very much had the knowhow to make the Islamic bomb. Both of them had visited the home of Abdul Qadeer Khan at Kahuta in January, and when the mastermind behind Pakistan's nuclear weapons programme was asked directly by the two journalists of whether Pakistan was capable of producing the nuclear bomb, he ofcourse very cleverly and flatly refused to answer yes or no. This only confirmed the fact that Pakistan well nigh had the capability of producing a nuclear bomb, but was reluctant to admit it. Shiraz having put two and two together therefore rang up his brother-n-law Salim Rehman in Islamabad to find out the truth and if what had been written by Monro in his interview with Zia had been denied by the Pakistan government.

According to Salim Rehman, though the government's official stand was that Pakistan nuclear programme was only for peaceful purposes, but President Zia's evasive answers to Ross Munro about what was going on at Kahuta, and then diplomatically denying Munro his request to visit the high security area had therefore further complicated the issue. Pakistan was on the threshold of getting a massive 4.2 billion dollar military and economic aid from the United States and Zia was apprehensive that Senator John Glenn and others like him in the US Senate who were against giving any assistance to any new member of the nuclear club would invoke the Symington Amendment and stop the bill from being passed by the Congress. Salim Rehman who was privy to all this therefore conveyed to Shiraz somewhat obliquely in Urdu that yes Pakistan if it so desired was now in a position to join the nuclear club, but were constrained to do so for fear of losing the massive aid from the Americans. This was now news to Shiraz since he was always under the impression that though Pakistan was making an all out effort to produce a nuclear bomb, but with pressure from Washington, the process had therefore been either delayed or stalled. But if what Salim Rehman said was true then it would pose a very great threat to India and also to the subcontinent, since India already possessed the bomb. Shiraz in good faith therefore considered it his duty to somehow inform India and convince them about this latest development. But the question was how should it be done and without any suspicion being aroused. Therefore in order not to show any anxiety on the subject over the telephone, Shiraz very cleverly said to Salim Rehman.

"Well on the 4.2 billion largesse from the United States, I don't think we need worry at all because the Americans having stuck their neck out very deeply through us in Afghanistan they can now ill afford to backout from it now. Moreover, President Zia had also told Munro categorically in the interview that the Senators and Congressmen on Capitol Hill should rather look to the higher interest of the country rather than to Pakistan's measly nuclear programme, and that I guess sums it all up, doesn't it?" Hearing Salim Rehman's chuckle over the telephone, Shiraz then casually asked him to confirm whether the information on the BBC regarding the troop withdrawals from both sides after Exercise Brass Tacks by India had been called off and whether that was correct or not.

'Inshallah it is all back to normal once again and hopefully with the men in uniform returning back to their barracks on both the sides peace will prevail," said Salim Rehman.

"Thank God it's all over," replied Shiraz as he gently put the receiver down.

That very evening after everyone had gone off to sleep, Shiraz took out his Olivetti portable typewriter and while pretending to finish some important official work wrote a plain four line matter of fact message on it. It was addressed to the Indian Embassy in Stockholm and it simply read. 'This is to once again confirm that what Kuldip Nayyar has already reported is absolutely correct. Though AQ did not spell it out in as many words, but Pakistan is are now fully capable of making its own Buddha and one that may give even a bigger smile, and Pakistan could do it at any time they want to." Though it was an unsigned anonymous letter, but in order to give more authenticity to it, Shiraz therefore wrote below the message. 'This is from a son of the soil and a well wisher from the subcontinent and one who sincerely desires peace and friendship between the two countries.' Late that night having put the anonymous letter in a plain envelope, Shiraz in capital letters and in inverted commas marked it as 'Private and Confidential' and addressed it to the Indian Embassy in Stockholm. Next day morning having fixed the required Swedish postage stamps on it, he while on his way to office dropped the letter in the mail box at Stockholm's main railway station.

The very next day, when the letter with Swedish postage stamps was delivered to the Indian Embassy at 12, Adolf Fredericks, Kyrkoghata, the lady receptionist on reading the words 'Private and Confidential' on it and as was routine promptly marked it to the Minister, who was India's number two man in the mission. On the third day in order to check whether the letter had reached the right person, Shiraz from a local private telephone in Stockholm rang up the Indian Embassy. Identifying himself as a student at Uppasala University and a Mohajir from Pakistan whose family had migrated to Karachi, from the erstwhile United Provinces he expressed his desire to speak to somebody very responsible and someone who could help him and his family to get a visa to visit India. Giving his place of birth as Lucknow and the excuse that his ailing grandmother from his mother's side was on her death bed, he was first connected to the officer dealing with the visa section. But when the Visa Officer having identified himself told him that he was not authorized to issue such visas and that it would be better for the caller to apply after returning to Pakistan through the Indian High Commission in Islamabad, Shiraz promptly dropped the Minister's name and that of his wife and children and giving the excuse that they were old family friends, the call was immediately transferred to the number two man in the Indian Embassy. In the small Diplomatic Community of Stockhoolm knowing the names of family members of those from the subcontinent was no big deal, and when the Minister came on the line and Shiraz simply said. "Sir, I sincerely recommend that the Indian government takes immediate cognisance about the smiling Pakistani Buddha that I had mentioned as a well wisher in my anonymous letter and please do not ask any questions." And when the voice at the other end asked for an identification, Shiraz promptly put the receiver down. He was now convinced that the message had reached the right man. Though indirectly Shiraz had violated the code of conduct by contacting the Indian Embassy and by giving them classified information on a subject that was suppose to be topsecret, but he did not feel guilty because he felt that by forewarning India, the chances of using a nuclear weapon by both sides would in fact be reduced and it was with that aim in mind that he had done it. He did not consider this to be a spying acititvity, but nevertheless he also knew that if he was caught it could be damn well dangerous for him and his family too. While driving back to his office at the Pakistan Embassy at 65 Karlavagen, Shiraz was reminded of the book that Shupriya had presented to him when he was posted in the Military Intelligence Directorate at Army Headquarters Delhi. It was the John Le Carre bestseller 'The Spy Who Came in From the Cold' and Shupriya without writing her own name on it had addressed it to 'My Very Own Loving Dablo.'

CHAPTER-5

The Smoking Gun That Backfired

On 16th April, 1987 and a day prior to Shupriya's departure from London to take up her new assignment in Colombo suddenly on that very afternoon at India House in London there was a big commotion. While Shupriya was being treated to a South Indian farewell lunch by one of her junior colleagues, there began a hunt to trace out Mr B.M.Oza, the Indian Ambassador in Sweden who it was believed had arrived with his wife and family from Stockholm to spend the short Easter holiday in England. The orders for his immediate return to Stockholm it seems had come directly from the PMO's office in Delhi, and it was with firm instructions that the diplomat must be traced, contacted and put on the next available flight back to Stockholm.

"I wonder where is the damn fire to trace Ambassador Oza and have him sent back immediately,"said Shupriya as she enjoyed the delicious vada and idly sambar with the mouth watering coconut chutney and dahi vada that only the South Indian Tamils could prepare.

"Well let me warn you that it is a bit chilly hot, but this is primarily to initiate you into the type food that you will be getting whenever you visit Jaffna or Battlcalao, or for that matter any other part of the northern and eastern region of Sri Lanka where we Tamils are in the majority," said the Second Secretary's wife whose great grand parents from her mother's side had migrated to Sri Lanka during the early British rule as tea pickers.And it was only after Shupriya landed at Colombo late on that Good Friday night of 17th April 1987, and rang up India House in London to inform them that she had reached safely, that she became aware of the reason for Ambassador Oza's to return to Stockholm immediately. It seems that on that very day of 16th April, a Swedish Radio broadcast had opened a can of worms for the Rajiv Government. Quoting senior company sources from Bofors, the radio alleged that the sale of the Bofors guns to India, which was the biggest export order ever received by that Swedish company had been won, but only after the company had paid bribes to senior Indian politicians and key defence officials in the Indian government. According to the source, a total of 30 million Swedish Kroners corresponding to 5 million US dollars were paid in four installments during the last two months of 1986 into secret Swiss Bank accounts for the deal, and which the radio said was highly irregular. That stunning revelation had now caused panic in the PMO's office and Ambasssdor Oza who was in London was finally traced and was asked to get back to Stockholm immediately. Poor Oza's Good Friday became a bad Friday and his Easter holidays with his family went for a huge six as he caught the flight back to Stockholm.

The Swedish radio broadcast was also heard by Shiraz, but he had paid little or no heed heed to it because he knew that paying bribes for such huge defence contracts to those in power was nothing very new or unusual. It was happening all the time all around the world and therefore he simply brushed it off as a routine matter.The fact that the Bofors had got that 1.3 Billion dollar Indian deal for the supply of 400 guns of 155 mm caliber plus 10 more guns as gratis was no longer a secret. Everybody in Sweden and especially those who were part of the company manufacturing the weapon were very happy in clinching the deal, but this revelation of having paid big bribes to the Indian politicians and bureaucrats came as a shock to the peace loving Swedish people. The Swedes considered themselves to be the apostle of peace and the arms export was guided by a strict government policy that clearly laid down that no lethal arms whatsoever were to be sold to communist countries, to rogue and dictatorial regimes, and regimes that suppressed human rights. And it also included countries that the Swedish Parliament considered to be in the war zone and it included Iraq, Iran and a few other countries of the Middle East, but India was not on that list. However, to educate himelf on this particular Swedish Gun, Shiraz went through the latest edition of Jane's Weapons and Equipment catalogue and was impressed by the gun's various characteristics. The Indian Army had ordered for the FH 77 B version that had a longer range and though it was a towed gun it had the capability to shoot and scoot.

Meanwhile in the PMO's office in New Delhi, the Swedish Radio broadcast on the 16th of April had created a panic situation and Rajiv Gandhi's government it seems had started running for cover already. On 18th April, after Oza was back in his chair he received a call from a Joint Secretary in the PMO and the caller categorically told Oza that he should not only get the exact and full text of the Swedish broadcast and send it immediately to the PMO's office, but the Indian Ambassador should also get an official denial both from Bofors and the Swedish government that no bribes were paid to any agents, officials or politicians. Simultaneously in order to convince the Indian people that no such bribes were ever paid and probably to hide their own guilt, Rajiv Gandhi's Congress government pressed the panic button, and conveniently blamed the foreign hand and who they said were bent upon destabilizing the nation.

Heeding to the Indian Ambassador's request, the Swedish Government asked Bofors who were a part of the Nobel Industries for an explanation regarding the alleged illegal payoffs. But before they could even reply, another bombshell rocked the scandal when on 22nd April, the influential Swedish newspaper 'Dagens Nyheter' while quoting reliable sources from the Bofors top management stated that the commission in the Indian howitzer deal were paid to the Hinduja family who had been acting as the middlemen in the deal.'Dagens Nyheter', the daily newspaper founded by Rudolf Wall in 1864 was the most popular daily and had the largest circulation in Sweden. So when a translation of that article from the newspaper accusing Bofors of paying bribes to the Hindujas was put up to Shiraz, he decided to find out a little more about the Hinduja family. He had heard that like other Sindhi families who originally hailed from Shikarpur in Pakistan were basically traders and businessmen, but for one family to have made so much of money in just one generation is what baffled him now.

Parmanand Deepchand Hinduja, the founder of the Hunduja Group was born in 1901, and he first came to Bombay when he was only 14 years old. With his prodigious drive in trading and a shrewd business brain, Parmanand after a struggle had established himself as an enterprising trader in the import-export market. During the fag end of the First World War, Parmanand started importing dry fruits from Iran in echange for tea from India which was then in good demand. A complete teetotaler and a pure vegetarian, both Parmanand and his wife Jamuna were deeply spiritual and had a spirit of humanitarianism and compassion for the poor. To start with, Parmanand in the name of his mother opened the Shrimati Pahunchbai Deepchand Hinduja Trust and during partition he also opened a free clinic for the Sindhi refugees in Bombay, and which later became known as the PD Hinduja Hospital and later in 1964 the Hinduja Foundation was formed. As the business kept growing particularly with Iran, the Hindujas established a good rapport first with the Shah of Iran and then with the Khomeini regime. After Parmanand's death in 1971, his four sons, Srichand, Gopichand, Prakash and Ashok took charge of the family business empire that soon grew by leaps and bounds. An interesting story of one of their many business deals with Iran in the mid 1970's was in the export of potaotoes and onions to that country. On instructions from his elder brother Gopichand who was looking after the family's business interest from Teheran, the youngest brother Ashok who was based in Bombay was asked to immediately dispatch 1,00,000 tons of the two perishable commodities at the earliest to that country. Ashok Hinduja who was then still a novice at the game having purchased the required quantity at a fairly high premium was stuck when it came to shipping it. Thanks to the on going Iraq-Iran war, the waiting period at the Iranian ports was a month, and by that time the consignment reached its destination it was bound to perish. Moreover, Iran wanted the delivery on top priority and something had to be done immediately. As Sindhis, the enterprising Hinduja brothers by using the good offices of Mr Bhutto, a fellow Sindhi and Mrs Gandhi they had the consignment delivered by road through Pakistan using Korean drivers and their fleet of the long 23 tonner air-conditioned trucks.

The Hinduja's first flagship company now in India was the Ashok Leyland at Madras. The factory produced heavy duty vehicles and had a good market both in India and abroad. In 1979, the two elder brothers Srichand who was born on 28th November, 1935 and Gopichand who was born on 29th February 1940 moved to London to expand their business. The third brother Prakash also followed them however he made Geneva in Switzerland as his base of operations, while the youngest Ashok held the fort in Bombay. According to Shiraz's information, the Hindujas by the early 1980's were hobnobbing with the high and the mighty not only in India, but also across the globe. As far as they were concerned any business was good enough for them as long as it raked in good money and it did not matter whether the deal was entirely legal or otherwise, because they with their battery of expert solicitors, financial advisers, tons of money and government contacts at the highest level knew how to circumvent them. Not only was the group into production of heavy vehicles, they were also into trading of sugar, tea, metals, textiles and they now also had a pie in the Bollywood business of film production. But now with the report in the Dagens Nyhter accusing the Hinduja brothers of also being arms agents in the Bofors deal, the possibility of the group being involved in gun running for Iran and possibly also Iraq and in the Iran-Contra affair could not be therefore ruled out thought Shiraz, while wondering as to why the Swedish paper was getting so very worked up about it. The paper had not only mentioned the

Hindujas by name, but it had also specified the amount and the time when the amount was secretly transferred into their alleged Swiss Bank accounts.

"Well unless they were absolutely hundred percent sure, the paper would not be so damn foolish as to publish the article and blatantly name the Hindujas as recipients of the bribe, because the Hindujas could well sue them for defamation." said Saira as she got little Tojo who was now little over four years old all dressed up to go to the park. On the very next day, Shiraz in order to find out if there was any truth to the many stories about Bofors having violated the Swedish laws in exporting arms illegally to other countries such as Iraq, Iran, Vietnam through freeports such as Singapore and Dubai contacted a few foreign shipping agents in Stockholm. Since the subject was now being openly talked about in public, Shiraz thought that getting such information in Sweden which was an open country would not be very difficult, but he was mistaken. He was politely told that this information was confidential in nature and could not be divulged, but if he so desired he could get the information directly from the concerned exporter. The fact that the Bofors were in deep trouble however became quite evident, when soon after the Dagens Nhyter newspaper report, Martin Ardbo, the Head Honcho and the Chief Executive of A.B. Bofors who was the mastermind and the Chief architect of the Bofors—India billion dollar deal resigned. Eversince January 1987, when Mr Alergnon the Swedish War Materials Inspector who was also the key person in the implememtation of the country's arms export policy was found dead on the rail track at a Stockholm subway station, Martin Ardbo had come under a cloud and now his place had been taken by Per Ove Morberg. Mr Alergnon had died under very mysterious circumstances and this only added to the speculation that Bofors were doing underhand arms business, which as per Swedish law was highly illegal.

In Sweden, while the Bofors illegal arms export stories kept getting murkier and murkier, Rajiv Gandhi's think tank inside the PMO in India it seems also started getting the jitters. To start with, the Swedish Governement by giving the plea that the contract was entirely between the A.B. Bofors and the Indian government and that they were therefore not prepared to issue an outright denial about the bribes having been paid had given the PMO a solid jolt. However on 24th April, Mr Morberg the new Chief of Bofors and Lars Gotlin the legal counselor from Nobel in their report to the Indian Ambassador very cleverly admitted that no commissions were paid to any Indian agents, but they made no mention if these were paid to any foreign agents. Both Bofors and the Rajiv Government were now in a tight corner and they both now got into a damage control mode. They knew that if there were any more such damaging revelations, it could well annul the huge contract and neither side could afford that. Taking the age old stance of attack being the best form of defence, Rajiv Gandhi who was known as Mr Clean now got into an offensive mode as he in no uncertain terms once again raised the bogey of the foreign hand being behind all this malicious propaganda to destabilize the nation.

On 27th April, 1987 after the Indian Ambassador in Sweden had informed the Ministry of External affairs in Delhi that the Swedish government was not prepared to issue an outright denial of the Swedish Radio report, but would consider making an official investigation into the matter and the suggestion had been agreed to by him, it looked like that the law would take its own course. But on that very day itself, when the Indian Prime Minister himself rang up Mr Ingvar Carlson the Swedish Prime Minister and conveyed to him that there was no requirement of any investigation by the Swedish Government since Bofors through the Indian Ambassador in Sweden had already confirmed that no commissions had been paid to any middlemen, it became quite obvious that Rajiv Gandhi was trying to scuttle the Swedish Government's effort in probing the matter any further. And it got further complicated, when Rajiv Gandhi made a statement in parliament saying that though the government had requested the Swedish Government for an official investigation into the matter, but now that the Swedish government had confirmed that there were no middlemen in the deal and the matter should therefore be laid to rest. But when to that statement by the Indian Prime Minister, the Swedish government retorted by saying that no such confirmation about the involvement of middlemen in the deal was given by them, Rajiv it seems was now caught in a whirlpool of his own making. By now the opposition too was breathing down the Prime Minister's neck, and to save his own skin when Rajiv gave the explanation that it was not the present Swedish Prime Minister, but the previous one, the late Olaf Palme who during his visit to Delhi in January 1986 had given him this clear cut assuarance that there would not be any middlemen and accordingly the contract had been finalised by the government and Bofors, that statement by the Prime Minister of India it seemed was not very convincing either. And with the recent resignation of VP Singh from the cabinet and his ouster from the Congress Party, things had indeed started hotting up as far as defence procurements and other such deals were concerned. There were now clear indications that things did not look as clean as they were made out to be.

VP Singh had also made public the allegations that even in the recent HDW submarine deal, commissions had been paid to middlemen and that had also damaged the credibility of the Rajiv Gandi government. On the television screen too it was no longer the self confident and smiling Rajiv anymore. He had become itchy and irritable whenever the name Bofors was mentioned and he seemed to be getting himself into knots.

"But do you personally think that the Prime Minister has a hand in all this, because I frankly don't think so. And before more damage is done to his good image and credibility, he should for his own sake and the Indian people who have given him such a big mandate come clean with the affair immediately. And I do not know who is advising him, but whoever it is, he is only doing him more harm than good it seems," said Reeta as she called out to Peeveee to get down to his studies a little more seriously. Peevee was now in his final year in school and Reeta was worried that with his music and extra curricular activites he might even fail. His weakest subjects were mathametics and science and she had even kept a good tutor for him during the summer vacations.

"Yes I also agree with you that personally the Prime Minister may not be directly involved in getting a cut from the deal, but it is very much possible that the Congress party may have utilized their own contacts so that the money comes into the party coffers and 3% of 1.3 billion dollars is certainly not a small amount if you ask me. And with Mr VP Singh's raids on the Ambanis and other top industrialists in the country, when he was the Finance Minister, the party coffers may have dried up, and this is like a jackpot for them and that too with no questions being asked. But this is only a conjecture," added Monty as he excused himself and with Reeta's permission drove down to the Press Club for a drink with Unni. Monty knew that with Unni's penchant for investigative journalism and with his contacts at various levels of the government, there could be much more to this sordid affair and he was therefore keen to find out how and when it all started.

"Well what I am going to say may not be gospel truth, but now looking back at hindsight and the way things are moving, all the pieces seem to be falling in place," said the 67 year old veteran journalist as he ordered Ramdin the waiter to quickly bring a chilled Golden Eagle beer for his guest.

"Firstly and according to some reports, the visit of the Swedish Prime Minister, the late Olaf Palme in January 1986 to Delhi it seems was not a very pre-planned or an official one either. But one that it seems had been finalised in a bit of a hurry. For some reason or the other and which I am afraid only Mr Palme can throw light upon if he comes back from his grave is the fact that the Swedish Prime Minister himself wanted the visit to be kept somewhat unofficial and informal. He also desired that it should be kept at a low key and without any protocol bullshit. In fact the day he was to leave Stockholm for India, someone from the Indian Embassy was surprised to see him standing in the queue waiting to get his boarding pass on the SAS flight, and for a Prime Minister of the country going on an official visit that indeed looked rather odd. On that visit Palme was accompanied by only his social secretary and his press secretary and according to the Swedes, Palme was going to Delhi primarily to discuss with the Indian Prime Minister the agenda for further action on the five continent six nation peace initiative, which was Palme's own brainchild. But unfortunately Palme on 28th February and after month or so on his return from Delhi was shot dead on the streets of Stockholm and nobody still knows as to why and who did it. It is therefore widely believed that it was during that January 1986 meeting with Rajiv in Delhi that the deal for the Bofors gun was more or less finalized and after Palme had given his word of honour that no middlemen would be included in the contract. And it was soon thereafter that the file on Bofors at the Defense Ministry kept moving at an unprecedented speed and the likes of which none had never seen before," added Unni somewhat sarcastically as he ordered another large rum for himself.

"But where was the damn frightful hurry?' said Monty as he put some chilled lemonade into his beer to make a shandy.

"Unfortunately after Palme was assassinated, and by the time Rajiv returned from the funeral, the Bofors file it seems was ready and waiting for the Prime Minister's final approval. On the 9th March 1986, and during his 24 hour visit to Sweden for Mr Palme's funeral, Rajiv Gandhi it seems had also conveyed to his incumbent Mr Carlson that he was very much in favour of introducing the Swedish gun in the Indian Army, but it was subject to certain clarifications regarding the financial terms of the contract from the Swedish side. Now what those clarifications were is a deep mystery. And on the very next day 10th of March, Ardbo in India, when he was asked he too gave in writing that there will be no middlemen whatsever in the deal. But soon thereafter I believe a new agreement was concluded by Martin.Ardbo with a company called AE Services. This agreement was performance related and was also very convienently termed as an 'Administrative Arrangement', but it had very short term validity till 31st March, 1986 only. Therefore, on that very evening after the funeral, Ghare Khan the Additional Secretary at the PMO's office who had accompanied the Prime Minister and Carl

Johan Oberg the Swedish State Secretary for Foreign Trade in the Swedish Foreign Affairs Ministry I am told had sat together and they had settled the matter to the satisfaction of both the sides and after both the sides agreed once again that there will be no middlemen. On 21ˢᵗ March, 1986, Arun Singh, the Minisiter of State for Defense who was on his way for an official visit to Bhutan that morning also gave his verbal approval, which was duly noted on the file, and the deal was more or less sealed. Three days later on 24ᵗʰ March 1986, the contract was signed by Mr Bhatnagar the Indian Defence Secretary on behalf of India and by Mr Martin Ardbo the Chief Executive on behalf of A.B. Bofors and Anders G Carlberg, the President of Nobel Industries that controlled AB Bofors. On 2ⁿᵈ May 1986, as per the terms of the contract the 20% advance amounting to Rs 296.15 crores in Swedish Kroners was paid to the firm and everything seemed to be in order. But according to one insider, one of the hidden terms for a separate payment at the rate of 3% was also concluded for the 'Administrative Services' that was to be rendered by this mysterious firm that called itself as AE Services. But it was only on condition that the deal must go through by 31ˢᵗ March, 1986 and failing which AE Services would forfeit the commission. This was not mentioned anywhere in the actual contract, but was agreed to as a gentlemen's agreement separately between AE Services and Bofors as a performance related clause in an appendix by the two sides. This behind the scene deal between AE Services and Bofors it seems took place on or about the time Sweden was getting ready for Palme's funeral, and since it was already mid March and 31ˢᵗ was not far away, everyone connected or concerned with AE Services were naturally worried. Hence there was it seems that terrible hurry to have the deal bull dozed through by that given dead line of 31ˢᵗ March," added Unni as he twirled his salt and pepper handlebar moustache and snapped his fingers at the bar steward to have his glass refilled.

"But what is this AE Services and how did they come into the picture at such a late stage, and who controls or owns it?" asked Monty feeling somewhat confused with the issue of whether it was a middleman or a registered company acting on behalf of Bofors, or maybe on behalf of somebody very powerful in the Indian government who were so keen and willing to offer its services administratively and therefore wanted its three percent commission on the deal.

"Well according to this insider, the AE Services Ltd was a company that was registerd in England and a contract between the company and Bofors was drawn up on 15ᵗʰ November 1985, and that was in and around the time, when Palme and Rajiv met at the United Nations in New York. Then in August 1986, the AE Services Ltd opened an account with the Nordfinanz Bank in Zurich and a few weeks later an amount of 7.3 Million Dollars from Bofors was creditied to that account. Well no sooner had the account been credited in the Swiss bank, then within a fortnight's time I believe it was transferred to a firm by the name of 'Colbar Investments' in Panama and though the insider mentions a certain Major RA Wilson from the AE Services as the MD of AE Services, but my gut feeling is that this is only a front company of that Italian Octavio Qattarocchi and his wife Mariah and who as everyone knows are very close to the Prime Minister and his Italian wife,"added Unni as he further lowered his voice so that the others could not hear what was being discussed and ordered another beer for Monty.

"But how do you know about all this?" whispered Monty looking rather surprised at the manner in which Unni with a sense of full authority kept giving the history of the gun deal.

"Ask no questions and you will be told no lies my friend," said Unni as he once again clinked glasses with Monty and continued with his story on how the Bofors officers, their workers with their wives and children at the Karlskoga factory in Sweden on getting the good news that the contract had been sealed celebrated the great event.

"Arre Baba It was like as if they had won an Olympic gold medal in the billion dollar arms race with a last minute spurt that had the Sofna from France retiring hurt and gasping for breath. Because till a few weeks ago the French Sofna gun was leading the two gun race, and now suddenly after Rajiv's reurn from Palme's funeral, Sofna was out of the race completely. And the senior officers at the Army Headquarters Directorate of Weapons and Equipment who were primarily responsible for the selection of the 155 mm gun were totally confounded, when Sofna was not even allowed to represent or give a fresh bid. The whole deal was finalized as if India's security was desperately at stake and as if the enemy was waiting at the doorstep to attack the country, and it seemed that only Bofors could provide the security and the answer to this so called threat. And as far as the financial security of those who were behind the deal are concerned, I am sure they may have already made their pile all right, but the Bofors deal as you can well see has turned out to be a smoking gun for the the government of India and possibly for the government of Sweden as well too. With only a handful of guns delivered, it has already started spitting political fire, and the way both sides are now trying to cover up with knee jerk responses, this shady deal I am afraid is going to create a lot more problems for our young Prime Minister," concluded Unni as he took out a few photographs from his old Khadi satchel to show them to Monty.

The photographs had been taken by Unni, when he visited the Bofors factory at Karlskoga sometime in April 1986. The sleepy small town with its population of only 40,000 was the Headquarters of Bofors and they were on that day celebrating the billion dollar contract that had given them a new lease of life. It not only gave employment to another 5000 Swedes, but the Bofors shares too in the Swedish stock market also had come back to life as it jumped to a new high.

"That day the small town had a grand festive look and at places it looked like a mini India. The Indian tricolour and the Swedish flag was everywhere and the shops were full of Indian curios and artifacts. Even popular Hindi songs were being played over the loudspeaker," added Unni as he pointed out a photograph of Martin Ardbo standing very proudly next to the Indian Ambassador Mr Oza who very rightly was the guest of honour that day. And while Monty perused through the set of photographs, Unni also mentioned to him about Martin Ardbo's famous 60th birthday party that was held at the luxurious Grand Hotel in Stockhom, and where the cream of Sweden's high and the mighty were all there to congratulate the hefty big built Swede.

"The happiness of clinching the deal with India was written all over Ardbo's face that evenng, but now that the Swedes have smelt a rat, Ardbo too I believe is beating about the bush and not talking straight regarding who had received those bribes, or rather the brokerage for the deal. And it is indeed rather strange that the man who till the other day was himself under investigation in Sweden for illegally exporting arms to certain Middle East countries was the very one who had successfully negotiated the billion dollar deal with the government of India. In other words I have a gut feeling that Martin Ardbo knows the real truth behind this shady affair, but he will be the last man to open his big mouth, because the Swedish government I guess is indirectly or in some manner is also connected with the deal. Do remember that India has so far received only six out of the 410 Bofors guns, and Ardbo will be a bloody fool to cut his own damn feet if he starts singing now. And with every new revelation and the manner in which our Prime Minister is personally taking so much of interest in the matter, I have a gut feeling that some very important people are behind this colossal scam, and if you think that by the Prime Minister just mentioning time and again about the foreign hand, the matter will die down, then I am afraid both the Prime Minister and his Congress Party are living in a fool's paradise. Now that the opposition in India too have smelt the rat, they too I am sure will be playing the cat and mouse game and they too will be going great guns to find out the real truth,"added Unni as he raised his glass and said 'Skol', the Swedish word for cheers.

On the 30th of April, 1987, some prominent members from the Indian opposition in the Rajya Sabha, the Indian Upper House of Parliament had raised a privilege motion accusing the Prime Minister of misleading the House on the Bofors contract. The Prime Minister, Rajiv Ganadhi in his statement to the Rajya Sabha on 28th April had stated categorically that the government had secured a confirmation both from Bofors and the Swedish Government that there were no middlemen in the deal. Whereas the fact was that at a press conference in Sweden a day later on 29th April, the Swedish Minister of Foreign Trade categorically said that the late Prime Minister Olaf Palme had only conveyed the assurances from Bofors to Rajiv Gandhi that there would be no middlemen, but there were no such assuarances from the government of Sweden to this effect at all. This statement from the Swedish Government once again had caught the government of India on the wrong foot, but luckily for Rajiv Gandhi the Swedish Ambassador in India on 18th April after the balloon had gone up had already sent a signed aide memoire which stated that the Prime Minister of India, Rajiv Gandhi, himself had demanded in his talks with Mr Olaf Palme in the autumn of 1985 and January 1986 that one of several conditions for Bofors to get the howitzer contract would be that the company eliminated all possible middlemen and that the contract must be finalised directly between Bofors and the Indian Defence Ministry. And based on that aide memoire, when the Chairman of the Rajya Sabha, Mr R Venkataraman dissallowed the charge of a breach of privilege motion against the Prime Minister, there was a big sigh of relief at the PMO. But the relief was rather short lived, when the opposition charged the government for backtracking on the questionable issue of illegal foreign currency transactions by the influential Indian businessman lobby that were believed to be close to the ruling government. While VP Singh was the Finance Minister and just before he was shifted to the Defence Ministry he had through his then Revenue Secretary, V C Pande had approved of Fairfax, a private detective agency that was based in the United States and was headed by Mr Hershman an ex-employee of the CIA to dig into this racket, but feeling the heat that Fairfax might generate after the already on going Bofors scandal, Rajiv Gandhi in order to diffuse the crisis cleverly announced that a government commission would examine the opposition's charges,"'added Unni again somewhat sarcastically as Ramdin the waiter rang the bell to give the signal that the bar was about to close.

While the Bofors scandal and the Fairfax probe rocked the Indian government of Rajiv Gandhi in India, in the United States of America, besides the Iran-Contra expose, some juicy political and sexual scandals concerning a formidable White House aspirant and the Marine guards at various American Embassies abroad and specially those posted to the US Embassy in Moscow and other Warsaw countries had also started hitting the headlines. It seems that Senator Gary Hart with his one night stand on board the yacht 'Monkey Business' with young Donna Rice a fashion model and a part time actress for good company had burnt his own boat. The Senator was a front runner for the Democratic Party nomination, but this small misdeameanour of his had now cost him rather dearly. Not only did he withdraw his nomination, but it also affected his martial relations with Lee his own wife though she very gracefully stood by him when she told the press. "If it doesn't bother me, I don't think it ought to bother anyone else." When Shiraz read about the Senator's fling with Donna Rice, he was reminded of Mandy Rice Davis and Christine Keeler the two high society call girls who in the early sixties had rocked the British government and one that had led to the resignation of the then Defence Minister John Profurmo.

And as far as the American Marines on duty at the American Embassy in Moscow was concerned, it was all thanks to the vivacious Violetta Seina, the Soviet receptionist at Spaso House, which was the official residence of the American Ambassador in Moscow. Working as a mole, the tall and slim Sienna with alluring big eyes was the most sought after lady at the annual Marine Ball and she it seems had very cleverly seduced Sargeant Claytone Lonetree, the seniormost Marine posted in the American Embassy. And as a result of which Soviet agents would quietly enter the embassy premises at night and especially on Fridays, when the marines not on duty would be indulging in their weekly orgies at the 'Marine House', which was the name that was given to the marine quarters inside the nine storeyed embassy building. While the marines, boozed, brawled and enjoyed their sexual escapades in their tiny rooms, the Soviet spooks would get busy planting the bugs at the most sensitive of places inside the vast complex.

A few days later, when Saira read about it in one of the latest issues of the Time Magazine and she jokingly said. "I hope the Pakistani Enbassy in Moscow is safe because you never know these Russian woman and specially that good looking Galya in our Military Attache's office and who I have been told has of late been seen quite often in the company of the newly posted First Secretary, and who too has very conveniently sent back his wife and children to her parent's house in Karachi," there was a mischievous smile on her husband's face.

"Don't worry my dear and though this is a well known modus operandi of 'Honey Trap'that the KGB often uses against foreign diplomats, but Pakistani diplomats as guests in that country cannot dare blame Galya, because that is her private affair. But you can be rest assured that incase what you have said is true, then I am afraid the new First Secretary is asking for trouble, because amongst our colleagues in the embassy in Moscow, there are a few from the ISI and the IB also. And they are there to keep a check on such activities and though they keep masquerading as diplomats and embassy staff members, but they will soon get after him. The First Secretary will be first asked politely to lay off, and if that warning by them is not heeded than he will be sent back home,"added Shiraz as he too glanced through the same magazine and to his horror found that on the long debate on the Fairfax matter in the Indian Parliament, the opposition had also raised a big hue and cry on this very sensitive issue. The opposition had argued that the probes on illegal foreign exchange dealings by influential Indian businessmen that had been initiated by the erstwhile Finance Minister VP Singh who had recently resigned from the Rajiv Gandhi government were now being deliberately scuttled because the financial dealings of the younger brother of the Indian superstar and film idol Amitabh Bachchan who was also a Member of Parliament and a dear friend of the Indian Prime Minister had to be protected.

"By God another big scandal after Bofors it seems is also in the making and I am afraid that though your favorite talented and versatile actor Amitjee has called the charges to be completely false, malicious and reeking of garlic, but I am afraid that this stink will linger on for a very long time and I only hope and pray that it should not in anyway affect the strong bonds of friendship that exists between the two families and the two brothers," said Shiraz as he followed Saira into the kitchen to help her in cutting the vegetables.

CHAPTER-6

A Gamble That Failed

While the Rajiv Gandhi government was feeling the heat that had been generated by the murky Bofors gun deal, and the opposition and the media onslaught on the young Prime Minister to come clean on the Bofors deal continued unabated, in Sri Lanka the ethnic conflict also became a source of worry for the Indian government. After the failure of the Thimpu talks and of the LTTE Chief Prabhakaran's refusal to come to a workable solution and understanding on the Tamil issue with the Jayawardhene government during the SAARC conference in last November at Bangalore, things had started hotting up again on the emerald island.

In January 1987, soon after Prabhakaran the LTTE boss returned back to Sri Lanka from Madras, his call for 'Eelam', full freedom for the Sri Lamkans Tamils in the north and eastern part of the country took a more determined and aggressive turn. His brave band of highly motivated young Tamil Tigers that included both girls and boys who had been armed and trained by India under the overall supervision of the RAW in various training centres including Dehradun and Chakrata were now ready to take on the Sri Lankan army. The LTTE was now not only the most organized, but also the most popular and respected revolutionary organization in the Tamil dominated areas of Sri Lanka. All the other such organizations like the PLOTE, People's Liberation Organization of Tamil Eeelam: TELO, Tamil Eelam Liberation Organization: EROS, Eeelam Revlutionary Organization and the ERPLF, Eelam Revolutinary People's Liberation Front who were also trained and armed by India had either become defunct, or had been completely subjugated by the more powerful and popular LTTE.

Meanwhile Shupriya having settled down in her new appointment at the Indian High Commission in Colombo, she in order to get a better perspective of this long standing ethnic conflict between the Sinhalese and the Tamils in Sri Lanka, went through all the relevant files, classified documents and correspondence on the subject and what she found was indeed quite revealing. According to one report it was after the ethnic riots in the island nation in 1981, that there was an upsurge in the sympathy wave for the cause of the Sri Lankan Tamils by the Indian people in general, and by the Tamils of South India in particular. There was no doubt that the bond between the Tamils in both the countries was always there and prior to 1963, even the Tamils of India wanted an independent state of their own. But in 1963 with the passing of the 16th Amendment of the Indian Constitution which made it mandatory for those running for public office to take an oath for upholding the sovreignty and integrity of the country that the regional parties in Tamil Nadu like the DMK and its offshoot the AIDMK came into the mainstream of political activity in the state. Both the DMK and the AIDMK which had split from its parent organization had now surfaced as political heavy weights in the state and their combined strength had completely overshadowed the erstwhile Congress Party that had been ruling the state for decades. During the state and general elections in 1967, 1971, and 1981 the two regional parties had contested for practically all the assembly seats and therefore they were now a force to reckon with. Both the DMK and the AIDMK during this period had tasted power intermittently and their sympathies rightly so were with the thousands of Tamilian Sri Lankans that had crossed over to the mainland as refugees. In 1983, Mrs Gandhi while conducting negotiations with the Sri Lankan government had directed RAW to take full responsibility in giving military training and also of arming the Tamil militants who had taken refuge in India. Her aim it seems was to step up the armed struggle by the Tamil militants so that more diplomatic pressure could be brought upon the Sri Lankan government and a workable solution could be arrived at, and one that would be acceptable to both the sides. As directed by the advisors to Mrs Gandhi, the training of Tamil militants under the overall supervision of the RAW started in right earnest. This was initially supposed to be a top-secret operation and one that was to be carried out without even the knowledge of the Tamil Nadu State Government and its intelligence agency, but soon the state government too got involved in this exercise. The Tamil Nadu Chief Minister, MG Ramachandran himself donated Rupees 4 crores from his Chief Ministers' Fund to the Tamil militants and soon thereafter practically the whole of Tamil Nadu was dotted with numerous training camps and with each one being conducted by their own respective militant organizations. The LTTE cadres were being trained in six camps with the largest being at Kumbarapatti in the Salem District, while the TELO had five, PLOT had 18, EROS-2 and the EPRLF—7. Besides these, there were a few camps of the other minor Tamil militant groups such asTEA, the Tamil Eelam Army etc.

Initially they were all accepted with open arms, but as time went by the rivalry between the various groups and factions also surfaced, and soon the various militant groups started infighting among themselves. As a result of this, their criminal activities in Tamil Nadu kept increasing and the common people also got fed up and were keen that the government must do something to send them back. Though the Indian government had taken the diplomatic initiative to solve the matter between the Sri Lankan government and the Tamil militants peacefully with a give and take policy, but because of intransigence on both sides an impasse had now been created. Whereas, the Jayawardhene government was not ready to grant the necessary concessions to the Tamil minority in the country and give them equal rights that were applicable to the Sinhalese, the LTTE, the predominant Tamil militant group and others were also not willing to reach an agreement that would be short of Eelam, full freedom.

The intention of the Sri Lankan government to open the strategic Trincomalee Harbour that was located on the Island's eastern coast to outside powers who could then convert it into a strong naval base had serious security implications for India. Moreover, Sri Lanka had also started utilsing the services of the Israeli Mossad to train their own commandos and this too was not a good sign as far as the interests of the Tamil militants trained by India were concerned. And by the time Shupriya could just about settle down in her new appointment, the yearly monsoon clouds from the south-east had already began to darken the horizon. The rains would now only spell more misery for the Tamilians in the north of the island who had already started feeling the heat of the Sri Lankan army. The sky soon turned into a dirty war cloud as the Sri Lankan Army got ready to launch a final offensive into the heavily Tamil dominated Jaffna Peninsula. Announcing his decision to fight and fight to the finish, when President Jayawardene on 27th May declared to his people that 24 hours earlier he had ordered his armed forces to attack Jaffna and the troops were already on the job, it took the mandarins in the South Block by complete surprise.

That day of 27th May, 1987 also happened to be Pandit Nehru's 23rd death anniversary and though Shupriya was aware that the balloon would burst one day, but she didn't expect it to happen on the death anniversary of the architect of 'Panchsheel' and the statesman who was one of the founders of the world's non-align movement. So when, Mr JN Dikshit the Indian High Commissioner in Sri Lanka informed Delhi about the Sri Lankan offensive and about their intention to economically blockade Jaffna, alarm bells started ringing in the Indian capital. With his vision to make India a power to reckon with in South-East Asia, the policy of Indian neutrality for the time being took a complete U-turn as Rajiv Gandhi, the grandson of Pamdit Nehru and his coterie of advisers decided that it was time for India to intervene with a show of force if necessary.

On that day of 27th May, Shiraz having heard about the crisis in Sri Lanka over the BBC radio felt somewhat upset and wondered how India who had been backing the Tamils of the island would react. That same very evening he with his family took the late evening flight from Stockholm to Moscow. They had been invited to the the annual prize distribution function of the Moscow International School that was scheduled to take place the next day afternoon and on the occasion of which their daughter Gammy who had topped her class was to get a plethora of prizes. Soon after the prize distribution ceremony at the school was over, Shiraz at Gammy's request first took her shopping to 'Detski Caad' the big children's toy shop on Derzhensky Square. And after Gammy and her little brother Tojo had picked up their choice of toys, all of them decided to walk back to their hotel room at Hotel Rossiya via the Red Square and the big departmental store called 'The Goom' that was nearby. It was summer time and the Red Square as usual was full of people, when suddenly a drone of a low flying light aircraft was heard in the near distance.

"My God what the hell is the mad guy trying to do," said Shiraz as he looked up and waved out to the pilot who looked indeed very happy as he flew around the great historic plaza. The time was nearing 7.30 PM and Shiraz could make out that the pilot was indicating to the people on the Red Square to move away so that he could land there. And minutes later, when it actually landed on the cobblestones behind the onion domed St Basil's Cathedral, which was not very far from Comrade Lenin's revered mausoleum there was pandemonium all around as the local policemen on duty tried hard to keep the people from getting close to the blue and white Cessna Skyhawk aircraft.

"My God this is not a Russian aircraft at all and if I am not mistaken it has West German markings on it, and I wonder how the hell it managed to land of all the places plumb on the Red Square," said Shiraz to his wife Saira as the young teenage pilot jumped out of the cockpit and smiled at all the onlookers who had gathered around him. No one till date had ever seen a feat like this before, and even during Hitler's 'Operation Barbarossa' when the Germans in 1941 were at the gates of Moscow, the Luftwaffe never had the guts to land on Red Square, and here was this guy coolly signing autographs and adding the words Hamburg—Moscow below it. Shiraz was also very keen to meet the guy in person, but seeing the huge crowd and with his two kids and wife in tow he gave up the idea of being pushed around in the crowd. And a few minutes later when a couple of Russian police cars with its sirens blaring arrived and picked up the young pilot, Shiraz knew that the adventurous young pilot was in serious trouble.

Mathias Rust, a 19 year old amateur pilot from Hamburg for the sake of sheer adventure had penetrated the most heavily guarded airspace in the world as he flew in undetected for 400 miles from Helsinki and touched down at the most tightly guarded centre of the Soviet capital. And by doing so he had also broken the myth that Moscow was not invincible. But now not only he, but even the Russian Defence Minister would have to pay for it. A few days later, when the Soviets announced that Marshal Sergei Sokolov, the Russian Defence Minister and Marshal of Aviation Alexander Kuldunov had been replaced, Shiraz knew that it was all thanks to Mathias Rust who had found the Soviet Air Defence system to be rather rusty.

By early June, with the Sri Lankan economic blockade being further tightened and the fresh fighting between the two warring sides continued unabated, this resulted in more and more Tamil refugees fleeing their homes in Sri Lanka and seeking refuge in Tamil Nadu. As the Sri Lankan armoured and infantry columns launched their attack through the Elephant Pass that was the southern gateway to Jaffna, and passed through the village of Valvaditturai, which was the birthplace of the LTTE leader Prabhakaran, the Tamil Tigers resolve to defend their motherland became for them now a fight unto death also. As the heavy fighting entered the fifth day, the Indian Prime Minister having shown his displeasure to President Jayawardhene to stop the hostility against the Tamilians, got into a huddle with his advisors. MG Ramachandran, the Chief Minister of Tamil Nadu fearing more influx of refugees also flew to Delhi to confer with the Indian Prime Minister. Cautioning the Sri Lankan President that the calculated slaughter of thousands of Sri Lankan Tamil citizens by their own government troops would never solve the problem and that it should promote a peaceful solution, Rajiv Gandhi was now contemplating to reach an accord with the Sri Lankan government, while using the Indian Armed forces as the referee. But before reaching that stage of sending a peace keeping force, he also decided to test and warn the Sri Lankans that if the blockade and the onslaught continued, then India may perhaps be forced to intervene on humanitarian grounds.

On the 3rd of June 1987, the government of India dispatched a flotilla of 20 fishing boats escorted by an unarmed Indian Coast Guard vessel with relief supplies and a host of correspondents to cover the fast developing events in the Jaffna Peninisula. This nearly resulted in a stand off between the small Indian flotilla and the frigates of the Sri Lankan Navy. However, before the Indian boats could approach the Sri Lankan coast, it was already getting dark, and when the Sri Lankan Navy radiod the message that they should go back or else would be fired upon, the small flotilla made its way back to the Indian coastal port of Rameshwaram. And while the Sri Lankan forces continued with their so called 'Operation Liberation' to capture Jaffna, the Indian government undettered by the set back to the small Indian flotilla on the very next day as a show of force decided to lift the economic blockade on Jaffna. Consequently India dispatched five Soviet-designed jumbo military transport aircrafts, the AN-32's that were based in Bangalore on a so called mercy mission. Escorted by five Mirage 2000 fighters, when the AN-22's dropped their payloads of relief supplies consisting of food and medicine to the beleaguered Sri Lankan Tamils at a dropping zone three miles north of Jaffna, it took the Sri Lankans completely by surprise. To Colombo this was a naked violation of Sri Lankan airspace and a gross interference in the internal affairs of their country, but with the limited defensive capabilities at their disposal and the Tamil guerrillas fighting it out with them, the Sri Lankan government had to perforce overlook this big brotherly bullying attitude of her powerful neighbour to the north. The manner in which the Indian government was trying to show its teeth by its gunboat boat diplomacy and in total violation of the Sri Lanka's airspace, it now looked as if India was hell bent in coming to the aid of the Sri Lankan Tamils. This bullying attitude by India against a weak neighbour therefore now came under a scathing attack from those who were once considered to be friends of India. Shupriya herself was perturbed by this sort of big brotherly attitude, but she could not go against her own government's policy and directions. On seeing the belligerent attitude of her powerful neighbour, and the success of the relief air-drop operations that the Indians airforce had carried out under 'Operation Poomalai', which was the Tamil word for garland, President Jayawardhene of Sri Lanka developed cold feet. And not wishing to escalate the matter further, he therefore decided to call off the offensive and to begin talks with the Indian government.

According to Shupriya's own assessment this was entirely Sri Lanka's internal problem and India had therefore no right to interfere militarily both directly or indirectly in this affair. And the only manner by which India could play a part while keeping her own interests in mind was to bring the two sides once more to the conference table. Though she knew that the Thimpu talks in 1985 were a failure, but there was no harm if India again took the initiative and looked for a peaceful solution to the problem. She felt that if Prabhakaran and his LTTE were not going to see reason, then India should wash her hands off completely, rather than try and solve the problem with a military presence in the area.

"To hell with bloody Prabhakaran," wrote Shupriya in her diary as she kept circling the date 6th June with the red pencil. That day Peevee had turned 15, but with the problems in Sri Lanka, Shupriya's proposed rendez-vous to celebrate her son's birthday with him and Monty's family at Bangalore where he was born had perforce to be cancelled at the last minute. Reflecting on her own life, the middle aged Shupriya took out the small photograph of her late husband, Major Shiraz Ismail Khan, PVC and kissed it tenderly. Then in order to pen down her own thoughts and views on the proposed Indian government's decision to send an Indian Peace Keeping Force to Sri Lanka if need be, Shupriya wrote in her diary.

"I wonder whether the same analogy would be accepted by India in the case of Punjab, Nagaland and Mizoram if an outside power which is militarily more powerful than us rallied to their cause. These Indian states too have been clamouring for independence and have also taken up arms to fight for what they feel is a just cause and had that been the case then maybe 'Operation Bluestar' against the Sikhs would have become a non starter, and military operations that are still being conducted regularly against the Naga and Mizo rebels in the north-east of the country could have escalated into something much more bigger than just a low intensity conflict that it presently is being referred to now. After all like we clandestinely armed the Tamil militants to fight for their own motherland in Sri Lanka, these militant groups too are being aided with the arms and ammunition by third countries and our immediate neighbours, who keeping in mind their own geo-political interests in these regions want to keep the fight going. And I only hope that we do not stumble in our quest for peace by sending the Indian Army over to Jaffna to sort out the muddle," concluded Shupriya as she booked a call to Monty and informed him that no further plans be made for a family reunion in Colombo till the present crisis in Sri Lanka was over.

Meanwhile in Stockholm, Shiraz on reading about the Iran-Contra affair in the United States and the Bofors scandal in India in one of the recent issues of the Time magazine drew a parallel to the problems that was now being faced by the two top leaders of both the nations. Both were arms deals and basically concerned the clandestine methods that had been used by those in power in not only procuring arms, but to also make a quick buck on the quiet it seems. While in the case of the Iran-Contra deal these lethal weapons were supplied to the Contra rebels by the Reagan Administration as a quid pro quo for the release of American hostages that were held by Iranian militant groups in Lebanon, whereas in the case of the Bofors deal it was alleged that top Indian politicians including the Indian Prime Minister had been paid off through third parties that had brokered the deal. In both cases though the two top leaders, Reagan of America and Rajiv of India had categorically denied their involvement and stated that they were ignorant of any such deals having been made by their respective governments, but the fact remained that both were now under a cloud. In America, while President Reagan was under fire from the Congress for the Iran-Contra deal, in India, Rajiv Gandhi's Congress Party and his inner coterie of advisors inside the PMO were trying desparately to save the image of 'Mr Clean' from being tarnished further.

"I think in both cases the massive cover up seems to have begun because the two leaders with their contradictory and often off the cuff remarks are trying desperately to hide the truth and plead complete ignorance. But I am afraid in the long run somebody will have to pay for it and quite dearly too if you ask me," said Shiraz while handing over the Time magazine to his wife Saira to go through the article,

"Yes such things at that level and with so many hangers on from within the inner circle of these VVIP's who are always snooping and hovering around the two leaders, it may well be very difficult to hide the facts. And one fine day the truth will eventually come out. You remember Watergate don't you? And look how Nixon was hopelessly cornered and he had to shamefully resign or else they would have certainly impeached him," said Saira as she rolled her big eyes and sternly told her four year old son Tojo to stop playing with his food and to eat it quickly.

"But Mamma there is too much of mirchi (chillies) in the dal," complained Tojo as he sat back in his tall dining chair and waited for his mother to come and feed him.

"What nonsense there is no mirchi in the dal and don't act like a little baby all the time," said Gammy as she scolded her little brother and then put a spoonful of sugar into his plate. This resulted in a fight between the two children because an adamant Tojo wanted only his mother to come and feed him. Ultimately it was Shiraz who had to personally intervene and separate the two of them with a promise that if they ate their food quietly then he would take them on a picnic to the zoo during the coming weekend. While the children quickly gobbled their food down, Saira in her inimitable style whispered into her husband's ear that bribing the children in this manner was not conducive to good upbringing and discipline and that it was time he as a father became a little stricter with them.

While the Indian and Sri Lankan Government continued their talks to reach an accord on the never ending ethnic problem on the emerald island, the Tamil refugees kept pouring into India from the Jaffna peninsula. Those injured and wounded including the militants were admitted to hospitals and those among the young, both boys and girls were sent to the camps for basic militay training. And with the Sri Lankan government now having put the brakes on 'Operation Liberation,' there was some respite in the fighting between the two warring sides, but there was now trouble brewing for India in the far extreme north of the country also.

To resolve the dispute over the Siachen Glacier which the Pakistanis claimed was their territory, the troops from the Shaheen Company of the elite Pakistan SSG, the Special Service Group under their Brigade Commander, Brigadier Pervez Musharaff had for the past two months in freezing weather successfully infiltrated into the massive glacier. This also resulted in a small group from the SSG setting up a new Pakistani army post at an important tactical feature. The new post that was located on the Saltoro Ridge and at the height of over 21,000 feet had been named as the 'Quaid Post' in honour of the Quaid-e-Azam, the late Mr Jinnah. The well sited post overlooked the Indian defences at the Bilafond La Pass and the Indians troops deployed there were now being constantly sniped at. So much so, that the Indian posts at Sona and Amar, which were maintained by air, had also become untenable. Even the Indian helicopter sorties to the pass were now in constant danger of being fired upon. On 18th April, 1987 Quaid Post had fired on the Indian post deployed at Sona and as a result of which one JCO and one Indian soldier from the Bihar Regiment had died. By end May, the Indian High Command had decided that the Pakistani Quaid Post come what may had to be eliminated and a daring plan to capture it was thus made. On 29th May, 1987 an Indian patrol led by the young and daring 2nd Lt Rajiv Pande from the 8th Battalion of the

Jammu and Kashmir Light Infantry Regiment made its way very stealthily to reconnoitre a route that could be subsequently used for the main attack on the post. The route was a hazardous one and entailed scaling over a virtual vertical 1000 feet icewall. Using their pick axes to get a proper foothold on the ice, the patrol slowly and steadily made its way across the deadly obstacle. After Lance Naik Mulk Raj Sharma had made it across, and when the patrol was hardly 30 metres from the enemy defences, they were detected and it came under heavy Pakistani fire. This resulted in the instant death of their patrol leader 2nd Lt Rajiv Pande, Mulk Raj and two others, while the remaining three survived to tell the tale. But Rajiv Pande and his boys did not die in vain. They had fought back heroically and had managed to leave the rope behind on the icewall, which would now be used by the subsequent Indian attackers.

On 23rd June, 1987 a task force led by Major Virender Singh launched 'Operation Rajiv.' The operation was named not after the Indian Prime Minister but after the gallant young officer 2nd Lt Rajiv Pande who had no doubt sacrifced his life, but had also shown the way on how to get at those Pakistanis. Having located that vital rope, the first attack was launched on the night of 24th and 25th March, by Subedar Harnam Singh's team, but by 0330 hours they were detected and fired upon. The enemy post at Quaid was now on full alert, but the indomitable Company Commander, Major Virender Singh was not the one to give up so very easily. It was the question of the battalion's honour and to avenge the death of young Rajiv and his colleagues. Even under those severe adverse conditions of biting cold weather and with limited food and water at their disposal, a second attack was launched by Subedar Sansar Chand's team, but this also proved abhortive. It was now a do or die situation and with the weapons jamming at night because of the low temperature, Major Virender Singh now decided to put in a dare devil daylight attack the next day. On that afternoon of 26th June at around 1.30 PM, a small force under Naib Subedar Bana Singh, a Sikh from the village of Kadyal in Jammu and Kashmir with just four jawans led the attack. It soon resulted in a bitter hand to hand fighting as Naib Subedar Bana Singh leading the ferocious charge soon got the better of the enemy. The Pakistani troops of the famed Shaheen Company from the 3rd Commando Battalion of the SSG Brigade no doubt also fought back heroically, but it was Naib Subedar Bana Singh and his gallant soldiers from the 8th Jammu and Kashmir Light Infantry who finally came out victorious. The Pakistani Quaid Post had ultimately been captured and with Naib Subedar Bana Singh having won the battle on the world's highest battlefield, not only was he immediately promoted to the rank of a Subedar, but he was also recommended for the country's highest gallantry award, the PVC, the Param Veer Chakra. The post was therefore aptly renamed as the Bana Post in his honour. But there was no doubt that the Pakistani troops led by Naib Subedar Atta Mohammed had done Pakistan proud too. For three consecutive nights they had successfully repulsed the Indian attacks and with no more ammunition to fight with they took on the Indians in a hand to hand combat. Though Naib Subedar Bana Singh and his four gallant riflemen Chunilal, Laxman Das, Om Raj and Kashmir Chand had made the Regiment and India proud when they unfurled the tricolour on the 'Quaid Post,', and did a Bhangra to celebrate the victory, a unhappy Brigadier Pervez Musharaff, a gunner himself ordered the Pakistan artillery to open fire. But when it did, it was already a bit too late. The Indians artillery too now retaliated, but the fact was that Pakistan had lost the Quaid Post.

Brigadier Pervez Musharaff was commanding a newly raised SSG Group from his base at Khapalu in the Siachen Glacier and with this set back, he was now preparing a plan to attack the Indian post at Bilafond La. When Shiraz at Stockholm came to know that the Quaid Post had been retaken by the Indian troops, he indeed felt very happy. And with his earnest desire to know a little more about the Pakistani Brigadier who was in charge over there, he therefore rang up his brother-in-law Salim Rehman Khan in Islamabad.

"Oye mere Saale Sahib ye toh bataiye ke ye Brigadier Musharaff hai kaun jisne humme marwa diya Siachen mein?" (Dear brother-in-law who is this man Musharaff who has landed us in bloody shit in Siachen) said Shiraz as Salim Rehman's voice on that long distance call to Islamabad became faintly audible.

"Arre thodha aahista bol meri jaan, kyun ki yahan dewal bhi subh kuch dhyan se soonte rahte hain aur ek din tu mujhe bhi zaroor marvayaga."(Please talk softly my friend because here even walls have ears and one day you will definitely get me into big trouble too) said Salim Rehman as he quickly changed the subject and told his wife Aasma to go back to sleep. The call had come in when it was well passed midnight in Pakistan, but it was stilll bright sunshine for Shiraz in Sweden.

"Now just don't get worried my love and go back to sleep. There is no war on I can assure you," said Salim Rehman as he lovingly patted his wife Aasma and then went to the adjoining drawing room to take the call.

"Humne sirf suna hai ke ye Brigadier Musharaff Sahib ek Mohajir hain, magar hain badi tez cheez. Profession mein hain toh ye gunner officer, lekin pahele bhi SSG mein naukri kar chuke hain aur ye bhi suna hain ke General Zia Sahib ne unne specially select kiya tha issi command ke liye."Inki paidaish toh Hindustan ke rajdhani Delhi mein hui thi aur partition ke samay inke pitta jo ki government mulazim the who apne purre khandan ko Karachi mein leke aaye. PMA ka banda hai, England mein bhi course kiya hai aur lagta hai bahut ambitious bhi hain."((I have only heard that Brigadier Musharaff is a Mohajir, but he is quite sharp and is thoroughly professional in his work. Though he is a gunner officer, but he has served in the SSG earlier also and the rumour is that President Zia had personally selected him for this prestigious command. He was born in Delhi and his father who was a government official at partition had brought the family to Karachi. He passed out from PMA and has also done a course in England and is supposed to be very ambitious too), said Salim Rehman while wishing Shiraz Khuda Hafiz.

By the time half the year was over, Shiraz in his diary made a short summary of how the long drawn out conflicts in Afghanistan, in the Iran-Iraq war, in neighbouring Kashmir, Punjab and at other places had started affecting the world in general and Pakistan and India in particular. In Afghanistan the war between the Russians and the Mujaheedens had entered its eighth year and there was still no let up in the fighting. The Iran-Iraq conflict was now in it seventh year and the Iranians having seized the initiative were now pressing hard to capture the strategic Iraqi port of Basra. As a consequence of this a stray wayward missile had unfortunately landed on the USS 'Stark,' a naval warship that was patrolling the oil rich and strategic Persian Gulf area resulting in the death of a large number of Amercan sailors. It was a horrible error on the part of an over enthusiastic Iraqi pilot who mistook the American frigate for an Iranian tanker and President Saddam promptly apolgised while reiterating his country's earnest desire to establish peace and stability with the Americans in the region. Saddam also agreed to pay heavy compensation to the families of the Americans killed in the unfortunate incident.There was saber rattling too by both India and China on the North East Himalayan border with each side accusing **the** other of nibbling into each other's territory. Nearer home the insurgency situation in neighbouring Kashmir and Indian Punjab was also hotting up with the Pakistan ISI providing both moral and military support to the insurgents to keep the fire burning.

With the failure of the Akali Dal to eliminate terrorism in Punjab, the Governor Siddhartha Shanker Ray had dismissed the Barnala government and President's Rule had been imposed and the tenure of Julius Rebeiro the tough Punjab Police Chief who was to retire on 5th May was extended by another year. There were widespread Hindu-Muslim riots in Meerut, the birthplace of the famous 1857 Indian Mutiny and it soon became a ghost town after four days of blood letting that killed over a hundred people and injured many more till the army had to be called in to restore the situation. The air dropping of relief supplies by the Indian Air Force to the Tamils of Jaffna had further complicated the ethnic problem on the island. The only positive sign as far as Shiraz was concerned was the thaw in the Cold War between the two super powers with Reagan challenging Gorbachev to breakdown the Berlin Wall and the delay by the Americans in not fulfilling the promise of supplying the Pakistan Airforce with the AWACS, the sophisticated Airborne Warning and Control System.

After the induction of the Stringer missiles, the Russians had suffered very heavily and in retaliation they had now started targeting areas that were well inside Pakistan and also on the Afghan-Pakistan border. The other encouraging news was that Maggie, Margaret Thatcher had achieved a hatrick by winning three general elections in a row and her visit to Moscow in April and talks with Gorbachev had further cemented ties between the two countries. The announcement by Moscow that they would be eventually withdrawing their troops from Afghanistan was another positive sign of the rapprochement between the two super powers. But what really thrilled Shiraz was the fact that the 38 year old Indian cricketer, Sunil Gavaskar had become the first man in cricket history to cross the 10,000 run mark in test cricket.

The last fortnight of July 1987 saw a spate of political changes in India. On 17th July, VP Singh resigned from the Congress Party and on the same day R Venkatraman was elected President of India. On the very next day Arun Singh too resigned and on the 19th VP Singh was expelled from the Congress Party. Rumours about the outgoing President Zial Singh having conspired to dismiss the Rajiv Gandhi government during the fag end of his own Presidential tenure on corruption charges also seemed to be true. Zial Singh, the man who had once said very openly that he would even sweep the floor for Indira Gandhi however did not want to embarrass her son by seeking re-election for a second term. Dissidents like VC Shukla, P Upendra, Arun Nehru and others had been feeding the out going President with all kinds of stories and rumours, but despite the rift between the President and the Prime Minister, Zail Singh on 25th July gracefully vacated his chair.

On the 18th of July, 1987 when Monty learnt that the Prime Minister's old buddy Arun Singh who was looking after the Defence Ministry had also put in his papers, but without giving or assigning any convincing reason, he surmised that this could well be a fallout of the on going Bofors scandal. A few days earlier,Amitabh Bachchan another dear friend of Rajiv Ganndhi and a Member of Parliament on being persistently hounded by the opposition had also put in his papers. And therefore putting two and two together, Monty was now of the view that the Bofors deal was far from clean and that the possibility of the Prime Minister's hand in clinching it for monetary gains either by him, his family or by his friends or his party could not therefore be ruled out completely. In order to get some more information on the subject, Monty for a change invited his old friemd Unnikrishnan as his guest for drinks and dinner, and the venue this time was the newly opened bar cum restaurant on the top most floor of Charanjit Singh's five star Hotel Le Meridien in New Delhi.

"Well your guess is as good as mine my friend, and with two stalwarts and both being very dear friends of the Prime Minister resigning in quick succession one after another, there must be some truth in what the opposition has been harping at. But my own hunch is that these two gentlemen who are supposed to be very close to Rajiv and his family probably do not know the real truth about who got the money from the Bofors deal. But there is no denying the fact that they were definitely disillusioned by the government's persistent stand in trying to cover it up, and what is even worse is that most of this cover up is being orchestrated by the PMO's office. And one thing is for sure and that is the top military brass are definitely not involved in this shameful and murky affair, but the role of some top bureaucrats from the Ministry of Defence in the South Block and maybe from the PMO's secretariat cannot be ruled out," said Unni as he requested the barman to put one more large rum into his glass.

"But what makes you say that, and that too so very confidently?" asked Monty.

"Well firstly my source in the Defence Ministry told me categorically that when the Bofors stink started rising, General Sundarjee was very upset about it and he himself recommended to Arun Singh that if the Bofors do not disclose the truth then for the sake of the honour of the country and its Prime Minisiter, the deal should be scrapped because by then only six guns had arrived. Arun Singh who had heard him patiently then told the Chief that he should put it all in writing and submit the same to Mr SK Bhatnagar the Defence Secretary and Sundarjee did that. But a few days later, when

Bhatnagar walked into the Chief's office and told the Chief to redraft it and to change his stand, the Chief was totally surprised and he simply refused to do so. Sundarjee then called on Arun Singh and asked him very categorically as to why the government was insisting that the deal should go through. To that when Arun Singh told him that the PMO was of the view that the cancellation of the order would jeopardize India's security, it was like a big joke to the very man in uniform who was responsible for India's security. And when the very top most General of the Indian Army retorted by saying that the Bofors gun in no way would affect the nation's security and defence preparedness and and that he was willing to guarantee that, I believe Arun Singh's face fell and all he said was that these were the orders from the very top and it had to be obeyed. So Sundarjee like a good obedient soldier and probably not wanting to ruffle any more feathers on this very sensitive issue reluctantly agreed to do so," added Unni as he gave a sly smile from the corner of his lips and tried to light his new Dunhill pipe that Monty had presented him with.

"But what is your own gut feeling, and why is the Prime Minister of India and the PMO trying so desperately to shield the Bofors,?' asked Monty.

"It is because of the simple reason that very big and influential people and their friends are involved, and the issue is so very sensitive that if Arun Singh who has very gracefully resigned opens his mouth then I am afraid that will not only be the end of Rajiv's political career, but his government too would fall. And all this bullshit about the foreign hand destabilizing the country that is now being sung will be thrown back straight into the Prime Minister's face and his so called 'Mr Clean's image would then be blackened forever. Even the former President of India who was also the Commander-in-Chief of the Indian Armed Forces and who had been asking for the relevant files on the subject has been refused access to them by the Prime Minister and thus the bonhomie that existed between the two of them has also turned sour. Yes and let me tell you one more thing in strict confidence and that is about the credibility of Martin Ardbo, the man who was primarily responsible to bag the muti-million dollar contract. Martin himself was under investigation in his own country since 1984 for illegally selling arms that were manufactured by Bofors and unless he had the late Prime Minister of Sweden Olaf Palme's blessings, he would not have been allowed to negotiate the billion dollar deal. And if he too now opens his big mouth then both governments may fall. So if at all Mr Ardbo does talk or is questioned, he will probably talk in riddles, but there is no doubt in my mind that he is the man who holds the secret at the Swedish end, while the

Prime Minister Italian friend Qattarochi and his AE Services probably hold the secret at our end," said Unni as he called for one more large rum and continued with his arguments.

"Now just take the case when the Swedish National Audit Board conducted their own official investigation into the matter and submitted the same to the Government of India. That report categorically stated that Bofors had paid commissions to brokers/agents/middlemen or whatever you may call them, and in that report they had also mentioned the amounts that had been paid to them, but they also very conveniently blanked out the names of the recipients on the plea that Bofors had invoked the clause of commercial confidentiality and that it could sue the government for making that information public and therefore the Swedish government was helpless in the matter. Now this clearly indicated that the Swedish government was also keen to wash its hands off the deal and keep it under wraps. But they were not averse if at the Indian Government's request, Bofors themselves were willing to divulge that information. Therefore based on that, Mr Oza, the Indian Ambassador then suggested that the best course of action for India would be to initiate legal action against Bofors for breach of contract, but there was no response to his suggestion from the powers that be in India. A few days later Mr Anders Carlberg, the CEO and Vice Chairman of the Nobel Group of Industries himself called on the Indian Ambassador and having said that middlemen in such contracts always existed, but since there was an understanding with the Government of India that Bofors should eliminate all existing Indian agents/middlemen, and that they should deal directly with the Indian government the same was done. But Carlberg had also stated to the Indian Ambassador that regarding the foreign agents or companies registered outside India and who looked after Bofors global interests including that of India, they had to be paid as per the contract agreement with them that had been made and finalized prior to the undertaking that was signed by Bofors with India and these therefore had to be honoured. And these were therefore those names of individuals and companies that had been blanked out in the NAB report. But when Carlberg who was naturally not willing to loose the huge contract agreed that if the Indian government so desired and if he could take the Governemt of India into confidence and he was willing to show all the books of transaction to them, it seemed that the mystery would finally be solved. But when Ambassador Oza requested permission from India if he could on behalf of India see the transactions or else a high level Bofors team could go to India with the documents, initially there was no response at all from Delhi. And a few days later, when the Indian Ambassador personally spoke to the Indian Defence Secretary and he agreed, and the Ambassador then asked Carlberg with his team to rush to Delhi; it looked as if things were moving in the right direction. Therefore without wasting time and over the weekend, visas were issued to the Bofors team with the relevant transactions to visit India. But surprisingly on the very day the team was to leave for India, an urgent message arrived from the government to hold them back. The explanation given was that the Indian Parliament was fully seized of the matter and that the visit would serve no useful purpose and since the security of the nation was at stake, a JPC, a Joint Parliamentary Committee would be constituted to go into the matter on priority. Therefore my dear friend you may now draw your own conclusions because as long as Rajiv's government is in the chair this murky deal will never see the light of the day. But the fact remains that the man has lost his credibility and the more he hides, the murkier it will get," added Unni when another friend of his who was also a veteran journalist with leftist leanings having overheard Unni's monologue also joined in the discussion.

"Yes I thing you are damn well right Unni, but eversince the young man came into politics and became first the Congress General Secretary and then the Prime Minister, we have been drifting from one crisis to another and except for his vision to open up the Indian economy, and project India as a future regional power there is little else to show for his achievements in the last four years. First it was 'Operation Blue Star' in which Rajiv was very much a part of the Punjab think tank, but which unfortunately for him ended in a total fiasco both politically and militarily. Then followed the Rajiv-Longowal accord which I am afraid has still not made any headway whatsoever, and we are back to square one as far as militancy in Punjab is concerned. The current political situation in Kashmir which is again of Congress making is also drifting the state towards militancy, which is also rather sad. Then India's saber rattling against the Chinese in NEFA last year by launching 'Operation Falcon' in the area of Somdorong Chu that the Chinese claimed was their territory could have well have become another repeat of the 1962 Namka Chu debacle for us. This was followed by 'Operation Brass Tacks' that nearly led to a fourth round with Pakistan, and now comes the Sri Lankan affair where I believe we will if required even send our own troops to fight somebody else's dirty war. And now this disgraceful thing called Bofors. So in short my friend if you frankly ask me there has been no worthwhile achievement by this government in any major field except ofcourse in the field of telecommunications and in corruption," said the elderly journalist somewhat sarcastically as he in utter contempt cursed all those who were now part of the Prime Minister's inner circle.

"But I don't fully agree with you on that score Sir. Yes Rajiv has messed up a few things no doubt, but he has also achieved some. For instance the Assam accord and the Mizoram accord with Laldenga was a step in the right direction and so was the Longowal accord which unfortunately just did not take off because Longowal was killed. And moreover, the man is young and is new to politics and mistakes under such circulstances are bound to occur," said Monty while trying to take the Prime Minister's side.

Late during that month of July 1987, while there was still tension in the highest battlefield in the world between India and Pakistan, and Rajiv Gandhi was still reeling under the impact of the Bofors scandal, the 54th Indian Division which was one of the reserve fighting formations of the Indian Army that was based at Secunderabad was given the warning order to move at very short notice for a likely peace keeping mission to Sri Lanka. The 54 Indian Infantry Division was being commanded by Major General Harkirat Singh, a high career profile officer from the Brigade of Guards and he was given the honour to lead the first Indian Peace Keeping Force, the IPKF to Sri Lanka. During the months of June and July, while negotiations on the Indo-Sri Lanka draft accord was being worked out, sporadic fighting between the Sri Lankan forces and Tamil militants in Jaffna continued. Simultaneously the relief supplies by the government of India on humanitarian grounds to the Tamils of Jaffna through the Red Cross channels were also allowed to pass through. But with President Jayawardhene bending to Indian pressures and sabre rattling, there was now more trouble for his government in Colombo and in the south of the island where the Sinhalese Buddhists from the Sri Lankan Freedom Party and the JVP, the Janata Vimukti Peranuma, (Peoples Liberation Front) started massive demonstrations against the government for buckling against the threat from India and for calling off 'Operation Liberation' that was launched against the Tamil disruptionist forces in Jaffna and in the north-east of the country.

"I think President Jayawardhene is now caught in a Catch-22 situation of his own doing," wrote Shupriya in her diary as she broadly analysed the approach to the Sri Lankan ethnic problem that was made initially under the directions of Mrs Gandhi and what was now being projected by the present government of Rajiv Gandhi. According to Shupriya, Mrs Gandhi had always generated pressure and she was not willing to mediate. She always sided with the cause of the Tamils, armed them to fight for their cause and she hoped that someday the Sri Lankan government would compromise and come to a just agreement with the Tamils in the island. Whereas in the case of Rajiv, he now wanted that the problem should be solved through mediation only, and that it should be done honestly and with a sense of purpose so that all parties were satisfied. Rajiv also expressed to his own advisors that he was averse to giving any more military aid to the LTTE or to any of the other Tamil militant groups. However, at the same time the Sri Lankan Ambassador to India was summoned to the Ministry of External Affairs and was told very categorically that the relief measures taken by India was a symbolic act of humanitarian support to the Sri Lankan Tamils and that India would retain the option to intervene actively if the Sri Lamkan army carried on with its offensive. Thus faced with the likely possibility of an active Indian intervention, and a hostile population at home, President Jayawardhene decided that it would be better to hold talks with India and arrive at an acceptable solution. And with Mr Jayawardhene having given his consent for talks at the highest government level with India, J N Dixit, the Indian High Commissioner in Colombo immediately started interacting with the Sri Lankan government, and very soon the draft agreement was ready and it was now waiting to be signed by the two respective heads of states. Shupriya while going through the final draft felt very happy that the agreement was fair to both the sides and she hoped that finally there would be cause for celebrations by every Sri Lankan and irrespective of his caste, creed or religion. Among the salient points was the devolution of power to the Provinces, the merger of the northern and eastern provinces that was however subject to a referendum, official status to the Tamil language, termination of 'Operation Liberation.', withdrawal of all Sri Lankan troops to their barracks in the north, and the total disarming of all Tamil militants. Finally it was also agreed to that India would also withdraw all support to the Tamil separatist movement and recognize the unity and sovreignty of Sri Lanka.

On that historic day of 29th July 1987, when the Indian Prime Minister Rajiv Gandhi with his Italian wife Sonia landed at Colombo for the signing ceremony, the welcome by the local people was far from enthusiastic. A day before their arrival there were widespread riots all over Colombo and at other places too. These were mainly organised by the JVP and it soon spread to the other cities. To show their displeasure they even burnt down the Sri Lankan's President's private house in the capital. Though generally the agreement was welcomed by the common people of Sri Lankan and gave hopes of a lasting peace on the island, but there were under currents within the various political parties in the country, the Buddhist clergy and the Tamil militants of the LTTE who were not signatories to the agreement and they were not happy with it.

While Shupriya, standing in a far corner watched the historic signing of the document, she was very impressed with the manner in which the Indian Prime Minister conducted himself with dignity and pride. Having firmly shaken President Jayawardhene's hand, the ever smiling, Rajiv Gandhi for whom humility and impeccable manners was always a plus point congratulated JN Dikshit the Indian High Commissioner to Sri Lanka for his magnificent effort. However, before signing on the dotted line, when the Sri Lankan President confided to the Indian Prime Minister that due to the on going agitation and riots in the south of his country, he would very much like to withdraw his regular forces from the north as they were needed to control the unrest, and requested whether India could help by sending a peace keeping force to ensure the security of Jaffna and Trincomalee, the Indian Prime Minister was somewhat surprised. Though this was not part of the agreement, but contingency plans for such an eventuality had already been worked out by the Indian government. However Rajiv was apprehensive and he asked the Sri Lankan President to first complete the formalites of signing the agreement, and if the President still desired the need for India to send a peace keeping force to the north and eastern provinces then he would require a formal letter in writing from the President himself on this issue indicating that the Indian troops were required for the speedy and efficient implemetation of the accord. Rajiv, however also cautioned the President of Sri Lanka that this could draw a lot of flak from both the governments, but if the Lankan President still felt that it would help, then Rajiv would favourably consider it.

That evening, Shupriya having heard about the Sri Lankan request for an Indian military contingent that had been more or less agreed to by both sides felt rather unhappy about it. The very fact that these Indian troops were to be used to disarm the very people that the RAW under the aegis of the Indian government had armed and trained seemed rather odd to her. Moreover, there were also a few unconfirmed intelligence reports that some responsible elements within the LTTE who were the main beneficiaries of the Indian arms largesse and aid were unhappy with the accord. And that was because they were neither signatory to the accord, nor were they consulted in a manner that their top leaders desired. It had hurt Prabhakaran's ego and the LTTE leader feared that he who had been the most vociferous voice of Tamil Eelam would now be sidelined. According to Shupriya's assessment the manner in which the Prime Minister of Sri Lanka,

Ranasinghe Premadasa had reacted to the signing of the accord was not very encouraging either. Premadasa being an ambitious man was a person to reckon with in the ruling United National Party and being a Sinhalese Buddhist from the south, Shupriya feared that the north-south divide in the island would further widen. Though Premadasa was the Prime Minister, but Jayawardhene was the Executive President and it is he who had all the powers under the constitution. The very fact that the Prime Minister of Sri Lanka was not even present during the signing ceremony was indicative enough to show that Premadasa was not in favour of it.

In those first few months of her stay in Colombo, Shupriya having interacted socially and officially with the Sri Lankan people had realized how much religion played a part in the politics of the island. The south was predominantly Sinhalese Buddhists who were anti-Tamils, the north beyond the Elephant Pass were mostly Tamil Hindus who were anti-Sinhalese, while the eastern seaboard had a majority of Tamil Muslims and each one of them for whatever be the reason only had their own interests in mind and axe to grind. However, the Sri Lankan President and his Prime Minister were both Sinhalese Buddhists. The President of Sri Lanka, Juius Richard Jayawardhene was born on 17th September, 1906. The eldest of 11 children whose father was a Judge of the Ceylon Supreme Court had converted from Christianity to Buddhism in his youth. A lawyer by profession, he joined the Ceylon National Congress in 1938. During the outbreak of the Second World, JR as he was popularly called together with Dudley Senanayeke had held secret discussions with the Japanese with the aim of ousting the British from the island. After gaining independence he became the country's first finance minister and in 1973 after the death of Dudley Senanayake he took over as the foremost UNP leader. In 1977, he was elected Prime Minister and in the following year became Sri Lanka's first Executive President. During his tenure the country was embroiled in two civil wars, one in the south was by the Marxist JVP and the other in the north was by the Tamil militants and as a result of which the country's economy had suffered very badly. He was now 81 years old and wanted peace at any cost. On the other hand his Prime Minister, Ranasinghe Premadasa was much junior in age to him. He was also born in Colombo on 23rd June, 1924 and unlike JR came from a family of modest means. He too was a Sinhalese Buddhist, but belonged to the Hinna caste. Though his rise to political power was resented by the Govigama caste families that had been ruling the country since independence, but Premadasa was a man of action. In January, 1967, as the Minister of Information and Broadcasting, he had converted Radio Ceylon into the Ceylon Broadcasting

Corporation. Premadasa also was instrumental in introducing the mobile secretariat concept, wherein the central bureaucracy was made to visit the villages and look into the problems of the villagers on the spot. The man who intended to become a journalist and had also transalated Pandit Nehru's autobiography into Sinhalese had a very simple life style. Being the number two man in the hierarchy he was now waiting in the wings to take over the UNP from the ageing Jayawardhene and from the clutches of the Govigama caste who had been in the forefront of Sinhalese politics eversince the British left the island.

On the next day morning, while arrangements were being made to give the Prime Minister of India a formal farewell with a guard of honour, there were very disquieting reports that the accord had not been well accepted by the people, both in the north and in the south. The general feeling in the predominantly Buddhist south was that too many concessions had been given to the Tamils and the idea of getting the Indian Army to control the north and the eastern region was like a total sell out. In the Tamil dominated north, the LTTE and their supporters were also feeling cut up because not only were they left out and ignored, but being one of the main players they felt that they too should have been a signatory to the accord. Seeing the general mood of the public who had been on the rampage for the last two days, the Indian High Commission's office was also now apprehensive about the security of the Prime Minister. In fact soon after the signing in ceremony was over, the Indian High Commissioner JN Dixit who was a very experienced Foreign Service officer and who had served in very many countries including Afghanistan and Bangladesh had cautioned NK Seshan, the man who was in charge of Rajiv Gandhi's security to be extremely alert and careful. The Indian Prime Minister's departure by air after an overnight stay was scheduled on the next day morning at 10.30 AM. The date was 30th July and it happened to be a Thursday, which was Sai Baba's day and Shupriya having prayed to the Saint from Shirdi for the safety of the Prime Minister, she with some other senior officials from the Indian mission made their way for the formal guard of honour ceremony that was to be held at the Presidential Palace. Looking as handsome as ever, when Rajiv Gandhi immaculately dressed in a closed collar coat and well creased trousers with his shoes shining like a mirror got on to the dais to take the salute, Shupriya with her newly acquired Sony video camera got ready to record the event for posterity. Once the national anthems of both the countries had been played and the guard of honour had presented arms to the Indian dignitary, the Prime Minister escorted by the guard of honour commander made his way along the red carpet to inspect the 72 men strong Sinhalese guard of honour contingent. During those few minutes, Shupriya zoomed in her camera on the VVIP spectators. The Prime Minister's wife Sonia Gandhi seemed to be in a pensive mood and so were all the others who were sitting next to her. Everybody looked somewhat worried and Shupriya was surprised to notice that only a few had smiling faces amongst those who had the privilege of occupying the first row iof the spectator's gallery that was only meant for the VVIP's. When the band struck the slow march for the inspection to commence, Shupriya automatically started panning her camera from left to right. Everything was going fine, but then suddenly when a young Sri Lankan sailor who was in the very first row after having been inspected by the VIP reversed his personal weapon and holding it by the barrel with both his hands swung the rifle like a baseball bat with full force and brought the heavy butt down on to Rajiv's back, Shupriya was stunned. "Oh My God,"exclaimed Shupriya as Rajiv lost his balance for a few seconds, but luckily did not fall down. All those who were watching the ceremony were simply shocked. This was something unprecedented and had never happened ever before when a visiting foreign dignitary while inspecting the guard of honour had been so blatantly targeted in such an insulting and crude manner. The Sri Lankan Naval Chief who was escorting the Indian Prime Minister and other security personel following him quickly overpowered the Sinhalese naval rating and Rajiv was lucky not to have been hit on his head or neck. Because had that been the case as had been intended probably by the attacker, then the injury could have been far more serious and could have been even fatal too. Thanks to his quick reflexes, his side vision and alertness that Rajiv had acquired as a pilot, the Prime Minister ducked in the nick of time and as a result of which the blow had landed on his left shoulder and just below his left ear. There was no doubt that for a few seconds the Indian Prime Minister was unnerved, but he somehow kept his cool and carried on with the ceremony. By that dastardly act by a serving Sri Lankan serviceman, it became quite obvious to Shupriya that the peace pact brokered by India was not at all to the liking of even those who were supposed to be better disciplined and in military uniform.

By the time Rajiv was given first aid and he boarded the flight back to Delh, there were already a few big blue welts and a swelling on his left shoulder. During the flight, while his wife Sonia seated beside her injured husband looked somewhat tense and perturbed and very rightly so, the Prime Minister took matters more calmly. On landing at Palam, when he told the waiting press and the hordes of other well wishers who had come to receive him that he was perfectly alright, and there was even that usual friendly smile on his handsome face, but the fact was that he was in great pain. When he also jokingly told the press that if they so wished he was even willing to take his clothes off to show them the lump on his left shoulder, everybody took him rather lightly. And though the injury was not very serious outwardly, but it did restrict the Prime Minister's left shoulder movement and made it difficult for him to sleep on his left side. He never complained about this and this fact was only own to his wife and maybe to his children.

Back in Colombo, though the Sri Lankan government profusely apologized for the ghastly incident, Shupriya once again realized that the accord that was signed by both the nations twenty four hours ago was full of pitfalls and the chances of its success to bring about a lasting peace on the island was also rather dim. Nevertheless, she decided to probe a little more into the antecedents of the young Srl Lankan sailor who had dared to attack the Indian Prime Minister in full view of the public, the press and the TV. The 22 year old assailant, Vijayamuni Rohana was a naval rating who had joined the Sri Lankan Navy only two years ago. Following the shameful incident, he had been immediately arrested and a court-martial had been ordered. But there was also a strong runmour that it was not just an act by the individual himself but a conspiracy that could have resulted in the death of the Indian Prime Minister. According to one source, it was a plot by a group of disgruntled Sinhalese naval ratings who were anti—Tamils and who were not happy with the concessions that had been granted to the Tamils in the peace accord. The plan was for Rohana to swing his rifle butt and hit the victim hard on his head or on the nape of his neck so that the victim collapsed and fell on the ground and thereafter his two other comrades would bayonet him because the rifles had no ammunition in the magazines. But Rohana could not achieve the first part of the sinister act and the other two conspirators it seemed had chickened out at the last moment, when Rajiv very adroitly deflected the blow on to his left shoulder. In those few seconds thanks to the alert Sri Lankan Naval Chief and the security men who were following behind, the attacker had been overpowered.

"Just imagine what could have been the consequences had the Indian Prime Minister been killed. This could have even resulted into an Indo-Sri Lankan-LTTE conflict, and maybe even to a more deadlier civil war in that country," wrote Shupriya to Monty a few days later as she once again viewed the bizarre incident that she had filmed on her video camera.

On that same very day of 30th July, 1987 when the Prime Minister of India was on his way back to Delhi, Lt General Depinder Singh, the GOC-in-C of India's Southern Command flew into Jaffna to discuss the necessary arrangements with the Sri Lankan military command for the induction of the Indian Peace Keeping Force. And soon thereafter on the very next day, the first contingent of the Indian troops from the 54th Indian Division under the command of Major General Harkirat Singh also landed at Jaffna. Thinking that it was going to be only peace time duty of disarming the Tamil militants and to stop the fighting between the two warring sides, the IPKF had not even been briefed properly on their likely role as peace keepers. Though a temporary ceasefire had been declared, but the Tamil militants were wary of voluntarily laying down their arms. They were afraid that if they were challenged and captured by the Sri Lankan forces, they would be left with nothing to fight with, and maybe they would be even tortured by them. They were also apprehensive whether the IPKF would be capable enough to guarantee them and their families the necessary protection. Moreover, the most important and the key man in the LTTE, Prabhakaran was still in Delhi. He had been summoned to Delhi and was a guest of the Indian government and was staying at the Ashoka Hotel, while the accord was being signed. He had met Rajiv Gandhi before the Indian Prime Minister left for Colombo and was assured by him that the interest of the Tamils and the LTTE would be looked after. But when he witnessed the signing ceremony on TV and heard about the Indian government's commitment to disarm the militants by sending in Indian troops as a peace keeping force, Prabhakarn was far from happy.

The ink on the accord had hardly dried up, when the 54 Infantry Division was ordered to pack up and move to Jaffna immediately. By the very next morning, when 3000 Indian troops landed by sea and air, the leaders of the LTTE and their representatives openly showed their displeasure to Major General Harkirat Singh, the GOC IPKF when they rocked his jeep and openly kept yelling that they would not lay down their arms unless their leader Prabhakaran was permitted to return back to Jaffna. Judging by the hostile reception to the Indian troops by the LTTE militants, Prabhakaran was released on the promise that he would prevail on his Tamil Tigers to lay down their arms peacefully and on Sunday 2nd August he too was back in Jaffna.

Looking at the manner in which the Indian units and sub-units landed, it was obvious that they had come for the delicate mission without doing any worthwhile preparations. It was a hurriedly prepared military plan that had no meaningful intelligence inputs. Moreover, it was without any proper war gaming, and without working out the likely contingencies that may well arise both politically and militarily once they landed on the two Northern and Eastern provinces of the beleaguered island. The presence of the IPKF it seems was therefore to act more or less like a referee or as an umpire till an election as envisaged for the devolution of power was held in the Tamil dominated areas of the nation.

Shupriya on learning that the advance party from the IPKF had landed at Jaffna felt indeed very proud and happy, and later when she interacted with the officers from the main body and found out that most of the troops had arrived with only their personal weapons, limited ammunition, light beddings, tentage and rations, she too felt that the task given to the IPKF would propably be over at the maximum by the end of the year and they would then all go back to Secunderabad or to their respective peace stations to be with their families. With the RAW's perception that there was nothing to fear from Prabhakaran and that the LTTE who the RAW claimed were good friends of India and that they would when ordered lay down their arms voluntarily, Shupriya took it for granted that it would be all smooth sailing and the ethnic strife that had been lingering for years would also now be over soon. But this was all plain wishful thinking.

The first few weeks in August passed of peacefully with the LTTE and other Tamil Militant organizations laying down their arms as and when told, but not totally. There were certain elements within the LTTE including their leader Prabhakaran who kept showing their reluctance to do so. The hardliners in the LTTE were not too happy with the Indo-Sri Lanka deal and they feared that they being the most popular entity in the north and east of the country and whose writ had been the mainstay for Tamil Eelam during these past few years they would lose their power and prestige. It would get eroded and once the IPKF was withdrawn they would probably be the first ones to be targeted by the Sri Lankan forces and the Sinhalese people who were seething with revenge. With no weapons to fight with, they would then be left at the mercy of their adversaries and their dream for Tamil Eelam after such heavy sacrifices would never be fulfilled ever. With all those apprehensions in mind, Prabhakaran very wisely and cleverly and in order to keep all his options open held back a large cache of arms, ammunitions and explosives and then slowly deployed some of his forces with those very arms to the safety of the nearby jungles.

In that month of August 1987, when Shupriya saw the arms surrender ceremony on the Sri Lankan television-Rupavahani-she was thrilled. It was done in typical fauji style and with all the bullshit, pomp and show that had now become very much a part of the Indian Army's way of life. With the presence of the Indian Southern Army Commander Lt General Depinder Singh and his Divisional Commander Major General Harkirat Singh smiling, shaking hands and backslapping with some of the senior Tamil militant leaders, it all looked very honky-dory, and everything it seems was progressing well and as per plan, but a few days later things began to sour. The old rivalries and rumblings between the various Tamil Militant groups had once again started surfacing out into the open, and this now spelt danger signals to the Indian-Sri Lankan accord. The differences among the militant groups soon took on a political colour as each one of them started demanding their own pound of flesh and representation in the proposed devolution of power. When the Indian Government's proposal to give the three main militant groups, namely the LTTE, EROS and TULF two representatives each and the others one only for the running of the interim administration in the northern and eastern provinces of Sri Lanka and till such time elections could be held, the LTTE leaders were visbly upset. According to them it was they who had been in the forefront of all the fighting and it was they who had made the maximum sacrifices and it was their writ that had been running all these years and they therefore felt that they were now being sidelined and being equated with the same very militant groups that they the LTTE themselves had disarmed and exiled from their motherland.

On 12th August, 1987 the IPKF suffered it first casualties, when a Sapper team consisiting of Major Dalip Singh, Lieutenant Vikram and Mohinder Rao from the 8th Engineer Regiment died while trying to neutralize a booby trap at a house in a village near Jaffna. When Shupriya learnt about this tragedy, her heart went out to the families of those unfortunate soldiers. She was reminded about her late husband Major Shiraz Ismail Khan who too had lost his life while raiding an ammunition dump inside Pakistan way back in 1971, but that was war while this was a peace keeping duty and the loss therefore for the bereaved families was even greater she thought.

In that very month of August, while the wounded Indian soldiers from Sri Lanka were being evacuated for treatment to the army hospital in Madras, the dreaded Sikh terrorist Harjinder Singh Jinda, the killer of General Vaidya, Lalit Singh Maken and Arjun Dass was fighting for his own life at the Army hospital in New Delhi. Jinda who had escaped from police custody was seriously injured in an encounter with the Delhi Police that took place in the Civil Lines area of the Indian capital. Thanks to the army doctors, Jinda's life was miraculously saved and he lived to tell Ved Marwah, the Delhi Police Chief who personally went and met him in the Army Hospital about Pakistan's involvement in training the Sikh terrorists and the ISI's plans to forment a Hindu-Sikh divide. Jinda was however not repentant for his many crimes and he was prepared to die for the sake of Khalistan.

And while Jinda was being treated in the Army Hospital in Delhi, the seeds of a terrorist movement in Kashmir were also being sowed. This was as a result of the tie up between Faroukh Abdullah's party, the National Conference and Rajiv Gandhi's Congress when they joined hands once again to fight the State elections. In the Seventh State Assembly elections that were held in end March 1987, Farouk's National Conference had got 40 seats, the Congress (I) 26 and the Muslim United Front secured only 4. Calling the elections a bloody fraud on the people and a totally rigged one at that, the angry younger generation of Kashmiri Muslims in the valley felt that they had been cheated and therefore they had now decided to take up arms and fight against this gross injustice. This also once again gave Pakistan the golden opportunity to indoctrinate and train these disgruntled young people to take up arms as Jihadis and raise the flag of freedom.

In that month of August, 1987 Monty while visiting the valley for his usual export business order of carpets and Kashmiri artifacts was taken aback by the sudden change of attitude of the young local men and even women from the villages that were located further to the interior and closer to the Line of Control. During his business visit to Bandipore, Kupwara and the picturesque Lolabh Valley the attitude was even hostile and they were openly cursing Faroukh Abdullah and his government of being the stooges of the Indians. This kind of anti Indian outlook Monty had never ever witnessed before and in a few villages he even saw some Pakistani flags flying. Some of them amongst the younger and educated lot even refused to take any more orders from him and openly said that they would rather starve then work for the people from Hindustan. While waiting for his Indian Airlines flight back to Delhi from Srinagar which as usual was late because of bad weather over the Pir Panjal Ranges, Monty in a letter to Shupriya somewhat jokingly wrote that if she thought that the militancy in the south of the country was bad enough thanks to the RAW arming and training the Tamil militants, then up north in Kashmir thanks to the rigging of the elections, the Pakistan ISI was now only waiting to motivate, arm and train the young Kashmiris to wage a proxy war in the valley and that too in the not very distant future.

A few days after his return to Delhi from Srinagar, Monty was surprised to read an article in the Time magazine dated 7th September about an alleged plot by the CIA to oust Rajiv Gandhi. This was a fall out of a secret letter that had allegedly been written by Whilliam Casey, the Director CIA on the 10th of December, 1986 and which had recently been published by the Indian weekly 'Blitz" in their issue dated 1st August 1987. With the sensational heading of 'CIA Dagger Behind Plot to Oust Rajiv' in bold capital letters that was on its front page, the Blitz had no doubt raised an hornet's nest in the Indian parliament, but Monty who at times suspected the veracity and the credibility of the weekly magazine was not convinced. He knew that Rajiv's government was still reeling from the severe barrage that the opposition had unleashed on him on the on going Bofors gun scandal, and the supporters of Rajiv Gandhi in the Indian Parliament and the Prime Minister himself who had been attributing time and again the malicious charges to a foreign hand needed someone to raise the bogey, and Blitz it seemed had obliged. Because there were also well confirmed reports that the Indian government to save the Prime Minister's skin by hook or by crook had launched a massive disinformation campaign and that this letter too was part of the massive cover up. Despite the fact that the American Embassy officials in Delhi had categorically stated that this was a clear case of a crude and total forgery and pointed out the many flaws in it, Rajiv Gandhi however kept insisting that he believed that the letter was authentic. Finally when the elderly Parsi editor of Blitz, Mr Rusi Karanjia himself admitted to Amrita Singh, the Time correspondent that he as a responsible editor would have never published the matter without getting it tested and verified by the responsible intelligence agencies of his own country, the cat it seems was now out of the bag. There was no doubt in Monty's mind now that the Rajiv Gandhi Government in their quest to keep the Bofors affair under wraps and to promote their own theory that it was the foreign powers who were hell bent in destabilizing India, that he with the copy of the Time magazine called upon his old friend Unni at the Press Club in Delhi.

"Well my friend you can well see that those in power in India will clutch to every damn straw to keep themselves afloat and that is exactly what this government has been doing eversince the Bofors scandal surfaced in April 1987," said Unni as he rolled up the sleeves of his khadi kurta and attacked the tender tandoori chicken with both his hands. In order to further prove his point that both the Indian and the Swedish Government were now partners in the great cover up plan, Unni ripped open the two leg pieces from the whole chicken and presenting the bigger one to Monty said.

"Though the breast and the neck piece are still left, but the chicken like this government I am afraid have no legs to stand on." This was probably

Unni's way of saying that all good and bad things must be shared and shared alike both with bouquets and brickbats and that the Bofors deal between the two governments was no exception either. To further amplify that it was a shady deal, when Unni said that the Rajiv Government had even sent Mr Natwar Singh who was an ex IFS man, but who was now a Minister of State in the External Affairs Ministry to Sweden to ensure that the enquiry that was being conducted independently by Lars Rineburg at the Swedish end should not see the light of the day, and that Natwar Sinbgh had held a series of meetings on this very score with the Swedish Foreign Minister Anderson, Monty was flabbergasted and asked.

"'Do you therefore mean to say that it was because of the pressure from top by the Swedish government on Rineburg that his investigation was scuttled?"

"Ofcourse my friend or else what could be the bloody reason for this sudden turn around by the eminent Swedish prosecutor who has now decided to close his investigation on the grounds that there was lack of sufficient evidence from the various authorities concerned," said Unni as he broke the chicken neck piece into two. This was Unni's way of symbolically reiterating that the present disinformation and propaganda campaign that had been launched by the Rajiv government would one day not only backfire very badly, but it would also make some people scapegoats in this whole sordid affair and those poor chaps someday for no fault of theirs and to save one person's skin would probably get it in their bloody necks. Unfortunately Unni's prediction about somebody getting it in the neck proved to be quite the opposite, when tax and revenue officials started carrying out raids in the offices of the Indian Express newspaper all over India. The paper off late in its editorials under the bold editorship of the 45 year old Arun Shourie had been repeatedly accusing Rajiv Gandhi of deceiving the Indian Parliament and the public on the tainted Bofors deal. The young editor with a PhD in economics from Syracuse University, USA had also earlier exposed the rift between the Prime Minister and the former President Zial Singh. Shourie had also been targeting the alleged illegal foreign currency dealings of a few well known personalities who were very close friends of the Gandhi Family and had therefore it seems earned the government's wrath. The raids by the tax authorities on charges that the Indian Express had violated customs regulations on import duties was nothing but a way of intimating to the owners and editors of this widely circulated newspaper that such anti-government columns would not be tolerated. It was also to warn the others obliquely that the government would come down hard on them too if they dared to write against the government and its revered leader. This smacked of the measures that Mrs Gandhi had adopted when her younger son Sanjay and she were both accused of corruption and dictatorship. As a result of this the opposition parties had now started chanting slogans accusing Rajiv of goondiasm.

Meanwhile in Sri Lanka, to further make matters worse for the government of India and the IPKF, both Amirithalingam Thileepan, the head of the LTTE's political wing and Prabhakaran the LTTE's fiery military commander together with their other senior commanders like Mahatyya and Pulendran made no bones to voice their displeasure to the locals whose support they stiil very much enjoyed. They thought that they were being scuttled both politically and militarily by the Indian government through the RAW and the IB who undoubtedly were not only the Chief Players and Umpires in ensuring the implementation of the accord, but also the prime intelligence gathering agencies for India. Soon the distrust between the Indian intelligence agencies and the LTTE started growing more and more hostile as reports of the fraternization between the RAW and the newly formed Tri-Star, which was a merger of TELO, EPRLF AND ENDLF started making the rounds. Fearing that the LTTE would now be completely sidelined, the LTTE leaders decided to go not only on a propaganda offensive, but they also became wary of totally surrendering their arms.

Slowing down the process of handing over their own weapons and ammunition, the LTTE now started utilizing the 'Eelamurasu'; which was an LTTE controlled daily tabloid, and also the local radio and television station that had been set up by them to air their resentment to the brokered peace plan, while at the same time they kept establishing secret military camps in the nearby jungles. The LTTE was apprehensive that incase the RAW started rearming the Tri-Star and other Tamil militant groups, because the Tamils Tigers as they were called were becoming a headache for the implementation of the accord, then in that case they would be left without any arms to fight and defend themselves with, and their call for Eelam would only remain a distant dream.These militant groups had also now been allowed to open their own offices under the protection of the IPKF, and this also constituted a direct threat to the LTTE's own power base on the island and in the Jaffna Peninsula in particular. Keeping all these factors in mind, the LTTE started getting ready to take on the rival Tamil militant outfits if need be. A clear indication of this was the abnormal increase in the sale of grease and polythene in Jaffna and Trincomalee. These were needed by the LTTE to grease and cache their weapons at safe hiding places for use when required.

While Shiraz sitting in Stockholm read about the problems that were being faced by the IPKF in Sri Lanka and in which some of the units that were now being commanded by his old erstwhile coursemates from NDA and the IMA, he was filled with nostalgia. But what bothered him even more was the brickbats and humiliation that Rajiv Gandhi the Indian Prime Minister was now facing from his own people and in the Indian parliament on the smoking Bofors gun. Shiraz always considered Rajiv Gandhi to be a perfect and forthright gentleman of honour, but the manner in which he was now ducking corruption charges, and the way he was trying to prove his own and his family's innocence in the tainted Bofors deal only made him more suspect. There were also confirmed reports of some well to do and important Indian politicians from the opposition parties, as also of some journalists from India having arrived in the Swedish capital to snoop around and get more details on the subject.

At around this time in August 1987, when Lars Ringberg the Swedish prosecutor incharge of the Stockholm region and of which Karlskoga was very much a part announced his intention of carrying out a criminal investigation into the dirty Bofors-India deal, provided India as the injured and defrauded party was willing to cooperate, and the same was recommended by the Indian Ambassador, it resulted in shockwaves at the PMO. And on 19th August, when Ringberg made a public announcement stating that since no request from India was forthcoming, but he as the public prosecutor will still go ahead and hold prelimininary investigations into the deal under the relevant portions of the Swedish law, that literally sent the PMO into a tailspin. And it got even worse, when Ringberg sent a personal communication to the Indian CBI requesting for cooperation in the matter, which resulted in a panic situation at the PMO. Mohan Katre the CBI Chief was therefore quietly instructed to lie low and not to even acknowledge Ringberg's request. The cover up operations at the PMO now had got into the fire fighting mode as an all out attempt was made to scuttle the murky and dirty Bofors scandal at all costs. The Government of India's total silence on the Swedish Prosecutor's request and the persisitent manner in which the Prime Minister was opposing the investigation further blackened Rajiv Gandhi's face and badly tarnished his image. He was now being referred to as a con man and his guilty conscience showed, when he instead of going himself, he deputed his senior minister Narisimha Rao to represent him and the country at the 'Festival of India' in Sweden. When Narismha Rao, who always had a perpetual frown on his face and who was therefore known as 'Mr Morose' in the Ministry of External affairs was nominated, the reason was quite obvious thought Shiraz. The Indian Prime Minister was probably too scared to face the Swedish public and the press. However a few day later when Shiraz learnt that a Canadian citizen of Pakistani origin by the name of Arshad Pervez had been recently arrested in Philadelphia on charges of trying to export 25 tons of a special steel alloy that could be used in the enrichment of uranium for producing nuclear weapons, he felt rather happy. This also gave the Reagan administration and the U S Congress not only the stick to beat Zia with, but to also withhold the much promised delivery of the AWACS aircraft that Pakistan very much wanted for early warning of the Soviet and Afghan air raids into the Pakistan border areas that had now become a daily routine affair. Later in the week, when Shiraz further learnt that a retired Brigadier by the name of Inam-ul-Haq had also been indicted for conspiring with Pervez to illegally export strategic material that was probably meant for Pakistan's topsecret nuclear facility at Kahuta, Shiraz was convinced that Pakistan was now hell bent in becoming a nuclear power.

CHAPTER-7

Caught in a Tangled Web

In the meantime an assassination attempt on the Sri Lankan President Jayewardhene in Colombo by a totally unknown group that called itself the People's Patriotic Movement had got Shupriya worried. She was aware that the Buddhist Sinhalese majority was bitterly opposed to the peace accord, but for this unknown group to so very openly target the President and get away scot free was rather surprising. Jayawardhene was presiding over the the ruling United National Party's first major caucus that was being held after the signing of the accord and everyone was in a very happy mood. But then suddenly the mood changed to one of utter despair, when the assailants having burst through the thick glass door of the adjoining storeroom fired directly at the President. By a stroke of goodluck an aide at that very moment came between the gunman and the seated President, and as a result of which the aide was critically wounded. Simultaneously two grenades were exploded by the assasins and this resulted in the death of one minister and injuries to 10 others including Premadasa, the Sri Lankan Prime Minister. It thus proved that despite the accord to foster peace and harmony in that trouble torn nation, nobody was safe.

By mid September 1987, Jaffna was once again in a grip of internecine warfare as clashes between the LTTE and their rival groups started gaining momentum, and by 22nd September it had claimed more than 120 lives. The LTTE had also now started initiating a campaign to discredit the presence of the IPKF on what they claimed was their motherland and that the Indian forces were unwanted. As the fratricidal rivalry between the rival militant groups kept spreading into the major towns and villages of the Northern and Eastern Provinces, the LTTE made a dramatic announcement by stating that they had lost faith in the accord and that it was not willing to surrender any more arms to the IPKF. Though the LTTE were now offered three out of the eight seats in the Interim Administrative Council, but they were still not satisfied. And to add more fuel to the fire, the matter got further aggravated when the bespectacled fiery orator and the head of the political wing of the LTTE, Thileepan announced on 15th September that he would go on an indefinite fast unto death if the five demands made by him on behalf of the Tamils were not met speedily. And these demands included the immediate stoppage of the Sinhalese colonization of what was the traditional homeland of the Tamils, release of all Tamil prisoners held under the Prevention of Terrorism Act and other such emergency regulations by the Sri Lankan government, formation of the Interim Administative Council, holding of the referendum for the merger of the North and Eastern Provinces as one region, and the withdrawal of all Sri Lankan Security personel from all the Tamil schools and colleges that was still under occupation by them. And when Shupriya came to know about Prabhakaran's volte face on the question of surrendering arms, she in her first and only remark to her superiors said.

"Yes looking at the negative way things are shaping, I too had a hunch that a situation like this could well soon arise, and it is now all once again back to square one it seems. And before it is too late and on the plea that inspite of trying our very best, if the concerned people are themselves not interested in peace and unity, then I feel we should gracefully walk out of this deal and leave all their internal problems to be sorted out among themseves. Failing which we might get into a Viet Nam like, or maybe an Afghanistan like situation and that would be disastrous for us," concluded Shupriya as she also made a note of this likely scenario in her own private diary.

Though the mandate that was given to the IPKF did not initially include the maintenance of law and order in the region, but looking at the manner in which things were now moving, some 4000 personel from the Indian Central Reserve Police with riot equipment were flown in, and the strength of the IPKF was also substantially increased when the 36 Infantry Division from Saugor in Madhya Pradesh was also inducted. And as far as Thileepan was concerned, he was a well trained Tamil Tiger, but in the month of May and during Operation Liberation by the Sri Lankan Army he had been shot at and had been seriously wounded. But when he began his fast unto death, the government of India and the RAW took it somewhat casually it seems. They thought it was another gimmick to divert the people's attention from the political killings in the Eastern Province and concluded that he would soon give it up. But they were mistaken. Thileepan was a diehard militant who was well respected and whose cry for Tamil Eelam had motivated a large number of young boys and girls to join the ferocious band of Tamil freedom fighters. Some of them like him had been inducted into the elite group and they were now known as the Black Tigers who were ever ready to even die for the cause of their motherland. The RAW it seems had highly underestimated the fighting qualities of these highly motivated dare devil young Tamils and made no attempt at all to cool the tempers which was slowly rising to a boiling point.

Under the special stage that had been erected at the Nallur Kandaswamy temple in Jaffna, while Thileepan continued with his fast and kept up his tirade day in and day out against the Indian Government for failing to protect the interests of the Tamils, and accused both India and Sri Lanka of having shoved the accord down the LTTE's throat, it was time for the Indian High Commission in Sri Lanka to take notice of it. Thileepan's fiery speeches that were being telecast live by Nidarshanam, the television network that was run by the LTTE was having an adverse affect on the population and it had started stirring anti-Indian feelings amongst the locals too. Soon people from all over the Jaffna peninsula started marching to Nallur. They too wanted to join their leader in the fast and to show their solidarity towards him and his call for unity. As the fast entered its second week and Thileepan's condition kept on deteriorating, the people's resentment and anger towards India and the IPKF also began to grow stronger. In order to guage the situation for herself, Shupriya made a hurried trip to Jaffna on the 21st of September, and according to her own assessment the matter was more than serious. As she stood in one far corner of the temple with her hands folded and prayed to the diety to make the young Tamilian leader change his mind and break his fast, she also had the uncanny feeling that she and those Indian in plain clothes who were sent to protect her were unwanted in that gathering. Thileepan during the last seven days of his fasting had not even touched a drop of water and his life was slowly waning away. Shupriya therefore felt that in order to save the man's life and bring about a quick change of heart in the people's mind, all that was required was an assurance and a guarantee by the Indian government to safeguard the interest of the Tamils and for the senior most representative of India in Colombo to come to Nallur and reassure the Tamil leader that the Indian government would do all it can to fulfill its pledges to the Tamilians. That would have not only been a good humane gesture, but it would have also boosted the flagging spirit of the locals who were desperately crying for peace. Only the other day, when the Indian troops had landed they had welcomed them with open arms and garlands as saviors, but now the hatred for them whether in uniform or otherwise could now be clearly seen on the faces of all those who supported the LTTE.

Though on the very next day of 22nd September, the Indian High Commissioner Mr Mani Dixit did arrive at Jaffna to study the situation and was met by Prabhakaran at the Palally airport, but he did not personally go to the Nallur temple to reassure and request the dying man to call off his fast. To do that Mr Dixit wanted a written guarantee from the LTTE leader that the man would yield to his request, but Prabhakaran was not willing to guarantee that. Nevertheless, had Mr Dixit done that, things may have turned out a bit differently. But he made the matter even worse by saying that the fast was a provocative act, which was aimed at instigating the Tamil masses against the Indians and that seemed to be last straw, wrote Shupriya in her diary. Four days later on 26th September, 1987 Thileepan died and now there was hell to pay. The death of this single individual who was an idealist soon became a rallying point by the LTTE to ask for more concessions and for more power in the running of the proposed Interim Administration. On 28th September an agreement was reached and an official statement issued. It was agreed that the LTTE would now have a maximum of eight representatives out of the total 12 on the Interim Council and that they would submit 15 names in writing including a list of three for the post of Chairman and the final selection of the eight would be done by the President of Sri Lanka. The agreement was signed by Mahatayya on behalf of the LTTE and by Hardeep Singh Puri, the Indian First Secretary in Colombo. With that aspect having been finally sorted out and which put the LTTE in the driver's seat, Shupriya was confident that the accord was once again back on its rails, but another ghastly incident on the 2nd of October on the high seas literally sealed the aspirations of the Tamil Tigers and they soon once again became maneaters.

On that Mahatma Gandhi's 118th birthday, a Sri Lankan Naval vessel that was patrolling off the coast of Point Pedro apprehended 17 LTTE men who were traveling in a fishing trawler. Among them were Pulendran, the Trincomalee Regional Commander and Kumarappah, the Jaffna Regional Commander. The Sri Lankans were delighted as both of them were prized catches and it also carried a solid reward of a million rupees each. The Sri Lankan navy therefore quickly disarmed all of them and having taken off the cyanide capsules that were hanging from their necks; they brought them under escort to the Pallaly airfield, which was the headquarters of both the IPKF and the Sri Lankan army in Jaffna. When the 17 LTTE men under heavy escort reached Pallaly, the news spread like wild fire and the

LTTE immediately cried 'foul' and demanded for their immediate release. According to the LTTE it was a gross violation of the accord and under which all militants had been granted amnesty. The Sri Lankan government was however adamant and wanted them to be sent for interrogation to Colombo immediately. They claimed that the 17 militants were transporting arms in the trawler which they had picked up from Tamil Nadu and that being a breach of the accord, and a voilation of the Sri Lankan immigration formalities, they were therefore guilty and had to be sent to Colombo for further questioning. The LTTE then pointed out that as per the latest agreement that was signed on the 28th of September with India, one of the clauses in it permitted the Tigers to retain their weapons. Thereafter a war of words followed between the two sides. The LTTE now appealed to the Indian government to intervene and to prevent their comrades from being taken to Colombo. The Sri Lankan President too went on TV and spoke to the nation, which made matters still worse. According to him, the 17 LTTE militants detained at Pallaly were arms smugglers who were caught red handed on the high seas and that was not covered under the accord. But surprisingly the Sri Lankan government did not exhibit the alleged arms and ammunition that had been seized by them. The LTTE now gave the excuse that their men had gone to Tamil Nadu to collect office equipment and only the two regional commanders were carrying arms and that too only for self defence. Seeing the shit that the LTTE had landed in, and in order to prevent a further rift in the already fragile accord, Lt General Depinder Singh flew to Colombo and urged President Jayawardhene not to insist on the dispatch of the captured militants to Colombo. Meanwhile Mani Dixit the High Commissioner of India who was in Delhi on a spot of leave also rushed back. But he too could not prevail on the Sri Lankan President to change his stand. In the meantime on the 5th of October, 1987 and after three days of higgling and hagglng, the Sri Lankans finally only agreed to allow the LTTE's Second-in-Command Mahataya to meet the detainees at the Pallaly airbase. That was also the day the detainees were to be flown to Colombo in the evening. In order to stop their deportation, the IPKF had even threatened to block the runaway with armoured cars, but at around 4.30 pm that evening, when instructions from Delhi arrived directing them and the Indian High Commission to abandon all efforts and allow the events to take its own course, the die was now cast. On that evening of 5th October, as thousands of Tamils from every walk of life flocked to the Pallaly airbase to have a glimpse of the detainees and to protest against their deportation, a terrible tragedy that probably had no other precedent in history took place on the tarmac. It was one incident that would put the clock back for very many years and make the LTTE to become the Indian Army's worst enemy ever.

At about 5.30 pm and minutes before the detainees were about to board the aircraft for their journey under a Sri Lankan army escort to Colombo, all 17 of of them swallowed the cyanide capsules. 12 of them who bit into it including Pulendran amd Kumarappah died on the spot. And the others who only swallowed it were rushed to the nearby IPKF hospital, but three more died a few days later. A pall of gloom now fell over the terrible incident as each side started blaming the other. The IPKF blamed the Indian Diplomats and vice versa. Jawawardhene's government in Sri Lanka felt vindicated, while the LTTE leaders were livid and blamed both India and the IPKF for being muted spectators in this pact of mass suicide that was committed by their erstwhile brave comrades in full view of the general public. When Shupriya learnt about it, she just could'nt believe that 12 of them had died on the tarmac itself, and the rest kept simply watching the macabre spectacle. Though there were some reports that the Sri Lankan troops guarding them did make some effort to prevent it, but they had failed. They were all motivated fighters and dare devil Tamil Tigers and it must have been the fear that they would be tortured brutally to death by the Sri Lankans that had made them take this drastic step thought Shupriya, as she read the official report on the dreadful incident. But from where did they get the cyanide capsules, because according to the Sri Lankans, the group had been completely disarmed and even the cyanide necklaces round their necks had been confiscated, wrote Shupriya in her diary as she helped herself to a frugal lunch of plain sandwiches and ice cold fresh sweet lime juice that day.

Therefore in order to find out a little more about this terrible incident, Shupriya decided to carryout her own discreet investigation. As far as the Indian High Commission was concerned, Nirupam Sen who was officiating as Ambassador had also done his best to prevent the 17 LTTE detainees from being sent to Colombo and so did Dixit when he returned post haste from Delhi. Both had met the Sri Lankan President to change his rigid stand, but Jayawardhene was adamant. Therefore what made the Indian government in Delhi to allow the events to take its own course baffled her completely. Going about the tragic event logically, the IPKF and the Sri Lankan Forces were definitely not keen to see all of them dead under such ghastly circumstances. Infact the IPKF had tried their level best to prevent their deportation to Colombo by blocking the runaway, but the Sri Lankan

Brigade Commander on the spot was only too keen to obey orders and to send them alive to Colombo or else his own future would have been in jeopardy. Therefore the cyanide capsules had either been smuggled in by some LTTE sympathizers working in the Pallay airfield, or by Mahataya and Bala, the two LTTE representatives who had been permitted to visit the detainees prior to their being flown to Colombo. Well whosoever had delivered them, it did sow the seeds of hatred and mistrust between the LTTE and the IPKF and that would now be hard to reconcile with. Maybe it was a master stroke by the Sri Lankan intelligence to create that mistrust and make the Indian army and the LTTE take on each other militarily, while the Sri Lankan Forces could then be free to deal with the situation in the south of the country. This would not only eliminate the threat to the Sinhalese from the Tamils in the north, but also from the Marxist elements in the south, and thereby ensure the integrity and unity of the people of Sinhalese origin in the country thought Shupriya as she made a note of the major players from outside Sri Lanka who had off late been showing a lot of more interest in the fast developing geo-political changes in the Indian Ocean in general and in Sri Lanka in particular.

With major multinational oil companies now expressing their desire to explore oil in that strategic region, and the government of India fearing that the Trincomalee harbour next door could be turned into a possible military base by some big foreign power, it was therefore in India's interest to show her strong military presence in that area also. Moreover, the reports of the Pakistan army and the Israeli Mossad being involved in the training of the Sri Lanka armed forces, and the presence of some LTTE elements hobnobbing with the PLO in Lebanon were also now a cause of major concern for the Indian government. Exactly two months ago on 5th August, the Indian Army had got it in writing from Prabhakaran that the LTTE would surrender all arms and though he himself was not present during that ceremony, but the arms and ammuition in lorry loads kept piling in. But from 21st August it dried up completely, because the LTTE started alleging that the RAW had started arming their old rivals the EPRLF, and that therefore had further vitiated the existing goodwill and trust between the two sides.

While Shupriya kept digging deeper into the circumstances and the reasons why the detainees who were now being referred to as martyrs and heroes by the LTTE had taken such a drastic step of commiting mass suicide, the situation in the Tamil dominated Northern and Eastern provinces took an ugly turn for the worse. The worst hit was Jaffna where the LTTE openly blamed the IFKF and the Indian government for letting them down so very badly. On 6th October 1987, General Sunderji the Indian Army Chief with his Southern Army Commander, Lt General Depinder Singh had flown to Jaffna to assess the deteriorating situation on the ground and following their return back to India, when the orders for 'Operation Pawan' was given, the die was cast. That was the codeword for the capture of the LTTE's tactical headquarters and its chain of command in Jaffna, and for Major General Harkirat Singh, the GOC 54 Infantry Division in Jaffna that order had to be obeyed.

The Indian troops of the IPKF who had initially arrived with no defence stores like barbed wire, mines and explosives, and who did not even possess proper maps of the area were now tasked to launch a military offensive operation against the very people whom they had come to protect. Even the maps that were given to them were of the Second World War vintage and they were all completely outdated. The Indian officers and soldiers who were required to disarm the LTTE and other militant groups did not even know who they were by name or by face. Except for the troops from the Madras Regiment that were limited in number, the majority of the others at the lower level had to use the sign language to communicate with the locals and their Sri Lankan counterparts, and at the same time also be ready to defend themselves. In such operations, battle field intelligence, signal intelligence and operational security were of vital importance, but these aspects because of the limited time factor to launch 'Operation Pawan' at the earliest had perforce now to be overlooked. But it would be with tragic consequences.

While 'Operation Pawan,' the battle for the capture of Jaffna was cleared by the Indian government, and the Indian Army was given the green signal by Army Headquarters to launch it, simultaneously the Reliance Cup for supremacy in world cricket also began with a bang. The cricket world cup was being hosted jointly by India and Pakistan and it was inaugurated by the Prime Minister of India. The eight teams were divided into two groups and according to the new rules all matches were to be played as day matches in traditional whites and only with the red ball. Each team was now required to bat for a maximum of 50 overs instead of the earlier 60. With the first match between Pakistan and Sri Lanka that was scheduled to be played at the Niaz Stadium, Hyderabad Sind on 8th October, the entire Rehman family from Peshawar and elsewhere had congregated there to witness it. The match turned out to be a real cliff hanger as the hosts Pakistan beat the visitors by just 15 runs and the victory for the Pakistanis was primarily due to the dashing century by Javed Miandad who was also adjudged as the man of the match. Later that very evening in order to celebrate Pakistan's victory, the two brothers, Brigadier.Aslam Rehman Khan with Fazal Rehman Khan who had come all the way from Dhaka for the event, together with their wives Farzana and Samina hosted a grand party for the elders at the Karachi Club. Though Karachi had recovered from the sectarian violence that had created havoc a few months ago, but it was still not safe as the forthcoming municipal elections were due to be held in the coming month of November. Since the next match was to be played between Australia and India in Chennai on the very next day, Salim Rehman Khan as usual acting as the family bookie gave odds at three to one for an Australian win.

On that very day, while the Rehmans in Karachi were celebrating Pakistan's victory, Monty with Peevee landed in Chennai. Having promised his father that he would do well in his school leaving final exams, Peevee a diehard Indian cricket fan whose favourite now was Asharuddin had accompanied him. When they checked in at the Connemara Hotel, Peevee was surprised to see that Mom number two was also there to welcome them. This was Monty's last minute idea and he had purposely kept it a secret from Peevee, because he was not very sure whether Shupriya due to the very short notice and the fast changing scenario in Sri Lanka would be able to make it from Colombo or not.

"My God, Mom Number 2 what are you doing over here," said a delighted Peevee as he touched Shupriya's feet and then hugged her tightly.

"Well frankly speaking it is not for cricket certainly, but simply to be with you all and it is only for a few hours because I have to get back to Colombo by lunch tomorrow positively," replied Shupriya as she kept smiling and looking at her handsome son. Peevee now in his seventeeth year was a ditto replica of his father Shiraz. He was already a strapping six footer, had the same jet black long hair, the same tenor voice and that very captivating smile that had swept Shupriya of her feet when she was of Peevee's age. In order to spend as much time as possible with one another, they decided to have all their meals in the room. The topic under discussion that evening was mainly the crisis in Sri Lanka, and while Shupriya and Monty kept discussing about the deteriorating situation on the island and the mess that the government of India had landed themselves in with their stupid carrot and stick policy, Peevee kept listening quietly. But when Shupriya concluded by saying that the war was now not between the LTTE and the Sri Lankans, but between the LTTE and the IPKF and that it would be a long drawn out bloody affair, Peevee also butted in by saying.

"I don't know why we cannot mind our own damn business, and why do we have to get into such awful messy affairs everytime. This is entirely Sri Lanka's internal problem and let them bloody well sort it out themselves. After all the IPKF was sent there at President Jayawardhene's own request to restore peace and stability in his country, and if the Indian soldiers are unwanted there, they should simply be withdrawn. There is no damn point in getting our soldiers and officers to fight somebody else's dirty war on that island and be killed, maimed and humiliated in this maner. I do not know why we must put our finger in every damn pie. Just look what is happening in Bangladesh now. We sent in our army in 1971 and gave them their freedom, but they proved to be an ungrateful lot. The same Bangladeshis who earlier blamed the Pakistanis for genocide in their country are today once again their best of friends. The same thing I am sure will happen in this case too. As it is some of the influential political leaders of Tamil Nadu including their leader MG Ramachandran, the ailing Chief Minister of the state who is now in the United States for medical treatment has of late been condemning the actions of our troops against the LTTE and other Tamil militant organizations, and the Sri Lankans are having the last laugh. Their own leaders like Premadasa and others are unhappy too with the IPKF sitting in their midst. They fear that it will become an occupation army and there will be more trouble for them in the future. I therefore simply do not understand as to why we had to get ourselves into this shit and I think the sooner we get out from there, the better it will for everybody," said a highly worked up Peevee as Shupriya kept nodding her head in appreciation in all that Peevee had to say but at the same disapproved of the kind of language that Peevee had used.

"But tell me why are you so concerned at your age for the troubles in Sri Lanka"? asked Monty as Peevee helped himself to another giant size masala dosa and then and gave his reasons. At his own Lawrence School Sanawar and in his own senior most class there were a fairly large number of his classmates who were from the services background. Some of them were sons and daughters of both retired and serving Generals, Brigadiers and Colonels of the Indian Army and Peevee had been hearing all sorts of stories from them about the sporadic fighting in Sri Lanka and the manner in which the Indian troops were handicapped in every damn possible way to deal with the insurgency movement in that country. According to some of them whose fathers were now in the thick of it, the IPKF was being made to fight as a fire brigade and that too with one hand tied behind their backs and that was because all major military decisions were being dictated not by the Commanders on the spot, but by the Generals sitting in Delhi, Pune and in Chennai, and who had no no clue whatsoever about the political amd military reality on the ground There were it seems merely following the dictates of their political masters and our so called experts from the Ministry of External Affairs and the RAW. Finally when Peevee concluded his assessment of the situation with the thought provoking sentence that this was entirely an internal problem between the Sinhalese and Tamils of that country and India had no bloody business whatsoever to interfere militarily, Shupriya got up and hugged him. And when Peevee ordered another chilled beer for his father and a round of some more fresh lime soda for Mom number 2 and said. "I don't think we should put our foot in any further, because by doing so we will only be cutting our own damn feet and nobody will be any the wiser," Monty too was impressed by the young lad's logic.

"Well son come to think of it you are not as dumb as I thought, but what India needs today is a military man like General Thimayya or Field Marshal Sam Maneckshaw, but unfortunately we do not have one at the moment who could stand up and tell the political bosses where to get off," added Monty in good humour as he switched the topic from that of politics to cricket. Early next morning, while Peevee and Monty accompanied Shupriya to see her off at the airport, the headlines in one of the local English newspapers carried a very gruesome story about the death of five Indian soldiers in Sri Lanka. According to the paper, the five Indian soldiers who were traveling in a jeep had been hijacked by a group of armed LTTE militants. Later they were publicly humiliated and brutally killed. According to one reliable source this was in retaliation to the IPKF's ineptness and bungling in not being able to save their comrades in arms who were forced to commit suicide while under detention at the Pallaly air base.

"My God I think this is the beginning of the end," said Shupriya as she opened the copy of the 'Hindu' to check whether that very popular and premier English daily too had carried that grisly story or not. And she felt really sad as she wished Monty and Peevee a final goodbye.

There was still half an hour for the match to begin, when Monty and Peevee took their seats at the MA Chidambaram stadium at Chepauk.

"But Papa who is this M A Chidambaram after whom the stadium has been named and did he ever Captain India?" asked Peevee as he bought a scorecard and a brochure that had the photographs of all the Australian and Indian players inside it.

"Captain India ? are you crazy! I don't think the gentleman ever played competitive cricket at any worthwhile national level at all, but yes he did

Captain the BCCI, the Board of Control for Cricket in India, and which as we all know is the controlling body and of which he was the President in the early sixties. And like most other discipline of sports in India, you do not have to be a player at all to sit on that hot seat, and all that is required is some clout, money power and a bit of political backing or patronage and MAC as he was popularly known had all the three it seems He was the third son of Sir Annamalai Chettier, a well to do businessman and the founder of the Annamalai University and since MAC headed the Tamil Nadu Cricket Association for 32 long years and was instrumental in having this stadium constructed, it was therefore named after him," said Monty when all the clapping began and the two umpires entered the field.

'Though India's Captain Kapil Dev had won the toss, he elected to field first. But when the Australian opening pair of Geoff Marsh and David Boon gave their team a fabulous start, and the first wicket partnership crossed the century mark, Peevee cursed Kapil Dev for not having batted first. Luckily and because of some good tight bowling and good.fielding by the Indians, when the Australians in their allotted fifty overs were restricted to a modest total of 270 runs for the loss of six wickets, there was a slight smile on Peevee's face. According to Peevee 270 was not a very difficult target, and when India began their innings with Gavaskar and Srikanth, and they gave the team also a fairly good start, Peevee was confident that with India's strong batting line up it would give them victory. And with the score reading at 131 for two wickets, when Peevee thought that India would surely win, the Australians started putting the pressure on. And thereafter this match too became a cliff hanger as wickets kept tumbling at regular intervals. It was 246 for 5, when Shastri was out for 12 and then 10 runs later Kapil Dev also left after scoring just 6 and he was follwed by Binny who was run out for a duck. With the scoreboard now reading at 256 for eight, and with only 15 runs to win and with two wickets still in hand, Peevee prayed to his Wahe Guru as Manoj Prabhakar walked to the crease. He was an all rounder who could bat well too and everybody in the stadium had high hopes on him. But he too in that tension filled atmosphere was also run out after scoring just 4 runs. There were now only 5 runs to equalize and six to beat the Aussies, when India's last man, Maninder Singh, the young Sikh spinner took guard. With the score reading at 269 for nine and with only two balls to go and two runs to win, Peeveee at the top of his voice got up and shouted. "'Oye Praji Maninder pape, just do a bloody Miandad Yaar." But when Steve Waugh with his short run up bowled to Maninder and knocked his wicket off, Peevee was simply stunned. India had lost her opening match of the world cup aganst the formidable Australians who were led by Allan Border by just one solitary run and with just one ball left to be bowled.

"By God this was even better than an Alfred Hitchcock suspense movie," said Monty as they got into a cab and made it back to the hotel. And as soon as Peevee reached his room he booked a call to his Mom number two in Colombo. He wanted to be the first one to convey to her that India had lost the match by a whisker, but the operator in the hotel just could not get the call through. All lines it seems were busy. The civil telephone lines to the emerald island it seems were now given on priority to the Indian army who were getting ready to launch 'Operation Pawan'.

Initially the Indian troops and their senior commanders at all levels thought that it would be a simple cake walk to capture Prabhakaran and his men who were inside the Jaffna University and therafter it would all be over in a matter of days. But they were totally mistaken. They had hopelessly under estimated the fighting capabilities of the LTTE and were now going to pay for it very dearly. With a hostile population and a determined enemy fighting on their own home turf, 'Operation Pawan' meaning 'The Wind" was definitely not going to blow India's way so very easily as the troops of the elite 10 Para Commandos and the 13th Sikh Light Infantry of the Indian army got ready to launch the first phase of the operation.

The Indian Army Chief's perception and that of the DGMO, the Director General Military operations that the IPKF would probably at the most take only a fortnight and maybe a little more to sought out the LTTE seemed rather optimistic. And even the initial assessment by Mr Anand Verma from RAW that the LTTE being their very own boys will not betray the Indian government was also given a rude shock, when on 8th October, 1987 the LTTE carried out a number of mortar attacks and ambushes on the IPKF. On the night of October 9/10 as a preliminary operation, the IPKF captured the LTTE radio station at Tavadi, the TV station at Kokkuvil and destroyed the printing presses of the two leading LTTE sponsored newspapers also. This also led to the capture of nearly two hundred Tiger rebels. Following these raids, the LTTE too retaliated with vengeance by ambushing a CRPF convoy and then by launching an attack on the IPKF post at Tellipalai. This was further followed by the hijacking of a 10 Para Cammando jeep and the ruthless killing of all its five occupants. These Indian soldiers were not only publicly lynched, but were also brutally tortured by having burning tyres put around their necks.

The deaths of the 15 LTTE militants at Palally air base by biting those cyanide capsuless was the turning point of the accord, wrote Shupriya in her diary as President Jayawardhene too revoked the amnesty order and announced a reward of one million rupees for the capture of Prabhakaran. On 10th October, the 91 Brigade under Brigadier J K. Ralli began to push forward towards the Jaffna City and 'Operation Pawan" had therefore now begun in real earnest. The GOC, Major General Harkirat Singh was now tasked to neutralize the operational capability of the LTTE in and around Jaffna, and this also included the capture of the Tamil Tigers chain of command that was operating from its tactical headquarters from inside the Jaffna University premises. Since the Jaffna University was located in a thickly populated built up area of the city and in order to reduce civilian casualties and also to keep the surprise element in mind, the General Officer Commanding the IPKF had therefore decided to launch a heliborne assault on the night of 11th/12th October by using the elite troops of the 10 Para Cammandos and the 13thh Sikh Light Infantry Battalion. The plan was to land 70 men from the 10 Para Commandos and first secure the university football field. Thereafter a second wave with a company from the 13th Sikh LI was to follow and both the subunits were tasked to carry out a lightening raid on Prabhakaran's den. Subsequently these heliborne troops were to link up with the 4/5 Gurkha Battalion and with the rest of the Sikh LI troops who were tasked to advance along the given axis and on the road leading to the university.

The IPKF however had no idea that all radio communications regarding the impending air assault was being closely monitored by the LTTE. They had little or no idea that the LTTE also possessed very sophisticated wireless sets and monitoring equipment, and therefore when the first wave of helicopters landed, the Indian troops were like sitting ducks as a volley of rapid accurate fire from LTTE automatics greeted them from every conceivable direction.The LTTE had very cleverly laid an ambush and the operation ended in a veritable disaster for the Indian forces. While the battle lasted throughout the night, it resulted in very heavy casualties to the IPKF. The advance of the ground forces to link up with the heliborne troops also got bogged down very badly as the Tamil Tigers fighting from well fortified built up areas targeted the leading columns of the advancing Indian forces with their well sighted automatic weapons. The most deadly were the LTTE snipers who with the use of their highly sophisticated telescopic sniper rifles that were fitted with night vision devices zeroed in on the Indian officers and their signalmen. By now the LTTE had also mined all the major approaches to the city by using the deadly claymore mine and they had also mastered the art of laying booby traps and the technique of detonating IED's, the improvised explosive devices by using remote control mechanisms. One such massive explosion killed 29 IPKF personel, but none the less the advance along the five major roads leading to the city continued. Inside the university campus heavy fighting was now taking place as the 10 Para Commandos and the Sikh Light Infantry troops doggedly held on and despite the very heavy casualties suffered by them they kept holding on to the ground till next morning, when Lt Colonel Dalbir Singh the brave Commanding Officer of 10 Para Commandos personally led a column of T-72 tanks to relieve them. Needless to say that the Indian Air Force and their intrepid pilots from the transport and helicopter squadrons did a marvelous job too in providing close air support, logistic cover, and in ferrying the assault troops, tanks and equipment into the battlefield. On their return air journey they also carried out the evacuation of casualties. The 44 Squadron that in the 1962 operations against the Chinese had flown in the AMX-13 light tanks to Chusul in Ladakh was now under the command of Wing Commander AG Bewoor and the squadron had also flown in the T-72 medium tanks in their IL-76 aircrafts. The pilots and crew of the IL-76, which was also known as 'Gajraj' not only ferried the tanks, but they were also the mainstay of the logistic cover that was required in the fast changing battle situation on the ground.

While the the battle for Jaffna continued unabated and both sides showed their valour, courage and determination to slug it out, the news over the All India Radio on that unlucky 13th of October 1987 told the lovers of Kishore Kumar around the world that the great versatile singer and artist had died of a massive heart attack. That day Shiraz who every evening religiously listened to the All India Radio's overseas programme for the news in English was shocked. Kishore Kumar was undoubtedly his favourite singer when he was regularly dating Shupriya in the late sixties. In fact the popular song 'Mere Sapnon Ki Rani Kub Ayegi Tuh' from the 1968 hit film Aradhana that made Kishore not only a singing star, but it also gave him his first filmfare award as the best singer was the very song that Shiraz had sung on Shupriya's 19th birthday and soon they were madly in love with each another. The other Kishore Kumar song that Shupriya loved was 'Ye Sham Mastani' from the film 'Kati Patang' and tragically it was this very song that Shiraz sang first to her on their wedding day, and then later in the taxi, when Shupriya saw him off at the Old Delhi railway station on that fateful day of September 1971 when he boarded the train to go and fight the Pakistanis in Kashmir. And when the Indian announcer in memory of the great artist who had become a legend in his lifetime played the same song over the radio, Shiraz very discreetly opened the locket that was around his neck, kissed that old small childhood photograph of Shupriya sitting on his lap and closed his eyes. Thereafter as he hummed the words of the song 'Ye Kiya Hua-Kaisse Hua' that was sung by Kishore Kumar in the film 'Amar Prem', he felt sorry for the loss of that great Bollywood showman.

Born Abhas Ganguly on 4th August, 1929, Kishore Kumar was the youngest brother of the veteran actor Ashok Kumar and was a natural born gifted singer whose trademark was yodelling. It was thanks to the talented music director duo of Sachin Dev Burman and his son Rahul Dev that had made Kishore a versatile and popular singing star of India. However, Shiraz felt rather sad that the Hindu from Bengal who was married not once but four times and whose second wife was the beautiful and vivacious Madhubala, a Muslim should have died so untimely. That evening Shiraz also fondly remembered his younger sister Loveleen who often teased him about Shupriya whenever he sang the song "Mere Samne Wali Khidki Mein Ek Chand Ka Tukda Rehta Hai" from the film 'Padosan". And it was in this 1968 film that Kishore Kumar besides literally lending his voice to Sunil Dutt for the scene in the film, he also established himself as one of the greatest comediens on the Indian screen.

For Shupriya too the 13th of October was a sad day. The news about the IPKF air assault on Jaffna University proved to be a total disaster and the fact that the Indian troops had suffered very heavy casualties in the bargain came as a total surprise to her. She could not imagine that the Indian army that always prided itself in being the fourth largest standing professional army in the world would lose so much face in just one night's battle, and that to against an enemy that was not only far less in numbers numerically, but it wasn't even a regular force. And added to that was the death of Kishore Kumar, the singer who was also a big morale booster for the soldiers of the Indian army and whose old popular songs like 'Hum Hai Rahe Pyar Ke, Humse Kuch Ma Boliye' and 'Ye Kiya Hua Kaise Hua, Kuyun Hua' was always on the lips of the Indian soldiers. Ironically it was this very song from the film 'Amar Prem' (Immortal Love) that was being played over the Vivid Bharathi, when the announcement was made that the great singer had died. This was the same song that Shiraz had serenaded her with soon after the film was released in 1971 and it was also the day that he had officially proposed to her. One day after seeing the movie, the two of them on his Lambretta scooter had visited the Bangla Sahib Gurudwara and it was there that they both of them decided that come what may they would get married and a week later they did. But like Pushpa the tragic role that was so brilliantly portrayed by Sharmila Tagore in the movie and that of Anand Babu by Rajesh Khanna in that poignant love story, this was no different except that Nandu's role that was played by Vinod Mehra was now being played by their only son Peevee. And the Indian Jawans no matter from which part of India they hailed from, they too simply loved Kishore Kumar's golden voice that came over the popular Vividh Bharathi and over the Special Forces request programme everyday. Whether he was a Naga from Nagaland, a Gurkha from Nepal, a Malayalee from down south or even a Ladakhi from Ladakh, for the Indian Jawan's lonely existence on the borders, picquets and in the far flung frontiers of the country, it was the melodious voice of Kishore Kumar over the transisitor radio that kept their morale high and Sri Lanka was no exception either.

But with the failure of 'Operation Pawan' in the very first round itself, the top Indian military commanders must be now wondering 'Ye Kiya Hua, Kaise Hua' thought Shupriya as she played some of the other old Kishore Kumar favourite numbers like 'Pal Pal Dil ke Pas' and Mere Sapnon Ki Rani' on her audio cassette player. The songs brought back to her those wonderful unforgettable days and she wondered how different life would have been for her and Peevee had her husband Major Shiraz Ismail Khan not volunteered to go to the battlefront and to die there as a hero. Though their married life had lasted only for 36 hours, but she could never ever forget him. As she took out an old photograph of her departed husband and put it softly to her lips, a few tear drops were indicative enough of her immortal and eternal love for him.

And while Shupriya on that night of Kishore Kumar's death kept thinking of her late husband and their short lived marriage, in Pakistan, Benazir Bhutto the pretty and charmimg daughter of the late Pakistan Prime Minister Zulfiqar Ali Bhutto at the age of 34 had finally decided to get married to the man who had been chosen for her by her family. And it all started a year ago in November 1986 after Benazir had returned to Pakistan, and soon thereafter the ball was set rolling by her dear cousin Fakhri who invited the bridegroom for an informal dinner party to her house. The prospective bridegroom was as old as the bride and though the proposal was first sounded to Benazir by her mother and her aunt two years earlier when the entire Bhutto family was holidaying in Cannes, but Benazir did not show any interest in marriage at that time. She had already embarked on a mission to revive the PPP that her dear father had founded and therefore had no time for marriage it seems. The handsome man was a Sindhi like her and he also came from a very affluent family. The Zardaris were originally from Iranian Baluchistan, but they now hailed from Nawabshah in Sind. A product of Petaro Cadet College, which was one of the prime educational institutions of Sind, Asif Ali Zardari was both a playboy and a good sportsman and had his own polo team that was known as the 'Zardari Four'. The well to do Zardari family was into agriculture, real estate, construction business and they also owned cinema halls. However, it was only a few months ago in July, 1987 when both Benazir and Zardari were in London that the proposal was finalized. It all happened when Benazir was invited by Asif to witness a polo match at Windsor Park and she was stung by a bee. Seeing her hand swollen the next day, Asif insised that she must see a doctor at once and he arranged for one immediately. He had even very thoughtfully brought the prescribed medicine for her. And seeing such care and devotion towards her, Benazir had given her nod. The very next evening the handsome Sindhi with a Omar Sharif mustache took Benazir, her sister Sanam, his mother-in-law to be Nusrat Begum and a few of his close friends to dinner and by the time the week was over they were officially engaged. In mid November, when the date for the wedding and reception that was to be solemnized at Karachi on 17th and 18th December was officially announced, Shiraz remarked to his wife Saira somewhat jokingly.

"Well finally now that your schoolmate from the Convent of Jesus and Mary at Murree has decided to take the plunge, I wonder wether she will take the surname Zardari or remain a Bhutto ?."

"Well to my mind I feel that for her own political future in the country, she should remain as Benazir Bhutto, because the name Zardari does not have that kind of charisma and appeal that the name Bhutto carries, and specially so in Sind. After all even today the name Bhutto in Pakistan is synonymous with her party the PPP and she should therefore cash in on it,'said Saira.

"Yes and undoubtedly so, because in India too the name Gandhi in politics has a special flavour and significance." added Shiraz with a mischievous smile as he got ready to help her daughter Gammy with her Mathematics home-work.

On the day the official announcement for the Bhutto-Zardari wedding was made, Ruksana Begum was at her weekly ladies kitty party at the Peshawar Club, and according to the local gossip in Peshawar, Asif Zardari it seems had an eye on the young Bhutto lady ever since she was a teenager and a few years later, he had even sounded his father about his agreement to the match. But somehow or the other, and maybe because of various political and other constraints, the Zardaris had kept postponing the matter till Asif's stepmother on 22nd July, 1987 while visiting her son in London dropped in for a cup of coffee at Tariq's flat. Tariq was Benazir's cousin and her Aunt Manna it seems was very keen on the match too. The mother was accompanied by her son and the idea was to atleast let the two meet and know each other a little better.

"Oh my God, I never knew that and now suddenly this name Zardari has become the talk of the town it seems," said Ruksana as she with her husband Arif Rehman dropped in as usual for their regular evening tete-a-tete with Gul Rehman and Zubeida. That month of November 1987 however was not a very happy one for Pakistan. On 1st November following serious differences with Prime Minister Junejo on the troublesome Afghan issue, the Foreign Minister Sahibzada Yakoob Khan had resigned, and three days later on 4th November, Pakistan lost the semi final match in the Cricket World Cup when the Aussies beat them by just 118 runs. The Pakistanis were playing on their own home turf at the Gaddaffi Stadium, Lahore and despite a fighting 70 runs by Javed Miandad, the Pakistanis chasing a not so big a total of 267 runs were bundled out in the 49th over. Gul Rehman with his brother Arif Rehman were very much there on the ground that day and despite a bad start by Pakistan, the team had scored 150 runs for four wickets when Imran Khan the Captain was out for 58. There were 6 wickets still in hand and Javed Miandad was at the crease and all that was needed was another 118 runs for a win and both Gul and Arif were confident this the target could be achieved if the remaining Pakistani batsmen played sensibly and did not throw away their wickets away. But then Craig Mcdermott the Australian pace bowler showed his true colours as he ripped through the Pakistani tailenders and gave the Australians victory. For his five wicket haul, Craig was rightly adjudged as the man of the match. The other factor which boosted the Australian total was the 34 extras that were conceded by Pakistan and of which 13 were wides and 19 were leg byes.

A day later in Bombay, when India too lost her semi-final match against England in the other semi-finals by thirty five runs Gul Rehman felt even sadder. With the prestigious tournament being played in the subcontinent, he was looking forward to a grand Indo-Pak encounter in the finals, and when Australia lifted the cup with a meager seven run win over England that was played at the famous Eden Gardens in Calcutta on 8th November, Gul Rehman who was glued to his TV till the very last ball was bowled remembered those wonderful days when he as a young boy in the company of his old departed friend Ismail Sikandar Khan made passes at the two good looking Pugsley twin sisters Debbie and Sandra. Whether it was a kind of premonition, telepathy or otherwise, Gul Rehman was taken aback when two days later in the obituary column of the newspaper Dawn, he read a four line write up about the death of Debbie. Debbie had died in Perth, Australia at the age of 67 on that very day when Australia lifted the World Cup in Calcutta. Later during that month in the Municipal elections in Karachi that were held on a non party basis, the emergence of those candidates being backed by the MQM had now become a cause of serious concern to the PPP whose hold in the urban cities of the Sind Province had shown a considerable downslide. And later that day when there was call from Fazal Rehman from Dhaka to give the sad news that his father-in-law Shamshul Haq who had earlier served in the Pakistan Foreign Service had died in a very mysterious manner and under very tragic circumstances it came as a shock to the Rehman family. The retired diplomat had off late been vehemently objecting to General Ershad's controversial bill of nominating military officers as non voting members to the District Councils. This according to him was not democratic and was only a subterfuge by President Ershad and his Jatiyo Party leaders to keep the military in their pockets and use them as Gestapos and informers as and when required. The controversial District Council Bill that was also known as the Zilla Parishad Bill had already raised a storm that had reunited the opposition and Ershad it seems was gunning for those who were fuelling the fire to get rid of him. Though Shamshul Haq and a few other elders had no political leanings, but their letters to the editors on the subject and comments in public had whipped up a strong anti Ershad feeling amongst the intellectuals in the country and it was they who were now demanding his ouster. Mr Shamshul Haq with three other like minded friends was returning by car from a protest meeting at Narayanganj. When the car stopped at a manned level crossing in the middle of nowhere and they waited for the train to pass, suddenly a tea vendor appeared from nowhere. Though it was only five in the evening but being winter, it was already dark and they all decided to have his tea. Giving the excuse that there was still time for the train to pass and that he would like to serve it really hot, the vendor lit a small fire to heat up the kettle. And no sooner was the train whistle heard in the far distance; the vendor quickly served the tea in the small earthen clay pots, took his money and disappeared. A little while later and after the train had passed by the journey was resumed. But a few minutes later all of them all of them except for one elderly person who was diabetic and who did not drink that heavily sweetened tea complained of severe chest pain. Suddenly the young driver collapsed at the wheel and though he did manage to apply the brakes, but it was too late. The car which was traveling at a fairly good speed swerved, skidded, dashed against a big tree and fell nto the khud. The post mortem revealed that all of them except for the diabetic patient had died of some kind of poisoning and there were no survivors. The diabetic patient who was sitting in the front seat next to the driver had died of severe head injuries. Though the hunt for the mysterious tea vendor was still on, but according to the railway man on duty at the level crossing this was the first time that somebody had sold tea at that place. He however did notice that the tea vendor had been picked up by a motorcyclist and the duo had followed the car for some distance till it disappeared from his view.

Having heard the tragic story, both Gul Rehman and Arif Rehman conveyed their heartfelt condolences to Fazal Rehman and the bereaved family over the telephone,and when Arif remarked very prophetically to the others that General Ershad's days it seems were also numbered, that prediction was vindicated soon thereafter, when a mass movement gripped the nation. Fearing that he would be toppled and to cool tempers a clever but shaky General Ershad on 6th of December 1987, dissolved the Bangladesh parliament and called for fresh elections in early March 1988.

By this time, the situation in Sri Lanka had also become a full time military operation for the IPKF as more troops and special forces were airlifted directly into the battle zone, and Shupriya wondered how many more lives of the poor Indian jawans and officers would be lost in this thankless and fruitless military venture. According to her, India's involvement was a total misadventure and it was turning out to be both a diplomatic as well as a military debacle for the country.Though the Jaffna Peninsula was in the hands of the IPKF, but the emormous casualties that were being inflicted by the LTTE had got the Indian High Command fairly worried. The LTTE by now also had young teenage children, both boys and girls fighting in their cadres and this too had become a cause of great concern to the Indian Military Commanders on the spot. While the fighting continued and progressively the Tamil Tigers tactically withdrew into to the jungles of Vavuniya to fight another day, in the United States of America, the ailing Chief Minister of the Indian State of Tamil Nadu was also fighting for his own life. Popularly known as MGR, Muruthur Gopalamenon Ramchandran was born on 17th January, 1917 in the village of Nawalapitiya near Kandy in Sri Lanka and ironically it was he who had during his long tenure as Chief Minister since 1977 had given the LTTE and the Tamils of Sri Lanka the moral, material and arms support to fight for their rights and for their freedom. The thrice married charismatic leader who had no issues and who was himself a displaced person from Sri Lanka was in a serious condition and it pained him even more when he was told that that the Indian Army and the LTTE had now become sworn enemies. Once the doyen of the Tamil Cinema and a remarkable actor who had dominated Kollywod for several decades and whose super hit film 'Rajkumari' of yesteryears had catapulted him into stardom was practically on his deathbed. In 1967, he escaped death when he was shot by a fellow actor and political aspirant M.R. Radha and though it resulted in a bullet being permanently lodged in his neck, but that was not the cause of his hospitalization. MGR had suffered a severe stroke and was inside the ICU, the intensive care unit for treatment. Strangely the screenplay of the film 'Rajkumari' was written by non other than Karunanidhi, the man who was now his political rival and from whom he had broken away. In 1972 MGR had formed his own political party the AIADM, The All India Anna Munnetra Khazagham Party which was named after the actor's mentor Annadurai and it was by now a very powerful political outfit in South India. While MGR was still fighting for his life, the succession struggle within his party it seems had already begun.

On 15th November an article in the India Today magazine together with a few photographs had given Shupriya a little more insight into what the IPKF would now be getting into. The courageous photographer Shyam Tekwani who was there during the Battle for Jaffna had spent 5 days with the LTTE fighters, and when he saw them in real action he was all praises in the manner in which the young Tamil militants took on the Indian Army. According to his report, the morale of the Tamil Tigers was exceptionally high and their motivation level to fight for Eelam had reached such a high pitch that they had now decided that they would rather die fighting or swallow the cyanide capsule incase they were badly wounded or were taken as prisoners, but under no circumstances would they ever surrender. The Indian Army too had their own heroes as they in a hostile country and in an environment where it was difficult to even distinguish between friend and foe; they kept on relentlessly attacking the numerous LTTE defences, camps and hideouts. Late on the night of 25th November, 1987 Major Ramaswamy Parmeshwaram from the Mahar Regiment while returning from a search and destroy mission with his column was caught in an LTTE ambush. Led by the gallant officer, the intrepid Indian jawans charged the enemy very boldly. It resulted in hand to hand fighting and though Major Parmeshwaram was critically wounded, he snatched the rifle from a Tamil militant and shot him dead. He nevertheless kept on fighting and inspiring his command and managed to finally clear the ambush. But in the bargain he also laid down his life and became the first recipient of the Param Veer Chakra in Sri Lanka. The Indian Navy too was not far behind. Their specially trained Marine Force led by Lt Arvind Singh had successfully carried out three daring raids deep inside the Jaffna Lagoon. The Naval commandos that were trained on the lines of the U S Navy Seals had swam for more than a mile underwater and despite being engaged by the enemy had destroyed their fleet of boats. And for this gallant action, bravery in the face of the enemy and leadership, Lt Arvind Singh had been awarded the Maha Veer Chakra.

And while the IPKF got more and more involved in their thankless task in Sri Lanka, far away in Karachi as the 17th of December 1987 came nearer, the preparations for the much politically hyped Bhutto-Zardari wedding was put on top gear. Simultaneously on the orders of President Zia, the close surveillance on the Bhutto's, the Zardaris and other senior PPP leaders too was also increased. To derive full political mileage from the event, Benazir had decided to have two weddings. The first would be in traditional style with family and friends, but with no extra frills attached and that would be at their family home at 70, Clifton, while the other would be held later as a public reception for her devoted PPP supporters and the poor of Karachi at the Kakri sports field in Lyari, which was also the stronghold of the party in the very heart of the city. Though the tradition demanded that the bride to be should wear yellow clothes and put no make up and remain in seclusion for atleast a week if not more, Benazir simply did not have the time and she decided that this custom known as 'Mayoom'should be done away with as a special case for her. Therefore, in order to ensure that the arrangements for the reception at the Kakri Ground were going as per her desired plan, Benazir herself having donned a burqua to conceal her identity from the snooping ISI and other agents, quietly slipped out of the house and went on an inspection tour. But it was not before long that the men from the CID at the reception ground knew who the lady was, when she kept making searching enquiries about the reliability of the heavy duty generator and the working of the large number of big TV sets and screens that had been installed for the grand event at the venue.

Next morning for the traditional Mehndi ceremony at 70, Clifton when the relatives of the bridegroom to the sound of drums and wooden sticks and carrying a big platter of henna that was beautifully shaped like a peacock arrived at the Bhutto residence and the singing began, an agent from the ISI posing as as a member of the press together with the host of other photographers and correspondents from the world media kept continously video recording the ceremony and of the people attending it. An important face that the ISI thought would be there and maybe in disguise was however missing. Benazir's brother Murtaza on the advice of his mother had decided not to take the risk. Mir as he was known in the family could not even attend his sister Sanam's marriage earlier and Benazir naturally was missing him. During the Nikah ceremony, when the handsome couple under the green and gold see through shawl looked into the mirror at each other as was the custom, a loud cheer went up. When the bride's mother and aunts showered them with grounded sugar cones to add to the sweetness of their soon to begin married life and then lovingly knocked the heads of the couple together to signify the blessed union, another round of cheers and ululations followed. Once the ceremonies at home came to an end and the couple in a big cavalcade made their way to the Kakri Ground, the cries of 'Long Live Bhutto' rented the air. On the next day, when the photograph of the couple and the huge crowd greeting them was splashed in all the leading newspapers of Pakistan, Ruksana Begum sitting at Peshawar very aptly remarked to her husband Arif Rehman.

"Well looking at the manner in which Benazir and her husband has been felicitated by the common people, it must be giving the Mulla General in Islamabad the jitters. And Zia I am sure must have gone through the entire video recording already with a fine comb and now must be cursing himself for allowing the Bhuttos to get back to main base. And I therefore won't be the least surprised if the man with his trademark toothy smile and double handshake will ever call for democratic elections in this country. It has already been over a decade since he took over the reins and that must have by now gone deep into his damn Khaki head," added Ruksana as she laid out the frugal breakfast of oats, fresh fruits and sprouted lentils for her dear husband.

As the year 1987 came to an end, Shiraz sitting in Stockholm also took stock of some of the important events that had taken place during that year. These were those events that he felt could shape the future of the world in general and it also included the role of certain important world personalities who had played a significant part in it. There were also the names of those who lived in glass houses and whose lives had been badly smeared by gossips and scandals by the world media. This was a summary of all the good, bad and the ugly events that took place and which Shiraz had religiously noted in his diary. With the new leadership of Gorbachev in the Soviet Union and his future vision of bringing about a radical change for a faster and better economic progress to his country coupled with his ardent desire to become friends with the west, all these were seen as positive signs for a better world. The decision of the Russians and the American to put a brake on the nuclear arms race was also a step in the right direction to bring to an end the Cold War that had started soon after Hitler was vanquished. As a result of this new found friendship between the two super powers, there was also now a hope that the long on going war in the volatile and strategic region of the Persian Gulf between Iraq and Iran that was being constantly monitored by the two super powers who were patrolling the area would soon end. The Russian leader's repeated hints that he would withdraw his forces from Afghanistan provided a just and fair solution to the problem was evolved by the two warring sides was also seen as a positive move. That bloody conflict had been raging for over seven long years and had resulted in the deaths of thousands of innocent people. However, the murky Iran-Contra deal by the Americans and the scandal in India of purchasing the Bofors gun even from a neutral country like Sweden with alleged kickbacks had already started having negative fallout on their respective leaders and the party that they belonged to. The continuing CIA support to the Afghan Mujahideens through the ISI who were now being supplied with the sophisticated Stinger missiles and other lethal weapons, together with India's involvement in Sri Lanka against the same very LTTE militants whom they themselves had trained and armed had added a new dimension to the proliferation of such conventional arms to radical groups, and Shiraz now feared that these very arms may well one day find there way through clandestine channels and deals by unscrupulous gun runners to other terrorist organizations around the world and Pakistan and India were no exceptions either The fact that Pakistan and India were both heading towards a nuclear hegemony in the subcontinent was also a cause of great concern to all.

On the lighter side the very fact that the manufacturer of condoms were now allowed to advertise their products through commercials on TV was a positive move to curb the spread of the deadly AIDS desease around the world. But the news that Shiraz's once favourite actor Rock Hudson may have died of this very AIDS was rather saddening. The fact that the world's population had crossed the 5 billion mark and both India and Pakistan were making no worthwhile efforts to bring it down in their respective countries was also a very disturbing factor. Even the rift between Prince Charles and Princess Diana was out in the open, and the fact that despite having two lovely young boys they were staying separately was a blackmark on the British royal family who were suppose to set examples of martial bliss to their own subjects. On the other hand the conviction of Britain's ace jockey

Sir Lester Piggot to three years imprisonment for tax evasion showed how impartial and quick the British justice system was. And had there been a similar case in India or in Pakistan, the court case would have gone on and on and on and the chances of the VIP culprit being honourably acquited, rather than being convicted was very much a possibility noted Shiraz, as Saira presented him with a new leather bound diary for the year 1988.

With the Bofors Gun scandal still belching fire in the Indian Parliament, the pro Rajiv top heavy Congress Party members of the Joint Parliamentary Committee appointed by the government and who were in complete majority got busy looking into the murky arms deal. The manner in which they went about conducting their business in the most unprofessional manner, was proof enough that it would as predicted by Unni become an exercise in total futility. It was quite obvious that Rajiv's government was not in the least interested in going deep into the bottom of the whole dirty affair and that it was more of a show and a cover up to convince the illiterate and gullible Indian public that the Prime Minister and his party were in no way involved in giving the contract for monetary gains But no matter how much they tried to cook up stories and hoodwink the people who had voted them into power, the Indian inteligentsia and the media had by now seen through the entire game. Thus the New Year of 1988 brought no cheer at all to the young Indian Prime Minister as the Bofors scandal kept rocking his government and the IPKF operations in Sri Lanka against the LTTE became a veritable death trap for the Indian jawans and officers serving there. The JPC, Joint Parliamentary Committee that was appointed by the government was becoming nothing but a complete eyewash operation as some of the influential Indian newspapers like the 'Hindu' and 'The Indian Express' started probing deeper into the Bofors scandal. Some of their revelations had not only further lowered the credibility of the government, but had also caused a lot of embarrassment to the Prime Minister, his family and friends too. In the elite clubs and hotels of India the only topic under discussion was Bofors and whether the Prime Minister and his family were in any way involved in getting a cut from the deal. The opposition parties had already started coining slogans like 'Gully Gully Mein Shor Hai, Rajiv Gandhi Chor Hai.' They were now openly accusing the Prime Minister of being a damn thief and a crook. And with the cry in the streets by the opposition that Mr Clean was not clean at all and that he was a crook and a thief getting momentum had also upset Shupriya. She had very high regard for the Indian Prime Minister and such cruel attacks on the honour and integrity of the man was not warranted she thought. Therefore to find out the real truth, she decided to probe a little more into the matter. Her only aim it seems was to impartially go into the history of the Bofors deal and from the inputs that were available from various sources and to arrive at a fair and logical conclusion as to who was guilty and who was not, and whether people in the top echelons of the Indian government working in the Defence Ministry and the PMO had received hefty kick backs in the deal. Her main source of information was the 'Hindu" and the "Indian Express" newspapers. These were the only two widely read newspapers published in India who it seems had smelt a rat and were now going the whole hog in getting to the bottom of this murky affair. An investigative Indian journalist and a woman at that by the name of Chitra Subramanium who was based in Geneva and who was working for the Hindu newspaper was undoubtedly the main source of this shocking information and it was her lucid reports and a few others by Arun Shourie of the Indian Express that had got Shupriya deeply interested in the matter.Piecing together whatever information that she could gather from the newspaper reports, and from other reliable sources in Delhi and elsewhere, Shupriya chronologically started jotting down every bit of information, big or small on the Bofors contract. Her start point however was not the day on which the deal was signed that was on 24th March, 1986, but the day when Bofors signed a rather innocuous but important agreement with the company called AE Services Ltd and that was on 15th November 1985. That agreement was signed by Martin Ardbo for Bofors and a gentleman by the name of Myles J Scott, a solicitor for AE Services Ltd. The agreement provided for a payment of 3 % of the total value of the contract to AE Services Ltd and it also specified that the payment would be made only in the event of Bofors winning the contract. It also had a cut off date till midnight 31st March, 1986 and failing which the agreement would automatically stand null and void. Shupriya therefore rightly surmised that the period between 15th November 1985 and 31st March, 1986 were crucial factors in the deal. It was in October 1985, that Rajiv had met Palme in New York where the clause of not including any Indian'middlemen in the deal was first put by Rajiv as a pre—condition for the contract, and this was reiterated again in January 1986 by the Indian Prime Minister, when Palme visited Delhi and once again soon thereafter, when Rajiv attended Palme's funeral in Stockholm. In early February 1986, Palme was assassinated and General Sundarji had just taken over as the new Army Chief. Rajiv went for the funeral ion 9th March and thereafter on his return the Bofors file in the Defence Ministry started moving at lightening speed. So much so, that Arun Singh who was looking after the Defence Minsitry and who was flying to

Bhutan on official work did not even have time to put his signatures to it and was asked to give his verbal approval, which was noted on the file that was sent to the PMO's office for the Prime Minister's final approval on 14th March, 1986. However, the information that was available to Shupriya from some other reliable sources both within the Defence Ministry and the PMO were somewhat different. It was in May 1984, while Mrs Gandhi was still in power that the Ministry of Defence had set up a seven member negotiating committee with the Defence Secretary as the Chairman to evaluate the suitability of a medium gun for the Indian Army and the French Sofna and the Swedish Bofors guns were both very much in the running. Then at the meeting held on 12th March, 1986, the committee was of the opinion that the Bofors offer was a better one and this was just after Rajiv Gandhi returned from Palme's funeral in Stockholm. The recommendations of the committee on being approved by the Defence Minstry officials was also now promptly given the green signal by the Finance Ministry, and then by the four concerned cabinet ministers and also by the ministers of state in the respective ministries. Once it had the approval of the then Defence Minister KC Pant, and his deputy Arun Singh, it was sent to VP Singh through his deputy Sukh Ram to the Finance Ministry who also gave their approval and finally the Prime Minister Rajiv Gandhi on 14th March also put his signatures to it. On that very same day a letter of intent to Bofors was also promptly issued. Supriya therefore concluded that it was probably this letter of intent that also gave a further assurance that no middlemen was involved in the deal and to which the Swedish government had also agreed when Rajiv had discussed it with his counterpart during Palme's funeral. Now that the deal was practically through, but there was only a fortnight left to officially have it signed and sealed by both parties because failing which the deadline of 31st March, 1986 would expire and the AE Services Ltd would not get their 3% cut. Therefore it was probably a race against time and hence soon after Rajiv landed back in Delhi from Palme's funeral, the file started moving at breakneck speed. On 21st March, Bofors submitted a revised offer which probably was meant to scuttle Sofna's chances and after Rajiv Gandhi gave his final approval, the deal was signed and sealed on 24th March and everybody it seems was happy thereafter concluded Shupriya as she made a note of all these crucial dates in her diary. Thereafter the deal having been signed by both parties on 24th March 1986, and which was well before the crucial April Fool's Day of 1986 everything seemed to be honky-dory till the Swedish Radio blew the whistle in April 1987. Following the signing of the contract in March 1986, the first installament of 20% for the full contracted amount of 1.4 Billion Dollars was also paid by India to Bofors, and six months later in September 1986, the AE Services Limited was credited with 7.3 Million Dollars in their Swiss Bank account with Nordfinanz in Zurich. This sudden monetary windfall that the AE Services had received looked somewhat strange to Shupriya since AE Services Ltd was based in the UK and had done nothing at all to qualify for this staggering commission and that too only six months after the no middlemen request was once again formalized between India and Bofors at the final signing of the contract. The fact that AE Services Ltd was not even based in India and Major Wilson, the frontman was an Englishman and not an Indian, and that this payment would have never come to light had not the Swedish Radio on 30th September 1987 blew the lid off again by confirming that this payment of SEK 50,463,966 had been made to AE Services Ltd by Bofors in early September, 1986 and it was this revelation that had got Shupriya thinking again. Thereafter delving deeper into the payment that was made to AE Services Ltd, Shupriya found that the company was registered in Guilford, Surrey, England but had no office. It had a paid up capital of only a hundred pounds sterling that was divided into hundred shares of one pound each and and of which Major Bob Wilson owned one share while the rest was owned by the mother company in Liechtenstein and the nature of work that was done by the AE Services was mentioned as consultancy. Therefore what intrigued her was what kind of consultancy did it provide and to whom in order to clinch the billion dollars contract for Bofors, and how come it received the colossal payment even before the guns had even landed in India. Technically the Prime Minister's repeated statements in parliament that no commissions were paid to any Indian middlemen was probably technically correct, but the fact that commissions had been paid was now in the open and that too in black and white, and not even the Prime Minister could deny that. But there was one major difference that had struck her and that was the fact that till date nobody had raised the question of whether a foreigner acting as a middlemen was entitled to a cut in the deal.

Earlier, when the Defence Minsiter, VP Singh had ordered an enquiry on the commission that was allegedly paid to an Indian agent in the HDW submarine deal and Bhatnagar the Defence Secretary who had headed that inquiry commission had on his noting on 9th April, 1987 indicated that most probably the agents were the Hindujas, but there was no subsequent follow up on that either. This was just before the Bofors scandal had surfaced, and soon therafter when the Swedish Radio had made that damaging broadcast, Martin Ardbo it is believed flew to London for an urgent meeting with the

Hindujas that was held on 21st May 1987. Shupriya therefore came to the conclusion that the Hindujas too were probably very much into this very lucrative arms brokerage buisiness. In June 1987, the Indian Army Chief, General Sundarji had taken a very tough stand. He had even recommended the cancellation of the contract if the Bofors refused to reveal the names of those who had been paid commissions, and he even reiterated to Bhatnagar the Defence Secretary that for the sake of national honour, the delay in getting a new gun was acceptable to him. On 12th June, 1987 Sundarji on the advise of the Defence Secretary had even put it down on paper. He had categorically stated that if India threatened to screw the contract, everything would come out pit-a-pat. But that coming from the Army Chief must have really shaken the Prime Minister and the PMO thought Shupriya as she chronologically tabulated all these events in her diary.

In mid 1987, when the Bofors scandal got murkier and murkier by the day, Martin Ardbo though he was no longer with Bofors, it seems had visited Geneva on 2nd July and had met Myles Scott of AE Services Ltd. Fearing that the Indian government might well put the screws on and cancel the contract, the Vice President of Bofors on 3rd July, 1987 also arrived in Delhi to suggest a meeting between the Government of India and a responsible delegation from Bofors. By this time Martin Ardbo was already in the dumps for his alleged involvement in the illegal export of arms to certain Middle East countries and was no longer an employee of Bofors. Nevertheless, he was still was very much in contact with AE Services and the Hinduja brothers and this to Shupriya seemed rather odd. And when on the very next day 4th July 1987, Rajiv Gandhi returned from Moscow and was told about the meeting proposed by the Vice President of Bofors with the Government of India, he outrightly rejected it and Shupriya now smelt something even fishier.

"Maybe he was afraid that Bofors in order to save the contract may reveal certain names of individuals who were close to Rajiv and that itself could be indeed very damaging and embarrassing to the Prime Minister and his Congress Party, and he therefore could not risk it because both he and his government had been all the time harping that no commissions whatsoever had been paid to anybody and the opposition was only waiting to take full advantage of such revelations by the press. And if any names were revealed and irrespective of the fact whether they were Indians or otherwise then they would mostly certainly crucify him," thought Shupriya as she got back to complete the rest of the New Year's greeting cards for dispatch the next day. Later that evening Shupriya wrote a long letter to Monty giving her own reasons and assessment about the shady Bofors deal and since they had discussed the issue, when they had met in Madras, she requested him to give his own comments on it and to also keep it confidential.

A week later, Monty having consulted his friend Unni at the Press Club replied some what candidly. And in his letter he wrote. "Well it seems that with Bofors not willing to lose the lucrative contract and Rajiv Gandhi and his government not keen to lose their power and credibility, both sides therefore according to Unni's assessment it seems have now decided to play ball and scratch each other's back. They have probabaly realised that the only way to get out of this terrible mess and save their own damn skins was to cooperate with one another and go in for a massive game of cover up mutually since the scandal had gained momentum from the day when the name of AE Services Ltd was revealed as one of the beneficiaries of the murky deal and that was in late September 1987. The aim thereafter was to confuse the issue in such a manner that even Sherlock Holmes and Hercule Poirot by putting their heads together would not be able to figure out as to who got how much from whom and when. As it is the disinformation campaign by the government in its ugliest form to shield the corrupt politicians and their close friends and relatives has reached its zenith in this country, and it is now a question I guess of throwing in a few more red herrings into this bizarre and dirty affair. This is probably the main reason I feel as to why Arun Singh decided to quit and may have made Amitabh Bachchan to also go back to the celluloid world of Bollywood. The very fact that Arun Singh on 10th June, 1987 had written a note to KC Pant the Defence Minister stating that since the Swedish National Audit Bureau had confirmed unequivocally that payments had been made and since such payments were grossly violative of all stated policy as communicated to and was understood by both Bofors and the Swedish Government, therefore the Government of India was duty bound to pursue the matter to its logical conclusion and that logical conclusion according to Arun Singh's noting was that the Indian Government must inform the Swedish Government and Bofors that unless they part with that information, the contract will be cancelled. And three days later on 13th June, when General Sundarjee in a separate noting further reiterated Arun Singh's views and said that he was prepared to live with the delay, these two notings therefore had further got the Prime Minister and the PMO looking for excuses on how best to honour the contract. On 15th June, 1987 in reply to Arun Singh's noting, the Prime Minister in his own hand and while citing that the security of the nation and the credibility of his government was at stake he not only rejected his Dosco buddy's proposal, but he also wrote that knee jerk reactions and stomach cramps would not serve any purpose. Therefore to my mind it was this noting from Rajiv that had probably got Arun Singh thinking that his own buddy was far from clean and he therefore put in his papers and cleverly washed his hands off and got away as far as he could from Delhi," concluded Monty in his long letter to Shupriya while adding a few more details in it as a post script.

According to Monty it was on 4th July, 1987 after Rajiv Gandhi returned from his Moscow visit when he called for an urgent meeting in his house and it was attended by Arun Singh, SK Bhatnagar and NN Vohra. They were the ones who were controlling the Defence Minstry and an angry Rajiv wanted to know as to why the Ministry of Defence was adopting a threatening posture towards Bofors and forcing them to divulge information about the recipients of the so called alleged kickbacks. It seems that General Sundarji's noting was the cause of all this, but strangely enough the Army Chief was not called for that particular meeting and asked to explain. On 14th July, 1987, a visbly rattled Defence Secretary, SK Bhatnagar had barged into Sundarji's office in South Block with a letter from the PMO's office that was written by Sarla Grewal, the Prime Minister's Secretary. According to that letter, the Prime Minister was very upset as to why the Defence Ministry had not sent the assessment on the Bofors Gun that he had asked for and the implications that was likely to follow incase the contract was cancelled or annulled. With that letter in hand, the Defence Secretary with the Army Chief then went and saw Arun Singh and four days later Arun Singh resigned. When the question of activating the legal option so that Bofors would automatically spit out the names was put to the Prime Minister, and he gave the excuse that such legal matters would take years and years and that it would jeopardize India' security and serve no worthwhile purpose, it was quite evident to Arun Singh that his erstwhile Dosco friend was trying to brush the whole thing off under the carpet and he therefore decided to put in his papers. Bofors naturally was delighted and knew that with the Prime Minister of India having said that India's security was at stake, the contract was therefore absolutely safe.

"In his last noting to the Defence Secretary, Sundarji had also very categorically stated that the screw should be tightened on Bofors to reveal the names or else the contract should be cancelled, but it was now quite evident that the Prime Minister was not at all in favour of cancelling it and he therefore very cleverly kept saying that it was the Ministry of Defence that was against the cancelling of the contract since the security of the country would be put in jeopardy. Since no valid reason was given for Arun Singh's sudden resignation and the government having conveniently attributed it to personal reasons, which was hardly convincing, the rumours doing the rounds in the elite circles of Delhi was that it was probably because of the two lady wives who were also neighbours and were once very close friends but were now not pulling along with one another. Whether this was a fact or a part of the disinformation campaign it was difficult to tell at this stage. However, there was no doubting the reality that the two Dosco buddies had decided to part ways. The Bofors gun it seems had taken its first victim as Arun Singh with his wife Nina like Ram and Sita decided to get lost in the wilderness of their country home at Bindsar near Ranikhet and Almora. It was probably to find peace and solace in the Kumaon Hills of Jim Corbett and get away from the maneaters of New Delhi. The Ex Minister of State for Defence it seems had followed his own conscience. He was not willing to go along with the Prime Minister and his government on this very sinister and sensitive issue and therefore to save further embarrassment to himself and to his old friend he had quit honourably."

Relating to the likely causes that led to the sudden resignation from the Union Cabinet by Arun Singh as was pointed out by Monty in his letter, Shupriya decided to dig into some of the old articles that had featured in the Hindu and other leading newspapers regarding the on going Bofors scandal. This also included the 10 questions that the fertile brain of Ram Jethmalani, a leading Sindhi lawyer of India who had two wives and who was from the opposition Bhartiya Janata Party had been asking the young Indian Prime Minister on a daily basis. As she rummaged through those tricky questions, she found some more interesting details. In August 1987, following the resignation of Arun Singh and during a heated discussion on the subject in Parliament a visbly worried Rajiv Gandhi had categorically declared to the House that neither he nor any other member of his family had received any consideration on the Bofors deal. A few days later, when the JPC through the good offices of Mr Oza, the Indian Ambassador in Sweden asked for Martin Ardbo and Moberg who had replaced him to come and depose before the JPC, Ardbo point blank refused, while Moberg agreed somewhat reluctantly. Therefore on 14th September, when Mr Moberg the Senior Vice President with Lars Gotlin the Bofors Chief Legal Advisor arrived for discussions in Delhi and had a long secret meeting with Bhatnagar, the Defence Secretary, NN Vohra the Additional Seretary in the Minsitry of Defence, the Law Secretary PK Kartha and Gopi Arora the Special Secretary to the Prime Minister, the massive cover plan it seems had already started rolling. And on 19th September, 1987 when the Hindu wrote that Bofors had disclosed that a total of SEK 319 Million had been paid to three non Indian companies at the rate of SEK 188, 81 and 50 million respectively and that these companies were all domiciled outside India and that these payments were for terminating the international consultancy agreement with them which though they were relevant to the sale of the guns to India but since the money had been paid in 1986 prior to the agreement being signed, tongues had once again started wagging. The visit and the disclosure by Bofors was dubbed by the opposition as a crude effort in trying to absolve and clear the Prime Minister's name and that of his family and it was like getting a certificate for him from the arms manfucturer and supplier.

With Rajiv Gandhi now changing his stance and admitting that yes, termination/consultancy charges by Bofors as admitted by them had been paid, but it was not to Indians, it complicated the matter even further. And another twist to this tale was given, when the Defence Secretary, Bhatnagar on 15th October 1987 wrote to Morberg asking for the credibility credentials of Pitco, Moresco, Moineau, AE Services and Svenska and the nature of services that these companies had rendered to Bofors. These were the names of the companies that had been disclosed by Bofors during Moberg's visit to India a month earlier and the most surprising part was that a copy of this letter had allegedly been sent to the Hindujas also, and who in turn it is believed had informed Martin Ardbo. And as a result of which a damage control meeting was believed to have been hurriedly held in London and in which the participants were the two senior Hinduja brothers, Moberg, Gotlin and Ardbo. This was during that third week of October 1987 and it was now becoming quite apparent that the base for crisis management to keep the names of the recipient's top secret would now be London since most of these so called companies it seems were all were based abroad and the services of a some good lawyers to safeguard the name of the Gandhi family confidentially may also be required.

Digging into the credentials of these companies further, Shupriya found that Pitco was closely linked to Sangam and Sangam was the Hinduja's flagship company in London. AE Services Ltd was a UK registered company, but it also had certain linkages in Switzerland and in the tiny principality of Liechtenstein. The company was formally known as 'Target Practice Ltd' and that name sounded so funny to Shupriya that she kept wondering that if they had targeted India now, whom they had targeted earlier and whom would they target in future. This company was based in Vaduz the capital of Leichtenstein and there also it had a very funny and unusual name. It was known as Ciaou. A.Anstalt and the Ciaou stood for" Consortium for

Infromation Assimilation and Output Unit'. It was definitely a very funny acronym for a company and since it sounded more Italian like the word Ciao meaning hello in that language, Shupriya decided to probe a little more into its functioning. This was the mother company of AE Services Ltd and which according to Monty was probably linked to Rajiv and Sonia Gandhi's close Italian friends the Quattarocchis. Whereas Moineau SA and maybe a few others could be decoy companies that had probably been introduced as red herrings and which could now send all those people snooping around to get to the real truth on a merry wild goose chase thought Shupriya as she opened the Atlas and looked for Vaduz. The sleepy small town in that tiny principality of Liechtenstein was situated in the north western fringes of Switzerland and not far from the Austrian border. Its total area was around 18 square kilometers and it had a population of around 5000 only and the major landmark was the Vaduz Castle that overlooked the tiny city. Therefore and not surprisingly when a letter from Major Bob Wilson to Ardbo's lawyer Bertil Sodermark that was dated 10th October, 1987 categorically mentioned that under no circumstances should Ardbo reveal the real identity of Chiao Anstalt, Shupriya had a hunch that this company could probably be the key to the whole story, but she unfortunately had no resources of her own to find out. And as far as the C.B.I. was concerned, Shupriya knew very well that it was only a tool of the government and they would only do what they were ordered to do.

While in that month of January 1988, Shupriya racked her brains in Colombo over the ever confusing Bofors scandal, in Stockholm Shiraz was surprised to to see the presence of the Indian Prime Minister with his Italian wife Sonia and their two young children Priyanka and Rahul in the Swedish capital. They were on a three day official visit to Sweden and the best part was that there was not a word about Bofors in the Swedish Press, and nor were their any questions asked on this very sensitive subject by the media. Was the Indian Prime Minister's visit to Sweden a public relations exercise by both the governments to bury the Bofors issue once and for all? And while Shiraz kept thinking about it he also quietly got ready to go for the wreath laying ceremony by Rajiv Gandhi at the grave of his old friend Olaf Palme, and the man who had probably started it all in good faith, but never realized that it would snowball into such a major issue both in India and in Sweden. Giving the excuse to his wife Saira that he would be busy in a day long meeting at the Pakistan Embassy and that she should not call him up, Shiraz first drove to the embassy and having parked his car there took the tube train to Gamla Stan. On reaching the Adolf Frederick Church where the ceremony was soon to begin, Shiraz found that there was unprecedented security all around. There was a genuine fear that with the on going insurgency in the Punjab, there could be a possibility of Sikh extremists abroad targeting the Indian Prime Minister and his family in a neutral and peace loving country, and the Swedes were not taking any chances whatsoever. As it is the Swedish Government had been under constant fire by its own people over the illegal sale of arms by Bofors to countries in the Middle East and though Lars Ringburg, the Swedish Public Prosecutor too had also raised his hands for good and had given up his pursuit to dig into the scam tainted Bofors-India deal, the Swedes did not want Palme's partner Rajiv to follow him to the grave. Moreover, the question of who killed Olaf Palme was yet to be solved.

Flashing his diplomatic credentials, Shiraz had no difficulty in getting entry to witness the solemn ceremony. The Swedes had erected a special bullet proof canopy over the church courtyard to ensure that no sniper from the top of the buildings overlooking the church could take a pot shot at the Indian Prime Minister. This reminded Shiraz about the book and the movie 'The Day of the Jackal'. It was a masterpiece of suspense by the author Frederick Forsythe and this particular ceremony was also taking place at the church with the same first name thought Shiraz as he noticed TN Sheshan, the man in charge of Rajiv Gandhi's security and who was also known as the 'Big Bull' making last minute security checks with his staff and his Swedish counterpart.

"Thank God that nothing untoward has happened," said Shiraz to himself as he got back to his embassy desk and rang up his wife Saira to tell her that he was back from the meeting. Shiraz too had been following the Bofors scandal with a lot of interest, and that was eversince he heard that a certain Indian lady from South India by the name of Chitra Subramanium was determined in getting to the bottom of that murky deal. Chitra was married to a foreigner and had a five month old baby boy and was based at Geneva in Switzerland. And she was the one who had the guts and was instrumental in writing all those sensational stories under her own maiden name. There was no doubt that the young Indian correspondent from Geneva with her penchant for digging into the truth on the Bofors gun scandal payoffs and with her investigative journalism had created quite a stir in the Indian press, and off late she had also been spotted quite often on the streets of the Swedish capital. Besides Chitra who was representing 'The Hindu' newspaper, there were also a host of others from the Indian media, the government, and from among the members of the Indian opposition parties and parliament who too were now constantly hopping in and out of Stockholm with the sole purpose of carrying out their own snooping activities on the stinking Bofors affair. And though most of these witch hunts to get to the real truth was being done very discreetly, but the fact remained that it was not going to be easy at all.

CHAPTER-8

Playing With Fire

In mid February 1988 and much to her disappointment Monty and Reeta's daughter Rohini Bajwa was posted as Third Secretary to the Indian High Commission at Dhaka. She was very keen to go to Colombo since Aunt Shupriya was there, but there were no vacancies in that mission. Though her close friends still addressed her as Dimpy, but being a diplomat now she was always addressed as Miss Rohini Bajwa. At 23, she was comparatively very young and attractive but had no plans to get married so soon, though her mother Reeta was very keen that she should. While under training at Mussoouri, she became friendly with a good looking South Indian Brahmin boy who was undoubtedly brilliant because inspite of having qualified for admission to the IIT, Karagpur and the IIM at Ahmedabad, he had opted for the IFS and Reeta felt that the boy whom she also met a couple of times at home would be a good match for her daughter. The boy was tall good looking and in some ways he even resembled Shashi Tharoor and Monty would often pull his daughter's leg whenever he got the chance.

Bharat Padmanabhan came from a very good intellectual family and both his parents were professors at the JNU, the Jawaharlal Nehru University in Delhi. Bharat also had two years experience as a lecturer in economics at St Stephen's College and Monty too was fond of him. It was not that Dimpy was against the marriage as such, but both had decided not to rush into it since they were aware that it would well nigh be impossible for the Ministry of External Affairs to give them common postings everytime. Moreover, having spent so much of the government's money in being trained it would be highly unfair if she or he resigned at the very outset thought Dimpy very wisely. The young couple therefore decided to give themselves a little more time before tying the knot. Bharat who was popularly known as Paddy had been posted as the Third Secretary to the Indian Embassy in Moscow and he felt indeed very lucky to get such an important station because the USSR was on the threshold of a different kind of revolution, and Paddy very much wanted to be there in the very midst of it all. Paddy wanted too see for himself how Gorbachev's dream of 'Perestroika and Glasnost' would transform the lives of the 250 million Soviets behind the Iron Curtain that had so far been so rigidly and strictly controlled by the Communist Party of the Soviet Union for the past 70 years. Though the Soviet people in general and the Russians in particulars were hard working, but they had now got used to a much laid back life style. The ordinary working class people known as the 'Rabochee Class' had been mollycoddled so much by the Communist Party that it had badly affected the entire Soviet economy, and Paddy was of the view that though the younger generation may welcome the change, but for the elders it would be somewhat difficult.

And while Paddy was getting used to the lifestyle in Moscow, it was election time in Bangladesh when Dimpy reported for duty in Dhaka. With the two main political party's the BNP and the Awami League having decided to boycott the elections, General Ershad's Jatiyo Party simply romped home with a massive majority of 251 seats. A few days later it was Fazal Rehman's turn to pack bag and baggage as he with his wife Samina and six year old son Shafiq caught the Bangladesh Biman Flight to Delhi. Having done his stint with SAARC, Fazal Rehman at 44 had now been posted as Counselor Political to the Bangladesh High Commission in the Indian capital. While on the flight he jokingly told Samina.

"Darling I will now not only show you the beautiful Taj-Mahal at Agra, but will also take you to Fategarh from where because of my undying love for you I risked my life and escaped from the prisoner of war camp and came back to marry you."

"Well in that case I suggest let us also carry a marble plaque to be installed there and with the wordings 'It was from here for the love of his beloved Samina in Dhaka escaped Prisoner of War number 2095 Captain Fazal Rehman Khan of the Pakistan Army in 1972,'replied Samina jokingly as she drew a caricature of her husband dressed in a prisoner's uniform complete with a cap and a medal of honour and then wrote below it in Roman English 'My Quadi Number One-Shreshto Bir Fazal Rehman Khan' (My Prisoner Number One, the one and only war Hero Fazal Rehman Khan)

On 25th February, 1988, the day Fazal Rehman reported for duty, India test fired the Prithvi, their first indegeniously developed short range ballistic missile. And it not only sent shock waves across the border into Pakistan and

Bangladesh, but also to the countries of the Western Bloc who also showed their anger by immediately enforcing a technology embargo on the country. The launch of the surface to surface missile with a range of 150 kilometers and with a circular probable error of only 50 metres from the designated target had catapulted India to the big league, and the man behind its success was simple soul and that too a Muslim from South India with a very long name. Avul Pakir Jainulabdeen Abdul Kalam was born on 15th October, 1931 in the small island town of Rameshwaram in the erstwhile state of Madras. The son of Jainulabdeen and Ashiamma was from an ordinary poor middle class family and had started life as a teenager collecting and selling tamarind seeds. Later while studying in an elementary school he earned his first wages by daily collecting newspaper bundles from the railway platform. A product of Schwartz High School, Ramanathapuram, and St Joseph College, Trichi, the unassuming brilliant student with his Bachelor of Science degree having completed his engineering degree from the prestigious MIT, the Madras Institute of Technology wanted initially to become a pilot in the Indian Airforce, but luck was not on his side. There were only eight vacancies and he was ninth in order of merit. However the IAF's loss was a gain for the Minstry of Defence. After qualifying as an aeronautical engineer from HAL, Hindustan Aeronautics Limited, the young Abdul Kalam joined the DTD&P(Air), the Directorate of Technical Development and Production as a Senior Scientific Assistant in 1958 on a monthly basic salary of Rupees two hundred and fifty. Four years later in 1962, and after being interviewed by none other than Dr Vikram Sarabhai, the father of the Indian Space programme, Abdul Kalam was appointed as a a Rocket Engineer at INCOSPAR, the Indian Committee for Space Research which was setting up a rocket launching station near the small fishing village of Thumba near Trivandrum. The site was chosen because it was close to the earth's magnetic equator and surprisingly it was the prayer room of St Mary's Magdelene Church in that village that became his first laboratory, and on 21st November, 1963, independenent India launched her first sounding rocket from there.Unknown to many, it was Tipu Sultan's army while fighting the British that had first used rockets as a weapon of war, and even the western world and the United States had accepted that fact. The NASA's sounding rocket programme that is based at Wallops Island in Virginia even has a mural painting at its reception lobby that depicts the battle scene of Tipu's rocket forces engaging the red coated English soldiers. On 20th November 1967, India had launched the Rohini rocket from Thumba and on 18th July, 1980 India's first Satellite launch Vehicle, SLV-3 lifted off from the small island of Sriharikota, that was located a 100 kilometers north of Madras. It was a hundred percent indegenious effort by the dedicated Indian scientists and to which Abdul Kalam was proud to belong, and now at the age of 57, he was on the threshold of making India a self reliant country in the field of guided missiles.

In early March, while the Indian scientists were still celebrating the success of the Prithvi missile, in Pakistan Prime Minister Junejo convened an All Party Conference to solicit support for the government's stand on the sensitive Afghan issue, but he had kept President Zia out of it. And as a result of which the relationship between the two had started becoming a little awry. By the end of March there was a spate of postings of senior bureaucrats and senior army officers who had served more than their required terms in Islamabad and Rawalpindi respectively. As a result of this policy decision, both Karim Malik and Salim Rehman Khan together with a few others from the Pakistan Foreign Office were given their marching orders. Karim Malik was posted back to Moscow as the Number Two man in the Embassy, whereas Salim Rehman was ordered to move to Beijing as Counselor Political, and since both were important assignments they generally welcomed it. Brigadier Aslam Rehman too having successfully completed more than two years of his command of an infantry brigade in the strategic Hajipir Area of Jammu and Kashmir had been posted as the BGS of a new Corps that was to be raised shortly at Bhawalpur. His future appointment as the Brigadier General Staff of a new Corps was indicative enough that he would if all goes well Inshallah he would get his General's rank in another two to three years time. He was only 48 years old, and his record of service during the last 24 years of service in the Pakistan army was impeccable. Overall he was second in seniority amongst all those who had passed out from the Pakistan Maílitary Academy, Kakul in the class of 1964 and his promotion board to the General Cadre was due earliest in 1990.

It was early on the morning of 10th of April, 1988, that Brigadier Aslam Rehman Khan having finally handed over his charge to the new incumbent and after been given a rousing send off by the officers and men of his Brigade, made his way by staff car to Islamabad. Enroute he stopped at the Headquarters of 12 Infantry Division at Murree for a farewell breakfast with the GOC, and then picked up his son Vovka (Samir Rehman Khan) from his school at Ghora Gali. It was nearing 9.30 on that sunny bright spring morning with the fragrance of wild flowers in the air that the father and son duo while singing away merrily crossed the last miltary traffic checkpost between Murree and Rawalpindi. Then suddenly when they were about 10

Kilometres from Rawalpindi, a series of very loud explosions were heard and soon thereafter it literally started raining rockets, shells and mortars all over the place. But luckily these projectiles were not exploding on impact and that had got Aslam Rehman thinking. Ordering the driver to stop, he got out of the car to observe. One rocket narrowly missed the car by only a few feet as it landed in a nearby khud and luckily that too proved to be a dud. Fearing that this could be an attack by the Indian Air Force on the sensitive nuclear plant in nearby Kahuta, Aslam Rehman ordered the driver to reverse the staff car and get back to the T CP, the military traffic check post. A little while later as the noise of the explosions continued intermittently, a huge ball of black smoke could be seen rising like a giant mushroom in the sky. The rain of rockets and missiles however did not stop, but observing the direction from which the dense black smoke was emanating, Aslam Rehman came to the conclusion that something terrible must have have happened at the ammunition dump at Ojhri camp, and about which he had fairly good knowledge, and he was dead right.

For the next two days, the people of Rawalpindi and Islamabad were witness to a spectacular display of fireworks that the Pakistanis had never ever seen before, but which unfortunately also claimed a very large number of innocent lives. On that morning, when the fireworks started, the roads leading to Ojhri and the camp were initially thronged with inquisitive onlookers, but soon thereafter as the rockets and other lethal missiles came raining down from the skies, it became a graveyard for many. The scene was simply chaotic as people scrambled for safety to avoid the deadly unpredictable attack. The true facts however emerged a fortnight or so later after the Junego Government had ordered an immediate high level court of inquiry into the disaster that was headed by Lt General Imranullah Khan, the 2 Corps Commander at Rawalpindi. On 22nd April, after the findings of the court of inquiry that was highly confidential in nature was submitted to the government, Brigadier Aslam Rehman through his contacts at the GHQ had managed to have as they say a quiet 'Dekho' of it and he was more than shocked.

On that day of 10th April, 1988 at the Ojhri Camp, boxes filled with ammunition were being manually shifted from the old world war vintage sheds by a group of hired civil labour to the waiting transport for onward dispatch to the Afghan Mujahideens. The work on that particular ammunition shed had started at 8 o'clock that morning and since the boxes were stacked nearly ten feet high, they were therefore for easy convenience and for saving time were being pushed down haphazardly by the untrained labour for subsequent loading into the waiting vehicles. At 9.30 AM, a box containing 122 mm rockets while it was being slided down from the top of the stack accidently fell down and hit the ground with a big thud and it exploded on impact. It resulted in an instant fire and caused immediate panic among the labourers who ran for safety. This resulted in a chain effect of fire and explosions and soon that particular shed and those in its near vicinity were set ablaze. The intensity of the heat that was generated by the blazing inferno now resulted in the sympathetic detonation of all the other rockets in the neighbouring sheds and literally the rockets had started flying like lethal bombs in all possible directions causing havoc and panic all around. By the time it was brought under control, a colossal 10,000 tons of ammunition and explosives, including some 30,000 rockets were destroyed and a very large number of vehicles both civil and military that were detailed for transporting the ammunition to Peshawar and elsewhere to the Pakistan-Afghan border for the Mujaheedin fighters were completely written off. More than a 100 people had died and over a thousand were wounded including five staff members and twenty others from the ISI who were solely responsible for the functioning of this massive arms depot that was being used to keep the Jehadis fighting the Russians inside Afghanistan and also in Kashmir.

"But how could it happen just like that and that to in a large ammunition depot that was located practically in the midst of the two important twin cities of Rawalpindi and Islamabad, which was the very capital of the country. Was it an accident or was it a well planned act of sabotage," thought Aslam Rehman as he reported to the GHQ for briefing on the new raising of the Corps. Having served with the ISI not so very long ago, Brigadier Aslam Rehman was familiar with the conditions inside the old ammunition dump and since he had good contacts with those in authority at the ISI Headquarters, he decided to probe a little deeper into this terrible tragedy.

Lt General Akhtar having relinquished his appointment as DGISI a year earlier had handed over charge to Major General Hamid Gul. The flamboyant new DGISI was born in Sargodha on 20th November, 1936 and as a teenager had witnessed the brutal 1947 communal riots. That had a very deep impact on his mind. He was commissioned in October 1958 and joined the 19th Lancers, an armoured regiment of the Pakistan army. A India hater to the core, he was actively also backing the Khalistan movement in Punjab, and according to him a destabilized Indian Punjab was equivalent to having an extra division and at no extra cost to the exchequer. The ammunition dump at the Ojhri Camp was exclusively the ISI's baby and on the day when it blew up, it was not only stocked to its maximum capacity, but it also held excess stocks that were much above the Jehadis immediate requirements. Under General Hamid Gul's new policy of replenishment of arms and ammunition to the various Afghan Mijahideen Commanders, the consignments to them were now required to be in composite packages, but because of the severe winter conditions in most sectors of the Pakistan-Afghanistan border, a large number of consignments had been held up, thus over burdening the holding capacity at Ojhri. These very consignments were now being readied for dispatch, when the dreadful accident occurred. Typical of any such major mishaps, the questions that were now being asked were firstly,why so much of ammunition was stocked in such a densely populated area, and secondly who was responsible for it. The Prime Minister and the civil authorities finding that this could be a good stick to beat the army with, had raised a hue and cry and a blame game had now started with the Army accusing the ISI and vice versa. Caught in a jam, President Zia very conveniently blamed neither, because he needed both the ISI and the Army's support to remain in power. Following Zia's diktat, the court of inquiry too did not blame any individual or organization, and to make matters even worse, the findings of the court of enquiry were not even made public. This was on the plea that the procurement and issue of those arms and ammunition were highly secretive in nature and therefore keeping the national and the defense interest of Pakistan in view, such sensitive information therefore could not be divulged for public consumption. This now resulted in a further rift between the President and his Prime Minister.

According to a reliable inside source from within the ISI, a similar fire had broken out in the same very ammunition warehouse at about the same very time last year, but luckily it was quickly brought under control and without any serious damage. In that particular case, it was because of some old Second World War vintage smoke grenades from which the white phosphorous had leaked out and had caught fire. But luckily the vigilant NCO on duty that day disregarding his own safety had pulled out the entire box from the warehouse and had put out the fire in quick time. Since there was no explosion, the court of inquiry that was held only recommended improved precautions and the matter had ended there. But in this case, when Aslam Rehman went into more details, he found that the fire had started from one of the boxes that contained Egyptian rockets that had been sent by the CIA for the Afghan Mujahideens. Contrary to safety regulations these rockets had been armed with the fuzes before shipment, and when it fell from the stack accidently there was an explosion followed by a fire. As a result of the explosion some of the labourers and staff were injured and thereafter everybody got busy in evacuating them. The fire then spread rapidly and within ten minutes the first gigantic bang was heard. And ofcourse the rest was history.

While the blast at Ojhri Camp shook Islamabad and Rawalpindi, in New Delhi a political dynamite that was allegedly planted by the opposition and the President of India very nearly brought down the Rajiv Gandhi government. Gian Zail Singh the outgoing President had become very embittered by the manner in which he was been treated by the very Congress and the young Prime Minister whose mother and the very party that she had created he had served so very loyally. With the Bofors scandal in the forefront and Rajiv's reluctance to have the Fairfax probe going to unearth the shady foreign exchange deals allegedly by some members of the Congress and of those industrialists who were close to the ruling party, the President in a letter to Rajiv it seems had called him a lair. Then according to his own admission the President who was aspiring for a second term in office very foolishly said that he had been offered huge sums of money to stand for re-election. This had now set the cat among the pigeons and there were therefore strong rumours that a conspiracy had been hatched to dismiss Rajiv and his scandal mired government, but it had finally fizzled out.Meanwhile on 14th April, 1988, the Geneva Accord on Afghanistan was signed between the warring sides, and realizing that the Soviet military venture was a totally miscalculated move by his predecessors, Gorbachev in his resolve to stop more further bleeding of this self inflicted wound on his already demoralized troops and sinking econmy had therefore decided to finally call it quits.

It was also around this time that President Zia addressed a top secret meeting of some specially selected senior military commanders and staff including the DGISI. At that meeting he spelt out in very clear terms his future policies and plans on Kashmir. With the accord on Afghanistan already signed, President Zia having carried out a very detailed analysis of the present situation in India and particularly so in neighbouring Kashmir and Punjab, now in very lucid manner unveiled his plan for 'Operation Topac.' He had arrived at this ingenious plan after considering some very important factors that were both political and military. Firstly there were very reliable reports about the unhappiness among the leaders of the Muslim United Front Party in Kashmir who felt cheated with the results of the last state elections and they were now absolutely against the Faroukh-Rajiv combine who they said had so blatanly rigged the election results. Secondly, there were also clear indications and feelers that had now started trickling in from across the Line of Control asking Pakistan for help in starting an insurgency inside Kashmir. Thirdly, with the covert arms aid and training that was already being given to the Punjab militants by the ISI, the same could also be given to the disgruntled Kashmiris. And fourthly with most of the Indian Army reserve formations already heavily committed in Sri Lanka, this could be the ideal time to set the ball rolling and build it up progressively. And lastly, once the Soviet troops were completely withdrawn from Afghanistan, those Jehadis who had been inducted from outside for the Afghan cause could now also well be utilized to fight for the cause of their Muslim brothers inside Kashmir. Thanks to the CIA and with the surfeit of arms and ammunition available, Pakistan could arm the new Kashmiri Mujahideens to the hilt and they would then be the ones to spearhead the movement. Having concluded his talk, when the President of Pakistan gave his million dollar toothy smile and asked if they were any questions, there were a few no doubt, but generally everyone was in agreement with the General's well thought out assessment and long term plan.

While the think tanks in the Pakistan army got busy in giving shape to 'Operation Topac,' the two elderly Rehman brothers and their wives were feeling a little cut up because most of their children and grandchildren would once again be many thousands of miles away from them, and they would not probably see them for another year or maybe more. They therefore decided to host one big family get together before they all finally left for their respective destinations.

"Alright in that case it will be my diamond jubilee birthday celebrations in advance," said Gul Rehman who at 74 plus was suffering from high blood pressure and diabetes and he had this uncanny feeling that he may not reach 75. The Medical Specialist at the Peshawar Military Hospital had very confidentially conveyed to him that his last few ECG's, electro-cardiagrams were not good at all and had warned the General that he should be very careful. Being highly diabetic, going in for a bypass operation at his age Gul Rehman thought would be both a waste of time and money. He had lived his life to the full and he did not wish to become a liability in his old age to his dear wife and children. He had suffered from a mild stroke a few months earlier, but he had kept it a secret even from his wife Zubeida. Since Mehmuda and family were scheduled to depart first for their second Moscow assignment on 25th April, Gul Rehman decided that the party should be held on the 23rd, which was a Saturday and an invitation should also be sent to Fazal Rehman who was now posted in Delhi and also to Riaz and Saira in Stockholm to grace the occasion if possible.

On receiving the invitation on telephone, Shiraz and Saira with their children decided to leave for Peshawar the very next day. It was a coincidence since Shiraz's home leave was also due and he had been granted the same from the 20th of April. And though they had planned to spend a week enroute in Greece, but they now decided to give everyone a surprise by landing up unannounced and a few days before the grand party.

The homely party at the old Haveli of late Colonel Attiqur Rehman at Peshawar was a grand family affair and there were no other guests or invitees. The large congregation of sons, daughters, their spouses and children reminded Gul Rehman of his own childhood days when he with his parents visited Aunty Suraiya's house in Calcutta. But there was one big difference. Whereas the gathering in Calcutta was always a cosmopolitan affair with the Sen's, the Ghosh's and the Pugsley's joining in the merriment as one big family, in this case it was restricted only to the Rehman family only. That evening with all the ten grandchildren ranging in age from Mehmuda's daughter Tarannum who was the eldest at 20, to Salim Rehman's son Shabir Rehman who was just 4 years old, it was more of a children's party as all of them kept kissing and cuddling their loving grandpa. A deeply touched Gul Rehman could not hide away his inner feelings as the veteran soldier kissed and hugged each one of them turn by turn and then said loudly. "I think that this is the best birthday I ever had in my life." A little while later, when it came to the ceremony of blowing the candle and cutting the big diamond shaped cake, there was literally a stampede as every grandchild and especially the toddlers wanted to do the honours. Therefore, to give everyone of them an equal opportunity and to bring in total impartiality in the proceedings that were soon to follow, Shiraz had very cleverly quickly arranged for 10 plastic cake cutting knives and these were placed around the table. The children were now required not only to cut the cake but also help Grandpa in blowing off all the 75 colourful candles, while the rest of them were to keep singing happy birthday to him. "Hooray" said all the children in unison as the entire Rehman family crowded around the big cake and got ready to begin the ceremony.

"Well I must say that our dear brother-in-law Riaz (Shiraz) is a very seasoned diplomat Abbajaan or else there would have certainly been a riot here," remarked Aslam Rehman as Shiraz acknowledged the compliment with a big smile while all the grandchildren kept hovering around their loving grandfather who was now ready to cut the cake and blow out the candles with them. As soon as the singing was over and after everybody had got a piece of that special Black Forest cake, Salim Rehman having taken over as the master of ceremonies raised a toast to his beloved uncle who was a father figure to all of them. Thereafter in order to convey to all the young children about their own heritage and also to project the true values of family bonding between all the brothers, sisters, cousins and the parents, Aslam Rehman and Fazal Rehman gave a very interesting power point presentation with a running commentary about the history of the Rehman family right from its origin. The two brothers, Gul and Arif Rehman together with their wives, children and grand children were all were part of the third, fourth and fifth generation and they indeed felt very proud and lucky to be of part of that great but humble Rehman family. Aslam and Fazal Rehman had worked really hard in scanning through all the old photographs of their forefathers and the many mementoes and memorabilia that were now very much a part of their great grandfather Haji Abdul Rehman's Haveli. The presentation started with a photograph of a one year old Gul Rehman sitting in his grandfather's lap and waving out. It was taken on the day, when his father Captain Attiqur Rehman from the Indian Medical Service left for France in 1915 to give medical cover to the Indian troops during the First World War. The second photograph showed Cadet Gul Rehman at the PWRIMC standing with his dearest friend Ismail Sikandar Khan and flanked by Major Attiqur Rehman on one side and Colonel Reginald Edwards on the other. And when the third photograph came on the big screen and the commentator gave out the names and the year when it was taken, Shiraz was totally moved. The photograph was captioned 'The Three Musketeers' and Shiraz now realized how very close the friendship must have been between his adopted father Ismail Sikandar Khan, uncle Daler Singh Bajwa and Uncle Gul Rehman. That photograph was taken on the day the three friends had passed out as Second Lieutenants from the IMA, and that was nearly 45 years ago. It was the same photograph with the same very caption that he had seen in the old Bajwa family album and he now remembered how very fondly Bibiji used to talk about the undying friendship between the three friends till the partition of the country ruined everything. Sipping the cocktail with a champagne base that Salim Rehman had specially prepared for the occassion and which was aptly named by him as the 'Rehman Fireball', Shiraz could never imagine that he was now a part of the same Rehman family. That evening the world had come full circle for Riaz Mohammed Khan, and his only desire now was to see that India and Pakistan lived as good friends and neighbours and not as enemies and adversaries.

But for Pakistan's military dictator General Zia-ul-Haq and his coterie of close military advisors, the bell to begin the fourth round for Kashmir it seems had already been sounded and 'Operation Topac,' the brainchild of the Pakistan President for launching a war by proxy in the valley had also received the green signal. This was a three part action plan for the liberation of Kashmir and the codeword Topac it seems was derived from the name of Prince Tupac Amru II of Peru who as a guerilla leader in the 18th century had led a war of liberation against the Spanish conquerors of that Latin American nation. In that month of April 1988, after the Geneva Accord was signed by the Pakistan Foreign Minister Zain Noorani and his Afghan counterpart Abdul Wakil that spelt out the withdrawal of all Soviet troops from Afghanistan by February 1989 and which was due to commence from 15th May, 1988 President Zia in his opening address to his Generals spelt out the importance of 'Operation Topac" when he said.

"Gentlemen, as you all know that due to our preoccupation in Afghanistan, in the service of Islam, I have not been able to put these plans before you earlier. However, let there be no mistake, and our aim remains quite clear and firm, and that is the liberation of the Kashmir Valley. Our Muslim Kashmiri brethren in the valley cannot be allowed to stay on with India for any length of time anymore and therefore something has to be done and done quickly. In the past we had opted for hamhanded military options and therefore had failed. So as I have mentioned before, we will now keep our military options for the last moment as a coup de grace, if and when necessary. Sheer brute force in any case is not needed in every type of warfare and especially so in the prevailing situation in the Kashmir valley. Therefore, to begin with there must be a well planned and a well coordinated use of moral and physical means other than military operations to destroy the will of the enemy, damage his political capability to rule over Kashmir and expose him to the world as an oppressor. 'Operation Topac' therefore gentlemen will be carried out in three main phases. In Phase One that may well last a couple of years if not more, we will have to assist our Kashmiri friends and brethren in getting hold of power from within the state and that will be done by a well directed method of political subversion, intrigue and defections. Therefore, in this phase it will be a low level insurgency movement against the present regime so that it is put under constant siege, but does not collapse, because any central rule by Delhi will upset the applecart. We have therefore to carry out this phase of the operation in a very subtle and careful manner, and to achieve our aim the following things have to be implemented simulataneously. We have to plant chosen men in all key positions to subvert the police force, the financial institutions, and the communications network, and also within the other important government and quasi government organizations inside Indian occupied Kashmir. Simultaneously whip up anti Indian feelings amongst the students and peasants and preferably so on sensitive religious issues that could lead to riots and anti-government demonstrations. Systematically organise, provide arms and train subversive elements and groups to initially deal with the Indian para military forces in the valley. Thereafter adopt and develop means to stealthily cut off the vital lines of comminication within the state itself and to Ladakh, while giving special attention to cutting off the road over the Zojila Pass to Kargil and beyond. In collaboration with Sikh extremists, create chaos and terror in the Jammu region and thereby create a greater Hindu-Muslim divide. Subsequently establish virtual control in the Southern Kashmir Valley and in other such depth areas where the Indian Army is not presently deployed or is thin on the ground."

"In Phase Two, exert maximum pressure on Siachen, Kargil and the Rajauri-Poonch sectors to force the Indian Army to deploy their reserve formations located inside the valley and in the depth areas of the state. Thereafter by covert actions, and at an opportune time attack and destroy base depots, headquarters of military formations that are located at important places like, Srinagar, Pattan, Baramulla, Kupwara and Chowkibal. This will be followed by carefully infiltrating some of the Afghan Mujahideens to expand deeper into the areas of influence that is expected to be created in phase I. Finally a Special Force consisiting of selected retired officers from Azad Kashmir together with the hardcore Afghans who have settled there will be poised to attack and destroy airfields, radio stations, the Banihal Tunnel and the Kargil-Leh Highway, while at the same time the bulk of the Pakistan Army will adopt an offensive posture opposite the Punjab and the Jammu Sectors of India.'

"In the Third and Final Phase, detailed plans for the liberation of the Kashmir Valley and the establishment of an Independent Islamic State would then follow. In the meantime maximum pressure must be exerted while the Indian Army reserves are fully committed in Sri Lanka." Before closing his address, the President of Pakistan once again while admitting that it would be disastrous for the country to take on India in a straight contest and therefore according to his assessment it was imperative for Pakistan and specially its military to maintain a low profile during the conduct of the first two phases of 'Operation Topac,' while ofcourse being vigilant all the time. The idea was not to give India an excuse and a chance to prempt and attack Pakistan at a time and place of its own choosing.

A week or so later, when Shiraz went visiting old friends and colleagues in the Pakistan Foreign Ministry at Islamabad and one of them discreetly mentioned to him about President Zia's ingenious plan to start a possible fourth round by proxy in order to liberate Kashmir, Shiraz was rather skeptical about it. Nevertheless, to find out if there was any truth to it, he called on Brigadier Aslam Rehman Khan who luckily was also visiting the GHQ in connection with the field trials of the new American Abrahams tanks that was scheduled to be held at the tank firing ranges near Bhawalpur in the coming month of August 1988. That evening over a round of good 18 holes of golf at the Pindi Golf Gulf, when Brigadier Aslam Rehman Khan casually gave a few more details regarding 'Operation Topac' and how it differed from 'Operation Gibralter' that in 1965 had ended in a bloody fiasco, it became very evident to Shiraz that the matter was indeed very serious and that the chances of Pakistan ultimating liberating the valley under the present political scenario in the state was indeed very high. The alleged rigging of the state elections by the National Conference had so angered the MUF, the Muslim United Front that some of their leaders were once again openly talking about secession and for complete Independence, while a few others were more than keen to become a part of Pakistan. While enjoying a drink with Brigadier Aslam Rehman at the Rawalpindi Club, Shiraz was also keen to find out from him a little more in detail as to how the Pakistan ISI functioned and when Aslam Rehman willingly obliged, Shiraz kept listening very intently. Having served in the organization, when Aslam Rehman also narrated to Shiraz some of the major success stories and failures of the ISI it was all very revealing to Shiraz.

According to Brigadier Aslam Rehman, the ISI dealt in three separate fields that included, Political, External and General Intelligence and these were headed by three Deputy Director Generals who reported directly to the DG ISI. The organization was divided into seven main departments and included the JIX, the Joint Intelligence Department which acted as the main coordinator of gathering the intelligence inputs from all the other departments and sources and after having thoroughly processed and analysed all the information, it was they who then prepared the final report. Next in importance was the JIB, the Joint Intelligence Bureau which basically gathered intelligence on the political parties within Pakistan and included operations in India, as also anti-terrorism operations, besides providing security to VIP's also. Then came the JCIB, the Joint Counter Intelligence Bureau and these also included selected Pakistani Diplomats who were very much a part of this department and who therefore reported directly to it. The JIN, Joint Intelligence North was exclusively responsible for gathering of intelligence in Jammu and Kashmir, while the JIM, Joint Intelligence Miscellaneous conducted specified espionage operations, spy missions, surveillance and such like activities. The JSIB, the Joint Intelligence Signals Bureau was the monitoring authority for all wireless communication and intercepts, while the JTI, the Joint Intelligence Technical was primarily responsible in developing various types of gadgets, explosives and such like monitoring equipment that would further supplement the ISI's requirement.

"But tell me how does one get into this organization and what is the recruitment policy for such an important and sensitive set up ?'" asked Shiraz as he ordered another round of drinks.

"Well as far as the recruiting procedure to the ISI is concerned, it follows two main channels, the armed forces and the civilians. The civilians after a thorough scrutiny are selected by the FPSC, the Federal Public Service Commission and if they qualify in the interview that is jointly conducted by the ISI and the FPSC then they are taken as employees of the Ministry of Defence. They are initially sent for their basic training to the Inter-Services Intelligence School and thereafter are kept on probation for one year. Their promotions however are restricted and they are not allowed to rise above the equivalent rank of Major in the Pakistan army," added Aslam Rehman while thanking the waiter for the drink.

"And how is the selection of the regulars from the three services carried out. I mean how are they screened, vetted and selected to become part of this very powerful arm of the government?" asked Shiraz as Aslam ordered the waiter to get a plate of sizzling sheek kebabs to go with the drinks.

"Well as regards the regulars from the armed forces are concerned, they are required to first apply through their respective channels. Thereafter depending upon their age, record of service, aptitude and the vacancies available, they are sent to the Inter-Services Intelligence School for the basic course. After successful completion of the course and if found fit with the right aptitude for intelligence duties, they are then posted initially to the Field Intelligence Units or to the Directorates of army, air and naval intelligence at the GHQ. Finally depending upon their overall performance and if found competent enough they are inducted into the ISI, albeit first temporarily and are made permanent later. Ofcourse some also find their way in through contacts at the right places and with the usual 'sifarish', (requests/ recommendation) from those who have the clout, but these are only exceptions. Needless to say that the selection of the top most man to head the organization is the government itself and that as you know in the present circumstances is none other than President Zia," said Aslam Rehman somewhat matter of factly.

"Well I must say that they are very choosy in selecting the right people and that I think is the right manner to go about it if we are to safeguard our own national and international interests,"said Shiraz as he ordered another round of drinks and then asked somewhat casually if Aslam Rehman was aware about some of the recent success and failure stories of the organization.

"Frankly speaking not very many, but I do know that the ISI was involved in sucessfully unearthing the plot to assassinate General Zia-ul-Haq during the Pakistan Day Parade on 23rd March, 1980 and of foiling the military coup that was to follow. The main conspirators in this case were Major General Tajammul Hussein Malik, his son Captain Naveed and his nephew and your namesake Major Riaz and all three are presently undergoing stiff jail sentences for their involvement in it. Then there was also the case of the Afghan Charge-de-Affaires Mansoor Ahmed of the Afghan Embassy in Islamabad who thanks to the ISI turned his back on the Soviet backed Afghan government and gave very important information regarding the Afghan intelligence agents from KHAD who having come in as refugees were indulging in espionage and gathering of information regarding the Mujahideens. However, in exchange for the vital information about Afghan agents operating inside Pakistan, Mansoor and family were secretly whisked out with a new identity in a British Airways flight to London and they are now believed to be living incognito and under a new identity somewhere in this wide world," added Aslam Rehman while instructing the Club steward to have the supper laid out in the dining room.

"But how are we doing against the Indian agents and sympathizers. I hope they are being kept under tight surveillance all the time, because they are the ones who are likely to cause all the mischief," said Shiraz very cleverly as he requested the steward to ensure that the soup was served hot at the table.

"I am aware of only one recent case and that concerns a lady teacher who was employed in the Indian School at Islamabad. According to our own intelligence agency source, she was a RAW agent and was involved in obtaining secret information about Pakistan's Nuclear Project at Kahuta from a Pakistani engineer and if I am not wrong she is now working as a double agent for us. I believe that the ISI has also unearthed an arms smuggling racket between two American private arm dealers and some of the Afghan tribal groups. The two dealers so I have been told were being aided by an American diplomat and a teacher in the American International School at Islamabad,"added Aslam Rehman as the butler walked in to announce that supper was ready.

"And what about the failures of the ISI ?" I am sure they must have had some failures also since in such cloak and dagger business the adversary sometimes has an upper hand," said Shiraz while enjoying his grilled fish and chips.

"Well the Pakistani bid to prempt the Indians in getting to Siachen first, was one such terrible failure, when we failed to perform a background check on the firm that had supplied the Pakistani Army with all the Arctic weather gear and equipment. The same company had also supplied India with her requirements, and when India came to know about our demands they simply put two and two together and beat us to it. Then another prominent failure by the ISI that I can recollect was during the 1965 war when we were clueless about the deployment of India's First Armoured Division," added Aslam Rehman as he smiled at Shiraz and jokingly remarked. "I hope as a seasoned diplomat you are not contemplating in working for or joining the ISI, are you?"

"Well if there is a vacancy where is the harm, and moreover in a country like Sweden where I am presently posted there is fuck all to do except watch the good looking Swedish women some of whom are carbon copies of bombshells like Anita Ekberg and the Gabor sisters," added Shiraz in good humour as he signed the bar and snack chits, while Aslam Rehman insisted on paying for the supper.

On the 29th of May 1988, with his two months long home leave about to get over, Shiraz and Saira with their two children Gammy and Tojo were waiting at the Islamabad airport to catch the British Airways flight to London, when Arif Rehman accompanied by his wife Ruksana who had come to see them off told them that the three year, two months and seven days old Junejo government had been dismissed that very morning under the 8th Amendment by President Zia.

"But why and where was the need to do that?" asked Shiraz who did not have a clue even as a diplomat that such a move was already in the offing. He was aware that on the very next day, Zia was to proceed on an official visit to China and was totally surprised by this sudden dismissal of the country's Prime Minister. Moreover the Prime Minister had just landed that very day on 29th May from his visit to the Philipinnes, and even the Vice Chief of

Army Staff Lt General Mirza Aslam Beg who was at the airport to receive him had no idea of what was on Zia's mind, when the dismissal order was handed over to Mr Junego at the airport itself.

"Well it is the usual excuse of corruption, nepotism, maladministration, procrastination, inefficiency and the Prime Minister's failure to enforce Islam I guess," said Ruksana Begum somewhat sarcastically as she presented her two grandchildren with their gifts.

"And it also could be a fallout from the Ojhri explosion, wherein the Prime Minister I believe wanted to make the findings public and punish the past and the present DG's Lt General Akhtar and Lt General Hamid Gul respectively of the ISI for their negligence, and this had caused a serious rift between the President and the Prime Minister I am told," said Arif Rehman as he too hugged his two grandchildren and presented them with the two boxes of their favourite Black Magic chocolates.

Zia it seems had also received an intelligence report that the Prime Minister was sincerely contemplating to have a resolution passed by the National Assembly by which the President would be asked to retire as the Army Chief and a new Chief appointed, but the plan had now back fired as Zia dissolved both the assemblies. Soon after announcing Junejo's dismissal and to avoid any mischief by the Prime Minister, Zia personally ordered his Signal Officer in Chief, Major General Hamid Hasan Butt to take all the telephone monitoring equipment installed at the Prime Minister's residence and at the Inspection Bungalow into his custody and prevent the Intelligence Bureau from tampering with the Bureau records.

With the withdrawal of the Soviet troops having begun on 15th May, and President Zia back in control of his country, winds of change were blowing in the Soviet Union. The Central Committee of the once all powerful Soviet Communist Party had accepted the many reforms of Perestroika and Glasnost that had had been advocated by their progressive leader Mikail Gorbachev, and on the day when Junejo was dismissed, President Reagan in Moscow held his fourth meeting with the Russian leader and the two signed nine agreements that included amongst others, the exchange of students, inspection of each other's nuclear sites, and the right of the Soviet Jews to migrate to Israel if they so desired.

As the summer got hotter in Pakistan, the heat now was also being generated and felt in the Indian States of Punjab and Jammu and Kashmir where the ISI had already started to implement the first phase of 'Operation Topac.' While in Punjab the Sikh militants were once again on the rampage, in the Kashmir valley the anti-India tirade had been stepped up considerably and the mushrooming of a large number of underground militant organizations like the old JKLF and the relatively new Hizb-i-Islami and other such pro-Pakistan and anti-India outfits aided and abetted by the ISI had also started surfacing. The Muslim United Front members too had resigned their membership from the State Assembly and they too had started supporting the underground and the anti national activities openly in Kashmir. And while on his yearly summer visit to the valley for placing his orders for the coming year's requirement of Kashmiri carpets and other artifacts for export, Monty Bajwa was also completely flabbergasted by the wholesale change of attitude of the Kashmiri Muslims and specially those from the far interior of the valley. Not only had the resentment against India grown considerably, but the local youths were now openly criticizing Faroukh Abdullah and his National Conference of becoming bigger stooges of India. These young men were also advocating an armed struggle to fight the bloody Indians and were even prepared to sacrifice their lives for the cause of freedom. Everywhere and even in the village schools and mosques the cry was to free the Kashmiri Muslims from the Brahmin imperialism of Delhi and to break the hegemony of the Abdullah family who had not only brought economic ruin to the state, but were also now being accused of running the state like a fiefdom of their own, and one that was even worse than that of the last Maharaja Hari Singh. The Kashmiri Muslims were also openly threatening the Kashmiri Pundits to quit the valley, but in India nobody it seems were taking these things seriously. To Monty this was quite an eye opener and he was quite surprised to find the indifferent manner in which the Faroukh Abdullah government and the government at the centre were handling the worsening volatile situation. As usual the Faroukh Government now being actively supported by the Prime Minister, Rajiv Gandhi and his Congress government in the centre paid little or no heed to the resentment of the people that had started growing from the day the election results in 1987 had been announced. Charged with blatant rigging, Faroukh Abdullah it seems had decided to walk the tight rope by speaking the language of Islamic fundamentalism in the valley, posing as a pseudo secular leader in Jammu, and posturing as a staunch nationalist while visiting Delhi, wrote Monty in his fortnightly letter to Shupriya.

On the 2nd of June, while emplaning at Srinagar for his return flight to Delhi, Monty heard the sad news about the death of the great Indian showman, Raj Kapoor. The versatile actor who was also an asthma patient had died at the age of only 63. Starting his career at the age of eleven as a clapper boy, and the man who at 24 had established his own RK films and studio was no more. Monty felt sad. He was only 10 years old in 1951, when the film 'Awaara "The Vagabond was released and that was the first time that his parents had taken him to see a Hindi movie with them. The famous song 'Awaara Hun' in that film had always haunted him and it became such a craze that even the Russians had started singing it and that to in Comrade Stalin's era. On his return to Delhi, when Monty on his regular Saturday afternoon beer session with his friend Unni at the Press Club debated the worsening situation in Jammu and Kashmir, Unni was even more critical of the central government's stand on the subject. He was off the view that by rigging the elections and by not giving the MUF a chance to show their real strength democratically, both Rajiv and Faroukh had lost a golden chance and an opportunty of bringing peace and stability in the state. Since the MUF in their manifesto had not challenged Kashmir's accession to India or else they would have been disqualified, the Centre should have monitored the elections more openly and impartially with independent observers from different states. This would have not only soothed ruffled feathers all around, but would have also negated Pakistan's claim for a plebescite in the valley.

"I am afraid our so called politicians at all levels whether it be local, state or national, they unfortunately have only their own personal interests in mind, and they are just not bothered about the long term consequences," said Unni as he like a cricket umpire waved his arm sideways at the barman to indicate that he needed his fourth and last large gin and bitters for the day. And in order to further substantiate his accusation against the politicians that they were not only disinterested in seeing the reality, but were more interested in subverting the truth in order to stay in power, Unni cited the findings of the sham JPC, the Joint Parliamentary Committee that the Rajiv Gandhi had appointed in August 1987 and that took nearly eight months only to throw wool into the eyes of the people, whereas one single lady by the name of Chitra Subramanium sitting in Geneva through her investigative journalism had blown open the Bofors scandal far and wide. According to Unni, Chitra with her fact finding reports that were further substantiated with photocopies of authoritative Bofors documents had with one stroke of her pen nailed the truth. Unni was referring to the story in the Hindu newspaper that was dated 4th June, 1988 and a copy of which he was carrying in his pocket and in which Chitra had debunked the government's story about the no-middlemen, no commission, and the no Indians involved theory, and to which Bofors was now very conveniently referring to as winding up charges.

Placing the copy of the Hindu newspaper on the bar table, Unni showed Monty how Chitra with irrefutable documentary evidence had logically analysed and proved how an amount of SEK 81 Million in three separate payments of SEK 37 million, SEK 12 million and SEK 32 million were paid by Bofors to the Hinduja Brothers as commissions for the deal, and how they with names like 'Moresco-Tulip-Lotus-Mont Blanc-Pitco etc had found their way into the Hinduja's many Swiss Bank accounts.

"So do you now also think that the Hindujas, the Win Chaddhas and the Quattarochis are all in the same league, and if it is so then what is your assessment of this sordid Bofors deal," asked Monty as he carefully went through all the documentary evidence that the Hindu had published.

"Well to begin with, the JPC report is nothing but a damp squib, and it is also very much a part of the big cover up that is still being orchestrated by the government to save their dear leader's skin. Because according to the JPC, not only did Bofors not give any information of the individuals who had received commissions, but the CBI too very conveniently did not succeed in tracing out the actual account holders of these companies to whom commissions had been paid. Infact the JPC gave Rajiv and his government a clean chit and it even concluded that there was no bribe or commission taken at all from Bofors. But the real facts are that the present top management of Bofors had themselves deposed to the JPC in September 1987 that they had two agents in India and they had named Pitco, which was a Hinduja company and the other was Svenska that belonged to Win Chadda. However, they also during their deposition had very conveniently added that the services of these two agents were terminated before the agreement was signed. Then if that was the case and when they were asked by some members of the JPC as to why they had been paid, the Bofors management very conveniently said that the payment was not a commission, but payments for winding up charges. Now that I think was rarher stupid of them because when they were further questioned as to why a third agent AE Services had been hired by Bofors if the contract with the previous two had already been terminated, the Bofors representatives were absolutely stumped and they came out with the lame and stupid excuse that they had forgotten that they were not suppose to hire agents. And that I think was rather childish of them because from the little that I know from my own source is that the AE Services was into this murky deal eversince November 1985 and that it had the 'sunset clause' of no contract-no payment and a deadline of 31ˢᵗ March, 1986 added to it. Therefore if the damn deal was signed in March 1986, it is logical that the 3% commission that was due to

AE Services must have been paid for the services rendered and there is no disputing that fact either, because Bofors had credited the required amount of SEK 50 million to the AE Services Swiss Bank account in September 1986 as was disclosed later by the Swedish Radio in the broadcast on 30th September 1987 which blew the lid off completely. Therefore for the JPC to say that no bribes or commissions were paid is nothing but bloody eyewash, and which undoubtedly has been orchestrated. by the PMO, and it has now become a game of a massive cover up and crisis management in which according to my own reading has the Hinduja brothers too now in the lead roles. And the manner and frequency with which these bothers with their vast wealth I am told open, close and operate these secret accounts from their many banks that are spread all across the globe, it will be a buggers muddle for anyone to find out as to how, where, why and who got those fat commissions," added Unni sarcastically as he tipped the barman with a new ten rupee note and finally called it a day.

In India while the Rajiv Gandhi government was being bombarded by the Bofors gun scandal, in Sri Lanka the IPKF that had by now four full fledged infanrtry divisions supported by armoured tanks, armoured carriers, and attack helicopters under the command of Lt General Amarjit Singh Kalkat kept the LTTE constantly on the run. From April to June 1988, the IPKF had launched two major operations. The first codenamed 'Operation Trishul,' was immediately follwed by 'Operation Viraat' and it was spread over the entire northern provinces extending from Mannar to Mullaitivu and from the Elephant Pass to Vavuniya.After 'Operation Pawan,' the LTTE had retreated to the dense jungles of Vavuniya. This was a key area and through which ran the North-South and the East-West communication routes and therefore was vital for the conduct of all operations by the IPKF in the north and eastern provinces of the Tamil dominated island. With the 4th Mountain Division and the 57 Infantry Division of the Indian Army having now taken over control of Vanni and the Batticalao Sectors, and the 36th Infantry Division and the 54 Infantry Division operating in the areas of Trincomalee, Jaffna and Vavuniya, the LTTE had also now started feeling the heat very badly. The doctrine of jungle bashing by strong patrols that was employed initially by the Indian Army to flush out the militants from the dense forests had now been replaced by search and destroy missions against the LTTE camps and bases. On 21st June, 1988 the IPKF launched 'Operation Checkmate' in the Vadamarachi area, which was Prabhakaran's home town and it forced the LTTE to retreat to their stronghold of Nithikaikulam and the riverine area adjacent to it. The fallout from these operations against the LTTE in Sri Lanka was now also being felt in the state of Tamil Nadu where Tamils sympathetic to Prabhakaran and the LTTE had started targeting the Indian army by throwing crude bombs on their vehicles and by planting bombs in the military compartments of trains, buses etc. The death of MG Ramachandran had also split the AIADMK vertically with one faction supporting the late leader's widow Janaki, while the other threw in their lot with the actor's old co-star Jayalalitha, and as a result of which President's rule had been imposed in the state. On 1st June, 1988 an organization that called itself the LTSO, the Liberation Tigers Solidarity Organization during a procession that was organized by them at Coimbatore publicly criticized the Central Government, the Prime Minister of India and the IPKF. So much so that they even warned the centre that they would not hesitate to create total chaos in the state and also vowed to attack the Congress leaders and even the Prime Minister of India if any harm was done to V Prabhakaran. Some of them even threatened to kill the Indian Prime Minister and other senior Congress (I) leaders if they dared touch Prabhakaran. Even some AIDMK leaders like Aladi Aruna and RM Veerapan in their speeches had started threatening large scale violence and a blood-bath if Prabhakaran was killed. A few days later various political parties also staged a joint demonstration in front of the Area Headquarters of the army in Madras condemning the Central government and calling for the withdrawal of the IPKF from Sri Lanka.

When Shupriya in Colombo heard about the deteriorating law and order situation in Tamil Nadu, and the open threat given by the LTSO that they would even kill the Prime Minister of India if Prabhakaran was captured or eliminated, she took the matter quite seriously and wondered why India had to put its foot in a neighbouring country militarily, when it was not wanted by the Tamils themselves. She had earlier been an eye witness to one attempt by the Sri Lankan naval rating on the life of the Prime Minister during the guard of honour ceremony and knowing fully well the LTTE guerrilla leader's charismatic popularity with his own highly motivated cadres, she reckoned that the matter should not be taken lightly at all. On the other hand there was now constant pressure from Mr Jayawardhene; the President of Sri Lanka for the holding of elections to the North East Provincial Council, and Shupriya was off the opinion that without the LTTE participating in it, the elections would be an exercise in total futility. Therefore while Shupriya in Colombo was trying to apply herself on how to stop this ugly war, the news arrived that Second Lieutenant Rajeev Sandhu from the 7th Battalion of the Assam Regiment had succumbed to his wounds.

Rajeev had only six months service but had died a hero in Sri Lanka. On 19th July he was on his way to collect rations, when his jeep and the one ton vehicle that was following him were caught in a deadly ambush. A LTTE rocket had directly hit his jeep and though it had turned turtle, the militants kept firing their AK-47's at him and his men. A badly wounded but undaunted Rajeev with both his legs smashed, and with his body ridden with bullets got hold of his 9 mm carbine and waited in silence. He had practically lost all his men and he was determined to avenge their loss. As some of the militants came looking for weapons, Rajeev sprayed them with bullets, till he was no more. Shupriya felt sad for young Rajeev's parents. Like her dear husband Shiraz, Rajeev at 22 would also not see the day when the country would honour him with the gallantry award of Mahaveer Chakra. Strangely enough the young intrepid officer's first name was also Rajeev.

"I think this name Rajeev seems to be jinxed. First we lost one Rajeev on the mighty Siachen glacier and now another Rajeev down south in Sri Lanka. And both were brave young officers. And now with the diehard supporters from Tamil Nadu braying for our own Prime Minister's head and whose name is also Rajeev, it may well be so," thought Shupriya while praying to the Sai Baba of Shirdi to end this dirty war.

CHAPTER-9

Sabotage or Accident?

Meanwhile in Pakistan, following the withdrawal of some of the Soviet forces from Afghanistan and having set 'Operation Topac' in Kashmir in motion, when President Zia on 21st July, 1988 announced that elections on a non party basis would be held on 16th November, Ruksana Begum as usual remarked sarcastically.

"Yes and that will be the day, when the Mulla General will once again preside over the country's destiny and will add more confusion to the already existing political chaos that is prevailing today."

"But why are you always so very anti-Zia? I agree that as an armoured corps officer he looks and acts like a misfit at times, but one should not take him lightly. His military gait may not be very impressive, but he is undoubtedly a shrewd person. However, my gut feeling is that he too one day I am afraid will buy it nice and proper. I think after having ruled for eleven out of the forty one years of the country's miserable existence, which is a record by itself, he should now gracefully retire and let the civilians run the show," added Gul Rehman as Zubeida cautioned him to go slow with his drink.

Meanwhile faraway in Stockholm in that beautiful summer month of July, Shiraz having based his information on the likely impact that Zia's 'Operation Topac' may have on India in general and on Kashmir in particular in the near future, he wrote a short brief on the subject and signing his name simply as a friend of India, posted it through the civil post office to the Indian High Commision in London. His only intention was to warn the Indian government to be on guard and thereby prevent a fourth round in the near future. Since he was not passing any military or state secrets and was doing it in good faith, he therefore did not feel guilty about it.

On 14th August, to celebrate Pakistan's Independence Day and in order to show their solidarity, the pro Pakistani elements in Srinagar and elsewhere in the valley openly hoisted a number of green Pakistani flags. This was a clear indication that 'Operation Topac' as envisaged by General Zia had now been set in motion. But it seemed that Zia was not destined to see his liberation of Kashmir because three weeks later on 17th August he died in a mysterious aircrash that had all the trappings of a good 'who done it' suspense story. Early on that morning of 17th August 1988, an ebullient and happy Zia on board the four engined Hercules C-130 Pak-One had taken off from Islamabad on the VVIP flight to Bhawalpur. He was on his way to the Tamewali Field Firing Ranges to personally witness the field tests of the US made M1 Abrams Tank that Pakistan was keen to accquire. The evaluation for the tanks induction into the Pakistan Army was being carried out by Major General Mehmud Ali Durrani, the GOC Pakistan 1 Armoured Division. It was not only Zia, but a host of other Pakistan army senior officers who that day had assembled at the range for the important demonstratation. Also present among the VVIP's was Arnold Raphael the young 45 year old United States Ambassador to Pakistan and Brigadier General Herbert Wassom, the Head of the U S Military Mission in Pakistan.

Brigadier Aslam Rehman Khan the BGS of the new Bhawalpur Corps that was under raising was also present there and he felt rather proud, when he too was introduced to the President and the American Ambassador. Impressed by the trials, Zia returned by a chopper to the new Corps Headquarters where he was briefed on the progress of its raising by the Corps Commander and this was followed by a sumptous lunch.

That 17th of August happened to be a Wednesday and it was also Farzana's birthday that day and Aslam Rehman after the demonstration and lunch was hoping to get a lift in the Presidents' aircraft to Islamabad. He had been granted four days casual leave and wanted to give a big surprise to his wife. She had turned 40 that day and though he had wished her over the phone that morning, he was very keen to get there by evening so that he could celebrate the event with his family. For the sake of the children's education and with no good schooling facilities available at Bhawalpur, Farzana had stayed back at Rawalpindi. But unfortunately because of some immediate requirements that had been given by the Army Chief to Major General Durrani regarding the submission of the trial report, Aslam Rehman Khan departure was also held up and he was literally cursing himself for not being able to get on that VVIP flight. Soon thereafter, when the Vice-Chief, Lt General Mirza Aslam Beg's small executive jet also took off for the

Dhamial military airbase near Rawalpindi that aircraft too had no place for an extra passenger and Aslam Rehman was feeling miserable about it and cursing his bad luck.

But a little later, when he returned to his office and got busy organizing the preparation of that trial report, he thanked his stars and realized how lucky he was. Because minutes after the jumbo Hercules with the President on board took off from the Bhawalpur airfield, it crashed killing all on board and there was not even one single survivor. It was 4.30 PM, when the Pakistan Air Force One took off with 31 passengers on board, and three minutes later all contact with the VVIP flight had been lost with the Bhawalpur air traffic control. Near the tiny village of Basti Lal Kamal, a young boy of ten who with his father was tending cattle in a nearby field had seen it all happening before his very own eyes, while his father was having a quiet snooze. Hearing the noise of an aircraft, the boy had instinctively looked up, but seconds later the sturdy C-130 turboprop that was known for its reliability and safety record had plummeted with its nose down, and it was not even three hundred meters from where the boy was standing. The engine had hit the ground so very violently that it had gone several feet deep into the ground and the impact resulted in a big explosion and a massive fire that went up like a giant red ball and soon rose like a huge mushroom into the clear sky. It was rather strange that on that clear and cloudless summer afternoon in that semi arid desert region with no obstacles whatsoever, the aircraft had crashed and there was not a single survivor. Seeing the bloody limbs and torsos of the passengers some of whom had been burnt beyond recognition lying all over the place, the father and son who were indeed lucky to escape from that blazing inferno ran back to the village to get help. While they were on their way, the boy and his father noticed another aircraft approaching. It was an executive jet, but much smaller in size and as it came low and circled over the burning wreckage a few times, the father and son ran for cover. A few minutes later, when the same aircraft once again gained height and flew away, the little boy waved out to it.

Noticing the wreckage, the pilot of the executive jet carrying the Vice Chief, the DGMO, Major General Jehangir Karamat and Brigadier Ejaz Ahmed, the MA to the Vice Chief immediately contacted the Bhawalpur control tower and told them about the terrible accident. A few minutes later a chopper landed not very far away from the wreckage itself. This was the same helicopter that had ferried the President to the demonstration area and it was on its way back to its base at Multan, when it was diverted to the accident site. A little later the Corps Commander together with Brigadier

Aslam Rehman and a rescue party arrived on the scene. But it was all in vain. There were no survivors. All 31 on board including 5 very senior Pakistan Army Generals including the President and the two Americans, the Ambassador and the Brigadier General from the American Army had all perished.

"But how the hell could it happen just like that," thought Brigadier Aslam Rehman as he with his team started looking for secret and classified papers from among the debris that was strewn for miles around. According to Aslam Rehman's logic, if the pilot was in trouble or even if he had sensed trouble and had lost control, he could have atleast made an attempt to send an SOS or a May-Day signal over his radio. Neither did it make an attempt to return to Bhawalpur and nor was there a May Day signal. And surprisingly there was no radio communication at all from the pilot or from one his crew members and that looked rather strange and unusual since the accident took place just minutes after the aircraft had taken off and it was a VVIP flight. Therefore to Aslam Rehman it now looked to be a very well planned, deliberate and an expertly executed act of sabotage. But unfortunately, there was not a single survivor who lived to tell the tale and who could have at least given a small lead or some hint as to what had actually happened after the aircraft was airborne. According to the young boy and some of the other villagers who had also seen the aircraft plumetting down, there was no major explosion while the aircraft was in the sky, and then it suddenly went on a roller coaster ride and nose dived with a loud bang. And what was still more surprising was that it all happened in just within a few minutes of the aircraft being airborne reflected Aslam Rehman, while ordering the search party to muster the remains of the dead bodies and other belongings of the unlucky 31 that could be salvaged from the wreckage.Brigadier Aslam Rehman therefore was indeed very lucky not to have been on that flight or else Farzana's happy birthday would have become a day of mourning for her and his family too. It was providence and Allah's blessings that had saved him from this terrible disaster and as the sun was about to set, Aslam Rehman with the search party knelt down and prayed for the departed souls.

But for Lt General Mian Mohammed Afzal, the CGS of the Pakistan Army and for Lt General Akhtar Abdur Rehman, the Ex DGISI and now the Chairman of the Joint Chief's of Staff Committee, for both of them that 17th of August it seems was destined to be their day of reckoning. The CGS who had arrived a day earlier to oversee all the arrangements for the trials was scheduled to take the commercial PIA flight back to Islamabad late that evening, but on President Zia's request he boarded the VVIP aircraft at the very last minute instead. The Vice Chief Lt General Mirza Aslam Beg would have also suffered the same fate had he too accepted the President's offer, but seeing the small executive jet of the Vice Chief waiting for him, Zia did not insist. In the case of Lt General Akhtar Abdur Rehman however, he it seems had actually summoned his own death. On the previous day, the General as usual was taking his evening walk on the Rawalpindi Golf Course, when he bumped into the Vice Chief who was enjoying his round of golf too. The General being the Chairman of the Joint Chief's of Staff Committee was a little upset on not having been invited for the tank trials. Beg had conveyed to him that the trial was exclusively for the President but he and the other Corps Commanders would also be invited for the repeat performance that was scheduled to be held after a few days. But on the very next day, when Akhtar landed with Zia, General Beg was also surprised. Lt General Akhtar though he was senior to Zia and had been superceeded by Bhutto, but he was however very close to the President and having known that the American Ambassador had accepted Zia's invitation to witness the tank trials, he too expressed his desire to accompany the President and that was that. So was the case with the American Ambassador whose personal embassy aircraft was also waiting at the Bhawalpur airport to take him back to Islamabad, but he chose to fly back with the President instead.

With the sudden death of the President who was also the Army Chief and the ouster of the Prime Minister a few weeks ago, Pakistan now found herself to be in a very peculiar situation. On seeing the wreckage, the Vice Chief initially wanted to return to Bhawalpur, but on realizing that there was now no President, no Prime minister and no Army Chief and that there was now a complete vacuum in Islamabad, he had very wisely returned to the capital. And immediately on landing at Dhamial, Lt General Aslam Beg who was now the senior most General in the Pakistan army very wisely drove straight to the GHQ and summoned Lt General Ikramullah, the GOC 10 Corps, Rawalpindi, Lt General Imtiaz Wahraich who was now with the Joint Staff Headquarters and Major General Hamid Gul the DGISI for consultations. Then all of them including Major General Jehangir Karamat the DMO sat down and coolly considered the options that were available to them. General Zia after the dismissal of Junejo and the dissolution of the National Asembly had appointed a cabinet and the options were now two. The Army if they so desired could either once again take over control and impose martial law, or under the provisions of the constitution invite the Chairman of the Pakistan Senate who as per protocol was the second senior most in the heriarcy and request him to take office as the new President of the country. After some serious in house debate and deliberation in which the Pakistan Air Chief, Air Marshall Hakimullah Khan and Rear Admiral Saeed Mohammed the acting Naval Chief also contributed their bit, it was unanimously decided that under the present circumstances, the second option would be by far the best for the country. With the three service chiefs having reached a consensus, Lt General Aslam Beg at 7.30 that evening requested Ghulam Ishaq Khan the Chairman of the Pakistan Senate to visit the GHQ immediately and to take over as President. And having given his acceptance, the new President immediately summoned the cabinet for an emergency meeting and announced the news about the terrible crash to them. Late that very evening in the new President's address to the nation on television and radio, when the people of Pakistan and the world were told about the terrible tragedy, some refused to believe it, while most thought that Zia had been deliberately eliminated. Announcing a ten day period of national mourning and declaring a state of emergency, Ghulam Ishaq Khan however assured the nation that the election date of 16ᵗʰ November as had been announced by the late President would not be changed.

Though some genuinely mourned the death of the Mulla General, but those from the PPP celebrated the occasion by distributing sweets to their supporters. With the election dates having been confirmed by the new President of the country, Benazir's party immediately started gearing up for it The news of Zia-ul-Haq's sudden death had set tongues wagging not only in Pakistan, but also in neigbouring India and the world. With a new civilian as head of state, the majority of the Pakistanis generally felt happy and there were only a few who genuinely felt the loss of the Mulla General. All the same the protocol demanded a proper funeral ceremony befitting a head of state and therefore it was planned accordingly. As far as the air disaster was concerned which had taken away the lives of so many senior Pakistani army officers, the finger of suspicion had now started pointing in all possible directions.While some blamed the Russian KGB, others attributed it to the KHAD of Afghanistan, a few even to the American CIA, and the rest to the Al-Zulfiqar Organization and to the Indian RAW. When Shiraz sitting in Stockholm heard the terrible news, he however felt happy and believed that with Zia's passing away and with a new civilian head of state, Pakistan would at least now think twice before starting a fourth round with India. But with 'Operation Topac' having received the green signal for the first phase, the Kashmir Valley was once again in the grip of Muslim fundamentalists and radicals, and they together with the Mullahs were now getting ready to start a low intensity conflict in the region and thereby force the Kashmiri Pundits and Hindus to quit the valley.

On 26th August, after the Friday special prayers at the Hasratbal Mosque in Srinager to offer 'Fateh' to General Zia, when the pro Pakistani elements got violent and the police opened fire that resulted in the the death of three, the stage it seems was set to fan the call for Jihad in the valley. And on 31st August, when a crude bomb exploded in a public bus in Anantnag and claimed its first casualty and for which the JKLF claimed responsibility, it was now evident that terrorism had come to stay in what was once considered to be a heaven on earth, but would soon become hell for the Kashmiri Hindus and Sikhs who were in total minority, and whose voices hardly mattered to those in power in the troubled state.

Inspite of 'Operation Bluestar' that the Indian Army undertook in 1984, and which was followed by 'Operation Black Thunder I and II' by the NSG, the National Security Guard in 1986 and May 1988 respectively, there was still no substantial decline in the militant activities of the disgruntled Sikhs who were still dreaming of their own Khalistan. Shiraz had also heard that the Pakistan Armed forces were now planning to hold their ever biggest military exercise 'Zarb-e-Momin' (Sword of the Believer) in the near future and all these were indeed very disturbing signs and one that could spark off another conflict between the two adversaries and bring more misery to their own people, thought Shiraz. Shiraz was also aware that Zia with his fundamentalist Islamic policies and with his penchant to make Pakistan a nuclear power had fallen out of favour with the Reagan admininistration. And now that the Soviets had started withdrawing from Afghanistan, Zia to the Americans had once again become a pariah and the Americans having had a taste of Khomeini in Iran were now seriously thinking of replacing Zia with some other senior General Officer who would be more conducive to the United States interest in the region. But now that Zia was no more and a rapprochement having been reached between Gorbachev and Reagan to bring an end to the Cold War, America's interest in Pakistan it seems had also started waning.

While all kinds of stories and rumours about the aircrash kept floating, the remains of those who perished in the air crash or whatever little was left of them together with their belongings were put in coffins and wooden boxes and were dispatched to their next of kin for the final burial. The remains of the two Americans had been flown to the United States, but some boxes were later returned with the remarks that some of the bones and articles did not belong to two dead Americans. Brigadier Aslam Rehman who had accompanied the caskets of the late President and the other senior Pakistani Generals who had died in that crash wondered what would have been the reaction of his wife Farzana and his children had he also been a victim of this terrible tragedy. There was little or nothing left of the bodies that had been charred beyond recognition and they were only identified by the individual's personal belongings and the accouterments that were found on their person. Quite a few of of them were even faceless, but the rituals had to be performed.

While the preparations for General Zia's funeral on the 20th of August was under way, Brigadier Aslam Rehman who had all along suspected foul play was not in the least surprised, when at the request of the Pakistan Government, a high level team of six senior Airforce officers from the United States Airforce arrived in Rawalpindi to assist the Pakistan Airforce authorities in conducting the court of inquiry into the crash. Aslam was also aware that some crates of mangoes had also been loaded into the aircraft at the last minute, and he now wondered whether these crates contained some poisonous gas or a bomb inside them. Two of those crates were from the Mayor of Bhawalpur, but from where the other two crates had arrived nobody it seems knew. There was also another theory that had started making the rounds and it concerned the recent Shia versus Sunni sectarian war that was now raging in the area of Gilgit and Baltistan. Moreover Wing commander Mashud Hasan was a very experienced VIP pilot who had been flying the President for the past five years and surely if there was something wrong he would have atleast sent a distress signal. The very fact that there was no radio transmission as the aircraft plunged to its doom was therefore even more intriguing.

In May 1988, the Kashmiri Shias who were in majority in the Gilgit region had revolted against the Sunni dominated administration in that area and as a result of which Brigadier Pervez Musharraf who was the man incharge had not only let loose his SSG's on them, but he had also inducted some thousandss of armed Wahabi Pakhtoon tribesmen into the area to teach the Kashmiri Shias a lesson. As a result of this the low intensity political rivalry and sectarian tension had ignited into full scale carnage and which had led to the death of hundreds of innocent Shia inhabitants of that place. In order to reduce the Kashmiri Shias of Gilgit and Baltistan to a minority, the Government of Pakistan it seems had started inducting Punjabis and Pakhtoons into the area, and quite a few of them were reported to be Mujahids from the Arab world who had fought against the Russians in Afghanistan. One intelligence report also indicated that the crash could well be an act of sabotage that had been perpetrated by a Shia airman who belonged to Gilgit and who wanted to take revenge for the May, 1988 carnage on his fellowmen.

Brigadier Aslam Rehman was also aware that Brigadier Pervez Musharraf who was his contemporary at the PMA in Kakul was actively involved at some stage in the training of the mercenaries that had been recruited by the various Islamic extremists groups for fighting against the Soviet troops in Afghanistan and it was during this period that the man had also come in personal contact with Osama Bin Laden. The wealthy Arab and a civil engineer by profession, Osama was a diehard Muslim and he was in Pakistan initially to construct bunkers and tunnels for the Mujahideens who were fighting the Russians in Afghanistan. Aslam Rehman had also briefly come in contact with the tall and handsome Arab, when he was posted to the ISI and he now wondered whether these Mujahids would be used in future to implement the late Zia's Topac Plan for liberating Kashmir. Like Aslam Rehman, Brigadier Pervez Musharraf was also lucky not to have been in the same aircraft that day. Musharaff had been selected by Zia to be his next military secretary but at the last minute Brigadier Najeeb had pipped him to the post and as a result of which Brigadier Najeeb too lost his life in the air crash.

On the eve of President Zia's funeral, when the elders from the Rehman family arrived at Rawalpindi to be with Aslam and his family, and when the topic whether it was an act of sabotage or an accident came up once again for discussion, both Arif and his elder brother Gul Rehman had no doubts whatsoever that it was a clear case of sabotage and nothing else.

"Well the manner in which the aircraft came down minutes after being airborne, and that too without sending an S.O.S. it is a clear case of sabotage. Bbut who was behind it is anybody's guess," said Gul Rehman.

"Agreed," but the question still remains is who was responsible for it,' said Zubeida as she put two more ice cubes into her husband's whisky glass.

"I think it is a bit too early to speculate and though people have already started pointing fingers at the Indian RAW, the KGB, the KHAD and the AZO, the Al-Zulfiqar Organization, but it could well be the CIA too and frankly speaking I personally think it was also time for the Mulla General to go," said Ruksana Begum as Aslam Rehman's son Vovka who was now 16 years old with his 6 year old sister Nasreen walked in with two big bouquets of flowers and two greeting cards for their dearest grandparents.

"I must say that thanks to Farzana, the grandchildren are being well brought up in a manner that is fully befitting of the Rehman clan," said

Gul Rehman as he read the greeting card and hugged his two grandchildren. The greeting card had a quote from Allama Iqbal in Urdu that read. "Aata Hai Yaad Mujko Guzra Hua Zamana, Woh Bag Ki Baharen Woh Saab Ka Chah-Chahana." (I Remember those days gone by, those beautiful gardens and everyone's love and affection) That evening while the Rehman family sat down for a quiet dinner there was a call from the Pakistan GHQ for Aslam Rehman. It was the duty officer on the line and who conveyed to him the good news that not only had he been nominated for the next National Defence Course, but he had been also selected to ensure that all protocol formalities for the visit of the Indian President, Mr Venkataraman who was scheduled to arrive next morning for the funeral were thoroughly looked into.

The 20th of August 1988 was a very sultry day, and while Brigadier Aslam Rehman waited in the blazing Sun for the President of India to arrive in his special aircraft, at the Army House in Rawalpindi where President Zia in a very modest manner had spent the last 12 years of his life presiding over the destiny of Pakistan, preparations were underway to give the man a ceremonial burial. It had therefore been decided that the coffin would be first flown in a helicopter to the helipad at the President's House in Islamabad and from there it would be carried to the designated transfer point in an ambulance. At the transfer point it would be draped in the green and white national flag of the country and then placed on the freshly painted gun carriage for the final journey to his grave.

Even after being elected as the President of Pakistan, General Zia never occupied the President's House in Islamabad, and Aslam Rehman always wondered why. According to his aunt Ruksana, the Mulla General was probably afraid of Bhutto's ghost haunting him there. Afterall it was Bhutto who had made him the Army Chief and the same Chief had stabbed him in the back. While Aslam Rehman waited for the arrival of the Indian President, he looked back into the luck factor, and how important a part it played in one's professional life in the Pakistan army. Because right from the time Ayub Khan the self syled Field Marshall was appointed as Pakistan's first Muslim Chief everyone down the line too had made it by superseding his seniors. Ayub was promoted over the head of atleast two that included Major General Mohammed Akbar Khan and NAM Raza and he would not have been in the reckoning had General Iftiqar not died in an aircrash. Then came the turn of General Musa who superseded Sher Ali and Latif Khan and both of whom were Sandhurst products. And Musa was followed in 1966 by Yahya Khan who superseded Altaf Qadir and Bakhtiar Rana. After the debacle in Bangladesh, Bhutto made Gul Hasan Khan the Chief who was hand picked by Bhutto to replace him and he superseded quite a few who were senior to him including Tikka Khan. Then once again thanks to Bhutto arrived General Zia who superseded not one or two but six other Generals including Sharif and Jilani, and now it was the turn of General Mirza Aslam Beg who had struck the lucky patch thanks to the aircrash.

General Beg was born in Azamgarh in India and thus was the second Mohajir after Zia to become the Pakistan Army Chief. Though Aslam Rehman was not a Mohajir, but a thoroughbred Pathan, he therefore felt that his chances of climbing up the hghly competitive and steep promotional ladder to reach the very top was far better, because with the passage of time there were now only a handful left in the Pakistan army who could justly claim that they were born in pre-partition India thought Brigadier Aslam Rehman as the Indian Airforce special aircraft carrying the Indian President touched down at the Islamabad International airport.

The funeral of the departed General was conducted in an extremely dignified solemn manner and in typical army style. The entire route was lined up with contingents from all the three services who were smartly turned out in their ceremonial uniforms with full medals glittering on their chests. Leading the funeral cortege were the three service chiefs followed by other senior officers from the Pakistan army, navy and the airforce. As they all slow marched behind the gun carriage to the beat of the massed military band, Aslam Rehman took some photographs of General Zia's last journey. A hundred yards short of the burial place that was inside the beautiful compound of the elegant Faisal Mosque, the coffin was removed from the gun carriage and thereafter it was carried on the shoulders of the mourners till it was finally placed on the platform next to the grave site. A minute or so later the final prayers for the man who ruled Pakistan for eleven long years were performed in accordance with the Muslim rites. Thereafter as the 21 gun salute echoed over the Margalla Hills, the coffin was slowly lowered into the grave that had been dug by the very soldiers the man had the honour to command. Mr Junejo, the ex Prime Minister of the country who had been dismissed not so very long ago by the President had also very gracefully lent his shoulders. And as the many VIP's, friends and relatives started putting the earth on the grave, the smart tri-service honour guard fired the three salvoes in quick succession. Meanwhile the squad of a dozen military buglers sounded the last post and soon the grave was submerged in a massive heap of floral wreaths. The man who loved his uniform and who had been promising time and again for the past couple of years that he would be soon hanging his boots had unfortunately and literally died with his boots on and that too under very suspicious circumstances.

A month or so later, when the findings of the the Court of Inquiry that had been ordered on that tragic air accident was placed before the government, for reasons best known to those now in authority it was decided not to make the matter public. Maybe the promise to hold free and fair elections in November was weighing on their minds. However, with his own contacts in the GHQ and in the Pakistan Air Force; Brigadier Aslam Rehman did come to know that it was not an accident at all. According to the findings of the court of inquiry, a low density detonation had occurred inside the cockpit minutes after the aircraft was airborne and this was immediately followed by the bursting inside of some innocous containers that contained some deadly poisonous gas, and which within seconds had incapacitated all the passengers, the pilot and the crew inside the aircraft. This resulted in the experienced cockpit crew of the Pak One being instantly paralysed and they just could not give the May Day signal. Aided by the air force technical team from the USA, some parts of the wreckage of the the aircraft had also been sent for forensic testing and the reports indicated that there were strong traces of PETN, also known as Pentrite which was a form of deadly explosive that is normally used for such sabotage operations.

"But it could also be a deadly chemical weapon that had been used and the type that Saddam's army in Iraq had been regularly using against the Iranians and the Kurds and which is no secret either. And procuring a canister or two and concealing them in the mango crates that were loaded I believe at the last minute, and that too without carrying out a proper security check could have also resulted in that disaster," said Gul Rehman as Brigadier Aslam showed him the photographs that he had taken after the plane had crashed and at the funeral of Zia that follwed soon thereafter. Commenting on the use of chemical weapons by Iraq, Arif Rehman then added "'The little that I know is that during the initial stages of the Iraq-Iran war, the Iraqis had used only riot control agents to repel the mass Iranian attacks, but thereafter as the war progressed Saddam Hussein I believe had started procuring vast quantities of chemical weapons from whosoever was willing to supply, and the American and other western nations were no exceptions either. Or else how could the Iraqi Airforce on 16th March, 1988 drop those deadly chemical bombs on the Kurdish town of Halabja which killed thousands of innocent civilians, and it was simply because they were pro Iranian. And according to experts, the Iraqis in that attack had used deadly nerve agents like mustard gas, SARIN, TABUN and the deadly

VX too. And if my memory serves me right, it was in March 1986 that the United Nations Secretary General Javier Perez de Cuellar had formally accused Iraq of using chemical weapons against Iran and called on Baghdad to end its violation of the 1925 Geneva Protocol that forbids the use of such chemical weapons in war. And what bugs me still more is that just four months after the chemical attack on Halabja, the Bechtel Corporation, a giant organization in the United States had won the contract to build a huge petrochemical plant in that very country, and which would now give the Saddam Hussein regime in Baghdad the capability to produce more such deadly chemical weapons. And since the Americans are using Saddam to fight their own dirty war against Khomeini, like the manner in which they used us in fighting the Soviets in Afghanistan, therefore a couple of such deadly chemical weapon cannisters surfacing inside the Pak-One on that fateful day to get rid of Zia and his coterie of Generals cannot be simply ruled out. Moreover, there were also very strong rumours off late that the Reagan government were on the lookout to have the Mulla General replaced by some other senior army man who was not so very rigid and a staunch fundamentalist like Zia," added Arif Rehman.

"But from where did the Iraqis get all these deadly chemical weapons, if not from the Americans. I am sure the Iraqis were not capable enough to produce them in such large quantities, and with the Reagan administration's love for the Iraqi dictator Saddam Hussein, which was amply evident only recently when on September 8th despite the US Senate having passed the Prevention of Genocide Act, which could have imposed sanctions on the Saddam regime, the White House not only stalled the bill in the House of Representatives, but they even called it premature. In fact there are very strong rumours that the Americans are also giving millions of dollars as underhand loans to the Iraqi strongman and I wonder whatever for," said Gul Rehman as he took another sip of his favourite Black Label whisky.

"Only to make them fight the Iranians and to keep their lucrative arms business going I guess," said Ruksana Begum a little sarcastically as she emerged from the kitchen with a plate of sizzling chicken tikkas which she knew was her brother-in-law's favorite snack with the drinks.

"Well thanks to the CIA, the ISI and the pull out of the Soviet troops from neighbouring Afghanistan, we are not doing too badly either, because as far as the manufacture and supply of arms are concerned and which has now become a lucrative small scale industry in our own very neighbourhood," said Aslam Rehman as he fixed a small skotch and soda for his uncle Arif Rehman.

242

"But how is that possible Dad ?' asked young Vovka who having completed his schooling from Lawrence School, Ghora Gali was now preparing to sit for the Federal Service competitive examination for admission to the PMA at Kakul. Samir Rehman (Vovka) had decided to follow his father's and grandfather's footsteps to become an army officer and he also hoped to join the First First Punjabees.

"It is all very simple my son and all that one has to do is too drive up to Darra Adam Khel, the small dusty town that is next door and get a weapon of one's own choice ranging from the sophisticated American Stinger missile and the Russian Kalashnikov rifle, better known as the AK 47, or one of those crude shotguns that are now being manufactured in bulk in that sleepy town and are being sold at throwaway prices too," said Aslam Rehman who having been nominated for the prestigious NDC, the National Defence College course was now looking forward to it.

"Yes and the manner in which these weapons are now being procured and are been used by the rival sectarian groups, the Muslim fundamentalist organizations and others within the country to get at each others throats, it may well lead to further chaos. And it is therefore high time that the government took a serious note of it or else another army general backed by the Americans may once again take over the country," said Ruksana Begum mockingly as she handed over a mocktail to her dearest sister-in-law Zubeida.

"Yes and she may well be right because the manner in which these lethal weapons are now being used in the province of Sind in particular to settle old scores between the Mohajirs and the Sindhis and which is widely being supported by the respective political parties that are now gearing up for the promised general elections in November, this could also lead to political assassinations that will further polarize the country. And these very same weapons I hate to say will one day backfire on us and I only hope and pray that I do not live to see that miserable day," said Zubeida Begum as she fed her six year old grand daughter Nasreen her favourite vanilla ice-cream with lots of chocolate sauce.

With the passing away of General Zia, the Shariah Ordinance that had been promulagated by the late President in June had already come under heavy fire from the Joint Action Committee, which wanted it repealed and there was now a general feeling that the country that had been ruled for years by the military would now revert back to civilian rule and without the kind of Islamisation that Zia had in mind. But there was also now serious ethnic trouble in Sind, when unknown snipers on 30th September in Hyderabad brutally massacred 120 people and on the very next day 70 more were killed in Karachi alone and the army had to be called in to restore order. Three days earlier on 27th September 1988, the Lahore High Court had declared Junejo's dismissal by Zia as unconstitutional and there was now hope that the forthcoming elections too would be party based, but with the ethnic violence erupting in Sind there was a feeling that the army might once again step in.

CHAPTER-10

Sleeping With The Enemy!

During that turbulent month of September 1988, while the street battles in the Province of Sind between the Mohajirs on one side and the rest of the Pakistanis on the other became a regular daily feature, a British Indian novelist and a Muslim at that with the publication of his fourth novel titled 'The Satanic Verses' drew the wrath of the Khomeni and other fundamentalist groups in the Muslim world including Pakistan. Ahmed Salman Rushdie who was born on 19th June 1947, in Bombay and whose early education began at the elite Cathedral and the John Connon School in that city where the school motto was 'Studies Make Famous', had certainly lived upto it. He had already achieved worldwide fame with his second novel 'Midnight's Children' that was published in 1981, and this one that was titled 'The Satanic Verses' would now make him a worldwide figure. A product of King's College Cambridge, who began his career with advertising agencies and whose first novel 'Grimus,' a part-science fiction tale in 1975 had made no impact on the public whatsoever was now an international celebrity in his own right. Having divorced his first wife Clarissa Luard, he had recently married the American novelist, Marianne Wiggins and was now based in England. Angered by the Booker Prize winner's irreverent depiction of the Holy Prophet Mohammed in the book and terming it as sheer blasphemy, the Ayotollah had issued a 'Fatwa' (religious edict) against the author. He wanted his death and had also announced a rich reward for it. With the book having kindled the fire of violence by the orthodox Muslims, Salman Rushdie was now on the run.

With the worldwide controversy that was generated by the book, Shiraz who was fond of the author also bought a copy. He had earlier read 'Midnight's Children' and 'Shame,' a book that depicted the political turmoil in Pakistan during the Bhutto and the Zia regime, and though a Muslim himself, Shiraz did not find the book to be so very offensive that the radical

245

Muslims should threaten the very life of the young author whose works had now opened an avenue for the other English authors in the subcontinent. Nontheless, the very fact that the book had sparked off a spate of violence by the Muslims around the world who were now demanding a worldwide total ban on it was also not a good sign thought Shiraz, as he read a few passages from it to his wife Saira.

"'Well being a Muslim himself and the manner in which the Muslim clergy in various Muslim countries including Pakistan have now started showing their clout, I think Salman Rushdie could have been a little more discreet and respectful to the Holy Prophet," said Saira as she got her nine year old daughter Shezadi dressed like a fairy queen. An excited Shezadi was all set to take part in the annual school concert that was scheduled for that evening. That day also happened to be the 2nd of October, and since Shiraz was very keen to watch the closing ceremony of the 24th Olympic Games that was being held in Soeul, South Korea, Shezadi felt very disappointed, when her father giving the excuse that there were no babysitters available that day to look after her little brother Tojo, decided to stay back at home.

Though the Seoul Olympic Games had produced quite a few stars and made people like sprinter Florence Griffith Joyner of the USA and Krisrin Otto the swimmer from East Germany household names in the world of sports, but what bothered Shiraz now was the manner in which athletes had started taking high performance enhancing drugs to win medals. Ben Johnson of Canada who had won the coveted 100 metres race to set a new world record had been disqualified and disgraced publicly, when he was stripped of his gold medal for testing positive. Two Bulgarian weightlifters also suffered the same fate after they failed the doping tests. But there were many more who must have got away, thought Shiraz as he with his five year old son Tojo enjoyed the beautifully choreographed closing ceremony by the ever smiling South Korean hosts. However, what fascinated little Tojo was the antics of the Korean tiger named 'Hodori' which was the mascot for the games and he demanded one from his father immediately.

Going through all the results of the games, Shiraz was highly disappointed with the performance of both India and Pakistan as they came back empty handed. Even the hockey gold was won by Great Britain, while the silver and the bronze medals went to West Germany and Netherlands respectively. Even a small little country like Surinam which was also once known as Dutch Guiana and whose population of just five hundred thousand comprising of Indians, Indonesian and Africans who had been brought there a few centuries ago as slaves for agricultural labour had won a gold medal when Anthony Nesty surprised everybody by winning the 100 metres butterfly title in swimming. Soon thereafter, when the curtains on the 24th Olympiad was about to close and Saira and Shezadi returned from the school function, Shiraz said somewhat emotionally.

"You know Saira even if India and Pakistan were to once again become one country, but thanks to our politicians who control most of our sports, we even with all our combined talent put together I am afraid will not be able to win a single gold medal in the next Olympics either."

"Yes, and with their supremacy in field hockey also now over, forget about winning a gold, they will not even be able to bag a silver or a bronze in that discipline also," added Saira as Shiraz in order to make up with his daughter who was still in a sulking mood presented her with ar scrabble set and kissed her on the cheek. Moreover, from that very day they also decided that Shezadi will not be addressed by her pet name Gammy anymore.

"But Papa now that Pakistan has such talented cricket players like Imran Khan, Javed Miandad, Wasim Akram and India has Gavaskar, Kapil Dev, and Vengsarkar, I am sure our combind cricket team will beat anybody in this world,"said a happy Shezadi rather proudly.

"Yes may be, but unfortunately cricket is not an Olympic sport and as far as cricket is concerned we need not look across the border, now that we have beaten even the mighty Australians led by Allan Border and who are currently touring the country. And we have beaten them on our own soil and that too by an innings and 188 runs in the first test match that was played at Karachi only a fortnight ago, and it was all again thanks to Miandad's dashing double century and Iqbal Qasim bagging nine wickets," said Saira, who thanks to her husband's interest in cricket had also now become a keen follower of the game.

"But with the deteriorating law and order situation in Sind, I only hope that the two one day internationals that are scheduled to be played at Karachi and Hyderabad Sind on 14th and 15th October respectively are not abandoned. In any case the first ODI at Gujranwala on 30th September was literally washed out thanks to the ground being flooded, and let us hope and pray that the other two should not be cancelled because of the on going riots in the two major cities of Sindh,"added Shiraz as he gave a brief history of Sindh, its people and the current ethnic conflict that had gripped the province to his young daughter.

"Sindh also known as the land of the mighty River Indus was the cradle of one of the greatest ancient civilizations of the world. Popularly known as the Indus Valley Civilization it flourished hundreds of years before even Christ was born and which rivaled the contemporary civilizations of ancient Egypt and Mesopotamia. The excavations at Mohen-jo-daro, near Larkhana, Lakhueen-jo-daro near Sukkur and at Kot Bala along the coast of the Lasbela District with their well planned grid cities and sewer systems bears ample evidence to the prosperity of the region and the Harappan civilization that once dominated the entire and once flourishing area of the subcontinent Then as time went by, the region passed through various era's starting from the Vedic times to the Magadh and the Mauryan rule and that was also followed by a brief period of Greek domination under Alexandar the Great. Then came the Kushans followed by the Gupta and the Chola Empires and then arrived the Muslim Arabs in 711 AD. Led by Mohammed Bin Qasim the Arabs established the Ummayad Caliphate in the province. The Arab rule however ended with the ascension of the Soomru dynasty who were local Sindhi Muslims and thereafter it came under the hegemony of the Delhi Sultanate and that was followed by nearly 300 years of Mughal rule. In 1747, Sindh became a vassal state of the Afghan Durrani Empire and subsequently was ruled first by the Kalhoras and later by the Baluchi Talpurs. In 1843, the British with the help of the first Aga Khan and under General Charles Napier conquered Sindh and soon it became a part of the Bombay Presidency. Though in the battle of Miani, the Talpurs fought valiantly, but unfortunately they lost. In 1936, it became a separate province and at independence a province of Pakistan. Till the time the British arrived on the scene, it was not Karachi, but Hyderabad, which was the capital of the province. The city of Hyderabad was founded in 1768 by Mian Ghulam Shah Kalhora who was also known as the saintly ruler of that dynasty and it continued as the capital under the Talpurs. Karachi became the capital of Sindh after it was conquered by the British and it was because the East India Company had its headquarters there. Then during those terrible days of partition began the mass exodus of the Hindus from Sindh into India and of the Urdu speaking Muslims of India into Sindh," added Shiraz as he got hold of an atlas and showed his daughter the location of the two cities.

"But Pappa, now that the province has a majority of Muslims and only a handful of Hindus then why are the Muslims fighting each other," asked Shezadi as she underlined the two cities with a red pencil.

"Yes and that is rather unfortunate because the fight is now between the Muslims who migrated from India as refugees against those who did not have to feel the pangs of partition. The migratory Urdu speaking Muslims now known as Mohajirs were probably better educated and more enterprising and with the adoption of Urdu as the national language they certainly did have the advantage as they took control of the federal government offices in the province. This was resented by the local Sindhis who in 1972 to resurrect their dying culture introduced the teaching of the Sindhi language in schools and when it was made compulsory in the entire province, the spark that was lit has now become an inferno. The recent riots has already claimed hundreds of lives not only in Hyderabad, but also in Karachi and other towns of Sind and ironically this has led to another mass exodus of the Mohajirs from the new townships of Qasimabad to Latifabad and of the Sindhis from Hyderabad and Latifabad to Qasimabad. And the manner in which these two Muslim communities are being armed and backed by their political leaders to get at each others throats, I wont be the least surprised if Pakistan is further cut to size. Moreover, had the enterprising Hindu Sindhis who were the mainstay of the economy in Sindh not been ousted by the Mohajirs and had remained in Pakistan, the province would have seen better days," said Shiraz as Saira fixed him his second and last whisky for the evening.

"But do you think that India would be foolish enough to try and cut us to size again," asked Saira, sounding a little surprised with her husband's last comment regarding the Hindus of Sindh.

"Well if we keep fingering them in Punjab and in Kashmir like we are doing today by proxy, then they too could finger us in Sindh and I may be totally wrong in my assessment, but I do believe that none other than the Indian Army Chief General Sundarji had conveyed this to Major General Nishat Ahmed in 1986 when both of them were attending a military seminar in USA and Sundarji it is believed had sounded Nishat that if Pakistan aided the Sikhs in Punjab then India too could play the Sind card," added Shiraz as he quickly once again changed the subject to that of cricket and of Pakistan's chances of beating the Australians in the forthcoming two ODI matches.

Shiraz's prediction about the situation in Sind was vindicated, when both the ODI's that were scheduled to be played at Karachi and Hyderabad had to be cancelled because of the ethnic riots in the two cities. For the final ODI the venue was therefore shifted to the Gaddaffi Stadium at Lahore and that too surprisingly ended in a tie with both teams scoring 229 runs in the 45 over match. But since Australia had lost three more wickets, Pakistan was declared as the eventual winner. By that win, Pakistan had created history because not only did they beat Australia in the Test series but also in the ODI's.

With the elections round the corner, the month of October saw the realignment of various political parties in Pakistan. On 6th October, eight political parties led by Nawaz Sharif of the Pakistan Muslim League teamed up together to form the IJI, the Islami Jamhoori Ittehad and it was soon joined by the Jamaat-e-Islami. This had now set the tongues wagging and the rumours were that it was the ISI Chief, Major General Hameed Gul who had engineered this coalition in order to keep the PPP getting back into power And in that month of October 1988, while the Pakistanis were celebrating their cricket victory over the mighty Australians, Major General Tajamull Hussain Malik was released from prison. He was the man who on Pakistan Day, 23rd March.1980 had planned to topple General Zia in a military coup, but had failed. He however was now once again a free man and Shiraz as a soldier felt indeed very happy for him and his family. The Major General was from the Awan community, a community that was always regarded as a martial race and one of the finest in soldiering by the British colonialists. The retired General officer was a seasoned soldier who refused to surrender to the Indian Forces during the Bangladesh War and he was also the only Brigadier from General Niazi's disgraced army in Bangladesh to get promoted to the rank of Major General. It was during the Battle of Hilli in December 1971, that Tajamull as the Brigade Commander of Pakistan's 205 Brigade truly proved his worth and was therefore justly rewarded. Throughout that battle he kept motivating his troops to fight to the bitter end and even on the16th of December, 1971 when the orders to surrender had been issued, the Brigadier in his staff car with his flag flying proudly and with his star plate uncovered was seen moving around the town of Bogra motivating his soldiers to fight on till he was finally captured by the Mukti Bahini and was badly beaten up by them. Luckily for him he survived and was taken as a prisoner of war by the advancing Indian forces. Even Hamoodur Rehman, the Chief Justice of Pakistan and a Bengali Muslim who was born in Patna, India had in his report praised the General for his bravery and had also recommended him for the country's highest gallantry award. With the release of the General Officer from prison and those who were part of the conspiracy that was led by him, it was generally believed that Pakistan was now slowly limping back to the time honoured judicial system of giving every one a fair trial.

Meanwhile in India, the Bofors controversy took another serious turn, when General Sundarjee as the Army Chief having hung his boots in a hard hitting interview to the India Today magazine reiterated his stand. According to him if the government had taken his advice of threatening Bofors with the cancellation of the contract, then the arms giant from Sweden would have had no other option but to reveal the names of those who directly or indirectly were responsible for swindling the nation of the millions of dollars that were paid as kickbacks to them. He also stated that had the contract being cancelled and as had been recommended by him, he as the Army Chief was ready to take the risk and the responsibility for the country's territorial integrity. But unfortunately the powers that be for some reason or the other felt otherwise. The scandal was given another peculiar twist, when a so called Hindu tantric by the name of Nemi Chand Jain who was also known as Chandraswami and who considered himself to be a 'Godman" claimed that he too had evidence about the Gandhi family's involvement in the Bofors payoff. And while this accusation triggered off another war of words between the government and the opposition in the Indian parliament and with the former accusing the opposition benches of using the so called 'Godman' to tarnish the image of their revered leader, elsewhere in London a beautiful young lady of Indian Haryanvi origin from the state of Rajasthan had opened a pandora's box with her many secret liaisons with those in power in Westminster.

Pamela Bordes, who was born in 1961 as Pamela Singh Chowdhury was the daughter of an Indian army officer. After finishing her schooling from the Maharani Gyatri Devi Public School for girls at Jaipur and college from Lady Sri Ram in Delhi, she in 1982 was crowned Miss India and had also represented the country in the Miss Universe pageant that followed. Subsequently she moved to Europe and married Henri Bordes. With her name now also being linked with that of Adnan Khashoggi, the big fun loving billionaire arms dealer from the Arab world who was purported to be also a good friend of the Indian 'Godman', tongues in India had also started wagging. There was no doubt that the good looking young Indian lady with her captivating smile and social connections had got the British tabloid papers and the paparazzi going gaga over her. And since her activities gave a whiff of a similar scandal, which in the early sixties linked Profumo to a call girl named Cristine Keeler, and one that had rocked the British government, Monty in order to find out whether the Bordes-Khashoggi-Chandraswami triangle had anything to do with the Bofors arms scandal, decided to call on his old friend Unnikrishan at the Press Club.of India.

"Oh no, I don't think that the Bordes-Khashoggi-Chandraswami link has anything to do with the Bofors affair, but there is no doubt that Khashoggi and the so called 'Godman' did have a hand in the Iran—Contra arms deal,'" said Unni while ordering a chilled beer for Monty

"But how are they connected with the Iran-Contra deal?" asked Monty looking a bit surprised.

"Well it was not exactly that kind of a deal concerning the shipment of arms to the Nicaraguans, but the two it is believed were responsible for financing the arms for the hostages deal between the Americans and Iranians. The Iranians who were fighting the Iraqis desparately needed sophisticated weapons like the Hawk and Tow missiles and which America was willing to provide in exchange for the American hostages who were being held by the Hezbollah. The key man being held hostage was Whilliam Buckley who was the CIA's Station Chief in Beirut and the United States therefore agreed to clandestinely ship these missiles through Israel and for which Khashoggi became the banker and the underwriter for the sale of those deadly weapons. But it was not all Khashoggi's money and that is where the so called 'Godman' with the big red dot on his forehead used his good offices with the rich Sultan of Brunei who was also the Swami's close friend and who considered the 'Godman' as a spiritual leader," said Unni.

"Well I must then say that the big portly 'Godman' has become quite a high flyer because I was also told that in October 1986, when Khashoggi threw a grand party for Elizabeth Taylor in Los Angeles, the Swami too was also there as his guest. And after the party they all flew in the Arab playboy's private jet to Las Vegas," said Monty as Unni showed him a photograph of the arms dealer who was also popularly known as AK by his dear friends dancing with the famous Hollywood actress Brooke Shields.

"'Well let me also tell you that this photograph was taken during AK's 50th birthday party that was held at his palatial home located on 5000 acres of rolling land in the beachtown of Marabella on the Mediterranean Coast, and to which I believe Chandraswami whom I consider to be only a 'Conman' was also invited," added Unni as he called for his third large rum of the evening.

"But tell me what is the latest on the murky Bofors deal and has Chitra Subramanium and N Ram been able to zoom in on the real culprits," asked Monty as Unni added another cube of ice to his rum and water

"Well not exactly, but Chitra I believe is conducting her own sting operation to get hold of a copy of Mr Ardbo's diary which though it looks like an ordinary one that was given to him from Wah Nobel, and which ironically is also a subsidiary of the Nobel Industries in Pakistan located at Wah, but the diary I believe does contain some very incriminating notings And though the notings are written in stupid pigeon English and in some childish code by Mr Ardbo in his own hand, but which if proved to be genuine could indeed be very explosive and damaging both to the Indian Prime Minister and to his Italian friend Mr Quattarochhi," added Unni as the barman rang the warning bell for the diehard tipplers to order their last drink for the evening.

"Then what is your gut feeling, and who do you think got all that money?"asked Monty.

"Well going by the whole set of documents that was published by the newspaper Hindu on 23rd June, 1988 linking 'Tulip,' 'Mont Blanc' and 'Lotus' to the secret payments that were made by Bofors as kickbacks to the Hinduja brothers and others, the chief beneficiary according to my calculations or rather inference is none other than the Italian friend of the Prime Minister. And that according to my mind was the political payoff that was made by Bofors to the mysterious AE Services for services rendered, and which is linked to Mr Quattarocchi. But whether the Prime Minister and his family or the ruling Congress Party benefited from it or not is still a million dollar question. But looking at the manner in which AE Services came into the deal and got it sealed by the given deadline, and then cooly walked away with the largesse is indicative enough that the payment was made to those people who had the power to also close the deal. Then as things started hotting up, the money from the Swiss accounts kept moving from one country to another to avoid detection, and then both the countries and Bofors very conveniently scratched each others back in covering it up and which is still very much in progress. And I am now apprehensive that the vital November 1985 'Sunset Clause' mentioning that no payments will be made if the deal is not sealed by the deadline of 31st March, 1986 will eventually be the main cause of the sun setting on our young Prime Minister's short and expolsive political career," added Unni as he took out some few press cuttings from various newspapers that he had in his satchel and then read out a few important and relevant portions from it to Monty.

While the Bofors scandal kept firing on all cylinders in India, in Sri Lanka the war between the IPKF and the LTTE showed no signs of abetting either as the casualty rate on both sides kept increasing day by day. Despite India's overwhelming superiority both in weapons and manpower, the LTTE with the support of the local Tamilians literally fought like wounded tigers. And with more than three Indian Infantry Divisions fully committed on the island, the ISI in Pakistan also stepped up their activities in the Indian states of Jammu and Kashmir and Punjab to once again kickstart "Operation Topac.'

Sitting in her office in Colombo, Shupriya now wondered whether the Indian Army's involvement in Sri Lanka and the attack on the Golden Temple in June 1984 was worth the effort. According to her own perception, the steady increase of the newly raised Rashtryia Rifles and other troops of the Indian Army into Punjab and the Kashmir valley would serve no worthwhile purpose unless the local population in both these states were fully with them in mind, body and soul to curb the terrorist movement that Pakistan had already started orchestrating in the valley and elsewhere. She therefore felt very strongly that the need of the day both for the government in the centre and in the two states was not to put up a show of force and do sabre rattling, but in being constantly vigilant and introducing such proactive measures in quick time to win back the hearts and minds of the people. What they urgently required was a genuine big doze of the healing touch and rapid economic measures that would prevent the young men and women in joining the terrorist movement that was now being actively and covertly aided by the Pakistan ISI. Reflecting on her thoughts and on how to get back those who had taken to the gun into the mainstream of life, she jotted them down and then wrote a long letter to Monty. After all Monty and his ancestors were Kashmiris who hailed from Bagh near Muzzafarabad, but which was now a part and parcel of Pakistan occupied Kahmir. And with Monty's export business of Kashmiri handicrafts and carpets increasing yearly, together with the influential contacts that he had now cultivated in the valley and within the state government, he could perhaps be the right person to sound the warning at the right quarters and thus bring about the much required harmony between the Muslims, the Sikhs and the Hindus that had now started deteriorating rapidly and especially so in the fertile and beautiful Kashmir valley. Some recent reports about the Kashmiri Pundits being threatened and being forced to leave the valley for good had upset her considerably,and she therefore felt that they must be protected at all costs, or else another exodus of a different kind altogether could start and which would be detrimental to the country's interest in that region.

Meanwhile in Pakistan, with the death of Zia and with elections round the corner, winds of change had already started blowing from various directions, and it also had its effect on the people from all walks of life. After the demise of Zia, the Shariyar Ordinance had died its own death and the common man too felt free to do what he wanted or desired. And all this became all the more evident when PTV, Pakistan Television started televising a plethora of political plays and dramas that had a flavour of anti Zia propaganda. Not to be left behind were the various talented theatre groups in the country who through their street plays openly castigated Zia and his policies and were now being highly applauded by all and sundry. Prominent among them was the Ajoka Theatre Group whose play "Neelay Haath' had taken the country by storm. The play was written by Shaheed Nadeem while he was imprisoned by Zia during the military regime and during his subsequent exile in London. The play was first performed on stage on International Women's day in 1987 in London itself and had drawn rave reviews. It was based on the discriminatory laws against women in Pakistan and was initially titled as 'Bari' (Acquittal). The lady behind this powerful play however was Madeeha Gauhar the wife of the the man who wrote that play and she was also the one who played the central character in the much acclaimed television serial that was now been televised by the PTV. Born in Karachi, the 32 year old Madeeha a product of the Convent of Jesus and Mary School and with a Master's degree in English literature from Government College, Lahore had been in the forefront of the WAF, the Women's Action Forum during Zia's military rule and as a result of which she too had spent time behind bars in the Kot Lakhpat jail. The Ajokha Theatre was born in 1983 and Madeeha was one of its founders.

"I am sure that with every episode of 'Neelay Haath', Mulla Zia must be also turning in his grave," said Begum Ruksana as she kept herself glued to the television serial. And once the episode for the day was over, she very seriously commented to her husband Arif Rehman that Benazir Bhutto and the PPP could not be taken lightly. And according to the Begum Sahiba with the current mood in Pakistan, Benazir could well emerge as the winner in the forthcoming elections that were scheduled to be held in mid November.

"Therefore don't be surprised if women power takes over the reins of ruling this beleaguered country that has been plagued with instability from the very day Jinnah died,"added Ruksana in lighter vein as her brother-in-law Gul Rehman with his wife Zubeida dropped in for a chit chat session over a cup of coffee.

"Yes that will indeed be a welcome change and moreover it is only because of you women that we two brothers are still alive and kicking, but ofcourse with certain restrictions now," said Gul Rehman jokingly as he winked at his younger brother and requested him to add a spoon full of brandy to his coffee.

"And as far the Bhutto girl is concerned, yes I agree that she could be the right choice, but with Nawaz Sharif of the IJI hobnobbing with Altaf Hussein the leader of MQM party, it may not be all that easy going for her. And God forbid if we have a fractured government that will be ruled by the majority, but will be remotely controlled by a minority group and without whose support in the national assembly the government could fall like a pack of cards, then we will be once agaihg asking for trouble," added Arif Rehman as he gave out his predictions of which party will win and with approximately how many seats in the National Assembly.

But when the final results were announced, Arif's prediction was not entirely correct. He had predicted that the PPP would win with an absolute majority but it fell a little short of the required target in the National Assembly. The PPP had secured 93, the IJI 54 and the MQM 13 seats respectively. And therefore it was now Benazir's turn to woo Altaf Hussein as a coalition partner and thus secure a majority in the National Assembly. Ruksana was however proved right, when on 2nd December, 1988 an elegant Benazir Bhutto who had already started calling herself as the daughter of the east was sworn in as the Prime Minister of Pakistan. She thus became the first Muslim women in the world to occupy that exalted post in a Muslim country and that too at the young age of 35.

On the 2nd of December, 1988 Benazir Bhutto dressed in a traditional shimmering emerald green salwar-kameez and with a spotless white dupatta covering her head, both of which were the colours representing the colours of Islam and Pakistan took the oath of office as the democratically elected Prime Minister of the country. The little girl from Lady Jennings Nursery School who once aspired to join the Pakistan Foreign Service had vindicated her father who the military had overthrown and then hanged. Administering the oath was none other than President Ghulam Ishaq Khan who at one time was her father's Defence Secretary. Seated in the front row was her proud mother, and across the aisle were the military top brass that included General Mirza Aslam Beg the Pakistan army chief and Lt General Hamid Gul the Chief of Pakistan ISI. For Benazir the world within one decade had come full circle and as she pledged by the constitution that ironically was rewritten by the late Zia, Gul Rehman who was watching it live on television wondered whether she would be able to complete her full term. Watching the proceedings was another fair and plumpish young man in his early forties who now kept wondering as to when his turn would come. Mian Mohammed Nawaz Sharif was the leader of the opposition and his party the IJI had stolen part of the thunder by winning the provincial elections in Punjab, the most populous province that was also the buckler and of which he was now the Chief Minister.

But since the election of a woman as a prime minister of a Muslim country was something unheard off and it therefore triggered off a great debate in the Islamic world. Infact during the election campaign itself, the Mullahs backed by Nawaz Sharif's IJI and in connivance with the ISI had started a smear campaign against the mother and daughter duo who were now in control of the PPP. To woo the voters away from them, they had even dropped thousands of leaflets and also some photographs of Benazir dancing in night clubs and her mother in a western evening gown doing the waltz with President Gerald Ford of the United States in the White House. Therefore the Mullas had termed all these activities as anti Islamic. But for people like the Rehman family and others, including the common man and woman on the streets of Pakistan they were all thoroughly fed up with the Zia brand of Islamization and military rule in the country. They now wanted more liberalization and freedom of speech and they therefore were now eagerly looking forward to that welcome change.

The return to democracy by Pakistan was generally welcomed by India too, but it was marred when Brigadier Zahirul-Islam Abbassi, the Pakistani Military Attache in New Delhi was caught red handed in a Delhi hotel while receiving some sensitive and secret defence documents from one of his contacts. He was therefore charged with spying and declared persona non grata. The Pakistani High Commissioner to India Mr Niaz Naik had also been summoned by the Indian Ministry of External Affairs and orders for the immediate expulsion of the Brigadier therefore also followed. The Pakistani Brigadier's desire to spend a happy New Year's Eve in the Indian capital was therefore dashed as this sensational news was highlighted by the Indian press and he had to leave the country immediately. Abbassi had earlier worked as a senior intelligence operative with the Jehadi groups who had fought against the Soviets in Afghanistan. He it seems he had been deeply influenced by the late President Zia's Islamization programme and was very much a part of the ISI, when he was arrested a day before Benazir was sworn in.

Reading about Brigadier Abbassi's exploits in Delhi that was communicated to Shiraz by Brigadier Aslam Rehman who was now attending the National Defence College course in Islamabad, Shiraz felt somewhat apprehensive and wondered what would happen to him and his family incase his true identity was ever revealed and he was unmasked. Moreover, though Stockholm was very far away and was considered to be a neutral country, but with the Bofors issue and revelations about the Nobel Group selling arms clandestinely to Iran, and officially to India with huge kickbacks being paid to the wheeler dealers who were probably being used as conduits by the politicians and the decision makers of that country, all these factors had also now started playing on his mind. The Swedish arms company had also made inroads into Pakistan and the probability of these weapons and those that the CIA had secretly pumped into the country finding their way through unscrupulous gun runners to other Muslim fundamentalist groups and terrorist organization that had now mushroomed in the Middle East, the Gulf Region, in Afghanistan and in the Indian subcontinent therefore could not be ruled out. While Shiraz was pondering over these issues, the news arrived that a commercial aircraft belonging to the Pan American airways on a flight from London to New York had crashed near Lockerbie in Scotland killing all the 243 passengers, the crew of 16 and also 11 civilians on the ground.

"But do you think this could be another case of sabotage by some disgruntled Muslim anti-American terrorist organization, since ninety percent of those killed according to the BBC are believed to be Americans," said Saira as Shiraz hurriedly booked a call to his counterpart in the Pakistan Embassy at London in order to get more details about the tragic accident and then said.

'Well my dear the Muslim terrorist angle I guess cannot be completely ruled out because only the other day there was a talk in the diplomatic circles here in Stockholm that a warning to this effect about an American aircraft likely to be targetted by some disgruntled Arabs had been received by the American Embassy in Helsinki and that as you know is right next door and therefore it may well be so," replied Shiraz.

Coincidently, but unknown to Shiraz, Monty by some good luck of fate was in Frankfurt that day for a meeting with his German importer. He was scheduled to catch the Pan Am feeder flight 103A to London that very evening and then board the regular Pan Am 103 that would take him to New York. Luckily for him that being the festive Christmas season, his jovial German host insisted that he join his family for the special dinner and then catch the late evening flight to London and Monty therefore obliged. When Monty got the news at Frankfurt airport that the Boeing Jumbo 747 that was named 'Clipper Maid of the Seas' had crashed, he just could not believe it. This was the third time that he had been saved by providence and when he landed at Heathrow, he found that there were also a few others like him too who by some stroke of goodluck had missed that ill fated flight. One of them was an Indian by the name of Jaswant Basuta. Jaswant it seems after checking in had one too many drinks while sitting in the lounge at Heathrow and he did not hear the final announcement for the departure of flight 103 to New York. And by the time he realized and ran to the gate it was already too late. The aircraft door had already been closed and despite his pleadings to the pilot and the Pan Am duty manager at the airport, the authorities refused to open the door. Similarly the American musical quartet known as the 'Four Tops' were also very lucky to have missed that flight. They were to return to the United States for Christmas that evening, but were delayed at the recording studios. So was the case with John Lyndon and his wife Nora. John was a band member of the group called 'Sex Pistols' and it was thanks to his wife Nora that they had lived to see another day. Nora hadn't packed her bags in time and by the time they got to the airport the flight had already taken off. But that was not the case for another Indian family who were rather unlucky. The Dixit-Rattan family had five members including the three year old Suruchi Rattan who was dressed in a bright red kurta and salwar and they were on their way from Delhi to Detroit. They were booked on the Pan Am flight 67 from Frankfurt and had already boarded the aircraft. But when the plane taxied for the take off, one of the children fell ill and complained of breathlessness. Taking no chances, the pilot returned to the gate and the family was allowed to disembark. They it seemed were destined to die that day, because the boy soon recovered and they were all transferred to the feeder flight PA 103. Realising that the news of his lucky escape would only upset his wife and daughter, Monty decided not to tell them about it. He however did ring up Reeta in Delhi and Dimpy in Dhaka to assure them that he was safe.

A couple of days later, when the so called accident was being investigated by the FBI, the local constabulary and Scotland Yard, it became quite evident that it was a clear case of sabotage. It seems that the warning received by the American Embassy in Helsinki had been conveyed in time to the FAA, the Federal Aviation Administration and they in turn had also issued a security bulletin on 5th December as a warning to all the United States carriers. The State Department too had alerted its embassies abroad. But this being the Christmas holiday season, there was a heavy rush of bookings and the warning it seems was taken somewhat lightly. Infact according to one reliable source the security team at Frankfurt airport found the warning hidden under a pile of papers a day after the Pan Am jumbo blew up in mid-air. With the amount of publicty that was being given to the crash by the media, and with all kinds of speculation doing the rounds as to why and how it happened, Monty just for the sake of sheer curiosity decided to visit the site of the accident and by the time he reached the small town of Lockerbie, the place was full of relatives of those who had perished.

The Pan Am Boeing 747 with Captain James MacQuarrie, First Officer Raymond Wagner and Flight Engineer Jerry Avritt in the cockpit had taken off from Heathrow at 1825 hours GMT. At around 1900 hours and cruising at an altitude of 31,000 feet the aircraft was given the oceanic clearance by the Scottish Control Centre at Prestwick and thereafter all contact was lost with the aircraft. A minute later the wing section of the Jumbo containing some 90,000 kgs of fuel hit the ground and exploded at Sherwood Crescent, Lockerbie. The explosion had punched a big 20 inch hole on the left side of the fuselage. The tail section with the cockpit recorder was however found in an open field, but there was no evidence of a distress call. Fragments of a Samsonite suitcase together with some parts and pieces of a circuit board of a radio cassette player indicated that a high intensity time bomb that was inside the Samsonite suitcase was probably the cause of the aircraft being blown up and disintegerating rapidly. This according to investigators was probably due to the fact that an unaccompanied baggage that was routed on to the aircraft through the interline baggage system had found its way inside the Jumbo. The suitcase it seems had made its way first to Frankfurt from Malta on the Air Malta Flight KM 189 and from there to the feeder flight PA 103 A to London and finally landed up on the ill fated flight to New York. This indicated that it was a clear case of sabotage and the perpetrators behind this dastardly crime were probably some Arab terrorist organization in the Middle East. This was further substantiated by the facts that on board the aircraft were four or five United States Intelligence officers and they were all from the CIA. It included Matthew Gannon who was the CIA's Deputy Station Chief in Beirut and therefore the likelihood of these CIA officers being targeted by the Abu Nidal Group, or the Hizbollah or the Libyans who were waiting to take revenge for the American air attack on Tripoli therefore could not be ruled out.

However, what impressed Monty the most was the helpful attitude of the locals. Though 11 of them had died and their houses and property were completely destroyed, the warm hearted Scots from Lockerbie who had lived with the dead bodies that lay in their gardens and on their streets had now opened their homes and hearths to the breaved families from abroad. The only house that was left standing at Sherwood Crescent was that of Father Patrick Keegans, the Roman Catholic priest of Lockerbie. Surprisingly those inside the cockpit and a fairly large number of passengers who were seated in the first class section and near the nose of the aircraft were found still strapped to their seats. So was a young mother who had her child in her arms. God it seems had ordained it for them thought Monty as he placed a bunch of flowers at the small little village church at Tundergarth and said a prayer. When it was reported that two small Scottish farm boys had found half a million dollars in the debris, Monty wondered whether this was the cash that the CIA may have set aside as ransom money for the American hostages who were being held by the Hezbollah in Beirut. However, there was no doubt in Monty's mind that with the death of 189 Americans, which was the largest so far, the targeting of Americans by the Arab fundamentalists had now begun in right earnest. The US after all was the strongest ally of their arch enemy the Israelis and they had to be therefore taught a lesson.

With the New Year approaching, Dimpy who was posted in Dhaka was feeling very homesick and lonely. Bangladesh having declared Islam as the State religion had been devastated with the worst floods of the century. Ironically, a devastating cyclone had struck the nation on the very day Benazir was sworn in as the Prime Minister of Pakistan. The tropical storm with all its fury had rendered millions homeless and the death toll was now in the tens of thousands and nearly three fourth of the riverine country was under water. The rice fields which were the lifeline of the people and which were ready to be harvested had been completely destroyed. Running water in most of the cities and towns had been polluted and the fear of an epidemic loomed large on the horizon. Dimpy who had visited some of these devastated villages with relief teams from the UNOCHA, the United Nations Office for the Coordination of Humanitarian Affairs was shocked beyond belief on what she had seen with her very own eyes. There were dead copses lying all around and most of the villages that were made of mud huts and from bush material had been flattened. The few lucky survivors of men, women and children half naked were on their knees begging for food and shelter. Their plight and misery had shaken her so very badly that she wanted somebody from home to come and cheer her up. Dimpy's letter describing the horrible scenes with photograps to her parents and to her aunt Shupriya had convinced the family that under the circumstances a quiet get together for the family at Dhaka for bringing in the New Year would therefore be highly appropriate.

With only four days leave that was granted to her, Shupriya decided to fly directly from Colombo to Dhaka, while Monty with Reeta and Peevee who was now in junior college took the Bangladesh Biman direct flight from Delhi. On board the same flight and seated across the aisle was the Fazal Rehman family. They too had decided to spend the New Year in Dhaka with Samina's mother who was now a widow. When Monty intrduced himself and said that he and his family were going to Dhaka for the first time and that his daughter was in the Indian Foreign Service and was posted there as the third secretary, the friendly hand shake by Fazal Rehman and a warm smile by Samina made the flight even more pleasant for all of them. And when the aircraft crossed the Indo-Bangladesh border and Fazal Rehman invited them all over for a meal to his mother-in—law's house the next day, it seemed as if both the families had known each other for a long time. This was actually true as far as their parents were concerned, but it was not known to them.

"Well that can only be possible after I get an approval from my daughter. I am sure that with you too being in the foreign service there must be some sort of a protocol that has to be observed and followed, Isnt that so?'said Monty as Fazal' Rehman's 13 year old daughter Sameera and 6 year old son Shafiq who were sitting in the row behind their parents invited Peevee to come and sit with them, so that the two ladies and the two gentlemen could sit next to each other for easy conversation. When Monty and Reeta both came to know a little more about Fazal Rehman's background and how the couple had met and got married, and how Mrs Haq's wonderful Bengali fish and prawn curries helped Fazal and Samina in swinging the match in their favour, they were simply delighted with the genuine warmth and friendliness of the Bangladesh diplomat and his wife. Having been reminded of the Sen Family and the late Aunty Mona's delicious Bengali dishes, Monty and Reeta therefore accepted the invitation very graciously. And while the two men folk debated the pros and cons of lowering the voting age from 21 to 18 as India had recently done on 15th December by passing the constitution amendment bill in the Indian Parliament, Peevee who too loved his prawn curry and rice cooked in Bengali style also quickly invited himself.

"Ofcourse and that goes without saying my boy and the invitation also stands for your sister and your aunt who I am told is expected to join you all from Colombo," said Fazal Rehman as he noted down Rohini Bajwa's residential address and telephone number.

On 30th December 1988, while Benazir Bhutto and Rajiv Gandhi, the two young Prime Ministers of Pakistan and India at their maiden meeting in Islamabad were busy discussing ways on how to improve the relations between the two countries, in Dhaka, Mrs Abida Haq was happy treating Monty, Reeta and Peevee with her many mouth watering fish preparations. Very diplomatically both Miss Rohini Bajwa (Dimpy) and Yeshwant Kaur Bajwa(Shupriya) giving the excuse that they had both already accepted an official invitation by the Indian High Commissioner, which was also a fact, they therefore had backed out from it. Moreover, Shupriya being a Bengali herself was also afraid that too many questions by the host about her own antecedents may well turn out to be somewhat embarrassing both to her, Monty and the hosts, and she therefore very correctly and politely had declined Mrs Haq's invitation.

"Oh the two of you really missed some delicious Bengali food," said Monty when he returned from the sumptuous meal and showed a few photographs of the hosts that he had taken that evening with his video camera.

"Well I must say that Mr Fazal Rehman and his wife Samina do make a very handsome couple and the very fact that he is a thoroughbred Pathan and she a charming Bengali is clearly written on their faces," said Shupriya as Peevee noticing the eagerness on Dimpy's face to see the video butted in with the remark 'Lekin Mera Bharat Mahan.'. Peevee was referring to Dimpy's boyfriend and colleague Bharat Padmanabhan who was presently posted as the third secretary in Moscow. Strangely enough that night and just before going to bed, when Shupriya as was her habit took out the small cut-out of her late husband's face from her purse and kissed it goodnight, little did she know that he was still very much alive and was married to none other than Fazal Rehman's own first cousin Saira.

The 31st of December, 1988 for the Bajwa family and Shupriya in Dhaka was rather a quiet affair as they sat at home and rang in the New Year with a sing song session and a simple but delicious Punjabi food that Dimpy had requested her mother to cook. With the country still reeling from the terrible devastation that was caused by the recent cyclone, they were all against the idea of celebrating the New Year Eve at the Dhaka club or at a five star hotel or restaurant. After the plain and simple fare of makki-di-roti, sarson-da-sag and dahi-vada that was followed by some delicious gajar-da-halwa, Peevee with a guitar in hand livened the evening with some old but ever popular English and Hindi hit songs of the late fifties and the sixties. When at Shupriya's request Peevee sang the old Kishore Kumar number 'Ye Kiya Hua, Kaisse Hua' from the film "Amar Prem", she was visbly moved. Besides the good looks that Peevee had inherited from his father, his mature baritone voice and his mannerisms too were exactly like that of her late beloved husband. Noticing the tears that were swelling up in Shupriya's eyes, Monty very cleverly got up, shaked his head in typical Rajesh Khanna style and having done a jig that was remniscent of the late Kishore Kumar in the film 'Padosan' it soon had everybody in splits. And when he requested Peevee to sing his own favourite Pat Boone number 'Love Letters in the Sand' it reminded Reeta of her first date with Monty at the Standard Restaurant on Connaught Place.

Early next morning on that New Year's Day of 1989 and having taken prior permission from the elders, Peevee flew back to Delhi. He had an important appointment to keep that evening with the Jana Natya Manch, a revolutionary theatre group who were to stage a street play titled 'Halla Bol' at an industrial area that was on the outskirts of Delhi. Also known as the People's Theatre Front, the Manch was founded by the young activist Safdar Hashmi in 1973 and the plays produced and performed by this group were primarily to educate the common man and the working class of India on how to fight against exploitation. There was no doubt that the factory workers in such industrial areas in a quite a few cases were being exploited by the politicians and the business class and Safdar felt that such kind of domestic exploitation must stop and the workers must be told about their rights through such kind of educative street plays. Safdar Hashmi was born on 12th April, 1954 in Delhi and was a member of the Communist Party of India, Marxist Group. Last year the group had performed the play 'Moteram Ka Satyagraha' and Peevee was highly impressed not only with the acting talents of the Manch, but also the dedication with which Safdar Hashmi and his Bengali wife Moloyashree produced, directed and conducted such kind of plays for the masses. However, the kind of revolutionary signals and messages that the Manch was sending out to the Indian working class at large it seems was not to the liking of some politicians. Moreover, with the Bofors scandal already playing on the minds of the common man, the play 'Halla Bol" meaning 'Attack' was being seen by some in the ruling Congress (I) as an attack on them. The Manch was however only trying to tell the people on the street not to simply take things lying down. Unfortunately at that time the Municpal Elections were also due in the State of Uttar Pradesh and one of the candidates was Mukesh Sharma, a local factory owner and a small time goon who was close to the ruling Congress (I). That evening while the street play was in progress, Mukesh Sharma with his procession of supporters arrived on the scene. He and his folowers were canvassing for his candidature, but when Safdar Hashmi politely requested them to take a different route, an argument followed. This so angered Mukesh Sharma and his goons that they decided to 'Halla Bol' on the actors with the sticks and iron rods that they were carrying with them. Their main target was Safdar whose head was bashed. It was a sad New Year's Day for Peevee and many others as they witnessed a helpless Safdar Hashmi and his group of actors being beaten up mercilessly by Mukesh Sharma's hoodlums. It was local 'Dadagiri' at its worst with the main target being Safdar himself whose head was bashed and who died of his injuries the next day. If this type of goondaism and cold blooded murder of a defenceless stage artist by a two bit local politician could take place in broad daylight and that to on a public street in the neighbourhod of India's capital city, Peevee wondered what must be happening in the interior of this vast country. The tragic death of Safdar Hashmi at the hands of a two penny local politician whose writ ran in that area was enough to convince Peevee that it was only muscle power and money power that was required to rule this nation and no amount of protests of any kind could change the mindset of those who were in a position to wield such power. Both the local police and the judiciary it seems were helpless. The law was in the hands of such like ruthless politicians cum hoodlums and for the common man and a bystander to launch an FIR, a first information report against them was like asking for trouble. But when Peevee with the thousands of Delhites that included intellectuals, poets, writers, stage artiste, journalists and renowned painters of India attended Safdar's funeral on 3rd January, he realized that the actor's untimely death was not all in vain. His killing had unleashed a wave of grief and rage in the whole of India and it gave a clear message to the powers that be that they cannot get away with such cold blooded murders. Undettered by the loss of her husband, a grief stricken Moloyashree within 48 hours was back with her troupe at that same very spot to complete the disrupted performance. The play 'Halla Bol' that was done in support of the striking workers was thus given even more impetus as Moloyashree in defiance raised her fist at that very spot where her husband had been felled and Peevee who was once again there felt very proud of the young lady.

While Peevee in Delhi mourned the death of Safdar Hashmi, the ten day short holiday with the family in Bangladesh had done a lot of good to Shupriya as she visited some of the locaties in Dhaka and Chittagong that her late parents often used to talk about. This also gave her an opportunity to do some saree shopping of the famous Dhakai and Tangail sarees, and it also gave her time to mix and talk to the locals freely and thereby get a first hand impression about their attitude towards their own government, towards the Indians who had helped them in attaining their freedom and towards the Pakistanis who now had a lady Prime Minister and whose late father, Zulfiqar Ali Bhutto and the coterie of Pakistan Generals led by Yahya Khan were undoubtedly instrumental in creating Bangladesh, though albeit most ruthlessly.

It seems that the present government that was being ruled by General Ershad and his Jatiyo Party was on its last legs as the common people were now cursing them for all the miseries that had befallen the country and the corruption at every level that had engulfed the nation. The attitude towards the Indians in general was that off 'Please just do not interfere in our internal affairs'. And as far as Pakistan was concerned, that being a Muslim country and of which they were once very much a part off, it was let bygones be bygones. Like most of the countries in the subcontinent including India, the poor in Bangladesh too it seems were getting poorer, while the rich were becoming richer.

It was in the early second week of January 1989, that Shupriya returned to her desk in Colombo and took stock of what India and the Rajiv Gandhi Government had achieved diplomatically and politically both at home and abroad during the past twelve months. With the Bofors gun scandal still simmering and belching fire, the political equations in India too were undergoing radical changes. Politicians both within the Congress and outside who were once friends of the young Indian Prime Minister and of her late mother Mrs Gandhi were now gearing up to challenge his very authority at the hustings. VP Singh, who was once Rajiv Gandhi's Defence and Finance Minister with the backing off the newly formed Janata Dal Party was waiting to fire the final salvo with the corruption angle as its main plank. The new party was a centre-left coalition that had been hurriedly formed in October 1988 with the merger of the major Janata Party factions, the Lok Dal, the Congress (S) and the Jan Morcha and was being led by none other than VP Singh himself who was now determined to gun down the corrupt Rajiv Gandhi government.

According to Shupriya's own assessment, Rajiv's government as far as the home front was concerned had really nothing much to show or rave about. In Punjab and in Jammu and Kashmir the ugly head of terrorism had shown no decline whatsoever. The ruling Congress (I) was also losing support in various important states as regional parties of every hue, shade and colour kept mushrooming by the dozens. As far as India's foreign policy was concerned, the only silver lining was Rajiv's recent visit to China and Gorbachev's visit to India. On the 3rd of November, 1988 on an SOS from the Maldive government, India had launched 'Operation Cactus,' when the Indian Air Force airlifted a Parachute Battallion and flew them non stop from Agra to Hulule, a distance of over 2000 kilometres. The group of mercenaries who had led the invasion failed in their attempt and within hours of the Indian paratroopers landing on the island, the government rule at Male was restored. A fortnight later on 16th November, 1988 India also gave full recognition to the government of Palestine. But as far as Sri Lanka was concerned, India was now on the backfoot as it continued to deal with

the Tamil militants in an ambivalent manner. Supriya was very upset, when
157 LTTE militants in October 1988 who had been arrested and detained in
Tamil Nadu under the NSA, National Terrorist Act were suddenly released
and deported to Sri Lanka. They were flown in Indian Airforce aircrafts and
were kept in custody by the IPKF at the detention facility centres at Jaffna
and Trincomalee. This gesture was meant to be a diplomatic move and by
which the Indian Government hoped that not only would the anti Indian
activities by the LTTE in the state of Tamil Nadu cease, but it would also
pave the way for the LTTE to lay down their arms and take part in the
provincial council elections in Sri Lanka that was scheduled for the 9th of
November.

A few months earlier in mid September, when India announced a five
day ceasefire and then extended it further by another 5 days, there was
however no positive reponse at all from the LTTE. And on 12th October
1988, when Kittu who was one of the 157 detainees and who had been
deported from Tamil Nadu and who was reputed to be very close to the
LTTE supremo together with a lady activist were both released in the
presence of the world media in Jaffna there was still a hope that this political
decision by India could still defuse the tension between the IPKF and the
LTTE and keep the possibility of a peaceful solution open and alive. And
despite the big publicity that was given to this event and the brief public
speech of reconciliation that was delivered by Major General Kahlon, the
IPKF's senior most Commander in Jaffna, it simply had no effect on the
LTTE leadership. A further ray of hope that the LTTE may yet give up the
militancy and fight the provincial elections was given a further boost, when
the IPKF in order to ensure that the elections would be free and fair called
off 'Operation Checkmate,' But it was all in vain. Not only did the LTTE
not take part in the elections, but they also carried on with their militant
activities and even threatened to disrupt it. And to make matters worse, the
release of Kittu and others that followed not only encouraged the locals,
but it also incresed the active support that the LTTE was receiving from the
DMK and other such pro Tamil chauvinistic groups in Tamil Nadu. And
on the 9th of November, when the elections in Sri Lanka were finally held
under the aegis of the IPKF and the results were declared and Vardharaja
Perumal of the EPRLF was made the Chief Minister, it only further angered
Prabhakaran and his ardent supporters both in Tamil Nadu and in Sri Lanka.
Lt General A.S. Kalkat who was overall incharge of the IPKF operations
however felt happy that his troops and commanders at all levels had carried

out the thankless and difficult task most admirably and under very difficult conditions and without any major casualties.

In January 1989, the elections to the Tamil Nadu state assembly was held and a new government led by Mr Karunanidhi of the DMK had now come to power. But what irked Shupriya the most was that this very government was now patronizing the LTTE who were fighting our forces in Sri Lanka. Politics really make some strange bed fellows wrote Shupriya to Monty as she in her letter praised the manner in which the Indian army soldiers and officers who were serving in the IPKF daily risked their lives trying to bring about peace on a foreign land where they themselves were now unwanted. And to add to that Kurananidhi's Tamil supporters and some other such like pro LTTE Tamil Groups in the state were also hand in glove with the militants. According to Shupriya they were infact sleeping with the enemy.

With Ranasinghe Premadasa having taken over as President of Sri Lanka from Jayawardhene on 2nd January, things were now getting worse by the day. Premadasa had no love lost for India and was infact not at all in favour of the Indo-Sri Lanka accord that his predecessor had signed with Rajiv Gandhi. He was also facing a rebellion in the south where the JVP, a Marxist group had shown its ugly head once again and the Sri Lankan army had to be deployed in force to quell it. Premadasa always considered the IPKF as an occupation force and was waiting to get rid of it. Shupriya's diplomatic assignment in Sri Lanka was therefore not a bed of roses either as the LTTE and the JVP had now started targeting vital communication centres and VIP's in the capital city of Colombo.

Meanwhile in Pakistan though democracy had been restored, but with Benazir Bhutto in the hot seat things were not going as smoothly as one wanted it to be. Some people were still debating whether a woman had the right to rule in an Islamic country, and there was also the fear that some disgruntled lot in the army may once again stage a coup and throw her out from office. Moreover, she did not have an absolute majority in the National Assembly nor was her party in control of the most populous province of Punjab. Within weeks of her taking office, the rift between the PPP and the IJI surfaced in right earnest, when the Governor of Baluchistan retired General Musa dissolved the provincial assembly. But thanks to the intervention by the Baluchistan High Court it was soon restored with Nawab Akbar Bugti as the Chief Minister. Though Benazir had the backing of the United States, she was still wary about the military and the ISI. As a safety measure she had decided to remove Lt General Hamid Gul the

DGISI whom she thoroughly distrusted and have him replaced by the low profile Major General Shamsur Rehman Kallue who had already retired from service and would have to be recalled. The biggest factor in Kallue's favour was that he was a good friend of her late father and she could trust him. But she wanted to first establish herself and then have Lt General Hamid Gul posted out as a Corps Commander. She was also aware that if she had to remain in power, she would need the support of the Army Chief and other bigwigs in the Pakistan army and it was too early to ruffle feathers.

With an educated woman at the helm of affairs in Pakistan, and a chauvinistic male population backed by the Muslim clergy showing their utter disapproval, Ruksana Begum and other liberal women like her in the country wondered whether Benazir would be able to last for very long. However, her daughter Saira who knew Benazir from her school days at the Convent at Murree was confident that she would be able to wither the initial storm and Inshallah put the country back on the rails again. On receiving the news that her beloved Uncle Gul Rehman had suffered a severe heart attack and had been put on the DI list, the dangerously ill list by the army doctors at the Peshawar Military Hospital, Saira with her husband Shiraz and their children immediately flew down to Peshawar and landed there on the 20th of January. It was on that very day that Mr George Herbert Walker Bush was also sworn in as the new President of the United States.

CHAPTER-11

Pakistan Bushwhacked

Born in Milton, Massachusettes on 12th June, 1924, George. W. Bush whose father was a Senator from Connecticut became the youngest pilot n the US Navy at the tender age of 18, and he saw active service in the Pacific Theatre during the Second World War. On one daring mission as a torpedo bomber pilot, when he was shot down by the Japs and landed in the ocean, he was lucky to have been rescued by a US submarine. A decorated war hero and an excellent sportsman from Yale University, Bush had started his career in the oil industry of Texas before getting into politics. With his vast experience as the head of the CIA and as the country's Ambassador to the United Nations that was followed by the Vice Presidency of the greatest power in the world, he had now been sworn in as the new President in a dramatically fast changing planet. The 40 years of the bitter Cold War with the Soviets and their allies was about to end, and it was also nearing the end of the communist party rule in the Soviet backed Warsaw Pact countries of Europe and in the Soviet Union itself. With Perestroika and Glasnost having been initiated by Gorbachev in his own country, the seeds of democracy had also been sowed. And with the total withdrawal of the Soviet Forces from Afghanistan about to be completed, a new world order for the Russians, and those of the Eastern Block countries was fast emerging. While Bush hailed the march of democracy, he however decided to tread with caution on the future US policies while dealing with this new group of emerging nations.

"But what is your assessment of the new American President. And now that the Soviets have practically pulled out from Afghanistan, do you think the American policy towards Pakistan will undergo a radical change?" asked Gul Rehman as Shiraz with more than half the Rehman clan crowded around his hospital bed. The retired General on that very day at his own risk and request had moved out of the ICU to the officers' ward, and when the doctors objected, he in good humour told them that he had already lived his life to the full and if he was destined to kick the bucket, then no power and no doctor on earth would be able to go against Allah's wishes

"Well if you ask me frankly and now that our usefulness to the Americans in their proxy war against the Soviets in Afghanistan is practically over, the Americans will probably once again down grade us to a poor third world nation and will tighten the screws on us both economically and militarily as and when it is required,' said Shiraz somewhat mockingly, while his daughter Shezadi planted a kiss on her loving grandpa's cheek and presented him with a get well card. Not to be left behind, her younger brother Tojo also handed over a bouquet of beautiful red roses to an ever smiling Gul Rehman.

"Yes and I think Riaz(Shiraz) is right, because according to a dear friend of mine, a Brigadier who till recently was serving with the ISI and who is currently attending the NDC course with me, there are already very strong rumours that the Americans are now demanding the return of the Stinger missiles that they had so generously supplied to us for the Jehadi war in Afghanistan," said Brigadier Aslam Rehman as hs son Gentleman Cadet Vovka (Samir Rehman Khan) who had come from PMA, Kakul clicked his heels and saluted his grandfather very smartly.

"Yes and those missiles do not come cheap, and neither do the gun factories at Dera Adam Khel have the know how to duplicate them. They cost a whopping hundred thousand dollars a piece and maybe more I am told and that is indeed a lot of money. But God forbid if these weapons should fall into the hands of terrorists and Islamist militant groups that have now started mushrooming in every nook and corner of the world and Pakistan is no exception either, then there will be hell to pay,"added Arif Rehman Khan while presenting a set of books by his current favourite author Tom Clancy to his dearest eldest brother. Born on 12th April, 1947, at Calvert County, Maryland, Thomas Leo Clancy better known as Tom Clancy was a contemporary of the Indian born author Salman Rushdie. Both were practically of the same age, and while Salman had created quite a storm with his latest novel 'The Satanic Verses,', Tom was riding the waves with his novels on espionage that was set during the Cold War period and and which was now slowly crumbling away. His first novel 'The Hunt for the Red October' was published in 1984. Based on a story about the defection of a Soviet nuclear submarine with its captain, it became an instant best seller and had made Tom a celebrity overnight. This was followed by 'Red Storm Rising' which was published in 1986, and his current novel 'The

Cardinal of the Kremlin' that had just hit the stands were also highly rated by the critics.

During the next two days, Gul Rehman had a lot of more visitors from his large family. On 23rd January, his younger son Fazal Rehman with his family flew in from nearby Delhi, and a day later his nephew Salim Rehman and son-in-law Karim Malik with their families from Beijing and Washington DC respectively also arrived. On 25th January, which happened to be a Wednesday, Gul Rehman wishing to be close to his near and dear ones got himself forcibly discharged from the hospital. He had a premonition that his end was nearing and he wished to die at home. That very evening for his home coming the entire Rehman family had got together at the big Haveli for a grand party and a jovial Gul Rehman was at his very best as he reminisced about his young days at the PWRIMC, his great friendship with his bosom pals Ismail Sikandar Khan and Daler Singh Bajwa at the IMA, His marriage to Zubeida, his experiences during the great war, the tragic breakup of the country, and the mess that the generals and the politicians had created during Pakistan's 42 years of existence. That evening he also drank a toast to all his children and grand children and urged them to become good human beings and to keep the Rehman flag always flying high. Then as he ended the toast with words from the Holy Koran, Gul Rehman probably realized that he only had a few more minutes to live. It was on the subject of compassion and as he quoted from Chapter 90, the verses 12 to 17 everyone listened to him with rapt attention. 'And what will examine to you what the steep path is? It is the freeing of slave from bondage: or giving the food on a day of famine to an orphan relative, or to a needy in distress. Then will he be of those who believe, enjoin fortitude and encourage kindness and compassion.' Having said those beautiful words, Gul Rehman smiled at all of them and quietly sat down on his chair and passed away. It was a painless death that he had always wished for and Allah had granted it to him most graciously. He was 75 years ol and had lived his life truly as an officer and a gentleman.

Next day, while Monty and family watched the might of the Indian armed forces at the grand annual Republic Day parade in Delhi, in Peshawar a gun carriage with the coffin of Major General Gul Rehman Khan from the first IMA course of the famed 'Pioneers' draped in Pakistan's green and white national flag slowly made its way to the burial ground. As the honour guard from the First Punjabees presented arms and fired their volleys, and the buglers sounded the last post, there were tears flowing down from everyones eyes. For Shiraz, Gul Rehman was not only a fatherly figure, but also his own real uncle from his mother's side. But this fact neither he nor anybody else knew. That evening, when he saw the framed phtograph of the three musketeers in their second lieutenant's uniform that was always kept displayed on the General's writing table, Shiraz wondered whether the celebrations were now also being held in heaven for the General's home coming by the three old musketeers.

On the 15th of February 1989 when Shiraz with his family returned to Stockholm, and the news over the BBC confirmed that the Soviets had officially initimated that all Soviet troops had been withdrawn from Afghanistan, Saira felt indeed very happy.

"Thank God this nine year old dirty war in our neighbourhood has ended," said Saira as she requested her husband to apply for a home posting. She felt that with a democratic government in Pakistan now firmly in the chair, and with Shiraz's experience in the Soviet Union that was now undergoing a radical change politically, he could probably contribute a lot more sitting in Islamabad than in Stockhom. Saira also knew that Sweden as a country for a career diplomat was not considered to be an important one. It was equivalent to that of a Grade 'B' appointment in the Pakistan Foreign Service.

"Well if you can sound your old school friend Benazir, and if she agrees then I would love to get back right now," said Shiraz jokingly.

"Well now that she is the Prime Minister, she may not even remember my name. Afterall it has been nearly 25 years since we left school, but I could definitely sound my dad who had worked under her father," replied Saira happily.

"Well in that case, let's call him up right now," said Shiraz as he booked a PP, a personal and private call by name to his father-in-law Mr Arif Rehman Khan in Peshawar.

On that very day of 15th February, as the last long convoy of the Soviet armored vehicles made their way back home through the treacherous snowbound Salang Pass in the Hindu Kush Mountains, and as the last giant Ilyushin 76 transport aircraft with the remnants of the Soviet soldiers in Kabul took off for their journey back to Russia, the 30,000 Mujaheedins who had been trained and armed by the CIA and the ISI, and who had surrounded the capital from all sides fired their weapons in the air and rejoiced with joy. Though the American game plan to create a Vietnam like situation for the Russians in Afghanistan had indeed succeeded to some extent, but it also created a few devils in disguise from amongst those radical and fanatical Muslim jehadis who had volunteered to fight the Russians.

One such amongst them was the tall and handsome Arab by the name of Osama Bin Laden who was now ready to take full control of all the Jehadis and of all those who were willing to fight and sacrifice their lives and spread Islam all around the word. And thus was born a rejuvenated Al Qaida.

Osama who had proved himself during the Battle of Jaji that he was as much a dare devil fighter as the other Mujaheedins was now a highly respected man. He had already parted ways with his mentor Abdullah Azzam. The two of them together in 1984 had established the Maktab-al-Khadamat in Peshawar. And it was this organization, which had funneled money, arms and the Muslim fighters from around the world to come and fight for the Afghan cause. But the duo had now split. Osama desired a more militant role for his Arab fighters who would fight under their own commanders against the infidels and he would be their overall boss, while his mentor Ayman al Zawahiri would provide the ideological and strategic guidance to the movement. The Arabic word Al-Qaida meaning 'The Base' was thus established and the deadly militant Sunni Islamist Organization was now soon to become the most dreaded terrorist organization as far as the Americans were concerned. And while the Soviet Union was getting ready to bring in the much required electoral reforms in their country, Saira kept praying for her husband's home posting.

And her prayers were soon heard. On 27th March, the day the results of the first ever free elections to the Soviet parliament was announced and which went against the Communist party, the posting of Riaz Mhammed Khan (Shiraz) to Islamabad as a Joint Secretary in the Ministry of Foreign Affairs was received. And three weeks later on 15th April 1989, while the young Chinese students and the people of China were mourning the death of one of their revered leaders and were getting ready to demand greater political freedom from their communist political masters, Shiraz with his family landed in Islamabad. But on that very day a human tragedy of a very different kind led to the deaths of 94 football fans in a stadium at Sheffield in England.They were all from Liverpool and they had come all the way to the Hillisborough Stadium at Sheffield to cheer their team who were playing 'Nottingham Forest' that day. The match had just started and the Liverpool fans were still in the process of getting inside the special enclosure that was reserved for them, when the stampede started and within ten minutes or so with the match being abandoned, dead bodies were being collected. On the very next day, when Shiraz took over his assignment as Joint Secretary Russia and he read about the terrible tragedy at that football match, he just could not believe it. He knew that the English were football crazy and hooliganism on the field was not uncommon, but this was a man made tragedy that could have been averted with proper access control.

On 18th April, when the BBC reported that tens of thousands of Chinese students demanding democracy had stormed the Communist Party Headquarters in the Chinese capital Beijing, Shiraz just could not believe that either. So he called up his brother-in—law Salim Rehman to verify the report.

"'Yes that is a fact and the way things are moving, it might even get worse in the days to come," said Salim Rehman who was now the Counselor Political in the Pakistan Embassy in China. Since China too was considered to be a country behind the Iron Curtain, Shiraz therefore consulted his counterpart who was looking after the China Desk in Islamabad to find out exactly what was happening in that big country. After all China was a mighty powerful neighbour and the Chinese had always been good friends of Pakistan and therefore any major political repercussions in that country would also have its effect on Pakistan and on India too, thought Shiraz as he glanced through all the current monthly political reports that were routinely and periodically received from the Pakistan Embassy in Beijing.

The recent spate of demonstrations by the Chinese people that was led by students, intellectuals and labour activists was sparked off by the death of the former Secretary General of the Chinese Communist Party, Hu Yaobang. The Chinese government had officially stated that Yaobang had died suddenly of a heart attack on 15th April, but some sections of the people, and especially the student community suspected foul play. Hu had resigned or rather was eased off from that powerful post in January 1987, when his call for rapid reforms both for economic and social restructuring in the country was rejected by Deng Xiaoping and others in the party hierarchy. Though it was a fact that since 1978, Deng did start some economic and political reforms that had led to the gradual implementation of a market economy and political liberalization, and he had also relaxed in some small measure the rigid system that was set during Mao Zedong's long rule, but everyone was not satisfied. It had only satisfied the farmers and the factory workers who were compensated with a slightly higher yearly income, whereas the intellectuals and others got practically nothing at all. The students and the intellectuals now were also demanding the loosening up of the social and political controls and they had also started accusing the Communist Party bigwigs and their cronies with rampant corruption. Taking the cue from the recent reforms that Gorbachev with his doctrine of 'Glasnost', and 'Perestroika' had introduced in the Soviet Union, they were therefore now demanding rapid changes and a faster roadmap towards democracy. There was no doubt that China with its huge population and size and with its vast mineral resources, nuclear know how and military potential was a power to reckon with, but this kind of open and mass dissent that was now being displayed by the students and the intellectuals of the country against the leaders of the powerful Communist Party of China was unheard off. Yes there were pro democracy student protests in 1986 and in 1987 also, but they were not on such a massive scale thought Shiraz while deciding to keep a close watch on the recent developments of political upheaval in that country.

The Tiananmen Square located in the centre of the capital city was a very historical place. Built in the fifteenth century during the reign of the Ming Dynasty it was the door that led to the Forbidden City. At the northern end was the Tiananmen Tower, a revered tower that only the royal family and the Chinese nobility could enter. In good old days, the square was only opened to the general public whenever a new Emperor and Empress were to be proclaimed as rulers. After the Communist take over, a massive granite monument to honour the heroes who died for the cause had been constructed in 1952. And in 1959, to the west of the square was built the Great Hall of the People and inside which the Communist Party leaders were now debating on how to diffuse the crisis that had now started to snowball into an unprecedented nationwide stir.

In the middle of May 1989, while the student's movement and the political unrest in China gathered momentum, the Soviet leader and reformist Gorbachev paid an official visit to China. This was the first ever visit by the Secretary General of the Communist Party of the Soviet Union in nearly three decades, and the very fact that it had come at a time when the iron curtain was slowly being lifted by the Communist Bloc countries, his visit to Beijing was welcomed by both the east and the west and was covered extensively by the world press and television that had gathered at Beijing. On 13th May, 1989 and just two days prior to Gorbachev's visit to Beijing, approximately a hundred thousand students and intellectuals took to the streets of the capital city and occupied the Tiananmen Square demanding free media reforms and a formal dialogue with the authorities and their own elected representatives. With no response from the government, the students now decided to go on a mass hunger strike and that had now become the defining moment as the common people too now rallied behind them. On 19th May, seeing the volatile situation, Zhao Ziyang the General Secretary of the Communist Party of China went to the Square and addressed the students and urged them to end the hunger strike, but the students were adamant and the standoff therefore continued.

Then on 22nd May, when India successfully tested the Agni, an intermediate range ballistic missile and joined the exclusive club that was hithertofore being dominated only by a handful of the the world's military giants, and it was followed by the Chinese government declaring martial law in China, it sent shock waves not only to Islamabad and Washington, but to Moscow also.

On learning about India's rapid progress in developing such sophisticated long range missiles, Shiraz in his heart of hearts felt happy and proud. And it was more so because the man behind the project was also an eminent Muslim scientist by the name of Abdul Kalam, who was a simple unassuming soul and who had risen from very humble beginnings. But Shiraz was also aware that Pakistan too was not lagging behind in this field. A group of scientists under the leadership of Dr Abdul Qadeer Khan who was also a Muslim, but of the boastful type had successfully developed the Hatf and the Unza missiles and therefore what bothered Shiraz now was whether the missile race that had now started in earnest between the two nations of the subcontinent would lead to a final destruction of one another in the times to come. Moreover in 1974, India had already detonated a nuclear device, and as per the late General Zia's and Dr Abdul Qadeer's own admissions, Pakistan not only possessed the necessary know how to produce one, but it was also ready to test it as and when it was nececessary. Therefore in order to find out the actual position on the ground, Shiraz decided to go a little deeper into this subject.

According to Shiraz's information, it all started off on a beautiful sunny winter morning of 20th January 1972, on the lawns of the stately old colonial mansion at Multan, when Bhutto while addressing the cream of Pakistani scientists and physicists who had gathered under a coloured canopy secretly told them about his future plans for a nuclear Pakistan. The new President and CMLA of the country was still smarting at the loss of East Pakistan and the humiliating defeat that was suffered by Pakistan both militarily, politically and diplomatically at the hands of the Indians, and he had therefore vowed to take revenge. Seated among the 50 top scientific brains of Pakistan were Professors Abdus Salam, the Chief Scientific Officer and a future Nobel Prize winner, Dr Ishrat Usmani the then Chairman of the PAEC, Pakistan Atomic Energy Commission and the 46 year old Dr Munir Ahmad Khan, who had come all the way from Vienna for that very important meeting. On that historic day, when Bhutto discussed the serious issue with his scientists and asked them whether Pakistan given the full resources by him was capable of building a nuclear bomb in three years time, most of the junior scientists who were present there said yes. And when the two top scientists of the country, Abdus Salam and Dr Usmani tried to dissuade him from diverting the resources from the peaceful uses of nuclear energy that Pakistan had already embarked upon, Bhutto immediately appointed Dr Munir Ahmad Khan as the new Chairman of the PAEC. The new chairman and the very man who as part of the IAEA in Vienna was responsible to stop the spread of nuclear weapons immediately took up the challenge and thus the process to manufacture the Islamic bomb was born.

Dr Munir Ahmad Khan was born on 20th May 1926 at Lahore and had completed his college education from the prestigious Government College in his home town. He was also a Fulbright Scholar with a master's degree in electrical engineering from North Carolina University, USA and had started his career as a research engineer at the Argonne National Laboratory in Illinois and thereafter in 1958 had joined the IAEA in Vienna. It was he who had secretly initiated Project-706, the Kahuta Enrichment Project in 1974 and that was much before Dr Abdul Qadeer Khan landed up on the scene from Holland with his briefcase full of nuclear secrets. Meanwhile a secret group that was known as the 'Wah Group' in March 1974, under Dr Munir's guidance had already initiated the project and even the tunnels at Chagai that were dug under his supervision were completed in 1980, but they were now being kept sealed. Brigadier Mohammed Sarfaraz had provided the necessary support to the Pakistan Atomic Agency survey team for the tunneling of the projected test site in the Ras Koh range that was in the Chagai Division of Baluchistan. Shiraz had also come to know that Pakistan had carried out a series of successful nuclear cold tests since 1983, and was therefore convinced that Pakistan was in possession of the bomb though they had not physically tested it on the ground. The first 'cold test', a test of the implosion using inert natural uranium instead of highly enriched uranium was conducted on 11th March 1983, inside the tunnels that were bored in the Kirana Hills near the important Pakistan air force base at Sargodha. A second cold test soon followed and it was witnessed both by Lt Gen KM Arif and President Ghulam Ishaq Khan in the presence of Dr Munir, the Chairman of PAEC who was responsible for it.

Needless to say that Pakistan's desire to have an Islamic bomb was given a further boost after India's Buddha smiled on 18th May, 1974 at the Indian Army's field firing ranges at Pokharan in the desert region of Rajasthan where it was successfully tested. Initially Pakistan had decided to follow the plutonium path, but with the arrival of Dr Abdul Qadeer Khan from Holland in 1975 and who had clandestinely brought with him the plans for uranium enrichment centrifuges, the Pakistani scientists decided to follow the uranium enrichment process, and thus in 1976 was founded the Engineering Research Laboratories in Kahuta and which was now known as the Dr Abdul Qadeer Khan Research Laboratories.

Eversince the Soviet invasion of Afghanistan in 1979, Pakistan had been given a front line status by the United States and the Reagan administration had very conveniently through those years of Soviet occupation overlooked Pakistan's progress towards the development of the Islamic bomb. But now in 1989 things were different. The 1985 Solarz Amendment which prohibited giving economic aid to countries that attempt to import nuclear commodities had put the screws on Pakistan, and Pakistan was therefore forced to seek nuclear assistance from China for its requirement of highly enriched uranium and this was indicated by the presence of the many Chinese technicians at the highly sensitive Kahuta plant.

Though the new Prime Minister Benazir Bhutto during her recent visit to the United States in April 1989 at the invitation of President Bush had categorically announced that as per the new Benazir doctrine, Pakistan would not put together the components for a nuclear device unless its own security was threatened and that it would not export nuclear technology to any third country, but the United States it seems were not fully convinced and nor was Shiraz. Moreover the recent testing of the Agni long range ballistic missile by India had spurred the Pakistanis to also produce missiles to match that capability and China was willing to help in achieving that also. The two countries in 1986 had signed the Sino-Pakistani atomic cooperation agreement and with Dr Qadeer Khan having succeeded in ousting Dr Munir Ahmad from the hot seat and with the set up at the Kahuta complex having the necessary infrastructure for producing such missiles, Pakistan's ambitious Ballistic Missile Development Programme had already begun. But the two Hatf series missiles that were tested in February 1989 were both short range solid fuelled missiles that had only a payload of 500 kilgrams and had a limited range of only 70 to a 100 kilometres and that was far below the range of the Indian Agni.

The fact that Pakistan had an Islamic bomb was further also confirmed indirectly by the now ever boastful Dr Abdul Qadeer Khan, when the Indian journalist Kuldeep Nayyar had interviewed him a year or two ago. Though the propaganda campaign in Pakistan hailed Dr Abdul Qadeer Khan or AQ as he was popularly known as the father of Pakistan's nuclear projects, and the likely father of the Islamic Bomb, but that was actually not true at all. For according to Shiraz, the man who really deserved that honour was none other Dr Munir Ahmad Khan. But unlike Dr Abdul Qadeer, who always wanted to hog the limelight, Dr Munir was a quiet unassuming man who was also secretive by nature and therefore his achievements had remained unsung.

On having learnt from reliable sources that the Wah Group had been conducting such cold tests regularly inside long tunnels that had been bored deep inside the Kirana Hills at Sargodha, and that the big PAF, Pakistan Air Force base at that station had also started evolving delivery techniques of such like nuclear bombs by using thieir fast flying combat aircrafts that were based there, Shiraz was now worried. He was also in two minds whether he should put India on the alert with all his findings, but the problem was how to do it discreetly, and in a subtle manner and without raising any suspicion. After all he was a much married man with two little children and any false move by him could spell disaster for him and his family and he could be even shot as a spy and a damn a traitor That would be a disgrace to the Rehman family and could also lead to his true identity being uncovered. At the same time time he also thought that since he was not passing any top secret papers or information, but was only trying as a well wisher to warn the Indians of the nuclear and ballistic missile capabilities that Pakistan was capable of attaining in the near future, and which in turn could lead to a disastrous holocaust if both the nations decided to go in for a fourth round. And with late Zia's 'Topac Plan' for clandestinely grabbing the Kashmir Valley already in progress, the possibility of another Indo-Pak war in the near future therefore could not be ruled out. Keeping all those factors in mind, Shiraz therefore decided that he would go ahead and warn the Indians. But the question was how would he pass on this vital information and convince the Indians that it was genuine. He had once tried it earlier, when he had wrapped an anonymous letter containing some secret information in a golf ball and tossed it over the wall of the Indian High Commission office that was located at G-5, Diplomatic Enclave, Islamabad, but that may now be too risky he thought. Therefore the best way of doing it he felt was to simply ring up a responsible senior Indian diplomat from a busy public telephone telephone booth in Rawalpindi and convey whatever he had to say and in as few words as possible and without disclosing his real identity, and then leave it to the Indians to take it or lump it. Ofcourse there was every possibility that the diplomat's telephone may be bugged, but that hardly mattered as long as the call was not traced back to him. Fearing that the

Indian High Commission may have the facility to record all such telephonic conversations, Shiraz therefore decided to ring up the senior diplomat at his residence on a Sunday.

The Sunday that Shiraz chose happened to be the 4th of June, and that morning after a good round of 18 hole golf at the Rawalpindi Golf Club that was followed by a heavy breakfast of scrambled eggs on toast and fried liver, Shiraz first drove down to the Saddar Bazaar and having parked his car there, he took an autorickshaw to Raja Bazaar that was inside the old bustling city. There having found a public telephone booth that was enclosed from all sides, he made his call. Having first cautioned the Indian diplomat in a very serious tone not to ask any questions and that he wont be told no lies, Shiraz rattled off all that he had to say about Pakistan nuclear capabilities and about 'Operation Topac' in two and a half minutes flat. Despite the din of the traffic outside, the Indian diplomat kept listening to the monologue very attentively, and since it was evident that the call had been made from a public booth, and the person making it seemed to be well educated and well versed with nuclear jargon, the Indian Diplomat it seems was convinced that the caller was not playing the fool and and was a genuine well wisher. The Pakistan sponsored terrorism by proxy in Kashmir had already fired its first salvo, when the JKLF, the Jammu and Kashmir Liberation Front during the month of May launched the Quit Kashmir Movement.

CHAPTER-12

The Toppling Game Begins

That evening at around 8 PM, Shiraz feeling a little guilty on having made that call to an Indian diplomat, he tried to get it out of his chest by playing a game of monopoly with his family. And as he was about to throw the dice there was a call for him on the landline. It was a long distance call from his brother-in—law Salim Rehman in Beijing and he seemed very agitated and excited in what he had to say.

"Arre no Barkhurdar, I am not kidding at all. It is a damn fact. The Chinese troops have opened fire on their own people who have been agitating for more freedom and the Tiananmen Square demonstrations has led to a massacre of innocent people whose protests against corruption and demands for more freedom for the press it seems has fallen on deaf ears and the situation in the capital is indeed very tense indeed and more trouble is also expected as tanks and armoured cars are now patrolling the city. It all started at 10.30 PM last night and has now become a free for all for the Chinese armoured troops who have been gunning down the protestors indiscriminately. And to prove the point I have also managed to videotape a few such bizarre incidents and will send it to you threw the next diplomatic mail bag," said an excited Salim Rehman as Saira picked up the phone that was on the parallel line in the bed room and cautioned her brother to be very careful.

"My God I think the Chinese leaders have gone mad," said Saira as Shiraz narrated to her about the killings in Beijing.

"Yes, and that is what happens when power goes into ones head I guess. It was all building up gradually since mid April and the Communist leadership under Deng it seems was bent upon crushing it, but nobody and no guns can stop the power of the people and Deng should have realized it by now. The Tiananmen Square protests of 1976 had led to the ouster of the gang of four, and this may now also lead to the ouster of Deng Xiaoping,

Li Peng and other such hardliners in the party," added Shiraz as he threw in the dice and having passed 'Go' collected his 200 dollars. But when his turn came to play again and he landed in the square that said 'Go to Jail,' the saddest person was little Tojo who was partnering his father and he very aptly said that it was the the Chinese leaders who should be going to jail and not his dear father.

And it was only after a week or so and having listened to the extensive coverage that was being given daily by the BBC and the Voice of America and by the reporters of the world press and television who had seen it all happen in front of their very own eyes, did Shiraz realize that his assessment about the people's power in China to oust Deng was wrong. In fact with the crack down, the 45 days of protests and demonstrations by the students and intellectuals of China that had commenced from 16 April and kept gaining momentum had infact fizzled out rather tamely. Zhao Ziyang the General Secretary of the Party who was strongly in support of a soft approach towards the demonstrators had been removed from his post. The hardliners who had ordered the crackdown were worried that the abandonment of the single party rule would be disastrous for the country and for them such lengthy demonstrations were a threat to the very stability of the country. The crudely sculped thirty three foot high'Goddess of Democracy' statue made of styrfoam and papier-mache over a metal armature that the students of the Central Academy of Fine Arts had sculpted, and which was carried surreptously in three separate segments on three wheeler bicycle flat rickshaw carts and was erected and unveiled ceremoniously in the centre of the historic square on the morning of 30th May with shouts of 'Long Live Democracy'did draw a very large number of spectatators for the next few days, but at 1 AM on 4th June after the armed soldiers from the PLA, People's Liberation Army reached the Square and an armoured tank knocked it down, the Democracy Movement was also given the death blow. The frenzied cries of 'Down with Fascism' and 'Bandits Bandits' that were being made by the protestors only made the soldiers who had been ordered to clear the Square by 6 AM angrier. This resulted in clashes and in the deaths of many in the city. The deathly defiance of the man in a white shirt standing in front of tank on the morning of 5th June at the intersection of what was known as the Avenue of Eternal Peace that had been widely publicized by the world press and that was shown live on television by the CNN had no doubt stirred the nation and the world, but with his disappearance the morale of the students and the hunger strikers and their supporters to face the Chinese army and for the fulfillment of their demands had also vanished. The famous

Tianenmen Square that had become a shanty town and was smeared with blood was soon restored to its pristine glory, but the movement did shake the Chinese leaders and brought home to them the lesson that the Square that was known as the 'Gate of Heavenly Peace' may lead to hell if they do not initiate more economic reforms at a faster pace and give the people a better life. The world was changing, Communism was crumbling and they needed to change too thought Shiraz as he watched the video that Salim Rehman had sent to him from Beijing.

It was also on the 4th of June 1989 that Poland first hit the nail on the Communist coffin as the Solidarity Party of Lech Walecsa contesting the parliamentary elections for the first time routed the Communists by capturing 99 out of the 100 available seats and thus heralded the dawn of a new democratic era and the death knell for their communist ruled neigbours of the Eastern Bloc.

While the Cold War between the two rival blocs was about to end in Europe, the transfer of Lt General Hamid Gul from the ISI to command a Corps, and the appointment by Benazir of retired Major General Shamsur Rehman Kallue in his place had now triggered off another kind of cold war between the senior generals of the Pakistan army and Benazir's young and newly formed coalition government that was still trying to find its feet in the murky and cut throat world of Pakistani politics. Even the Army Chief General Mirza Aslam Beg who was primarily responsible to bring back democracy to the country felt peeved, when the powerful post of the head of Pakistan intelligence was given to a retired Major General. Lt General Hamid Gul who was aspiring to become the next chief initially blamed the Americans for the change over and the rift between her and the three service chiefs grew even wider, when she wanted to have Admiral Sirohey removed from his position as Chairman of the Joint Chiefs of Staff Committee and have him replaced by her own man. But this was beyond her perogative and as per the constitution only the President was empowered to dismiss or appoint Generals and Admirals. But Benazir it seems was adamant to have her own way and this led to a long stand off between her and the President also. The army was worried that if she had her own way and got away with this act, a precedent would be set and by which she would be able to then sideline all those senior officers whom she was suspicious off and have them replaced by her own trusted favourites. The very fact that Benazir at her very first press conference after taking her oath had pledged to abrogate the eighth amendment, which would curtail the powers of the President had made President Ghulam Ishaq Khan wary of her intentions.

He did not wish to become just another figure head or a rubber stamp president. There were also unconfirmed reports or rather rumours of the likelihood of some elements from within the ISI who were reportedly close to the deposed DGISI and Nawab Sharif were plotting to destabilize the Benazir government by buying off a big chunk of the elected members in the National Assemby from her own party and bring down her coalition government.

"But don't you think that will be rather unfair to the young woman Prime Minister who has been elected democratically. She should atleast be given a fair chance to prove herself and if this rumour is true then God help Pakistan," said an angry Ruksana Begum as she helped herself to some more of the 'Bhel Puri' that little Shezadi had especially made for her loving Nanni.

"Well as the saying goes all is fair in love and war and as far as horse trading with hard cash is concerned, it entirely depends upon how much one is willing to pay for someone to change his colour and side. It is like buying potatoes and onions from the market where rates change daily and our polticians I regret to say are no better than a sack of lousy potatoes who don't even know their damn onions," said Arif Rehman somewhat sarcastically as he helped little Tojo to tie his shoe laces and then got ready to play indoor cricket with him.

"'But Abbajaan wasn't Benazir's father the man who was responsible for creating a political cell in the ISI in order to closely monitor the activities of the opposition thereby giving a domestic role to them and which Zia very conveniently and cleverly manipulated during his rule?" asked Saira.

"Yes you are very right my dear, and now it has come to stay. And this will carry on irrespective of who controls the reins. And I regret to say that our politicians today are more worried about their own damn chairs and how to make a quick buck, than to legislate in the interest of the nation. They simply care two hoots for those who elected them and will change sides at the drop of a hat. These turn coats and pardon my saying so will even sell their mothers and sisters too for that extra buck," said Shiraz as Saira seeing her husband's belligerent mood tried to calm him down.

"But come to think of it what Shiraz has stated is quite correct, because even after 40 years of independence, the poor people of this country forget about getting two, but they cannot even get one square meal a day, and I won't blame just the politicians for it. The big businessmen, the bureaucrats and even the generals who ruled this country were all hand in glove in bringing about this sorry state of affairs and therefore they are equally to be blamed for the dirty mess that we are in today," said Ruksana Begum as she like a dutiful grandmother showed Shezadi the finer points of knitting a sweater for Lara, her favorite giant size Russian doll.

Meanwhile in Sri Lanka with President Premadasa putting on the political pressure and the heat on the IPKF to quit and go back to India, and with ugly rumours circulating that he had even opened up secret channels to arm the LTTE to fight the Indians, Shupriya in Colombo wondered whether more innocent Indian soldiers will be sacrificed for the stupid adventure that the Rajiv Gandhi government had undertaken quite unneccasarily as a so called peace keeping mission. As it is the Rajiv Gandhi government was in a big fix because the Bofors gun scandal was now practically out in the open and by now had done enough damage to his reputation as a so called 'Mr Clean'. Added to that with the Sri Lanka-India accord turning out to be an utter disaster and one that would be a veritable tragedy for him if he pulled out the IPKF under such threatening circumstances as was being demanded by new Sri Lankan President, the credibility of young Indian Prime Minister was also now at stake. According to one reliable source President Premadasa had even ordered his army generals to throw the Indian forces out of Sri Lanka and in response to that Lt General AS Kalkat had warned that the IPKF would retaliate if fired upon by the Sri Lankan forces. Therefore, with Rajiv Gandhi refusing to withdraw the IPKF and Premadasa insisting that the IPKF must get out of his country at the earliest, the Indian army who had sacrificed so many lives was now put in a very embarrassing position. It was like a Catch 22 situation for the Rajiv government because if India pulled out the IPKF then it would be considered a big diplomatic failure, and if the IPKF remained in Sri Lanka against the wishes of the Sri Lankan government, then not only would it be condemned and branded as an army of occupation, but it could also face the wrath of both the LTTE and the regular Sri Lankan armed forces. It was therefore a no win situation as far as India was concerned. Added to that the Rajiv government was already reeling by the incriminating disclosures and documentary proofs that Chitra Subramanium had been constantly unearthing from time to time and these were now making the headlines practically every other day. As it is the new DMK government led by Karunanidhi in Tamil Nadu with their anti IPKF stance was proving to be a hindrance to the whole military operation in Sri Lanka and Shupriya now wondered whether all the sacrificies made by the Indian army and the colossal amount of money spent was worth the effort. According to her assessment the Indo-Sri Lankan accord had achieved nothing at all. It was an all round failure diplomatically, politically, economically and to some extent even militarily and she therefore now feared that the LTTE that was nurtured by India with the active involvement of the RAW that had trained and armed them would now look for support from elsewhere. As it is they were feeling let down by Rajiv and his government and therefore the possibility of the LTTE supreme Prabhakaran taking his revenge someday on the Indian Prime Minister could not be ruled out.

With all those thoughts racing through her mind, Shupriya wrote a long letter to Peevee. The letter was nothing but a resume of the sacrifices that young Indian army officers and jawans who had laid down their lives for the honour and integrity of the country eversince the day India got her independence. Major Somnath Sharma the first recipient of India's highest gallantry award, the Param Veer Chakra was only in his early twenties and so were Arun Kheterpal, Albert Ekka and Major Shiraz Ismail Khan who was just 25. As a mother Shupriya was a little apprehensive about her son's ambition to become a Bollywood actor and a singing star. There was nothing wrong in making that as a profession, but one had to be indeed lucky to reach stardom. The careers of the super stars like Amitabh Bachchan, Uttam Kumar, Dilip Kumar, Sanjeev Kumar and such others like him did not bloom overnight. They had to really struggle and at times struggle hard to prove themselves till the public made them icons of the tinsel world. In fact she wanted Peevee to join the army as an officer. That was a noble and honourable career and though it did not bring in much money but it had its own lifestyle of glamour, pomp and show and bullshit as some called it. But then she was still his mom number two and could only give a hint and it was upto Peevee to decide what he wanted to do with his life. He was soon going to be eighteen and she therefore left it to him to chalk out his own career path.

Meanwhile in India with the Bofors stink of corruption polluting the nation and the amateurish manner by which the Rajiv Gandhi's government was trying to cover it up gave the members of the opposition in the Indian Parliament a longer and harder stick to beat the government with. The Monsoon session was soon to begin and the oppsition now had all their guns trained on the Prime Minister. In that month of July 1989, Shanti Bhushan a former Law Minister and an eminent constitutional lawyer had written to the President of India seeking his permission to prosecute Rajiv Gandhi under a relevant section of the 'Prevention of Corruption Act, 1947', but the new President R Venkataraman in his reply citing the clause that the advice tendered by the Council of Ministers to the President could not be enquired into by any court had rejected it. And on 19th July 1989, when the CAG's, the Comptroller Auditor General's report was tabled in Parliament, it shook the nation like a devastating earthquake. The report by TN Chaturvedi, the CAG had blown a large hole in the stand that was taken both by the government and by the Joint Parliamentary Committee that the government had convened for the very purpose of getting to the truth. The CAG report now revealed that the government's warning to the various companies that were competing for the contract to eliminate agents in the howitzer deal referred to only Indian Agents and no information was sought on agents who could have been living abroad and working for the lucrative contract. And as a result of this 319.4 million Swedish Kroners as a settlement of commission following the signing of the deal were paid to three companies that were not domiciled in India. The report also questioned the technical and final assessment of the Bofors offer thereby refuting the government's claim that the guns were bought at the lowest possible price. Moreover the Indian Army Headquarters on six occassions between the period December 1982 and October 1985 had given its preference for the French Sofna gun, but in February 1986, the Army Headquarters revised its preference and on 14th March the letter of intent was given to Bofors and on 24th March, 1986 the contract was signed. But till as late as October 1988, the Bofors had not even supplied a full regiment's worth of guns. The CAG report further castigated the government by mentioning that the rules had been flouted, procedures had been bypassed and the credit terms had also been bent in favour of the supplier. Morever, the detailed project report was submitted by Bofors only in April 1987 and that was also a good nine months after it was due.

With more ammunition fodder in their hands, the opposition now demanded the immediate resignation of the Rajiv Gandhi government. According to them with the indictment that was made by the CAG in his report, the Rajiv Gandhi government had forfeited its right to rule and on 23rd July 1989, 106 members of the Lok Sabha, India's Lower House of Parliament belonging to the non Congress (I) decided to quit the house. There were still five months for the government to complete its full five year term, but the combined opposition were now adamant to bring it down. Electing VP Singh as their star leader the major opposition parties therefore decided to join hands and waited for an opportunity to give the final knock out punch to the Congress led Rajiv Gandhi government.

But on 20th August 1989, when the Kuwait based 'Arab Times' published a sensational story alleging that the Janata Dal leader, VP Singh was the main beneficiary of a secret bank account with deposits amounting to US dollars 21 million which was held in a bank in St Kitts, a small island in the far away Carribean Sea, and the story was promptly picked up by the Indian media, Monty smelt a rat. He just could not believe that VP Singh who had always been shouting against corruption in the Rajiv Gandhi's government could have been a beneficiary from the ill gotten Bofors deal also.

"May be this could be a ploy by someone outside, but who is close to the Indian government to belittle the Janata Dal leader and take some of the steam out from the on going Bofors scandal that had tarnished the name of the Congress and their leader Rajiv Gandhi. Or it also could be a tit for tat that has probably been cleverly engineered by the Rajiv Gandhi government with help from outside,"thought Monty as he tried to contact Unnikrishnan, his correspondent friend from the Press Trust of India to throw some more light on it. But unfortunately Unni had gone home to his village in south India and was incommunicado and was expected back in Delhi only by the second week of September.

And on 26th September, 1989 when AP Nandy a Deputy Director in the Enforcement Directorate was appointed to probe into what the government had now termed as the St Kitts scandal involving VP Singh and his son Ajeya Singh, it was evident to Monty that come what may the Rajiv Gandhi government it seems was now out to fix the ex Finance Minister of India who had switched sides. Therefore when within a fortnight after visiting the bank in St Kitts, Nandy submitted his report to the government and the government in turn without wasting any more time tabled the report first in the Rajya Sabha on the 11th of October, and then followed it up two days later by presenting it to the Lok Sabha, Unni was convinced and told Monty that the report was nothing but a cock and bull story that had possibly been concocted by the government to belittle the opposition leader and his family. But it looked that the government was already cornered as far as the Bofors issue was concerned because on 9th October 1989, 'The Hindu' had already landed its knock out punch. On that day the paper had published in facsimile form the Swedish National Audit Bureau Report which both the Swedish government in collusion with the Rajiv Gandhi government had kept suppressed for two long years. The secret part of that explosive report revealed that the Bofors payments were entirely proven commission payments to companies/accounts in Switzerland and those were all in relation to the Bofors FH-77 deal. And the report further added that these payments unquestionably related to this business and was based on the fact that this had been communicated in writing by AB Bofors to the Bank of Sweden.

With the dye having being cast, Rajiv Gandhi's own credibility and those of his friends and others who were helping to cover up the Bofors scam was given a further resounding blow, when three Indian leading newspapers, the Hindu, the Indian Express and the Statesman on 31st October, 1989 published excerpts from Martin Ardbo's 1987 private diary. The entry of 2nd July 1987 in that explosive diary mentioning that Ardbo had met the Gandhi Trustee lawyer was very revealing and damaging too for the ruling party who had kept denying their leader's role in the deal. And a week later, when Mr Ram of the Hindu released the transcript of his April 1988 conversation with GP Hinduja, and in which Hinduja claimed that he knew who the real recipients of the kickbacks were, but he could not reveal it in national interest, Monty in order to get more definitive and authentic inputs on the subject immediately contacted Unni at the Press Club of India. That 31st October 1989 was also the fifth death anniversary of Mrs Gandhi and on that day, when the Ardbo diary revelations made headlines in the Indian Press, the death knell of Rajiv's government was also sounded. And following the Hinduja transcript, the Indian Defence Minister KC Pant who was a key player in the Bofors cover up therefore very cleverly announced that he would be opting out of the coming general elections that was due in December.

At the Press Club of India as Monty with his chilled beer in hand kept listening to Unnikrishnan's deep analytical appreciation of the Bofors scandal and its subsequent cover up, and who were the likely culprits who had taken those hefty kickbacks, he was convinced that though Rajiv and his family may not have received the cheques in their individual names, but the involvement of the Prime Minister in giving Bofors the lucrative contract, and then trying to cover it up could not be denied or simply wished away. He was ubdoubtedly the main player in not only finalizing the deal, but also in trying to cover it up in a ham handed manner after the Swedish Radio broadcast on 16th April, 1987 had blown the first whistle alleging hefty underhand payments had been made by Bofors to Indian politicians and government officials for the multi-million dollar arms contract. And as Unni chronologically brought out the facts while collaborating them with what Chitra Subranamium had been revealing from time to time through the press, Monty was more than convinced that Rajiv Gandhi, the PMO and the Congress(I) were all hand in glove in the deal and that they were now trying desperately to hoodwink the nation. So while Unni in his own lucid style that was laced with humour gave a short resume on how it had all started and added to that his own personal assessment on the likelihood of who took how much and why, and then followed it up by his own critical analysis as to what made the two governments of Sweden and India so frantically to run for cover, Monty kept listening to him with awe.

According to Unni's version, it all started when Rajiv and Palme first met at the United Nations headquarters in New York in the autumn of 1985. By then the French Sofna gun was India's first choice and Bofors who had also bid for the big billion dollar contract were it seems now out of the race. But for Olaf Palme getting that lucrative contract would have meant not only giving a new life to the failing and dying Bofors arms industry, but it would also give a strong fillip both to his own political party and also enhance his image as a socialist leader. Palme's promise therefore to Rajiv that Sweden was willing to offer the gun at the lowest possible price and also give a few pieces as gratis and without any middlemen in the deal as Rajiv had desired had got the Bofors back to the negotiating table. There was no doubting the fact that till then Bofors like any other arms manufacturer had their agents already working on the deal and there were two of them. At the lower government level it was Win Chaddha's 'Anatronics Corporation,', while at the higher political and bureaucratic level to swing the deal and if it was at all necessary to do so they had Pitco of the Hindujas as their representatives. The Hindujas were past masters in this game and with their clout and and their agents they were always at the right place and at the right time to swing such deals. They were already in this business as they had already helped Bofors in selling their arms clandestinely to Iran during the Iraq-Iran war and also to some other countries. But with the Rajiv government, the four Hinduja brothers were practically persona non grata and Bofors therefore desparately needed someone in Delhi to push the deal through at the earliest and that is how Rajiv and Sonia Gandhi's good Italian friend Octtavi Qattarocchi was probably roped in. His close proximity to the Gandhi family was already well known and the Snam Progetti man whose clout in government circles could even make or break a senior bureaucrat or even a junior minister was it seems the right choice to broker the deal. But whether this choice was brokered by the Hindujas or by Rajiv Gandhi himself is difficult to tell. The Italian wheeler dealer was already well known in the Indian government circles both in the north and south blocks for swinging such deals for his own chemical fertilizer giant, and he therefore probably jumped into it most obligingly. The Hindujas and Win Chaddha as per the government of India's requirement were therefore sidelined thus adhering to India's demand of no Indian middlemen. So Bofors to ensure that the billion dollar deal did not fall through at any stage and that it would be in their hands not later than 31st March, 1986, when the Indian financial year was scheduled to close, they therefore very cleverly signed the 3 percent commission contract with the sunset clause of no deal-no pay with AE Services. This was a shady foreign based company that Qattarochi had hurriedly floated with a bank account at the Nordfinanz Bank in Switzerland. Thus technically the clause that no 'Indian' middleman would be involved in the deal was also met.

"Now as per the documentary proof that Chitra Subramanium and the Hindu had unearthed and as per Bofors own declaration, tha Arms Company had paid SEK 319 million to three non-Indian companies that they admitted were domiciled out of India. But these payments of SEK 188, 81 and 50 million respectively Bofors said were made to terminate their consultancy agreements as was desired by the government of India and they were thus paid off prior to the signing of the contract in March 1986 as winding up charges. But this was now proved to be a blatant lie, when the Hindu published that these payments were made soon after the deal was signed and was paid as commissions to the 'Pitco-Moresco-Lotus—Mont Blanc-Tulip accounts of the Hindujas, the Svenska Incorporated account of Win Chaddha and to the AE Services account of Mr Qattarocchi in Swiss Banks. In fact the SEK 50 million amounting to 7.3 million US dollars was paid to Major Wilson who was Qattarocchis front man in AE Services on 11th September, 1986 and was depositied in the company's Nordfinanz Bank account in Zurich, Switzerland. This had been admitted by Bob Wilson himself," said Unni as he showed the various paper cuttings from the Hindu that he had in his satchel and ordered one more rum and water for himself.

"Well if that be the case then why is the poor Prime Minister's name being dragged in everytime? asked Monty.

"Well it is simply because he is being stupidly advised and because he has been denying his total involvement in the deal at every damn stage. And even when these bare facts were staring him at his face, he kept opening his big mouth. You see eversince that Swedish broadcast of April 1986, he has been tying himself into knots and now that very rope is hanging around his own neck. One lie had led to another and then the cover up began with the Hundujas playing the key role in it. And since their services for the cover up were badly needed, they were therefore probably now in the good books of the Gandhis and the Indian government," added Unni somewhat sarcastically as he chronologically and step by step analysed how the deal had been made and till it became a national scandal and a cover up that was even worse than America's 'Watergate'.

"The Boforsgate as I now call it gave its first stink when Win Chadda soon after the deal was signed on 24th March, 1986 threw a lavish party at the luxury five star Hotel Maurya in Delhi and where the posters that day blatantly read 'Win Wins Again.'. And at that party, when Win Chada also openly boasted to his many guests and I also happened to be one of them, and he proudly declared that his family for generations had now been set up and that they had nothing more to worry for their future, he had inadvertently let the cat out of the bag. But by now such deals by the government of India was common place and nobody cared a hang till the Swedish Radio on that Good Friday of April 1987 made that sensational revelation of big money having changed hands to get the contract. And thereafter as more true facts started tumbling out of the cupboard, and the Rajiv government foolishly kept blaming it on the foreign hand, I knew that the government was trying to hide something. And to add to that, when the Prime Minister himself by his many pronouncements and actions started shielding the deal at every stage and reiterating quite uneccassarily that neither he nor any members of his family were involved in getting a cut, it was quite evident that he had more than a major role to play in trying to prove his innocence,"said Unni as he took out his note book and made a Bofors scandal tree together with the ham handed manner in which the Prime Minister himself and his staff at the PMO tried to cover it up.

"In mid November 1985, and soon after AE Services had been roped in to ensure that the the deal must be finalised by 31st March 1986 and failing which they would loose their three percent commission, the procurement of the Bofors gun for the Indian Army was put into high gear. And in January 1986, when Palme the Swedish Prime Minister made his semi-official trip to Delhi and met Rajiv Gandhi and gave him his assurance that no middleman would be involved in the deal, the Defence Ministry in Delhi now also got into top gear to give Bofors the top slot. Till December 1986, the Army Headquarters had given their preference to the French Sofna gun, but on the plea that the Bofors were now willing to reduce their prices and also give 10 guns as gratis, the Defence Minsitry decided to do a quick about turn and give the contract to Bofors. With the sudden assassination of the Swedish Prime Minsiter in February 1987, Rajiv Gandhi flew to Stockholm for the funeral of his departed friend and later when he called on the new Swedish Prime Minister and the two once again agreed that there will be no middlemen in the deal, the ball was once again set rolling and that to at a much faster pace. Immediately after Rajiv's return from the funeral, the Bofors file now started moving at lightining speed in the concerned ministry and on the 24ᵗʰ of March, and just one week before the 31ˢᵗ March 1986 deadline, the contract was signed and sealed. And it was all very honky dory till the Swedish Radio and media in April 1987 burst the bubble. On that Good Friday after the Swedish Radio on 16ᵗʰ April, 1987 had made that sensational broadcast, Mr BM Oza the Indian Ambassador to Sweden who was on a short Easter holiday with his family in England was immediately ordered by the PMO's office to return to Stockholm and he was instructed to get a denial both by the Swedish government and Bofors that no hush money had been paid to anybody on the deal. That was the first knee jerk panic reaction by the PMO's office, and when a week later on 22ⁿᵈ April, the influential Swedish daily Dagens Nyheter quoting sources in Bofors top management alleged that the Hndujas had been paid commissions on the deal, it gave another twist to the story and people were convinced that it probably was true because by then the HDW submarine scandal had also surfaced and VP Singh the Defence Minsiter had ordered a court of inquiry into it. The Defence Secretary Mr SK Bhatnagar who was to head that inquiry had in his noting on the HDW file on 9ᵗʰ April had also said that the Indian agent in that HDW deal was probably the Hindujas. And to make matters even worse, when the Swedish radio broadcast on 13ᵗʰ May, 1987 said that the Bofors contract that was signed by all the concerned parties had a clause that Bofors would pay three percent commission of the total amount for the contract, it took the government of India by complete surprise and they vehemently denied it. The government of India it seems had not done their homework properly because though the main contract of some 100 odd pages did not have such a clause, but there were a thousand pages of several appendices that were attached to it and it was in one of those appendices that the clause in fine print had figured. By now a panic stricken PMO had already started their propaganda campaign by telling the nation that some foreign hand were trying to destabilize the nation and which ofcourse nobody in the media world nor I was willing to believe. Thus smelling a rat and that there was something indeed very fishy about the deal, some enterprising journalists from the media world like Chitra Subramanium, N Ram and yours truly with their own contacts in the government and elsewhere started probing a little deeper into it. Likewise the opposition parties too got into the act when they started demanding that the government must come out with the truth,"said Unni as he took out a few photo copies of some important notings that he had procured from his friends in the government.

"No but I just can't believe it that the Prime Minister could be so naïve in his judgement,"said Monty as he read aloud to himself the noting that General Sundarjee as the Army Chief and Arun Singh in his capacity as the Minister of State for Defence had sent to the Prime Minister through Mr KC Pant the Defence Minister and which subsequently led to Arun Singh resigning from his office on 18th July 1987. An extract from the note by Army Chief dated 13th June 1987 read as follows. 'In the interest of vindicating National Honour we should apply full pressure on Bofors to part with the information needed for legal action against the culprits and accept the risk that this might in the worst case lead to a cancellation of the contract.'The noting by Arun Singh that was dated 10th June, 1987 and one which was approved and endorsed by his immediate boss the Defence Minister KC Pant was even more lucid and it stated. 'We as GOI, Government of India must pursue this matter to a logical conclusion. The Indian Ambassador in Sweden should be instructed to inform both the Swedish government and the company that unless they give the information we want, we will have no alternative but to cancel the contract for the FH 77B 155 mm Howitzers. I am fully cognizant of the fact that this cancellation will have some negative impact on our defence preparedness, but you may like to reconfirm with the COAS (Chief of Army Staff) whether we can live with that. In my view we must be prepared to go to this extent of cancellation because our very credibility as a government is at stake and what is worse the credibility of the entire process of defence acquisitions is also at stake.'

"And now look what our Prime Minister had to say in his reply to Arun Singh's noting,"said Unni as he took another paper, which was also a photocopy and gave it to Monty to read. That noting though it was dated 15th June 1987, it however looked that it had been probably antedated in order to cover up the Prime Minister's embarrassment over his good friend Arun Singh's parting of ways with him on the scandalous Bofors issue because Arun Singh's resigned only after a month of his having sent that noting to the Prime Minister and to which the Prime Minister replied rather curtly like a school teacher reprimanding an erring student who had not done his homework. And this is what the Prime Minister wrote. 'It is unfortunate that the Minsiter of State has put his personal prestige above the security of the nation before even evaluating all aspects. I appreciate his feelings as he had been dealing with Defense almost completely on his own and with my support, but that is not adequate reason to be ready to compromise the security of the nation. Has he evaluated the actual position vis-à-vis security? Has he evaluated the financial loss of a cancellation? Has he evaluated the degree of breach of contract by Bofors, if any? Has he evaluated the consequences for all future defence contracts if we cancel a contract unilaterally? Has he evaluated how the rival manufacturers will behave in the future? Has he evaluated how GOI prestige will plummet if we unilaterally cancel a contract that has not been violated? To the best of my belief the Swedish Audit report upholds GOI's position and does not contradict it. What we need to do is to get to the roots and find out what precisely has been happening and who all are involved. Kneejerk reactions and stomach cramps will not serve any purpose. RRM, the Rahtriya Raksha Mantri has run the ministry fairly well but there is no need to panic, especially if one's conscience is clear.'

"Well if his own conscience was clear then where was the need for him to convene the JPC?" asked Monty.

"Exactly, it was because his own conscience was not clear and to save his own skin and that of his own family and his Congress (I) Party, he had to do something to prove that he was innocent, and what better way to do it than to get his own pliant members of parliament from his own party and a handful from the opposition whose palms were probably greased to bail him out so called honourably," added Unni as he took out a copy of the JPC report and on which Monty noticed that it had the word "Bullshit !" written on the top in block capital letters.

"You see this idea of convening a JPC by the Prime Minister was triggered off when the Swedish Public Prosecutor Lars Ringburg started contemplating to carry out a criminal investigation into the sleazy Bofors-India deal and this had really jolted the Prime Minister very badly. And on 19th August 1987, when the Swedish Public prosecutor sent a formal communication to the CBI asking for its cooperation, the CBI Chief Mr Mohan Khatre was specifically told by the PMO's office not to even acknowledge that request. Thereafter in order to ensure that the Swedish Prosecutor did not come out with his report, the Prime Minister sent Mr Natwar Singh, the ex IFS officer who was now the Minister of State in the Ministry of External Affairs to Stockholm to have it scuttled at all costs. It was a very lucrative contract and the Swedish government therefore was not willing to lose it either, so they too decided to play ball. So giving the excuse that since no evidence was forthcoming from either government, the Swedish prosecutor simply raised his hands. But let me also tell you that before the Swedish prosecuter raised his hands, there was another interesting development that made the Prime Minister chicken out. On the 3rd of July 1987, when the Vice President of Bofors intimated to the Indian government that the Swedish firm was ready to send no less a person than Anders Carlberg the Chairman of the Nobel Group of Industries and a few other senior officials and that they would come and give further details of the payments, Arun Singh gladly accepted the offer. The team was scheduled to arrive on 6th July, but on 4th July when Rajiv returned from his Moscow trip and was told about it, he panicked. That very evening Rajiv held an emergency meeting in his house and it was attended by Arun Singh, Mr Bhatnagar the Defence Secretary and by NN Vohra the Additional Secretary Defence, and when Arun Singh's decision of getting the Bofors team over was immediately turned down by the Prime Minister, Arun Singh to it seems had smelt a rat. For Rajiv Gandhi to have the Bofors officials coming and disclosing the names and details of the payments that had been made by them as commissions for striking the deal would be like putting his own head, his family's head and that of his Italian friend Quattarocchi and his own Congress Party squarely on the chopping block. Though his personal name and those of his family members he knew may not directly feature in that list, but the other names if they were revealed by the Swedes would be nothing less than a catastrophe for him and his government. Not only the opposition, but the entire country too would chew him and his party up like this," said Unni as took another big bite of the the tender and delicious chicken lollipop to demonstrate what he meant.

"By God and I must say that you deserve nothing less than a Padma Bhushan, but that won't certainly be under the present government," said Monty as he ordered another chilled beer.

"Then in September 1987, when the small coterie around Rajiv Gandhi, and which included powerful senior bureaucrats like Gopi Arora, S K Bhatnagar, NN Vohra and a few others met the Bofors officials secretly and coached them on how to depose before the JPC and what to say and what not to say, it was quite evident that the government was bent upon covering the whole thing up by hook or by crook," added Unni as he looked at the bar clock and signaled the barman for his last drink.

"But since Rajiv was repeatedly saying that he and his family was in no way involved in getting any commission from this deal, then where was the damn need for him to play this cat and mouse game ?" asked Monty.

"Because as the saying goes guilty conscience pricks the mind and there is no doubt in my mind that the man was guilty because he despite the advice of his close friend and colleague Arun Singh and the Army Chief to scrap the deal unless the Bofors came out with the names declined to do so by giving the lame excuse that the country's security was at stake. However the real fact was that his own existence and credibility and that of his family, his close friend Qattarocchi and his other friends and colleagues in the PM's office and inside the Congress Party were also at stake. Just imagine the man had even forsaken his old friendship with Arun Singh for the sake of that damn gun and he was now even willing to catch any straw to save his own damn skin," added Unni as he ordered for another plate of the succulent chicken lollipop.

"But I still can't believe that the Prime Minister could be so naïve in his judgement. And what do you think he will do now ?" asked Monty as the barman put another large Old Monk Rum into Unni's glass, while Monty very minutely went through the excerpts from Martin Ardbo's diary that the Hindu had published.

"Well if you study the entries in the diary and relate it to the corresponding dates on which they were written by Ardbo and that too in such a childish manner that even a high school boy having knowledge about this case would have easily deciphered as to who was who, then you will find that it all adds up to the gun now pointing squarely towards Rajiv, his Italian friend Quattarocchi and the Congress (I). So you can now very well see and deduce for yourself that since the day the Swedish radio blew the whistle, Rajiv and his coterie at every stage tried their level best to scuttle the investigations. They simply did not want the truth to surface and they all kept on telling all kinds of lies and for what. It was only to save one person's skin and isnt that a real shame,",id Unni.

"Shame? That is a gross understatement my friend. It is a bloody Maha shame and especially for the man who the people of India had so overwhelmingly voted for as a leader and the future of this country," said Monty somewhat in disgust.

"Yes and that unfortunately today is what politicians and politics is all about in this country. And if you frankly ask me the country does not deserve the motto 'Satya Mein Ho Jayate'(Let Truth Prevail).'n fact it should now be changed immediately to "Jhoot Mein Hai Jayate'(Let Lies Prevail). And as far as your question on what the Prime Minister should do now? I think the only course of action for him would be to either take the blame for the inept manner in which the case had been handled by him and his government, apologise to the people and gracefully resign. At the same time he can call for fresh elections, but this scandal will haunt him and his Congress party for years to come and his chances of making a quick comeback I am afraid is therefore rather doubtful. But you never know with our Indian mentality of forgive and forget he may still do so like his mother had done, but for the time being he has burnt his boats. And if he knows what is good for him, he should lie low on the Bofors issue because the more he tries to prove his innocence, the more flak will he get. Because one thing is for sure, he cannot become Mr Clean again," concluded Unni as he did a bottoms up with whatever little was left in his glass and then requested Monty to drop him home in his car.

Later that night with the Ardbo diary entries in his hand, Monty tried to visualize as to why the big Swede firstly needed to keep and maintain such an explosive diary. There was no doubt in Monty's mind what those few alphabets and names stood for. The main players 'R' and 'Q'" undoubtedly stood for Rajiv and his Italian friend Quattarochi. 'Nero' stood for Arun Nehru, 'Hansons" were the Hinduja brothers. 'GPH' was Gopi Chand Hinduja. Bae was probably Bob Wilson of AE Services because as per the diary entry of 30th Janury, 1987 Ardbo had met GPH and Bae in London on that day. But it was the entry of 2nd July, 1987 in which Ardbo mentioned that Bob Wilson had met Gandhi's trustee lawyer in Geneva is what had got Monty thinking. Bob Wilson was Quattarocchis front man and his meeting Gandhi's trustee lawyer in Switzerland could only make sense if money was required to change hands and Ardbo was propably witness to it. As per his diary and record, Ardbo was in Geneva on 1st July therefore he too must have met that illusive Gandhi trustee lawyer also. By 2nd July 1987, the Bofors scandal stories was bursting at the seams in India and having been put in a corner so that the deal should not be scrapped the Swedish team led by the Chairman of the Nobel Industries were also planning to visit India on the 6th of July and they were willing to give the name of the recipients. This could have therefore prompted the meeting of Ardbo with the Gandhi trustee lawyer so as to ensure that the Gandhi name does not in anyway figure or gets linked to the payments that Bofors had made to the Swiss Banks. Or maybe those entries were made by Ardbo since he feared that he too could be prosecuted in his own country for violating Swedish laws on the terms and conditions for such sales. Another revealing entry in the Ardbo's diary that stated very categorically that Q's involvement may be a problem because of his closeness to 'R' had also got Monty thinking. There was no doubt in his mind that 'Q' was Quattarochhi and 'R' was Rajiv and that did substantiate the role Q had played in swinging the deal for Bofors.

Next morning, when Monty discussed the entries in the Ardbo diary that had already started making waves in the capital with his wife Reeta and also told her what Unni had conveyed to him the previous night about his own contention that the SEK 50 million that was equivalent to 7.1 Million US Dollars was most likely the political payoff that was made to secure the billion dollar contract, Reeta immediately agreed. According to her perception that payment to AE Services and of which Quattarochhi was unquestionably the boss was thereafter probably split three ways and with a equal share going to the Gandhi's, the Quattarochhis and to the Congress Party coffers as beneficiaries, or else why should the name of the Gandhi trustee feature in the diary, she argued. Therefore by doing that and sharing the loot equally they would not only be happy individually but it would also help if need be in protecting each other's backsides and that of the Congress Party too. But these are my own personal views and I may be wrong," added Reeta as she poured a second cup of tea for her husband. But, Monty who was still not convinced by Reeta's logic said.

"But it is also quite possible that by feeling the heat that the controversy had generated since July 1987, Rajiv may have decided to forfeit his share and give it to the party instead and that is where the trustee lawyer's role came in I guess. Because by doing so he would also ensure that the Congress (I) party members remained loyal to the Gandhi family in future too and his own image was not sullied further," added Monty.

"My God you have now started thinking like Sherlock Holmes, but for heaven's sake please don't carry on giving publicity to this angle because one never knows what may happen tomorrow," said Reeta.

"But I am only conjecturing," said Monty as Peevee's booming loud voice was heard from the adjoining room. He was seriously rehearsing his role in the new Hindi play 'Unche Log' that his college was to stage for the inter college Hindi drama competition that evening.

"Oye Paape subah subah zara ahista bol. Ek Italian ne tho Rajiv Gandhi ka kunda karwa diya aur hamare Italian padosan ki Biwi tumhara unchi awaaz sun kar phir ek aur written complaint bhej degha." (Please it is still very early in the morning therefore do not rehearse so very loudly. As it is one Italian has got Rajiv Gandhi in a fix and if you dont lower your voice, our Italian neighbour's wife will send me another complaint for noise pollution) said Monty with a smile as Peevee came out of his room bowed his head in respect and said a very good morning to the two of them.

A few days later feeling totally cornered like a lion in a cage, but before any more further damage could be done to his reputation and credibility by the smoking Bofors gun, Rajiv Gandhi tendered his government's resignation to the President and called for fresh general elections in the country. In that second week of November 1989, while India was busy preparing to conduct her forthcoming general elections, Monty arrived in West Berlin with another big consignment of Kashmiri carpets that his client and old friend Herr Gunther had especially ordered for the coming Christmas festive season. On that very evening Herr and Frauline Gunther feeling very happy and satisfied with their order decided to take Monty out to dinner to one of the more sophisticated restaurants in West Berlin and one that also had a live band and cabarets as added attractions. While they were on their way to the restaurant and having heard that the Sovier leader Mikhail Gorbachev had visited East Germany only two days ago to mark the 40th anniversary of the German Democratic Republic, and with the current revolutionary wave that was sweeping across the Soviet Union and in the other communist countries of Central and Eastern Europe, Monty asked. Fraulein Gunther.

"Tell me Fraulein, I believe some of your family members including your maternal Uncle and a few others are still in East Germany, but with this new wave of glasnost and liberalization now being advocated by Comrade Gorbachev do you think that such families like yours who have been separated for no fault of their own for so many years will once again be reunited. And is it possible in the near future that your dream to once again see a united Germany will come true?"

"Well if they have an open referendum today and both sides are allowed to vote without fear, then I am sure we will all overwhelmingly vote for one unified Germany. But with Comrade Honecker and other commies like him on the other side of the wall that will be like commiting suicide for those damn pigs. They simply want to hold on to their power and are not bothered about anything else. Their so called brand of socialism under the Soviet umbrella has been an utter failure and even Gotbachev has admitted that it was now time for change. As it is the East Germans are fed up with the strangle hold that the Communist Party has had on them for the past 40 years and they want to break that shackle, but they are not being allowed to do so unfortunately," said the angry Fraulein as she pointed out on a tourist map her late maternal grandparent's house inside East Berlin.

"Yes she is damn well right. These so called pseudo commies have ruined the economy of East Germany and if given the chance the common people from the other side would like to run away and come to the west right now. And mind you eversince the nation and Berlin got divided by the super powers after the war, some two and a half million if not more of East Germans have already crossed over to the west and more are also waiting to do so. Therefore, in order to check that outflow of labour and blue collar workers migrating in droves and crossing the border, Comrade Ulbricht was forced to erect that ugly wall which aptly symbolizes the 'Cold War,' said Herr Gunther.

"Unfortunately I never got a chance to visit East Germany and I wonder what kind of a life do they have on the other side of the wall," said Monty expressing his desire to one day visit that part of Berlin too.

"Well if you are really keen to have a glimpse of it, then I suggest let us first go to Café Adler'for a drink,"said the burly jovial German as they took the road towards 'Checkpoint Charlie.' Checkpoint Charlie was one of the important crossing points from the west to the east and vice versa. it could be crossed both by foot and by car and was meant only to be used by foreigners and by members of the allied forces. It was located at the junction of Frederickstraffe, Zimmerstrafe and Mauerstraffe, which when transalated into German ironically meant 'Wall Street.'The checkpoint was manned by armed soldiers and border guards from both the sides and the Berlin Wall also ran alongside it. Café Adler was located bang near the checkpoint and had been made famous by the author John Le Carre who it is believed had spent considerable time in that café writing his many thrilling spy novels. And though it was a smallish dingy place, nevertheless it was also now one of the many tourist attractions for those who wished to have a peep into East Berlin and have a closer look at that ugly wall.

"What an eyesore and I wonder what Hitler in hell must be thinking about this monstrous manmade obstacle that has divided the capital city and a city that the Fuhrer had tasked his able minister Albert Speer to make it as one of the the most beautiful capitals of the world,"said Monty as Herr Gunther recalled the tragic death of Peter Fechter. It was on 17th August, 1972 that the teenage Peter while making a bid to escape from East Berlin was shot at by the East German guards and thus became the first victim of that infamous wall. As his body lay in the tangled barbed wire fence, everybody watched like mute spectators, while the poor boy slowly bled to death. Fear of provoking a retaliatory action by the allies that could have resulted in a shoot out as had occurred a few days' earlier and in which an East German border guard was killed, the East German sentries on duty were reluctant to approach the fence that day. Fascinated by the strategic importance of the café and in order to see whatever little was happening on either side of Checkpoint Charlie, Monty who was not very fond of cabarets and floor shows requested his host if Café Adler could be the place for dinner too that evening.

"As you please," said Herr Gunther as he ordered another large pitcher of Monty's favourite Lowenbrau German beer and some more sausages with baked ham on toast to go with it. As the evening got longer, the disparity in the life styles of the two Germany's also became more and more apparent as Monty took a few photographs with his zoom lens camera. Whereas, the West Berliners sang and danced inside the many beer halls and young couples were seen holding hands and kissing each other in public, and while some others did some window shopping in the well lit shops on Freidrichstrasse, but on the other side of 'Checkpoint Charlie" it was all dim and dark and there was hardly anybody on the streets. But then suddenly after a few hours everything changed as thousands of East Germans kept congregating near the checkpoint gate and kept shouting and demanding that the gate be opened for them to cross over into West Berlin. Watching from their ringside seat at Café Adler, Monty and his hosts just could not believe what was happening.

"This must be some sort of a damn miracle," said an excited Fraulein Gunther as her husband quickly payed the bill and they all ran towards the checkpoint to have a closer look of what was taking place. The huge crowd on the other side were now scolding the East German Border Guards and demanding that the gates be opened immediately since the government had announced a few minutes earlier over the East German radio that all border restrictions had been lifted and that the people of East Germany if they so wished could go over to the other side.

"'But I only hope it is true and not a political propaganda stunt to get rid of the riff raffs and their spies to cross over to our side,'said Herr Gunther.

"But with so many men, women and children and all of them so very arrogantly demonstrating it must be true," said Monty as he with his flash camera took a few more photographs of that historic evening.And with similar scenes being enacted at the other border crossings at Checkpoints Alpha and Bravo, practically the whole of West Berlin was now congregating to see what was happening on the other side of the great divide. Some of them had also heard the proclamation over the GDR radio and were now eagerly waiting to welcome their long lost loved ones with open arms. Soon thereafter, when the flood gates were opened and as thousands of East Germans broke the shackles of communism and once again became citizens of a free world, Monty was the happiest man. Early next morning Monty with his hosts and camera was once gain at the wall where history was now being created as the West Germans and the East Germans hugged and cried with joy. It was also a sight to see as Berliners from both sides climbed the wall, painted graffiti on it and also removed fragments from it as souvenirs. Not to be left out from this revelry, Monty to collected a fewl chipped stone peices from what now clearly signaled the end of the 40 year old Cold War.

The Second World War had created the two Germany's and had brought with it the existence of the two power blocs of communism and capitalism and the bloody Cold War. This had at times even threatened the very existence of the world with a nuclear holocaust as the Warsaw Pact and the NATO forces with their huge nuclear arsenals kept threatening one another. This fortunately had the emerging third world countries uniting together as non aligned nations. Soon after the war, the British had divided India into two separate countries and this was soon followed by the Korean War and the war in French Indo-China. Thus was created the north—south divide that split Korea and Vietnam into two separate nations. The world had also given the Jews their holy state of Israel, which was carved out from what was once known as Palestine, but the Palestinians themselves eversince that day had become unwanted refugees and without a land that they could call their own. Monty however now felt happy that a beginning had been made and one that could lead to the reunification of Germany in the near future. He therefore wrote a long letter to Shupriya about his visit to Checkpoint Charlie and also sent her a few photographs of that historic 9th of November evening in Berlin.

However, it was only a few days later while still in West Berlin to see what the exodus from the east would lead too that Monty came to know the real truth about the government controlled East German radio broadcast that was made on the late evening of the 9th of November. According to a reliable East German government source whose family had also crossed over to West Berlin, that announcement was made by mistake. It was an error of judgement or shall we say a faux pas that was inadvertently made on that day and which took even Moscow by surprise. On 18th October, Erich Honnecker the strongman of East Germany had resigned and he had been replaced by Egon Krenz. Meanwhile a large number of East German refugees had made their way to the west via Czechoslovakia and this it seems was a gentleman's agreement that was made with the communist controlled government of that country. Therefore realizing that such kind of exodus could not be stopped any longer and that private travel should be allowed, the East German Politbureau that was now led by Krenz in their meeting on 9th November had decided to allow their subjects to directly cross over to the other side from their own crossing points if the so wished to do so, but only with prior permission. This notification was to take effect from the next day, but Gunter Schabovski, the East German Minister of Propaganda who had been tasked to announce this had only rejoined from his leave on that very day. That evening he had been handed over the note from the Politbureau that said that East Berliners would be allowed to cross the border with proper prior permission, but he failed to give the modalities on how and when it would come into effect done. The East German Border Guards at the various checkpoints had also not been briefed properly and they were also taken by complete surprise. For them to retaliate against the huge crowd with their weapons would have led to a mass massacre of innocent people some of whom were their own kith and kin. Therefore using discretion as a better part of valour they had opened the gates and watched in silence as the grand spectacle unfolded itself.

The day Monty returned to India it was the 14th of November, the late Pandit Nehru's birthday and a day that was observed in India as 'Children's Day'. But with the election fever in full swing it was the political leaders from various parties who were behaving and fighting like children. Some of them who till yesterday were known adversaries of each other had suddenly become friends as they joined hands to oust the ruling Congress (I) government of Rajiv Gandhi from coming back into power. Calling themesleves as the 'Janata Dal', it was nothing but a rag tag of small centre-left coalition partners that hardly had any all India base, but was now prepared to fight it out with corruption as its main plank. It comprised mainly of various small regional parties like that of the Lok Dal (B), the Congress (S) and the Jan Morcha. They had joined hands and were being backed from the outside by the Bhartiya Janata Party and the Communist Party of India, and their leader was none other than VP Singh. VP Singh was India's ex Defence and Finance Minister in Rajiv Gandhi's cabinet and the man who had led the revolt against the corrupt practices of the ruling Congress (I) government. Citing the Bofors scandal, the murky HDW submarine deal and of the Congress (I) party being hand in glove with India's big business houses, the newly formed Janata Dal was now openly accusing the Congress (I) and its leader Rajiv Gandhi for economically ruining the country and of making the rich richer and the poor poorer. The new party was therefore now appealing to the Indian masses to vote for them and with the promise that they would give the people a scandal free clean and transparent government.

"But do you sincerely think that these so called leaders if they do come to power will live up to their so called promises and to the expectations of the poor Indian masses who have been at their mercy for the last 42 years," said Reeta somewhat sarcastically as Monty showed her and Peevee the prized photographs of the Berlin Wall and the various souvenirs that he had brought along with him.However,commenting on the broadside that Reeta had fired on the politicians of the country, Monty said.

"Yes, these so called Netas and leaders I am afraid are nothing but total opportunists. These turncoats except for a handful like VP Singh and a few others maybe exceptions, but by and large they have no scruples whatsoever and once they are voted to power they will be no different from the others I tell you. They are all from the same stock of the old Congress and it is like putting the same old wine in a new bottle. As it is the leaders from the various groups have already started jockeying for power so that they too can fill their own coffers when and if given the chance, and God help this country if it is a hung parliament. And though the general prediction in the country is that this new rag-tag combination may be able to form a new government with outside support, but the question is for how long will they be able to run it. With the kind of horse trading that goes on nowadays in politics, I am afraid it will suffer the same fate as that of the Morarjee and Charan Singh governments of the late seventies and the early eighties," said Monty.

"Yes and all this thanks to the to the 155 mm Swedish Bofors Gun, a gun that will probably bring to an end the Nehru-Indira-RajivGandhi legacy of ruling India if another salvo of the government's lies, deception and cover ups of the scandal is fired by Chitra Subramanium and Mr Ram of the Hindu," said Peevee as he opened the champagne bottle with a loud bang that the Gunthers had presented with a set of six beautiful cutglass tall champagne glasses as a Christmas gift to the family.

"Well then let us say cheers to the future of India's democracy and let's hope for the best," remarked Monty while allowing Peevee to have a sip from his glass.

By the end of the month the Indian masses had given their verdict and though the Congress (I) had won the largest number of seats in the Indian parliament, but it was not good enough for them to form a government. The number of seats from a massive 400 that the party had won in the last general elections had plummeted to a measly 196, and with no party having the required majority to form a government on its own strength, the dawn of coalition politics had now descended upon India, thought Monty as he rang up Shupriya in Colombo to give her the good news that Peevee had been awarded as the best actor in the inter-university Hindi play competition that was held in Delhi recently. For his remarkable histrionic talent on stage, Peevee had also been awarded a scholarship by the National School of Drama, but since Peevee was not a full fledged college graduate, which was the minimum educational qualification for admission to the NSD that offered only 20 seats for the course, Peevee felt rather disappointed. Monty in his letter also conveyed to Shupriya that one of the judges at the competition who was also a renowned film director had made Peevee an offer to act in his next film that was expected to be launched sometime in August next year. And since it was going to be an off beat film on the lines of the late Bimal Roy's immortal 'Do Bigha Zamin' and not the usual run of the mill of the hero and heroine running around trees singing songs, he on her behalf had therefore given his blessings to him. Monty also emphasized in his letter that Peevee by then would have crossed the new voting age of 18 years and would be considered as an adult and since he was bent upon becoming an actor and a singer there was therefore no point in curbing his life's ambition of becoming a star. But whether he would make it to Bollywood and Hollywood was still a million dollar question.

On 29th November 1989, after Rajiv Gandhi handed over his letter of resignation to the President of India, the decks were cleared for VP Singh and his newly formed Janata Dal to form the new government. And on 2nd December 1989, when VP Singh was sworn in as the new Prime Minister of India, there was once again hope that he would not betray the trust of the people and that he will bring in the honesty and transparency of good gvernance that was promised by him and by his new party in their manifesto. The people of India could not afford to have another 'Mr Clean' playing dirty politics and they looked forward to a dirt free, progressive and efficient government. But on 8th December, and just six days after the VP Singh government had been sworn in, the Janata Dal faced its first test when the ISI backed Jammu and Kashmir Liberation Front militants in broad daylight kidnapped Rubaiya Saeed the twenty three year old daughter of Mufti Mohammed Sayeed, the new Home Minister of India. Not only was Mufti Mohammed Sayeed the first Muslim Home Minister of India, but he was also the first Kashmiri Muslim to be given that powerful portfolio.

Dr Rubayia Sayeed was an intern doctor at the Lal Ded Memorial Women's Hospital in Srinagar. At around 3.45 in the afternoon of Friday the 8th of December 1989, when she was on her way home from the hospital in a local public matador van, she had no idea that she was being followed. And when the van was roughly half a kilometer away from her house in Naigom, it was stopped by four militants at gun point and Rubaiya was forced to get into a waiting Maruti Van and she was whisked away to some unknown destination. The dare devil kidnapping of the daughter of the Home Minister of India and who himself was a Kashmiri immediately had the alarm bells ringing. Faroukh Abdulla the Chief Minister of the state was away on a holiday in London, and when he was contacted, he immediately booked a return flight back home. The Home Minister too on being informed about his daughter's abduction expressed his deep anguish. This was the first instance of its kind, when a woman had been abducted in Kashmir by militants, but she was not an ordinary woman, she was the daughter of India's new Home Minister, a ministry whose primary responsibility was to ensure law and order in the country. For the next couple of hours Rubaiya's abduction and disappearance had everybody on the run in Srinagar and a frantic search was launched for the culprits. Then at about 5.30 that evening her abductors rang up the office of the local Srinagar daily 'The Kashmir Times'and spelt out their demands. Calling themselves as Mujahideens they demanded the release of five of their comrades from the JKLF, the Jammu and Kashmir Liberation Front, in exchange for the Home Minister's daughter. It just so happened that Moosa Raza the Chief Secretary of the Jammu and Kashmir State happened to be in Delhi on some official work that day and therefore a high level cabinet subcommittee of ministers was immediately formed to deal with the crisis. The ministers included were Arun Nehru, Arif Mohammed Khan and Inder Gujral, and in exchange for Rubaiya, the militants were demanding the release of Sheikh Abdul Hameed, a self syled JKLF 'Area Commander' who had been wounded and arrested in an encounter and who was now undergoing treatment at the Sher-i-Kashmir Institute of Medical Science, together with Ghulam Nabi Butt, the younger brother of the late Maqbol Butt, Noor Mohammed Kalwal, Mohammed Altaf and Javed Ahmed Zangar all of whom were undergoing jail sentences.

By early next morning Ved Marwah, the Director General of the NSG, the National Security Guard also flew down to Srinagar and the possibility of launching a commando raid to rescue Rubaiya was therefore also on the cards. In the absence of the Chief Minister who was yet to arrive from London, the Kashmir government's initial reaction was to give in to the demands of the militants and get the whole thing over with as quickly as possible. But that would be playing into the hands of the militants and setting a wrong precedent for the future. Thanks to Mohammed Sofi the Editor of Kashmir Times and Zaffar Meraj an enterprising journalist who was with the same paper, the contact that had been established by them with the militants was not broken and a continous dialogue was kept open in order to strike at an honorable deal. On Sunday the 10th of December, the militants sent an ultimatum demanding the release of their colleagues by 1900 hours the next day and failing which they would kill Rubaiya. With the militants having reiterated their demand for the release of five of their colleagues in exchange for the Home Minister's daughter together with a death threat on her had further aggravated the situation. The ball was now in the new VP Singh government's court. For the next 48 hours and while the government debated their next move of whether to give in to the militants demands, Faroukh Abdullah returned from London. The central government it seems was by now reconciled to the exchange offer, but the Chief Minister was totally against it. In a confidential letter to the Governor, General KV Krishna Rao, Faroukh Abdulla stated that such an exchange would only open the floodgates for the future and would further boost anti national activities that would be difficult to control. Meanwhile, the Home Minister Mr Mufti Mehmood through his old friend Moti Lal Bhat who was a Judge of the Allahbad High Court had opened another channel to the militants. Finally on 13th December, the government buckled when early that morning Inder Gujral and Arif Mohammed Khan the two Union Ministers flew to Srinagar with the orders from the centre to release the five JKLF militants in exchange for the Home Minister's daughter and by 7 PM, Rubaiya was back home.

Late that evening while listening to the news over the BBC about the shameful swap over and that to at the ratio of five militants for one woman, and the jubilation of the locals of the valley that followed hailing the militants as heroes was a bit too much for Monty to swallow. As a Kashmiri Sikh whose ancestral village of Bagh was now a part of Pakistan occupied Kashmir and whose business of exporting Kashmiri carpets and handicrafts depended heavily on peaceful conditions in the valley, this kind of utter surrender by the government to the diktat of the militants he thought would only encourage more such abductions and hold the state and the country to ransom also.According to Monty the rise of militancy in the valley began from the day the polls were allegedly rigged during the 1987 state assembly elections, and the National Conference of Faroukh Abdulla and Rajiv Gandhi's Congress(I) once again joined hands to form a coalition government in the state. On 14th August, 1989, Pakistan's Independence Day in open defiance of the goveement orders there were Pakistani flags flying all over Srinagar, and on the very next day, 15th August, India's Independence

Day was observed with a complete 'Bandh' during the day and a blackout at night in the valley. Three weeks later, when on the death anniversary of the the late Sheikh Abdullah, who was once revered by his own people as the 'Lion of Kashmir,' his effigy was burnt on the streets of Srinagar, it was quite evident that the militants had now started calling the shots. And while the writ of the militants in the valley became more and more evident, the government both in the state and in the centre simply turned a blind eye to all that was happening in front of their very own eyes. And now with the release of the five hardcore militants not only had the new government of VP Singh played into the hands of the Kashimiri terrorists, but it had also lost its credibility to act tough with them, which was the need of the hour, thought Monty as he discussed the repercussions that may follow with his journalist friend Unni.

Meanwhile in Islamabad, Shiraz too was very unhappy with the rise of militancy in the valley. He knew that the release of the five JKLF militants had given the Pakistani military high command a further boost in maintaining the momentum of phase one of 'Operation Topac' that they had already launched in the trouble torn Kashmir. The armed forces of Pakistan were also now in the midst of their largest military exercise ever held. Code named Zarb-e-Momin',the exercise in offensive-defence was the brainchild of the Pakistan Army Chief, General Mirza Afzal Beg and was being conducted not very far from the international border adjoining the two troubled Indian states of Punjab and Kashmir where militancy was constantly now on the rise. The Pakistan airforce too in close coordination with the army and Exercise Zarb-e-Momin had also just conducted their own biggest national level air exercise code named 'High Mark 89.'Therefore the release of the five JKLF militants so very tamely by the Indian gvernment was like a shot in the arm for the ISI and the Pakistan army who were only too happy to set up more terrorist training camps inside Pakistan occupied Kashmir. A month earlier on the 4th of November, the militants had shot dead N K Ganjoo the retired District Sessions Judge who had sentenced the JKLF leader Maqbool Butt to death and plans were now being made not only to subvert the bureaucracy inside the valley and make them tow their line, but also to let loose a reign of terror against those who opposed it. Their slogan now was Kashmir for the Kashmiri Muslims only and with the Kashmiri Pundits and Sikhs in the valley as their number one target, Shiraz was therefore worried that all this could lead to another long war of proxy and that would not only be economically disastrous for both the countries, but would also result in the deaths of thousands of Indian soldiers and civilians.

By the time the year 1989 ended, the one year old Benazir's coalition government too was facing its first tremors of uncertainity and instability. To start with there was a serious attempt made to destabilize her government, when 'Operation Midnight Jackal' was clandestinly launched by retired Brigadier Iqbal and Major Aamir. They had been video taped by intelligence operatives, when they tried to bribe members of the National Assembly to vote against their leader Benazir in a no-confidence motion. There were also reports of Nawaz Sharif the Chief Minister of Punjab having a hand in that ham handed affair. The appointment of retired Major General Kallue as DGISI by Benazir had so irked the military high command that the new ISI top boss was not even being invited to the high level Corps Commander's conferences that was presided over by the Army Chief. The military was of the view that Benazir was bent upon civilianizing all the intelligence departments in the country and come what may the Pakistan Army was not prepared to accept that. Benazir had also clashed with President Ghulam Ishaq Khan over the appointment of the Chief Justice of the Supreme Court and also that of the Chief Election Commissioner. The violence and the law and order situation in Karachi in particular and in Sindh in general, which was Benazir's home province had been going from bad to worse everyday. Business in the city of Karachi that provided nearly two thirds of the country's revenue was practically at a standstill and a fear psychosis had gripped the factory workers who often stayed away from their work. Cases of corruption and sanctioning of huge loans by the government to those who had the right political connections had also started making the rounds. Overall it seemed that Pakistan was once again in a state of turmoil and that was definitely not a healthy sign for a country that had only recently returned to democratic rule.

According to Shiraz the only silver lining to the deteriorating situation in Pakistan was the death of Abdullah Yusuf Azzam who was considered to be the central figure in the global development of the militant Islamist movement. The Muslim cleric from Jordan's West Bank who with Osama Bin Laden in 1984 at Peshawar had founded the 'Bait-ul-Ansar,'the House of Helpers, and which had brought in hordes of young Muslim Jehadis from all over the world to fight the Soviet occupation of Afghanistan had after falling out with Osama bin Laden was trying to perpetuate his vision of global Islamic revolution and had been killed by a landmine. It happened in broad daylight on the 24th of November, when the cleric with his two sons, Ibrahim and Mohammed were on their way in a vehicle for the Friday prayers at the the same very mosque on Gulshan Iqbal Road, Peshawar that Sheikh Azzam had also converted into a Jihad Centre. The powerful landmine that was detonated by the unknown assasins to get rid of the man who regularly promoted Muslim fundamentalism with the gun as his main weapon took everybody by surpise. He was both a radical and an inspirational figure for his highly motivated young Jehadi fighters and they were now calling for revenge. But who was behind that brutal assassination was a million dollar question. Some suspected the CIA, the KGB, the Pakistan ISI and even the Israeli Mossad, while a few also pointed a finger to Osama Bin Laden's newly created Al Qaida.

CHAPTER-13

A Fast Changing World

As the year 1989 drew to a close, Shiraz as was his habit ended the entries in his diary with his own observations about how various important political events both international and domestic during the year had changed the world in general and the subcontinent in particular. While the bloodless revolutions of 1989 in the Soviet Union and its allies in Eastern Europe greatly altered the balance of power in the world and marked the end of the Cold War, it also brought to an end the many years of Communist rule in those countries. The Russians had repealed the old Brezhnev Doctrine and were now no longer interested in intervening in the internal affairs of their erstwhile Warsaw Pact comrades. Countries like Poland, Czechoslavakia, Bulgaria, and Hungary had reverted back to a multi-party system with democratic values. The Berlin Wall had fallen. The Romanians and the Albanians too had expressed their desire to be free from the strangle hold of their dictatorial rulers. On Christmas Day the people of Romania watched happily on television the summary execution of their tyrant ruler Ceausescu and his wife Elena. While all these changes heralded a new world order in Eastern Europe, it also heralded further Balkanization of a few others like Yugoslavia where ethnic considerations were now becoming the order of the day and as hatred between the Croats and the Serbs and between Muslims and Christians started taking centre stage. In the Middle East the on going war between the Muslims and the Jews aided and abetted by various Muslim Fundamentalist organizations on one side and the CIA backed Israelis on the other only spawned more terrorist groups to become bolder and bolder in executing mass scale killing of innocent people around the world. A further twist to American diplomacy in the oil rich Gulf Region was added, when President George Bush Senior on 2nd October, 1989 signed the top-secret National Security Decision Number 26 and declared that not only normal relations between the US and Iraq would serve America's long term interests better and promote stability in both the Gulf and the Middle East region, but more political and economic incentives to Saddam Hussein would be in America's favour in the long run. And in November, when the American President approved the one billion dollar loan guarantees for Iraq, Shiraz wondered what the Americans were upto now.

"Maybe the Americans need more oil in future and Iraq I believe has plenty of it and so do the Saudis and the small Emirate countries in its neighbourhood, and all of them I am told are flushed with reserves of that black gold," said Saira rather matter of factly while presenting her husband with a copy of retired Lt General Attiqur Rehman's autobiography that was titled 'Back to the Pavilion' and which had just been published. The retired General was the 1939 sword of honour winner from the Indian Military Academy, Dehradun, and was a true living example of courage, modesty and one who firmly believed in an officer being a gentleman. The foreward in his book was written by his dear old friend Admiral Ahsan, the man who in 1971 quit his governorship of East Pakistan because he was against the reprisal policy that Yahya Khan wanted him to initiate against the Bengalees. Jokingly the two friends Atiq and Ehsan were addressed as HerrGeneralfieldmarchall Attiq Von Rachmann and Herr Grossadmiral Von Ahsan respectively and Shiraz had a very high regard for both of them. Shiraz also had a very high regard for Hesky Baig, who was the sword of honour winner in the 1936 batch that had passed out from the IMA. As he read through that fascinating book about the author's life and experiences, Shiraz was reminded of his own career in the Indian army. It had a lot of similarities as far as their lives as young officers were concerned and it reminded him of the wonderful time that he had with many of his course mates during the training at IMA. Some of them his course mates with nearly 25 years of commissioned service were in command of infantry and armoured brigades and whose headquarters were located close to the international border and the line of control in Jammu and Kashmir. At times he wondered what would be his fate if his true identity was ever discovered.

However as the year 1989 came to a close there was again trouble for Pakistan again. Though Benazir had taken Pakistan back into the folds of the Commonwealth by reversing her late father's decision, and she also had the USA's backing behind her, but her government was far from being a stable one. In neighbouring Afghanistan after the withdrawal of the Soviet troops it was now the Afghan warlords who with the backing of the ISI, the CIA and Benazir's blessings were hell bent in overthrowing the pro-communist Najibullah government in Kabul. But the stupid frontal attack on Jalalabad that was launched by them with the Mujahideeens in the late spring of 1989 and that had the full support and blessings of Mr Oakley the American Ambassador to Pakistan and Lt General Hamid Gul the boss of the ISI had unfortunately proved to be a military disaster. The Americans and the ISI had underestimated the fighting capabilities of Najibullah's Afghan army who thanks to the Soviets were well equipped with modern tanks, artillery guns and helicopter gunships. They were under the impression that since the Russians had left, the already demoralised Najibullah's forces would soon capitulate, but they were sadly mistaken. The set piece frontal attack on Jalalabad that had the full support of the Americans and also that of Lt General Hamid Gul, the ex DGISI only resulted in heavy casualties to the attackers. This was one of the reasons that gave Benazir the lever and opportunity to post Lt General Hamid Gul as a Corps Commander and fill the slot with his own man, retired Major General Kalhue.

The instability in Afghanistan after the withdrawal by the Soviets, and the fiery rhetorics by the Mullas from across the Durand Line had already started influencing and polluting the minds of the young Pathans and Pashtuns in the already volatile tribal territories of Baluchistan and the North West Frontier Provinces, and Shiraz was now apprehensive that this could one day become a real headache for Pakistan and India too. As it is General Zia's eleven long years of rule had made Islam in Pakistan the most dominating factor not only in promoting the importance of the Mullahs, but these Mullahs were also now being used by various political parties and militant organizations as vote catchers. Their weekly Friday sermons in the many mosques that were under their control were now not only openly promoting radical Islamic thoughts and ideas, but quite a few amongst them were also demanding total Islamization of the country and calling for another Jihad in Kashmir. According to Shiraz, the only sobering factor that had put the brakes on the growing fundamentalism in that region was the assassination of the radical Muslim Palestinian cleric Abdullah Yusuf Azzam at Peshawar in last November and the return to Jeddah of the Arab millionaire Osama Bin Laden. Unconfirmed reports of the rapid growth of the Al-Qaida movement under the leadership of the big moneyed radical Osama Bin Laden were also becoming a disturbing factor. It had its original roots in Pakistan and had now started spreading its tentacles from its base in Sudan, where Osama Bin Laden having been refused permission to return to Saudi Arabia by the King had taken refuge in Khartoum. The word Al-Qaida which in Arabic was the word for 'The Base' was now gearing up to change the world with its own methods of violent Muslim radicalism.

And the year 1990 for Pakistan in general and for Brigadier Aslam Rehman Khan and his family in particular began rather tragically when the Bahauddin Zakaria Express in which the Brigadier's in-laws were traveling crashed into a stationery goods-train at Sanghi railway station killing over three hundred passengers and injuring hundreds of others. This was the worst ever rail accident in Pakistan's history and on getting the sad news Aslam Rehman immediately rushed to the spot to collect the dead bodies, while the rest of the family air dashed to Karachi to make arrangements for the burial ceremony. But Karachi that was once the city of happiness and laughter was not the same any longer either. It had become a city of gun toting hoodlums and an arena where different political partiess aided by their hired goons fought pitched battles on the streets. The big land owners, the so called political leaders and other feudal lords inside Pakistan had become a law unto themselves. They were like the Mafia who in their quest for power kept enhancing the Kalashnikov culture that had already killed so many thousands of innocent people in the local wars that had now become a regular feature in the Sind Province and particularly so in the busy financial capital of Karachi. And as the law and order in Sind worsened, so did the relationship between the military and the Prime Minister. And it finally came to a head when the army maintained that the PPP's reluctance to take action against their own party members who were instigating their followers to take punitive action against the MQM was the main cause of all the law and order problems. The army therefore had now started taking things into their own hands and on 11th February 1990, when the Karachi Corps Commander, Lt General Asif Nawaz Janjua oversaw the messy business of the exchange of 27 political workers who had been abducted by the two rival parties in a tit-for tat exchange operation, it was quite evident that the Pakistan Army was not prepared to remain a silent spectator any longer.

"My God, when will we ever be able to live with each other in peace if the PPP and the MQM keep on fighting like this," said a sad Farzana as she recalled her wonderful young days in that city.

"Yes and it is becoming more like the wild west and if this kind of lawlessness and killings continue, I am afraid even the army will be helpless in restoring law and order," said Aslam Rehman as he with his family drove around the city and pointed out the various prominent landmarks of Karachi to his eight year old daughter Nasreen and which also included her mother's old school and college.

Meanwhile in Bangladesh, the government of General Ershad and his Jatiyo Party were also being castigated for incompetence and corruption by all and sundry. The people were calling for his ouster and with every passing day, the anti-Ershad movement also started gaining momentum. It was now only a question of time and Dimpy wondered what the future would be for the poor people of this country if another military dictator took over the country. Bangladesh was a country of poor peasants whose main occupation with their meager land holdings was agriculture and while the politicians and the clergy kept exploiting them politically, the monsoons and floods as a yearly ritual devastated their lands and added to their miseries. Suddenly realizing that the 26th of January was only a week away and feeling somewhat lonely and despondent, Dimpy wrote a long letter to Aunty Shupriya in Colombo and wished her a very happy 40th birthday.

Shupriya's 40th birthday was rather a quiet affair as usual because she after the death of her husband never ever celebrated it. For her life in Colombo was also becoming a little boring. But she was very happy that the VP Singh government had decided to pull out the IPKF from the island and the process of de-induction had already started. With Premadasa having been sworn in as the new President of Sri Lanka, the Indo-Sri Lanka accord that had been signed not even three years ago had become a big diplomatic, military and foreign policy failure for India. Not only was Premadasa dictating terms by ordering the IPKF to stay put in their barracks, but he was also threatening that he would dub them as an occupation army if they dared to disobey the order.

The induction of the IPKF had resulted in the loss of more than a thousand Indian soldiers and had cost the Indian exchequer more than two billion rupees. But what was even worse was the blatantly marked increase of the LTTE activities in Tamil Nadu itself where the militants with the patronage of the Karunanidhi government were openly defying the authority of both the Central and State government law enforcing authorities in the state.

"My God what a mess we have got into for nothing over here in Sri Lanka," wrote Shupriya in her reply to Dimpy as she explained to her that it was pointless for India to act as a big brother to her immediate small neighbors and Bangladesh was not an exception either. Having completed the letter, Shupriya opened the secret numbered mini locker that was inside her big Godrej almirah, and took out the copy of the holy Guru Granth Sahib. It was the same book that Monty had presented her with when they had both converted to Sikhism. Inside the folds of the holy book was a photograph of Shiraz in military uniform, the Param Veer Chakra medal that was awarded to him and also a photograph of little Peevee in her arms that Monty had taken a week after the boy was born. Those were all her priceless possessions and as she put her lips to them, closed her eyes and said a prayer, tears of both joy and sadness trickled down her beautiful face. She was missing the family and did not mind a home posting now. She had been out of the country for more than fifteen years and was also due to become a Joint Secretary soon, and therefore a tenure on home turf in that important rank was considered essential for further advancement as a career diplomat. In April, 1990 she was due to complete three years in Colombo and was now keen to go back to Delhi. Then as she with her new short hair style looked into the mirror and saw those many strands of grey hair and the few wrinkles on her face, she was confident that even in the many social gatherings that she in her official capacity may have to attend with the glitterati of the capital, she would easily pass off as Miss Yeshwant Kaur Bajwa.

During those early months of 1990, while the world was undergoing a radical change of attitude towards the old communist regimes of the Warsaw Pact countries and the apartheid rule by the White Afrikaners in racist South Africa was also slowly coming to an end, the situation in the Kashmir Valley was becoming worse by the day. Pakistan's Lady Prime Minister, Benazir Bhutto with the active support of the ISI and her military generals it seems had launched phase two of 'Operation Topac'. And as thousands of Kashmiri Hindus under the threat of the Pakistan backed Kashmiri militants left their ancestral homes, businesses and properties in the valley to become unwanted refugees in their own country, VP Singh's government decided to send back Jagmohan Malhotra as Governor again. Faroukh Abdullah the Chief Minister had raised his hands and had resigned and President's rule had once again been declared in the troubled state.

Jagmohan was born on 25th September, 1927 at Hafizabad in Pakistan. He started life as a young bureaucrat in government service and was the Vice Chairman of the DDA, the Delhi Development Authority during the infamous 1975 Emergency in the country. And it was he who under the orders of Sanjay Gandhi had mercilessly bulldozed the hutments at Emperor Shahjehan's Moghul capital in order to beautify the old city of Delhi. That had made the poor occupants of Turkman Gate and from such other places of the walled city to look for shelter elsewhere and in the outskirts of the capital. In 1980, he was appointed the Lt Governor of Delhi but was now feeling quite helpless as Governor of Jammu and Kashmir to stem the tide of militancy that had gripped the beautiful vale. This was his second tenure as Governor of the state where the Kalashnikov culture had set in and it was quite evident as masked militants toting their weapons prowled the streets of the state capital giving their orders to the locals to rise against the Indian government. The walls were plastered with posters and handbills that conveyed the grim warning to all non Muslims to either quit the valley or embrace Islam, or be ready to face death. During his first tenure as Governor, Jagmohan in 1987 with the blessings of Rajiv Gandhi had thrown out the elected government of Faroukh Abdulla and through defections had installed his estranged brother-in-law, Ghulam Mohammed Shah into the hot seat. But now Faroukh Abdullah who had once again been reinstated by the same Rajiv Gandhi's Congress as the Chief Minister it seems too had started feeling the heat. Probably realizing that he did not have a role to play and fearing that he and his family may also be targeted by the militants, he had therefore thrown in the towel and left the valley with his English wife and children for a long holiday in England, while Kashmir burnt.

While in the chair as Chief Minister, the Faroukh Abdulla's government in the State and Rajiv Gandhi's government in the centre it seems had not taken the threats that were being orchestrated by the Pakistani backed militants very seriously. They were probably under the impression that it was a passing phase and that it would die its own death and they therefore it seems had turned a blind eye to it. Moreover, the recent kidnapping of Rubaiya and the subsequent release of the five hardcore militants in exchange for the Home Minister's daughter was also taken as a sign of weakness of the VP Singh government and the militants were now taking full advantage of it. Though some feared that Rubaiya's kidnapping and her subsequent release was all stage managed, but whatever it was, it had only encouraged the militants to carry on with their anti national activities even more vigorously. The militants now not only wrote threatening letters of reprisals to the Kashmiri Pandits, but they also blatantly started eliminating them if they voluntarily did not leave the valley by the given deadline. They had also issued their diktat to the people not only not to pay any taxes, but to also refrain from making any deposits in the banks. They had also forced the women too compulsorily wear the burkha and directed that all liquor shops to be closed. The local shopkeepers were made to fly green flags on their shops and it was quite evident that it was the militants who were now calling all the shots in the valley. It seemed that the mass migration of the Kashmiri Hindus from the enchanted valley was of no concern to the National Conference of Faroukh Abdulla and to the Congress (I) of Rajiv Gandhi, because compared to the Muslims of India, these Kashmiri Hindus were only a handful and their votes hardly mattered. To the politicians and the political parties the vote of the Muslims of India it seems was far more important than the safety and honour of the Hindus in Kashmir thought Monty whose export business had also been hit very badly. Monty was also surprised to learn from his old friend Unni that Governor Jagmohan had written a very strong letter to Rajiv Gandhi who was now the leader of the opposition for ignoring the warning signals that Jagmohan had sent to him in 1988 and in 1989, when Rajiv was the Prime Minister. In fact Jagmohan even accused Rajiv of being totally averse to the insurgency movement that had now engulfed the entire valley. Jagmohan also criticized Rajiv for siding with Faroukh Abdullah who was now openly propagating that the Governor was a 'Hallaqu,' a 'Chengez Khan,' and an anti-Muslim and one who was bent in converting the valley into a vast Muslim graveyard. Therefore, in order to see the situation on the ground and to expedite his pending export orders, Monty decided to pay a flying three day visit to Srinagar and the valley.

It was on the beautiful spring morning of 11th April 1990, when Monty landed in Srinagar by the Indian Airlines flight. A day earlier the bullet ridden body of Musher-ul-Haq, the Vice Chancellor of the Kashmir University who had been kidnapped on 6th April was found on the roadside and the city looked like a ghost town. However, it seems that Jagmohan's tough attitude against the militants and their supporters had started paying dividends. With his aggressive and hard-line actions, he had managed to break the back of not only those anti national political parties who were clamouring for an independent Kashmir, but also of those who wanted the state to merge with Pakistan. The prolonged spell of curfew restrictions imposed by him in the militant affected areas of the state capital and in other important towns inside the valley, together with the simultaneous conduct of massive search operations by the Indian army and other para military forces to flush out the militants had also started having its positive effects as quite a few misguided youths surrendered voluntarily to the security forces. But that was only the tip of the iceberg. According to one reliable intelligence report, the militants had planned by 26th January, 1990 to declare Kashmir as an independent republic, but with Jagmohan's timely arrival on 19th January as Governor and his subsequent tough and strong actions against the militants and their supporters it had upset the militants applecart.

After promising his suppliers that he was willing to pay another twenty percent more for his pending orders, but only on condition that they would have to meet the required deadline of 30th June, Monty on 16th April afternoon boarded the Indian Airlines flight to Delhi. That very morning the Governor also declared that militant outfits like the Jamait-e-Islami, the JKLF, the Hizbul Mujaheedin, the Students Liberation Front and a few others as unlawful and imposed a total ban on them. India's war against terrorist outfits in Kashmir and Pakistan's nefarious proxy war codenamed 'Operation Topac' that was now being covertly supported by the Benazir government had thus entered a new phase.

There was however a pleasant surprise for Monty, when his aircraft landed at Palam airport that evening. Waiting to greet him was Shupriya with his wife Reeta and Peevee. Shupriya was now posted as Joint Secretary in the Ministry of External Affairs and she had been assigned the Soviet desk. Mikhail Gorbachev had been recently elected as the new executive president and Shupriya was happy and she hoped that the Soviet Union under his leadership for the sake of their own people would realize that communism and the one party rule by the CPSU was a total failure. Prior to her arrival in Delhi, one of her last duties in Colombo was to ensure that no more IPKF personnel remained on Sri Lankan soil. On 23rd March 1990, at Trincomalee she had wished the last contingent of the Indian troops a fond goodbye and a happy journey back home, but felt very sad, when she came to know that besides the Governor of Tamil Nadu, Mr P C Aexander and Mr Raja Ramanna the Defence Minister from Delhi, there was not a single minister from the ruling DMK government to welcome them at Chennai. Even the Sri Lankan army had given the last IPKF contingent a ceremonial send off, when it sailed from their shores, but when it arrived at Chennai, besides the two civilian VIP's and a few top brass from the Indian army, there was nobody else to greet them on their home coming. According to Shupriya, the honourable Indian army officers and soldiers had done their duty to the best of their ability, but when they came home unsung that she thought was a bloody shame both on the part of the government and the media. And what was still worse was that they were now been made scapegoats by some sections of the press that was under the control of the local Tamil politicians and who were mostly all pro LTTE in their attitude. The bodies of the Indian soldiers, except for the officers who died in that conflict were not even sent home for cremation. They were all simply buried or cremated on Sri Lankan soil where they had died fighting somebody else's bloody war. According to Shupriya, the Indo-Sri Lanka Accord was not only a colossal failure of India's premier intelligence agencies, the RAW and the IB, but also of the Rajiv Gandhi government. All of them had not only completely under estimated and miscalculated the fighting capabilities of the LTTE Supremo, Prabhakaran and his highly motivated Tamil Tigers, but they had also misjudged the ungrateful attitude of the new Premadasa government in Sri Lanka. After the Indian troops were withdrawn, the fighting between the Sri Lankan forces and the LTTE had once again resumed with full fury and it was once again all back to square one thought Shupriya as she handed over her charge to the new incumbent in Colombo on 13th April, Baisakhi Day and took the next morning's flight to Delhi.

Meanwhile in Benazir's political stronghold of Sind, when she as the Prime Minister directed the military to restore peace to the two riot torn cities of Karachi and Hyderabad and the army asked for a quid pro quo that they be allowed to also carry out similar operations in the country side and with the powers to set up military courts under Article 245(4) of the constitution, Benazir refused. She knew that Sind was her main support base and she could not allow the army to arrest her own people. But on 27th May, when the Sind government of the PPP launched a crackdown in Hyderabad, which was the power base of the MQM and a shoot-on-sight curfew was imposed, the rivalry between the two warring communities took a more sinister turn. And when the police started a house to house search to apprehend the culprits, the fuse was lit. Defying the ban, as hundreds of Mohajirs with their women and children in front and holding the Holy Quran over their heads emerged from the old Hyderabad Fort that was known as the Purana Qila, it resulted in a massacre of innocent men women and children. This sparked off a chain reaction not only in Karachi, but also in other cities and towns of the province. And as the civil war between the PPP and the Mohajirs kept escalating further, it became a free for all for everybody. This resulted in the deaths of hundreds of others as the supporters of the MQM and the PPP fought pitched battles on the streets, while the gangs of local goondas looted the city. Once again the army had to be called out to restore peace and order, and when certain sections of the population starting praising the army and others were seen holding banners calling for restoration of martial law, Benazir Bhutto knew that if she had to remain in the hot seat she could not afford to antagonize the Generals and that she needed someone as the next Army Chief whom she could trust and one who would be totally loyal to her. General Mirza Aslam Beg was due to retire in August 1991 and fearing that her arch enemy Lt General Hamid Gul could well step into that chair, Benazir therefore tried to secure an extension for Lt General Alam Jan Mahsud, the Corps Commander at Lahore, but this only further upset the bigwigs in the army.

However, Benazir at the same time having recently toured the eight member states of the Organization of Islamic Conference that included among others Syria, Turkey and Egypt, she was very keen to internationalize the Kashmir issue once again and therefore pleaded to all the member states in the name of Islam to once again rake up the Kashmir issue in the United Nations. On 26ᵗʰ April, when the Pakistan Foreign Minister, the retired General Sahibzada Yaqub Khan submitted to the President of the United Nations Security Council a memorandum accusing India and the Indian Army of violating human rights in Kashmir, Shiraz knew that this concerted anti Indian campaign of vilification, disinformation and hostile propaganda that the Pakistan government had launched in an aggressive manner was also a part of the overall 'Operation Topac' plan. The plan had received a set back ever since Governor Jag Mohan returned as Governor off the state, and with Benazir Bhutto's popularity now on the downslide, it may well be a ploy by her government to side track her own people and play the usual perennial threat from India card in order to stay in the chair, thought Shiraz as he made a note in his own code of all the militant training camps that had been set up by the ISI inside Pakistan Occupied Kashmir and where the Kashmiri militants were now being trained.

But on 21ˢᵗ May 1990, when Mirwaiz Maulvi Mohammed was killed in Srinagar and later his funeral procession that grew violent was fired at by the Indian security forces and which resulted in the death of 50 other civilians, Governor Jag Mohan too was given his marching orders. His sudden and unexpected departure it seems was because of the hue and cry that some members of the opposition had been voicing in the Indian parliament about Jagmohan's high handed policies against the Muslims of Kashmir and Shiraz was rather upset about it. His replacement Girish Chandra Saxena was an ex policeman who had also headed the RAW and Shiraz wondered whether an ex cop as Governor was good enough to stop the militant menace that had gripped the valley. And on the 3ʳᵈ of June, when the dead body of Mohammed Gujjar, the loyal Kashmiri nomad who had first warned the Indian Army in 1965 about the presence of Pakistani infiltrators in the Gulmarg area and for which he was awarded the Padmashree was found on the roadside near Baramulla, it was apparent to Shiraz that the militants now really meant business.

Meanwhile in Delhi on 25ᵗʰ May 1990, with the CBI registering a FIR, a first information report against KL Verma, the Director Enforcement Directorate, Nandi his deputy, Chandraswami the self styled godman, his aide KN Agarwal also known as Mamaji, Larry J Kolb the son-in-law of the notorius arms dealer Adnan Kashoggi and George Mclean, the managing director of the bank First Trust Corporation Limited, Unni's prediction that the St Kitts affair was all a forgery was vindicated. According to one reliable source it was Kolb who had planted the story in the 'Arab Times' and he with Chandraswami had also arranged to fly Nandi to St Kitts in a private aircraft. Having obtained the letters and documents showing the details of the bank account allegedly opened by Ajeya Singh and which allegedly carried the signatures of Ajeya Singh and VP Singh, Nandi had them attested by RK Rai, the then Consul—General of India in the United States, and also by Deepak Sen Gupta, the Deputy Consul-General and then returned to India post haste. But the Central Forensic Laboratory had found that the documents bearing the signatures of VP Singh and his son were all forged and Unni very rightly concluded that all this could not have been achieved without the active connivance of the Rajiv Gandhi government. During that period Narasimha Rao was his External Affairs Minister and KK Tewari was his Minister of State and Narasimha Rao was close to the godman Chandraswami. That evening over a drink with Monty at the Press Club when Unni remarked casually that in India only the small fries get caught and the big politicians always get away scot free, Monty too very aptly added. "'No wonder only the seasoned crooks in India want to become politicians."

In early June 1990 during the children's summer holidays, when Shiraz with his family accompanied by Brigadier Aslam Rehman and his family suddenly landed up at the old ancestral family Haveli in Peshawar, both Arif Rehman and his wife Ruksana Begum were simply delighted. Shiraz and Saira's daughter Shehzadi who was going to be ten years old on 6th June wanted to celebrate her birthday with a moonlight picnic at the famous Khyber Rifles Officer's Mess at Landhikothal and of which she had heard so much from her Uncle and her grandfather. The 6th of June also happened to be the day when the allied forces launched 'Operation Overlord' in Europe forty six years ago and it also happened to be the project study that Shiraz was assigned at the NDA when he was in his final term. The day was also known as the 'The Longest Day' and an epic film by that very name had also been made by Hollywood highlighting the many sacrifices that were made by the soldiers on that momentous day, when the allied troops landed on the beaches of Normandy to take on Hitler and Field Marshall Rommel's army that was defending the strongly fortified Atlantic Wall. That evening under a cool moonlit night sitting on the beautiful lawns of the famous Khyber Rifles Officer's Mess when Shehzadi got ready to blow off the ten candles on the cake, her proud father Shiraz presented her with her first Sony walkman and a music cassette that had a medley of all the popular old English songs in it. The first song, was the Joan Baez number 'Blowing in the Wind,' and as the pretty birthday girl listened to it through the earphones she was simply thrilled with the words and kissed her father tenderly. Then as everybody sang happy birthday to her and she cut the big 'Black Forest' chocolate cake, her mother Saira presented her with her first ladies Omega wrist watch. And finally when Shehzadi put the first piece of cake lovingly into her grandmother's mouth and the second one into her grandfather's, both the grandparents were indeed very touched by that gesture and they blessed her with an 1887 Victorian gold guinea. When Shiraz had a look at it, he was reminded of the gold guinea that he had inherited from the late Colonel Ismail Sikandar Khan and which he had left in the safe custody of Monty on that 15th of September 1971, when he boarded the Kashmir Mail at the Old Delhi Station to fight the Pakistanis. That guinea too was minted in 1887 and Shiraz had heard the story of how Colonel Ismail Sikandar Khan had inherited it from his father Naik Curzon Sikandar Khan. That story was told to him many a times when he was a young boy by the late Colonel Daler Singh Bajwa.

While Shiraz was engrossed in his thoughts, Shehzadi's cousin brother Vovka who was now eighteen and who had especially come all the way from the PMA at Kakul for the occasion jokingly plastered her pretty face with the chocolate icing. Though Shehzadi was not the least amused, she took it rather sportingly. But her seven year old younger brother Tojo was up in arms as he gave it back in style, when he threw a big piece of that cake straight into Vovka's face. Not to be left behind when Vovka's eight year old sister Nasreen also joined in that cake fight, Zubeida Begum now seventy years old very sternly said. "Let me remind you all that the "Officer's Mess is not a children's playground and its sanctity must be maintained at all times.' With that message from her being loud and clear, the children quietly went indoors for a game of table tennis, while their parents and grandparents got engrossed in a serious discussion about the future of the Benazir government.

"Well looking at the manner in which she and her party the PPP has been running this country where law and order has taken a complete back seat and where horse trading has become the order of the day, I wonder if she will be able to serve her full term. And with her fun loving polo playing husband Asif Zardari who I believe is now popularly known as 'Mr Ten Percent' together with some others who have the right political connections raking in the moolah and looting the country, she may be given the boot even earlier," said Arif Rehman Khan as he added a few more ice cubes to his single malt whisky.

"But I only hope the army won't step in again, because if General Aslam Beg who I have been told in private is not entirely averse to the proposal does so even in good faith, then God help this country. Because past history has clearly shown that once these jack booted Generals take over the country and promise the people that they would soon restore it back to democracy, they never actually do so," said Ruksana Begum in her usual sarcastic tone as Shiraz opened the bottle of champagne to celebrate his daughter's birthday.

"That is true, but Benazir by appointing her father-in-law Hakim Ali Zardari as the Chairman of the Public Accounts Committee has also made a mockery of the whole thing. That appointment is traditionally held by a senior member from the opposition in the National Assembly and whose prime duty is to scrutinize the government accounts, but all that the elderly Zardari is busy doing is targeting the leader of the opposition, Nawaz Sharif and others from the IJI party and propagating to the press that they are ones who are totally corrupt and are fleecing the country. It is not that the likes of Sharif and others like him in the opposition are more 'Sharif' and less corrupt, but for the Bhuttos and the Zardaris to claim that they are the only holy cows in this country is really a bit too much to swallow. And if 'Mr Ten' percent carries on with the same tempo for another couple of years, while his wife Benazir is still in the chair, then I am sure he will get into the Guinness book of records of having scored the fastest billion both in American dollars and Sterling pounds," said Zubeida Begum somewhat in a lighter vein.

"Yes Bhabhiji, you are damn well right. Because the manner in which horse trading is being done in our very own provincial assembly of the NWFP and where I believe the PPP in order to stay in power is offering members of the IJI not only the mind boggling amount of five million rupees to defect, but it is also giving them four plots each as bonus and that money has to come from somewhere, isn't it?" added Arif Rehman as his son Brigadier Aslam asked the handsome Pathan Mess Havildar in his ceremonial uniform to lay the dinner in the air-conditioned VIP dining room of that legendary officer's mess that the British had built and one that was now also a big tourist attraction for those old retired British officers and their families who had served in the North West Frontier. And besides the historical radial clock the big chained walnut tree in the garden was also one of the major attractions.

While Vovka very gallantly escorted his grandmother to the dining room and helped her to be seated on the well laid dining table, and elderly Englishman who was immaculately dressed in a pin striped three peice and with a regimental tie of the First Punjabees around his neck kept staring at her all the time. The Englishman with his wife was seated on a nearby table, and while he kept staring at her Zubeida naturally also started feeling a little embarrassed. Then a minute or so later, when the Englishman after having whispered a few words to his wife got up and gracefully walked up to where Zubeida was sitting and having first wished everybody a very good evening said." Please do pardon me Madam but if my memory is not very wrong aren't you Mrs Gul Rehman Khan?" Hearing those words coming from the elderly Englishman, there was total silence on the table. And when the gentleman further added that he too had served with her husband in the First First Punjabees during the war in Burma where he had been wounded during the ding dong 'Battle of The Tennis Court' that was fought inside the DC's bungalow at Kohima, and from where he was rescued by her husband, all that Zubeida could respond with was a stony smile. But that was some 46 years ago and Zubeida too had now grown fairly old. But after the elderly British officer having surveyed the long family table finally asked. "But where is my dear friend Gulu? I don't see him around." Brigadier Aslam Rehman broke the ice and introduced himself. And when Aslam Rehman conveyed the sad news that his father was no more, the British officer who had introduced himself as Major Mitchell felt indeed very sad. Then like a true First First Punjabee when Aslam Rehman requested Major Mitchell and his wife to join their table and congratulated the elderly Englishman for having recognized his mother after 43 long years, there was a big smile on Major Mitchell's face as he got up from his chair and having raised a toast to his departed friend said very candidly. "Well this is what is called true regimental spirit my son and let me confess that your mother is still as pretty and as graceful as she was then when I first met her. She was then a devoted young mother of two unruly toddling brats and that was soon after the war when the First First Paltan was stationed at Bannu in the North West Frontier Province and I as a bachelor conveniently made it a habit to drop in for some delicious mutton curry and rice on every other weekend at your father's bungalow inside the Bannu fort. But then followed the terrible damn partition of the country and it spoiled the entire party. Thereafter I left India and lost touch with him and his family. But I am glad that my wife and I today are honoured to be with the family once again." And when it suddenly dawned on Zubeida that the gentleman could be nobody else but Captain Bruce Mitchell who always used to address her as Zubi, she immediatelty requested her son to order for a bottle of champagne to celebrate the happy reunion. As soon as the bottle was popped open and Aslam Rehman did the honours, Arif Rehman on behalf of Zubeida raised a toast to the elderly

British couple who had come all the way from England and whom they had only by chance met that day. And while everybody said cheers to the happy reunion, Zubeida closed her eyes and remembered those lovely beautiful days. She was then a young wife and whenever she and her handsome husband with their two chubby little sons Aslam and Fazal who were then five and one year old respectively went for their daily evening stroll to the Company Bagh inside the small army cantonment at Bannu all eyes would be on them. And even during the monthly ball at the officer's club whenever a tag dance was announced and though she was one of the handful of ladies in a sari, all the young bachelor British officers would make a bee line for her and Captain Bruce Mitchell who was a war time emergency commissioned officer was no exception either. That evening before retiring to bed, when Shiraz remarked to Saira somewhat seriously what a great institution the Indian Army was and then added that had it not been for partition it would have today become the single largest standing army in the world and that the Indian subcontinent would have been a power to reckon with, Saira who was pleasantly taken by surprise asked.

"But tell me darling, why is it that you always have such a weak point about the army and the so called traditions of espirit de corps and comradeship that go with it. Because to my mind this very army has ruined this country and it is high time that the Generals kept themselves away from politics and looked after the defense of the nation which is their prime responsibility, isn't it?."

"Yes there you are absolutely right, but if the politicians having been given the chance to rule democratically as is the case right now, and they start indulging in promoting religious fundamentalism, sectarianism and corruption at the highest possible levels in order to stick to their chairs, then you don't expect the Pakistan Army, which is still a very disciplined force and which has tasted power thrice earlier to just sit idle and twiddle their thumbs, do you? As it is there are strong rumours that the President Ghulam Ishaq Khan is very upset and unhappy in the manner in which the Benazir government is functioning, and I will not be surprised if one fine day he uses his powers under the eighth amendment to the 1973 constitution that General Zia had introduced and dismisses her without any further adieu and fanfare," added Shiraz as he walked to the children's bedroom to kiss them goodnight.

While the Benazir government in Pakistan and the VP Singh government in India were still trying to find their feet, the LTTE stepped up their activities to eliminate their own Tamil rivals who had fled from Sri

Lanka and who had now sought refuge in the Indian state of Tamil Nadu. On 19th June 1990, when a LTTE hit squad assassinated K Padmanabha the Secretary General of the EPRLF and 14 others who were gunned down in broad daylight in an apartment in the centrally located colony of Kodambakkam in Madras and later escaped to Sri Lanka, Shupriya was shocked. The apathy of the DMK government that was being led by Mr Karunanidhi to take no action at all to apprehend the culprits was proof enough that they were either in league with the LTTE or they had simply decided to close their eyes to such like activities in the state thought Shupriya as she made a note of the modus operandi of the hit squad that had done the job so very daringly inside the state capital. 'My God if such like merciless killing by the LTTE to eliminate their rivals continues in our own backyard and they manage to getaway scot-free, then I am afraid one day they may even target our own political leaders with the same weapons that we had provided them with and that would indeed be a sad day for the country that had once supported the LTTE both politically and militarily,' wrote Shupriya in her diary.

In mid June 1990, Arif Rehman Khan expressed his desire to go for Haj to the Holy City of Mecca and that too during the forthcoming Eid-ul-Zuha, the Muslim 'Feast of Sacrifice' that was due in early July provided somebody was ready to give him company. Arif Rehman was now seventy years old and he was aware that Mecca during such Muslim holy festivals was always a sea of people in spotless white who congregated there to offer their prayers to Allah and atone for their sins. But he also knew that with the millions of devout Muslims heading for the Holy City from all corners of the world and the Saudi administration at times unable to control the huge crowd, his going there alone would not be permitted by the family.

"Don't worry, I will keep you company Abbajaan because I have never been on Haj before and as a good Muslim I think I need to do so also and before it is too late. However, there is one small condition and that is after the Haj, you will have to accompany me to Rome to witness the World Cup Football finals that is scheduled to be played on the 8th of July and I would not like to miss it for the world," said Shiraz somewhat excitedly.

"Certainly I would love to see the finals myself, but provided we are able to make it to Rome by the 7th of July and get a decent place to stay in," said a delighted Arif Rehman as he lovingly looked at his wife Ruksana to give her final approval.

"Don't worry Abbajaan, the stay in Rome will not be a problem at all since my colleague and a dear friend in the Pakistan Embassy will be our host and I am sure he will be able to get us the tickets for the finals through the diplomatic channels," added Shiraz as he promptly booked an urgent international call to the Pakistan Embassy in Rome to talk to the Counselor Political there.

Besides witnessing football, Shiraz was also keen to visit the town of Cassino where the great battle of Mount Cassino was fought during the Second World War and where his adopted father, Colonel Ismail Sikandar Khan met and fell in love with an Italian Jew girl and had married her. They also had a son, but unfortunately by the time the war ended, the Germans had killed the mother and the son and Colonel Ismail had wowed thereafter never to marry again. The late Colonel Daler Singh Bajwa's wife whom Shiraz addressed as Bibiji had narrated to him that tragic story and Shiraz very much wanted to see that historic site which had also now become a big tourist attraction.

It was on the evening of 30th June, 1990 when Arif Rehman and Shiraz took the special PIA Haj flight to Jeddah. The Holy Quran exhorts all men to make the pilgrimage as a religious duty and Shiraz went well prepared for it also. On the very next morning having donned the 'thram', the pilgrim's dress of two plain unstiched lengths of white cloth, Shiraz and Arif Rehman waited for their turn to enter the newly constructed air-conditioned tunnel. Shiraz was thrilled by the fact that he too would perform the ceremonial journey between the two hillocks called Safa and Marwa and renew his pledge to devote himself to the call of God, as Ismail and his mother had done many centuries ago. It was a hot sunny day and by the time it was their turn to enter the tunnel, the crowd of devotees had swirled to an unprecedented number. As the devotees surged forward to enter the tunnel, Arif Rehman felt a little uneasy and claustrophobic, but all the same he kept moving forward while holding on tightly to Shiraz's hand. But as they kept going, the pressure from the rear also kept increasing and Arif Rehman who suddenly had a black out inside the tunnel was indeed lucky to have survived. Had it not been for Shiraz's ingenuity and initiative both of them probably would have become victims of that terrible man made tragedy in which more than a thousand pilgrims died. They were fortunate that they were not very far from the exit to the tunnel, when the stampede inside started and Shiraz using his full height, built and strength while firmly holding on to his father-in-law's hand managed to crawl out from the finishing line. Luckily an alarm had already been raised and with a few ambulances waiting outside, Shiraz rushed him to the nearby hospital and where Arif Rehman was immediately put under oxygen

The newly built air-conditioned tunnel named 'Moessem' was meant only for pedestrian traffic and was part of the 15 billion dollar development plan of the holy city that the Saudi government had undertaken. The tunnel was constructed to facilitate the move of the millions of pilgrims in an orderly fashion to the holy site. It had a capacity to hold not more than a 1000 pilgrims at a time and it connected the city of Mecca to the tent city of Mina on the other side. But on that hot summer Monday of 2nd July with the temperatures soaring high and the sun beating down mercilessly on the pilgrims, the large crowd waiting to get inside the air-conditioned comfort of the tunnel soon became impatient. With the crowd surging forward, the entry to the tunnel could not be regulated in the desired manner and it soon became a free for all as the pilgrims pushed and jostled their way in. And as the crowd grew larger, it only got worse. Unable to take the pressure of the human bodies that thronged the tunnel, it resulted in severe congestion and soon became a death trap. With the lack of oxygen in the tunnel and with more than four times the capacity of human beings inside the enclosed space, it was now the survival of the fittest as people trampled over each other in order to reach the exit at both ends. Ironically the rituals on that very day that commemorated Prophet Abraham's offering of his son in sacrifice to God, resulted in the painful deaths of nearly 1400 others who had come all the way from across the globe and most of them were either from Malaysia and Indonesia. The irony of the senseless tragedy however was that from the millions of Muslims who had come from all over the world to pray at the holy shrine, around 1400 of them had been sacrificed like helpless sheep in a suffocating manger.

Arif Rehman's fifteen suffocating and traumatic minutes inside the 'Moessem Tunnel 'and his subsequent hospitalization for 72 hours inside the ICU where he was kept under close medical observation was reason enough for Shiraz to cancel the trip to Rome and return back to Peshawar. Though he was not particularly disappointed in not being able to see the World Cup Football finals between West Germany and Argentina, Shiraz however felt sad that the home team and the hosts Italy whom he was backing had to bow out in the semi-finals when they lost to Argentina in a penalty shoot out. So was the fate with England for whom Arif Rehman was rooting as they too lost their semi-final match against West Germany and that too once again in a penalty shoot out. Shiraz was still more disappointed because the surprise tour of Mount Cassino and Naples that he had planned for had also to be cancelled.

Nevertheless, in order to compensate for the World Cup Finals that he missed seeing at the stadium in Rome, Shiraz on the 8th of July hosted a grand football finals evening for the entire Rehman family and their close friends on the lawns of their spacious and elegant Rehman Haveli at Peshawar. For the occasion, Shiraz had set up a giant screen and also established a mini betting booth with Vovka in charge for those who were interested in placing a few bets on the team that they fancied would win the coveted world cup and on the player who would score the final match winning goal. With Diego Maradona still showing glimpses of his fantastic dribbling and ball control, almost everyone was of the view that he would be the architect of Argentina's win, but it proved otherwise. To make the venue look like a mini stadium, Vovka with his sister Nasreen and his cousin Shehzadi had even put up four giant size paper cut outs of 'Ciao', the mascot. The four stick figures with a football head and an Italian tricolour body and with the Italian word 'Ciao'meaning 'Hey' written boldly in English were lit with bright halogen lamps and as the three great Italian tenors including Pavarotti began the proceedings with their rich voices to welcome the people, Vovka announced the last and final call for any more bets. And as the song ended he also closed the betting booth.

When the game began, most of the Rehman family and their guests were rooting for the Argentineans to win and every time Maradona had the ball the cheering would get even louder. But with lacklustre performance by both the teams and with no goals scored till half time by either side, Aslam Rehman was very disappointed, and when he remarked loudly that his going to Rome would have meant a colossal waste of time, money and energy, everybody by and large agreed with him. And even after lemon time when the same dull defensive football continued, Shiraz too thanked his stars that he was not there in person to watch such a disappointing World Cup final. But as the game progressed, it soon became a game of rough and tough football and which the Mexican referee, Eduardo Mendez at times found hard to control. In the 65th minute after he awarded the first red card to Pedro Monzon of Argentina and four minutes later blew his whistle and pointed at the Argentina penalty spot, those watching the match were simply astounded. It was a hotly disputed penalty kick that had been awarded to the West Germans and the entire Rehman clan was up in arms shouting against the decision of the referee. But the referee's decision could not be disputed. And as the West German striker Andreas Brehme placed the ball to take the spot kick, only Vovka prayed for a West German win. With most of the Rehman's and their guests having wagered on the Argentineans, Vovka as the bookie knew that a German win could now well turn out to be an unexpected windfall for him. And after the goal was scored when the referee handed over another red card to Gustavo Desotti and the Argentineans were now left with only nine players on the field, the match was well nigh over. And a few minutes later when the referee sounded the long whistle, and West Germany emerged as the world champions having scored that one and only controversial penalty kick goal, the entire Rehman clan except Vovka were very disappointed. But the West Germans had taken their revenge that evening because four years ago in Mexico they had lost in the finals to Argentina and when they lifted the trophy it was celebration time once again and this time in both the Germanys. However, Shiraz was very happy, when a relatively unknown Italian by the name of Salvatore Schillachi who was popularly known as Toto with six goals to his credit was declared the best player of the tournament and was awarded the golden boot.

During the Haj and while interacting with the Pakistan Consulate in Jeddah and also with some of the other Muslim diplomats who had come as pilgrims from the nearby neighbouring countries like the Emirates, Iraq and Iran, Shiraz was constrained to learn that Saddam Hussein was planning to invade Kuwait. There were strong rumours floating about a likely confrontation between Iraq and its oil rich small neighbour of Kuwait, which had earlier been part of the Ottoman Province of Basra, but had later become a protectorate of Britain. But after gaining independence, it was now being ruled by the Al-Sabah dynasty and was a free nation. However, Iraq had always refused to accept Kuwait's separation and Saddam Hussein was now claiming it to be a part and parcel of Iraq. There was also no doubt that the long drawn out war with Iran that had finally ended in August 1988 had made Iraq virtually bankrupt and it was heavily indebt both to Saudi Arabia and Kuwait. Moreover, in 1989, when in open defiance of OPEC quotas, Kuwait increased its oil production by forty percent and it resulted in the overall collapse of oil prices, and one that had a catastrophic snow balling effect on the fledging Iraqi economy, this had further infuriated Saddam Hussein who considered it to be a form of economic warfare that would further weaken his country. According to one confirmed source, though the two governments of Iraq and Kuwait had started negotiations to resolve the border dispute, but Saddam it seems had also ordered mobilization of its armed forces. But what bothered Shiraz even more was the confidential report from a friend of his in the Pakistan Mission in Washington that stated that President George W Bush had recently approved 4.8 million dollars in advanced technology sales to Saddam Hussein's Iraq and whose end users would be the Iraqi Ministry of Industry and the Ministry of Defense for military industrialization. According to another inside source, the massive American aid that George Bush and his administration had been pouring into that oil rich country and which now amounted to a billion dollars a year was also being used by Saddam Hussein to illegally obtain technology for Iraq's nuclear weapons and ballistic missile program and that could be rather dangerous to the world felt Shiraz as he made a small brief of his talk with various Arab diplomats who had come to Mecca for the Haj in his little red diary.

It was on 2nd October 1989, and not even a year ago, that President Bush had signed the National Security Directive Number 26 and in that he not only stated that access to Persian Gulf oil and the security of key friendly states in the area were vital to US national security, but with respect to Iraq he had further added that normal relations between the United States and Iraq would also serve America's long term interests and promote stability in both the Persian Gulf and the Middle East. While concluding his brief with the assessment that President Saddam was quite capable of invading Kuwait, which would be a cake walk for him, Shiraz wondered how the United States and the rest of the world would react to such an eventuality if Saddam actually did so. There was no doubt in Shiraz's mind that such military jingoism and strong arm tactics by a militarily powerful country like Iraq against a weak and defenseless Kuwait would set a wrong precedence, but he wondered if the US keeping its overall interest in the oil rich Gulf Region will be able to dissuade Saddam Hussein from undertaking such a misadventure. This would result in a blatant invasion of an independent but militarily weak nation and of which there were many such in the area including Saudi Arabia and if it was not checked in time, it could well trigger off a larger conflict in the region and that would be disastrous for the world noted Shiraz in his diary while he casually perused through the political map of the Gulf States.

However, by the time the month of July was over, Saddam Hussein's tanks were all set to overrun Kuwait and on 2nd August 1990, Iraq without caring a damn about world opinion invaded the small nation and took over its many rich oil fields. Fearing an Iraqi hegemony in the Persian Gulf that would effect the future oil supplies to the United States and to the western world, the US and Kuwaiti delegations in the United Nations immediately requested for a meeting of the United Nations Security Council and which under resolution 600 condemned the invasion and demanded an immediate withdrawal of all Iraqi troops from Kuwait. On the very next day, fearing a foreign intervention, the Arab League called for a solution to the conflict from within the League and warned against any foreign intervention in the region. On 6th August, with Saddam refusing to pull his troops out of Kuwait, the United Nations under resolution 661 placed economic sanctions on Iraq. Fearing that Saddam Hussein may well be emboldened to escalate the conflict further into neighbouring oil rich Saudi Arabia, which would be disastrous to the Americans, the United States immediately launched 'Operation Desert Shield'. And as leading contingents from the United States armed forces landed on Saudi Arabian soil, Osama Bin Laden the hero of the 'Battle of Jaji' that took place during the fag end of the Soviet occupation of Afghanistan and who had now left Pakistan was not too happy with the American move.

Meanwhile on that very same day of 6th August, 1990, while Saddam Hussein's troops consolidated their hold on Kuwait, there was political turmoil in Pakistan. And as had been correctly predicted by Shiraz a month earlier during the world cup football finals, Benazir and her government was also now given the boot. But it was a boot of a different kind, when the Pakistan President Ghulam Ishaq Khan dismissed her government on charges of rampant corruption, nepotism and gross misconduct. The President also dissolved both the National and Provincial Assemblies and called for fresh elections in late October. During the interim period, the President of Pakistan appointed Ghulam Mustafa Jatoi, a leader from the opposition as the interim Prime Minister.

"By God, you were dead right," said Saira to her husband as he returned home that evening from his office while his mother-in-law Ruksana Begum criticized the arbitrary manner by which Benazir was shunted out from office. The 6th of August happened to be a Monday, and when on that late afternoon Shupriya sitting in her Ministry of External Affairs office in South Block, New Delhi was given the news about the sudden change of guard in Pakistan, she could not believe it either. Only twenty months ago Pakistan had returned to democratic rule and had elected Benazir Bhutto as the Prime Minister, and her sudden dismissal now did not augur well for stability in the subcontinent thought Shupriya as she too noted the day in her diary. And two days later on 8th August, when Benazir at a press conference in Karachi categorically blamed the military for her dismissal, Shupriya was not the least surprised. But an unstable Pakistan was not in India's interest and with militancy and religious fundamentalism gaining ground in that country and being constantly exported from across the border to our own neighbouring states of Jammu and Kashmir and the Punjab; this was now a very serious issue and could not be taken lightly by the Indian government.

On 6th August 1990, and immediately following the dismissal of the Benazir government, the Army Chief General Mirza Aslam Beg appointed Major General Asad Durrani who was the Director General Military Intelligence to handle both the MI and ISI concurrently. On that very day Yasin Malik, the self styled Commander-in-Chief of the JKLF and other top militants of that group were also arrested by the Indian security forces. Soon thereafter the militant outfits in Jammu and Kashmir at the point of the gun sponsored a 72 hour strike by the state government employees in the Kashmir valley. The deteriorating law and order in Srinagar had further affected Monty's export business and he wondered as to when the situation would improve.And in India too VP Singh's mishmash Janata Dal coalition government in Delhi that had been in power only for nine months had also now started feeling the heat from within. The heat however was not from the Indian armed forces whose officers and soldiers kept battling the militants in the valley and in Punjab, but from the opposition forces in Parliament. Having been humiliated and disgraced by VP Singh on the Bofors scandal issue that led to the fall of the Rajiv Gandhi government, the Congress (I) led by the former Prime Minister and his supporters were hell bent in redeeming their honour. They also knew that the memory of the illiterate masses of India was always rather short livid and to forgive and forget was part of the Indian culture. A classic example of this was Indira Gandhi's return to power in 1980. So while the VP Singh government kept limping along, the Congress (I) as a tit for tat started a vilification campaign against him.

VP Singh's fragile and so called National Front government was in a minority and it had to rely heavily on the support of the right wing BJP, the Bhartiya Janata Party and the left wing CPI(M), the Communist Party of India Marxist group. Moreover, VP Singh's own deputy Devi Lal had also started sulking for not being made the prime minister of the country. There was also the Ram Mandir issue in Ayodhya that the BJP and the Sangh Parivar wanted to cash on, but they could not risk doing so. They knew that by toppling the VP Singh government would only bring back the Congress (I) back into power and that would be suicidal for them. But when the BJP and Devi Lal began playing politics of caste, creed and religion and Devi Lal on 7th August, 1990 made false charges of corruption against his own cabinet ministers that engineered his own ouster from the government, VP Singh to counter the threat dug out the ten year old Mandal Commission report. The report that had been gathering dust dealt with 27 percent reservation of jobs in the Central Government for the backward classes was the handy work of BP Mandal, a former Chief Minister of Bihar. Though the man whose report on job reservation redefined class-caste stratification in the country had died in 1982 and was buried with him, but his ghost was suddenly resurrected, when VP Singh on 7th August as the messiah of the down trodden very triumphantly announced that his government would honour and implement its recommendations. This resulted in a caste war as nearly 75 upper class youths in protest immolated themselves. Amongst them was Rajeev Goswami a twenty year old college student from Delhi who set himself on fire. And when the entire national and international media and the television channels played it up, there was hell to pay. The decision to implement the Mandal Commission report had triggered of a bloody caste war as people came out on the streets to protest both for and against it and which resulted in police firings and caused the deaths of many. VP Singh's strategy to finish his arch rivals like Devi Lal and thwart the design of the communal forces in the country had sent shock waves through the BJP's rank and file since it directly hit their upper caste based vote bank. To counter the Mandal offensive, LK Advani the fiery President of the BJP launched his Rath Yatra. In order to checkmate the 'Ram Rath' that the BJP had initiated with LK Advani in the lead, VP Singh decided to launch his own 'Mandal Rath.' It seems that Sharad Yadav and Ram Vilas Paswan the two ministers in VP Singh's cabinet had assured the Prime Minister that the 'Mandal Rath' would crush the 'Ram Rath", but that was not to be. The confrontation between the two sides only resulted in increasing communal tension in the country and as the BJP chariot made its journey across the length and breadth of India to its final destination Ayodhya, Hindu-Muslim riots erupted everywhere. To stem the tide of violence, VP Singh goaded Lalu Prasad Yadav, the maverick Chief Minister of Bihar to arrest Advani as soon as he entered Bihar. This further resulted in the arrest and deaths of a large number of Sangh Parivar activists who were now even more determined to march and destroy the Babri Masjid and build the Ram Mandir there at Ayodhya.

To avoid a direct confrontation with the BJP, VP Singh had earlier pinned his hopes on the decision of the Allahabad High Court that had been sitting on the disputed Babri Masjid case for the past 41 years. Any decision for or against would have given him and his government the moral and legal authority to force the court's ruling on both the contending parties, but the court kept sleeping on it. For the fragile National Front government of VP Singh and his hurried decision on 7th August to announce the implementation of the Mandal Commission report prematurely and without consulting his allies and without initiating a debate in parliament was a blunder of the highest order and he would now have to pay heavily for it. When on 14th September 1990, the BJP announced its decision to support the temple agitation and further resolved to build the Ram temple at the disputed site, it was now only a question of time for the government to fall. VP Singh's momentous decision to implement reservations in government jobs had also opened a Pandora's Box as caste based politics now took centre stage and created regional satraps of the likes that of the Mulayams, Mahawatiis and the Lallu's in the country. They were now only eagerly waiting in the wings to get on to bandwagon of coalition politics that had come to stay.

In that month of August, while the young men of India in protest against the Mandal Commission Report were setting themselves ablaze, in England a 17 year old young Indian cricketer was setting the English pitches on fire.

"Didn't I tell you that last year, when India toured Pakistan that this young lad who was just 16 then would one day be the toast of Indian cricket? Well to me it seems that the day has come because he has scored his first maiden century against England at the Old Trafford and believe you me there will be many many more such centuries to come," said a delighted Monty to Peevee as he showed him the photographed of the curly haired, baby faced Sachin Tendulkar in the newspaper "The Times of India' that was published from Bombay.

"Yes Papa and he is a real genius and I believe his father named him Sachin in honour of the great music maestro Sachin Dev Burman and now the young budding cricketer is already a master of the willow," added a delighted Peevee as he kissed the photograph.

Born on 24th April, 1973, in Bombay, the dimunitive Bombay batsman with a squeaky voice who could bat, bowl and accurately throw with his right hand but who wrote with his left was a cricket prodigy right from the day he as a toddler came under the eyes of his coach Ramakant Achrekar. The boy from Sharadashram High School and the son of Ramesh Tendulkar, a Marathi novelist had created cricket history in 1988, when he with his team mate Vinod Kambli in the inter school Harris Shield tournament had notched up an unbroken partnership of 664 runs. And then in his very first Ranji Trophy match scored a maiden hundred against Gujrat. He further established his greatness when at 16 he made his test debut against Pakistan.

Though he only scored 15 runs but the manner in which he faced the fast bowling of Waqar Younis who was also making his debut showed the kind of guts the young boy had. Although he was hit on the mouth by Waqar Younis, Sachin kept batting with his blood drenched shirt. The lad who wanted to become a fast bowler and who had attended the MRF camp under Dennis Lillee was now the 'Little Master' when it came to batting.

And while Sachin Tendulkar with his bat was going great guns, the political leaders of the country were getting ready to once again destabilize the country. On 23rd October 1990, when Monty with his wife Reeta, Shupriya and Peevee were on their way home after watching the evening show of the sensational block buster film of the year 'Maine Pyar Kiya' that had a handsome young Salman Khan as the hero and a relative newcomer by the name of Bhagyashree as the heroine, Peevee who loved good Moghlai food suggested that Karim's at Nizamuddin would be an ideal place to end the day with. When they entered the restaurant and Monty overheard from someone that the BJP had withdrawn support to the VP Singh government, he was not the least surprised. It had been triggered off by the arrest of LK Advani at Samastipur in Bihar that morning, but VP Singh had not resigned. He had decided to test his strength in parliament. And when Peevee jokingly remarked that VP Singh instead of weeping should send his own 'Kabootar' (Pigeon) with the message to the opposition that he was willing to sacrifice his own government for the sake of unity, love and secular credentials of the country like it was shown in that hit movie, everyone laughed. But they all knew that VP Singh's days were numbered.

Meanwhile in Pakistan with only a few days left for the elections to the Provincial and National Assemblies, rumours were rife that the ISI and the military in the country were not at all keen to see Benazir and her PPP back in the driver's seat. And in order to ensure that that did not happen under any circumstances, a very large sum of money of Rupees 14 crores for horse trading and rigging the elections had been transferred from the Mehran Bank to the ISI by Yunus Habib who was the owner of that bank. According to Brigadier Aslam Rehman who confidentially had told Shiraz that the entire Rupees 140 million had first been deposited with the 'Survey Section Account Number 202' of the Military Intelligence that was headed by Major General Javed Ashraf Kazi and later from there 60 million was also paid to President Ghulam Ishaq Khan's election cell mates, while the remaining 80 million was transferred to the ISI account to ensure that Benazir and her party did not win, Shiraz refused to believe him. But with big money in their hands, the ISI it seemed had managed to have their way because when the election results were officially and finally declared, Benazir and her PDA, the Pakistan Democratic Alliance were a distant second. The IJI, the Islamic Jamhoori Ittehad led by Nawaz Sharif of the Pakistan Muslim League not only secured a two third majority in the National Assembly, but the alliance had also acquired control of all the four provincial assemblies. And to top it all it also enjoyed the full support of the military.

Mian Mohammed Nawaz Sharif the Prime Minister designate was born in 1949 at Lahore on Christmas Day like Jinnah. He came from a family of Kashmiri immigrants who had migrated and settled in Punjab in the late 19th century. His dominating father who had started a modest cast iron parts business was now a prominent industrialist and the family owned the Iteefaq Group of Industries. Nawaz Sharif became politically prominent after General Zia in 1977 took over the country. He had served both as the Finance Minister of Punjab and subsequently also became the Chief Minister of that important province. And as he waited to take his oath as the eleventh Prime Minister of Pakistan, the ISI sponsored militants in Kashmir which incidentally was also once Nawaz Sharif's ancestral home were getting ready to unleash a fresh round of terror in the valley.

Meanwhile on the 30th of October, 1990 with the security forces opening fire on the crowd that was marching toward the disputed Ram Janmabhoomi-Babri Masjid site and which resulted in the deaths of several people and injuries to many, the end of VP Singh's government was in sight. On the 5th of November, there was a vertical split in the Janata Dal when a breakaway group of 58 Members of Parliament elected Mr Chandrashekhar as their leader and VP Singh having lost the no confidence motion in parliament resigned. Three days later on 8th November, when the Congress (I) extended support to Chandrashekar to form the government, the political cat and mouse game had once again begun. As Chandrashekar who was once a 'Young Turk' during Indira Gandhi's first Congress government took his oath of office as the new Prime Minister of India, in Islamabad a radiant and elated Nawaz Shariff waited for the 10th of November to be sworn in as the new Prime Minister of Pakistan. Elsewhere in Bangladesh, Dimpy was witness to another change of guard. In November with large scale disturbances in the country, General Ershad had declared emergency. But as the situation further deteriorated and in the face of a mass uprising, he too threw in the towel and on the 6th of December formally quit office. The power was transferred to Chief Justice Shahbuddin who as an Acting President called for fresh elections in February 1991.

While India, Pakistan and Bangladesh, the three nations of the subcontinent were looking forward to a new beginning in 1991, the crisis in the Gulf region took a more sinister turn. On 29th November, 1990 the United Nations Security Council having passed resolution 678 authorised military intervention in Iraq if it did not withdraw all its forces from Kuwait and free all the hostages by Tuesday, 15th January, 1991. The blatant Iraqi violation of Kuwait's territorial integrity was not acceptable to the world body. A day earlier John Major having succeeded Margaret Thatcher was appointed as the new Prime Minister by Queen Elizabeth II. On the 6th of December 1990, Saddam Hussein released the western hostages, but he was in no mood to withdraw his troops from Kuwait.

And as the year 1990 came to a close and the world waited with baited breath to see if Iraqi forces would retract their steps, the combined military might of 34 countries led by the United States of America got ready to launch their offensive against Iraq. Though Pakistan was a part of that 34 and had promised to commit a full brigade, but it was only on condition that the Pakistani troops would only be deployed in guarding vital areas in depth including the Royal Palace of the Saudi King who was a dear friend and a true well wisher of Pakistan.

During the first week of 1991, though various peace proposals had been floated to avoid the armed conflict in the Gulf Region, but none were agreed upon. Whereas the United States kept insisting on Iraq's unconditional withdrawal from Kuwaiti soil, Iraq kept reiterating that it should be linked to a simultaneous withdrawal of Syrian troops from Lebanon and Israeli troops from the West Bank, Gaza Strip, the Golan Heights and from southern Lebanon. Though Syria had joined the coalition, Israel with the tacit support and blessings of the United States remained totally neutral. And on 12th January, with the US Congress having officially authorized the use of force and as the war clouds darkened further, Shiraz sitting in his office with a map of the region on his table tried to figure out as to how the war was likely to be fought. He had correctly surmised that with the preponderance of air power in favour of the coalition forces, the offensive had to commence with a massive air campaign to begin with and which would then be followed by a mass scale ground attack with mechanized forces and he was dead right.

During the early hours of 16th January and 17th January 1991, with the deadline having passed, 'Operation Desert Storm' went into action. And as US helicopter gun-ships and attack helicopters blasted the Iraqi radar sites near the Saudi Arabian border, the 22 F-15 fighter aircrafts attacked the Iraqi airfields in western Iraq. At 3 AM in the morning, 10 US.F-117 Nighthawk Stealth fighters bombed the Iraqi capital of Baghdad. Concurrently the deadly accurate Tomahawk Cruise Missiles from the US Naval ships also came raining down on Iraq's capital city destroying strategic targets that included the TV station, the government headquarters, buildings and the Presidential Palace. As the deadly air assault continued relentlessly it destroyed the Iraqi Air Force and its anti-aircraft capabilities both on the ground and in the air. Feeling the heat, Saddam Hussein in a radio broadcast to his people urged them not to give up hope. He told them that though the mother of all battles had begun, the victory would be finally theirs. But he was only fooling himself. With precision guided munitions, also known as smart bombs and cruise missiles targeting strategic objectives at will, all that Saddam could retaliate with on the first day was by launching 8 Scud missiles into Israel. He was hoping that Israel would retaliate and the neighbouring Arab countries would come to his rescue thereby escalating the conflict to another Arab-Israeli war. But his hope that it would draw other Arab states out of the coalition miserably failed when Israel very cleverly refused to hit back.

Unknown to Saddam Hussein and his coterie of Generals, most of the Iraqi targets had been located by aerial photography and they were all in reference to the GPS coordinates of the US Embassy in Baghdad. This had been determined by an US Air Force Officer way back in August 1990, when he visited the US Embassy for this very important task. And as the air war with sophisticated American stealth fighters dominated the skies over Iraq and the Tomahawk cruise missiles and cluster bombs called 'Daisy Cutters' continued raining death and destruction on the ground, an adamant Saddam Hussein waited for his turn to strike. And he did so with his ground forces on 29th January, when Iraqi tanks and infantry attacked the lightly defended Saudi city of Khafji. But after two days of heavy fighting and superior air power, the Iraqi troops were driven back. Had Saddam Hussein captured that strategic city that was located in the Eastern region of Saudi Arabia, he would have not only secured a major portion of the oil fields in that area, but it would have also enhanced Iraq's defensive capability against the coalition ground forces who were now getting ready to launch the ground phase of 'Operation Desert Storm'. A few days' later three eight man patrols from the British Special Air Services landed behind Iraqi lines to gather intelligence on the movement of Soviet built Scud mobile missile launchers and other battle field tactical intelligence about the Iraqi defensive deployment on the ground.

During that month of January 1991, while the Gulf War was in progress, there was some very disturbing news both from the Indian States of Tamil Nadu and from Jammu and Kashmir. As per reliable intelligence reports after the withdrawal of the IPKF from Sri Lanka more than a lakh of Tamil refugees had made their way to Tamil Nadu. And according to the Indian Intelligence Bureau, there was now a diabolical plan by a group that called itself the Tamil Nadu Retrieval Troops, which was a front organization of the LTTE in India to start a secessionist movement in the state. As a result of this and for the DMK government's alleged support to the LTTE, Karunanidhi's government had been dismissed and President's rule had been imposed in the state. There were also reports that the LTTE had also developed links with several Indian terrorist organizations that included the PWG, the Peoples War Group of Andhra Pradesh and the ULFA, the United Liberation Front of Assam. And when all this came to Shupriya's notice she was naturally very upset and she decided to check back with a friend of her's who was now a senior officer in RAW and was posted in the Cabinet Secretariat.

Known more commonly as the Research and Analysis Wing, the RAW had been organized on the lines of the American CIA. The Chief of RAW whose official designation was Secretary (Research) in the Cabinet Secretariat was therefore a part of the PMO, the Prime Minister's Office. The officers serving in RAW were designated as 'Research Officers' and it had a fairly large number of lady officers even at the operational level. The main functions of this organization which had now become a full fledged cadre based service was to obtain information that was critical to India's strategic interest, sift the data so collected and classify them appropriately according to the threat perception. Thereafter, based on all the inputs, RAW was required to make a reasonably sound assessment and keep the Prime Minister regularly informed. All this was carried out by their trained sleuths through aggressive intelligence gathering as well as by carrying out effective counter intelligence against the enemy's intelligence collecting agents and organizations. To facilitate them to carry out their tasks both overtly and covertly they were generally posted as first and second secretaries in the Indian diplomatic missions abroad, as also in certain other government and non government organizations that do business with foreign companies, and even in multinational companies, cultural organizations and the media too when and if required. It was entirely a cloak and dagger business and while Shupriya was being briefed by her friend about the latest political scenario in Sri Lanka and in Tamil Nadu, she was reminded of her late husband Shiraz who always wanted to become an Indian James Bond and she had therefore in her letters always addressed him as 'Dablo' meaning Double O.

Acording to Shupriya, It was nearly twenty years ago during the 1971 war that Shiraz had died fighting the Pakistanis in Jammu and Kashmir, but now it had become a war of proxy that was being fought practically everyday in that troubled state. 'Operation Topac' as planned by the late General Zia-ul-Haq was moving along its charted course, but what was worse was the kind of noise that was allegedly being made by Faroukh Abdullah who was sitting pretty in London. According to one source, he had been instructing his party members not only to lie low, but if need be to cross the line of control and arm themselves to take on Governor Jagmohan who he claimed because of his anti Muslim stance was now Kashmir's greatest enemy. When Shupriya discussed the veracity of this report that had been sent by some source in London with Monty, Monty dug out an extract of an old letter that Sheikh Abdullah had written to his Highness Maharaja Hari Singh on 26th September, 1947, the day he was released from prison. A copy of this extract had been kept by his father Colonel Daler Singh as proof of what was going through the Sheikh's mind and that of the Maharaja after India had already been divided and the Maharaja was still to make up his mind. The letter read as follows.

"May it please Your Highness? In spite of what has happened in the past, I assure Your Highness that myself and my party have never harboured any sentiment of disloyalty towards your Highnesss person, throne or dynasty. The development of this beautiful country and the betterment of its people is the common aim and interest and I assure your Highness the fullest and loyal support of myself and my organization. Not only this but I assure your Highness that any party within or without the State which may attempt to create any impediment in our effort to gain our goal will be treated as our enemy and will be treated as such."

That evening reflecting on that old letter which finally ended with the sentence 'Your Highness' most obedient servant, SM Abdullah,' Shupriya wondered whether the Sheikh together with the Maharaja had reconciled to the idea of having an independent Kashmir and they may well have got it had Pakistan not sent in the Pathan raiders to spoil the party that ultimately gave most of Kashmir to India instead. It was only a month later on 27th October. 1947, a day that was now celebrated by the Indian Army as 'Infantry Day' that the Maharaja and the Sheikh having reconciled that there was no other option left but to sign the instrument of accession and in return to seek India's help militarily. Monty had also heard from his late father that the Maharaja fearing his life was in danger had left Srinagar for Jammu on the previous night and though he had signed the instrument of accession before departing for his winter capital, but he still nursed hopes of getting back his kingdom once the raiders were thrown out by the Indian army But according to Monty what was still worse was the fact that 47 years later Faroukh Abdullah whose father was made the first Prime Minister of the State by Jawaharlal Nehru and which finally brought to an end the Maharaja's rule in Kashmir was now with his irresponsible statements from London encouraging the secessionist elements in the state, and that was unacceptable to him.

"Pardon my being a little blunt but both the Nehru-Gandhi family and the Abdullah family have made a mess of the Kashmir problem and it is high time they realized it," said a visibly angry Monty whose export business was one of the worst hit.

"But Dad though the old Maharajas with royal blood are all now dead and gone, but it this new breed of young Maharajas from the dynastic political families that India should now be bothered and worried about. Having been catapulted into the murky and corrupt world of Indian politics through their family trees and lineage, it is they who need to be watched and kept under control, both by the Indian intelligentsia and the masses or else there will be hell to pay if there is another war over Kashmir," said Peevee as Reeta announced that dinner was ready.

The next day was 26th January, and as Shupriya with Peevee, Monty and Reeta watched the impressive military parade and the pageant on the Rajpath, there were tears in her eyes. Exactly nineteen years ago on that day of 1972, which was also her twenty second birthday, she had watched the same parade on the television screen in Bangalore. On that day with Peevee in her womb, when Monty during that parade received her husband's Param Veer Chakra posthumously from the President of India she had collapsed and fainted. But today with 19 year old Peevee sitting beside her, she felt indeed very proud. On 29thh January, after the beating of the retreat by the massed bands of the Indian Armed Forces on Vijay Chowk was over, a lonely Shupriya silently walked towards the India Gate and laid a bouquet of red roses at the cenotaph of the 'Unknown Indian Soldier.' And as she silently read the names of all those Indian army men who had sacrificed their lives fighting for the British Empire during the First World War, she was reminded of her late husband Major Shiraz Ismail Khan who had been decorated with the Param Veer Chakra. That was the highest award for bravery no doubt, but she wondered at what price was that glory. As the brother of the highest gallantry award winner in the Indian army and whose late father Lt Colonel Daler Singh Bajwa and Uncle Colonel Ismail Sikandar Khan were also decorated soldiers who had laid down their lives for the country, Monty felt rather sad in the manner in which these heroes living or dead and their families were being so shabbily looked after by the government. And as he too kept reading the names of India's war heroes of the First World War he said to Shupriya.

"I think it is a bloody shame. Whereas an athlete or a national shooter having won just a single medal in the Asian Games, or for that matter a cricketer having scored a few centuries in international cricket were being monetarily rewarded and honoured with tons of money and free accommodation by their respective state governments and the central government, the poor decorated soldier fighting and dying for his country was in comparison being given a pittance for his bravery and valour. While all kinds of lucrative advertisement contracts by various sponsors showcased the smiling face of such sporting heroes with their products that could now be seen on giant size hoardings, and on the television screens, the poor soldier with his gallantry award went unsung and was soon forgotten. And I am afraid that if this trend continues then not only will the army suffer in the long run but the country to."

That evening over a frugal dinner of plain soup, toast, omelet and cheese at Shupriya's apartment when Monty once again brought up the topic as to why young men were shying away from the glamour of the uniform, Shupriya said.

"Well, as far as the jawans and other ranks were concerned, that was not the case at all, but that could be attributed to the unemployment in the country and therefore the young men from the villages were still keen to join the army. But as far as the officer cadre was concerned, it was indeed a very serious issue and it was high time that the government took a serious note of it." And when Shupriya further added that the officer deficiency in the Indian Army was a staggering thirty percent, Reeta just could not believe it.

"Well what do you except, if you only give them peanuts as a starting salary and forget them when they retire so very young. And that is the one main reason that today's young educated men and even those coming from service backgrounds have started looking for brighter pastures elsewhere," added Monty.

"And to such young, ambitious and educated people what mattered now was not the glamour of the uniform or the regiment that his father and grandfather had served in, but the kind of money and perquisites that the multinationals and big Indian business houses including the foreign banks were now offering in the civvy street. And therefore very few were willing to join the army," added Reeta as the new state of the art cordless telephone that Reeta had presented Shupriya with on her forty first birthday rang. It was a new gizmo with a voice control and a recorder and as Peevee's loud tenor voice came on the line, Shupriya was thrilled.

"I am sorry I will be a little late, but I must also tell you that my performance as Hamlet in the play at Sapru House was highly applauded by the audience," said an excited Peevee while informing that he will soon be home. And a little later when Peevee still with his make up on entered the room with a big bouquet of tube roses for his Mom Number 2, Shupriya was amazed at the similarity with her late husband. It was not only just the good looks and the voice, but also his mannerisms.

That night before going to bed, Shupriya prayed for her son's success in the profession that he had chosen for himself, but was still waiting to step into it. Peevee was determined to become an actor on the Bollywood screen and though Shupriya was aware that successful screen heroes in the filmy world of Bombay made tons of money, but she also knew where most of that money usually came from. The underworld of Bombay with their black money had made deep inroads into Bollywood and Shupriya was afraid that her son would get into wrong company. The extortion racket known locally as the 'Hafta', together with the 'Hawala' business of laundering black money combined with smuggling of gold, silver, and drugs with the help and connivance of some unscrupulous policemen and customs officials who in the underworld parlance were known as 'Dresswallas' had become such big business that the 'Dons' of Bombay who were commonly known as 'Bhais' or big brothers had now started dictating terms in Bollywood too. As big time producers and distributors it was they who now dictated and decided who should be the hero and heroine of the film, how much they should be paid in black and how much in white since quite a few films with big stars were being financed by them.

And as the month of February progressed, and a different kind of a war of terror was unleashed on England's capital city of London, Monty was shocked beyond belief. On 7th February 1991, the IRA, the Provisional Irish Rebublican Army had launched a dare devil mortar attack on 10, Downing Street where the new Prime Minister John Major was holding his cabinet meeting. Luckily the bombs missed the target. And when this was followed by the bombings of the Paddington and Victoria railway stations on the 18th and Peevee nonchalantly remarked and said my God what is this world coming to, Reeta who had just come in with a the tall glass of milk for Peevee simply looked at him and said somewhat jokingly. 'Now please drink the milk fast or else Gabbar Singh will come.' Hearing that Monty who was enjoying his beer was immediately also reminded of Peevee's fourth birthday. The date was 6th of June, 1976 and Peevee was refusing to have his milk that day, till Reeta repeated the dialogue that actor Amjad Khan as Gabbar Singh had immortalized in his debut film Sholay and little Peevee that day immediately gulped his milk down.

"But don't you think that it is time that Peevee graduated from drinking milk to drinking lassi (buttermilk) or may be a little beer instead," said Monty as he winked at Peevee and opened another can of imported Carlsberg beer, while Peevee like a good boy very reluctantly drank his milk.

"Now for heaven sake please do not start giving him such ideas. There is no better substitute for milk to a healthy mind and body and with his big manly physique, I think he should have more of it everyday," said Shupriya.

"Yes I agree but only if it is pure milk. Because nowadays I regret to say nothing is pure in this country. Even our political parties and their leaders are all a bunch of adulterated goons who keep changing sides at the drop of a hat or even rather at a drop of a coin should I say," added Monty with a look of sheer disgust in his face as he made a direct reference to the newly formed coalition government of Mr Chandrashekar at the centre that had been propped up by the Congress(I) and predicted that it would be miracle if it lasted even for ninety days, if not less.

"But do you think that with the Bofors issue now placed on the back burner and in case fresh elections are held, Rajiv Gandhi and his Congress (I) will still be returned to power?," asked Shupriya.

"Well the manner in which these politicians keep changing their colours and sides like chameleons and with the money power that the Congress (I) commands today, I will not be in the least surprised if he does. But yes, one thing is for sure and that is it will not be a glorious second innings entry for him. The last time it was more because of the sympathy wave on his mother's assassination that gave him the brute majority in parliament and which thanks to the Bofors scandal also resulted in his downfall. And with the kind of regional politics that is now being played in the country, it may even be a coalition of mutual convenience," added Monty as he poured himself another can of imported Carlsburg beer that he had bought in the black market from a bootlegger in Khan Market. It was from a small shop adjacent to a grocery store that was run by a sophisticated gentleman in what was considered to be one of the posh shopping centers of the capital and which had now become a regular dumping ground for all kinds of imported liquor. Some unscrupulous staff members working in the foreign embassies in connivance with their bosses from the diplomatic corps in the capital in order to make a quick buck had become regular suppliers. And the Delhites with their money power and craze for foreign goods and specially scotch whisky were willing to pay any price for it. But not everybody had direct access to the man who ran it. Khan Market was only a stone's throw away from the quarters of the senior government of India officers at Bharti Nagar and where Shupriya too had been allotted a flat. And whenever Monty with his family dropped in, which was at least once a week if not more, Monty would replenish his stock from there. However, to be on the safe side 'Operation Bootlegging' could only be carried out during the hours of darkness and that to only after most of the other shops in Khan Market had pulled down their shutters.

And by the time Monty replenished his next stock of imported booze, 'Operation Desert Storm' under the overall command of Lt General Norman Schwarzkopf of the United States army had moved into its fourth week. And while the American air force pounded the Iraqi capital and the ground troops and tanks kept throwing the Iraqis out from Kuwaiti territory, it provided a new kind of live thrilling entertainment for even those who were thousands of miles away from the battlefield. The live broadcast of the war through satellite cable TV by the intrepid CNN correspondents who were on the spot had revolutionized the art of reporting. Every afternoon over a glass of chilled beer at the swanky Le Meridien's rooftop bar while Monty with his journalist friend Unnikrishnan watched the progress of the battle on television and discussed the pros and cons of America's involvement in the strategic Gulf region, Shupriya sitting in her office wondered whether the latest ceasefire proposal by the Russians would be acceptable to the Americans. The Russian proposal envisaged a temporary ceasefire and a total withdrawal of all Iraqi forces to their pre-invasion positions within the next six weeks and it was to be followed thereafter by a total ceasefire in the region. The withdrawal and the monitoring of the ceasefire were to be undertaken under the aegis of the United Nations Security Council and though Iraq agreed to abide by it, the coalition rejected it. However, the coalition agreed that incase the Iraqi forces started withdrawing within the next twenty four hours, it would not be attacked. But when the Iraqis refused to budge, US armoured columns on Sunday 24th February, 1991 with massive air and artillery support launched their attacks. On 26th February, as the Iraqis started retreating while setting fire to the Kuwaiti oil fields, Monty who was watching it all on TV saw an unusual spectacle of precision bombing and destruction. The long Iraqi military convoys that had formed on the main Iraq-Kuwait highway were bombed so very extensively that the road soon became known as the highway of death. Hundred hours later after being briefed by General Colin Powell, the first coloured American to head the American armed forces, President George Bush at White House declared a unilateral ceasefire and on 27ᵗʰ February Kuwait was liberated. By then the allied forces had also penetrated deep into Iraqi territory and were only 240 kilometers from Baghdad.

That evening over a drink at the Press Club, when Monty called George Bush Senior a bloody fool and argued that the coalition forces should have pursued Saddam Hussein's elite Republican Guards to his doorstep and forced his ouster, Unni simply remarked that such a move would have fractured the coalition since the mandate given by the United Nations was to only liberate Kuwait. And when Unni added that maybe the CIA sleuths who were adept in plotting such internal coups may soon engineer one in Baghdad too, Peevee who had just entered the bar gave the good news that he had been selected for the two year course at the NSD, the National School of Drama in Delhi.

"Well then cheers to that,"said Monty as he offered a glass of shandy, a mix of beer and Limca to him. That day nineteen year old Peevee had his first taste of sweetened beer and when he remarked very confidently that one day he would become the brand ambassador either of that soft drink and maybe of that beer too, Monty patted him on his back.

"Yes, and now that India is on the road to liberalization this could be the best way to begin with," said a delighted Unni as all of them happily clinked glasses.

Keeping in step with India's mood to go in for economic liberalization, the Nawaz Sharif government in Pakistan also decided to follow suit. On 7ᵗʰ February 1991, he had announced the government's twenty five point economic package program and which among other measures relaxed the country's stringent foreign exchange control rules and permitted foreigners to repatriate profits as well as principal, thereby encouraging them to invest in the local market. As a result of this, the business at the country's foremost stock exchange at Karachi had started booming. Commenting on the sudden rise on the KSE Karachi Stock Exchange index, when Brigadier Aslam Rehman who had started dabbling in shares while he was posted as a Colonel with the ISI at the Embarkation Headquarters at Karachi suggested to Shiraz that he too should put some money into the bullish market to rake in a good profit, Saira was absolutely against it.

"But Bhaijaan, this is only a passing phase and until this country is both politically and economically stable and which I am afraid it is not at the moment, I don't think dabbling in shares will be such a good idea at all. Moreover, the Benazir government was thrown out because it was reported to be corrupt, and who knows, the Nawaz Sharif government too may also tow the same line," added Saira as she looked disapprovingly at her husband.

"Yes I think she is right and one must wait and watch to see if this boom is sustainable or not before putting in one's hard earned money into the share market," said Arif Rehman who considered the share market to be a gambler's den of some big time brokers who were also friends of some of the more important politicians and feudal lords of the country and had money to throw around.

Meanwhile the invasion of Kuwait by Iraq and the subsequent presence of the massive United States war machine in his own country Saudi Arabia had upset Osama Bin Laden. After the Soviet withdrawal from Afghanistan, Osama had returned to Jeddah and wanted to start his own kind of Jihad. In fact when Saddam Hussein invaded Kuwait, Osama even volunteered to bring all the Arab Mujahideens who had fought with him in Afghanistan to come and fight the Iraqis. But his religious sermons and lectures extolling the Muslims of the world to unite, rise and fight was not appreciated by the Saudi Royal family who considered him and his diehard fanatical followers to be a threat to the monarchy. Moreover, Shiraz during the 'Umrah' and on his visit to Jeddah last July had heard that not only Osama's movements in Jeddah had been restricted, but he was also under constant surveillance by his own government. Lately the National Guard from the Saudi King's army had even conducted a raid on his farm house in Jeddah and as a result of which Osama had written a protest letter to King Abdullah. But what was bothering Shiraz now was the fact that the hero of the 'Battle of Jaji' was now planning to return to Afghanistan with all his followers. In Afghanistan, Najibullah the puppet of the Soviets was still holding fort and a civil war to oust him was already in progress and the presence of Osama Bin Laden and his jehadis in the neighbourhood would only worsen matters for Pakistan and India, thought Shiraz as he made a note of it in his little red diary.

In March 1991, Dimpy having completed her tenure in Bangladesh was eagerly looking forward to her next posting. She and her steady boyfriend and batch mate Paddy, Bharat Padmanabam who was also completing his tenure in Moscow had decided that it was time that they got married. They had decided that it would be a simple civil marriage followed by a reception and that it would be held in Delhi on the 21ˢᵗ of May, 1991. In order to ensure that their next posting should be in New Delhi they had also decided to take their home leave in early April so that their combined request to the powers that be in the Ministry of External Affairs could be considered favourably. With general elections due in Bangladesh, Dimpy off late had also been kept very busy trying to ascertain which political party and of which there were now many would eventually emerge as the winner. In its short two decades of existence, Bangladesh like Pakistan had been ruled mainly by the military generals and some of whom subsequently had floated their own political parties. With General Ershad and his Jatiyo Party now in the dumps, the fight Shupriya reckoned would now be between Kahleda Zia's Bangladesh National Party and the Awami League, the party of the late Bongobodhu, Sheikh Mujibur Rahmen and which his daughter Hasina Begum was heading. While Khaleda was the wife of the late General Ziaur Reham and Hassina was the daughter of the father of the nation, but the sad part was that both the General and the Bongobdhu had been assassinated by the military. With Bangladesh having seen turbulent times, all that India was hoping for was a free and fair election and the formation of a democratically stable government in the country. During these last twenty years of their existence this predominantly poor country of Bengali Muslims had been victims of internal rivalry and political feuds, and as a result of which it had spawned a large number of fundamentalist groups and some of whom had also taken to the gun. The Presidential form of government had been a failure and it had only added to the miseries of the people. Therefore the two main political parties who had now expressed their desire that if voted to power they would amend the constitution and reintroduce the parliamentary form of government was indeed a healthy sign.

"Things are going faitly well and with the many foreign observers and local bodies also monitoring the elections, let us hope there will be no rigging," wrote Dimpy to her aunt Shupriya on the day the Bangladeshis went to the polls. The results that followed were also very encouraging. Khaleda Zia's BNP had won 144 seats and it was followed by the Awami League which had bagged 88. This was followed by the Jatiyo Party with 35 and the Jamaat-i-Islam got only 18 seats, while the rest with their single digit seats were in the also ran category. But these 18 seats that were won by the Jamaat-i-Islam a party with fundamentalist ideas were vital for Khaleda Zia to form the government and she therefore did not hesitate to seek their support. And while Khaleda Zia and her the BNP in Bangladesh were celebrating their victory, in India Rajiv Gandhi and his Congress(I) were waiting to pull the rug from under Prime Minister Chandrashekar's feet. With the instability in the centre, the Indian people by and large were now also fed up with the dirty and selfish politics that was being played by all the political parties both big and small. They people wanted stability at all costs and sensing their mood the Congress (I) was now waiting for another opportunity to form the government at the centre.

A few days later, Fazal Rehman the Counsellor Political in the Bangladesh mission in New **Delhi** in his monthly report to his Ambassador very categorically stated that the minority government of Mr Chandrashekar that was fostered by the Congress (I) had started losing its shine and therefore could fall at any moment. And in case fresh elections were held, then despite the Bofors scandal, the chances of Rajiv Gandhi and his government coming back to power could not be ruled out. Fazal Rehman's assessment was not based on any inside information, but on his constant endeavour to interact with some of the leading luminaries of the country and these included disgruntled politicians, respected journalists, writers, artists, jurists, retired bureaucrats and also some retired senior officers from the Indian armed forces. All of them as members or as guests were regulars at the Delhi Gymkhana, the Delhi Golf Club and in the many five star hotel twenty four coffee shops that had sprung up in the capital. For those who were from the disgruntled lot, all that was required to be done was to have their egos pepped up by a few pegs of good whisky and make them talk, and after a few pegs of good Scotch most of them invariably did. It always started with the usual monologue by them of 'Oh I did this and I did that, or had I warned the government, or had the government taken my advice etc etc.'. And while all this self aggrandizement continued, Fazal Rehman sitting in a corner with Samina and a glass of wine would quietly keep listening to their animated conversation.

The aura of VP Singh being the messiah of the downtrodden had already taken a beating and as the second coalition government kept wobbling, and India's economy went on a downward spin with the GDP growth rate falling to a dismal level, and inflation kept rising to unprecedented heights, it seemed that the time had come for the people of India to wake up from their slumber and try and put back the economy into forward gear. Though India was now on the verge of producing its own super computer called 'Param' but her foreign exchange reserves had reached a crisis level. And then there appeared a man who would with his ideas and brains reverse the trend and save the country from being branded as a defaulter. That man was none other than Dr. Manmohan Singh.

Born on 26th September, 1932, in Gah, which was now in the Punjab province of Pakistan, and a product of Cambridge and Oxford, Manmohan Singh had worked earlier with the International Monetary Fund. An economist by profession, he had also served as the Governor of the Reserve Bank of India. Unassuming by nature he knew that India's economic woes lay in getting rid of the several unrealistic socialist policies, the corrupt 'License Raj' and conversely bring about an economic liberalization with foreign direct investment. And while Dr Manmohan Singh and his team of economists got busy trying to find solutions for India's economic woes there were more problem for the government. As predicted earlier by Fazal Rehman on the 6th of March 1991, the four month old Chandrashekhar government fell. The Prime Minister had developed some serious misunderstandings with Rajiv Gandhi and his Congress (I) party and without whose support he knew that he could not survive. This was triggered off by an allegation that the Omprakash Chautala government in Haryana had put Rajiv Gandhi under police surveillance and to confirm this, when two Haryana policemen were shown sipping tea outside Rajiv Gandhi's 10, Janpath Road residence the battle lines between Chandrashekar's ruling coalition and the Congress(I) were drawn. It was a replay of the same situation not very many years ago, when Indira Gandhi withdrew support to the minority Charan Singh government in the centre. But now with no political party willing to form a third coalition government, the President of India dissolved Parliament and announced fresh elections for the tenth parliament in June.

Soon the country was once again gripped with the election fever and though Unni predicted that the Congress party led by Rajiv Gandhi would come back to power, Monty was of the view that it would be a hung parliament. Monty reckoned that since Bofors was still not a dead issue, the bribery scandal would therefore be played up again by those power brokers who were anti Rajiv. And then there was also the issue of President's rule that had been imposed in the volatile South Indian state of Tamil Nadu where the LTTE being averse to Rajiv Gandhi's returning to power had become again fairly active. The LTTE high command feared that Rajiv Gandhi's return may once and for all finish off whatever chances there were for an independent Eelam in the trouble torn north eastern region of Sri Lanka and this was not acceptable to them. According to Shupriya's information, Kasi Anandan an important emissary of Prabhakaran through the good offices of Malini Parthasarathy of the English daily 'Hindu' had met Rajiv Gandhi a day before parliament was dissolved, but had returned very disappointed when the former Prime Minister who was expected to come back to power rejected any plans for an independent Eelam. But this was only a rumour. However, after the parliament was dissolved and Shupriya conveyed to Monty that a few more pro LTTE supporters including a London based chartered accountant of Sri Lankan origin had been meeting Rajiv Gandhi to seek his support, Monty could not believe it. It was however quite apparent that the LTTE big wigs were quite upset, when they realized that the Congress and the AIADMK had joined hands to fight the forthcoming elections The AIADMK was the arch rival of the DMK in Tamil Nadu and its leader Jayalalitha Jayaram was at daggers drawn with Karunanidhi, whose party the DMK were strong supporters of the LTTE. The situation was no better in the north of the country either, where the ISI backed Kashmir and Sikh militants had stepped up their terrorist activities in a big way also.

During that month of March 1991, while the political parties in India were busy framing their respective manifestos for the forthcoming general elections that were to be held in June, at the Bombay House of Tata Sons the 87 year old Chairman Emiritus of the giant Indian company was getting ready to finally retire from the scene. JRD or Jeh as he was popularly known was always a perfectionist and he had made a perfect choice as to who would succeed him. On that Monday of 25th March, 1991 at the Tata Sons historic board meeting, JRD having spoken about his six eventful decades with the House of Tata's finally annointed the young and dynamic Ratan Tata as his worthy successor and Group Chairman. JRD always advocated that good human relations not only brought great personal rewards, but it was essential to the success of any enterprise and in Ratan Tata he had found the right man. The menu for the director's lunch that day was also a kind of a meal that Parsis normally prepare on festive occasions and this certainly was also a day for celebrations. The only person who was missing from that board meeting was the chubby Rusi Mody, the TISCO chairman who also loved playing the piano. The head honcho at Jamshedpur was also one of the strong contenders, but he missed out because he had spoken to early and out of turn to the press and had taken it for granted that he would be the one who would br heading the mighty Tata empire. Ironically the road on which the Tata Empire headquarters was located was on Sir Homi Mody Street and it was JRD who had it renamed after Rusi Mody's illustrious father who was a great friend of Jeh. The 1937 born Ratan Tata, the son of Naval Tata had in fact reluctantly joined Tata's after his return from the United States in

1962 and as the story goes he joined the company to please his grandmother Lady Navajbai, but now everybody will be pleased thought Monty who had only recently bought a thousand TISCO shares from the market. India was on the threshold of economic liberalization and there could not have been a better choice than the 54 year old dynamic bachelor.

Meanwhile as the Indian election tempo in the middle of April gathered momentum, Shiraz with his family decided to spend a few days first in Quetta and later in the nearby hill station of Ziarat. While in Quetta, Shiraz visited the Defence Services Staff College of which he had heard so much, but never had the chance to visit. The staff college that was set up by the British was the cradle of learning and leadership for those in the Pakistan army who aspired to become not only able and dynamic staff officers, but also capable battalion and unit commanders. The 44 week course of the student officers with their families not only gave them the opportunity to inter act with old friends and colleagues from their own armed forces, but also with those who had come from various friendly foreign countries. And though it was a hard grind for all of them, nevertheless, it was always an enjoyable year of both learning and socializing. The members of the directing staff in the college were all from the cream of the Pakistan armed forces and they ensured that their products one day would do them proud. The big brass bell that adorned the main entrance hall of the college building was testimony enough of the rich heritage of that premier military institution. The historic bell was a war trophy that was salvaged from a Russian warship during the Russo-Japanese war and was presented to the students of the staff college in 1907, when they visited Japan to see the battle sites of Manchuria.

"I must say this is a real priceless museum piece !" exclaimed Saira as the smart liaison officer, a Major from the Frontier Force Rifles who had been detailed to conduct them around remarked that it was nothing compared to the many artifacts and war trophies that were on display in his own regimental centre at Abbotabad. And when he also added very proudly that the museum also had on display the dog tag of Major Shiraz Ismail Khan from the Jammu and Kashmir Rifles of the Indian army who had been decorated posthumously with India's highest gallantry award, the Param Veer Chakra, during the 1971 war, there was lump in Shiraz's throat. He never dreamt that his dog tag, a small piece of oval shaped identification disc in aluminum with his Indian army commission number and blood group engraved on it would find a pride of place in a regimental military museum in Pakistan. But all the same Shiraz who was very keen to see it with his own eyes also wanted to know the Pakistani version of how and where it was found and what was so very great and heroic about the Indian officer's action that had made him a martyr and a hero of India. He therefore very casually asked.

"But tell me Major do you have any idea where that action was fought and how that dog tag was found?'

Feeling a little elated, Major Salimullah said."Certainly Sir, it is now part of my regiment's history." And then as Major Salimullah'in an excited tone narrated the battle for the POL dump that was fought near Kotli, a few of the officers who were doing the staff college course also joined in. While all his family members kept listening to the Major rather intently, Shiraz was convinced that it was all a fabricated story, and a story that only praised the bravery of the Pakistan army and the Frontier Force Regiment. And no sooner had Major Salimullah concluded his version by saying that though the Indian troops had fought bravely, but they were no match for the battle hardy soldiers of the Frontier Force Regiment whose battle cry was 'Nedar Hazar Ali'" meaning 'I am present before the Almighty' and whose regimental motto was 'Labbaik" meaning "Oh Lord I am at Your Service,.' Shiraz quietly walked away to see some other exhibits. These were the very words that are chanted annually by multitudes of Muslims from Mount Ararat as part of the annual rites of Haj. And when eight year old Tojo having heard that war story innocently remarked 'Agar hamari fauj ne unke Major saab aur unke sub Hindu kafiron ko maar dala, aur hum bigar kisi nuqsan ke jeet gaye, tho phir ladai kiya hui ?'" (If our soldiers killed the Indian Major and all his heathen Hindu soldiers and they could not kill a single one of ours, then what kind of a war was that?.) And on that comment, when Major Salimullah started elaborating further, Shiraz very diplomatically cut him short and told him that since time was at a premium, he could continue with the story later and requested him to proceed a little faster with the guided tour. It was nearly twenty years ago that providence had blessed him with another life and as he recalled that action and felt the scar under his trimmed beard, Shiraz said a small prayer and thanked Allah and the Saibaba of Shirdi.

Chapter-14

Does The Surame Gandhi Only Spell Disaster!

On 29th April 1991, a day after Dimpy landed in Delhi from Dhaka, a tropical cyclone once again devastated Bangladesh and it resulted in the death of over an estimated 100,000 poor people and more. On the next day, after watching the terrible destruction on television at home, when her fiancé Paddy invited her that evening for a quiet candle light dinner at the **"Dum Pukht'** restaurant at Hotel Maurya, Dimpy was not quite game for it. The suffering of the poor Bangladeshis was still n her mind, but after some coaxing by Paddy and when she heard him say that it was all God's will and that no one can fight Mother nature, Dimpy consented.

When they reached the restaurant and got to their reserved table, Dimpy who was still feeling a little down and out commented to her fiancée that Bangladesh as a country must have been born under the wrong stars or else why should it be ravaged every year with such natural disasters. On hearing that, Paddy simply smiled and replied somewhat in good humour.

"Well you could ask that question to Field Marshall Sam Manekshaw, because he and his army was the one who actually created Bangladesh." However, Dimpy was not in the least amused by that remark till Paddy conveyed to her that the hero of Bangladesh was sitting only a few tables away from them and was enjoying his chicken tikkas. Dimpy initially thought Paddy was trying to pull her leg, but it was indeed a fact when Paddy pointed him out and she was thrilled. Now in his early eighties, the immaculately dressed gentleman with his white handle bar moustache and looking much younger than his years with his ever smiling face was sitting in the company of a few more oldies and they were all enjoying the mouth watering tikkas with their drnks.

"I must say that even after he finished off General Niazi nearly twenty years ago and who I believe also had a penchant for chicken tikkas, the Field Marshall has kept himself very prim amd proper," said Dimpy.

"Undoubtedly so it seems," said a delighted Paddy as he too ordered a plate of those mouth watering succulent chicken tikkas as starters. And when Paddy added somewhat sadly that whereas the business world took cognizance of the expertise of such capable retired senior officers of the Indian army and made them chairmen and directors in their companies, but it was rather sad that the political parties completely ignored them, Dimpy too was in total agreement with him.

"Yes and you are absolutely right and what is still more surprising is the fact that none of these Generals, Admirals and Air Marshalls ever get even nominated to the Rajya Sabha, but some film stars of Bollywood fame somehow do. And I am sure with their experience and expertise in their own respective fields these senior officers from all the three services even after retirement could contribute a great deal. Their expertise can be utilized very profitabily not only in disaster management, but also during the debates on national security, internal security et al,' added Dimpy.

"'Undoubtely so but darling they are not film stars and crowd pullers who can get them the votes my love. They are all disciplined soldiers and the kind of lack of discipline that you sometime see in the Indian Parliament these days is not what it should be," said Paddy somewhat sarcastically as he ordered for a bottle of Dimpy's favourite Chardonay dry white wine.

As Dimpy closely kept observing the coterie of the immaculately dressed people on the Field Marshall's table enjoying the evening with sizzling kebabs to go with their drinks, she indeed felt very happy for them. But it was their suave table manners that impressed her the most. And when all of them stood up gallantly when a lady joined their table and Dimpy very candidly remarked. "I bet all of them must be all retired Faujis," Paddy very discreetly took out the diamond ring that was in a velvet box from his inner coat pocket. And when Paddy while saying that she was absolutely right very tenderly held Dimp's hand and slipped the ring down her wedding finger, a delighted and blushing Dimpy could only respond by gently squeezing Paddy's hand because kissing in public in India was simply not done.

On the evening of the 21st of May 1991, after the happy couple in the presence of the registrar of marriages signed on the dotted line that was witnessed only by a few of their close friends and relatives, Dimpy and Paddy were legally pronounced as man and wife. Thereafter, the celebrations on the lawns of the Delhi Gymkhana, which was the venue for the reception soon followed. The day happened to be Tuesday and quite a few of their guests and family members including Shupriya were either fasting or were on a strict vegetarian diet. As the many guests that included a large number of

VIP's and foreign diplomats with their gifts slowly moved along the never ending long line to wish the newly weds, Paddy and Dimpy kept standing and smiling like dumb mannequins, while the official photographer kept clicking away. After remaining in that standing and smiling mode for more than three long hours and after the last of the well wishers had wished them a very happy married life and had got themselves photographed with the happy couple by the official photographer and the video operator, a tired Dimpy and Paddy having got the chance quickly sat on the two hired red satin covered mahogany chairs that had been placed on the dais. As Paddy got into a semi reclining mode, he also checked the time on his new Rolex wrist watch that his father-in-law had presented him with. The time was ten minutes past ten, and noticing the sudden silence all around, Paddy instinctively remarked to Dimpy that probably the Angels were passing.

But unknown to him and to the rest of the world, at that very moment far away in South India and at a place called Sriperembudur it seems that the devil was passing. In that small sleepy town fifty kilometers south west of Madras, a young and dark complexioned bespectacled woman dressed in a green salwar and a mustard coloured kameez with a sandalwood garland in her hand was getting ready to perform her deadly sinister act. It looked as if she was possessed by the devil himself as she waited for her quarry to arrive.

A few minutes later at the wedding reception, when the army brass band from the Jammu and Kashmir Rifles Regimental Centre at Jabalpur, which was on official duty at Rashtrapati Bhawan and which Monty with the kind courtesy of his friend the Military Secretary to the President of India had arranged for started playing some old Dogri folk songs, Shupriya's mind flashed back to the days when Shiraz was secretly courting her. That was over two decades ago and some of the Dogri songs that the band played were the same old ones like 'Bhalla Sipaiya' and 'Aaje Di Rati' that Shiraz often serenaded her with. And as Shupriya with nostalgia and sadness listened to those old folk songs, Monty, Reeta together with their daughter and son-in-law also joined her. But since those Dogri numbers had a very slow beat, Monty in order to bring more life into the party walked up to the Band Major and said very softly to him.

"Oye chal Yaar is shub din par kuch fast Punjabi bhangra number hojaye, yaha tho kohi latest chalta phuta filmy dhun hi baja dey aur jis pur hum sub dance bhi kar saken."(Oh please on this happy occasion do play some fast Punjabi song or a latest Hindi movie hit song so that all of us can dance to it.) Seeing the Military Secretary giving his nod, the Band Major promptly obliged. And when the JAK Rifles band started playing 'Choli Ke

Piche Kiya Hai' from the latest Subhash Ghai blockbuster film 'Khalnayak' that had the handsome Sanjay Dutt and the beautiful Madhuri Dixit in the lead roles, the bandstand soon became the place to be in. Though the film was yet to be released, but that particular promotional song had already taken the country by storm. Some people however considered the lyrics of the song to be rather bawdy and vulgar, but the people of India and those among the young crowd who were present that evening at the wedding reception, they simply went crazy over it. While some felt that the words of the song had a lewd double meaning, but that hardly mattered as they all danced to its lilting beat. Then as it neared 11 PM that night and by which time most of the guests had already left and it was time for the band to pack up, Shupriya having had enough of that 'Cholike Peeche' requested the band as a grand finale to play her late father's old favourite song 'Que Sera Sera.' While everybody sang and danced the waltz to that age old Doris Day number from the Alfred Hitchcock film 'The Man Who Knew too Much,' suddenly a gentleman in a police officer's uniform barged in to announce that Rajiv Gandhi had been killed, and added that it was also time for the music to stop. But he could not elaborate any further as to who was responsible for it and all he could say was that it was a bomb blast some where in South India. With the large number of VIP's attending the wedding reception that evening, the police officer n the rank of an ASP, Assistant Superintendent of Police with his squad was on duty at the Delhi Gymkhana to oversee the security arrangements at the venue. And he had only overheard a transmission over the police radio network that Rajiv Gandhi had been killed in a bomb blast, but he had no idea as to how, where and who had triggered it.

"Don't be silly. I am sure it must be some sought of a bloody joke or a hoax. A similar ploy was also played up by some sections of the media, when during the 1977 election campaign it was reported that Sanjay Gandhi too while on his campaign trail near Sultanpur had been fired upon," said Monty's old classmate from Sanawar, Charu Brar who with his wife and children had come all the way from Ludhiana for the wedding.

"But it may very well be true, because Rajiv Gandhi has been on the hit list of not only the Sikh and the Kashmiri militants from the north, but also that of the LTTE and their sympathizers from the south too," added Dimpy as Monty abruptly stopped the band from playing any more numbers and called it a day.

It was however early next morning that some details, and that too in a speculative form of what actually happened at Sriperembudur on the night before was made known to the people of India. There was no doubt that Rajiv Gandhi had been killed in a massive explosion that had rocked the venue of the election meeting that he was scheduled to address. But who did it, how and why now remained the million dollar question. According to some eyewitness reports, Rajiv Gandhi as the leader of the opposition had landed at the Meenabakam airport in Madras at around 20.30 hours and by 2100 hours he with his motorcade of 14 vehicles were on the way to Sriperembudur. Seated in a bullet proof Ambassador car, the President of the Congress (I) looked happy and confident for an electoral victory in the state as Congress supporters who had lined the route kept cheering and shouting 'Rajiv Gandhi Ki Jai.' The election rally organized by the party at Sriperembudur was in support of the Congress candidate Maragatham Chandrashekar who was standing from that constituency. At 22.10hours that evening, the motorcade had halted for a few minutes at an important road junction, which was hardly 500 meters from the final venue and where Rajiv Gandhi garlanded the statue of her late mother Mrs Indira Gandhi. Little did he realize then that a few minutes later he too like his mother would be garlanded not with flowers, but with a deadly bomb and become a victim of some merciless diehard hardcore assassin.

A few minutes later, when Rajiv arrived at the venue, got out of the car and gave that million dollar smile of his and started waving to the large crowd of cheering women who were seated in a special ladies enclosure on the left side of the red carpeted pathway that led to the stage, everything seemed to be in order. While the traditional offering of silk scarves was in process and though RK Raghavan, the IGP in charge of security and other senior police officials as per the laid down drills surrounded the Congress President to form a security shield around him, the lone suicide bomber it seems had managed to avoid the security cordon and had quietly sneaked into the restricted area where three others who had been security checked earlier were waiting to garland the VVIP. As Rajiv Gandhi led by two party workers who were sprinkling flowers from their baskets moved forward along the red carpet and towards the stage, he received scarves from four persons. One of them was Latha Kannan a Congress lady activist whose young daughter Kokila also sang a small song in Hindi in Rajiv's honour. With only a few meters left to get on to the stage, and delighted with the little girl's gesture, Rajiv gave another big smile and moved forward. Then suddenly as if from nowhere a bespectacled young lady with the sandal wood garland in her hand propped up and she came face to face with her target. At 10.18 PM the loud explosion shattered the stillness of the night as both the bodies of Rajiv Gandhi and his dare devil assassin were flung high into the air The first suicide bomber of Tamil origin and that too a female had struck. The explosion had not only killed Rajiv Gandhi but eighteen others also including nine policemen besides injuring many more. The massive explosion that had produced a flash of high intensity light was soon followed a by a thick pall of smoke. It created a pandemonium and the blast had resulted in a total blackout as people sitting in the front rows ran for safety. Those sitting in the far rear thought it was part of the fireworks to welcome their leader, but as the smell of stench burnt human flesh and bones polluted the entire area, and the ripped off limbs and torsos were found littered all over the place, it was evident that the bomb was indeed a very powerful one.Late that very night as the news of the terrible blast that resulted in the instantaneous death of Rajiv Gandi spread like wild fire, his poor Italian wife Sonia and daughter Priyanka were in a state of shock as they boarded the special aircraft to bring back whatever little remains were there of the dead and respected leader's shrapnel ridden body.

'But who do you think was responsible for this dastardly and cowardly act?" said Reeta as the families of both the newly weds sat late into the night listening to various news reports and bulletins and kept discussing the pros and cons of the after effects of the terrible tragedy.

"Well whoever it is but the gruesome manner in which it was carried out only goes to show that the assassin was well prepared and that the perpetrators of the crime had done their homework very thoroughly," said Monty.

"But nevertheless it was a clear case of a massive security failure and someone will have to pay for it I guess," said Peevee who was upset that Dimpy and Paddy's's honeymoon at Ooty that was to begin early next morning with a flight to Madras had now to be cancelled.

It was at 4.45 on that early morning of 22nd May 1991, when a heartbroken Sonia with her daughter Priyanka landed at the Madras airport, and by 5.30 the special aircraft carrying the body of her beloved husband was on its flight back to Delhi. By the time it landed at Palam airport at the Ar Force technical area it was well passed 8 AM and the President of India, Mr Venkataraman was there to receive the body. As Monty and family watched the live telecast, they felt pity for Rajiv Gandhi's widow and their daughter. Shupriya too was badly shaken, but she admired the manner in which the young widow and her daughter took the tragic loss. For the next two days while the body lay in state, all of them paid their homage as they filed past the body of the departed soul. On 24th May, Shupriya was on protocol duty at the VIP enclosure for the funeral, which was attended by a large number of foreign dignataries including Prince Charles, Dan Quale the American Vice President and the Prime Minister of Pakistan, Nawaz Sharif. As the body was put to flames by his son Rahul Gandhi who had arrived from abroad to perform the last rites, Shupriya could not hold back her tears. This was the third political assassination of a national leader in the country and all of them strangely bore the same surname of Gandhi. The first one was the father of the nation, the second was Indira Gandhi and now it was her son Rajiv Gandhi. And all of them had been killed in cold blood. But while in the former two cases the assassins were immediately identified and arrested, in this particular case there were just no leads or clues to begin with. Even after 96 hours after the crime had been committed, the top Indian sleuths from the RAW and the IB who had started investigating into the case remained clueless. They had even contacted their counterparts in other countries to help them find a lead, but nothing was forthcoming. Shupriya thought that this too like the John F Kennedy assassination would remain unsolved, but then luck suddenly smiled on the investigating team when they thoroughly searched the site and found a double-layered denim cloth jacket with Velcro stripes at the two far ends. They also found pieces of the mustard coloured kurta and green coloured salwar that ladies normally wear and the two pieces of wire inside the Velcro belt that was attached to it. A nine volt rechargeable AAA size battery of UK make was also recovered from the blast site and some distance away from the battery and about 30 feet away from the stage was found a head with a face that was still identifiable. It was that of a dead woman. While the bodies of the rest of those killed had been identified and claimed by their next of kin, there were no claimants for this particular victim who happened to be a young lady.

On the 24th of May 1991, while Rajiv Gandhi's bomb shattered body was cremated with full military honours, one of the many foreign dignitaries at the cremation site that day was Nawaz Sharif, the Prime Minister of Pakistan. He too was a young man like Rajiv and dreamt big. He had taken over the reins of his country at the age of 42 years and was a couple of years younger to the man whose body now lay on the funeral pyre. Then with the chanting of prayers when the pyre was about to be lit by his only son Rahul, Shupriya broke down. Strangely the ancestors of both Nawaz Sharif and Rajiv Gandhi were both originally from Kashmir. And as the flames from the funeral pyre with the smell of sandalwood and ghee (clarified butter) leapt high into the air, Shupriya wondered whether the eternal problem of Kashmir would ever be solved. The valley too was now in flames that were much bigger, and what bothered Shupriya was the fact that it was constantly being fanned by the same very Prime Minister of Pakistan who was now desperate to once again internationalize the burning issue. His predecessor Benazir Bhutto during her tenure had given a fillip to the proxy war in the region, and with fundamentalism on the rise in Pakistan, the country had now become a safe haven and a place of pilgrimage for aspiring Islamist radicals from all over the world, and particularly so from the Arab nations of the Sunni Muslim countries that dominated the Middle East.

On that same very day of 24th May 1991, while Rajiv Gandhi was finally laid to rest, the investigation into his death was handed over to the CBI, and a SIT, a Special Investigating Team under D.R. Karthikeyan was constituted. Luckily it ran into another piece of good luck, when the team found a camera of one Haribabu, a photographer who too had died in that terrible blast. And when the reel inside the camera was developed, it gave a goldmine of information that the CBI would have never got had the camera like the body of the killer also been blown to bits. The photographs revealed a dark young bespectacled woman in her mid twenties dressed in a mustard coloured kameez and a green coloured salwar holding a sandalwood garland in her hand. Another photo showed the same woman moving closer to Rajiv Gandhi, and this particular photograph it seems was taken a few minutes before the explosion took place. The third photograph showed an unidentified man standing in kurta pyjama and with a cloth bag like the ones the journalists or artists normally carry and he had a notebook in his hand. There were also a few photographs showing Rajiv's arrival at the venue, and of a section of the crowd receiving him and finally a photograph of the explosion itself. Further investigations revealed that the two, the woman and the man in the photographs were neither part of the local Congress organizing committee, nor were they from that area at all. Some witnesses in hind sight on being shown the photographs also claimed that they had seen the bespectacled woman with the garland moving towards Rajiv Gandhi and then bending down as if to pay her respects to him by trying to touch his feet, but nobody knew as to who she really was.

It however became quite evident that the main assassin was definitely a woman and since the manner in which she carried out the dare devil suicide bombing was reminiscent of the deadly attacks by the young Tamil Tigers of the LTTE on the Indian troops in Sri Lanka, Kathikeyan who had been to Sri Lanka during the operations by the IPKF was more or less convinced that the needle of suspicion pointed towards Prabhakaran, the LTTE Supremo and his henchmen. But he still was not very sure since no identification of the suicide bomber had been categorically established. It was still all speculation, but there was no doubt that this was a meticulously planned operation that had been ruthlessly executed and without leaving any onward trail that could lead to the real perpetrators who were behind this heinous and deadly act. But when the photographs of the bespectacled woman and the man in kurta pyjama were published in the various newspapers including those of the vernacular press, the SIT office in Madras was flooded by callers. The woman was identified as Dhanu, alias Anbu, alias Kalaivani. But her real name was Gyatri and she was the daughter of one Mr A Rajaratnam. Her father was a former government clerk who was opposed to the Sinhalese government's attitude and step motherly treatment towards the Tamils. Later he with his dear friend K Sivananansunderam a fellow clerk during the late sixties and the early seventies had become active sympathizers and supporters of the Sri Lankan Tamils who had come as refugees. The father thereafter left the government service prematurely and in 1975 died a virtual pauper while living in Madras. The gentleman in the kurta pyjama posing as a journalist was identified as Sivarasan, alias S Packiyanathan, alias Raghuvaran. Having lost one eye while fighting the IPKF, he was also called one eyed Jack. But nonetheless the identification had no meaning unless they were caught and brought to justice and therefore the massive manhunt for them had now begun.

By carrying out a detail examination of the various articles and the physical remains of whatever little was left of Dhanu, the various experts including eminent doctors, forensic specialists and others it was proved beyond doubt that it was an IED, an Improvised Explosive Device that was used by the suicide bomber. It undoubtedly was a very powerful and sophisticated device that was carried on the body of the bomber in the form of a denim belt and was loaded with explosives. The belt was apparently shaped to neatly fit the assassin's body and was well hidden and cleverly camouflaged by the clothes that the woman was wearing. The device had a foolproof triggering mechanism with an electronic detonator and the explosive used was of the deadly RDX variety. To create an even more deadly impact, the bomb maker an expert had even used thousands of small steel balls that acted as pellets. Therefore it was little wonder that the epicenter of the blast was centered on the assassin and her victim and it resulted in both the bodies taking the first impact from it. This not only resulted in instantaneous death to both of them, but the very fact that some of the body parts had been found well away from the scene of the crime was proof enough that the explosion was indeed a deadly one.

A few days later, when Peevee came to know as to how the actual crime had been committed and that too by a young woman in her mid twenties, he unwittingly commented that the police would now also have to perforce frisk the ladies more thoroughly to find out 'Choli Ke Piche Kiya Hai" (What is behind a lady's blouse} and when he started humming the tune, Reeta did not find it funny at all and she berated him for being so naïve. Monty, however finding that the comment by Peevee was unintentional but practical, simply smiled and hoped that the Indian Home Ministry would make a note of it.

For Shiraz sitting in Islamabad, the assassination of the young Indian Prime Minister was not very surprising. According to his information, Rajiv Gandhi was already on the hit list of the Sikh militants from the day the Golden Temple was attacked, but the gruesome manner in which he was killed by a woman suicide bomber of Tamil origin and that too in general view of the people was nothing short of a public execution, said Shiraz to his wife Saira as he showed her the photograph of the young dark complexioned lady in spectacles with her front white teeth clearly visible waiting to garland her prey.

"Well if as you say that this particular photograph was taken just a few minutes before she committed that dastardly suicide attack, then I must say that with the smile on her face and with her front teeth clearly showing, she looked absolutely confident in achieving her aim of devouring her prey," said Saira as she with the help of a magnifying glass took another closer look at the photograph of the lady with the sandalwood garland in her hand that had been published by some Indian magazine. Then as she had a second look at that garland of death as Saira now called it and added that the reason for that gruesome killing of the man was beyond her comprehension, Shiraz in typical Sherlock Holmes style said.

"That's elementary my love." And when he explained to Saira that Rajiv Gandhi's decision to send the IPKF to Sri Lanka to take on the LTTE had simply backfired on his face and the LTTE was only waiting for an opportunity to strike and which they did rather unsuspectingly by using a highly motivated woman suicide bomber and that too once they were probably sure that the Government and its security agencies responsible for Rajiv Gandhi's security had lowered their guard, Saira was convinced. And when he futher explained to her the kind of indoctrination and motivation that goes in the making of a human bomb, Saira wondered whether the fundamentalists in Pakistan would one day bring in the same culture of fearless suicide bombers to the youth of the country.

"But do you think that with Rajiv's death there will be another sympathy wave for the Congress like it happened when Indira Gandhi was shot by her own Sikh guards," asked Reeta after Shupriya who had dropped in for her usual Sunday lunch remarked that the Congress party was up in arms and were blaming the caretaker Chandrashekar government for not providing their leader with the necessary SPG, Special Protection Group cover. It was a special force to provide protection that the late Rajiv Gandhi as the former Prime Minister and leader of the opposition was officially entitled to. According to Shupriya's information, this aspect of providing continued SPG cover soon after VP Singh's new Janata Dal government had taken over had been discussed at the highest level. And Mr TN Seshan, the out going Cabinet Secretary who also held the appointment of Secretary (Security) had in his noting dated 14th December, 1989 had also suggested that the SPG cover for Mr Gandhi should continue and Mr MK Narayanan the Director IB was also of the same view. But it was on condition that the law allowed such elaborate SPG cover to ex Prime Ministers. But with the change of government these two senior officers had been shifted from their posts and subsequently it seems that the SPG cover to Rajiv was diluted," added Shupriya.

"So in other words the Congress is now blaming the VP Singh and the Chandrashekhar governments for the death of their leader, but will that in any way evoke a sympathy wave to bring back the party to power at the centre," asked Peevee.

"Well it all depends on how the party plays it up on the run up to the polls, which is now just around the corner, and knowing how sentimental we are on such matters, this factor might well swing the votes in their favour, but it certainly will not be a landside victory like it happened after Madam Gandhi was killed," said Monty very confidently.

Monty it seems was dead right in his poll prediction and though the Congress (I) romped home victorious, but it did not get the necessary majority to form a government on its own. The new minority government that was headed by Prime Minister Narasimha Rao and which came into power on 21st June 1991 had therefore to rely on outside support. Though the economy of the country was now in a real mess and the foreign exchange reserves were abysmally low, yet on the advice of an optimistic Manmohan Singh, the government took a bold stand to kick start the on going liberalization program in the country. It was indeed a bold move that would set in motion the mechanisms to bring down the inflation rate, but for that the need at the moment was to ensure that the foreign hard currency reserves go up. India's disastrous economic policies and oppressive licensing controls on industry and foreign trade together with the rampant corruption and baneful long bureaucratic procedures during the last four decades had practically ruined the country. And it was now time to open up to external commerce and calculated foreign investments that would raise India's economic and political profile to the outside world Therefore the time for a radical change had come and the new government was bent upon implementing it by bringing down the inflation rate to the single digit level.

Besides the glaring poverty in the country, India was now also faced with the worldwide phenomenon called AIDS, the Accquired Immune Defficiency Syndrome. The menace of that dreaded disease and for which there was no cure had spread its tentacles far and wide and had resulted in the deaths of thousands of people in the country who were not even aware of what the disease was all about till they succumbed to it. Though a vivacious Pooja Bedi, the daughter of the actor Kabir Bedi and the renowned dancer Protima Bedi with her alluring looks and fabulous figure had launched the commercial range of condoms called Kama Sutra that was now being marketed by J.K. Chemicals, but even those sexy advertisements had in no way contributed to educate the illiterate masses of India of the fact that the use of the condom was one of the safest methods to avoid getting the killer disease. Fearing that Peevee who in a few months time would turn twenty and who was now determined to try his luck in Bollywood may with his good looks and manly figure be seduced not only by some unscrupulous woman, but maybe also by men, Monty one evening very diplomatically educated the young lad about how and why people contract AIDS and what sort of precautions should be taken, As an example, he also mentioned the name of the late Hollywood star Rock Hudson who was gay and tested HIV positive and had died of that dreaded disease not so very long ago.

It was during the month of July 1991, and while taking part in a singing talent competition in the capital New Delhi, that Peevee was spotted by a little known producer of an on going television serial and who offered him the lead role for his next production. It was based on a story of a poor 18 year old village boy from the foothills of Uttar Pradesh who had a good voice and wanted to become a Bollywood singing star and how he after being lured by his own uncle who was an underworld Don of Bombay was ruthlessly exploited and sodomised by him and which ultimately led to the young boys death in a police shoot out. But Peevee felt that though the story line would no doubt give him a good opening to display his histrionic and singing talents through the mass media of the government controlled

Doordarshan television that had spread its tentacles far and wide to the many villages and towns of India, but it would be by and large a negative role. He therefore suggested to the producer that he would accept the offer, but only on condition that he would not die in the serial, but would escape during the shootout and return a few years later as the new Don who would not sing or act in films, but would control Bollywood instead and take revenge on his uncle.

"My God, you do have ideas young man and in that case all I have to do is to increase the number of episodes," said the producer who was delighted with the suggestion and immediately gave Peevee an offer of Rupees five thousand per episode to begin with and for which the shooting schedule would commence from the 1st of October. Without asking any more questions, Peevee whole heartedly accepted the contract and from that day a new star with the screen name of 'Deepak Kumar' was born. It was the name of the boy in the forthcoming serial and Peevee decided to keep it as his future screen name too. He was confident that the serial would be a hit and would eventually catapult him to stardom.

CHAPTER-15

On The Road to Liberalization

In that month of July 1991, while Karthikeyan's SIT unearthed more clues to the sensational Rajiv Gandhi murder case and arrested a few people in India, in New York, USA a grand jury indicted Agha Hasan Abedi and his Chief Executive Swaleh Naqvi on several charges of fraud and grand larceny. Abedi who was once known as the respected Agha Sahib was now being dubbed as the Rasputin of the east. His maverick bank the BCCI having looted lacs of customers had gone kaput and he and his compatriots were now being accused of criminal dealings ranging from everything under the sun including blackmail, money laundering, gun running, fraud, espionage and even murder.Known as the Bank of Credit and Commerce International, B.C.C.I. for short, it was founded in London in 1972 by Agha Hasan Abedi, a wealthy Pakistani national and was registered in Luxembourg. It at one time operated in 78 countries, had 400 branches worldwide and had assets worth a staggering 25 Billion US Dollars. Abedi in 1959 had set up the United Bank of Pakistan but following the nationalization of Banks by Mr Bhutto he ventured in creating the BCCI with the main capital coming from the Emir of Dubai and the Bank of America. On 24th June 1991 and on the orders of the Bank of England to carry out a detailed enquiry, Price Waterhouse the auditors of the bank using the code name 'Sandstorm' submitted their report indicating that the BCCI had engaged in widespread fraud and manipulation of their funds. Even the Abu Nidal Group a terrorist organizatiom had held its account with the Sloane Street Branch, near Harrods in London. As a result of this on 5th July 1991, the Bank of England closed down BCCI.

When more details of this sordid business by the now defunct BCCI was sent to Shiraz by Mehmuda's husband Karim Malik who was the Political Counsellor in the Pakistan Embassy in Washington and also his co-brother-in-law, Shiraz was shocked beyond belief. He had also heard that a number of well connected and rich families of Pakistan both in the business world and in politics were in one way or the other also connected with the nefarious activities of this bank, but there was no concrete proof to nail them. Nevertheless, Shiraz through his influential contacts decided to dig a little more into its shady deals.

Simultaneously during the same very month of July, Nawaz Sharif having stepped up his diplomatic offensive against India over the Kashmir issue in a clever move had the resolution passed by the conference of Islamic countries and urged them to support Pakistan's stand on Kashmir in the United Nations. On his return from the conference, when there were unconfirmed reports and rumours that General Mirza Aslam Beg, the army chief whose three year tenure was to expire soon was planning to topple his government and usurp power, the President of Pakistan, Ghulam Ishaq Khan in a smart preemptive move made the official announcement that General Asif Nawaz Janjua on 16th August 1991 would take over as the new chief of the Pakistan army. With General Beg having retired, Lt General Asad Durrani the DG ISI who had been in that chair only for a year was also replaced by Lt General Javed Nasir who was the Engineer-in-Chief of the Pakistan army. The E-in-C was Nawaz Sharif's own choice and the change it seems was made at the Prime Minister's own personal request to the new army chief. Wishing to know a little more about the new appointments in the top hierarchy of the Pakistan army, Shiraz called on Brigadier Aslam Rehman Khan.

"May be the Prime Minister Nawaz Sharif wants to keep his flanks well protected," said Brigadier Aslam Rehman when Shiraz asked him what could be the reason for this sudden change over. According to Shiraz's information, the bearded Javed Nasir was an officer from the Corps of Engineers and though the Sappers were a fighting arm, but to have an officer from that corps to head the premier intelligence service of the country seemed a little odd to him. Javed Nasir was also known to be a staunch devout Muslim who was absolutely anti India and who advocated a more aggressive militant policy in Kashmir. And by his being elevated to that powerful slot, it had got Shiraz thinking.

"But do you think that the Prime Minister's new appointee will be able to do full justice to the cloak and dagger service," asked Shiraz as Aslam Rehman fixed him a tall Tom Collins.

"Well I think it is a bit too early to speculate about that, but nevertheless the appointment has definitely surprised many," said Aslam Rehman.

Brigadier Aslam Rehman having successfully completed the NDC course was now posted in the operations branch of the Pakistan GHQ. He had been cleared for the next rank of Major General and though this was only a stop gap posting for him, but nevertheless, it was a very important and sensitive one. The military operations branch known as the MO in common military parlance was the nerve centre from where all operational instructions and orders as per the governments policies and directives, both for internal security and against external aggression emanated from, and Shiraz was very keen to know on how far the government was willing to stick its neck out as far as Kashmir was concerned.

"Arre Just don't worry Yaar, twice bitten is thrice shy, and we are not going to fight this battle with our tanks and guns as was the case in 1965 and 1971, but are going to fight it by proxy as we are doing right now, and we will keep doing so till Kashmir is ours," said Aslam Rehmam very confidently as his wife Farzana looking as charming as ever rolled in the small drinks trolley with the snacks. Arif Rehman who was also listening to the conversation then added very intelligently.

"But the problem is that we just cannot trust the Kashmiris, both on our side as well as those who live across the border and along the LOC. While some of them keep advocating that they would love to become part of Pakistan, the others want full fledged independence or more autonomy, and the Hindus in the south want to remain with India. And as a result of which both the countries that have been fighting over this erstwhile Maharaja Hari Singh's kingdom of so called heaven on earth for the past forty-four years have made life hell for all of us. And I regret to say that the politicians are making the bloody man in uniform from both sides pay rather dearly for the late Maharajas indecisiveness. Had the Maharaja like the other princely states openly declared his willingness to accede to either of the two countries when he was required to do so, or took his people first into confidence to decide their own future, then there would have been no Kashmir problem at all. But he instead simply kept dilly-dallying over the issue and with the hope that he would have his own independent Kashmir and look what a bloody mess it has resulted into?' added the retired diplomat, as Salim Rehman rang up from Moscow to convey that he with his family had arrived safely in the Soviet capital.

Having completed more than three years in Beijing, Salim Rehman on 17th August reported for duty at the Pakistan Embassy in Moscow and took over as Counsellor Political. The erstwhile Soviet Union was fast crumbling and the Soviet Communist Party it seems by now had lost total control of the situation.Ever since Mikhail Gorbachev had introduced his policy of 'Glasnost' (Openness) and 'Perestroika' (Restucturing) in the country and repudiated the Brezhnev Doctrine of non interference in the internal affairs of the former Warsaw Pact countries, Communism had become the biggest casualty. And on 7th February, 1990 when the CPSU, the Central Committee of the Communist Party of the Soviet Union also had agreed to give up its monopoly of power, all the 15 republics that constituted of what was once known as the mighty USSR, the Union of Soviet Socialist Republic, they too therefore decided to go their own way. Faced with growing separatism from many of the republics that sometimes even led to Moscow using its strong arm tactics to keep them in check, Gorbachev was therefore left with no other option but to try and restructure the Soviet Union into a less centralized state.

On 20th August 1991, and three days after Salim Rehman's arrival in Moscow, all the republics were required to sign a new union treaty that would make them independent republics in a federation, but with a common President, centralized foreign policy and defense. And though most of the Central Asian Republics were in favour of it since they simply could not do away without the economic support from the centre and the benefits of the common markets of the Soviet Union, but there were others who wanted a more rapid transition to a market free economy and to them it did not matter if in that process, the USSR disintegrated. However, the hardliners within the Communist Party including some senior officers from the military establishment were completely opposed to anything which might contribute to the weakening of the Soviet state. On 19th August, a day before the new union treaty was to be signed, a group of four hardliners that included Gennadi Yannayev, the Soviet Vice President, Vladimir Kryuchkov, the KGB chief, Valentin Pavlov, the Prime Minister and Dmitry Yazov, the Defense Minister together with a few others acting in unison decided to put a spoke into Gorbachev's wheel. They therefore in order to prevent the signing of the new union treaty formed the 'State Committee on the State Emergency' to restore the union state to what it formerly was. As an opening move they put Gorbachev who was vacationing down south at Foros in Crimea near the Black Sea under house arrest and then quickly issued an emergency decree suspending all political activity and banning most newspapers. The group of seven who had expected popular support for their actions it seems had totally miscalculated the pulse of the people as the general public sympathy quickly turned against them. Though it started as a bloodless coup, but it soon became a fight between the pro and the anti communists who far outnumbered those who were supporting the coup leaders. Having tried but failed to arrest Boris Yeltsin who was leading the rally of mass opposition to the coup, it was now Bolshevism in reverse gear as people in thousands came on to the streets to defend the 'White House' which was Boris Yeltsin's office and the symbolic seat of Russian sovereignty.

The 19th of August happened to be a Monday and when Salim Rehman sitting in his office came to know about the coup and that the Moscovites in large numbers were congregating near the Kremlin to protest against the coup leaders, he too decided to go and see what exactly was happening there The Kremlin, which was the seat of communist power for the past 71 years and where outside its high walls was the mausoleum of their revered leader Vlladimir Ilych Lenin was now a sea of people of all shapes and sizes who with placards and anti communist slogans were demonstrating and protesting against any roll back. Having tasted the freedom of speech, these people were in no mood to set the clock back to the oppressive one party communist rule.

On 20st August 1991, while Moscow was witnessing a different kind of revolution, far away in Bangalore in India during the early hours of the morning, the police were closing in on the alleged mastermind and his team who had so brutally assassinated Rajiv Gandhi. It was practically three months to the date, when the Indian Prime Minister was killed and that day also happened to be Rajiv Gandhi's 47th birthday. Sivarasan whose real name was Raja Arumainayagam together with his female accomplice and second in command Subha who were the brains behind that heinous act after a massive man hunt had been finally cornered. Sivarasan with his accompliciries had taken refuge in a building at Kanankunte on the outskirts of Bangalore and the entire area was now cordoned off with hundreds of armed policemen and commandos to prevent them from escaping. The identity of the 35 year old Sivarasan standing with a notebook in his hand that had been taken minutes before the explosion on that fateful night of 21st May 1991, and which was clicked from the camera that the police had luckily found at the venue had established beyond doubt the involvement of the LTTE in the murder of the Indian Prime Minister. Monty who happened to be in Bangalore on that day on a business trip on hearing the news immediately hired a private cab from his hotel and rushed to where all the action was, but by the time he got there it was all over. It seems that the seven terrorists had been tracked to their hideout on the night before. They were heavily armed and were involved in a long three hour gun battle with the police force. The commando group from the NSG wanted to capture them alive, but fearing that the LTTE terrorists may all commit suicide they had therefore delayed their final assault while waiting for the delivery of the medical antidotes for cyanide poisoning to arrive. But at the crack of dawn, when the commandos from the National Security Guard burst into the house with the antidotes, it was already too late. All the seven terrorists were dead. Those who consumed cyanide were found locked in an embrace of death with one another, while Sivarasan had put a bullet through his head. Though the main culprit was no more, but it was hardly the kind of gift that Sonia and his family wanted on the man's 47th birthday, thought Monty. And while the grief stricken widow prayed at her husband's memorial that morning, a lot more important questions still remained unanswered. It was widely believed that the Indian army signal intelligence had been regularly monitoring the clandestine radio network of the LTTE cadres that were operating from Indian soil and it also included some crucial conversations between Sivarasan and his bosses Prabhakaran and Pottu Amman, and yet no proper security cover was given to the ex Prime Minister. The fact that the killers had even carried out a dry run when VP Singh the Indian Prime Minisiter visited the state of Tamil Nadu and which was only a fortnight before Rajiv's assasination was proof enough that neither the Indian Intelligence Bureau nor the RAW were aware of this diabolical plot.

And while Karthikeyan and his team were being eulogized for their efforts in getting their act together in such a short time, in the Soviet Union, events were moving at a very fast pace. During the last 72 hours inside the capital city while the anxiety and the uncertainty prevailed over which side would emerge victorious, one by one the three small Baltic Republics of Estonia, Latvia and Lithuania in quick succession declared themselves as independent countries. On 21st August, after the coup had completely collapsed and the coup leaders were taken under custody, Gorbachev once again returned as President of the Soviet Union. But by then the declaration of independence by the three Baltic States had set the ball rolling as others too one by one followed suit and by the time the month of August was over, half of the 15 Soviet Republics were no longer a part of the Soviet Union. They had declared themselves independent.

And as the mighty Soviet Union kept disintegrating, in that month of September in Karachi and in Sind, the infighting within the MQM had also led to a split in the party. It also resulted in fierce gun and street battles between the two warring sides. Earlier, Altaf Hussein the MQM leader had accused the media which included the newspapers Dawn and the Star for conspiring against his party and for spitting poison. This also resulted in the MQM taking law into their own hands as motorcycle gangs of MQM supporters and activists started confiscating the two leading newspapers of Karachi and Sind. As the law and order situation in the province grew from bad to worse, cases of dacoity, kidnapping and ransom also kept increasing. Though the Federal government had launched operations against such criminal elements in Sind, but with the alleged unholy nexus between the criminals and the politicians it was a task far beyond the police and the Pakistan Rangers.

And while the law and order situation in Sind was getting worse by the day, and the proxy war in Kashmir was gaining in momentum, these factors however had no effect on the cricket mania that had gripped Sharjah. On the 25th of October 1991, while Shiraz with his family sitting in front of the television set were waiting eagerly for the Pakistan versus India one day cricket match at Sharjah to begin, and while there was still time for the first ball to be bowled, Shiraz got busy reading the third quarterly intelligence report on the internal situation in Sind. According to the latest crime figures more than 1500 cases were that of kidnapping alone and the cases of armed robberies, extortion and ransom had also risen very considerably. Commenting on those figures, when Shiraz told his wife Saira that Sind had now become the wild west of Pakistan and Karachi its capital was no less than what Chicago was during the Al Capone days, and that there was a requirement to send the army to thrash all those hoodlums, eight year old little Tojo who was more interested in the cricket match simply blurted out by saying that Pakistan would thrash India and they actually did. Batting first Pakistan thanks to some fine batting by Zahid Fazal and Saleem Malik in their fifty overs had scored 262 runs for the loss of six wickets and then with Aaqib Javed bowling superbly, India were skittled out for a paltry 190 runs in 46 overs. Aaqib with his match figues of seven for thirty seven and a hatrick had thus created a world record. "But smoking is injurious to health," said Shiraz in jest as the Pakistan captain Imran Khan walked away with the handsome Wills trophy. But what surprised Shiraz was the manner in which Aaqib had achieved the hatrick. The first one to go was Sanjay Manjrekar who was caught by Waqar Yunis for a brilliant fifty two and then followed the Indian captain Mohammed Azharuddin and Sachin Tendulkar both of whom were out leg before wicket in the very first ball that they faced from the Pakistani bowler.

But no sooner had the cricket fever dyed down; there was more bad news from Sind. In the month of November, when the news about two women from respectable families in Sind on being abducted and raped was highlighted by a NGO, a non government organization that was run by a woman for the safety and honour of the weaker sex in the country, Ruksana Begum who had received a copy of it was shocked beyond belief. In the first case Khurshid Begum the wife of a PPP worker Essa Balooch had been raped, and of all people the culprit was the police inspector of Korangi Thana, the very man who was supposed to prevent crime. And in the second case, which was even more bizarre and which took place on the 27th of November was when five people gang-raped Veena Hayat and she was no ordinary girl. She was the daughter of Sardar Shaukat Hayat Khan, who was a close friend of both the Zardaris and the Bhuttos and in her case the finger of suspicion was pointed towards the son-in-law of another influential politician of Karachi. According to Veena Hayat it was at around 7.30 on the evening of 27th November, when five masked men broke into her Karachi residence and had gang raped her. And she also claimed that the terrible crime had been committed on the orders of Irfanullah Marwat who was the son-in-law of President Ghulam Ishaq Khan and the Interior Advisor to Jam Sadiq Ali who was the Chief Minister of Sind.

"My God if such heinous crimes that are being committed by the high and the mighty goes unpunished, then I am afraid the 'Goonda Raj' that has already taken deep roots in this country will one day see the end of Pakistan too," said a highly worked up Ruksana Begum as she reminded her daughter Saira and her son-in-law Shiraz not to ever send the children alone out anywhere whatsoever, and not even to the nearby park, which was just across the road.

"Yes, she is right and these are not normal times and anything can happen," added Arif Rehman while also suggesting that no domestic help should be hired without getting a proper police verification done.

And while the law and order problem in Pakistan had the rich and influential people constantly on their toes and they hired private bodyguards to keep them company, in the erstwhile Soviet Union with the country fast disintegrating, the law and order situation too was going from bad to worse everyday. According to Shiraz, the only good thing that happened to Pakistan during that month of November was the departure of Osama Bin Laden from its soil to Sudan. Fearing that he could be repatriated to Saudi Arabia, where he was not wanted, Osama had very wisely left in a private jet for Khartoum, the capital of Sudan.

"My God, I never expected that the mighty Soviet Union, which till yesterday was considered to be a world super power would crumble and disintegrate so very rapidly and meekly," said Salim Rehman to his wife Aasma as they on that New Year's Eve day while standing near the ramparts of the Kremlin watched the Soviet flag being lowered for the last and final time. A month earlier Boris Yeltsin the burly Russian who was now the boss of Russia, the republic that till a few months ago was the largest and the most populous in the Soviet Union had not only banned the CPSU, but he had also banned the dreaded KGB and had it replaced by the SVR. Known in Russian as 'Slushba Vineshnayi Rasvedki' and in English as the FAS, the new Foreign Intelligence Service carried out the same duties as that of the First Chief Dircerotate of the erstwhile KGB and whose former chief Yevgeny Primakov was now the appointed head of this new outfit. On Christmas day Gorbachev had resigned as the President, and a day later the Supreme Soviet finally and formally had dissolved the Soviet Union. At midnight of that 31st December, 1991 and 1st January, 1992 while the world celebrated the coming of another New Year, the once mighty Soviet Union had passed into history. And though the break up was generally welcomed by the people, but it also brought along untold economic miseries for them. The national economy that was already in a tailspin had sent the inflation rate of the ruble soaring to the skies and this had led to extreme shortages of food, clothing and other basic necessities of daily life. And as a result of all this, the law and order situation also had deteriorated very sharply and criminal gangs of thugs and black marketers were now on the prowl to make a fast buck.

On New Year's Day, 1992 a change of guard at the headquarters of the United Nations in New York saw Mr Boutros Boutros Ghali as the new Secretary General. He had replaced Javier Perez de Cuellar of Peru. Born on 19th January, 1920 Javier as he was popularly called was a Peruvian from Lima and a career diplomat. During his two terms that began in January 1982 and continued for a full decade, De Cuellar had successfully mediated in the Falkland crisis, in Namibia's quest for independence and on the Cyprus issue. The twice married Preuvian however declined when he was offered a third term. His new successor Mr Ghali was born on 14th November, 1922. He was a Coptic Christian from Egypt and also a career diplomat with a doctorate in International Relations from Cairo University. A Fulbright Research Scholar at Columbia University, he had served as Egypt's Minister of State for Foreign Affairs from 1977 and had played an important part in the peace agreements between President Anwar Sadat and the Israeli Prime Minister Menachem Begin, and Shiraz therefore hoped that the same man with his vast experience would now go all out to bring genuine peace in trouble torn Middle East. But for the Egyptian from the very first year of his having been appointed as the Secretary General of the United Nations the task was not going to be an easy one at all. Though the collapse of the Soviet Union and the dissolution of the Warsaw Pact had greatly reduced the threat of a nuclear war in Europe and had heralded the end of the Cold War, but it had also brought into focus an ethnic conflict in Central Europe and in those states that were once part of erstwhile Yugoslavia. On 25th June, 1991, after Croatia and Slovenia that was once an integral part of Yugoslavia also declared their independence, it led to the complete collapse of that country and resulted in a bitter civil war. It was not only a war between the Serbs, the Bosnians, the Croats and the Slovenes, but also between the Christians and Muslims, the two most dominant religions in that region, and as a result of which the call for a Jihad by Muslim fundamentalists groups to save their Muslim brothers from massacre soon became a rallying cry. And when reports of Mujahideens from the Middle East, Afghanistan and even Pakistan were getting ready to fight in Bosnia, Croatia and Slovenia started surfacing in the world press, it got Shiraz really worried. As it is with the rise of the various Mujahideen groups in Afghanistan, the situation in that neighbouring country was far from peaceful, and moreover with the unconfirmed reports of the presence of Osama Bin Laden's Al-Qaida fighters still in that region, the possibility of his exporting his Jehadi fighters of Pakistani origin to Bosnia and elsewhere therefore could not be ruled out.

The history of Pakistan's political involvement in Afghanistan had started from the day the Russian forces withdrew from the country in 1988 and it got a further boost in 1989, when under the Benazir Bhutto government, the ISI with the backing of the USA embarked on the disastrous Jalalabad offensive. The aim was to take that important strategically located city as a base for a Pakistan backed interim government in Afghanistan, but with the offensive resulting in a total failure and a fiasco, Pakistan's Afghan policy to have a friendly government in Afghanistan and one that would secure her western borders had therefore received a big set back. And now with the end of the very existence of the Soviet Union in sight, Najibullah's regime also had lost all its credibility. The internal strife for power within the country coupled with the deteriorating state of Afghanistan's crippling economy had given rise to mass scale desertions and dissatisfaction within the Afghan army, and as a result of which a large number of them had joined hands with the Mujahideen forces and factions of the various rebel warlords who were bent upon ousting Najibullah from Kabul. The civil war in Afghanistan was also now of major concern to Pakistan and Shiraz feared that with the country now on the verge of breaking up into small city states, this could may well be used by Pakistan to look for potential proxies from among the Pashtuns who could later be used to promote the on going proxy war in Kashmir.

Meanwhile on 17th of January 1992, during GM Syed's 89th birthday celebrations in Karachi, when the veteran Sindhi separatist leader was arrested once again for advocating an independent Sindu Desh and also for propagating a separatist Baluchistan, Pakhtunistan and Seraiki Desh, Ruksana Begum who with her husband Arif Rehman was in Karachi that day could not help but remark to her son-in-law Shiraz that though Altaf Hussein the MQM Chief had left Pakistan for London on New Year's Day, but this kind of blatant secessionist ideas coming from a Sindhi who was not even a Mohajir was simply unpardonable.

"Yes and I do fully agree with you Ammijaan and such people if you ask me frankly should be shot by a firing squad and that too in public,"replied Shiraz who with Saira had come to see them off. The elderly couple was on their way with their grandchildren Shehzadi and Tojo for a week's holiday to Nepal.

"And don't forget to climb Mount Everest for me," said Shiraz to his 9 year old son Tojo in good humour, as the final announcement for security check was made for the departing PIA flight to Khatmandu. On that very evening as Shiraz and Saira caught the evening flight back to Islamabad, Saira presented him with a book that had just been published and had started making waves in Pakistan. Titled 'My Feudal Lord' it was a kind of an autobiography and a true story of a 40 year old divorcee from a well to do family of Pakistan who had been exploited and used by her ambitious and ruthless husband who was also a great womanizer.

"But isn't the author Tehmina Durrani an accquaitance of yours from your school days at Murree and wasn't she the wife of Ghulam Mustafa Kar, the ex PPP leader who was made the Governor of Punjab by Bhutto and who later stabbed him in the back?" asked Shiraz as he browsed through the pages that also had some interesting photographs in it also.

"Yes that's very correct and as per the raving reviews that the book has received world wide, and if what she has written so very candidly about her ex husband and Mr Bhutto's sexual exploits is even fifty percent true, then I must admit that Tehmina is a woman of substance and guts to have put it all in black and white," said Saira as she recalled her days when the beautiful Tehmina was dating her fiancé and whom she ultimately married till the lecherous Ghulam Mustafa Kar swept her off her feet. And minutes later after the pretty and demure PIA airhostess handed over to Shiraz the latest issue of the Time Magazine that carried a report of President Bush's recent visit to Japan and his falling sick at a state dinner and vomiting into the lap of the Japanese Prime Minister. Shiraz couldn't help but remark somewhat loudly. "My God I am sure even the Japanese must have fallen sick seeing it all live on the television screen."

"Yes and Saddam Hussein who is desperately trying to keep the United Nations observers in Iraq off his back so that they do not discover his hidden nuclear weapons program must have wished that the American President had swallowed some of it and died," remarked the well dressed elderly gentleman who was sitting across the aisle in the business class section of the aircraft. He was a retired and decorated senior British officer from the Frontier Force Rifles who had served in Iraq and in the Middle East during the Second World War and where as a major he had been awarded the military Cross for gallantry on his 40th birthday and that was way back in 1941. But he had now on his 90th birthday come especially all the way from England to Pakistan to present all his medals and decorations to his old regiment.

"See that is what I call real and true regimental spirit and the man's love for his own regiment, and that can only be found in the army officers of yesteryears," said Shiraz very proudly to his wife Saira as he introduced her to the grand old man.

On 26th January 1992, while India celebrated her 42nd Republic Day, Shiraz while watching the military parade on CNN was reminded of Shupriya. It was also her birthday that day and had she lived she would have also been 42 years old today, thought Shiraz as he quietly went inside the bathroom to see the old photograph of the chubby two year Shupriya in his arms and which she had presented him with on their wedding day. Though with time it had faded a little but it was inside the old locket that was always around his neck. Observing the many grey hairs on his own head in the mirror, Shiraz realized that he was not very young either. He too was nearing fifty and had completed more than twenty years in the Pakistan Foreign Service and he wondered where his next posting would be. He only prayed that it should not be in Delhi.

That very evening, when Shiraz learnt that the great film director Satyajit Ray had been awarded the prestigious Oscar by the US Academy of Motion Pictures, Arts and Sciences for his lifetime achievements in films, he was thrilled.

"'This was the first time that somebody from India and the subcontinent has been given such a rare honour and we must all see atleast some of his award winning films if we ever get a chance to do so," said Shiraz as he narrated to his daughter Shezadi who was now 13 years old and in the ninth standard at the International School in Islamabad. The prestigious co-educational day school that was established in 1964 with its 23 acre campus was located on Johar Road and in Sector-H of Islamabad and it offered an American based educational program from kindergarten to the 12th standard. With its blue and white school colours they called themselves 'Cobras' and Shehzadi having had most of her education abroad wanted after completing her school to either take up advertising and mass media or journalism as a profession. When her father told her that the six feet four inches tall pipe smoking doyen of the Indian cinema now 71 years old was suffering from an acute heart problem and that he may not live long, Shehzadi felt very sad for the man and his family. On the day the award was announced, Satyajit Ray was working on the screen play of his 31st film and this information Shiraz had gathered from a write up in the 'India Today' magazine that was published from Delhi and a few copies of which was routinely sent by the Pakistan Embassy in Delhi through the regular weekly diplomatic bag to the Foreign office in Islamabad. The man who started his career as a junior visualiser in DJ Keymer, a British advertising company at rupees eighty a month and who wrote detective stories for children with 'Pheluda' as his Indian Sherlock Holmes was undoubtedly a whizkid. Cinema and the camera was his passion and by the time he was not even forty years old, he had achieved worldwide fame with his famous trilogy of Pather Panchali, Aparajito and Apur Sansar.

"I must say that the man who had rightly been decorated with India's highest award the 'Bharat Ratna' and now with the coveted Hollywood Oscar was undoubtedly a shining star that had brought Indian cinema to the realm of international glory and recognition and for which we should all be very proud," said Shiraz as Saira who was listening to the long monolgue on the life and times of Satyajit Ray asked her husband somewhat abruptly.

"But tell me darling, since when have you been so very fond of Bengali films and that to of such an eminent and renowned director like Satyajit Ray. The little that I know of you as far as Indian films are concerned is that you only had a liking for veteran producer-directors like Mehboob Khan, Bimal Roy and such like others, but you never told me ever that you were also a fan of Satyajit Ray," added Saira with a look of total surprise on her face.

"Well to be honest I saw his famous trilogy and a few others of his earlier films when I was first posted in London and before I met you there. There was a festival of the great master that had been organized by a group of Indian film lovers from the subcontinent and though they were in 16 mm, but they were subtitled in English and I was lucky to see quite a few of them," said Shiraz very confidently.

"Well Abbu in that case I am sure some of his films must be available on video cassettes also and I too would like to see them if you can get them through Fazlu Chacha who is now posted in the Bangladesh Embassy in Delhi," said an excited Shehzadi.

"No Sherry dear, you have to now first concentrate on your studies and such art films can be seen when you get a little more mature and older," said her mother Saira as ten year old Tojo with a cricket bat in hand walked in and demanded from his father that a bigger and better colour TV should be bought in exchange of the old one so that everyone could enjoy the cricket world cup that was soon to be played in Australia.

The Cricket World Cup that was being played in Australia and New Zealand had got the cricket crazy fans of the subcontinent in a mad frenzy and Shiraz was no exception. It was not only the first world cup with day and night matches, but a very colourful one too when all the nine teams turned out in their multi-coloured uniforms and the white ball instead of the red one was used for the first time. Though India did not reach even the semi-final stage of the tournament, but it had the consolation of beating their arch rivals Pakistan during the group stage at Sydney by 43 runs. But luck was on Pakistan's side and though Imran Khan's team had won only one of their first five matches they however qualified for the semi-finals when they beat New Zealand in their final round robin game. It was however all thanks to the weather when chasing Pakistan's paltry score of 74 and England at 24 for one wicket were crusing towards an easy victory, when the rain God's came to Pakistan's rescue and it earned them the crucial one point that was needed to gave them a semi final berth. On 21st March, when Shiraz with his family sat around the new big 29 inch screen Sony coloured television to see the Pakistanis take on the Kiwis in the first semi-final, an excited nine year old Tojo sitting with the autographed photo of his new found cricket hero Wasim Akram in his hand said to his father.

"Abbajaan if Pakistan wins will you take me to Australia to see the finals?'

"I wish I could but today it is already the 22nd today and the finals are on the 25th and we will never make it in time. However to compensate you I will buy you a new cricket set provided we win today," said Shiraz as Imran Khan led his team out into the field.

"My God he is really handsome," said Shezadi as she too took out a photograph of the well built Pathan that was inside the book she was reading.and came and sat next to her father.

Thanks to Inzamam-ul-Haq's fine 60 runs in 37 balls it was celebration time in Pakistan as they cruised to a four wicket win. In the other semi-final luck favoured England as the South African's after the delay by rain and chasing a total of 252 runs was set an impossible target of scoring 21 runs with the last ball.

"I think this is simply ridiculous and the International Cricket Control must revise their rules in such badly rain affected matches," said Shiraz as they all celebrated Pakistan's semi-final win with a grand dinner at the Daman-e-Koh, a popular restaurant on the Margalla Hills that overlooked the twin cities of Rawalpindi and Islamabad. Situated at a height of over 2000 feet above sea level the restaurant's mouth watering tandoori chicken was Tojo's favourite and that evening the nine year old boy had a full chicken to himself.

"If we win the finals then we will come again and I will have not one but two full chickens."said Tojo to the friendly waiter as Shiraz paid the bill and very generously to celebrate Pakistan's win gave a hundred rupee tip to the man.

On the 25th of March 1992, it was celebration time again at the Daman-e-Koh, when Pakistan defeated England by 22 runs in the finals and the man of the match award went to none other than Tojo's favourite Wasim Akram who not only took the three prized wickets of Ian Bothan, Allan Lamb and Chris Lewis, but he also scored a hurricane 33 of only 19 balls. Wasim Akram was born on 3rd June, 1966 at Lahore. The tall lanky and dashing 26 year old left arm pace bowler from Lahore who started his test career against New Zealand in 1988 was an allrounder and it was his swing bowling that had earned him the sobriquet of the 'Sultan of Swing'. He was now the toast of all Pakistanis.

And while the cricket world cup fever in India was still on, Peevee's first few episodes as 'Deepak Kumar' in the television serial 'Main Kisse Se Kum Nahin' was aired over Doordarshan TV. It however did not get a very favourable viewer rating and Peevee therefore was a little disappointed. The producer had chosen the title because he had seen the musical hit movie 'Hum Kisse Se Kum Nahin' starring Rishi Kapoor a number of times when it was released and that was a good sixteen years ago in 1976. He therefore thought that since his TV serial was also based on the life of a singer who wanted to become a hero, he simply changed the first word from Hum to Main and that was that. But luckily, by the time the ninth episode in early April was telecast, Deepak Kumar's rating as a talented singer-actor had shot up tremendously and there were now even offers for him to come and try his luck in Bollywood. But Peevee was on a contract and his getting to Bollywood therefore could only take place when the shooting for all the 52 episodes of the serial were completed and that would not be before the year end at the earliest. Being a little unsure of his future in the world of show business, Peevee therefore decided to consult his father and take his advice.

"Don't be a damn fool son and never even think of terminating the contract. That will be like cutting your own feet and now that your talent on the small screen is being recognized, you should cash in on it. In fact it is good for you, because only recently a relatively young and handsome new comer by the name of Shah Rukh Khan from Delhi who had also started his life on the small screen in a serial titled 'Fauji' is I believe now trying his luck in Bollywood also. Moreover, the other two up and coming Khans, Salman and Aamir are also very much in demand these days and breaking the contract at this stage would only give you a bad name," said Monty as Dimpy also advised Peevee not to take a hurried decision. According to her, self promotion together with good beginners luck in the Hindi filmi world was a must and she therefore felt that Peevee should not jump into a hero's role just because he was being offered one.

"I do not want that my handsome and talented brother Param Veer Singh alias Deepak Kumar should become only a one film hero and then fade away like a villain or as an extra like so many others who never could make it to the top in Bollywood. In fact I want him to be as great and big an actor and star like Amitabh Bachchan, Dilip Kumar, Spencer Tracy, Henry Fonda and the great Charlie Chaplin all rolled into one, so that someday besides being honoured with a couple of Filmfare best actor awards, we would also like to see him on stage getting the coveted Oscar from Hollywood too," added Dimpy with a big smile on her face, while her husband Paddy reminded Peevee that he should also be very choosy about the roles being offered to him and that he must carefully study the entire script before signing on the dotted line.

"Yes and one more thing and that is you must get a good dedicated secretary and a sound public relations man, because that too is a must in the sometimes bad and wicked world of glamour," added Dimpy as the doorbell like that in a movie hall rang twice. And while the debate that early morning on the breakfast table of whether Peevee should or should not join the tinsel world was still in progress, Shupriya walked in with a big bouquet of 47 red roses and a large Black Forest cake. It was not only Baisakhi Day that day, but also Reeta's 47th birthday. But everybody was so engrossed with Peevee's future in Bollywood that they all forgot to wish the lady of the house who as per the orders of the children and her husband was busy making those delicious hot alloo, mulli and gobi ka parathas for them in the kitchen. And too Reeta's utter surprise when everybody started singing loudly and in chorus 'Happy Birthday to You', she too having forgotten that it was her own birthday came out and asked."By the way may I also know whose birthday are we all celebrating?"

On hearing that remark by Reeta when everyone suddenly stopped singing and started laughing, she did not find it very funny till Monty got up and putting his arms around her whispered softly into her ears "It is your birthday darling, so let us all celebrate." And it was only then that an embarrassed and blushing Reeta also realized that she too was now getting old.

In May 1992, Monty once again made a trip to Srinagar. During his flight from Delhi seated in the front row was Girish Saxena, the very senior police officer who had also served in RAW and who was now the Governor of the State. Unknown to Monty and the Indian intelligence sleuths and traveling on the same flight was a well dressed person of Kashmiri origin and who claimed to be a rug dealer. Monty was very worried about his export business and wanted to make sure that all his orders for carpets and other Kashmiri artifacts that were being produced were as per the given specifications and would meet the deadline of 30th June. According to Monty and his sources in the Kashmir Valley, there was no let up in Pakistan's effort as far as the export promotion of militancy and terrorist activities from across the border and into the state was concerned. In fact the proxy war had been further strengthened with the reported induction of a new terrorist organization that called itself HUA, Hurkat-ul-Ansar. It was founded as Harkat-ul-Mujahideen in 1980 at Karachi primarily to fight the Soviets in Afghanistan, but had now moved its headquarters to Muzzaffarabad in Azad Kashmir with the new name and after it had merged with the Harkat-ul-Jihad-al-Islami. The HUA was now getting ready to target the area south of the valley and the Doda district that had a sizeable Hindu population. Information about the presence of Afghan fighters and a few from other West Asian Muslim countries from this organization had also been reported. It was only while talking to his manufacturers and dealers in Srinagar that

Monty came to know that the so called rug dealer on the flight was non other than Yasin Malik, a dreaded terrorist from the JKLF, the Jammu and Kashmir Liberation Front. And Monty wondered what would have happened had Yasin Malik taken the Governor of Jammu as hostage and hijacked the aircraft to Pakistan. He therefore decided that for the return journey he would not take a flight back, but would instead go to Jammu by road in a hired private taxi and with one of his main suppliers as an escort to keep him company. Moreover, he also wanted to go and pray at the famous Vaishno Devi shrine near Jammu for Peevee's future success in Bollywood and then catch the train from Jammu Tawi.

Meanwhile in the month of May 1992, Karim Malik having completed more than four years in Washington DC, was posted as Pakistan's Ambassador to Afghanistan. By end April, Kabul had fallen to the Mujahideen Forces and Najibullah who tried to escape had taken sanctuary inside the UN Mission in the war ravaged capital city. Fearing that Kabul was hardly the place for his family to be in, Karim had decided to leave Mehmuda and the children at Peshawar with her widowed mother Zubeida and go alone to Kabul. To delay his arrival at Kabul, Karim Malik also took two months long leave that was due to him and it was on the plea that he had to get his twenty three year old daughter Tarranum married and which was a fact. Tarranum had just completed her masters in economics from Harvard and had been engaged for a year or so to a tall and handsome Durrani Pathan whose family was also from Peshawar. They were both contemporaries at Harvard and after their marriage were planning to return to the USA to do their doctorate. Both of them being brilliant students had decided to take up teaching as a profession, because not only was it a very well paid job in America, but a highly respected one too.

"No wonder the damn Americans have all the best brains in the world," said Arif Rehman after the Nikah ceremony on the 17th of June was finally over and both Ruksana and her husband had blessed the couple with a few ancestral heirlooms that dated back to the days of the bride's great-great grandparents, Haji Abdul Rehman and his wife.

"Yes and do keep all these precious things very safely, and let me also remind you that as far as good English is concerned, the Americans are simply awful in their spellings. Because just the other day at a spelling bee contest at Trenton, New Jersey and that to in an elementary school, when a student correctly spelt potato, of all people Dan Quale, the Vice President of the United States opened his big mouth to correct him. According to Quale's dictionary the correct spelling of the word was potatoe and not potato and he kept insisiting that it should be spelt by adding that extra letter 'e' to it. And mind you I am not joking because I read about it in a popular American magazine," said Shiraz as the young couple and others had a good laugh at Mr Quale's spelling of 'potato' with that extra 'e'.

Unfortunately during that hot month of June with all the meticulous hard work that Zubeida Begum had put in for the Nikah ceremony and during the lavish receptions that followed at her first grand child's wedding, she soon fell very seriously ill with high fever. Thinking that the fever with the application of ice packs would subside, she refused to be admitted in the hospital, and on the evening of the 30ᵗʰ of June with all her children and grand children by her bed side, she passed away peacefully.

"My dear mother was 72 years old and had lived her life to the full," said Fazal Rehman who with his wife Samina and their children Sameera and Shafiq had luckily managed to arrive that very morning from Delhi.

"Yes and it is rather sad because only a fortnight earlier Ammijaan was so hail and hearty and full of life telling us all the old stories of her own wedding and guiding us in her inimitable style on how to conduct ourselves during the Nikah, and now all of a sudden she is no more," added a heartbroken Samina as Shiraz and Saira tried to console her.

"Yes we all have to go one day and the fact that she went away so very peacefully only goes to prove that Allah the kind and merciful probably felt that it was time for her to join my brother and her dear husband who I am sure must have been missing her in heaven too," said Arif Rehman as he with the others in family stood in line to thank all those who had come to offer their condolences.

Only a week earlier on 22ⁿᵈ June, when it was reported that two skeletons had been excavated at Yekaterinburg in Russia and that they were those of the last Tsar Nicholas 11 and his wife Tsarina Alexandra, Zubeida Begum had commented that the discovery would now only bring out more skeletons from the Communist cupboard and she was dead right. That day she also described to all her grandchildren as to how and why the Tsar and his wife and children were massacred so very brutally by the Red Guards.

"It was on 15ᵗʰ March, 1917, that Tsar Nicholas 11 was forced to abdicate his throne in favor of his brother Grand Duke Michael. Though the real heir to the throne was the Tsar's son Prince Alexei, but he was only 13 years old and was suffering from haemophilia. The First World War was still raging in Europe and after the Bolsheviks had seized power and in March 1918 signed a peace treaty with the Germans to end Russia's involvement in the war, the Tsar's fate was finally sealed. And soon thereafter, when the civil war between Lenin's Red Guards and the White Guards who were against the Bolsheviks broke out, the Tsar with his family was whisked away to Yekaterinaburg a city in the Ural Mountains. There the family was kept in a house of a wealthy Russian merchant that had been confiscated by the Communists. The responsibility of guarding them was now given to the dreaded Cheka, the secret police of the Bolshevik Party that was headed by Yalov Yurovsky. With the White Guards closing in towards Yektarinaburg and fearing that the Romanovs may be rescued by them or may escape, Yurovsky on 16th July, 1918 was given the order to kill the entire family. Giving the excuse that there was disturbances in the town and that they would all be safer in the basement, all of them were taken there and shot in cold blood. The dead bodies were then loaded into a lorry and taken to the nearby mine shafts and were thrown inside it. That particular mine shaft was not deep enough and when the locals started talking that the remains of the Tsar and his family had been buried in the mines, Yurovsky decided to recover the bodies and throw them down a deeper shaft. But unfortunately the lorry that was carrying the bodies got bogged down in mud and Yurovsky burnt and buried them where they were. Had he thrown them down the deep shaft, the bodies would never have been found. But now that they have been discovered, let us hope that Yeltsin's new Russia would give them a decent and proper burial, atleast,' added Zubeida Begum that day, as Shezadi requested her to narrate a few more such interesting historical events but without involving dead bodies because she was mortally scared of ghosts.

On that 30th of June 1992 if the passing away of Zubeida Begum at Peshawar left a pall of gloom on the Rehman family and her many friends, elsewhere in Karachi and in Sind, men, women and children of those from the Mohajir families were cursing the day when they opted to come and settle in Pakistan from India. The army's ruthless operations in that province had turned their guns against the MQM and their supporters. Earlier in the week, the army and the Pakistan Rangers stood like mute spectators as the Haqiqi dissidents kept targeting Altaf Hussein's MQM first in the PPP's stronghold at Landhi and then elsewhere in the city. The Haqiqi Mohajir Quami Movement was a splinter outfit of Altaf Hussein's MQM and it only surfaced recently when two prominent militant leaders Afaq Ahmed and Aamir Khan broke away from Altaf Hussein. Earlier on 19th May, at a high level conference that was presided over by the Prime Minister Nawaz Sharif and which was attended by the Chief Minister of Sind, Muzzafar Hussain Shah, Home Minister Chaudhry Shujaat, the Army Chief Asif Nawaz and the Corps Commander Sind, Lt General Naseer Akhtar together with other top officials at the GHQ, Rawalpindi, it had been decided that 'Operation Clean-up' in Sind would be carried out only by the Rangers and the Mehran Force, but with the full backing of the army. The MQM that once had a vice like grip over Karachi was now on the run. They were at the receiving end as their leaders who were now on the most wanted list were arrested and tortured. But the free hand that was given to the army to also end the dacoit menace in Sind was also being misused by some unscrupulous men in uniform to blackmail, and in a few cases to also extort money and settle old scores. In one particular case it unfortunately resulted in the deaths of nine innocent villagers and that had given the army a very bad name. It was on the 13th of June, when Major Arshad Jamil and his troops in cold blood murdered nine peasants in a village till it was later revealed that it was an act of reprisal committed by the Major in the garb of settling personal scores with them.

"My God I thought that Hitler's SS were bad enough, but this is really shocking," said Saira as Aslam Rehman narrated to her and Shiraz the true story of how Major Jamil in order to settle old scores on a land dispute killed those nine innocent people who belonged to Tando Bahowal, a village that was only ten miles from the city of Hyderabad Sind.

"By God this is even worse than the killings at My Lai that was so ruthlessly carried out by Lt Calley during the Vietnam war, and I hope the army authorities will set an example by having the bloody major court-martialled and if found guilty the bastard should be shot by a firing squad and nothing less," said Shiraz while shrugging his shoulders in sheer disgust.

CHAPTER-16

A Blast Bigger than Bofors

By the time half the year was over, and while the United States were fighting the menace of drugs in that country, and Pakistan was busy eradicating the dacoits of Sind, in India and in it's financial capital Bombay, the mighty Bombay Stock Exchange was reeling under the effects of a deadly securities scam that had been triggered of by a Gujrathi whose real name was Harshad Mehta, but who had earned the sobriquet of being the Amitabh Bachchan of the trading ring. It was also around this time in Miami that the former Panamanian leader, Manueal Noreiga was sentenced to 40 years in prison for drug running and racketeering, while far away in Medellin, the drug capital of Columbia, in South America, Pablo Escobar the drug lord fearing his extradition to the United States was successful in making good his escape from what was suppose to be a jail, but in reality was a luxurty villa.

However, it was Bombay, the financial capital of India that was more in the world news and was hogging the limelight. The millions of investors who had been taken for a ride by Harshad Mehta were now braying for his blood. The scam that ran into a few thousand crores in Indian rupees would have ruined many more had not an internal enquiry by the State Bank of India put a stop to it. Harshad Mehta's borrowing and speculating in the market had made him a multi multi millionaire, but now it was all over. With the scrutiny in progress, the man from Byron Bazaar, Raipur and with only a bachelor of commerce degree from Lala Lajpat Rai College, Bombay and who started his life with New India Assurance company was now in the dumps. He had been denied access to his millions that he rolled over everyday from his many accounts with India's largest bank, and as a result of which he could not liquidate his heavy investments to meet his dues to the bank. Known as the Big Bull who lured others in investing in the same very scrips was now like a running bear. Over a month as Harshad Mehta's exploits tumbling out of his cupboard, the BSE, the Bombay Stock

Market index like an avalanche also came crashing down. And while the small investors were the ones who had burned their fingers very badly, the market capitalization fell by a whopping hundred thousand crore. This was the biggest ever scam in India's history and as compared to it, the Bofors scandal was like a drop in the ocean. But unlike the stock exchange scam it was the Bofors scam that could still have a deadly political fall out and since it kept surfacing off and on, it therefore had the Narasimha led Congress government in the centre on its toes all the time. Since Harshad Mehta was not a political leader like Rajiv Gandhi but he too had taken the public for a ride and as a result of which on the 5th of June, 1992 he was arrested for his role in the scam.

In the last week of September 1992, while Fazal Rehman and Samina in New Delhi were still trying to figure out as to how an ordinary mediocre college graduate from Bombay could dupe so many people including the banks and make a bloody ass of them, there were also strong indications that some middle level bank officials from India's public sector banks were also very much involved in abetting the crime and in making quite a few fast bucks themselves. Commenting on a report in the papers that Harshad Mehta in order to get off the hook had also been hobnobbing with some influential politicians, Fazal Rehman said somewhat jestingly to Samina.

"Well in that case don't be surprised if the man in order to keep his golden goose in fine trim had also been regularly filling up the Congress party coffers, and maybe someday with his penchant for juggling with figures, they may even make him the Finance Minister of the country."

'Now that I think is hitting below the belt, and it is not that I believe that all Indian politicians are corrupt, but there are a few who are impeccably honest and I am sure that Narasimha Rao and his minority government will never allow that to happen," said Samina.

"Possibly not, but in politics anything can happen because its now only a question of money power and muscle power, and if one has the money then for ones very own survival even the politicians from the opposition parties can easily be bought off," replied Fazal Rehman as he with Samina and their nine year old son Shafiq got into the car to go to the airport. Their seventeen year old daughter Sameera having completed her schooling from the International School at Kodaikanal had with her school friends gone on an exchange program to the United States and was now finally returning home. Two days later while the family was discussing Sameera's higher educational plans, the news arrived of Fazal Rehman's posting on promotion and as Counsellor Political to the Bangladesh Mission in Washington DC.

"Well that calls for a celebration and Sameera will now go to Radcliffe," said a delighted Fazal Rehman as he called up Hotel Maurya and booked a table for four at the Dum Pukt restaurant.

In early November, 1992 while Peevee as Deepak Kumar was busy shooting for the final climax scenes in the last few remaining episodes of the television serial 'Main Kissi Se Kum Nahin,' he was surprised to receive a gift with a greeting card from an Indian girl fan of his in the United States. The college going girl a Bengali while on a holiday in India with her parents had seen Deepak Kumar by chance in one of the episodes on television where the rising star had sang the first four lines of a popular Spanish song in Spanish and then followed it up with the English and Hindi version of it, and the teenage girl was so very impressed both by his looks and by his singing that she immediately on return to the States sent him the card with a long playing record and a music video. The cover had the title 'Erotica' on it and it depicted Madonna enjoying a sexual intercourse. The album had been released only a month ago and had already been labeled as the most controversial album in music history. The greeting card also had a naked woman with a fig leaf in her hand and was attached to the music album, which simply read 'Just don't go by the cover, because love is only skin deep.'And the name below was signed in Bengali by someone who called herself 'Bidrohi' meaning revolutionary.

"Good Heavens, even some of the young Indian girls in America are now getting highly perverted by free sex in that country," said Peevee to Dimpy and Paddy while showing them the surprise gift that he had received from the Indian well wisher of the opposite sex in California, USA.

"Thank God the Customs in India did not open it or else you would have been in serious trouble my boy and by Jove if the press had by chance sniffed what was inside then that would have been the end of you dreams to become a Bollywood star. Because the press is always looking for such lurid and sensational stories and it would have played it up and branded you as the one with the perverted mind and that would have been disastrous for your career," said Paddy.

"Yes thank God and bless my stars,"said Peevee as he tore up the card and threw it into the waste paper basket.That evening Peevee who had heard about Madonna came to know a little more about the sensational American singer who was now a celebrity. Madonna Loise Ciccone was born on 16th August, 1958 in Bay City, Michigan and was raised in a Catholic family. A natural dancer who had taken ballet lessons as a young girl, she had moved to New York when she was not even 17 to pursue her dance classes. Working during the day with Dunkin Donuts and dancing with dance troupes in the evening, she had to indeed work very hard to make both ends meet in America's biggest city. Though she had come with only 35 dollars to New York, but she was now not only a sensational singing star but also a Hollywood actor who was now internationally known throughout the world. The latest album had three overtly sexual songs including the title song 'Erotica,' which had become a craze in America and after having heard it Peevee very confidently said to his sister Dimpy, "Well Didi if Madonna could make it to Hollywood then why cant I?"

Later that evening after seeing the recently released Hindi movie 'Deewana', starring the newcomer Shahrukh Khan with Rishi Kapoor and Divya Bharati, Peeveee was even more confident that he was destined to become a future Bollywood star and maybe even a Hollywood hero.Born on 2nd November, 1965 at Gurgaon, the young and unassuming Delhi lad from St Columbus High School and Hansraj College who always wanted to become an actor and who started his career with television serials had finally come of age in his very first debut film. Commando Abhimanyu Rai of the television serial 'Fauji' fame with his brilliant performance in 'Deewana' as Raja Sahai had made his mark in Bollywood and now there would be no looking back for him as producers lined up to sign him up for their films and Raja Sahai it seemed was destined to become the Raja of Bollywood. Like the legendary Yusuf Khan whose screen name was Dilip Kumar. Shahrukh Khan too was born to Muslim parents who were Pathans, and whose ancestors came from the Quissa Kahani Bazaar of Peshawar. His father Taj Mohammed Khan was a freedom fighter and so was his maternal grandfather the famous Major General Shah Nawaz Khan of Subhas Bose's INA fame. Unfortunately both his parents did not live to see their talented son as a Bollywod hero, but his Hindu wife Gauri the daughter of an Indian army officer whom he married in 1991 was thrilled, when Shahrukh's very first Bollywood film became a box office hit. Having seen the film that evening, when Peevee said that Shahrukh would become the next Badshah of Bollywood after Amitabh Bachchan, Dimpy was totally in agreement with him.

"Yes there is something in that actor that produces goose pimples in me and I believe his next movie titled Baazigar where the actor as the hero plays a negative role, and which I am told is going to be released next year will definitely catapult him into stardom," said Dimpy.

"Yes that I think is a gamble well taken and I am sure that Shahrukh Khan with his versatile talent will live upto it,' added Peevee who had seen him acting on the stage and on the Television screen and who also was aware that the up and coming star had studied acting under the versatile Theatre Director Barry John who ran the Theatre Action Group in Delhi.

With the advent of the Video camera and the Video Casette Recorder watching old movies in the comfort of one's home had now become a passion for young Peevee. And thanks to the internet while the whole wide world was getting perverted with pornographic photographs and films, in England Queen Elizabeth who during her long reign had produced four children was also getting worried about them. And it was because all of them were practically going through with some sort of a problem with their marriages. To add to that, on 20th November, a fire in the Private Chapel room of Windsor Castle had damaged a major portion on the northwest side of the magnificent building and the Queen therefore very aptly described the year 1992 as the most horrible for her and the Royal Family. To add to that the British tabloid press and the paparazzi who were always snooping around with their telephoto lens cameras to catch what the Royal siblings were up to only added to the Queen's woes and miseries. On reading about one such scandalous article that had a photograph of the Prince of Wales with his dear old girl friend Mrs Camilla Parker Bowles, a much married lady with two teenage children on the front page, Reeta who was very broad minded remarked rather angrily.

"Though the royal couple Prince Charles with Diana had visited India in early February and they stayed for six days, but there was nothing that indicated that they were not pulling along. And as far as the article goes I don't know why they are making such a hue and cry of it. If the two are in love so let them be damn it and I simply do not know as to why the world should be bothered about their personal lives. I remember that in the not too distant past even some of the Maharajas of the erstwhile rich princely states of India not only married half a dozen times, but they also had their own harems full of girls and young ladies and some of whom were probably of their daughter's age and maybe even of their grand daughter's age and nobody said a damn word. And mind you quite a few also had white skin foreign wives too. And now just because any royal family affair in England makes news the tabloids shamelessly play it up." Monty who had never seen Reeta so worked up and that too on an issue that practically had no relevance to their own family simply smiled and said.

"Well dear that reminds me of a joke about one such great Maharaja who had so many girls in his harem that he could not even remember all their names and he therefore decided to remember them only by giving them numbers. And to further ensure that nobody else had a good time with them, he kept a platoon of eunuchs guarding his big harem and also had a special eunuch ADC appointed and whose only duty was to go to the harem and get the girl of the Maharaj'as choice whenever he desired to have her in bed for sex. The harem was located quite some distance away from the palace and the Maharaja being a short tempered and an impatient man he always wanted everything in a jiffy. Therefore, if he desired a particular girl he would simply tell his eunuch ADC to go and fetch Number so and so and the eunuch ADC would then run, jump over the wall, run across the fence, piggy back the girl from the harem and present her to his highness. However on one hot evening, when the Maharaja at night was feeling a little more randy than was usual, he ordered the eunuch ADC to first go and fetch number 10 immediately. And the eunuch ADC without batting an eyelid jumped over the wall, ran across the fence and came back with Number 10 on his back. A little later the Maharaja having had enough of Number 10 asked the same ADC to take her back and get Number 33. Again the poor ADC jumped over the wall ran across the fence as fast as he could, and with number 33 saddled behind his back he returned panting. Having had his good time with number 33 and still not fully satisfied, the Maharaja then asked the ADC to take Number 33 back and return with his favourite Number 111 and that to in two minutes flat and failing which the ADC should be ready to face the guillotine. The poor eunuch ADC realizing that his life was in serious danger, he with 33 on his back ran at full speed dumped her inside the harem, picked up number 111 on his back and returned in a record time of one minute and fifty five seconds. The Maharaja was delighted and so was the ADC, but the smile on the ADC's face soon vanished as he kept gasping for breath and then suddenly fell flat at the Maharaja's feet, collapsed and died. But after having completed the story, when Monty asked Reeta if she knew what the moral of that story was, and Reeta with a blank face replied in the negative, Monty softly whispered into her ears. "My love the moral of that story is that it is not the fucking around that kills you, it is the damn running around." And when Reeta heard that and was about to hit him with that thick British tabloid magazine that was in her hand, Peevee suddenly entered to say that he had completed the shooting of the last television episode. But when he further added that a well known film producer from Bombay would be arriving the next day to sign him as a hero for his maiden Hindi feature film, Monty jokingly said.

"Well my son let me then advise you to play it cool, keep your distance, ask your price, but don't run around these producers because if you take on too many films at one go, then it will only kill you and nobody else."And as Peevee went to his room, Reeta with a wicked smile on her face said to her husband."My God for a second I thought that you were going to repeat that Maharaja's joke to him also, but thank God you didn't."

Late that evening, when Monty while sympathizing with Princess Diana's plight told Reeta a little more about the Charles-Camilla affair, Reeta was a little surprised. Camiila was born on 17th July, 1947 and was christened Camilla Rosemary Shand. She was the daughter of Major Bruce Shand and Rosalind Shand nee Cubitt. Major Shand was a British army officer turned wine merchant and Mrs Shand also came from a well to do English family from Sussex. Camilla after completing her schooling attended a finishing school in Switzerland and she first met Charles in 1970 at a polo match and that was well before either of them were married. In 1973, Camilla married Andrew Parker Bowles an army officer who was also a polo playing friend of the Prince of Wales and as their friendship grew so did the affair between the charming Prince and Camilla, and the rest of course is history, And with the popular saying that two is for company and three is a crowd, poor Diana probably felt completely left out and she will now I guess will have to live with it. And according to some who are close to the royal family, the Prince and Diana have already started living separately I have been told' added Monty.

"Yes Papa that's right, but neither is Diana an angel. I agree that she has been given a raw deal by the Prince of Wales who unfortunately has also admitted in public about his extra maritial relations with Mrs Bowles, but Lady Diana's alleged affair with her riding instructor Major James Hewitt has only added more juice to the scandal. After all she was a princess and a lady and she should have been more discreet about it,"added Dimpy as Peevee butted in to say that it was all in the game and nobody had the right to comment on anybody else's private affair. And while the sordid tales of alleged extra martial affairs of the Prince and the Princess of Wales hogged the limelight in the British tabloids and the pros and cons of having such grand fairytale weddings of the rich and the famous that normally ended in disaster became a subject of discussion in many well to do Indian families, in the Bajwa family the subject was taboo.

Early on the morning of Sunday, the 6th of December 1992, Reeta with her husband, Shupriya and Peevee went to the Bangla Sahib Gurudwara. Though this was a Sunday weekly ritual, but on that particular Sunday, the Bajwa family had especially asked the head priest to offer some special prayers and to invoke the blessings of all the Sikh Gurus since Peevee was due to sign his first contract for his maiden Bollywood venture that day. A few days earlier Shupriya had consulted an astrologer who had advised her that the 6th of December would be an ideal day for the contract signing since as per the Hindu almanac it was an auspicious day. Moreover, according to Peevee's horoscope, number six was also his lucky number and as such signing of the contract on that auspicious day was bound to bring great fame and fortune to the young budding actor. However, the astrologer also cautioned Shupriya that the signing must be completed latest before midday and preferably earlier in the day because thereafter the configuration of certain planets will undergo a change and that may not be all that lucky for the young man. After Shupriya had discussed it with Reeta, the time for signing of the contract was therefore fixed at around 10.AM so that all the other formalities connected with it could also be completed well before the given deadline. It was exactly at 10.10 AM, a time that is normally regarded by many as the time for the angels to pass, when Peevee signed on the dotted line. Soon thereafter as the cameras clicked away and the token signing amount was handed over by cheque and while the ladoos were still being distributed, Dimpy who was watching TV in the adjoining room came charging in to say, that secularism in India had taken a very bad beating. She was referring to the demolition of the Babri Masjid that had started early that morning by the Hindu zealots from the Sangh Parivar and which was now being shown live on TV.

On that day it seems that the Hindus from the Sangh Parivar, Bajrang Dal and the RSS calling themselves as 'Karsevaks" and voluntary workers had lost their heads as they went hammer and tong to demolish the 16th century mosque at Ayodhya that was adjacent to the town of Faizabad in Uttar Pradesh. The mosque commonly known as the Babri Masjid was built in 1528 by Mir Bagi, a general of Babar, the first Moghul Emperor of India at a spot where it was being alleged by the Hindus once stood an ancient temple that was reputed to be the birthplace of Lord Rama. Mir Bagi having destroyed the temple had built the mosque and named it after his master, the King Emperor and hence the name Babri Masjid. But the mosque which stood for more than four and a half centuries was now being reduced to dirty rubble, while the guardians of law who were duty bound to protect it sat like dummies. The matter was to be resolved by the Allahabad High Court, but for reasons unknown the court just kept sitting on it. Only a year ago the Ajoydha issue had dominated the electoral scene in the country, and though the Congress emerged as the single largest party, but it was a minority government under Narasimha Rao that took office in June 1991. The first

Kar Seva to build a temple adjacent to the mosque commenced on 9th July, 1992 and it continued for 17 days and nothing happened. But as months passed by and with the Narasimha Rao government's utter neglect of what was an explosive issue the matter it seems had now gone completely out of hand.

"Frankly speaking I think the political parties in this country have messed it all up, and it is all for their own political ends. Even during the British Raj and till we got our independence both Hindus and Muslims used to worship in the same complex and the place was often referred to as 'Masjid-e-Janmastan' meaning thereby that besides being a prayer hall for Muslims, it was also the birthplace of Lord Rama," said an angry Peevee while switching off the television set.

"Yes Peevee is right, but way back in 1883 and again in 1886 the Hindus who wanted to build a temple there had taken the matter to court but had lost the case. And thus the first round of the legal battle that was fought by the Hindus came to nought. Then during the communal riots of 1934, one of the walls and a dome was damaged, but the British had got it reconstructed. The problem became acute only after independence, when the country got divided on communal lines. At around midnight of 22nd December 1949, and while the police guards were fast asleep a group of Hindus planted the idols of Ram and Sita inside the mosque and trouble arose when on the following morning a large number of Hindus made a frantic effort to enter the Masjid to offer puja to the deities. Luckily KK Nair the District Magistrate with the help of the available police force had managed to keep them at bay and had promptly reported the matter to the higher authorities. And when Pandit Nehru was told about it he was livid and he ordered the Chief Minister Govind Vallabh Pant to have the deities removed immediately. Thereafter the Government of India declared the site to be a disputed one and a huge lock was put at the gate. In 1984, the Bhartiya Janata Party and its ally the Vishva Hindu Parishad started the movement for the creation of the Ram Janmabhoomi temple at Ajodhya and two years later in 1986, when the District and Sessions Judge KM Pandey of Uttar Pradesh gave orders for the opening of the disputed structure to the Hindus, the fire ball of communal violence was set rolling once again. To some this was considered as a political move by the then Congress government to off set the favour that was shown to the Muslims in the Shah Bano case. In 1989-1990 the VHP intensified its activities by laying the foundation of the proposed Ram Temple on the adjacent property and it got further aggravated when on 30th October 1990 members of the

Sangh Parivar stormed the mosque and planted a saffron flag on it, and as a result of which 50 people died in the police firing. The then minority Chandrashekar government immediately proposed negotiations between the Muslim Mullas and the Hindu Sants to solve the matter peacefully. The most contentious issue was the ownership of the land and if that could be proved then probably the problem would have been solved once and for all. But that was not to be. It is also believed that the people who were working behind the scene to work out a deal had also come to a consensus, and they wanted the matter to be referred to the Supreme Court, but when Justice VR Krishna Iyer took the proposal to Prime Minister Chandrashekar, the Prime Minister wanted more time. Since it concerned both the Hindus and the Muslims of India, the issue was therefore a very sensitive one. And when Chandrashekhar wanted advice from his law officers, the matter only got further delayed. In the meantime the matter had leaked out and the Congress President Rajiv Gandhi fearing that Justice Iyer's proposal would boost Chandrashekar's rating, he decided to scuttle it. The minority government of Chandrashekar that had only sixty members of parliament was being supported by the Congress from the outside, and when the Congress declared that no reference should be made to the highest court in the land, that golden chance was lost," added Monty who had heard about this story from his journalist friend Unni.

"Well it only goes to prove that our politicians no matter to which political party they belong to are more interested in their own vote banks and they could'nt care less what happens to this country. And I won't be surprised if the demolition of the Babri Masjid is played up by our Muslim neighbours who are only waiting for an opportunity, and this may well lead to more blood letting between the Hindus and the Muslims," said a visbly angry Reeta who had no love lost for the dhoti and kurta pyjama clad leaders of the nation.

While the debate over the destruction and demolition of the Babri Masjid took centre stage, and the major political parties started blaming each other for their incompetence, a group of Muslim fanatics in India aided by the ISI from Pakistan started conspiring to take revenge for the descecration of the old 16th century mosque. Following the demolition and as predicted by Reeta, there were Hindu-Muslim riots in many towns and cities of India, but the worst hit and where the Muslims suffered the most was in the financial capital of the country. Bombay had a very sizeable Muslim population of all sects and not only was the city a home to the likes of Dawood Ibrahim and other big Mafia Dons who were only waiting for an opportunity to strike, but it was also the home of Bal Thackeray and his Shiv Sainiks who were staunch Hindus.

Born on 23rd January, 1926 at Pune, Bal Keshav Thackeray who came from a lower middle class family was now a man to reckon with in Hindu politics. Having started his career as a cartoonist with the newspaper Free Press Journal, he founded the Shiv Sena, the army of Lord Shiva on 19th June, 1966. With an ideology based on the concepts of 'Bhoomiputra-'Sons of the Soil' and strong Hindu Nationalism spirit, the Balasahib as he was now popularly known with his headquarters at Dadar was now a big political figure in the nation's financial capital. His party the Shiv Sena with the springing tiger as its emblem had not only spread its wings far and wide within the city, but also in the entire state of Maharshtra. With the party's labour union that called itself Bhartiya Kamgar Sena (The Indian Workers Army) and the Akhil Bhartiya Vidyarthi Sena (All India Student's Army) together with its mouthpiece 'Samna' the Marathi newspaper published from Bombay, the 66 year old firebrand had now started giving more importance to the Hinduvta ideology and had drifted away from the earlier concept of the Marathi Manoos'. The island of Bombay that was given to the British East India Company in 1666 as part of the dowry by the Portugese King when his daughter Princess Catherine Braganza married King Charles theSecond was no longer a group of small islands. It was now a major bustling cosmopolitan city and the heart of India's financial world, and the Shiv Sena leader very rightly had now started realizing its vast potential and importance. But on that Sunday as the news about the demolition of the Babri Masjid spread throughout the city, it unfortunately became a day of rejoicing for the Shiv Sainiks as they organized themselves to take on the Muslims of the city. The first spell of rioting took place from 6th to 12th December 1992 and it resulted in the deaths of over 900 innocent people, and of which the majority were Muslims.

"I think the people have gone mad and the media must not publicise such killings, arson and looting because that will only aggravate matters," said Peevee to Monty while taking his permission to switch off the television set. Peevee was also worried that if such gruesome killings of innocent people just because they were from a particular minority community continued in a cosmopolitan city like Bombay, then not only will it effect Bollywood, but it would also spread like wild to the other big cities in the country.

On the very day the Babri Masjid was demolished, Aslam Rehman Khan was promoted to the rank of Major General and took over command of Pakistan's 12 Infantry Division at Murree. A few days later he selected his son, Vovka, Lieutenant Samir Rehman Khan temporarily as his ADC. Though Vovka had only two years plus service in the First Punjabees, the regiment that his father and grandfather had also served in, but since his battalion was part of the same field formation and was deployed in the Hajipir Sector of Azad Kashmir, his appointment as his father's ADC did not raise any eyebrows, though Vovka himself was initially reluctant to take on the assignment.

Meanwhile in Kashmir, the ISI backed Muslim terrorist organizations had also stepped up their activities. In the month of December alone, a series of daring operations by the Harkat-ul-Ansar had practically paralyzed the Indian administration in the state. The militant organisation had relentlessly attacked 25 police stations and as a result of which the police force in the valley was completely demoralized. And by the time the year 1992 came to a close, Shiraz wondered whether the destruction of the Babri Masjid and the meteoric rise of the Sangh Parivar advocating Hinduvta together with the volatile situation in Kashmir would sound the death knell of secularism in India.

On 8th January, 1993 the sudden demise of the Pakistan Army Chief, General Asif Nawaz Janjua while holding office surprised many. Though some said that he had died of a severe heart attack, but others including his wife Nuzhat Janjua suspected foul play. She claimed that her husband had been poisoned by the DIB, the Director of the Intelligence Bureau, which was headed by retired Brigadier Imtiaz and that it was done by lacing his tea with arsenic She therefore demanded an enquiry into it. As a result of this, the government posted a police guard at the general's grave in order to ensure that his body was not exhumed for medical examination. There were also rumours that the General's stomach had been removed prior to the burial in order to avoid possible detection of any foul play. Reacting to all such rumours and gossip that were being spread by all and sundry, Saira felt pity for the widow and said to her husband.

"I think it is rather sad that in this country not only will they not let the dead army chief rest in peace, but they won't even allow the next one in seniority to take over the reins smoothly either. And I believe though President Ghulam Ishaq Khan is in favour of General Abdul Waheed Kakar taking over as the next army chief, but the Prime Minister Nawaz Sharif wants his own man to fill that chair, and as a result of which there is already a cold war going on between the two of them," added Saira as Shiraz in a little sarcastic manner congratulated her for being so very up to date in what was happening around the capital.

"Yes, General Janjua's sudden death has indeed created a lot of doubts and stories, but whether he died of natural causes or otherwise is something that the medical doctors will have to determine However, it is also believed that the General off late was also quite upset in the manner in which the Prime Minister Nawaz Sharif had started interfering in the promotions and postings of some senior officers, and the CIA too was also unhappy with the lack of cooperation from the late General on the issue of buying back the stinger missiles that had been supplied by them through the ISI to the Afghan Mujahideens. None the less all said and done, I personally feel that the General's death was due to natural causes and not due to any foul play," said Shiraz as he got ready to take the family out for the weekend to Nathia Gali.

On 11th January 1993, when General Abdul Waheed Kakar the Corps Commander Quetta Corps having superseded quite a few senior generals was appointed as the new Army Chief, not every one was happy, and certainly not the Prime Minister who had only been told about the appointment a few minutes before the formal ceremony was about to take place. There were also reports that the Prime Minister had even threatened that he would not even allow the new Chief to discharge his duties. Fearing that this may further create problems, the President using his powers and constitutional privilege of appointing the service chiefs, had very clearly out maneuvered the Prime Minister. He was apprehensive that with Nawaz Sharif's lust for more power, he could pose a direct threat to his own authority and this had further widened the rift between the two of them and had brought the fight between the President and the Prime Minister of Pakistan right into the open.

But what bothered Shiraz even more was the fact that Lt General Nasir, the DGISI was not only against returning the FIM-92 Stinger missiles on a buy back basis to the USA, but there were also reports that these were now being given to organizations such as the Harkat-ul-Ansar and other such fundamentalist militant groups, and the possibility of these weapons being used against the Indian forces in Kashmir was therefore very much a possibility. Though the United States by now had placed Pakistan on the watch list of countries sponsoring international terrorism and had branded Harkat-ul-Ansar as a terrorist organization, but the fact remained that such sophisticated weapons were also a danger to Pakistan itself where Muslim fundamentalism was on the rise. Another information that was bothering Shiraz very much was the clandestine efforts that were being made by the ISI in procuring nuclear material and missile delivery systems from some rogue countries. According to a reliable source, the Pakistan Defense Attache in Moscow, Brigadier Sultan Habib who was also a high level ISI operative had been constantly procuring such like material from certain Central Asian Republics, North Korea and also from a few of the erstwhile Warsaw Pact countries of Central Europe.

And while Shiraz got busy in trying to gather more information on Brigadier Sultan Habib's modus operandi in procuring nuclear related material, Monty decided to make a trip to Mumbai. On 5th of January, 1993 with Bombay slowly limping back to normalcy after the horrible December riots, Monty flew into the city firstly to be close to Peevee who had started shooting his first Hindi feature film at Film City, and secondly to find a new tenant for his apartment at the Maker Towers in the fashionable area of Cuffe Parade. As per his builder friend's predictions, the property had appreciated manifold, but because of the recent riots in the city, it was also now very much in demand since it was in close proximity to the military station at Colaba and thus provided more incidental security to that area. During his stay in Mumbai, Monty had booked himself at the nearby Hotel President and while on his way from the airport to the hotel had found that the army was still very much visible in certain sensitive areas of the financial capital, and particularly so in the suburbs of Mahim and East Bandra, where there was a sizeable number of poor Muslim population. Though the city was relatively calm, but it was an uneasy one. There was still a lot of tension between the militant Hindus led by the Shiv Sena and the Muslims in certain parts of the city, and the government fearing a backlash had therefore kept the army standby. They could not afford to take any more chances.

But nevertheless after a gap of about three weeks, violence again erupted on the 7th of January. This time it was not only the Hindus who were targeting the Muslims and vice versa, but also the goondas of Bombay were also making hay as they too resorted to arson, looting and killing of the Muslims of the city and targeting their properties. The sectarian violence had once again engulfed the city of prosperity as Hndus and Muslims got at each other's throat, while a paralyzed Congress government in the state led by their Chief Minister Sudhakar Naik looked on helplessly. While the top Congress leaders squabbled, the army was again called in to restore order. The shaken minority government of Narasimha Rao at the centre had also by now air dashed the Defence Minister, Sharad Pawar, who was a powerful political bigwig from Maharashtra to take immediate charge of the deteriorating situation.

From the 7th of January to the 16th of January 1993, while Mumbai was in flames, the prospect of finding a reliable tenant for Monty's apartment became even more difficult. Though one broker had brought a well to do Muslim who was also willing to pay more rent and also a fat lump sum in cash to pay for the fixed deposit, but the housing society was not very happy with the gentleman' credentials. He claimed to be a well to do businessman who was based in Dubai and he wanted the apartment for his large family who were presently staying in Mahim West, which was one of the worst areas that was affected by the recent riots. Though Monty felt bad for the courteous and kind middle aged Muslim, but the housing society was not willing to take him on as a member. On the 18th of January after having failed to get a reasonably good tenant for his apartment, Monty returned back to Delhi.

Unknown to Monty and to the rest of the world, while Bombay by the end of January 1993 thanks to the Indian Army was once again limping back to normalcy, in Islamabad some of the top sleuths from the ISI and their agents in India got busy in cultivating those Muslim elements in Bombay and elsewhere who were willing to take revenge against the Hindus of the city. They had to however, first find a leader who would be able to identify and motivate other like minded Muslims to join in the retribution that was being planned against the Hindus for the destruction of the Babri Masjid. Needless to say that the team to be recruited had to be a small, but it had to be a very trusted and a selective one too. And one that would for the sake of Islam be prepared to even sacrifice their lives if need be also. It also had to be a complete in house operation and without any direct links to the ISI or their agents in Bombay and they finally found the man in Dawood Ibrahim, the great Mafia Don from Bombay who was now based in Dubai. Dawood Ibrahim Kaskar was the son of a police head constable from the Bombay police crime branch. The Muslim family from the Konkan coastal area lived near the Musafirkhana on Pakmodia Street that was not far from Bombay's famous Crawford Market. Coming from a very large family of seven brothers and three sisters, Dawood had studied up to class nine and then with his brother Shabir as his buddy started indulging in petty crimes of stealing, extorting money and into selling smuggled goods in Mohatta Market and Manish Market that were near their home. The first case against Dawood that was registered by the police was in early December, 1974 when he with eight others committed daylight dacoity by attacking a Hindu trader with country made pistols and choppers and decamped with a fabulous sum of nearly four lakhs of rupees. During the emergency years 1975-77, he together with other hard line criminals like Haji Mastan were detained under MISA, the Maintenance of Internal Security Act. And it was while he was in Arthur Road jail that he came in contact with Haji Mastan and Yusuf Patel, both of whom were the biggest gold and silver smugglers of the time. Haji Mastan and Yusuf Patel were impressed by young Dawood's earlier exploits, and after their release from jail they inducted Dawood into the syndicate. When an ambitious Dawood tried to expand the smuggling business and started trespassing on what was Karim Lala's exclusive territory, the wily Pathan who was also in the same business felt highly offended and it soon resulted in deadly gang wars.

It was in the early 1920's, when a group of Pathans from the North West Frontier Province landed in Bombay to seek employment. While some became taxi drivers and watchmen, others took to money lending and to the drug business. One of those whose thriving drug business flourished was Juma Khan Charaswalla of Dongri. Then in the early 1940's, and during the war came Karim Lala who with Charaswala's son Faroukh became a regular drug supplier and then slowly he graduated to become a dreaded Don. By the 1970's, Karim Lala with his muscle power and hit men together with his Godfather like figure and Robin Hood image had become a household word in Bombay. And then came the gang wars between the Dawood Ibrahim and the Pathan's gangs which inspite of Haji Mastan's best efforts to reach at some comprise it resulted in a failure. And when Haji Mastan with Karim Lala's help got Yusuf Patel bumped off over a smuggling deal, the gang wars became even more daring and violent. In January 1981, after Dawood's brother Shabir was gunned down near a petrol pump at Prabhadevi and Dawood was lucky to escape, he decided to take his revenge. And one night in October 1982, when Samad Khan, a trusted lieutenant of Karim Lala who had gone visiting his girlfriend at Grant Road got out of the lift, he was literally riddled with bullets by Dawood and his men. After this the message to the Pathan syndicate was loud and clear, but Dawood was still not satisfied. He was determined to find and finish off Alamzeb and Amir Zaada, the two brothers who had killed his brother Shabir and that day came on the 6th of September, 1983. In a daring daylight attack inside the court premises, David Pardesi a contract killer who was hired by Dawood shot dead at point blank range Amir Zaada while he was being escorted to the court room. That 'Supari' killing which was the local slang for contract killing had not only shocked the people of Bombay, but also its police force. Though Dawood was arrested, but he managed to obtain bail and was released in May 1984. But soon thereafter feeling the heat of the Bombay

Police closing in on him and his gang, Dawood Ibrahim jumped bail and ran away to Dubai. And from there the "Bhai" as he was now known with the help of local Bombay gangsters had started expanding his mighty syndicate and empire. Soon it became known as the 'D' Company. But in early 1992, when Ibrahim Parker, the husband of Dawood's beloved sister Haseena was gunned down and killed by members from the Arun Gawli gang, the gang wars were back in action again. To avenge his sister's death, two of Dawood's henchmen during the early hours of 12th September, 1992 stormed into a major hospital of the city and shot dead Shailesh Haldankar the hit man from Arun Gawli's gang who had made his sister a widow. Haldankar was admitted in the hospital for treatment and that daring attack in a public hospital also shook the police and the people of the city.

The indiscriminate killings of Muslims by the Hindus during the December and January riots in Bombay and elsewhere had angered the little man from Pakmodia Street who was now a very big man in Dubai and who hobnobbed not only with the Sheiks and Emirs, but also with the high and the mighty from India, Pakistan and elsewhere. And the elite circle included not only film stars and starlets from Bollywood and Lollywood, but also those who had good political clout with the people who mattered in the subcontinent. His well furnished big bungalow in the up market area of Zumera in Dubai which ironically was also known as the White House was home to many influential people and where entertainment with good food and with the best of French wines and Cuban cigars was a regular feature.As it is the barbaric manner in which the Babri Masjid was reduced to rubble by the Hindus of the Sangh Parivar had angered many in the Muslim world and some of whom were now determined to avenge the insult. And when more reports of the sufferings of the poor Muslims of Bombay at the hands of the Hindus kept reaching Dawood's ears and those of the other expatriate Muslim smugglers from the subcontinent who were also based in Dubai, they all decided that it was time that the people of Bombay at least to begin with should be taught a lesson of their lives. And seeing their belligerent mood the ISI of Pakistan therefore also decided to take full advantage of it.

The rampant killings of the Muslims of Mahim and the indiscriminate looting and burning of their shops and property had also affected another smuggler who was a resident of that very area. Mushtaq Abdul Razak Memon was born in Bombay and he too came from a large family of many brothers and sisters. A product of Beg Mohammed High School at Pydhonie, Mushtaq was also a good sportsman and a dare devil car driver who was willing to take risks. He was therefore also known in his close friends circle as Tiger Memon The family who earlier stayed in a small one room apartment opposite the post office on Mohammed Ali Road, not far from Crawford Market had because of poverty shifted in the late 1970's to the fisherman's colony at Mahim. But thanks to Tiger's lucrative silver smuggling business, the man who was now in his mid thirties had relocated the entire family into two spacious flats in the big Al-Hussaini building at Mahim. As a young man working as a chauffeur, Tiger Memon with his driving skills had once saved another big don by the name of Yakub Bhatti who had come from Dubai to visit the Dossa brothers in Bombay. Mohammed and Mustafa Dossa were also well known smugglers and Tiger Memon while chauffeuring Bhatti to the airport on realizing that he was being tailed by the police pressed on the accelerator. Fearing that capture of the Don from Dubai would also land him in thick soup, he outwitted the police forces who with their sirens blazing were chasing his car. His dare devil driving that day helped Yakub Bhatti to catch his flight to Dubai and that was the turning point in Tiger Memon's life. Not only had he saved Bhatti's life, but he too had managed to escape from the police dragnet that day. A few weeks later he was rewarded with an invitation to join Bhatti in Dubai. Thereafter there was no looking back and soon the young chauffeur became a gold carrier and whose only job was to ferry smuggled gold biscuits into Bombay.

Tiger Menon and his younger brother Yakub, who was an educated and well to do chartered accountant with their many influential contacts and wealth in Bombay were now well known and respected figures. But after the December 1992 Bombay holocaust that destroyed their office and other property, they were now like wounded tigers seething with anger and were waiting to take their revenge. Tiger Memon therefore once again made his way to Dubai to solicit support from his smuggler friends and well wishers who were only too willing to pitch in with their slush funds. And by the time the New Year arrived, the conspiracy by the dons of Dubai to take revenge had already been set in motion, and it got further fuelled, when the second round of riots, killings and arson took place in January 1993 and when the Muslim communities were once again the worst sufferers. Having received the financial backing and the final nod from Dawood Ibrahim, Taufiq Jaliawala, Haji Ahmed and a few more Pakistani smugglers including Aslam Bhatti most of whom were based in Dubai, Tiger Menon returned to Bombay in mid January 1993, and he soon got busy in planning the whole operation that would literally not only shake Bombay and India, but also the world.

While Tiger Menon was busy making his murderous plans to terrorize the 12 million people of Bombay with a series of bomb blasts, in the United States the handsome young man from the State of Arkansas was getting ready to take his oath of office as the 42nd President of the United States of America. Born in Hope, Arkansas on 19ᵗʰ August, 1946 with the name Whilliam Jefferson Blythe, the American public welcomed the change, as the 46 year old Democrat took his oath of office. The Americans had voted the young handsome man to power and they now had very high hopes in him to revive the country's fledging economy. Having grown up in a troubled home after his father died in an automobile accident three months before he was even born, the little baby was brought up by his grandparents, while his mother moved to New Orleans to continue with her nursing studies When his mother married Roger Clinton, Bill's surname also underwent a change and he became a Clinton. A good student Bill while studying international affairs at the Georgetown University also served as an intern to Senator J Whilliam Fulbright who was also from the State of Arkansas. He was however lucky not to have been drafted for service in Vietnam, because he had won a Rhodes scholarship to Oxford University. Though it was rumoured that Clinton had managed to escape the draft and had cleverly evaded his military sevice, but all said and done he was destined to get into politics. On his return from England, he joined the Yale Law School and graduated from there in 1973. On 11th October, 1975 he married Hillary Rodham, a fellow Yale student and thereafter having worked for Jimmy Carter's presidential campaign, he became Arkansas's attorney general and in 1978 at the young age of 32 years he was elected as the nation's youngest governor. When he announced his candidacy for president, the country's economy was in a state of recession and he therefore focused on the economy, the high unemployment and promised the people better health care, tax cuts for the middle class and reduction in defence spending. His winning the elections with a 43% of the popular vote was a landslide victory and it surprised most of the Pundits. It was after 12 years of Republican control that a Democrat was back in the White House and Bill Clinton was determined to take America forward and into the 21ˢᵗ Century.

As the good looking American President with his million dollar smile spoke about his future plans for his country and the world, Shupriya having listened to the inaugural speech of the world's most powerful man live on cable television, simply remarked that America may be a very powerful nation both militarily and economically, but that does not give them the right to dictate terms to others. Shupriya was referring to a news report on the Iraq disarmament crisis, wherein the US forces not even 24 hours earlier had fired 40 Tomahawk cruise missiles at factories in Baghdad simply because they thought that these factories were linked to Saddam Hussein's illegal nuclear weapons program.

"Yes I quite agree, but then as far as Iraq and the Gulf countries are concerned they are so bloody well rich in oil, that America simply cannot do without them either. Therefore they want complete control over that region and a nuclear Iraq with Saddam Hussein still in the chair could prove catastrophic for America in the long run," said Monty as Dimpy gave the good news that Peevee had rung up to say that Bombay was peaceful again and that there was no requirement for anyone to visit him, or worry about him. And since he was busy shooting at Film City in Goregaon, he would therefore call up later to speak to all of them.

Peevee alias Deepak Kumar's future in the highly competitive Bollywood's film industry depended entirely on the box office success of his first movie, and that too on debut as a hero. Topping the charts were names like Sanjay Dutt, Salman Khan, Aamir Khan and a relatively newcomer in the industry by the name of Shahrukh Khan. With the big Mafia Dons from Bombay and Dubai pitching in with their enormous slush funds to control Bombay's film industry, their demands too were on the rise and it ranged not only from asking for the distribution rights for the film and its music, but they also had started dictating the cast that they wanted for a particular film. This had also inflated the rates of the big stars and they too had now started demanding more mone,y and some of them were asking for payments not just in six but also in seven figures. But besides them, they were also many other players including some big stock market brokers who had also got into financing Bollywood films, because the banks were not ready to risk their money into it. There were also a few small time players who were generally satisfied with the video rights and music rights of the movie, but piracy in these two fields had reached such a sophisticated state that the industry had to perforce now seek the help of the police and other private detective agencies to stop this illegal practice. At times the pirated version and the music was out in the market even before the movie was released on the cinema screens and this at times resulted in a few of them hiring contract killers from Bombay's underworld to get rid of their rivals. Reports of many of the top Bollywood stars performing exclusively at private shows and parties for the dons of Dubai at the White House had also become an annual feature and reports of a few budding starlets aspiring to be heroines through the good offices of some of the bigger dons provided they slept with them were also being heard in the corridors of the many studios in Bombay.

In Bollywood, a budding star was no star at all till he proved himself to be a star attraction and one whose name itself would rake in good money. In fact he was considered a non entity till his face and name appeared on the bill boards, on the television screen, on the innumerable hoardings that dotted the streets of Bombay, and in the various film magazines that regularly flooded the market. In other words he or she had to be a big money spinner for those who controlled the cut throat industry. And ofcourse to get that break, luck also played a very important part. If your first film as a hero was a box office hit then one could say that he would probably make it to a star, but nothing in Bollywod was guaranteed or certain for a newcomer.

Unsure about his own future, Peevee had put his heart and soul into it. It was his first film that was based on a story of a dedicated police officer who was determined to prove the unholy nexus between a Mafia Don and corrupt police officers. The Don with his money and muscle power had become a big political leader. And while the Don continued with his nefarious activities in the guise of doing social work for the masses, Deepak Kumar In the role of a dare devil dedicated police officer who had been suspended earlier was required to unmask him. Therefore as the hero of the film Deepak Kumar with the help of a good looking freelance female journalist as his heroine, were required to carry out a successful sting operation and expose the nexus. Though as a story this was nothing very unusual, since such like films had already been made in Bollywood, but it gave Peevee a chance to really show and prove on the big screen that he was a face to be reckoned with by the general public. Morever the movie had a plot which he knew would appeal to the middle class, the lower middle class and the slum dwellers who in reality were the ones who were being systematically exploited by such pseudo political cum mafia leaders. And while the movie was still under production, Peevee rented a small dingy one BHK, one bedroom, hall and kitchen flat on Shirley Rajan road in Bandra West. It was a predominantly Christian locality that was adjacent to Carter Road and where other top stars like Rajesh Khanna had their palatial bungalows on the sea face. Early morning in order to keep himself fit, Peevee would daily run up and down the slopes of Pali Hill and go past the bungalows of Dilip Kumar, Sunil Dutt, Rajender Kumar, and the legendary "Girnar" where once lived Baburao Patel, the outspoken editor of the once very popular but now defunct film magazine called 'Film India.'. Peevee also hoped and prayed that someday he too would have a big palatial bungalow on Pali Hill and like

Amitabh Bachchan have fans waiting outside the gate at 'Pratiksha" to have his darshan.

On 25th February, 1993 while shooting outdoors inside a posh bungalow with a big swimming pool on the outskirts of Alibaug, a seaside weekend resort for the rich and the famous in Bombay and which as per the film script had been converted into a gambling den cum nightclub that was run illegally by the don turned politician's kith and kin, when the producer and director who were still undecided about what name that should be given to the movie during the lunch break asked for suggestions from the others, Peevee whose own future depended on the success of that movie promptly said somewhat matter of factly that keeping in view the story line and the final climax scene that is yet to be shot inside this makeshift gambling den cum nightclub,a catchy title like 'Gundagiri ka Raj Netaon ke Haath' would be I think ideal, there was a stunned silence for a moment as both the producer and the director got into a huddle. Unknown to Peevee the Don cum politician had also put in a major share of his black money also into the film. Moreover according to Bollywood protocol it was considered improper for a newcomer in the Bombay film industry to even open his mouth. But to Peevee's utter surprise, when the title was unanimously accepted by both the producer and the director, he indeed felt very proud about it. And he only hoped that for the sake of his own career it should not be a flop.Ever since the day the first shot was taken, Peevee had been thinking about it. To him it looked rather strange that though the shooting had commenced and the story was also fairly good and convincing, yet it was untitled to begin with. He was also aware that good and positive publicity during production was an important factor not only for the success of the film, but for his image building too and he was happy that his title for the film had been accepted.

Late on that night of 26th February, 1993 after the shooting schedule for that particular casino scene with a sexy song and dance item number was finally over, Peevee sat down under the open sky to enjoy a chilled glass of beer. And when he was told by somebody that the World Trade Centre in New York had been bombed and that six people had been killed and a very large number injured, Peevee just could not believe it. According to the BBC the bombing took place at around 12.17 in the afternoon New York time and though the massive explosion had created a huge 30 metre wide crater that had cut through four sub levels of concrete structure, but luckily the 110 story tower was still standing. Eighteen years earlier on the 13th of February, 1975 the 11th floor of the tall impressive steel framed building had caught fire but that was accidental, but in this case I think it is definitely a case of sabotage, and I wonder who could have done it said Peevee to his director who was of the opinion that it was probably just an act of revenge by some disgruntled elements from the multi-ethnic city that was more like a mini world. The World Trade Centre was also known as the Twin Towers by the New Yorkers and it was the pride of downtown Manhattan. It consisited of a complex of seven buildings that was largely designed by architect Minoru Yamasaki and engineer Leslie Robertson and was developed by the Port Authority of New York and New Jersey. Thanks to the rich Rockefeller family and to Nelson Rockefeller who was then the Governor of New York, the complex was completed in 1973, and it not only became the tallest building in the world, but also the main hub for global business.

In Islamabad having seen the destruction that was caused by the bomb on TV, Shiraz too was stunned. During his tenure in the United States he with his wife and children had often while visiting New York and the Statue of Liberty driven past that beautiful marvel of architecture and he wondered why someone would try to destroy it. And a few weeks later he got the answer. After going through the wreckage, the bomb technicians had luckily found the axle of the Ryder truck that was used for the bombing and the vehicle was traced to a Palestinian named Mohammed Salemeh who had rented it. On 4th March, Salameh was arrested and the trail further led on to Rahman Yasin of Jersey City. Both the arrested men then led the authorities to the apartment of Ramzi Yousef where the bomb making material was found. Ironically they also found the bomb making manual that was written by the CIA for the Mujahideen fighters who had fought the Russians in Afghanistan. It was a 1500 kilogram bomb that was made primarily from urea nitrate, but Ramzi Yousef the architect of the bomb had managed to escape from USA. According to the FBI, Ramzi Yousef was born in Kuwait and had entered the United States in 1991 on a false Iraqi passport. He had set up residence on Nicole Pickett Avenue in Jersey City and during his stay was in constant touch with Sheikh Omar Abdul Rehman, a blind Muslim cleric who regularly preached at the Al-Faroukh Mosque in Brooklyn, New York and who was now suspected of having conspired with the bombers for this deadly act. Sheikh Omar Abdel Rehman was born on 3rd May, 1938 in Egypt and had lost his eyes at a very young age because he was diabetic from childhood. Thanks to Braille he graduated in Quaranic studies from the Al-Azhar University, Cairo and was always considered a radical by the Egyptian authorities. Although he was not convicted of conspiracy in President's Sadat's assassination, he was however expelled from Egypt and had made his way to Afghanistan where he was reunited with his former

Professor Abdullah Azzam. And while in Afghanistan, Sheikh Omar joined his old mentor and Osama Bin Laden in the struggle against the Soviet occupation of that land locked country. After Azzam was assassinated in 1989, he landed up in New York in July 1990. Thereafter he kept preaching in three mosques in the city and though his sermons often condemned the Americans and the west for their pro Israeli stance, the FBI it seems took little notice of it. But after the WTC bombing he was now being kept under close surveillance. The Blind cleric was a known Muslim radical and a fundamentalist who was also instrumental in recruiting thousands of Mujahideen fighters from all over the world including the North West Frontier of Pakistan to fight the Russians in Afghanistan and according to Shiraz, the ISI and the CIA were also fully aware of his activities because at that time it suited them. Shiraz was therefore now not only worried but was also afraid that as far as Pakistan was concerned the bombing of the WTC may well give the Americans the excuse to once again turn the screws on Pakistan both economically and militarily.

Meanwhile in Pakistan, the love hate relationship between the President of the country and the Prime Minister that had surfaced openly from the day General Waheed Kakar was appointed as the new army chief got further aggravated, when General Kakar asked Lt General Asad Durrani and Lt General Javed Nasir to put in their papers for violating the channels of command. Both of them who once headed the ISI it seems were also hobnobbing with the politicians and this had infuriated the new chief who appointed Lt General Javed Ashraf Qazi who was the DGMI to take over as the DG ISI while Major General Iftikhar was assigned to look after the external wing of that same organization. And when Shiraz came to know that the two new incumbents had also been ordered by the Chief not only to cleanse that ISI of the "Islamists" but also to rein in the so called 'Jehadis' in Kashmir, he indeed felt very happy. This had resulted in not only recalling those officers who were still involved in Afghanistan's long on going and bitter civil war, but it also led to the retirement of many others who were fundamentalists in their views. Correspondingly it also led to the dismantling of some of the ISI's vast sophisticated intelligence network in that region. Unlike the CIA and RAW, the ISI was not a career service, but with the Army Chief controlling it, those who had a chance as senior officers to be seconded into it felt proud to be a part of that important policy making arm of the government of Pakistan.

And while the CIA was still in the process of tracking Ramzi Yousef the mastermind behind the deadly WTC bombing, Monty on Friday

12th March, 1993 caught the first early morning flight to Bombay. His broker had finally found a good respectable tenant and who luckily was also acceptable to the housing society. Since the initial paper work had to be completed on that very day of his arrival and the final legal formalities were to be completed on the following Monday, Monty decided to spend whatever little time he could with Peevee. Luckily for Peevee there was no shooting schedule for him till Monday afternoon, and when he picked up Monty from the airport it was only nine o'clock in the morning.

"Come Dad let me first show you my pad in Bandra and then we will both go to Hotel President and I will spend the entire weekend with you," said an excited Peevee as they got into an air-conditioned chauffeur driven hired Fiat 124. During the journey, when Peevee took out the photo album that had all his photographs and interviews, and which had appeared in various filmy magazines and newspapers, Monty indeed felt very proud in the mature manner in which Peevee had replied to some of the tricky questions that had been put to him. When one young lady correspondent asked Peevee whether he had ever fallen in love with somebody and Peevee told her of course and then added that he always kept falling in love at the drop of hat every time he saw a pretty face, the lady correspondent smiled and diligently noted it down. But when she asked him very seriously as to whose pretty face did he see last and when Peevee immediately replied with a big smile and said 'Yours of course,' the correspondent was completely bowled over and she gave Peevee a big thumping write up with as many of his photographs as she could in the popular glossy film magazine that she represented.

At about 10.30 AM, after having had a quick cup of tea at Peevee's pad they made their way to the hotel where the broker with the prospective tenant were waiting for them, While driving past the dargah(Tomb) near Mahim, when Peevee noticed a large gathering of Muslims and said "Oh that's Saint Makhdum Shah Baba's dargah dad, and they say that those who sincerely revere and worship him are granted with fame and fortune are always blessed. And though I have never visited him as yet, but I intend doing so in the near future," the Muslim driver gave a few more details about the history of the shrine and then added that the large crowd was because it was the 17th day of Ramzan and it was also a day for the Friday prayers. When Peevee told his father that his next shooting schedule was on Monday afternoon and that he desired that Monty should stay on till at least Tuesday evening so that he could show him a bit of his own talent and introduce him to the production team and his co-stars, Monty immediately agreed. Therefore with the change in Monty's departure schedule and while they were on their way to the President Hotel, they stopped by at the tall and impressive Air India building at Narriman Point where the Indian Airlines main booking office was located on the first floor. But little did they know then that they were literally sitting on a deadly time bomb. Luckily it was nearing lunchtime and Monty did not have to wait very long to have his departure for Delhi rescheduled and changed for the morning 9 o'clock flight on the 17th of March.

By the time they reached Hotel President, the time was nearing 1 P.M. and as soon as Monty had completed the initial formalities with his broker and the prospective new tenant, Peevee who knew about Monty fondness for good seafood said.

"Dad today let me for a change treat you to some really delicious and mouth watering Malvani sea food, but we will have to hurry or else we wont get a table because the restaurant is located in the congested Fort area and it is so very popular that by 1.30 PM it is always jam packed," Monty readily agreed. And when he told the cab driver to take them to 'Apoorva Restaurant 'by the shortest and fastest possible route, the driver immediately obliged by taking the route via the Colaba Causeway. 'Apoorva' was a restaurant that specialized in serving giant size crabs, lobsters and all other varieties of sea food that one could think of. All the preparations were cooked in Konkani, Malvani and Goan style and were served as per the individual's choice. Though it was a small air-conditioned restaurant, but it was very centrally located in the Fort area of Bombay and not far from the Bombay Stock Exchange, the Reserve Bank of India and the VT railway station. Moreover, it was reasonably cheap and they also served chilled beer. Thanks to the smart and enterprising cab driver, they reached the restaurant just in time to get a table for two and that too near the window facing the road.

It was around 1.30 PM in the afternoon and while they were enjoying the chilled beer with the delicious stir-fried masala tiger prawns as starters, suddenly there was an unusual rattling of the big window, and though it hardly lasted only for a couple of seconds, Monty thought that it could be a mild earth tremor since Bombay and the Konkan area were prone to such occasional and mild seismic shocks. But some five minutes later, when there was complete pandemonium on the streets, Monty realized that something was very seriously wrong.

"I only hope it is not communal rioting again," said Monty as they heard police jeeps, ambulances and fire brigade tenders with their sirens blaring speeding away on the road and they were all heading towards the nearby high rise Bombay Stock Exchange building on Dalal Street. And when both of them ventured outside to see what was happening and saw the thick black smoke bellowing from the high rise building they first thought that the building had probably caught fire. At first the rumours were that a gas cylinder in one of the many eating joints around the stock exchange had burst, while others said that a vehicle that was parked in the basement had accidently caught fire and exploded, and somebody even said that it could probably be part of a film shooting and the loud blast that was heard could well be a part of the scene. But nobody knew the truth and the truth was very different. Therefore in order to find out the truth and help in the rescue work if need be, Peevee having paid the bill with his father ran towards the massive Bombay Stock Exchange building and what they saw there was simply ghastly. Outside that tall and impressive building on what was also known as the Wall Street of India, the area was strewn with the severed heads, limbs and torsos of innocent people, some of whom were even beyond recognition. There was blood every where and the small street looked as if it was covered with thousands of pieces of red blood stained glass. Those who were lucky to survive watched in disbelief. They could never think that such a thing could ever happen to the financial capital of India and that too at its very nerve centre.

"'This is no accident but a criminal act by some fanatical maniac bomber' said Monty as he too joined in the rescue operations. Minutes later MN Singh, the Joint Commissioner of Police from Bombay's crime branch arrived on the scene and cordoned off the area. The people worst hit were those who were in the basement or were working in the mezzanine and on the ground floor of that high rise building or were simply loitering around the area. A large number of people were out in the open enjoying their lunch break with cigarettes and paans, while others were simply gossiping or talking about the rise and fall of their shares in the the stock market. The trading for the day at the stock market was about to close and quite a few were seen enjoying the large variety of food and snacks that the many food shops and vending stalls on the nearby streets and around the imposing building had to offer.

While Monty and Peevee with other civilian volunteer workers were busy helping to evacuate the dead and the wounded to the nearby hospitals, the news arrived over the police wireless net that two more such blasts had taken place. The first one was at Bombay's largest grain market at Katha Bazaar near Masjid Bunder, and the second one was near the portico of the

Air India Building at Narriman Point. And while the first blast took place at 2.15, the second was just 10 minutes later at 2.25. P.M.

"This simply cannot be a one man show by a maniac, but a well calculated conspiracy by some terrorist group I am sure," remarked Monty as the father and son duo kept evacuating the dead and the injured from the streets to the designated emergency ambulance pick up points that had been established near and around the stock exchange building.

"Yes and we should be thankful to Wahe Guru that we were not inside the Air India building at that time,"said Peevee as he lifted another unidentified dead body from Dalal Street and placed it with all the others. And within an hour's time he had counted nearly forty of them and more kept coming.

It was only around 5.PM that evening after the rescue work was practically over that Monty and Peevee got into a cab to go back to the hotel. On the way Peevee, kept thinking as to who could be responsible for such merciless killings and wanton destruction. And by the time they arrived at the hotel, there was still more bad news as reports of more such blasts from various parts of the city kept coming in. And when at around 5.30 PM they reached the hotel room and switched on the TV, practically all the channels were breaking news about the serial blasts that had shaken and paralyzed the financial capital of India. Within a span of just two hours plus starting at 1.30 PM when the BSE was targeted and till 3.35 PM that afternoon there had been a total of 13 such explosions all over the city and the worst one it seems was near the Century Bazaar at Worli where the casualties were reported to be the maximum.

"I hope it stays at that unlucky number 13'" said Monty as he rang up the room service and ordered for some snacks and tea since both of them had gone without lunch and were very hungry.It was indeed a Black Friday for Bombay and with panic spreading and rumors floating about another possible breakout of rioting and looting, the people were on the run to get to their homes as soon as possible. Monty now wondered whether this was a fall out of what began with the destruction of the Babri Masjid on the 6th of December at Ayodhya.

"Yes and you maybe right dad. That day was a Sunday and according to some Hindu astrologers it was an auspicious day for the Hindus of the Sangh Parivar to reclaim the birthplace of Lord Rama. But it only led to large scale sectarian violence in Bombay and resulted in the deaths of innocent people and most of whom were Muslims. And today is a Friday and that too a Friday afternoon in the holy month of Ramzan when Muslims all over the city would have congregated at the mosques and on the streets of the city for their afternoon prayers,"said Peevee as he made a second cup of tea for his father. Peevee had an uncanny feeling that the timings of the blasts therefore could be the handiwork of some Muslim terrorist group who wanted to take revenge, but he was not very sure.

"'However, the fact is that whoever carried it out, the involvement of locals and hoodlums from Bombay and especially those who knew the city well was very much in evidence. Because most of the bombs were either car bombs, scooter bombs and suitcase bombs and most of these had been detonated in crowded areas and the people involved therefore knew not only how to drive two wheelers and four wheelers, but they were also trained in arming such deadly devices,' said Monty as more news about the after effects of the blasts were shown on the various TV channels.

Late that evening at 9 PM in far away Islamabad, when Saira switched on the TV to listen to'Kabran," the news over PTV and heard the headline about the terrible serial bomb blasts in Bombay, she immediately called out to her husband Riaz (Shiraz) and said.

"Well if you think Karachi was bad enough then just come and watch this. Bombay it seems has been targeted by terrorists."

Shiraz, who was busy helping his ten year old son Tojo with his school homework immediately came running down the stairs and what he heard and saw was simply unbelievable.

"My God this is something incredible and it has never ever happened anywhere in the world before and whosoever is behind it must have meticulously planned and executed this very daring and outrageous operation in a most secretive manner. And it cannot be the handiwork of just one single person since the bombs were detonated in quick succession in various parts of the big sprawling and congested city," added Shiraz as he went looking for map of the city in the big Readers Digest Atlas that was in his library.

Late that evening and after Saira and the children were fast asleep, Shiraz kept listening to the news over All India Radio and the BBC. Then with cups of hot coffee and a tourist map of Bombay city that he had found in one of the many tourist guide books for foreigners, he kept plotting the exact places that had been targeted by the bombers. Since the news had confirmed that car and scooter bombs were used for the bombing and that at certain places even hand grenades had been thrown, Shiraz who had a fairly good idea of the geography of the city and of the various areas that were dominated predominantly by the Hindu and Muslim communities therefore marked each of those affected areas with the letter 'H' for Hindu, "M" for Muslims and 'HM' for areas and localities that had a mix of both. Under these alphabets, he also wrote the letter 'C' for car, 'S' for scooter, SC for suitcase and 'G' for grenade thereby indicating the kind of bombs and explosives that were detonated at these places. Having seen the destruction and devastation on TV that the bombs had caused and with his prior knowledge on the use of explosive and grenades, Shiraz decided to carryout his own appreciation and assessment and thereby arrive at some tangible conclusion. As he delved deeper into it, some sort of a pattern did emerge and which he thought could lead to some clear evidence as to who could have masterminded this senseless and macabre dance of death and why. And looking at the similarity of the recent bombing of the World Trade Centre in New York with that of the blasts at the Bombay Stock Exchange and the Air India building in Bombay, Shiraz first suspicion fell on some international Muslim terror organization that may have links with those in the Middle East. But the possibility of the LTTE having a hand in it could not be ruled out either, because in January itself, Kittu a top LTTE leader had been killed in a bomb blast on the high seas and since they suspected that it was the Indian Navy that was behind it, the LTTE cadre had sworn to take revenge. With the destruction of the Babri Masjid and the killings of Muslims in India and particularly so in Bombay by the Hindu fanatics from the Shiv Sena, and the Sangh Parivar that followed, the possibility of the ISI having an indirect hand in these blasts in connivance with certain Muslim fundamentalist organizations could not be ruled out either. Shiraz was also aware that the ISI was very active in sponsoring the on going militancy in the Indian states of Punjab and Jammu and Kashmir, but now after the destruction of the Babri Masjid and the killings of Muslims during the recent riots in Bombay, the political equation in India had also undergone a radical change. The BJP, Bhartiya Janata Party, the Shiv Sena in Maharashtra and other such like Hindu regional political parties in the other states of India with the support of the RSS, the Rashtriya Sevak Sangh, the VHP, Vishwa Hindu Parishad were practically now all a part of the Sangh Parivar and had started gaining ground politically. Their anti-Muslim stand had also started showing good results at the polls. The BJP whose only aim it seems was to promote 'Hinduvta' in the country had gained immense popularity and was soon becoming a dominant political force to reckon with in India. And maybe as a result of this that the ISI had stepped in to fan the flames of hatred between the two communities and create political instability in the country, thought Shiraz as he once again tuned in to listen to the late evening news over the BBC. After all, Bombay was the financial capital of India and it was in Bombay that the Muslims had suffered the most during the recent riots. That night having racked his brains for hours together, when Shiraz just could not figure out with firm conviction as to who could be the real culprit behind those well planned bombings, he fell fast asleep.

On Sunday afternoon and a good 48 hours after the Bombay blasts, Shiraz having returned home after a friendly game of golf was still unable to get over the terrible tragedy that had claimed hundreds of lives of mostly innocent civilians including men women and children from all communities and irrespective of their caste, creed and religion. That day he once again sat down with a paper and pencil and with no terrorist organization claiming responsibility for the heinous act, Shiraz became a little more suspicious and wondered whether it was a tit for tat by some fanatical Muslims who probably had suffered immensely during the Bombay riots and wanted to give it back with vengeance to the Hindus. Generally a terrorist organization after having carried out an operation of such great magnitude and so very successfully would have by now certainly claimed responsibility for it, but since nobody had, that itself seemed rather odd to him.

Late that evening and having got hold of a bigger map of Bombay City from the concerned department in his office, Shiraz once again sat down to plot those particular areas that had been targeted by the perpetrators of those devastating blasts. In the process, Shiraz had not only highlighted each area with a red coloured roundel, but he also added the alphabetical letters 'H', 'M' and 'H-M" against each to denote whether the area was predominantly Hindu or Muslim or were they common to both. Below the red roundel, he also noted the time of the attack After carrying out a thorough and detailed study of the sequence of events, he came to the following deductions and conclusions. Firstly, the blasts were triggered of starting from the South of the city and went progressively towards the North and were carried out at regular intervals of approximately 10 to 15 minutes each. This clearly indicated that the bombs had been armed and timed to go off in that particular sequence also. Secondly, the places that were worst effected were the crowded areas of south and central Bombay and included, bazaars, important commercial centers that had a predominantly Hindu population. Areas such as Dadar, Worli, and the Plaza Cinema, had been targeted by car bombs, whereas in places like Katha Bazaar and Zaveri Bazaar which were highly congested areas, the scooter bombs were used. The blast at the Lucky Petrol Pump at Dadar was very close to the Shiv Sena Bhawan, the headquarters of Bal Thakeray's political party and whose leader and his followers were reportedly the ones who had taught the Muslims of Bombay a lesson during the December-January riots. Thirdly, the BSE and Air India buildings were two very prestigious landmarks in the main business district of the commercial capital and there also the car bombs had been used. The three five star hotels of Sea Rock in Bandra, and the two Centaur Hotels at Juhu and Santa Cruz respectively were relatively close to the domestic airport, but the modus operandi was quite different from the others. Here the perpetrators had booked individual rooms and had used suitcase bombs. These hotels were generally patronized by those who either visited the city for a day or two on business, or by those who were connected with the film industry, the civil aviation and by the rich who resided in that area and could afford eating and drinking in luxury. Grenades were thrown at the Machhimar Colony at Mahim, which was predominantly a Hindu Fisherman's colony and also at the Sahar Airport. All the blasts in quick succession had all taken place between 1.30 and 3.30 PM in the afternoon when it was primarily lunch time and when the majority of the workers and office goers were generally expected to be out on the streets lapping up the delicacies that the many roadside vendors of the city had to offer. The month was that of Holy Ramzan and the Muslims who were fasting were either at their prayers or were indoors waiting for sunset to break their fast. By and large the areas that had been targeted had little or hardly any Muslim population worth the name and the predominantly Muslim areas like Dongri, Pydonie and the ever busy Mohammed Ali Road that had nurtured Dawood Ibrahim and others who followed his footsteps to become 'Dons' of the city were practically left untouched. Putting all these above factors together, there was no doubt in Shiraz's mind that this was definitely the handiwork of some syndicate with probably pro Muslim leanings. Moreover, the Bombay Police had by now also confirmed the use of RDX, the lethal and deadly Research Developed Explosive with sophisticated pencil timers by the persons responsible for the blasts and these were highly restricted items that were not easily available in the open market or elsewhere. Moreover, the possibility of RDX together with the cache of AK-56 Rifles and hand grenades that had been recovered by the police from a battered and abandoned old maroon coloured Maruti van near the Siemens factory close to the TV tower at Worli, was proof enough that either these items were smuggled into the city, or had been supplied by some enterprising gun runner. The police had also recovered from inside the glove compartment of the same maroon maruti car a green rosary that the Muslims normally use during prayers.

Suprisingly it was also on that very Friday, 12th March, 1992 that General KV Krishna Rao the retired ex Army Chief was sworn in once again as the new Governor of Jammu and Kashmir. For the General Officer from the Mahar Regiment this was going to be his second tenure in that trouble torn state. The first tenure was rather a short one of six months only and and it lasted from July 1989 to January 1990. During the 1971 Bangladesh operations the General as the GOC of 8 Mountain Division had captured Sylet and had acquitted himself well. He had also served as Governor of Nagaland, Mizoram amd Tripura from 1984 to 1989, when those states were facing insurgency problems and he was able to restore order. But in the state of Jammu and Kashmir it was now a different kind of ball game altogether. With the recent induction of the 'Lashkar-e-Toiba,' from across the Line of Control by the ISI, 'Operation Topac' was now given a completely new dimension. The members of this deadly terrorist group consisting mainly of Pakistani and Afghan mercenaries who were hard core fundamentalists and who called themselves as 'The Army of the Pure,' had fought against the Russians in Afghanistan and it was also widely believed that it had direct and strong links with Osama Bin Laden's Al-Qaida too. LeT for short, the Lashkar-e-Toiba with their headquarters at Muridke near Lahore had also established quite a few camps inside Pakistan Occupied Kashmir and their cadres were also very well trained and highly motivated. Shiraz was also aware that in the recent past atleast a dozen of them in tandem with the Islami Inquilabi Mahaz, a terrorist outfit that was based in the Pakistan Occupied Poonch District of the State had infiltrated into the state, and he was therefore worried that these battle hardened Muslim mercenaries with their sophisticated weapons may well in the near future become the driving force in perpetrating the massacre of the minority communities and which could lead to ethnic cleansing of the Hindus in and around Jammu, Udhampur, Khistwar and other such like Hindu dominated areas of the state. Meanwhile in Delhi, the series of bomb blasts in Bombay had got Shupriya and Reeta extremely worried also.

"I only hope and pray that your findings are wrong and the Muslims of Bombay are in no way connected with this ghastly crime and by chance if it is true then Allah help the Muslims of India, because it could lead to another serious round of rioting and killing not only in Bombay, but all over the country and I am worried about Peevee too," said Shupriya as Monty on the telephone gave out his assessment and also added that the involvement of the Pakistani hand in these deadly blasts therefore was very much a possibility. His reasoning was that RDX and AK 47 rifles were available at the drop of a hat in Pakistan eversince the Russians withdrew their forces from Afghanistan and these were also being used by militant groups inside Kashmir and who were being armed and trained by the ISI.

"Well let us only hope and pray that the culprits are brought to book and peace prevails, and let's also hope and pray that Pakistan is not involved in anyway since that would further worsen the already deteriorating ties between the two countries,"said Shupriya while requesting Monty to give the telephone to Peevee. In Delhi, the massive Bombay blasts had also rattled the minority Congress government of Narasimha Rao. Soon after the holocaust, the Prime Minister, the Home Minister, SB Chavan, Rajesh Pilot, the Minister of State or Internal Security together with a few other cabinet ministers hd landed in the city, but 48 hours had already passed and the famed Bombay Police had made no breakthrough whatsoever. But luckily there was no violence in the city and it was only late on Sunday evening, when luck smiled on the police force when they traced the owner of that battered maroon coloured Maruti van that had been found abandoned near the Siemens factory at Worli. The car belonged to Mrs Rubina Suleiman Memon, a resident of the Al-Husseini Building at Dargah Road Mahim, and when the police visited her flat and found that not only her apartment was locked, but also that of all the others who belonged to the large Memon family, DCP Rakesh Maira the dedicated police officer immediately smelt a rat. During the search of the flats, the police also recovered the keys of a scooter. This was the key of an abandoned locked scooter that had been found primed with RDX near the Naigaum Cross Road, but luckily had failed to explode. And when it was confirmed that the scooter was registered in the name of another member of the Memon family, Maira was convinced that he was on the right track.

Tiger Memon was considered to be a small time smuggler with a police record and had suffered during the riots, when his office was reduced to ashes. And therefore the possibility of his being the kingpin and the brains behind this sordid conspiracy was very much a possibility. And when on further enquires from the neighbours and others who worked for the Memons, it was revealed that the entire Memon family had left for some unknown destination a week or so ago and that the last one to leave was Tiger Memon who had taken the early morning flight for Dubai on that same Friday, the 12th of March, Rakesh Maria knew that he had homed in on his man, but the man unfortunately with his entire family had fled the country.

On Monday the 15th of March 1993, and despite the terrible tragedy that had befallen on the people of the city, Monty was surprised to see that Bombay was once again back on its feet and it looked as if nothing had happened. The stock market was buzzing with activity and it was business as usual. That evening as he witnessed the first ever film shooting in his life and that to with his son Peevee as the hero, he felt proud of the Bombayites and the 'Guru-Chela' attitude of those who were part of Bollywood.

"I must say that there is a lot to learn from these filmi people as far as respect for the elders are concerned and the disciplined manner in which shooting is conducted. In fact what touched me the most was when I saw every member of the unit irrespective of his status and starting right from the light boys to the producer and director all sitting together and relishing the same food, and mind you it was a very good spread too,"said Monty as he proudly showed to Shupriya and Reeta the photo album that Peevee had sent.

"Yes in that police officer's uniform he does look as handsome and dashing as Vinod Khanna in the film 'Amar Akbar Anthony," said Reeta.

"Yes he definitely does, but has the Bombay Police made anyway headway in the serial bomb blasts that rocked the city," asked Shupriya, as she quietly put her lips for a second to the photograph.

"Well all I can say is that the Bombay Police have indeed been very lucky. If they had not found those abandoned scooters full of explosives and the battered maroon Maruti van with its cache of weapons, they would still be running around in circles," added Monty as he narrated the terrible carnage that he had witnessed in front of the BSE building.

"But Dad do you think that Pakistan is in anyway involved in this dance of death," asked Dimpy as she fixed her father a mocktail of Virgin Pinacolada.

"Well you never can say, but with the kind of weapons, grenades and explosives, and the markings on them that have been found, there is no doubt that some foreign hand is definitely behind it amd my hunch is Pakistan," said Monty.

"But I believe that the kingpin who is absconding is only a small time smuggler but why should he stick his neck out in this diabolical murder of innocent people. Of course it is well nigh possible that he may have been used by the cartel of the big Indian and Pakistanis smugglers who are now based in Dubai and they I am told all have links with the ISI too," said Dimpy's husband Paddy who was now posted as a Deputy Secretary in the Pakistan Desk of the Indian Ministry of External affairs in Delhi.

During the month of April, as Shiraz went through the quarterly report from the Pakistan Embassy in New Delhi about the internal situation in India and particularly so in the terrorist infested states of Punjab and Kashmir, he was surprised to learn that there was a tremendous decline in the militant activities in both the trouble torn states and especially so in Punjab. It seems that KPS Gill, the tough police officer and the DGP of Punjab had got the Sikh militants on the run because the killings by the militants had declined very sharply and the people too were now very happy. This kind of determined and strong action it seemed also had its effect in the neighbouring state of Jammu and Kashmir, but to a much lesser extent though.

However, a few days later on 18th April 1993, when the President of Pakistan using his powers dismissed the Nawaz Sharif government, Shiraz thought it was rather unfair. According to his own perception, every government was corrupt in one way or the other, but to summarily dismiss a legitimately elected government would only lead to more instability in the country and which Pakistan could ill afford.

"May be Nawaz Sharif had opened his big mouth a bit too wide and had over stepped his limits. And yesterday while addressing the nation, when he accused President Ghulam Ishaq Khan of conspiring against his government and also defiantly reiterated that he would not take dictation from the President that must have really annoyed the big boss" said Saira as her 14 year old daughter Shehzadi walked in with a coloured picture poster of Sanjay Dutt and Madhuri Dixit. It was a poster from the yet to be released Subhash Ghai film titled 'Khalnayak', (The Villain) and the poster was presented to her by one of her school friend's whose father had set up an export business house at Sharjah in the United Arab Emirates.

"With your final exams round the corner, you should be studying and not collecting posters of these stupid Indian film stars," said her mother Saira rather sternly as she gave a very disapproving look to her daughter.

"But it is only a coloured poster from the film and not the video cassette of the film, which given a chance I too would love to see. After all Subhash Ghai does make good films,"'said the father with a big smile as he winked at his daughter and had a closer look at the poster of the film that was being promoted for release world wide.

"Yes, keep spoiling her and at this rate I don't think she will ever fulfill her dreams of doing her masters in journalism from the USA when she grows up," said an angry Saira as the whole family sat down in front of the television to watch the video cassette of the remarkably popular and evergreen Pakistani family serial titled 'Dhoop Kinare.' Haseena Moin's television drama starring Rahat Kazmi as Dr Ahmer Ansari revolved around a child specialist had created a sort of record on Pakistan Television. Since the play had the poetry of Faiz Ahmed Faiz in the background, Shiraz loved watching it time and again. There was no doubt that the television serials of such like family dramas on PTV were highly popular and most of them were based on the close knit family ties of love and sacrifice, which was the corner stone of good upbringing and which the older generation cherished and cared for. But it was now being eroded by the modern day hippy culture and the fast life of the new generation. Late that evening after the first part of the long episode was over and they all sat down to have their supper, when Shiraz casually remarked that Sanjay Dutt, the hero of the film'Khalnayak' was in some way or the other also involved with the Bombay bomb blasts, and that some of the Indian papers had carried that story as headline news a few days ago, Shehzadi refused to believe it.

"Oh come on Abbu, you most be joking. Yes he may be a 'Khalnayak", a villain in the film but certainly not in real life," said Shehzadi as her mother gave her another dirty look

"Maybe you are right my love, but his name is now making headlines in all the Indian papers, and though he has categorically denied it, the fact is that the police are waiting to question him,"said Shiraz rather matter of factly.

"Well I must admit that both the father and daughter duo are more interested in Bollywood than about the constitutional crisis that is raging in the country today and pray where did you get this news about the police waiting to question Sanjay Dutt'" asked Saira as she kept staring at her husband.

"Well, if you do not believe me then tomorrow I will bring home some of the Indian newspapers that come to us through the diplomatic mail bag from New Delhi and you could go through them yourself," said Shiraz rather abruptly.

Meanwhile the sudden dismissal of the Nawaz Sharif government in Pakistan and the appointment of an interim caretaker government under Balkh Sher Mazari, a feudal landlord as the new Prime Minister by President Ghulam Ishaq Khan had made a mockery of the political system in Pakistan, where governments were being elected by the people but were being dismissed by the President under the Eighth Constitutional Amendment.

"I wonder for how long this game of political roulette and vendetta will continue in this country, and it is indeed a bloody shame that even after 46 years of Independence we still have not learnt any lessons whatsoever,' said Ruksana Begum rather angrily to her husband Arif Rehman as the elderly couple discussed the chances of the appeal that had been filed by Nawaz Sharif against the dismissal of his government in the Supreme Court.

"Well I think both the President and the Prime Minister are to be blamed for this damn mess and it was all because of the 8th Amendment. Whereas, Nawaz Sharif wanted its abrogation so that he could become more powerful, Ghulam Ishaq Khan it seems was not at all keen to reduce his own powers," added Arif Rehman.

"Well whatever may be the reason but this is certainly not the way to run the country. This is even worse than a 'Banana Republic' and I wonder where was the damn need and the urgency to have Benazir Bhutto's husband, Asif Zardari whisked out of jail and inducted as a member of the caretaker Federal cabinet. This only smacks of political opportunism and nepotism by the President who probably wants to keep sitting on that exalted chair and I won't be surprised if the army steps in once again," said Ruksana Begum with a look of utter disdain in her face.

"Well I guess that is what politics in Pakistan is all about. It is you scratch my back and I'll scratch yours. It is as simple as that," added Arif Rehman when the telephone rang. It was from his son Salim Rehman in Washington who rang up to give the good news that their 13 year old daughter Nadia whom he had named after the famous gymnast Nadia Comaneci had won two gold medals in the floor and beam exercises during the inter school gymnastics championship finals and as a result of which she had also been offered a scholarship.

"That is all very well, but do please also remember that she is first a Pakistani and a daughter of a diplomat and though excelling in gymnastics while still in school is all very well, but she should not take it up seriously," said Ruksana Begum as she handed over the cordless phone to her husband who was more than thrilled with his grand daughter's achievement. And a little while later, when their other grand daughter Shehzadi rang up to say that she had just heard the news on BBC television that Sanjay Dutt who had earlier been taken for questioning by the Bombay Police on his arrival from Mauritius on 19th April, Ruksana Begun simply brushed it off with a shrug. But when Shehzadi further added that the film star had been shooting in Mauritius for a film titled "Aatish" (Fireworks) and was now in police custody, Ruksana Begum was quite taken aback with her grand daughter's interest in the Bollywood hero and she therefore said to her husband somewhat disapprovingly

"My God if at this young age this grand daughter of ours is so very infatuated with Sanjay Dutt, and I have been also told that at times she even sleeps with his photo under her pillow, then I can well imagine what will happen if she ever comes face to face with the young man."

"Oh these are all passing fancies which I am sure you too must have had of your favourite Indian stars of yester-years like Prithviraj Kapoor, Sohrab Modi., K L Saigal and such like others when you were her age, and like you and I am sure our dear Sherry too will get over it as she grows up." said Arif Rehman very confidently.

"Well let us only hope so, because nowadays with satellite TV ruling the waves, the idiot box is playing merry hell into the growing modern young generation and if they are not guided properly now, then they could well go astray, like it has been in the case of Sanju Baba, when he also fell into wrong company and got into drugs. And I only hope that this young man, the son of the illustrious couple, Nargis and Sunil Dutt is not in any way involved with the bomb blasts," added Ruksana Begum as she got ready to go for her once a week ladies kitty party.

Next morning on 20th April, when Shiraz arrived in his office there was some very disturbing news with regards to the on going war in Bosnia. Not only had the Serb forces captured Srebenica, but they had also started exterminating the Muslim population of men, women and children from that predominantly Muslim area of that war torn country. But what was even more disturbing was the report by the Pakistan intelligence bureau and the ISI regarding Osama Bin Laden's Al Qaida and his clarion call to his Pakistanis and Afghan brethen to join their Bosnian Muslims in their fight against the Kafirs, meaning thereby the Serbs and the Croats Christians. It was on 15th October 1991, after having declared their independence from Yugoslavia that the Republic of Bosnia and Herzegovina was formally recognized by the European Community. And that was on 6th April 1992, and on the following day the United States also recognized it as an independent nation. This was much to the dislike of the Serbs and the Croats and as a result of which a fierce struggle for territorial control among the Bosniaks, Serbs and the Croats had begun. As the Bosnian war erupted, the Serb forces that were much better equipped militarily attacked the Muslim population in Eastern Bosnia. Their aim was to gain control of the strategic area of Srebrenica and they had now finally succeeded in doing so. And though the United Nations Security Council on 16th April 1993, had passed a resolution that all parties and others concerned should treat Srebrenica and its surroundings as a safe area which should be free from any armed attack or any other hostile act, but the Serbs it seems were not bothered one bit as they kept killing and expelling the Muslim Bosnian population from their homes and out of Serbrenica. For the Bosniaks the ethnic cleansing had begun and Shiraz was apprehensive that this war could well lead to a bigger conflict of Muslims versus the Christians not only in Europe but also throughout the whole wide world. A week later, when the presence of Muslim mercenaries who had fought against the Russians in Afghanistan were reported fighting in Bosnia and that there were also quite a few Pakistanis amongst them, Shiraz was not at all surprised. However, the very fact that even in the late 20th Century the so called civilized world of European Christians could resort to ethnic cleansing of the minority Muslims and who till yesterday were both living in relative peace and harmony with one another only proved the point that not only might was right, but it also brought home the fact that the Muslims were now an unwanted race in Europe.

And while the dirty civil war and the ethnic cleansing in Bosnia continued in all its ferocity, Shupriya on the 1st of May 1993, invited Monty and Reeta for some Bengali lunch at her apartment. It happened to be May Day that day and a public holiday, and while the ladies were enjoying their soft drink of fresh mango juice and Monty his chilled beer, the news of the assassination of the Sri Lankan President Premadasa by a human bomb over the radio did not come as a total surprise to Shupriya.

"I knew it would come. First they got Rajiv, and last week the leader of the opposition in Sri Lanka and now Premadasa. And I wonder whom the LTTE will target next"said Shupriya as she showed a photograph of her shaking hands with the late President of Sri Lanka.

"I think the big political leaders of this subcontinent are all jinxed because eversince the British left our shores, there has been a spate of political assassinations in India, Pakistan, Bangla Desh and in Sri Lanka too, and it all started with the assassination of Mahatma Gandhi in 1948. Then it was Liaqat's turn in Pakistan, followed by Mujib and Zia-ur-Rehman in Bangladesh, Indira and her son Rajiv in India and now of Premadasa in Sri Lanka. And I am not counting Bhutto who was hanged and Zia-ul-Haq who died in that mysterious air crash," said Monty as he switched on the TV to listen to what the BBC had to say about the death of the Sri Lankan head of state.

According to the BBC it happened when Premadasa in order to celebrate May Day with his supporters was on a 'Padyatra'. He was walking along Armour Street in Colombo, when a tall dark man with tousled hair came pushing his bicycle, and as soon as he was close enough to the target, he detonated the deadly bomb that was strapped to his chest.

"Well whatever one may say but it requires real guts, courage and a high level of motivation to carry out such a dastardly act," said Reeta.

"Yes agreed but such killings will not solve Sri Lanka's ethnic problem with Prabhakaran and his LTTE. In fact this will only escalate the on going conflict between the two warring factions and lead to reprisals and more deaths on both sides," added Shupriya as she laid the array of half a dozen prawn and fish dishes that she had cooked herself on the table. These special dishes she knew were not only Monty's favourite, but also that of her late husband Shiraz.

"My God, this is indeed a real feast and like the true Hindu Brahmin does I too must keep some of it aside for my late brother Shiraz," said Monty as he surveyed the big spread on the dining table.

"Yes and while in heaven he must be missing all these delicacies and for all you know the wonderful whiff of the delicious prawn curry may well bring his spirit down to share this grand meal with us today," said Reeta with a smile as she helped herself to a big ladel full of the delicious tiger prawn curry that Shupriya had cooked in coconut milk and in typical East Bengal style.

During the third week of May 1993, while the Bajwa family with Shupriya in order to get away from the hot Delhi summer made their way by road to 'Flanders', Colonel Reggie's beautiful bungalow in Kasauli, in Pakistan Shiraz with his family at the invitation of Major General Aslam Rehman Khan visited Murree and other areas of Azad Kashmir. This gave Shiraz an opportunity not only to assess Pakistan's military capability to withstand a possible major offensive by India along the Uri-Hajipir and the Poonch-Hajipir axes, but also to gain first hand knowledge about the many Mujahid training camps that had sprung up in the area to train and infiltrate the so called freedom fighters into Indian occupied Kashmir. There was no doubt that the Divisional defended sector on the Hajipir Bulge was indeed very formidable and the gaps had also now been well covered by strong fortified contingency positions both in depth and in the flanks between the neighbouring brigades. It was not what it was like in 1971, when Shiraz with his troops had managed to infiltrate right up to Kotli and that too without being detected. The Pakistanis now had sensors established at important crossing places to check cross border infiltration and all these were also covered by long range artillery guns. The visit to the Kotli Brigade and to the battalion defended areas overlooking the Mendhar and Poonch townships was even more thrilling since that was the area through which Shiraz had infiltrated. The petrol dump that he had blown up near Kotli had been shifted to a nearby re-entrant and was now off the main road, well camouflaged and protected. During the formal lunch at the Headquarters of the Kotli Brigade Officer's Mess, when the topic of whether the Mujahids from Azad Kashmir and those from across the border who were being trained by the ISI would remain loyal if at all 'Operation Topac' proved to be a success in the long run, the opinion was divided. While some felt that it was worth the effort, Major General Aslam Rehman as the GOC however was of the opinion that the Kashmiris could no be trusted. According to his own perception, most of the militant groups like that of the JKLF, the Hurriat Conference and others who were based in the valley still wanted an independent Kashmir, while those like the Hurkat-ul-Ansar, the Hizbul Mujahideen and the Jamaat-e-Islaami wanted Kashmir to become part of Pakistan. And since all these militant groups were not united with a common cause and aim, that could very well be exploited by the Indians and could even result in one militant group fighting the other to gain control in the long run, like it is happening in Afghanistan today, thought Aslam Rehman. He was therefore of the view that the LOC should once and for all be made as the international boundry and the problem of Kashmir be resolved in a peaceful manner once and for all. Therefore there was no question of either India or Pakistan giving up whatever territory was under their respective control and it would be foolish to even think that India would ever part with the valley.

It was on the 26th of May, 1993 while visiting the old 'Naik Curzon Sikandar Khan, VC School' at Gilgit, when the news arrived that the Pakistan Supreme Court had declared the dismissal of the Nawaz Sharif government by the President as unconstitutional and that it had directed that the National Assembly be restored immediately, everybody felt happy

"Thank God for once good sense has prevailed," said Aslam Rehman as Shiraz with his family presented the school children with boxes of sweets and candies. Later that evening they visited picturesque Skardu and where a delightful moonlight picnic by the Headquarters of the NLI, the Northern Light Infantry had been organized for them on the banks of the River Indus. Sitting around the camp fire, Aslam Rehman narrated to all the children the bravery of Naik Curzon Sikandar Khan and Colonel Attiqur Rehman, their great grand father, both of whom had fought against the Germans during the First Great War in France. When Aslam Rehman also mentioned the name of Colonel Ismail Sikandar Khan the son of Curzon Sikandar Khan and who was a great friend of their grandfather Gul Rehman Khan, but who unfortunately had died fighting for the Indian army during the 1947-48 operations in Kashmir and at a place that was not very far from Skardu, Shehzadi who was very intently listening to the story innocently asked.

'But tell us also what happened to Colonel Ismail Sikandar Khan's family and why they the Rehmans did not keep in touch with them?'

On hearing that coming from none other than his own daughter, Shiraz feeling a little guilty quickly added that the Indian Colonel who was born in Gilgit had died a bachelor.

On his return to Islamabad on 4th June after that fascinating tour of Azad Kashmir, Shiraz in his own code jotted down in his little red diary all the important information that he had gathered. The quantum of troops since 1971 on the 'LOC', the line of control had not only more than doubled, but the northern sector too was now under the command of the newly raised Northern Light Infantry Division. The Pakistan High Command had also carried out many war games that signified the importance of the northern sector both for attack by major infiltration as also by conventional forces along the routes leading from those difficult areas into the valley and into Ladakh. The location of the many major Mujahid training camps near Muzzafarabad, Kotli, Skardu, Gultari, Tarkuti inside Azad Kashmir, and Muridke near Lahore, as also those at Batrasi and Sufaida in the NWFP and Tando Allahyar in Sind also indicated that Pakistan had intensified their efforts in waging the proxy war against India. And the fact that the young boys and men in these camps were being totally indoctrinated with fundamentalist ideas by the Mullas, that they would all ultimately achieve salvation through self sacrifice and 'Jihad" against non believers was even more frightening to him. "I only hope and pray that this adventure of indoctrinating and arming these young people does not spawn the growth of terrorism within the country and outside,'" wrote Shiraz in his diary.

The next day 5th of June,1993 Major General Aslam Rehman having returned from his holiday at Skardu was working late in his office at Murree when Shiraz rang up to say that 23 Pakistani soldiers from the 7th Frontier Force Regiment who were part of the UNOSOM-1, the United Nations Operational Group in strife torn Somalia had died in a bizarre, but tragic incident. The 7th FFR was a fine battalion that had served under Aslam Rehman when he was commanding a brigade and it had been hand picked by the Pakistani Army Chief after Pakistan volunteered to send its troops to render humanitarian aid to the suffering Somalians. In fact Pakistan was the first country to respond to the call of the United

Nations, and the first contingent of 500 troops had landed at Moghadishu on 14th September 1992. Since the early Nineties, the Somali Democratic Republic had been ravaged by not only a dreadful civil war, but also with an uprecedented famine and in which a million people had died and a lot many were on the verge of dying of starvation. The main duties of the Pakistan contingent included the securing of the seaport and the airport at the capital Mogadishu, escorting the food convoys, ensuring the smooth distribution of the relief supplies, providing medical aid and also in the recovery of unauthorised weapons from the local armed gangs who were terrorizing the villagers and looting the relief supplies that were meant for the starving population of that country.In March, 1993, the UNOSOM-1 was converted into UNITAF,(United Nations International Task Force) and it soon had over 37,000 troops from 12 different countries including the United States, France, Germany and Italy. And the largest operative contingent was from Pakistan and they were deployed in the most ravaged part of the capital city that was being controlled by the Farah Aideed faction. The other part of the city was under the control of the rival Ali Mahdi faction. Both these factions were authorized a limited number of weapons that were required to be kept in their respective authorized weapon storage sites. These measures were primarily to reduce incidence of violence and loot. But those who were to be disarmed were not happy to give up their weapons. On 5th June, the Pakistani troops were asked by the UN Force Headquarters to carry out an inspection of the weapons storage sites of Farah Aideed and Aideed had also been intimated about the date and time of the inspection. Taking advantage of the advanced information and in order to deny the United Nation's forces entry to their weapon storage site, Aideed's armed men had laid an ambush on the road to the site. And to make matters worse they even used children and women as human shields. Caught in the ambush the Pakistanis returned the fire. But Aideed's gang had also set up a road block to cut off the withdrawal of the Pakistanis and as a result of which the Pakistani troops were not only taken completely by surprise, but they were also massacred in cold blood. Unable to withdraw tactically the 7th FFR fought back gallantly. But in that deadly firefight 23 gallant Pakistani soldiers had laid down their lives, while fifty six were badly wounded and eleven were disabled for life.

On that very night learning about the betrayal by Aideed, Major General Aslam Rehman wrote a long letter of condolence to the Colonel of the Frontier Force Regiment expressing his grief on the death of so many brave Pakistani soldiers. It was ironical that the Pakistani soldiers, who with their humanitarian approach and helpful attitude towards the Somalians were once considered as their brothers, were butchered by the very people they had come to help. That night Shiraz too wondered what had happened to all that euphoria and love for the the Pakistani soldier by the Somalians who just the other day were shouting 'Pakistani-Somali Walal Walal' (Pakistani and Somalis are brothers.)

While Pakistan was mourning the terrible loss of their soldiers, in India the insurgency in Punjab by the Sikh militants was being deftly tackled by KPS Gill, the tough and no nonsense Director General of Punjab Police. The police officer who started his career in the north eastern state of Assam had it seems with his stick and carrot policy brought Punjab back to near normalcy. On Sunday 13th June, when Monty with his wife Reeta, Shupriya and Peevee visited the Golden Temple at Amritsar to pray for the success of Peevee's maiden film which was still under production they found the city to be very peaceful. There was a special langar that was organized and paid for by Peevee to feed the poor that day and Peevee was surprised to see the Hindus, Sikhs and others all sitting together, chatting and eating like long lost friends. Later that evening as they drove through the city and the villages around the sacred city, they not only found everything peaceful, but the people in general too had reconciled to the idea that militancy and Khalistan was not the answer to their problem. The state now needed economic progress and a change of heart for all to live peacefully. There was no doubt that the Pakistan ISI under their boss the bearded Lt General Javed Nasir was heretofore actively aiding the Sikh militants, till under pressure by the Americans he was prematurely and compulsorily retired from service on 13th May, 1993. The Americans had threatened to declare Pakistan a terrorist state unless Lt General Javed Nasir was removed from office. But Kanwar Pal Singh Gill's contribution was no less either when he to applied pressure and which resulted in the deaths of many Sikh militants in various encounters and consequently lowered their morale.

On the 23rd of June 1993, when Peevee resumed his film shooting schedule, there was a story on one of the foreign television news channels that a married woman by the name of Lorena Bobbit had cut off her husband's penis with a kitchen knife. And it was all because she was tired of being constantly abused sexually and being ill treated by him. But Peevee who was in the make-up room getting ready for the next shot simply could not believe it.

"I guess this can only happen in the United States, the only super power in the world where sex and crime go hand in hand it seems," said Peevee while instructing his make up man to lessen the shine on his face.

"Yes and undoubtedly so, and let me also tell you that according to another news channel that covered the same story, it was primarily because her husband John Wayne Bobbit had come home late after partying the whole night. He was absolutely sozzled and intoxicated, and when he tried to forcibly molest her she did not like it one bit. A little while later she went into the kitchen for a glass of water and came back with a carving knife. And seeing her husband fast asleep, she I believe chopped off half of John's big John and very aptly the news reader next day coined a new word and said that John had been 'Bobbittised' by his wife," added the make up man while laughing away merrily.

"'Yes and the irony of the whole thing is that the husband calls himself John Wayne, which is the name of the famous macho Hollywood actor who starred in so many western movies and which I would love to see again and again," said Peevee.

And while John got 'Bobbitised,' the Americans on the orders from President Clinton of the United States also got ready to catch Saddam Hussein by his balls. On 27th June, the Americans without warning and in response to an alleged assassination attempt on President George Bush that was planned by the Iraqis during his visit to Kuwait in April, Bill Clinton let loose his destructive and deadly cruise missiles on the Iraqi intelligence headquarters that was located in the Al-Masur district of Baghdad. And when Peevee heard about the deadly strike on the CNN news channel he was a little upset and he remarked some what angrily to his film producer.

"Don't you think it is highly unfair that the Americn President should use such barbarous methods to bring Saddam to his knees and which has only resulted in innocent civilian Iraqis being killed. And would it not have been far better and easier had he used his intelligence spoofs from the CIA to do what Lorena did to her husband. That would have not only bobbitised Saddam but it would have also given the Americans the opportunity to also cut his bloody balls off for good. And had they done that then that prick of a man who has ruined his country would no longer be able to fuck around with his neighbours any more."

"Well that I must say is a good one indeed, but to do that the Americans would have to first get hold of some pretty 'Jane Bond' to first bell the man's damn prick before bobbitising it," said the director in good humour as Peevee got ready to take the next shot.

And while the Bobbit case became a pathfinder and a fight for women's liberation all over the world, in Pakistan, Nawaz Sharif's second honeymoon as the Prime Minister of Pakistan was also over as he and the President once again were at loggerheads and General Kakar, the army chief had no other option but to intervene and force both of them to resign. On 18th July 1993, Moeen Qureshi a World Bank whizkid and Wasim Sajjad, the Chairman of the Senate, were appointed as the Caretaker Prime Minister and Acting President respectively. And when once again it was announced that another general election will be held on 6th October for the National Assembly and on 9th October for the Provincial Assemblies, Ruksana Begum did not find it funny at all.

"This is going to be the third general election in six years in this country and the world must be laughing at us," said the lady to her husband while predicting that though Benazir Bhutto may stage a comeback, but the political roulette and the proliferation of political corruption within the political parties and their quest for power that had eroded the political system would only lead to even more political instability in the country. And while Pakistan was gearing up for the October elections, and the big time bookie syndicates at Karachi and Lahore got busy setting up their illegal betting booths, in India Harshad Mehta the brains behind the massive Bombay Stock Exchange rip off surprised everyone with his 'Suitcase Scam.' The tainted stock broker in an affidavit had sworn that he had not only personally visited 7, Race Course Road in New Delhi, which was the official residence of the Indian Prime Minister, Narasimha Rao, but that he had also handed over to him rupees one crore in hard cash that he had carried with him in a suitcase. As the story made headlines in the Indian Press and TV, Monty in order to ascertain whether the sensational allegation had any evidence of truth at all called upon his old friend Unni at the Press Club.

"Well I am not quite sure and though the Prime Minister had categorically denied the allegation, but the very fact that the man Harshad Mehta could point a finger so very brazenly and openly against no less a person than the Prime Minister of the country, only goes to show that there must be some element of truth to it. Everybody in this country is aware that political parties do require cash and that they do solicit such like donations from their well to do well wishers, but the question now arises is whether that money paid by Harshad Mehta was to get him off the hook or was it simply a political donation. But the manner in which Harshad Mehta has given a detailed account of his meeting with the Prime Minister, it does smack of some authenticity in the minds of those who know how the system works. Personally the money may not have gone into Narasimha Rao's pocket, and though the Prime Minister has said that he will emerge out of this trial by fire in the same manner as Sita did, but what surprises me is the knee jerk response by the government and his own party to deny it. And if the Prime Minister is telling the truth than he or atleast his family members and the Congress party should have by now filed a case of defamation against the man,"said Unni while ordering another large gin with a dash of bitters for himself.

"Yes you do have a point there and may be the Narasimha Rao government which is in minority does not want to overplay the issue. As it is the Bofors scandal has not yet died down completely and if this scandal also get added to it then it could well lead even to the fall of the government," added Monty as he showed Unni photographs of Peevee in a police uniform as the new and emerging Bollywood Hero.

"Well if Amitabh Bachchan made it to the top in the role of fiery police officer and an angry young man in the film 'Zanjeer', then I am sure our Deepak Kumar will also get top most billing after his maiden movie is released too,"said Unni as he raised a toast to Peevee in absentia.

Soon after the Harshad Mehta's suitcase scam another sleazy revelation of a greater magnitude rocked the Narasimha Rao Congress (I) government when on 28th July, ten so called Honourable Members of the Indian Parliament from the JMM, the Jharkhand Mukti Morcha Party and the Janata Dal voted in favour of the ruling minority Congress Party in order to defeat the no confidence motion that had been tabled by the opposition. All the ten members had been heavily bribed and according to a reliable source the bribe money was deposited in the names of the MP's and their family members at the Punjab National Bank, Nauroji Nagar Branch in New Delhi. But the irony of this sordid murder of Indian democracy was that bribe givers and not the bribe takers were subject to criminal prosecution. It was a clear case of the Prime Minister Narasimha Rao and his Home Minister Buta Singh entering into a criminal conspirscy between themselves and others to abet Members of Parliament to demand and accept bribes in lieu of support to the minority Congress (I) government that was gasping for breadth for its own survival. But thanks to Article 105(2) of the Indian Constitution, no Member of Parliament could be made liable to any proceedings in any court with respect to any vote given by the MP in the Indian parliament.

And while the JMM bribe scandal shook the very roots of the so called democratic rule in India, on the night of 29th/30th July, 1993, Octavio Quattrocchi with his wife Maria and family like a thief and hunted by the law quietly fled from the country. Six days earlier the Interpol had alerted the authorities in India that among those who were appealing against the transfer of the incriminating Swiss bank documents in the Bofors payoff also included the Italian friend of the late Prime Minister and his widowed wife and therefore feeling the heat Octavio Quattrocchi had probably with the connivance of those in authority fled the country for good. According to a very reliable source, the CBI who had been alerted by Interpol had put up the relevant communication to Mrs Magaret Alva, the concerned Minister of State in the Narasimha Rao government on 24th July, 1993, but the minister for reasons unknown retained that file and noting till 16th August, and by then it was already too late.

"So the Italian bird has finally flown eh and what do you have to say to that," said Monty to his old journalist friend Unni when they met for lunch at the Le Meridien Hotel in Delhi.

"Well your guess is as good as mine, but this only goes to prove that Mr Quattrocchhi and his so called front company the AE Services were undoubtedly the real brains and beneficiaries of the political pay offs and now that he has vanished from the scene the Narasimha government must be feeling very relieved I am sure." said Unni.

"Yes, and I am sure the Gandhi family too must be breathing a lot more easy now that their Italian friend with his wife and kids have sought refuge in Malaysia. But I am quite sure that the Quattrochhis would not have left without saying atleast a goodbye to Sonia, afterall they were such close friends of the family," added Monty a little sarcastically while ordering a large gin and tonic water for Unni and the usual draft chilled beer for himself.

"In that case let me then once again run through in brief the complete sequence of action on the scandalous Bofors deal and then you can come to your own conclusions," said Unni as he took out his old little diary from his pocket. Then as he had the first sip of the gimlet, Unni step by step, and chronologically quoting important dates, methodically and meticulously narrated to Monty on how the deal was struck and how in the most amateurish and ham handed manner Rajiv Gandhi and his coterie inside the PMO tried to cover it up.

"According to my perception the entire 'Operation Bofors' kickback affair can be classified into three distinctive stages. The first was the decision making process and which was followed by the second and that is the arrangements for the pay offs. While the third was the cover up and crisis management, which thanks mainly to the investigative journalism by Chitra Subramanium of the Hindu newspaper had the PMO literally running in circles. So much so that Rajiv Gandhi and his advisers kept goofing up with every new revelation. Therefore going by these three stages, the first one was the decision to introduce the 155 mm state of the art gun into the Indian Army and this decision was taken sometime in 1980 and thereafter once the green signal was given, the ball started rollng. In December 1982, four foreign firms were shortlisted, but by November 1985 and based on the advice of the Indian Army Headquarters and on the recommendation by the Negotiating Committee, two firms, the French Sofna and the Swedish Bofors became the front runners and till mid February 1986, Sofna was in the lead. 'On 1st February, 1986, General Sundarji took over as Chief from General Vaidya and though the army had opted for the Sofna, but suddenly during the stages of final decision making the time factor was convieniently telescoped and the contract was hurriedly given to Bofors and it was signed on the 24th of March. And now you may well ask me as to why to Bofors and not to Sofna and where was the frightful hurry in giving the contract. Well it was for the simple reason because with that deal some middlemen and wheeler dealers would undoubtedly get their cut from the big Bofors cake, but the largest and the biggest peice would be for Quattrocchi who by then had very cleverly wriggled his way into the contract. And I am sure you will understand that the Italian was afterall a very close friend of the then Prime Minister Rajiv Gandhi and his family and had a clout in all the ministries too. It was on 15thNovember 1985, and a good six months before the deal was actually signed that Quattrocchi and his AE's Services had asked for a 3 percent cut on the total value of the contract and gave the assurance that they would even forfeit the commission if no contract was signed by 31st March, 1986. Realizing the Italian's closeness to the Prime Minister of India and his Italian wife, Bofors therefore very cleverly hitched on to the Quattrocchi bandwagon. In January 1986, the Swedish Prime Minister visited India and he too was very keen to get the contract. So when Rajiv told him that it could be possible but provided no middlemen were involved in the deal, Palme I believe also agreed. Unfortunately in February, Olaf Palme the Swedish Prime Minister was assassinated and Rajiv went to Stockholm for his funeral and where the Bofors gun contract was once again discussed with the new Prime Minister. The Sofna Gun was still then in the lead, but time was running out for Quattrocchi. Therefore immediately on Rajiv's return from the funeral, the file on the 155 mm gun started moving at breakneck speed. The crucial date was the deadline of 31st March and Quattrocchi was fully aware of its implication. Afterall 3 percent of a billion dollars as commission was no chicken feed and the Italian being a good friend of Rajiv Gandhi had to doubly ensure that the deal did not fall through. Hence, it was from the day Rajiv Gandhi returned from Stockholm that the real race against time began. On the 13th of March the two Ministers of State for Defence, Sukh Ram and Arun Singh and the Defence Minister KC Pant approved the deal and on the very next day 14th March the Finance Minister VP Singh and the Prime Minister too signed on the dotted line. On that same very day and without wasting any more time, the letter of intent was also issued and on 24th March, 1986 a week before the deadline, the billion dollar arms contract was signed by both the sides. After that everything for the next 12 months was absolutely hunky-dory. The Indian Army was satisfied with the terms of the contract and the additional six guns that would come gratis, Quattrochi and others had pocketed their hefty commissions and everybody was very happy till on 16th April 1987, the Swedish radio blew the whistle. Mr Oza, the Indian Ambassador to Sweden who was holidaying with his family in England was immediately asked by the PMO to rush back to Stockholm and to get an official denial from the Swedish government and also from Bofors that no bribes or commissions were paid on the deal to anybody whatsoever as had been alleged by the radio. From that day onwards for Rajiv Gandhi the Bofors gun became a total nightmare and with Palme's death it also led to his own political funeral."'

"Then began the second stage for the massive cover up, but it ran into foul weather, when on 1st June 1987, the Swedish National Audit Bureau confirmed that money had been paid by Bofors as winding up costs to some middlemen, but it gave no names. In fact the crucial references to the bribe takers had been blanked out very conveniently in that report. But it got even worse when a few days later Rajiv's close friend and Doon school buddy Arun Singh who was the Minister of State for Defence asked for the cancellation of the contract unless Bofors supplied the names of those who received the bribe money as commission. And when the Army Chief General Sundarjee also put his foot down and said that he too was prepared for the cancellation of the contract for vindicating national honour, it sent the Defence Secretary and the PMO's secreteriat on a virtual roller-coaster ride and tailspin. On 3rd July, 1987 the Vice President of Bofors who was in Delhi suggested a meeting with the Government of India and a high level delegation from Bofors, but on the very next day and fearing that the cat could be let out of the bag, Rajiv immediately vetoed the idea. The Prime Minister who was now caught in a 'Catch 22' situation and he therefore appointed a JPC, Joint Parliamentary Committee. The JPC was nothing but an eyewash to save the Congress (I) and their Prime Minister. On 18th July, when Arun Singh resigned from the government citing domestic reasons, it was evidently clear that he had decided not to be a party to the cover up. Meanwhile Sten Lindstrom the head of Sweden's National Bureau of Investigation who was leading the Swedish investigation into the Bofors scandal was also told by his own government to go slow on the investigation. In autumn 1987, Bofors offered to send a high level team to India with the names of the recipients who had been paid commissions/ winding up charges, but Rajiv Gandhi cancelled the trip at the last minute. He probably feared that Quattrocchi's name or that of his firm AE Services was bound to be on that list and that would have led to his political Hari-kiri. Then In September, 1987, some top officials from Bofors secretly met Gopi Arora, NN Vohra the two very senior bureaucrats in the PMO's secretariat as well as SK Bhatnagar the Defence Secretary in Delhi. They had come to depose before the JPC and therefore had to be tutored, coached and told what to say and what not to say to the Joint Parliamentary Commission. Rajiv Gandhi's unprovoked declaration in Parliament that neither he nor any member of his family was involved in the deal and his concerted efforts to cover up his own involvement together with his reluctance to call for a genuine investigation into the scandal while he was still in the Prime Minster's chair only made him more vulnerable. Then came the sensational documentary evidence of the pay offs that was unearthed by Chitra Subramanium and which the newpaper 'Hindu' periodically came out with headline news. In June 1988, with Mr Oza the Indian Ambassador to Sweden not willing to play ball, he was conveniently packed off to some insignificant third world country. And it was only on 20th February 1989, when Rajiv knew that he was badly cornered that he added another red herring to the cover up when his government very cleverly signed a MOU, a Memoramdum of Understanding with the Swiss government which granted the government to track economic offenders who were subject of investigations in India, but provided there was a request from the Indian government. However, there was a small rider that India attached to it and which meant that no fishing enquiries would be allowed. The Swiss authorities had told India that the available documentary evidence could be admitted under the clause of fraud or embezzlement provided India requested for it. Six weeks later on 4th April, the first Indian request for assistance in tracing the Bofors payment arrived in the Swiss capital, Berne, but that request pertained to certain charges of tax fraud by middlemen. According to Swiss law if this so called middleman had concealed his income then it was not considered as a fraud, but if that middleman had forged documents with intent to conceal his income, then it was valid. Therefore as far as the Bofors case was concerned under the Swiss law, it was obvious that the government of India's request would meet with a dead end and that was what the government actually wanted. The so called MOU was therefore a farcical attempt by the Rajiv government to unearth the Bofor's payments and it was only for public consumption of the Indians and to tell its people that the government of Rajiv Gandhi was keen to get to the bottom of the matter. But in reality it was the other way round. Then in February 1992, when Madhavsinh Solanki the former Indian Foreign Minister from the same Congress (I) party carried an unsigned and undated letter for Rene Felber, his Swiss counterpart requesting him to stop the Bofors investigation that the previous VP Singh government had initiated and which had led to the freezing of the accounts of the recipients, it only worsened matters. It was on the plea that no further steps should be taken in Switzerland till a final decision was arrived at by the Indian courts since the matter was already under litigation in India. But this only clearly indicated that the Congress (I) and the bureaucrats concerned with the Bofors deal were only doing all this to save the skin of their beloved leader and master, Rajiv Gandhi. But now with Quattrocchi having run away like a thief in the dead of night, and with Rajiv Gandhi in heaven, it only requires common sense to conclude who were the main recipients of that largesse. In other words and according to my own personal findings it is crystal clear that the 7-3 million dollar pay off to Quattrocchi's AE Services was a political pay off and of which Ardbo was fully aware off. Ardbo also knew fully well that he could not get the contract without accomodating AE Services in the payment schedule," concluded Unni while calling for another large gin with a dash of bitters this time.

"But all said and done do you think this government or for that matter any other government that follows will ever let the truth surface because as far as our politicians are concerned and irrespective of the party that he or she represents, most of them have their own small and large Bofors in their own cupboards and therefore it serves everybody's purpose to cover it up. In such like matters all of them and irrespective of their party affiliations become as the saying goes thick as thieves," added Monty.

"Undoubtedly so and the pity is that a person like Rajiv who came in as Mr Clean and had India at his feet, in just half a decade not only lost the trust of the Indian people but also that of some of his own close and busom friends like Arun Singh and Amitabh Bachchan to name a few," said Unni.

"Yes that indeed is rather unfortunate and though Rajiv is no more, but the ghost of Bofors I am afraid will keep haunting the Gandhi family and also the Congress (I) party for a long time to come and especially during election time,"added Monty as he paid the bill with his new Bank of India credit card.

While the efforts by the ruling Congress (I) party of the minority Narasimha Rao government went head over heels to protect the name of the Gandhi family and questions were being asked on the sudden disappearance of the Quattrocchis from Delhi, the Chief Election Commissioner of India, Mr TN Seshan on 2nd August, 1993 at 9.50 AM signed the historic order declaring that from 10 AM that day all elections in India would end unless the government acceded to the powers of the CEC which had every right to control the civil and state officers who were required to be deployed for the forthcoming state elections. The short and round statured 1932 born IAS officer who in 1965 as the District Magistrate of Madurai was responsible to ensure that Sheikh Abdulla, the Lion of Kashmir while under detention at Kodaikanal did not create any mischief was now dictating terms to the government. It happened to be Raksha Bandhan Day, a day when the sister ties a sacred thread on her brother's wrist and which symbolizes that the brother come what may will always protect his sister, and the Chief Election Commisioner too was ensuring that he should not be tied down discharging his sacred duty and therefore sitting in his office at Nirvachan Bhawan he wanted the government to recognize his powers and one that would empower him and his office to hold fair and free elections in future. Seshan also wanted the bond of protection to be extended to the masses of India during elections and his actions as the savior of democracy through a model code of conduct for the corrupt politicians to be introduced in India was being hailed by the common people.

"Well whatever you say Mr Seshan deserves all kudos for standing upto his principles and the firm manner in which he has sounded the government and the politicians that he would not hesitate to take action against them if they violated the moral code of conduct, speakes volumes of the man who I am told loves to eat politicians for breakfast, lunch and dinner," said Monty as he joined Unni for the weekly Saturday afternoon beer session at the Press Club.

"Yes and I must tell you something more about this fearless bureaucrat who loves listening to Indian classical music on the half a dozen radio and cassette players that he possesses. Crazy for electronic gadgets, wrist watches and fountain pens, Seshan was appointed as the CEC by the Chandrashekhar government on 12th December, 1990. He had earlier been Secretary in charge of Prime Minister's security during Rajiv Gandhi's tenure and was later appointed by him to the top most bureaucratic post of Cabinet

Secretary. But after Rajiv lost his mandate and VP Singh took over, Seshan was shunted out to Yojana Bhawan as member of the Planning Commission. A stickler for punctuality and a man with a great sense of humour, he once removed the clock from his office and sent it to the secretary planning commission with the remark that the clock was redundant since no meeting was ever held on time and no work was being done by the office staff. A few days later Seshan sent him the calendar also and it was because he found that most of the scheduled conferences were either cancelled or postponed at the last minute because the principal members of that august body never ever showed up on time. And I feel really proud that the young man who started his career in the IAS as the Sub Divisional Officer in Dindigul and who is now sitting on that powerful chair has lived upto his reputation of being an honest and straight forward person. But I wish more men from that cadre of what the British once called the heaven born should try and emulate him and rise up to the standards that have been set up by Seshan and who I have also told knows the Bhagwad Gita by heart," added Unni.

That afternoon, when Monty after the beer session while on his way home to Defence Colony drove passed Seshan's official bungalow at 4AB, Pandara Road, his thoughts went back to Uncle Ronen Sen and his wife Mona. The couple too had once lived there when Ronen was a Joint Secretary in the Defence Ministry and Shiraz was secretly dating their daughter Shupriya.

CHAPTER-17

Back to the Bhuttos

While the sudden disappearance of the Quattrocchis from India became the hottest topic in the corridors of power and in the circles of the rich and the famous in Delhi, in Islamabad the rise of sectarian violence in the country had got their political leaders rather worried. During the month of August 1993, when renewed clashes between the Shias and the Sunnis plunged the once peaceful Gilgit Valley into bloody violence that was even worse than what had taken place there earlier in 1989, Shiraz felt rather sad. For him Gilgit indirectly was the land of his forefathers and with news of curfew being clamped in many parts of the Northern Region and in Gilgit City in particular, he wondered whether the sectarian violence in that remote area would have a snow balling effect on the rest of the country. The Shias as compared to the Sunnis were once the dominant community in that far flung region, but in Pakistan they were a minority and such kind of violence had also erupted though intermittently not only in the two big cities of Karachi and Lahore, but also at places like Multan, Faisalabad and Rawalpindi. Shiraz therefore was apprehensive that this factor may also be exploited by the political parties during the forthcoming elections. While Pakistan was being rocked by sectarian violence, in India a massive earthquake of a magnitude of 6.5 on the Richter scale on 30th September, 1993 devastated the town of Latur and the surrounding villages nearby. It resulted in the death of over 10,000 people and Shiraz wondered as to why God always punished the poor.

And as Pakistan was gearing up for its third general elections in six years, sectarian violence, political killings and vendettas were once again on the rise. On 26th September, the former Punjab Chief Minister Ghulam Haider was killed, and on 1st October, 1993 when General Asif Nawaz's corpse was exhumed from his grave for autopsy, and Murtaza Bhutto while still in exile and having fallen out with his sister Benazir now deciding to contest the elections from Sindh, the common man on the street wondered how many more skeletons would come out of the cupboards of the unscrupulous and corrupt Pakistani politicians whose sole aim it seems was to somehow get to the seat of power and make more money. Though the caretaker Prime Minister Moeen Qureshi had issued a list of bank loan defaulters and most of whom were seasoned politicians and had warned them that they would be barred from contesting the elections unless they paid up, it only created a ripple. Even the sensational roster that was prepared by the Prime Minister's secretariat informing the people the measly amounts that were paid as income tax by some of the richest people in the country including the Sharif family it had no tangible effect on the diehard politicians of the country.

In the second week of September 1993, when orders for Salim Rehman's posting back to Islamabad was received, the happiest people were his wife Aasma and their two young children. After the disintegration of the Soviet Union, Moscow had become a very unsafe place to live in and with the high rate of inflation and poverty on the streets; the crime rate in the capital city too had risen at an alarming rate and no place was safe. One could even get mugged on the lift and the escalator while returning home and with the Russian rouble on the decline; those with dollars and pounds in their pockets therefore had to be doubly careful. Though the date for reporting at Islamabad was 15th November and Salim Rehman was going on promotion as Joint Secretary to the India desk, it was therefore decided that because of the deteriorating internal situation in Moscow, the family should leave at the earliest and they did so on 20th September, while Salim Rehman would follow a little later and after handing over proper charge to his reliever.

With the Russian President Boris Yeltsin having dissolved the country's legislature arbitrarily on 21st September, there was a big constitutional crisis that resulted in large scale public protests and violence in Moscow. The Congress of Deputies having rejected Yeltsin's decree had voted to remove Yeltsin from the Presidency through impeachment and they had also sworn in his estranged Vice President Alexander Rutskoy as the Acting President of the country. But Yeltsin was not the one to give up so very easily. On the 28th of September pro and anti Yeltsin supporters were involved in armed clashes inside the city and those legislators who were against Yeltsin had now been barricaded inside the White House of the Russian parliament building and that too without any electricity and water. Having heard from a reliable source that the Russian army tanks and armoured cars were likely to take up positions near the parliament building, Salim Rehman early on the morning of 2nd October, 1993 went and parked himself inside a suite on the top most floor of Hotel Rossiya. The hotel with 21 floors and with 3200 rooms was the largest in the world and it provided a panaromic view of the city. Salim Rehman wanted to get a bird's eyeview of what was happening on the streets below and near the White House. With the heavy presence of troops and tanks barricading the parliament building, it was quite evident that Yeltsin had the firm backing of the Russian army and the Ministry of Interior was also behind him. But what Salim Rehman witnessed during those next three days was something that he had least expected.

Salim had initially thought that the tanks were there only as a show of force, but when it started blasting the White House, it was like war. Russia was on the brink of a second revolution and a civil war with the pro and anti Yeltsin supporters battling it out on the streets. The ten day old conflict had already taken a large number of lives and it was the most deadly street fighting in Moscow since the Bolshevik Revolution of October 1917 and which Salim Rehman now feared could well spread to the other major cities and towns of Russia. On 3rd October, there was a pitched battle near the national television centre at Ostankino as both sides tried to gain control of it and though Rutskoy was himself a former army general, but his appeals to his former colleagues did not have any effect at all. By sunrise on 4th October, the Russian army had encircled the parliament building and a few hours later when the tanks began shelling the White House, Salim Rehman just could not believe his eyes.

"My God this must be recorded for posterity," said Salim Rehman to himself as he got busy video recording the battle for the White House. By lunch time the troops had entered the place and had taken over the battered building and with the subsequent storming of the White House all the top political leaders who were anti Yeltsin had been taken into custody and the popular resistance in the streets also died down. On the 5th October afternoon, when Salim Rehman returned to his apartment, all the fighting was over and Moscow was back to near normalcy. That evening when he dispatched his report of those ten days that shook Moscow by telex to Islamabad, Shiraz on reading it was convinced that communism as an ideology was dead, It reminded him of the book 'Ten days that Shook the World' by John Reed an American journalist, poet and communist activist. It was a first hand account of the Bolshevik revolution in Tsarist Russia and which he had read when he was first posted to Moscow. And while Shiraz sympathized with the plight of the Russians, he prayed that the people of Pakistan who were getting ready to go to the polls again should vote with a clear conscience and sincerely hoped that the elections would not be rigged

On that 3rd October, 1993 while the Russians were engaged in a bloody civil war in Moscow, in Somalia, the American Task Force Rangers raided the Olympic Hotel in Mogadishu. They had been tasked to capture the notorious trouble creator Mohammed Farah Aidid and on whom a reward of 25,000 US dollars had also been announced in June. And that was soon after the 24 Pakistani soldiers were killed by the the warlord's armed Somalis. In August, when more United States troops were targeted and in what ironically was called 'Operation Restore,' 440 elite troops from America's famous Delta Force were flown in for the special mission. Their mission was to capture Aidid. But at the same time and unknown to the top military commanders in Somalia, the Clinton administration was also simultaneously holding secret negotiations with the Somali warlord. Aidid was educated in Rome and in Moscow and had also served as Somalia's Ambassador to India. He was the one who was responsible in ousting Mohammed Siad Barre's dictatorial regime and it was during Barre's rule that he rose to the rank of a general and was later appointed as the intelligence chief. But the raid on the Olympic Hotel that day to capture the elusive warlord ended in a fiasco for the Americans. It was a long seventeen hour battle and the bloodiest since Vietnam and which resulted in the death of 18 US soldiers and wounded 84 others. Seeing the bodies of the dead American soldiers being dragged through the streets of Mogadishu and in a battle in which hundreds of Somalis had also died, Shiraz who was watching the news on CNN television channel was worried, because what began as a peace keeping mission to provide relief to the starving people of Somalia could now end up as a fight between David and Goliath, and this would only add to the miseries of the poor Somalian people.

Shiraz had heard this story while in school at Sanawar. It was a Biblical story when the Philistine army led by Goliath the giant took on the Israelis and King Saul of Israel permitted young David to take on the mighty Goliath. Armed only with a shepherd's staff, a sling shot and a pouch full of stones, the teenage David approached the nine feet tall armour clad Goliath and moved in for the kill. Aiming for his head, the stone from David's sling shot hit bulls eye as it got the giant on his forhead and he came crashing down and David then using Goliath's sword cut of his head. Thereafter, the Philistines turned and ran away from the battlefield. Now it was Aidid as David who had taken on the mighty Americans and there was no doubt that the American Goliath was feeling the heat in Somalia and President Clinton was keen to get them out from there as early as possible.

On the 6th and 9th of October, 1993 when Pakistan went to the polls it was evident that the common man in Pakistan was fed up as only forty percent turned out to cast their precious votes. But it was still a very close fight with Benazir's PPP winning 86 seats as compared to 75 that was won by Nawaz Sharif's PML, the Pakistan Muslim League. Surprisingly Murtaza Bhutto also while still in exile had won his seat from Sindh. But soon after the results of the elections in Pakistan were declared, a group of armed militants in a daring and bold move on 15th October in Kashmir took control of the famous Hazrat Bal Mosque in downtown Srinagar. This did not come as a surprise to Shiraz because there were reports earlier of the militant groups attempting to damage or destroy various other mosques in the valley. In the month of September, a mosque in the vicinity of the Maqdoom Sahib shrine was gutted by fire and four days later an attempt was made at night to set ablaze the historical Naqshband Sahib's shrine inside the capital city. On 3rd October, an attempt was also made on the old Asara-e-Sharif mosque which was also located in Srinagar. All these actions it seems was to instigate a fresh wave of violence in the valley by the Pakistan ISI so that the Kashmir question as promised by the incoming Benazir government could once again be highlighted in the international forum.

On 19th October, after Benazir Bhutto took the oath of office for the second time and addressed the nation with the same old polemics of promising to protect Pakistan's nuclear programme, mobilizing international opinion against Indian aggression in Kashmir, eradicating unemployment and corruption, recovering outstanding loans, and making Pakistan an egalitarian Islamic society, Ruksana Begum on hearing that speech simply said.

"It is all the same old story and this entire big talk that one has been hearing time and again from the same political and military masters is like an old worn out record because unfortunately nothing happens in this country and in reality the poor gets poorer and the richer gets richer all the time."

'Yes undoubtedly so, but let us atleast hope that good sense prevails and at forty the lady prime minister of the country and her husband, 'Mr Ten Percent' follow the rules and they don't play dirty, or else the army which is always waiting in the wings may step in again and General Waheed Kakar the Army Chief should not be under estimated," said her husband Arif Rehman as he got dressed to go for his farewell rotary meeting and which was to be followed by dinner.

With the motto 'Service Above Self,' Arif Rehman had become a Rotarian when he was first posted as a Third Secretary in the United

States. The Rotary Club was founded in 1905 in Chicago by attorney Paul. P. Harris and his three friends, Silvester Schiele, a coal merchant, G E Loehr, a mining engineer and HE Shore, a tailor. They chose the name Rotary because they took turns by rotation to hold the weekly meetings at their respective offices. The aim of such meetings was to promote and bring together business and professional leaders and promote humanitarian service to mankind in an honorary capacity, encourage high ethical standards in all vocations and disciplines and help build goodwill and peace in the world. The Rotary became international when in 1910 a branch was opened in Winnipeg in neighbouring Canada, and it was now a worldwide organization. At 74, Arif was not keeping in very good health and therefore could not devote much time to the Rotary's social programme of eradicating drug addiction that had spread rapidly in the various tribal districts of the North West Frontier during the last decade. This was a fall out from the Soviet invasion of Afghanistan and had now become not only a menace, but also a big business for wheeler dealers with both money and political power and Asif Zardari the Prime Minister's husband was no exception it seems. The fact was that the government of Pakistan and the military with the connivance of some of the tribal leaders and unscrupulous smugglers had made narco trafficking a means to raise funds for Pakistan's covert military operations and Arif Rehman was aware that without the help from the government, it would be futile and impossible to implement the Rotary Club's much desired drug eradicating programme.

"I think Abbajaan has taken the right decision and he should now take it easy, "said Shiraz while throwing some more light on the government's and the ISI's involvement in selling heroin to pay for the country's clandestine military operations. Acoording to Shiraz and his source it was in early 1991, and soon after Nawaz Sharif was in the chair that the Pakistan Army Chief, General Aslam Beg and the DG ISI, Lt General Asad Durrani had mooted this idea to the Prime Minister. They told him that the Pakistan army needed more money for such like covert operations and they wanted to raise it through the secret and large scale drug deals which could be manipulated by them. There was no doubt that after the Russians had got out of Afghanistan, the money and arms that had been pouring in earlier through the CIA, Saudi Arabia and other channels for the Afghan Mujahideen fighters had practically dried up, and Pakistan needed funds to pursue their goals in Indian occupied Kashmir and also elsewhere very badly.

Geographically, Pakistan along with Iran and Afghanistan lay on the so called 'Golden Crescent' and this was one of the world's biggest drug producing regions and where opium grew in abundance. And whether the policy to stop opium production was ever implemented or not, it was not very clear. But the manner in which mobile laboratories to refine opium mushroomed in the frontier region after the Soviets invaded Afghanistan was an eye opener to many. In 1980, there was only one such mobile laboratory in Landikotal, but now there were nearly a hundred. There were also reports of some junior level officers in the rank of Majors and Flight Lieutenants and even a high ranking serving Air Vice Marshall from the Pakistan Air Force who were all involved in this smuggling racket using military transport and aircrafts for carrying the precious cargo to Karachi and beyond the high seas. The involvement of Pakiatani armed forces personnel in drug trafficking was nothing new. Three days before the State visit of the former Prime Minister Mr Zulfiqar Ali Bhutto to Sweden in 1976, the Swedish authorities in Stockholm had recovered large quantities of hashish from two Pakistan Air Force's C-130 aircrafts. And during General Zia's tenure as many as 18 very senior officers both from the Pakistan Army and Air Force were sentenced to various terms in jail on drug related charges, and this was further substantiated, when Prime Minister Junejo admitted the fact when it was raised in the National Assembly in 1986.

"My God if all this is true and if the same trend continues, then I am afraid Pakistan besides being branded as a terrorist state, it will also be branded as the largest narco hub of the world," said Ruksana Begum while reiterating the fact that the country which Jinnah had visualised as a secular entity had been raped by the men in uniform, by the unscrupulous politicians, and also by the mullas in the name of so called religion, and now only Allah Talla could help this country."

On 4th November, 1993 when Murtaza Ali Bhutto, the brother of the Prime Minister having won his seat from Larkhana returned from exile in Syria and was promptly arrested at the Karachi airport on charges of terrorism and for the hijacking of the PIA aircraft in 1981, it was quite evident that the Bhutto family for selfish political gains was now heading for a split

"Well as far as dynastic rule is concerned it seems that India and Pakistan have the same problems. Whereas in the Gandhi family, Meneka was shown the door, in Pakistan the sister citing the good old cliché that everybody was equal in the eyes of the law has now very conveniently put the brother behind bars," said Monty as Shupriya walked in with a big bouquet of red roses.

"'So what are we celebrating, Murtaza's arrest or Benazir's return to power? After all India I believe was in some ways instrumental in helping the AZO, the Al Zulfiqar Organizsation too and which Murtaza had founded to avenge his father's death and for which Benazir had duly applauded him. But now I guess times have changed and I believe the mother too is not in the good books of the daughter either. As the Chairperson of PPP, Mrs Nusrat Bhutto during the elections I am told had canvassed actively for her son, and after his return she even tried too broker a deal between the sister and the brother, but it just did not work out. According to one reliable source she wanted the daughter to remain as the Prime Minister of the country and desired that Murtaza should take over as the Chief Minister of Sind, but Benazir was not in favour of such an arrangement,"said Monty.

"'Well I must say that you are fairly well informed as far as Pakistani politics and politicians are concerned, and as regards these beautiful roses, these were sent through interflora by Peevee to me on my promotion to Joint Secretary," said Shupriya as she tastefully arranged the flowers in the drawing room.

"Well in that case it calls for a celebration and we will go to your favourite 'Taipan Restaurant' at the Oberoi's tonight, and I will be the host," said Monty.

"'Most certainly but the champagne will be on me," said Shupriya.

Having completed more than three years in Delhi, Shupriya was due out for posting soon and the chances of her going as an Ambassador to some 'C' grade country was certainly on the cards

"I sincerely wish they sent me to Cuba, or to some of the erstwhile Warsaw Pact countries like Bulgaria, Romania or Hungary. And if it is Cuba then I can see and compare for myself and evaluate whether Communism under Fidel Castro is still flourishing there or is it only a myth. And if they send me to one of the erstwhile Balkan countries then that will give me an opportunity to find out whether the changeover from soviet style commuinism to democratic rule in the Balkan countries has been good or bad for the common man," added Shupriya as she did the honours of selecting the most exclusive and authentic Chinese starters and food from the well bound a la carte menu.

"And also please do serve us the best Dom Perignon champagne from your cellar and we would like to have it really chilled," added Peevee who in order to give everybody a surprise had flown in for the occasion from Bombay. So when on the 12th of November, 1993, the film 'Baazigar' was released in, Peevee decided that he must see it not only on the first day but also on the very first show also. The film starring the new comer Shahrukh Khan as the hero in a negative and a villain's role and Kajol as the heroine with debutant Shilpa Shetty in the supporting role was directed by Abbas Mustan. It was a story of a young man and a killer who was seeking revenge against the man who had cheated his family and made them paupers. It was a thriller that bore some similarity to the Hollywood film 'A Kiss Before Dying:' and with Shahrukh Khan the upcoming star in the role of a baddie it was quite a gamble for the young man whose ancestors like that of the legendary Dilip Kumar also came from the land of the Pathans. Although Akshay Kumar was initially offered the lead role, but he had declined it and it was now a personal gamble for ShahrRukh Khan to make it or break it in the tinsel world of Bollywood. And with 'Baazigar' (The Gambler) as its title, ShahrRukh Khan's gamble it seemed had also paid off. Though it was an off beat film, but the histrionic talent of the new hero together with the excellent screenplay and the lilting music by Anu Malik had made the movie a super hit. Early next morning Peevee went and prayed at Saint Maqdoom Shah Baba's's dargah at Mahim and sought his blessings. The visit was long overdue and with his first film about to be released shortly, Peevee as Deepak Kumar needed all the luck in the world.

While in India the film Bazzigar was running to packed houses, in Pakistan Benazir Bhutto and her Pakistan People's Party took the gamble and elected Farook Leghari as the new President. Farooq Leghari was the PPP nominee and he had won in a run off against Wasim Sajjad the Senate Chairman. Born on 29th May, 1940 at Dera Ismail Khan, Sardar Farook Ahmad Khan Leghari came from a well known family that served as hereditary chiefs of the Leghari tribe. A graduate from Aitchison College, Lahore and Oxford University, he joined the Civil Service of Pakistan in 1963, but after having served for fourteen years, in 1977 at the invitation of Zulfiqar Ali Bhutto joined the PPP. Later he was apppointed General Secretary of the party and during Zia's martial law regime was imprisoned for four years. In October 1993, with the PPP winning the elections, Leghari was appointed Federal Foreign Minister, but soon thereafter was elected as party president, when the rift in the Bhutto family for the control of the party became a very serious issue. Mrs Nusrat Bhutto's differences with her daughter Benazir on the arrest of her son Murtaza was now an open secret and therefore to keep total control over the party, the PPP on 5th December had the mother replaced by the daughter as the new Chairperson.

'So I think the split is now final and the daughter is in full command. But I think it would have been proper had Mrs Nusrat Bhutto on grounds of ill health resigned gracefully like Jehangir Khan, the greatest Squash player the world had ever produced had done at Karachi on 23rd November, when he lost his crown to Jansher Khan at the recent world open championship," said Shiraz to his wife Saira while presenting a new Dunlop squash racket to his fourteen year old daughter Shehzadi and a cricket bat to his ten year old son Tojo. Sherry had recently won the under 16 girls squash tournament that was conducted by the Rawalpindi Club, while Tojo had been selected for the sub-junior winter cricket coaching camp that was being conducted by the Pakistan Cricket Board at Islamabad.

Born on 10th December, 1963 in Karachi, Jehangir Khan was coached by his illustrious father Roshan Khan who himself was a legend as far as the game of squash was concerned, but his son was undoubtedly a bigger legend. During his career Jehangir had won the world open championship a record six times and the British open a record ten times. In 1981, when he was not even eighteen he became the youngest world champion when he beat Australia's Geoff Hunt in the finals. And when he lost to Jansher Khan in the finals at Karachi recently, he felt happy that it was another Pakistani who was also from his village in the Peshawar District and who had deservingly won the crown.

Meanwhile on 16th November, the month long stand off between the militants and the Indian army at the Hasratbal shrine in Srinagar luckily ended without any further bloodshed and Shiraz was very happy. To show their muscle power the militants had even held an arms exhibition inside the mosque and they also set fire to a part of the premises, but that did not provoke the highly disciplined troops of the Indian army who played it cool and showed admirable restraint in not resorting to force. And what was even more praiseworthy was the fact that even the locals residing near the shrine maintained peace and tranquilty during those tension filled and highly charged days. However, the death of seventeen civilians on 22nd October who were part of the procession organized by the Jamaat-i-Islami and who were demanding an end to the siege of the holy mosque by the Indian security forces had given India a bad name.

A month after the elections in Pakistan, some states in India also went to the polls, and while the Congress won in Himachal, Madhya Pradesh and Mizoram, the BJP bagged Rajasthan and Delhi. But what surprised many was the emergence of the Samajwadi Party and the Bahujan Samaj Party in Uttar Pradesh who as torch bearers of the poor had now formed a coalition government and where the Congress was completely routed. Shiraz who had been closely monitoring the state elections in India was also now worried about the rise of many such like regional parties in India and according to his perception this was not good for the country.

While coalition politics had now come to stay in the state elections also, there was sad news for India when on 29th November, 1993, JRD Tata died in a hospital in Geneva, Switzerland at the grand old age of 89. The illustrious son of India and the recipient of the Bharat Ratna, India's highest national award had many a first to his name and to Shiraz he had always been a role model. On learning that the legendary JRD would be buried in Paris, Shiraz decided to be there in person to pay his last respects to the man whom he considered to be the epitome of both an officer and a gentleman. Since his posting to the Pakistan Embassy in Paris as the Minister and the number two man had already been approved and issued and he was scheduled to report for duty by 1st February, 1994, Shiraz nevertheless decided to combine it with a short temporary duty to Paris for consultations. The 3rd of December happened to be a Friday, and when Shiraz reached the Pere Lachaise cemetery on the outskirts of the city, he was surprised to see the large number of dignitaries from all over the world that had assembled there to pay their last repects to India's first pilot and the man who introduced aviation to India. Considered to be one of the oldest cemeteries in Europe where famous men like Moliere, Oscar Wilde and Proust were buried, it was a fitting last resting place for the ever popular Jeh. When the ceremony began with JRD's two favourite hymms 'Abide with me' and 'The Lord my Shepherd', there was pin drop silence all around. And as the two Zorashtrian priests in their white robes began to chant a few selected passages from the Avestha, the holy book of the Parsis, Shiraz felt sorry for Mrs Thelma Tata. The old lady was bed ridden and she would now miss her dear husband who was always by her side telling her stories and reading to her the latest from the best sellers. As Ratan Tata led the congregation in a single file, Shiraz too joined the the long line of mourners. And when he touched the coffin his thoughts went back to some of the great man's achievements that were known only to a few.

During the Second World War with the need for heavy armour, the innovative Tatas had gone in for the production of special steel for the growing armament industry. Simultaneously they also developed products like armour piercing shots and shells, service helmets and harness for parachutes. The Tata research laboratory that was set up by TISCO had also developed high tensile alloy steel that was extensively used in the construction of the silver coloured Howrah Bridge. However their prized product during the war was the 'Tatanagar' an armoured car that was fitted with bullet proof armour plates and which saved many a soldier's life during the campaign in Burma and elsewhere.

On the 6th of December, 1993 while on his flight back to Islamabad, Shiraz felt happy when he learnt that the dreaded cocaine king and drug lord of the notorious Medellin Cartel of Columbia, Pablo Escobar had been gunned down. The man who started his criminal career by stealing tombstones and selling them to smugglers from Panama, and whom the Forbes magazine in 1989 rated as the seventh richest man in the world had been shot like a pariah on 2nd December, when the police tried to arrest him. However, the much married man who loved teenage girls in bed did not die without a fight. Though his hideout in the middle class borough in Medellin was tracked and identified with technical assistance from the sophisticated United States signal intelligence network, and Pablo knew that he was cornered, the El Patron of drug supplies to the world in general and the United States in particular died after a prolonged gun fight. Fearing Pablo's death may trigger off the need for Pakistan's ISI and the military to clandestinely boost their export of heroin for arms in their proxy war in the Indian states of Kashmir and Punjab, Shiraz very cleverly and intelligently on his return to office sent a secret note to his immediate boss indicating that since the US government was totally against the drug culture, it would be prudent for Pakistan to also refrain from such like activities and specially because of the fact that the Indian security forces in Kashmir had intensified their drive against the ISI backed Mujahideens who had infiltrated recently into the valley.

On the 19th of December, when Ahsan Dar the Supreme Commander of 'Muslim Mujahideen' and his colleague Ghulam Mohiuddin Lone were arrested at Jawahar Nagar and were later interrogated, there was good cause for the Indian intelligence network to celebrate. To save himself, Ahsan had readily confessed that he had been visiting Pakistan Occupied Kashmir very regularly and had infiltrated 250 of his compatriots from the 'Muslim Mujahideen' organization that he had formed after he was removed from the post of Chief Commander of the 'Hisbul Mujahideen.' Ahsan also said that he had held discussions with Brigadier Farhad, Colonel Raja Sajjad and some other Pakistani ISI officials and that they the Pakistanis wanted more action by the Mujahideens against the Indian army in Kashmir.

A few days later, while appreciating the good work done by the IB, the Congress government of Narasimha Rao at the centre was also given an unexpected boost, when 10 of the 13 members of the Janata Dal (A) led by Ajit Singh joined the Congress Party on 30th December. For the Congress

(I) it was like a new year's gift because with the party's a total strength of 266 Members of Parliament it now commanded a majority on its own in the Lok Sabha. The other silver lining was the non acceptance of the resignation of Mr Manmohan Singh by Prime Minsiter Narasimha Rao. As Finance Minister, Manmohan Singh had acknowledged full constitutional responsibility of his ministry's failure in the Harshad Mehta stocks and security scandal that had rocked the country and he therefore had put in his papers on 24ᵗʰ December, but very wisely realizing that Manmohan's exit would hamper India's move towards a market economy that had been initiated by the Finance Minister, his resignation was not accepted by the Prime Minister.

During the month of January 1994, while the Narasimha Rao Congress (I) led government with those extra 13 seats consolidated their political hold inside the Indian parliament, in Pakistan, Benazir's government was struggling to keep the Sunnis and Shias from killing each other. Both the religious sects were now not only targeting people, but their mosques also.

"My God is this what the Holy Koran and the Hadiths of Mohammed, the last messenger of Allah and peace be upon him has taught us," said a visibly angry Ruksana Begum, when she read about the attack on a Shia mosque in district Muzzafargarh on 21ˢᵗ January that killed six and injured twenty innocent worshippers. The sectarian violence was more prominent in the Punjab as militant groups belonging to the main parties, the Sunni Sipahe Sabha and the Shia Tehrik Nifaz-e-fiqh Jaffria took on each other in bloody clashes. And while the sectarian violence in Pakistan continued unabated, Arif Rehman and Ruksana on the eve of Shiraz and Saira's departure for Paris hosted a grand party for the entire Rehman clan. That day happened to be also India's Republic Day and Shupriya's 44th birthday and for Shiraz it was a day that he could never forget. On that day he resolved that come what may he would not ever abandon his wife and children and go back to India. But when Arif Rehman got ready to propose a toast for Shiraz's well deserved promotion and posting as Pakistan's number two man in Paris, Shiraz wondered what would happen if he was ever unmasked and his true identity revealed. He was now more worried about Saira and the children and he sincerely hoped that no harm should come to them.

That evening in New Delhi, Peevee was also hosting a birthday party for his mom number two at his favourite restaurant 'Dum Pukt' in Hotel Maurya. Coincidentally it was also a send off party for Shupriya too who had been posted to Havana, as the Ambassador of India to Cuba and was expected to take up her assignment by mid February.

"I regret I wont be able to be there in person for the premiere of your maiden film, but I am very sure that as Deepak Kumar the light that you have kindled in your heart to act in films as your profession will always shine like a bright star in my heart too," said Shupriya as she presented him with a Ronson cigarette lighter in a silver case and cautioned him to smoke a little less.

"'But what do the words 'Two My Dear Dablo' that is engraved on the lighter signify,' said Peevee as he thanked and kissed his Mom number 2 on her cheek. Knowing fully well that she would definitely be asked that question, Shupriya had come well prepared when she lied and said.

"Actually that was the nickname that I gave to you when I first saw you the day you were born. You were like a doll and very chubby with two big round drooping cheeks, but since the name Dolly sounded rather feminine, I named you Dablo. But then your parents did not like that name and we stuck to Peevee,"said Shupriya as both Monty and Reeta gave a smile of appreciation to that well thought out off the cuff explanation by Shupriya. That silver Ronson lighter was a gift that Shupriya had bought for Shiraz while he was away fighting the Pakistanis in the front and she wanted to surprise him with it when he returned, but he never did.

Meanwhile at Arif Rehman's party, when his son Major General Aslam Rehman who was commanding the Murree Division in Kashmir brought up the topic of the ISI and said that its role was now being sidelined and diluted under the new boss Lt General Javed Ashraf Qazi who had succeeded Lt General Javed Nasir and that was primarily because of the pressure being applied by the Clinton administration, everybody generally agreed with him and they all thought that it was a wise move. Having served in the ISI, Aslam Rehman had kept in touch with the organization and therefore knew a lot more than the others about all its nefarious activities. According to his perception it all started after Zia's death, when Benazir as Prime Minister tried to clip the wings of the ISI by inducting the retired Lt Gen Kallue to head the organization, and though his successor Lt General Azad Durrani tried to restore the situation, but he fell foul of the Army Chief. Then Nawaz Sharif brought in the fire brand Lt General Javed Nasir who was more interested in bringing in Islamization to the entire world and which only resulted in spawning terrorism. With Javed Nasir's penchant and love for the Afghan freedom fighters, whom the west now considered as potential terrorists, Pakistan's credibility as a front line state in the war against communism had taken a severe beating. So much so that it was now being branded as a nursing ground for Muslim terrorists by the Americans and others. As a result of this Lt General Javed Nasir was sent home and was replaced by Lt General Javed Ashraf Qazi who probably because of American pressure from abroad and political pressure from the government had started getting rid of those who were once considered to be the effective pillars of not only the ISI, but also of the Intelligence Bureau in Pakistan.

"But what about the role of the ISI inside Indian occupied Kashmir. Has that also undergone a serious policy change or are we still actively persuing 'Operation Topac,' asked Shiraz somewhat casually as he poured himself another large whisk.

"Well I won't say that we have given it up entirely, but it has definitely curbed our style, and as a result of which the required momentum of infiltrating and inducting the trained Mujahideen Groups including the Afghans has slowed down considerably. Moreover, the Kashmiri Muslims in the valley are also divided, and especially those who belong to the Hurriat Conference and some of them are completely against the idea of Kashmir becoming a part of Pakistan. They are still clamouring for independence of all the territories that was once Maharaja Hari Singh's erstwhile kingdom and to us that is only wishful thinking," added Aslam Rehman.

"'Yes indeed so, but this damn Kashmir problem economically has been milking both India and Pakistan high and dry, and it is high time that the matter is resolved amicably between the two countries. Because neither country is capable of achieving it militarily, and it would be foolish to even try and do so operationally, because by doing so we will only get involved in another bloody war like we did in 1965 and which frankly got us nothing as far as Kashmir was concerned," said Shiraz.

"'But do you think the politicians and the political leaders on both sides are interested. Frankly speaking I don't think so because nobody wants to give what the other side wants to take, and moreover this has become a forgotten issue as far as the world including the United Nations is concerned. And though India and Pakistan periodically keep holding talks to keep the issue alive, but it never makes any significant progress to sincerely resolve it once and for all," said Arif Rehman.

"Yes agreed, but for the politicians on both sides it will be like commiting harikiri, and they want to keep the issue alive. It has been their bread and butter eversince both countries got their independence, and to my mind the only sensible answer is to let bygones be bygones and both sides should agree amicably and truthfully to keep what they already have of that ill fated and unfortunate state of Jammu and Kashmir, and recognize the LOC, the line of control as the international border," said Ruksana Begum.

"Yes and that I also think is the only logical way to settle the problem, and by doing so it will not only promote goodwill and friendship between the two nations, but the colossal amount of money that both the nations are spending in arming themselves to the teeth and going nuclear could then be better utilized for the welfare, education and upliftment of the millions of poor people in both the countries,'" said Saira.

"How very right and then all of us will go on a holiday to Srinagar and maybe Sherry will also get an opportunity to visit Bollywood and meet her current favourite actor Sanjay Dutt of 'Khalnayak' fame," added Arif Rehman in a lighter vein.

CHAPTER-18

Towards Economic Prosperity

Though the New Year of 1994 began on an optimistic note with the seventh round of talks between Indian and Pakistan on Kashmir and on other bilateral issues at Islamabad, and where both the countries were represented by their respective foreign secretaries, JN Dixit and Shahrayar Khan respectively, but ultimately it yielded no worthwhile results at all. And by the time the month of January came to a close there were more violence in the valley. According to a Press Trust of India report, on 27th January some 26 people had died in secessionist related violence in Kupwara itself and the 'Bandh' that was called by the militants on the next day had virtually paralysed life in the entire valley. Meanwhile down south on the 19th of January at the Designated Court at Poonamallee near Madras, the trial of the 26 accused in the Rajiv Gandhi assassination case commenced with the examination of witnesses in camera. And on the 1st of February, as Shiraz with his family boarded the flight to Paris, he wondered whether the long standing Kashmir dispute would ever be solved, and whether the mastermind of the Rajiv assassination plot, Prabhakaran, the LTTE supremo and his intelligence chief Pottu Amman would ever be brought to book. The two main culprits Dhanu and the one eyed jack Sivarasan who committed the heinous crime were already dead, and those who were now being brought to book were only the small time conspirators who probably only abetted in committing that dastardly crime.

During the third week of Ferbruary, while Shiraz as Pakistan's number two man in Paris was still settling down to his hectic routine both official and social, he was shocked to hear about the involvement of an American CIA man who had been selling top secret and classified material to the Soviets in return for hard cash and that too since 1985, when he cooly walked into the Soviet Embassy in Washington and offered them his unique services. And what Shiraz found even more shocking was the fact that the man and his second wife were openly maintaining a life style of the rich and the famous, and which was well beyond the means of a normal middle ranking CIA officer and nobody had even pointed a finger at them all these years. Aldrich Ames began working for the CIA in 1962 as a low level operative when he was only 21 years old. His first assignment as a case officer was in 1969, when he was staioned in Ankara, Turkey and where surprisingly his job was to target Soviet intelligence officers for recruitment. His martial life with his first wife Nancy was already in shambles and by the time he became a little more senior, it was already over. In 1983, while on posting to the American Embassy in Mexico he had met Rosario Dupuy, she was an employee in the Colombian Embassy and ultimately married her. To meet the financial pressure of his divorce from Nancy and to cater for Rosario's binges while shopping and holidaying had turned him into a spy and a traitor. And it was he and his wife's high lifestyle together with his love for booze that had also led to his doom. Ever since the day Ames had walked in to the Russian Embassy in Washington in 1985, the CIA's network of Soviet Bloc agents had started disappearing at an alarming rate and it was Ames who was responsible for betraying them to the Russian KGB. And as a result of which a large number of KGB and GRU agents who were working for the Americans were either executed or jailed for life. And it was finally the FBI who having kept the CIA counter intelligence officer and his wife under constant surveillance picked them up on 21st February. Ames was the highest paid spy in American history That evening, when Shiraz narrated the exploits of the mole inside the CIA to his wife Saira, her only comment was that such traitors who sell their own countries secrets just for the love of money should be stripped naked and shot in public by a firing squad. That night Shiraz just could not sleep and he wondered what would happen if he was ever caught and betrayed.

Next morning there was still more shocking news, when his mother-in-law Ruksana Begum from Peshawar rang up to say that three masked Afghan terrorists in broad daylight had hijacked a school bus full of school boys from the very heart of the city and had taken them as hostages and that they were demanding money and food convoys to be sent to Afghanistan in exchange.

"My God what is Afghanistan coming to? Is this the way they pay us back after so much that we have done and sacrificed for them to get the Russians off their backs," said a visbly agitated Saira when she came to know that some of those young boys were from fairly well to do families and a few were also known to them personally.

"Yes it is indeed rather a pity, and it is all a fall out of our stupid policy of joining hands with the emerging Taliban in Afghanistan in order to keep our northern and western flanks secure. And the present civil war that is raging in that country between the many factions after the Soviets left the country, and the communist regime was removed from power will further ruin the nation. But let me also tell you that these so called young people from the madrassahs and their Mullahs, most of whom are Pakhtuns and who had come to Pakistan as refugees will become a big headache for Pakistan one day and that day I am afraid is not too far off either," said Shiraz as he got ready to leave for office.

Immediately on learning that one of his best friend's only son had also been taken hostage by the hijackers of the bus and that the bus was on its way to the Afghan Embassy in Islamabad, Salim Rehman kept his fingers crossed. And since he had served in Afghanistan earlier he therefore also volunteered to negotiate with the hijackers, but the Ministry of Interior was already on the job. There was no doubt that the International Red Cross had given a warning that food supplies for atleast 50,000 homeless people in Kabul could run out within a week, but the demand by the hijackers for five million American dollars in addition to a food convoy to be sent urgently to Kabul sounded a bit too far fetched. Pakistan's Interior Minister, Major General Nasrullah Babbar who initially started the negotiations with the hijackers was not one of those who would agree to those demands so very easily, and while the talks were in progress though the hijackers released 55 boys and 6 lady teachers, but they kept the rest of the older boys and one male teacher as hostage. The Interior Minister had even promised the hijackers with a helicopter and a safe passage back to Kabul and had reiterated that Pakistan was also eager to send food to Afghanistan, but paying that kind of big money was simply out of question. Later when Pakistan's acting Foreign Secretary, Zahid Saeed continued with the negotiations, his reading was that they were probably all terrorists and that they were only after the money. Finally when the Pakistan's Special Forces got into action and all the three hijackers were killed and all the boys and the teacher were rescued safely, Salim Rehman came to know a little more about the suave and polished Interior Minister.

Major General Nasrullah Babbar whose ancestors originated from Kandahar, Afghanistan was born in 1928 in Peshawar and the family had settled in the village of Pirpai, near Nowshera. His father was a Recruiting Officer of the British Indian Army and had given him a good education. A product of Presentation Convent, Peshawar and Burn Hall School,

Baramulla and Srinager, Nasrullah Babbar joined the PWRIMC in 1941 and passed out from there in 1946. He had joined the IMA but soon after the partition he was among those Muslim gentlemen cadets who were airlifted from Saharanpur to Lahore and became part of the First PMA course at Kakul.During his training at the PMA, he volunteered for service in Kashmir and also commanded a Tribal Lashkar Group in the Poonch Sector. Commissioned into the Regiment of Artillery, he later became an air observation post pilot and flew quite a few hazardous missions during the 1965 war. A graduate of Staff College Quetta, he was Commander of the 23 Division Artillery Brigade during the 1971 conflict and later also commanded the prestigious 111 Infantry Brigade. On 6th December, 1971, he was wounded by enemy shelling and in November 1972 as a Brigadier was posted as Inspector General Frontier Corps. Having also commanded the 14 Parachute Brigade at Silakot, he was promoted to the rank of Major General in August 1975. A close ally of the late Mr Bhutto, he retired from service on 1st March, 1976, the day Zia was promoted as Army Chief because Bhutto wanted Nasrullah to serve as Governor North West Frontier Province. After Benazir took over as Prime Minister for the second time, she appointed him as the Interior Minister. Later that evening after the hijackers were killed in a swift commando action and all the hostages were rescued, it was time to celebrate. That day when Salim Rehman was introduced to the Minister he indeed felt very proud. The highly decorated General officer was not only an old soldier but also a seasoned diplomat

While Pakistan celebrated the rescue of the school children, in New Delhi, Shupriya was getting ready to pack up her house and to fly to Havana on her new assignment as the Ambassador of India to Cuba and the Indian Embassy in Cuba was also accredited to the neighbouring Dominican Republic and Haiti It was comparatively a small mission and she was very happy that she was going as the number one. Since she was due to fly out on 1st March, Peevee had also arrived two days earlier from Bombay to help her pack her bags and to see her off at the airport. Peevee was also keen to witness the budget session in parliament and more so because it was predicted that it would be a historic one since India was already on the road to liberalization. Dr Manmohan Singh, the Indian Finance Minister had set the ball rolling in 1991 and which truly laid the foundation for a new era. The 28th of February 1994, a Monday was a historic day for an emerging India and as Peevee with Monty took their seats in the press gallery, kind courtesy of Mr Unnikrishnan who had managed the special passes through the Press Trust of India, all eyes were on that gentle and most unassuming

Sikh gentleman in Prime Minister Narasimha Rao's cabinet and who as also the Finance Minister of the country. There was no doubt that in less than three full years that the minority Congress (I) government had come to power, it had shown the road to recovery from a shattered economy that it had inherited. The foreign currency reserves which were at a dismal low of one billion dollars was now close to 13 billion and India's gold reserves, which earlier had been pledged abroad was also back in India's possession. As Peevee listened in the cool and confident manner to the Finance minister's historic budget speech, he felt proud as an Indian. And after the Minister concluded his speech with the words "Mr Speaker, Sir, this budget is inspired by a firm conviction that India has all the material and human resources to be a front ranking nation of the world," he was greeted with a thunderous applause from both the benches. Finally when he quoted from Rabindranath Tagore's prayer which said that to build an India where the clear stream of reason has not lost its way into the dreary desert sand of dead habit, and recommended the budget to be passed by the august House, there was no doubt in anybody's mind that the fiscal reforms that were initiated by Dr Manmohan Singh would bring in a new dawn for a vibrant and resurgent India.

That evening in order to celebrate the historic budget speech, and to bid a final goodbye to Mom number two, Peevee organized a farewell dinner with champagne at the Gaylords Restaurant on Connaught Place, which Monty knew was once upon a time also Shupriya's and Shiraz's favourite and where they often met on the quiet while dating one another. When Peevee very gallantly ushered Shupriya to her seat, Shupriya's thoughts went back to 15th January 1971, when Shiraz on that Army Day after the grand parade on that cold winter morning met her outside her college and took her for a long ride on his new Royal Enfield motorcycle and then treated her to a sumptuous lunch at Gaylords. It was on that very afternoon and while they were enjoying the gulab jamuns with ice cream for dessert and Shiraz while trying to put one more into her mouth suddenly proposed to her out of the blue, she was all smiles. And though she was not taken very much by surprise and accepted the proposal whole heartedly but the big gulab jamun almost choked her. During that exclusive candle light dinner for the family that included his sister Dimpy and her husband Bharat,(Paddy), when the topic of whether Castro's Cuba would also now break away from the shackles of 45 years of communist rule came up for discussion, Dimpy was of the opinion that the Cubans who had been taken for a ride by Fidel Castro's tall promises of Utopia and with the Russians having thrown communism out of the window, the time was not very far when the Cuban people would also call off his bluff.

"But whatever one may say, the bearded Castro, the ruler of that tiny island, which is only ninety miles from the Florida coast of America has never buckled even under mighty Uncle Sam's pressure and for that he definitely deserves all the credit,"said Peevee.

"But what really beats me is how does a small island like Cuba with its tiny population of not even ten million can produce so many world class Olympic medal winning athletes, while India, Pakistan, Bangladesh and Sri Lanka all put together have not yet produced even a single one so far," said Bharat.

"Yes that indeed is a real shame and as far as India is concerned, our not producing any world campions is primarily because sports in this country has become totally politicized and the pity is that the politicians and the bureaucrats who run these so called federations and boards most of them have never played any of these games, atleast not at any recognized level. And their sole aim in heading these organizations it seems is to wangle a few free trips for shopping on junkets abroad and that to at the tax payers expense,"said Monty.

"Yes and that is damn well right and the last time when India came close to winning an Olympic medal in athletics was way back in 1960 at Rome, when Milkha Singh from the Indian army literary lost by a whisker when he came fourth in the 400 meters men's finals," added Peevee as a young teenage girl who was having dinner with her parents on the adjoining table having recognized the budding young film star Deepak Kumar confidently walked upto him and requested him for an autograph.

"But today I am not Deepak Kumar; I am Param Veer Singh Bajwa. But nevertheless the very fact that I have been recognized in public and even before my first film which is still waiting to be released I do feel highly honoured and therefore for good luck young lady I will honour you with an autograph not just on a piece of paper but on a photograph of mine from my maiden film," said Peevee as he took out a few still photographs from his purse and having addressed it to 'My First Fan Anjuna' he signed it with a flourish. When a delighted Anjuna clutching the autographed photo to her chest went back to her table, Shupriya closed her eyes and silently said a prayer. She very well knew that Bollywood seldom offered a second chance to new comers unless he or she was from the same fraternity or was well connected to the stars, producers and directors of yesteryears and whose names still spelt magic in the celluloid world.

While the soup was being served, Shupriya gave a brief resume of how Cuba came into being and the irony of it was that it was the Americans who during the first insurrection on the island in 1895 had come to the assistance of the Cubans, when it was being unscrupulously exploited by Spain which was the mother country. And on 15th February 1898, when the American warship 'Maine' was mysteriously destroyed in the Havana harbour, America declared war on Spain and the American Congress declared that the people of Cuba are and of right ought to be free and independent. And it was as a sequel to this that the Treaty of Paris was signed on 10th December, 1898 and Spain finally gave up all claims to Cuba. In fact from 1899 to May 1902, it was the United States military governors who administered Cuba till a democratic constitution under President Tomas Estrada Palma took office. But into Cuba's constitution was also incorporated the Platt Amendment that specified that the Cuban government could not enter into any foreign treaty which might threaten its independence, and that the United States had the right to intervene and assume control of Cuba to protect its people or to preserve its freedom and which they did in 1906 when the national elections in Cuba stirred violence. The Platt Amendment also granted U.S. coaling and naval stations in southeast Cuba and that is how the Americans are still there in Guantanamo Bay. The Americans till 1909 had set up a military government and thereafter General Jose Miguel Gomez was elected President of Cuba. In 1933, there was an army revolt in Cuba that was led by Fulgencio Batista who deposed President Machado and as Batista's power grew under his absolute rule after he first took office as President in 1940 and then again in 1952, the Cuban people lost much of their personal liberty. In 1953, the revolution against Batista commenced and it culminated in 1959 with Castro coming into power and the rest is history, concluded Shupriya.

"But then why are the Americans always after Castro, and why cant they leave him alone," asked Reeta.

"That's a good question, but I am afraid in order to get the right answer we will have to ask all the successive American Presidents starting with President Eisenhower and who in turn was succeeded by President Kennedy, the man who gave the go ahead for the Bay of Pigs fiasco and the one who also initiated the Cuban blockade in 1962 and which could have well resulted in a nuclear holocaust," said Monty as he raised a toast to Yeshwant Kaur Bajwa and wished her a happy and eventful tenure in Castro's Cuba.

It was not even a fortnight since Shiraz with his family landed in Paris, when a dear old Pakistani friend of his called on him. Shiraz had first met

Maqbool Hussein when he was posted in London in 1973 as the Third Secretary and since Maqbool was also very fond of Urdu poetry they had hit it off very well. Maqbool had come to Paris from London on some official private business and when he learnt that Shiraz was Pakistan's number two man in France, he not only invited him and his family over for the weekend to London, but also for the premiere of Steven Speilberg's new film titled 'Schindler's List.' But what really surprised Shiraz was the fact that the man who had a master's degree from Cambridge University in English and who for over a decade was also a lecturer in a renowned college was now a leading restaurateur with a chain of fast food joints that only served tandoori snacks, tikka kebabs, kati kebabs and such like food both for non-vegetarians and vegetarians. This was the brainchild of Maqbool Hussein's second wife Taslima, a Bangladeshi Muslim. Maqbool's first wife Gulnar was from a rich Iranian family from Bombay and in 1972 as a 20 year old she had come to Cambridge for higher studies when she met Maqbool who was then a lecturer and they soon got married. It was much against the wishes of her parents because they were Shias while Maqbool was a Sunni Muslim. But that marriage only lasted for two years because Maqbool devoted more time to his lectureship in college and in going to 'Mushairas.' So one fine day Gulnar just walked out on him and went back to India. Maqbool met Taslima in September 1975 in London. It was at a friend's big Iftaar party during the holy month of Ramzan where Taslima as a hotel management trainee was looking after the catering for the breaking of the fast that evening. Originally her family was from Calcutta, but at partition had moved to Dhaka. Her grandfather was a great friend and admirer of Sheikh Hazan Raza, the ex peon of Calcutta Municipal Corporation who in the early 1900's gave up his career and got into the catering business and later opened the no-frills Nizam's restaurant near Calcutta's famous New Market and who also introduced to the world the mouth watering 'Kati Roll' and which to the western world later became known as the 'Frankie'. That evening at the 'Iftaar', when Taslima convinced Maqbool by giving examples of how Kentucky Fried Chicken, Wimpy's and McDonald's ventured into the fast food business and soon became household names, Maqbool was completely floored not only by her arguments, but also by her desire to start one in London provided someone was willing to become a partner in financing the project. Seeing the young lady's enthusiasm, Maqbool not only gave up his lectureship, but also became her partner for life when their first restaurant 'Tandoorian' which was a liitle more than a cabin to seat 12 people at Hounslow became an instant hit and thereafter there was no looking back for them. According to Taslima, the location of a restaurant was very important and one that would be able to cater to the palate of the local gentry residing in that general area, and Hounslow with its large Indian, Pakistani and Bangladeshi population and which was close to the Heathrow airport was ideally suited for the purpose. A very large number of these people were employed as sweepers, rest room attendants, porters and helpers at the airport and for them time was always at a premium. There requirement was that the food should not only be served in a jiffy, but it should also be hot, tasty and reasonably priced, and the end product should be such that it could be eaten while also on the move and without soiling one's hands or clothes. Therefore according to Taslima's logic, if Dick and Mac Mcdonald way back in 1940 in San Bernardino, California could open Mcdonald's and Colonel Harland Sanders from North Corbin, Kentucky in 1952 could introduce to the world the Kentucky Fried Chicken, and Eddie Gold of London in early 1950's could give the Londoners the Wimpy hamburger, then why could'nt the expatriates from the Indian subcontinent also give to their own people and the Englishman the delicacies from the tandoor.

With the release of the Spielberg film scheduled for the evening of Friday 18th February, Shiraz and family arrived well in time at Maqbool's palatial mansion near Kensington Gardens Throughout the entire journey from Paris, while Shiraz talked about the remarkable career of Steven Spielberg, Saira and the children were highly impressed about his knowledge of Hollywood. Speilberg was now undoubtedly the world's number one film director and whose latest film 'Schindler's List' was a resounding box office success in America where it was first released on 15th December, 1993. So enamoured were both his children with the man's life story and also that of his new film that his daughter Shehzadi who was soon going to be 16 decided that she too would now take up directing films as a full time profession. Born on 18th December, 1946, in Cincinnati, Ohio, Steven Spielberg, the son of Jewish parents it seems had film making in his blood. Even as teenager and a Boy Scout at the tender age of 13, Steven had won a prize for a 40 minute war movie that was titled 'Escape to Nowhere.' At 16, he wrote and directed his first independent movie, a science fiction adventure called 'Firelight'. But the irony of the whole thing was that after graduating from school when he applied for admission to a film school at the University of South California School of Theatre, Film and Television he was rejected not once but thrice due to his C grade average in high school. His actual career began in Universal Studios as an unpaid, eight-day-a week intern and guest of the editing department. Therefore, it was not at all easy going for the young man as far as Hollywood was concerned. And it was only in 1969, when he got a break as a professional television director for the pilot episode of 'Night Gallery,' and it was because of none other than the legendary Hollywood actress Joan Crawford who spoke very highly of this young twenty three year old rookie director. Finally it was in 1975 as the Director of the Peter Benchley novel 'Jaws' that Steven Spielberg came into his own and later gave the world a host of other hit films like 'ET-Extra Terrestrial' and 'Raiders of the Lost Ark', that were a class into themselves. And as far as Schinder's List was concerned, it was a biographical film that told the story of Oskar Schindler, a German businessman who saved the lives of over a thousand Polish Jews during the Holocaust. Roman Polanski was given the offer to direct the film and so was Billy Wilder, but they both declined because the matter was very sensitive to both of them personally. Polanski's mother was gassed at Auschwitz and so were quite a few members from Wilder's family But with the rise of neo-nazism after the collapse of the Berlin Wall, and on hearing stories of the recent genocide in Bosnia, Speilberg who was also a Jew took up the challenge and made a masterpiece of the book by Thomas Keneally. The shooting began in Krakow, Poland and in other real life locations on 1st March, 1993 and an exact replica of even the gas chambers at Auschwitz was also constructed outside the actual camp because permission was not given to shoot inside the premises. The entire film was shot in just 71 days and it was more like a documentary and that too in black and white in order to give it more authenticity, and there were no crane shots. Initially Speilberg was skeptical about the film, but when it became a box office hit even in Germany, he himself was surprised. And finally, when the film won seven Academy Awards including that of the Best Picture, Best Director and Best Music Score, Speilberg's name had become a household word everywhere.Though the film that evening was enjoyed by all, but for Shiraz's 11 year old son Tojo it was a big bore and therefore to compensate the young lad, Maqbool decided to take him and the family out on a picnic to the London Zoo next morning and followed it up with a special screening of Tom and Jerry cartoons in the evening at his private auditorium in the basement.

In mid March, with Dimpy and Bharat Padmanabhan expecting their first child in June, both of them had requested for an year's extension to stay on in Delhi, but the Ministry had not only turned it down, but it also rejected their request to post them to the same foreign station whenever it was due. They were about to complete their three years of home posting next month and when Dimpy's request was rejected, she immediately put in her papers and it was accepted. The following month, when her husband Paddy got posted to the Indian Embassy in Tokyo as First Secretary, Dimpy also left with him bag and baggage. When Shupriya in Havana got to know of her resignation she felt rather sad, but there was little that she could do sitting thousands of miles away. In a way the ministry was also right and bringing up a child was also the responsibility of both the parents.

And while Paddy and Dimpy got busy packing their bags, on 25th March, 1994, the entire Rehman clan with Karim Malik from Pakistan Embassy, Kabul and Fazal Rehman who with his family from USA was on his way to Dhaka for a holiday congregated at Lahore to witness the finals of the Champions Trophy with host Pakistan taking on the mighty Germans. The Pakistanis would have loved to see India playing them on their home turf, but India was not even a qualifying team in that six nation tournament of champions. The man who they all came to watch was their Faisalabad born hockey captain, the mercurial Shahbaz Ahmad who was also known as the Dhyan Chand of Pakistan hockey. It was a well fought match with Pakistan ultimately lifting the trophy 5-4 after a tense and nerve racking penalty shoot out. To celebrate Pakistan's win, Major General Aslam Rehman threw a grand party at the Lahore Gymkhana Club and where the topic for discussion that evening was non other than the civil war in Afghanistan and the recent emergence of Taliban as a force to reckon with in future.

"Frankly speaking if the young lady and by that I mean our honourable Prime Minister Benazir Bhutto and her party the PPP keeps actively supporting the Taliban movement and the ISI also once again vigorously starts imparting them with military training and it keeps supplying them with weapons and equipment, then I am afraid we will only be creating a medieval monster in our own back yard and one which will be worse than even Ravana," said Arif Rehman who was now nearing 74 and was the senior most member of the Rehman clan.

"Yes and if my information is correct, these were the same young people who had come as refugees during the Soviet occupation of Afghanistan, became diehard Koranic students in the many madrassas that were set up for them in the frontier region, who fought the Soviets with weapons given by us and the Americans, who were jointly trained by the CIA and the ISI, and now they want a helping hand from the lady in order to come to power. Moreover, there is also a strong rumour that Osama Bin Laden is also supporting the movement very actively while sitting in Khartoum," said Fazal Rehman as Karim Malik very diplomatically gave him a smile, but made no further comments.

"That can very well be true and I personally feel that Pakistan should have diplomatically stayed away from the PAIC, the Popular Arab and Islamic Conference that was held in Khartoum in mid-December 1993 under the aegis of the radical Sudanese leader, Turabi. But what was even worse was the fact that the official Pakistan delegation also included General Mirza Aslam Beg, the retired Army Chief and Lt General Hamid Gul, the former chief of ISI. This further confirmed that Benazir in order to consolidate her power with the Mullahs and the Muslim world was now eager to continue and persue her Islamist policies and which I am afraid could be detrimental to Pakistan's interest in the long run," added Arif Rehman when Karim Malik finally butted in to say that the bearded Osama Bin Laden who was a keen football fan had been spotted at a football match in London on 15th March and it was just one week after the Saudi Arabian government had withdrawn his citizenship. In fact after the match, which Arsenal won against Torino, Italy by a solitary goal, Osama had even bought a replica of the Arsenal shirt.

"But I thought Osama was now in Sudan but how the hell did he land up in London?" said Salim Rehman.

"May be to set up another Al-Qaida office there. After all London is Europe's financial capital and it could be an ideal place to set up another base for his followers under the guise of an Islamic charitable mission," said Aslam Rehman as all their lady wives who had gone out shopping after the hockey match returned with their many purchases.

"Now no more shop talk please," said Fazal's wife Samina as she presented her father-in-law Arif Rehman and her mother-in-law Ruksana Begum with a set of music cassettes that was aptly titled 'Shraddhanjali.' and which she had especially purchased for them when they were posted in New Delhi. It was a tribute paid to the immortal singers of the subcontinent who were no more in this world by none other than the legendary and the evergreen nightingale of India, Lata Mangeshkar and included hit songs of KL Saigal, Pankaj Mullick, Noor Jehan, Ameer Bai, Mohammed Rafi, Kannanbala Devi, Mukesh, Kishore Kumar and others.

"Oh how I wish those beautiful lovely happy days could come back again, and though we were being ruled by the British at that time, it was certainly a more peaceful country then and there was atleast a sense of discipline and well being among the people of all communities. And now whether it is Pakistan, India or Bangladesh it is the same old story of corruption, nepotism, chicanery and sycophancy at all levels of society and with the politicians and their unscrupulous political parties and leaders hoodwinking the illiterate poor masses and raking in millions for themselves and their kith and kin. This was the same old story also when both Pakistan and Bangladesh were being ruled by Generals, and I therefore sometime wonder whether by becoming independent nations we have achieved anything at all except to get at each other's throats both overtly and clandestinely and bring more miseries to our people," said Ruksana Begum who though she was now nearing 70, but she looked as charming and elegant as ever

"Yes and that is rather a pity and had we remained as one nation we too would have probably been a super power by now. And sometimes I wonder what happened to those families of our old friends like Ronen Sen, Debu Ghosh, the beautiful Pugsley sisters and where have they all disappeared," added Arif Rehman as he got into a nostalgic mood and talked about the two good looking Pugsley twins, Sandra and Debbie and about Uncle Edwin and his bawdy jokes.

Strangely enough on the very next morning, when Arif Rehman was routinely going through the set of Indian news papers that his son Salim Rehman had brought from his office, he found in the Bombay edition of the 'Times of India' dated 18th March, 1994 an obituary mentioning that Shaun Pugsley, the eldest son of Edwin Pugsley and ex foreman in the EIR, the East Indian Railway of India had passed away peacefully at Perth, Australia at the age of 80. Since there were no other names except those of Shaun's children and grandchildren mentioned in the obituary, Arif concluded that Shaun was probably the last of the Pugsley's from his generation and all of them were now in heaven.

A week later, when Arif with his wife returned to their big Haveli in Peshawar, he took out a set of old albums with black and white photographs that had now with time turned practically pale yellow. One group photograph that was taken sometime during the Christmas season of 1931 in Calcutta and titled 'Picnic at Diamond Harbour', showed a 11 year old Arif Rehman in an underwear standing in between the two 15 year old beautiful Pugsley twin sisters Sandra and Debbie, while their two brothers Shaun who was then 18 and who was about to join EIR as an apprentice engine driver with Richard who was a year older to Arif getting ready to fly the set of kites that Arif's father the late Colonel Attiqur Rehman had presented them with that day. Another photograph showed all the ladies including his mother, Suraiya aunty, Shobha aunty, Hena aunty all busy cooking the lunch at the picnic, while all the uncles and his father Colonel Attiqur Rehman enjoyed a game of bridge. There was also a photograph of his sister Shenaz with Mona Ghosh the sister of Debu Ghosh and Ronen's younger sister Purnima Sen all of whom were then little children in frocks playing hop skotch. That morning as Arif and Ruksana scanned through those old priceless photo albums and recalled those lovely days, it suddenly dawned on them that all their grand children now belonged to the fifth generation and that time was also running out for the elderly Rehman couple.

"Yes and my sister Shenaz had she lived she would have been 70 plus today and her son my nephew Imran Hussein would have been nearing fifty, but unfortunately Dr Ghulam Hussein's family did not go beyond the third generation and that indeed was rather sad," said Arif to his wife as he took out their old wedding album and then suddenly realized that they had been married for a good 48 years. Unknown to the elderly couple, to the Rehman family and the world, including their nephew Imran Hussein (Shiraz), alias Riaz Mohammed Khan by a strange fate of luck was very much alive and he was now very much a part of the same family.

CHAPTER-19

Full Circle

Imran Hussain, the infant boy was saved by an Irish nun way back in October 1947, when the Pathan raiders attacked Kashmir. It was also like a God's gift to Colonel Ismail Sikandar Khan who had found the abandoned child near the old Church at Baramulla and after the Indian army had recaptured the town in early November 1947. He subsequently legally adopted him and had lovingly given him the new name of Shiraz Ismail Khan. But the late Colonel Ismail did not know that the little boy was his best friend Colonel Gul Rehman's own nephew. He was the son and only offspring of Shenaz and Nawaz Hussain who had been killed by the raiders as they kept advancing towards Srinagar. The aftermath of the 1971 war was another quirk of fate that made Shiraz Ismail Khan to perforce change his name to that of Riaz Mohammed Khan and take on a completely new identity. The much decorated ex Indian army officer now masquerading as a senior Pakistani diplomat and unaware that his wife Saira was actually his own first cousin was now a happily married man with two lovely children and he had no intentions now of ever going back to India or letting his new country Pakistan down. His one and only desire now was to ensure that the two countries lived as good friendly neighbours and this ongoing war of proxy by the Pakistanis must not only end, but under no circumstances should it be allowed to escalate into an all out fourth round because with Pakistan also now on the verge of becoming a nuclear power that would be simply disastrous for the subcontinent and the world.

On 9th April, 1994, when Arif and Ruksana called up Paris to wish their son-in-law Riaz Mohammed on his 48th birthday, it was time again for celebrations. Unaware of what was happening around them, the entire surviving Rehman clan unknowingly it seems had come full circle. And on that early Saturday morning as Shiraz with his wife and children drove out for the weekend to visit the Palace of Versailles on the outskirts of Paris, he wondered who his real parents were and what was his real name and date of birth. As they approached the magnificent and historical palace, Shiraz as a good father acted as the guide. Built in 1624, by Louis XIII, King of France as a modest hunting lodge, the magnificent palace was now a grand museum. For the subsequent monarchs of France it was the seat of supreme power till the French Revolution together with the storming of the Bastille that led to the beheading of Louis XVI and his beautiful wife Marie Antoinette forced the seat of power to return to Paris. It was also the place where the famous Treaty of Versailles was signed and which ended the First World War. During that weekend stay at the Hotel Le Versailles which was practically adjacent to the magnificent palace, when Shiraz explained in detail to his children the history of the palace that also led to the French Revolution, Saira too was pretty much impressed by her husband's knowledge of French history. Maybe that was part of a good diplomat's way of knowing the French people better thought Saira as she purchased a few picture postcards.

According to Shiraz the seeds of the French revolution were sowed during the reign of Louis XV, when he in his desire to wage more wars left France virtually bankrupt. And when this was followed by King Louis XVI and his nobles continuing with their extravagant life style, while the common man on the streets and in the fields kept starving, it was then that the people decided that enough was enough and it led to the storming of the Bastille on 14th July, 1789. Thereafter followed a reign of terror between rival factions and which resulted in the deaths of thousands of French men, women and children and which some even termed it as genocide.

Later that evening, when Shiraz tuned in to listen to the BBC news on TV, he was shocked to hear about another genocide that had engulfed the small African country of Rwanda, and where a systematic cleansing of the Tutsi minorities by the Hutus who were in the majority had begun in right earnest. It had started a few days earlier on 6th April 1994, when the sleek executive jet carrying the Presidents of both Rwanda and of neighbouring Burundi was shot down by a missile near the Rwandan capital of Kigali and there were no survivors. But the shooting down of that unarmed VIP aircraft had angered the Hutus. According to the BBC, this was the worst kind of genocide in recent years and one that had already claimed thousands of innocent Tutsis. There was also a report that Hutu gangs were on a murderous mission to eliminate all Tutsis, and in one case they had even bulldozed a church at a place called Nyange and where more than 1500 Tutsis who had sought refuge there were mercileesly killed. And the fact that it was done with the connivance of the local priest was even more appalling. The well armed Hutus not only bulldozed the church and razed it to the ground, but they also brutally killed all those Tutsis who were trying to escape from there. With the use of their sharp machetes,rifles and guns they had started the genocide. And when the BBC started showing a video footage of the ghastly killings, Saira immediately switched off the TV and said.

"I wonder what this world is coming to, and if this is the state of affairs at the end of the 20th century, the I simply dread to see or imagine what our children and grandchildren will go through in the new millennium that is around the corner."

"Yes it is indeed rather sad, but thank God that finally the whites of South Africa have finally woken up to reality. And I am confident that when the results of the first ever fully multiracial elections that is scheduled to be held on 27th April is declared, it will be a Black native and not a White Afrikaner who will become the next President of that country," said Shiraz very proudly. And when he further added that if Mr Nelson Mandela and his party the African National Congress did win the elections, then to celebrate his victory he would take the family for a short holiday to Italy and which would also include a trip to San Marino to witness the Motor Grand Prix that was scheduled to be held on 1st of May.

'Oh that simply will be great Papa," said an excited 11 year old Tojo whose hobby now from collecting stamps had shifted to collecting Dinky toys and miniature F-1 formula racing cars.

"Well if both the father and son duo wish to go and watch the car race, then we have no objections at all because as far as Sherry and I are concerned we would rather spend more time on the beaches and take a day long cruise along the beautiful Adriatic Coast,' said Saira.

"Yes Papa and you must promise that you will take us to Venice and Florence also,"added Sherry who did not like to be addressed as Shehzadi anymore because she considered that name to be a bit too snooty and aristocratic.

While Shiraz with his family made their tentative plan to visit Italy, in Bombay on Friday 15th April, the much awaited release of Peevee's maiden film titled "Gundagiri Raj-Netaon Ke Haath,' with its catchy English title 'The Dons in Khadhi' opened at several of the leading theatres of the city. With the first week's box office collection surpassing all previous records, it catapulted both the newcomers Deepak Kumar and Shreya Salve as the rising stars of Bollywood. And when a popular Bombay weekly film tabloid heralded the debut of the new handsome and talented singing star Deepak Kumar with the headlines "A new Amitabh on the Hollywood horizon,' the Bombay's underworld promptly dubbed him as 'Chikna Mauna' meaning thereby the young shaven Sikh.And on that late evening far away in Havana, when Shupriya heard Peevee's voice over the telephone telling her that he had made it finally to the tinsel world and to Bollywood, her joys knew no bounds as she took out Shiraz's photograph in uniform from her small secret safe together with that of the Sai Baba of Shirdi and having touched them softly to her head and lips said a small prayer.

Meanwhile after the 7th round of the Indo-Pak Foreign Secretary level talks on Kashmir in early January, when there was a slight lull in the activities of the ISI sponsored militancy in the valley, Shiraz felt a little happy. But this was also attributable to the large number of foreign delegations, including the envoys of various countries and the Red Cross who had been visiting the valley during the months of February and March to check with the ground reality. But on the 29th of March1994, when a powerful blast in an Indian army ammunition depot inside the Badami Bagh cantonment at Srinagar resulted in the death of 13 army personnel including a Major General and four other senior officers, it was all back to square one. It was also another wake up call for the policy makers in South Block and those who were dealing with Kashmir to take stock of the deteriorating situation in the valley.The death of Major General EW Fernandes who was the Director of Military Intelligence at the Indian army headquarters in New Delhi came as a big shock to Shiraz. A gunner by profession and an ex colleague of his, Ferdie was also an air observation pilot. He was on an official tour to the Indian Army XV Corps headquarters in Srinagar and the blast only indicated that militants had also now infiltrated into some of the vital static units of the Indian army in the valley and which had a mix of both men in uniform and people from the civvy street and who were mostly local Kashmiris. However a week later a different kind of blast shook Pakistan too, when on the 7th of April, 1994, the ISI arrested Yunus Habib, the Chief Executive of the Mehran Bank and which brought home to the Pakistanis how deeply corrupted was the political system in their country. The Mehrangate scandal had brought into the open on how a banker with high political connections could siphon off a staggering five billion rupees, while doling out as bribes millions of rupees to the politicians in order to cover up the crime. And on 20th April, when the Interior Minister, Major General Nasrullah Babar gave more details about the various payments that were made to politicians, generals and political parties, it was quite evident that starting from the President to the Prime Minister and the Army Chief everybody had a cut of that big pie. Addressing the National Assembly, when Major General Babar openly said that the main beneficiary of the largesse was the former army chief General Mirza Aslam Beg who received Rupees 140 million, followed by the former Interior Minister Jam Sadiq, MQM's Altaf Hussein, Nawaz Sharif and a host of others, and that quite a large sum of that money had also gone towards bank rolling the 1990 election campaign of certain politicians, and that it had also been used by the ISI in the run up to the 1988 elections in order to ensure that the PPP was kept out of power, Arif Rehman and Ruksana Begum both of them just could not believe that all this could be true. They knew that the politicians by and large were corrupt, but for the ISI to be initially used as a political match referee and then as a match fixer to determine who should sit in the treasury benches and who should sit in the opposition was simply beyond their comprehension. And what was even more surprising was the fact that it was the ISI account in the Mehran Bank that had finally sealed the fate of that bank. Ever since its inception, the Mehran Bank was not doing well at all and In order to help Yunus Habib out, General Aslam Beg who was then the Pakistan army chief and Lt General Javed Nasir the DGISI had deposited the ISI's foreign exchange reserves totaling to a whopping 39 million US dollars into the Mehran Bank account. With that money in his kitty, Yunus Habib then decided to finance other lucrative deals on the side. But unluckily for him it got exposed, when Lt General Javed Nasir was prematurely retired and was replaced by General Javed Ashraf who took over as DGISI in January 1993. And the scam finally came to light, when General Javed Ashraf on taking over wanted to transfer the money back into a safer government owned financial institution as was the rule. But when Yunus Habib pleaded for more time and was unable to pay up that staggering amount with the accumulated interest, he was quietly picked up by the ISI. It was the same law enforcing agency which had deposited the amount and who now wanted it all back with full interest. Soon thereafter the grilling began. Finally Habib was arrested on 7th April by the FIA, the Federal Investigating Agency of Pakistan on a complaint that was made by the State Bank of Pakistan for having fraudulently misappropriated a very large amount from the sale proceeds of the DBC, the Dollar Bearer Certificates which also amounted to a whopping 36.7 million US dollars.

While the financial scandal in Pakistan kept hogging the headlines, the eyes of the rest of the world were now focused on the elections in South Africa. And on 27th April 1994, when the final results of the elections were announced, it created history. With the African National Conference having secured 62% percent of the votes, their revered leader Nelson Mandela was unanimously elected as the President of the Republic of South Africa. And soon after receiving the good news and as was promised, Shiraz with his family on the very next day took the first flight out to Florence.

Though Shiraz was personally not fond of fast cars, nevertheless to get the thrill of it he at his son Tojo's request hired for a whole week an Alfa Romeo 155 sedan, a compact executive car that was currently under production by the parent company Fiat. On 30th April, they visited the main tourist attractions of Florence and it included the many beautiful churches, palaces and museums But when later in the evening drove when the down to San Marino and were given the shocking news that the up and coming Austrian driver Roland Ratzenberger had been killed in a practice accident on that very morning they felt sad. On the previous day the newcomer Rubens Barrichello a protégé of Ayrton Senna the world champion was also involved in a serious accident during the afternoon qualifying session and he too was therefore now ruled out from the competition. And on hearing that when Saira casually remarked.

"Well I only hope that this competition for tomorrow is not jinxed and there should not be any more such accidents," Shiraz told her not to be so superstitious

On that Sunday morning of 1st May 1994, and in order to get a good ringside seat near the finishing podium, both father and son arrived at the Imola racing track well before the start of the race. And as a result of which an enthusiastic Tojo not only managed to get an autographed photo of the 34 year old Brazilian legend and the current world champion Ayrton Senna da Silva but also that of his nearest rival, the young German driver, Michael Schumacher. But when at the very start of the race there was another accident, Shiraz too wondered whether the race track was jinxed. And he did not have to wait very long for the answer because a few minutes later after Senna had set the pace with the third quickest lap and was being closely followed by Schumacher disaster struck. As the cars entered the high speed Tamburello corner, it turned into a bad fatal accident. Senna's car that was doing nearly 135 miles per hour sudddenly veered of the track and hit the thick concrete retaining wall. Shiraz who was closely following the leader with his powerful binoculars was simply stunned. After the massive right front wheel had shot up like a catapult and it came crashing down it resulted in a fatal skull fracture on the celebrated driver. When the medical team rushed to the accident site Senna was still alive, but with the small San

Marino principality having no major medical facilities, he was immediately flown by a chopper to Bologna and where he was later declared dead. The man who was often compared to the legendary Juan Manuel Fangio was born on 21ˢᵗ March, 1960, in San Paolo, Brazil. As the son of a wealthy land owner he developed an interest in motor car racing at an early age. The dare devil driver who was particularly known for attaining pole positions, the fastest qualifying time for a given race and who in his career had achieved it a record 161 times was a national hero. When the organizers of the San Marino Grand Prix found an Austrian flag in the wreckage of his car, it was the victory flag that Senna wanted to raise that day after the event in honour of Roland Ratzenberger who had died on the same track a day earlier. For Brazil the death of Senna was a great national tragedy and the government declared three days of national mourning in his honour. At his state funeral an estimated one million people lined the streets including practically all Formula One drivers who had raced with him and one of the pall bearers was none other than his fierce rival Alain Prost. When later on that evening of the tragedy Tojo very proudly showed his mother the autographed photo of the great Brazilian driver who was no more, Shiraz was convinced that both life and death was all in Allah's hand.

After their return from the tragic San Marino Grand Prix, when on the 10ᵗʰ of May, Shiraz heard the inaugural address by Nelson Mandela live over the CNN, he was reminded about the late Martin Luther King and his famous speech of 'I have a dream.' Speaking to his countrymen, the man who had served more than half his life in prison in apartheid Africa was a true disciple of Mahatma Gandhi. Using his charm and power of speech, he begged and exhorted his people to forgive and forget. Finally when Mandela concluded his speech with the golden words "Let there be justice for all. Let there be peace for all. Let there be work, bread, water and salt for all and let freedom reign," Shiraz wondered that if the blacks and the whites of South Africa could now live in peace and harmony, then why could'nt the Hindus and the Muslims of the subcontinent do the same.

Meanwhile with the induction of more Indian army troops and para-military forces into the Kashmir valley to check the ISI sponsored militancy in the state, Monty during mid May made another of his business trips to Srinagar. That day on the flight he met an old classmate of his from Sanawar who had joined the Indian Police Service and was now posted as the head of the Indian Inteligence Bureau in the valley. The Intelligence Bureau in Srinagar besides gathering internal and local intelligence was also responsible for tracking down Pakistani agents who had set up sleeper cells in the valley. According to his friend, though there was a lull in the ISI sponsored infiltration in the recent past, but that was primarily because of the hard winter conditions in the upper reaches of the valley and also due to the intense patrolling of the LOC, the Line of Control by the Indian army. However, the recent capture of Mohammed Ramzan, a Pakistani national from Faisalabad who was apprehended from Udhampur on 11th May, and his subsequent interrogation gave a clear indication that Pakistan's efforts to create further trouble was not only inside Kashmir, but also in the big important towns and cities of India.

Mohammed Ramzan's induction into Kashmir militancy took place in 1992, while he was undergoing religious training in his home town of Faisalabad in Pakistan. After his induction he was trained for a month at Maaskar-e-Taiba, a training centre for terrorists that was located at Kunnad in Afghanistan and he later also underwent a rigorous three months commando course with 200 hundred others at another training centre in Afghanistan. And though the trainees included a few Afghans, but most of them were from Pakistan occupied Kashmir. During the course they were trained not only in small arms, but also in the firing of stinger missiles, in the laying of mines, booby traps and also in the manufacture of high intensity indigenous bombs and explosive devices. In May, 1993, with his group of 15, Mohammed Ramzan who was now the Chief Commander of the Ansar-ul-Mujahideen had infiltrated into the valley from the Gurez-Kel sector. Prior to his departure, he had been briefed by one Colonel Salim of the Pakistan ISI at the 'Al Barq' office in Muzzafarabad. Before being inducted from that sector, they were equipped with arms, ammunition, explosives, and grenades and also with two computerized wireless sets. To sustain his group, Mohammed Ramzan was also handed over a sizeable amount in Indian currency, added the senior police officer as the aircraft touched down on the heavily guarded Srinagar airfield.

'But do you think that the majority of the locals who have been at the bitter end of this conflict since 1947 are still supporting this kind of activity, and what about the APHC, the All Party Hurriyat Conference, and on whose side are they on?"'asked Monty while taking a lift in the police officer's staff car that was being escorted by a group of armed policemen.

'"Well the word 'Hurriyat' means freedom, but the party that was formed on 10th March, 1993 as an alliance of 26 political, social and religious organizations is only a year old and they have no set agenda it seems. It is more of a splinter organization and like most political parties in the country their members are also waiting to have a taste of the Kashmir pie. While one group that is led by Mirwaiz Maulvi Omar Faroukh favours independence, the other led by Geelani favours the accession of Kashmir to Pakistan, and though some of their leaders during their recent visit to Delhi on 8th April did say that they were ready for talks without any reservations and without prejudice with peoples from all levels for solving the Kashmir dispute, but it is easier said than done my friend," said the police officer while inviting Monty to be his guest at his residence and more so because of the tension in the valley his and family was not staying with him in Srinagar.

Monty's three days stay at Srinagar as the guest of the police officer not only helped him to understand the difficult task the Indian intelligence agencies have to undertake in a hostile and thankless environment, but also the risks involved in trying to obtain information from an uncooperative and scared local population. And as far as his own business was concerned, the locals for the sake of money were most willing to supply him with whatever was required for Monty's export business but only at an additional cost. This was on the pretext that extorting money by the militants from them had become part of the business and it therefore only added to the cost. But what surprised Monty even more when he returned from Srinagar to Delhi was the warning that was issued by the Supreme Court to Mr TN Seshan, the Chief Election Commissioner of India to mend his ways. It seems that Seshan was in the process of unilaterally enforcing a non-statutory model code of conduct for the forthcoming general elections, and since he was getting rather powerful usurping the powers of the states and which at times included that of the judiciary too, he had therefore been cut to size.

"It is indeed a real pity that the man who was trying to bring in a semblance of honesty and fair play in the country's corrupt political system, has to be chided like an errant schoolboy and told not to mess around," said Monty to his old friend Unni when they met at the Press Club of India for their weekly pow-wow session.

"Yes it is rather unfortunate and especially when one sees the rapid criminalization of politics in this country, whereby even a hardened illiterate criminal serving his term in jail and in the garb of a so called 'Neta' and a two pice political leader is allowed to stand for elections," said Unnikrishnan somewhat disgustedly.

"That apart, but do you think that the stink from the Bofors gun scandal which is still in the air will be whipped up again for the forthcoming elections," asked Monty, as Unni ordered his usual gin with a dash of bitters,while Monty settled for his good old mug of chilled beer.

"Well the crude manner by which the Congress Party with the help of the bureaucracy has been scuttling the issue ever since the day Mr Quattarochhi with his family like a thief quietly sneaked out of the country, this factor may well be capitalized upon by the opposition and especially so by the BJP, the Bharatiya Janata Party who under the dynamic leadership of Atal Behari Vajpai seem to be gaining ground every day. And the recent high level meeting of the 36 leaders of that party at Sariska that was also attended by the RSS General Secretary H.V. Seshadri and Joint General Secretary K. Sudershan only further enforces the view that they will take a hard Hinduvta line in order to come to power,"said Unni

"But I wonder why all our big political party head honchos always want to go to the Sariska Tiger sanctuary to hold their important conclaves. Even when Rajiv Gandhi was in the chair, he too preferred that location to discuss important issues with his selected circle of close friends and advisers," said Monty.

"Well for one, the place is only 200 kilometers from Delhi. It is not only a secluded spot that is well guarded by the tigers inside the forest, but also by the human 'Black Cats' who prevent snoopy correspondents like yours truly to pry around. And lastly our great political leaders are no less than the tigers and the leopards that are found there. In fact some of them are even worse than some of the man-eaters as they keep changing spots for their selfish political gains," said Unni rather sarcastically and with a sly grin on his face.

Meanwhile in Bombay, on the morning of 20th May, 1994, while Peevee was busy signing a new contract with a top film production company to do three more feature films with them and the news arrived that Miss India had been crowned Miss Universe, he just could not believe it. That very evening when Peevee saw the crowning on TV and those tears of unbelievable joy on Sushmita Sen's beautiful face, he immediately called up his parents in Delhi and told them to switch on the idiot box.

Born on 19th November, 1975, the 19 year old daughter of Wing Commander Shubir Sen and Shubra Sen from the Indian Air Force had created history They just could not believe that their daughter had become the first Indian to beat 76 other world beauty contestants for the coveted Miss Universe crown and title. The girl who had once thought of taking up journalism as a career was now being thronged by journalists and photographers from all over the world, and with that stunning win by her, India was really on the road to liberalization too, thought Peevee as he wrote to his Mom number 2 in Havana while enclosing the paper cutting of the stunning Bangali girl with the million dollar smile.

In Pakistan too there were celebrations but in a different sort of way as Arif Rehman and his wife Ruksana Begum who were in Islamabad as invitees for a seminar on the role of United Nations Peace Keeping Force in third world countries joined the delegates for the farewell dinner. Their elder son Major General Aslam Rehman Khan was also one of the participants in that international seminar that had been organized by the Pakistan GHQ. However, the one person who impressed Arif Rehman the most was Major General Pervez Musharraf, the dashing DGMO, and Director General of Military Operations of the Pakistan Army. And though the panel of eminent speakers included Jamshed Marker, Pakistan's Ambassador to the United Nations, Lt Gen KM Arif a former Vice Chief, and Agha Shahi the former Foreign Secretary, but they all spoke with an anti-western stance. But when Musharraf came on the rostrum, he spoke frankly and factually and with competence and credibility.

"I must say the DGMO had done his home work thoroughly, and he not only spoke with facts and figures, but he also brought home the point that it was the vested interests of some of the more powerful countries who at times were more of an hindrance than an asset in such peace keeping duties and which is undoubtedly true," said Arif Rehman to a group defense attaches and advisors who had also been invited for the seminar.

'Yes and I also think that the role of such peacekeepers should be spelt out clearly by the UN and they should be completely impartial while carrying out their duties," said the Indian Military Attaché as a few others including Arif Rehman and his Begum Sahiba congratulated India for having produced a stunning Miss Universe.

And while the Indian press went all gaga about Sushmita, and the political parties in India, big and small geared up for the next general elections, India on the 4th and 6th of June, 1994 also successfully tested the short range surface to surface Prithvi missile from its testing range at Chandipur. Having achieved the required optimum range of 250 Kms, it not only got Pakistan worried, but also the United States, and as a result of which, Pakistan not only stepped up its own missile development program, but also it's militant activity in the Kashmir Valley. Three days later, when the controversial high flying Yogi, Dhirendra Brahmachari died in a plane crash, a lot of tongues started wagging. The Yogi's private aircraft had crashed not far from his ashram at Patni Top, near Udhampur in Jammu and Kashmir, but the rumours were that he had been conveniently eliminated by vested interests. However, some feared that it may have been shot down by Pakistani militants using a stinger missile. Two days earlier, when two British citizens were abducted by Kashmiri militants at Aroo, near Pahalgam, it looked that Pakistan was once again desperate to internationalize the Kashmir problem. To add to further woes of the Narasimha Rao's government, the opposition parties had also called for the resignation of Kalpanath Rai, India's Food Minister and two other ministers for their role in the sugar scandal and the Bombay stock market downturn that had shocked the nation. They alleged that while the Food Minister had willfully delayed a million ton of sugar imports so as to allow pro-Congress sugar lobbies and companies to rake in windfall profits, the other two ministers Mr Shankaran and Mr Thakur were held responsible in allowing 1.5 billion dollars of government securities that were held by Indian and foreign banks being diverted into speculating in the Bombay Stock Exchange. And while all these scandalous stories were being played up by the Pakistan and the Indian media, Fazal Rehman with his family having spent most of his home leave in Dhaka, boarded the long flight back to Washington DC. Enroute they stopped by for a few days in Paris to catch up with all the news from cousin Saira and her family.

With the football world cup about to begin in the United States, Fazal's young son Shafiq Rehman presented Tojo with 'Stricker,' a dog in red, white and blue uniform with a soccer ball, which was the official mascot for the competition. Not to be left behind Sameera who was soon going to be nineteen presented her cousin Sherry with a set of Elton John's music CD's and Ludwig Beethoven's famous sonatas. Sherry who had started learning the piano in Moscow as a hobby was now serious in completing her diploma from a recognized music school in Paris and she on an average therefore devoted a minimum of three to four hours every day practicing on the piano. That evening before supper, when she entertained all of them with a medley of songs that ranged from the age old favourite 'Que Sera Sera' to Bruce Springstee'n Hotel California, and finally ended up with the Elton John number 'Don't Let the Sun Go Down on Me,' even her father Shiraz was pleasantly surprised. Later that evening of 17th June, 1994 as they all watched the opening ceremony of the FIFA World Cup live on television, 12 year old Shafiq Rehman who was mad about football had his eyes firmly glued to the idiot box. When all the 24 teams that had qualified stood proudly in silence and took their solemn oath, Shafiq prayed that his favourite team Brazil should win. Little later as Diana Ross the famous American singer dressed in a red jacket and trousers took the penalty spot kick with her pointed toe, which was a part of the show and missed the target completely while the goal post split into two and the goalkeeper jumped out of the way, the crowd went delirious with that gimmick. And finally when Oprah Winfrey the compere for the event fell through the dais, the spectators including those watching the event did not find it very funny. But when the handsome young American President Bill Clinton declared the tournament open and the Germans got ready to take on Bolivia in the inaugural match everybody was surprised that it was a complete full house. With the USA hosting the finals for the first time and in a country where football was not at all a popular sport, this was indeed rather surprising. But it was a welcome sign for the organizers. FIFA had no doubt taken a big risk and gamble, but they were now confident that the nine venues that they had selected in the United States and which stretched from the east to the west and from the north to the south would give them the necessary financial returns and encourage more Americans to take on the sport more seriously.

On the 17th of July for the world cup football finals between Brazil and Italy, Salim Rehman and his wife Aasma hosted a party at their residence. Out of the dozen couples who were there, the majority of them favoured Brazil to win, but Salim Rehman was backing the Italians. Both the countries had won the world cup thrice and everybody was expecting a thrilling and hard fought final, but it turned out to be a lackluster performance by both the teams as both sides got into a defensive mode and as a result of which not a single goal was scored by either side even after 120 minutes of play. And for the first time in world cup football history the winner was required to be decided by a penalty shootout. With every spot kick as the excitement gathered momentum, even the ladies who were otherwise busy gossiping most of the time were excited. After four rounds, when Brazil was leading 3-2 and Italy's star player Roberto Baggio was getting ready to take the final spot kick that would have kept Italy's hopes alive, Salim Rehman in anticipation popped open the champagne bottle. But to his bad luck, when Baggio kicked the ball over the cross bar and that gave the Brazilians their fourth world cup win, the happiest person was little Shafiq who quickly took the bottle from his uncle Salim Rehman and filled up all the glasses. As all the crazy Brazilian supporters at the Rose Bowl in Pasadena, California went crazy with joy, the celebrations in Brazil continued for the whole week. For Diego Maradona of Argentina who was Salim Rehman's all time favourite it was however a sad ending to his career. He was expelled from the tournament after the very first match, when he failed a drug test. Another tragic story was that of Andres Escobar of Columbia who was shot dead in cold blood outside a bar in a Meddellin suburb. His crime was that he had scored a self goal against the lowly placed United States during Columbia's first round match and which Columbia eventually lost 2-.1 and was therefore eliminated subsequently.

CHAPTER-20

A Different Kind of War

No sooner had the war for world football supremacy ended; a different kind of war engulfed the world. On 5th August, 1994 when one of the main conspirators in the March 1993 Bombay bomb blast case, Yakub Abdul Razak Memon the younger brother of Tiger Memon was arrested by the CBI at the New Delhi railway station, the Narasimha Rao Congress government was totally upbeat. But when a happy S.B. Chavan, the Home Minister of India on Doordarshan TV reiterated that Pakistan's complicity in that horrendous massacre of the innocents was beyond doubt, Peevee wondered whether the real masterminds behind those awful massacres would ever be caught and brought to justice. According to one reliable source, Yakub Memon was tired of running from pillar to post like a fugitive and had therefore voluntarily surrendered because he and his family were on the run for nearly a year and a half, and they now feared that the ISI may also eliminate them. His wife Raheen was also expecting his child and moreover he was not pulling on well with his elder brother Tiger Memon who was the brain behind those deadly blasts. Another version was that Yakub after landing at Khatmandu on 21st July, 1994 by a PIA flight with a Pakistani passport in the new name of Yusuf Mohammed Ahmed had checked into at a hotel in the city. But three days later he it seemed developed cold feet and was back at the airport to catch a return flight to Karachi. But while conducting during the security check when two passports, one Indian and the other Pakistani were found in his brief case and since he also was on the Interpol wanted list, he was immediately arrested and after joint interrogation by the Nepalese and Indian police was handed over to the CBI who secretly brought him to Delhi for further detailed interrogation.

Reacting vehemently to the Indian Home Minister's charges, the Prime Minister of Pakistan, Benazir Bhuuto said very bluntly that there was no question of Pakistan's involvement in the Bombay blasts and that it was a pack of lies and a ruse by the Indians to divert attention from its own internal problems including that of gross human rights abuse in Kashmir. But a few days later in order to tell the world how deeply Pakistan was involved, when India aired a live interview of Yakub Memon over 'Doordarshan' the national television network and Yakub made no bones while implicating his brother and Taufiq Jalaiwala another Don who was also a close associate of Dawood Ibrahim, Monty and Reeta who were watching the interview now had no doubts whatsoever as to who were the real culprits behind those mass murders. In fact all of them together with the Pakistani ISI had conspired and master minded the Bombay blasts as revenge killings for the demolition of the Babri Masjid and the killing of Muslims during the Bombay riots that followed soon thereafter. And as Monty and Reeta listened to Yakub's version on how he and his family were duped into the conspiracy by his elder brother, it seemed more like a confession by the young chartered accountant and a plea for mercy for the family.

"Well now that Yakub wants to come clean, the family too I guess will also soon return and this will definitely help in the progress of the trial of all the others including the actor Sanjay Dutt who is also one of the accused," said Reeta.

"But what is the damn use of catching only these small fries who allegedly and probably unknowingly only conspired in that heinous crime, whereas the main culprits like Dawood Ibrahim, Taufiq Jalaiwala and Tiger Memon are sitting pretty in Karachi under the watchful eyes of the ISI, and which of course is being vehemently denied by Mrs Bhutto," said Monty.

"But may be Yakub has very wisely struck a deal with the Indian Home Ministry and based on his confession and information it could therefore now be possible for India to apply more pressure through the International forums and have these kingpins extradited to India," said Reeta.

"That I am afraid is all wishful thinking and even if Dawood volunteers to come back and face trial, the ISI will never allow it and they may even bump him off for good," said Monty as he explained to Reeta how some custom officials including a very senior Custom's officer from Bombay whose prime duty was to check smuggling of contraband goods had for the greed of money allowed the big consignment of the RDX explosives, arms, ammunition and grenades to be smuggled into the city.

And while the accusations and counter accusations between the governments of Pakistan and India continued unabated, there were problems on the other side of the world too. In Communist Cuba the pot was kept boiling by the anti Castro agitators who had started demonstrating against

their bearded leader and his socialist policies. Such protests in the capital
Havana and in other big cities of that small island nation were simply
unheard off ever since Castro came to power way back in 1959. However,
on 5th August, 1994, which happened to be a Friday and while Shupriya was
hosting a lunch for the trade delegation from India at the Nacionale Hotel
on the Malecon, she was surprised when all of a sudden she received a note
from the management requesting her not to leave the hotel till the all clear
was given by them. She was not told the reason why, and nor did she have
a clue about the massive protest demonstration that was taking place a few
kilometers away, till she overheard one of the stewards who was supervising
the lunch telling a waitress that Castro's days were probably numbered and
that more Cubans were joining the march on the Malecon. The Malecon
with its 7 kilometre drive along the sea shore was like the Marine Drive of
Cuba and with the monumental Hotel Nacional de Cuba on the waterfront,
it provided a bird's eye view of the capital. In order to check what was
happening on the Malecon, Shupriya with her Second Secretary went up the
lift to the top most eighth floor where in one of the double rooms the head
of the Indian trade delegation had been accommodated.The famous hotel
in the heart of the city centre and overlooking the grand Havana harbour
was opened in December 1930 as a posh tourist hotel for the rich Americans
visiting Cuba both for work and pleasure. While the going was good it was
patronized not only by eminent people like Winston Churchill, the Duke
and Duchess of Windsor, Ernest Hemingway, Errol Flynn, Frank Sinatra
and such like others, but also by the notorious Italian American gangsters
like Lucky Luciano and Frank Costello. Following the Cuban revolution by
Castro, and with no tourists from the American mainland coming to the
island, the hotel initially was mainly used to accommodate diplomats and
foreign government officials. After the collapse of the Soviet Union, and
with the Cuban economy in the doldrums, the hotel went through a difficult
period till it was renovated in 1992 to attract the wealthy foreign tourists
and foreign government delegations who could afford the five star luxuries in
Communist Cuba.

Armed with a pair of fairly powerful binoculars that the enterprising
Second Secretary had purchased from one of the shops in the hotel,
what Shupriya witnessed that day was something unbelievable as far as
Communist Cuba was concerned. The protest that began peacefully near
the Deauville Hotel, on the Malecon had suddenly turned violent. The root
cause of all this was the floundering economy of the country which began
from the day the Soviet Union disintegrated. Cuba was highly dependent on

its trade with Russia and the erstwhile Warsaw Pact countries, but with all that having dried up, it was now a hand to mouth existence for most of the Cubans. In the face of continuing political repression and an ever worsening economic crisis, a large number of Cubans since late 1993 had been fleeing the country. However, the mass protest by his own people on that day was not going to be taken lightly by the man who had been ruling over them for more than three decades. As the protests on the streets grew louder, Castro brought in his famous fast response forces that were also known as the Blas Roca Brigades. These were members of Cuba's state security that was organized, controlled, mobilized and put into action when required by the Castro regime.

When Shupriya from the hotel room witnessed the brutal manner in which Castro's henchmen went after the unarmed peaceful demonstrators, she was really shocked. Armed with thick chains and staves, they mercilessly beat up those that opposed them or came in their way. The protestors were demanding the right to emigrate and which Castro had forbidden. And when a few police officers tried to prevent a group of Cubans from launching a raft, the hostile crowd turned on them and seized their weapons. It now became a free for all as spontaneous riots followed in the downtown commercial area of the Cuban capital. Late that evening as Shupriya flying the Indian tricolor flag on her official car and escorted by an armed Cuban patrol returned to the Indian Embassy at Calle 21, Number 202, at Vedado Plaza, the crackdown on dissidents and opposition groups had already begun.

Feeling the heat and the unprecedented mass demonstration by the people, when the Cuban leader as usual accused the imperialists for plotting against his ouster, Shupriya was not at all surprised. And on the very next day, when Fidel Castro in an address to his people criticized the Americans for encouraging illegal emigration, it was nothing new either. But what was really surprising was the declaration by the Cuban leader that the government would no longer detain those who sought to leave on their own boats and rafts. At an internationally televised news conference, when Castro asserted that the rioting was caused by rumours of a US sponsored boat lift to Miami, Shupriya simply took it with a pinch of salt. However, during the next fortnight, when hundreds of Cubans started arriving daily in Miami, it spelt a crisis situation for the United States government also. With the Governor of Florida, Lawton Chiles refusing to accommodate any more Cubans, the Clinton administration had no other choice but to announce a major shift in U.S policy towards Cuba. Whereas, for the last 35 years the

United States welcomed any Cuban escaping Castro's regime as a refugee with open arms, but henceforth and as per Clinton's orders, no Cubans seeking to enter the country illegally would be allowed to step foot on US territory. As a result of this a large number of them were now being detained at the US naval base at the nearby Guantanamo Bay. But by the end of August 1994, with both the United States and Cuba willing to discuss the future emigration policy on a reciprocal basis, and with the tension having eased between both the countries, Shupriya wondered as to how a man like Castro had managed to survive for so long while sitting under the very nose of a super power.

Soon after the takeover by Castro and by the early autumn of 1960, the US government was engaged in a secret campaign to remove Castro from power. On 3rd January, 1961, President Eisenhower broke off all ties with Cuba giving the excuse that Fidel Castro had provoked him once too often. Then there was the American Bay of Pigs fiasco which was followed by the Cuban missile crisis in November 1962. No less than a dozen attempts at assassination had been made on the man, ranging from the use of an exploding cigar, to a mafia style shooting by the underworld of America that had the blessings of none other than Robert Kennedy, the then Attorney General. And though they also tried to kill him by poisoning his food through a Miami mafia syndicate, but yet the man was still living. And one day when the bearded Cuban leader himself admitted in jest that if surviving assassination attempts were an Olympic event, he would easily win the gold medal, he was simply speaking the truth and nothing but the truth. In one bizarre case when his own girlfriend and ex-lover Marita Lorenz aided by the CIA attempted to smuggle a jar of cold cream containing poison pills into Castro's room, and Castro having come to know of it even gave the lady his own gun so that she could kill him, it only probably showed how much he loved her. But it seems that her nerves failed to carry out that act. That was way back in 1960. There were also reports that Marita who was the daughter of a German ship captain and an American mother and who was born in Bremen. Germany on 18th August, 1939 had first met Castro in February 1959 in Havana. There were also reports that she had also borne him a love child. And if that was true then the child today would have been 34 years old thought Shupriya as she kissed Peevee's photograph in the latest issue of the Filmfare magazine and called it a day.

On the 17th of September, 1994 since the Indian mission in Cuba was also accredited to the two independent Caribbean nations of Haiti and the Dominican Republic, Shupriya as the Indian Ambassador to all the three countries landed at the Haitian capital of Port-au-Prince on an official visit. The small island of Haiti once known as Hispaniola was discovered by Christopher Columbus in 1492, and was initially a Spanish colony till the French in 1664 took control of the island and thereafter with the massive induction of African slaves during the 18th and 19th centuries; it soon had more blacks than whites. On 22nd August, 1791, the slaves staged a revolt and with that began the Haitian Revolution. On New Year's Day 1804, Jean Jacques Desallines having defeated the French declared independence and he gave back to the island its indigenous name of Haiti. It was the world's oldest black republic and the second oldest republic after the United States in the Western Hemisphere. During the early part of the 20th century, the small island country was plagued with a series of revolutions and bad debts and as a result of which the United States occupied the country. And it was only in 1934 under President Roosevelt's 'Good Neighbour Policy' that the US forces were withdrawn from the island. Thereafter there were a series of military coups and rule by dictators. And it was only in September 1957, that democracy was restored and which saw Dr Francois Duvalier elected as President. But the man who was also known as 'Papa Doc' however turned out to be a sadist and a ruthless dictator like Hitler and who with his para-military police that was known as the Tom Tom Macoutes he enforced a reign of terror on his people. The hated Duvalier family rule finally ended in 1986, when the old Doc died and his son Jean Claude who was also known as 'Baby Doc' took over country. But he too was soon forced to go into exile. After that followed a short period of uneasy calm till 1989, when General Avril staged another coup and came to power. And it was only after a general election was held, that Jean Bartrand Aristide, a former Roman Catholic Priest on 7th February 1991 was elected as the President. But his rule was also rather short lived and he too was ousted on 30th September 1991 in a military coup by the Haitian army. Aristide was being supported by the United States while in exile and the US government therefore enforced an economic blockade which further weakened the island's already tottering economy.The United States wanted democracy to be restored and Aristide reinstalled to complete his term of office. On 15th September 1994, when President Clinton in a television address reiterated that the military rulers of Haiti must step down, it was a veiled threat and knowing the likely repercussions that could follow, the military leaders agreed to hand over power. Therefore on 18th September, when Shupriya was in the Haiitan capital and Clinton announced it to the American people, she felt indeed very happy. But on the very next day, when the American marines landed in Haiti to put 'Operation Uphold Democracy' in motion, it only brought to focus that might was always right. And with Cuba not willing to toe the American line, the U.S. could not afford to have another small but belligerent island nation led by corrupt army officers as another next door troublesome neighbour. As it is the island was being used as a safe transit point by the powerful Cali drug cartel of Columbia and much of which was being smuggled into the United States.

During her four day stay on the island, Shupriya was shocked to learn that most of the Haitian senior army officers and the police officers were neck deep in the lucrative cocaine smuggling racket and that the kingpin not so long ago was none other than the Police Chief himself, Colonel Michel Francois who had been trained at the US Army School of the Americas that was originally based in Panama and in 1984 had moved to Fort Benning in Gerogia. Known by its initials as the SOA and in Spanish as La Escuela de Golpes, this school of coups specialized in training pro American forces from Latin American countries. But what also surprised Shupriya was the fact that it was Senator John Kerry of Massachusetts who not so very long ago as the head of the subcommittee on terrorism and drug trafficking in his report had very categorically pointed out that not only Haiti's military rulers were very much into this racket, but General Manuel Noriega of Panama was also in the same unholy business. Accordingly President George Bush then ordered military action on 20th December, 1989 against Panama and claimed it to be a major victory in the war against drugs. According to the US, Panama was acting as the banker and transit point for the cocaine smugglers from the cartels of Columbia and since most of it was finding its way into the lucrative United States market it had to be stopped at all costs.

In mid September, while Shupriya at Port-au-Prince was busy establishing better relations with the leaders of the pro Aristide group in Haiti, Shiraz with his past experience of having served in Russia earlier was sent to Moscow from Paris on a fortnight's temporary duty. This was primarily to foster better ties with Russia's new government leaders and ministers. After a shaky start, Boris Yeltsin, an engineer by profession who was born on 1st February, 1931 in the village of Butka in the Swerdlovsk District of Russia was now in full control of that massive landmass that stretched from the Baltic Sea to the Pacific Ocean. Despite losing his thumb and the index finger of his left hand in a grenade accident while in school when he with a few friends having sneaked into a Red Army base pilfered with the hand grenades that they had stolen, he was otherwise quite healthy. And the big booze loving and big built Russian in order to implement his radical economic reforms had now vested himself with special powers. Having inducted his own loyal followers into his cabinet, including a few from the erstwhile dreaded KGB, Yeltsin was confident of having his way.

Knowing that the Russian ladies loved designer wear dresses and French perfumes, while the men preferred expensive wrist watches and rare malt skotch whisky, Shiraz with a couple of suitcases full of Yves St Laurent and Pierre Cardin dresses of various sizes, Christian Dior and Coco Chanel perfumes and cosmetics together with half a dozen expensive Cartier wrist watches and a few crates of JB's rare malt whisky landed up in Moscow on the 17th of September, 1994. But having spent most of his time entertaining his Russian friends and making new contacts, Shiraz however felt sad for the ordinary Russian people and especially the elderly women folk whose only livelihood now was to beg on the streets. He could not ever imagine that the people of that once powerful country and a super power at that were literally on the verge of an economic collapse. The law and order situation in the capital that was once the pride of the Soviet Union and where earlier one could safely walk on the streets at anytime of the day or night was now a thing of the past. Moscow was now a mugger's paradise and where even for a measly one dollar bill one could even get killed. In good old days one was scared of being picked up by the KGB, but now they were afraid of the powerful Russian mafia, and ironically most of them were the same people who still not so very long ago were probably being supported by the communist party card holders and the KGB. The Russian rouble was valueless and there was a heavy demand for those in power for the American dollar and the pound sterling. Giving a bribe to get things done was nothing new in that country. It was present even during the erstwhile tight communist rule. Therefore as a gesture of goodwill and to keep all avenues open for the future, Shiraz without embarrassing his contacts at the government level, he gave each one of them a loan of a thousand dollars. And it was with the tacit understanding that it was payable when able. He of course knew very well that those 5000 dollars he would never get it back, but it was nevertheless a good investment for the future in Yeltsin's Mother Russia, thought Shiraz. And in any case it was not going from his own pocket.

During his stay in Moscow, Shiraz also learnt that the export of Russian arms clandestinely by the Russian mafia was also now big business and that some of the clients included both the CIA and the MI6 too. These foreign intelligence agencies were not doing it directly though, but through their agents covertly, and most of these were from the stockpiles that the

Soviet Armed Forces had left behind in the new independent nations of neighbouring Latvia, Lithuania and Estonia. All the three small nations which were earlier part of the erstwhile Soviet Union were now independent free countries and since they were all conveniently situated on the Baltic coast, it was therefore easy to carry out such kind of illegal activities from its sea ports. One of the ports that his Russian contact mentioned to him was that of Tallinn, the capital of Estonia. In order to probe a little deeper into the matter and in order to have a reasonably good cover story, Shiraz requested his wife to fly down with the children to Stockholm on 27th for a short holiday with their old Swedish friends and he promised to join them there on 28th September morning by taking the night boat ferry from Tallinn.

It was on 25th September evening, a Sunday that Shiraz landed in Tallinn and having made himself comfortable in Hotel St Petersburg which was in the heart of the town, he made a quick survey of the harbour. Next morning having booked his ticket on the MS Estonia, in the upper deck class for the 27th evening ferry to Stockholm, he took a long walk along the harbour to check the type of loads that were awaiting dispatch. Finding nothing very unusual, he did some sightseeing of that small little town and returned to his room in the hotel. Early next morning, when he again went for a casual stroll along the harbour, he found the massive ferry cruise ship MS Estonia that could carry 2000 passengers and 460 cars was already in the process of being loaded with various types of cargos that were packed in various sizes of both metal and wooden containers. At around 5 o'clock in the evening having spoken to Saira in Stockholm to have him picked up next morning at 9.30 which was the scheduled arrival time of the ferry at Stokholm, Shiraz checked out of the hotel and boarded the ferry two hours before the scheduled departure time of 1900 hours. Though there was a nip in the air and the sea was slightly rough that evening, but it was nothing unusual during that time of the year. With the cruise ferry offering a lot of entertainment and games for the passengers on board, Shiraz did not even realize when the anchors were away and the ship with its 989 passengers and crew was on the high seas to Stockholm. This was not the first time that he was doing an overnight ferry over the Baltic, He had done it twice before with his family, when he was posted in Sweden and that was not very long ago. The first time it was from Stockholm to Turku in Finland and subsequently from Malmo to Copenhagen in Denmark. In order to find out from the crew the type of cargo such ferries were generally allowed to carry on such overnight trips and the cost involved, Shiraz befriended one of the security officers, an Estonian who had served in the Soviet navy earlier.

"'Well Sir there is no specific restrictions and it all depends on the space available in the holds and as long as it has been cleared by the local customs, we ferry anything from tiny match boxes to giant size trailers. And since this is an overnight ferry, the cost of transportation of such cargo is very reasonable too, We generally however make our profits from the slot machines, the discos, the duty free shops, the cabarets shows and other games of skill that we provide on board,' said the security officer somewhat nonchalantly. Realizing that the security officer was rather secretive, Shiraz decided to spend his time at the bar and at the slot machines. At around midnight after a sumptuous buffet dinner and a few nightcaps Shiraz retired to his reserved single berth cabin on the upper most deck. And since he was not feeling very sleepy he kept reading Jeffery Archer's latest best seller 'Honour Among Theives.' It was a political thriller that was set against the 1991 Gulf war and having reached practically the climax of the story, Shiraz got so very engrossed with the book that he decided to finish it on that very night itself. Then suddenly at around 1:20 A.M. that night, when he was practically nearing the end of the book, he found that there was an unusual heavy starboard list and minutes later an alarm was also sounded. Realizing that there was drastically something wrong, he immediately changed into his trousers and shirt and with a sweater in hand rushed out of his cabin door and on to the deck only to find that the huge ship was capsizing rapidly and an alarm to abandon ship had been sounded. Seeing the massive vessel lurching some 30 degrees towards starboard, Shiraz having got hold of a life jacket from the deck and without waiting for any orders instinctively jumped into the cold waters of the Baltic Sea and swam as far as he could from the ill fated ship. But what seemed most strange was that the big cruise liner with most of its passengers who were Swedes and Estonians had within a span 40 minutes completely disappeared from the scene.

To the good luck of those few like Shiraz who at that time were on deck and had managed to jump out in the nick of time, there arrived on the scene at around 2:15 another ferry ship. It was the MS Martella that had received the S.O.S. call and had come to their rescue. Little while later helicopters were also on the job looking for survivors. Luckily for Shiraz, and thanks to the life jacket, he had been saved from what would have otherwise surely been a watery grave for him. At dawn he was spotted by a rescue helicopter and by the time it was daylight he was on board the MS Martella.On arriving at Stockholm, when he narrated that harrowing experience to his family, they just could not believe that a ferry cruise ship of that gigantic a size and that to without facing extreme rough weather conditions could suddenly disappear into the sea taking along with it 852 passengers and the crew to their watery graves.

And it was only months after an enquiry was conducted that the world came to know the cause of the disaster, but that was not the whole truth it seems. According to one official report there was a typical seasonal storm in the Baltic Sea and the accident occurred when the locks on the bow visor gave way under the strain of the waves. When the visor got separated from the ship, it damaged the ramp which covered the opening of the car deck behind the visor. The sudden surge of the water into the car deck destabilized the ship completely and it went down in a jiffy. But according to another source, the ship was also believed to be carrying a secret cargo of military equipment that had been smuggled on board as part of NATO's ongoing effort to monitor the technicalities and development of Russian made armaments and weapons. The fact that these operations were being carried out secretly and clandestinely by some vested groups with the help of the CIA and MI6 was already known to Shiraz, but there was no concrete proof. There was yet another rumour that the Russians having got wind of the smuggling of arms that was being carried out by the cruise ferry, they therefore had sabotaged it. Well whatever was the truth, Shiraz was indeed very lucky to have escaped unscathed.

A week later in end September 1994, with Saddam Hussein of Iraq adopting an attitude of non cooperation with the UNSCOM inspectors and once again mobilizing his forces for deployment on the Iraqi-Kuwait border, it looked as if a second round was in the offing in the tension filled region of the Gulf States. The UNSCOM, United Nations Special Commission was created to ensure that Iraq complied with the policies that were laid down by the world body in the production and use of weapons of mass destruction. This came about soon after the 1990 Gulf war ended and there were grave apprehensions that Iraq too was probably on the verge of becoming a nuclear power. There was no doubt that Iraq during the long Iran-Iraq war had used biological and chemical weapons against the Iranians and the Kurds, and the possibility of these being used against Kuwait and its American allies could not therefore be ruled out in future. As a result of this recent standoff, when the United States too started redeploying troops in Kuwait, Shiraz was worried that this sort of brinkmanship by both sides would only worsen the fragile peace in the Gulf Region. Luckily better sense prevailed, when the United Nations Security Council threatened the Iraqi regime with dire consequences and Saddam on 15ᵗʰ October, 1994 withdrew his troops from the border with Kuwait.

And while there was an easing of tension in the Gulf Region, a very charming and pretty girl from India was waiting to take the centre stage in Souh Africa. And on 17ᵗʰ November, 1994 when Aishwaraya Rai of India won the Miss World Contest that was held in Sun City, South Africa, it was a record double that no other country in the world had ever achieved before. By winning both the Miss Universe and the Miss World title in the same year, Indian women like the Venezuelans had been catapulted into the top most rung of the most beautiful women in the world. And it was not only the charming good looks and vital statistics of the Indian participants that had got them the coveted crowns, but also the dignified and confident manner in which they gave their intelligent answers to the panel of eminent judges.

Born in Mangalore on 1ˢᵗ November, 1973, the girl from Arya Vidya Mandir High School and Ruparel College, Bombay had walked away with the Miss World title in a trot, and the first one to congratulate her was none other than Nelson Mandela, the President of South Africa. When the crowning was telecast all over the world, Shiraz and Saira who were watching it live on television were both stunned by the good looks and the captivating smile of the beautiful and charming winner.

"It is indeed a real pity and I wonder why Pakistan, which also has some stunning beauties does not participate in such competitions. Because I personally do not find anything vulgar or degrading in showing off one's figure and brain power," said Shiraz somewhat casually to his wife.

"And neither do I, but to bring about such a radical change when our lady television news readers even today are required to follow the Islamic dress code and have their heads covered, this is next to impossible. And mind you though we have now a mod young woman Prime Minister in Benazir Bhutto and who for the second time is sitting on that chair and who had most of her education in America and England, even she I am afraid for her own political survival will never allow a 'Miss Pakistan' contest to take place in this country,' said Saira.

'Yes I agree and under the present circumstances one cannot ever imagine a 'Miss Pakistan' on the ramp parading in a swimming costume. But let us hope that times change for a more liberalized and progressive Pakistan in future," said their 16 year old daughter Sherry.

"However, I personally still feel that Shusmita Sen with her height and figure looked more elegant, graceful and charming than Aishwariya, though

Mamma feels that it is the other way round," added Sherry who was turning out to be even more beautiful than her mother and grandmother both put together.

"Well as far as Femina Miss India contest was concerned it was practically a photo finish between Shusmita and Aishwariya, and I must confess that both of them are indeed stunningly beautiful," said Shiraz as 11 year old Tojo walked in with his new hockey stick and told his father that it was time that he played with him. Tojo was celebrating Pakistan's world cup win in hockey. Led by the mercurial Shahbaz Ahmed, Pakistan at Sydney had won the hockey world cup after a lapse of 12 years.

And while Pakistan was celebrating their world cup victory, the Americans were desperately trying to rein in the Iraqi leaders with threats of dire reprisals if Saddam Hussein continued with the production of weapons of mass destruction. Simultaneously in Russia, the Russian President, Boris Yeltsin was getting ready to sort out the Chechens who were trying to break away from his Mother Russia.

Chechnya, situated in the Caucasian Region of Southern Russia was first invaded by the Russians during the reign of Catherine the Great in the 18th Century and was later incorporated first into Bolshevist Russia and then into the Soviet Union. In 1936, Stalin created the Chechen-Ingush Autonomous Soviet Socialist Republic. After the collapse of the Soviet Union in December, 1991 the Chechens, most of whom were Muslims under the former Soviet General Dzhokhar Dudayev decided to break away from Yeltsin's Russia, and in 1993 formed the independent Chechen Republic of Ichkeria with General Dudayev as its first President. This resulted first in a bitter civil war between the ethnic Chechens and the non-Chechens most of whom were Russians. In August 1994, a coalition force from the opposing factions that were based north of Chechnya and who were being supported clandestinely by the Russians launched an armed campaign to oust Dudayev and the Russian troops also joined in by setting up a military blockade of the new republic. In mid October 1994, the opposition forces with Russian troops launched a clandestine attack on the capital Grozny and when that proved disastrous, unmarked Russian aircrafts began bombing the city. On November 26-27, a second and a larger attack on Grozny was launched, but General Dudayev's forces repulsed the attack. And what became even more embarrassing to the leaders of new Russia was when the Chechens captured some 20 Russian army regulars and 50 other Russian citizens who were believed to have been working as informers for the Russian FSK, the state security agency that had replaced the dreaded KGB.

On 29th November, an angry and desperate Boris Yeltsin issued an ultimatum to all the warring factions in Chechnya to lay down their arms and surrender, and when Grozny refused, the stage was set for a massive Russian intervention. On the 1st of December, 1994 the Russians forces carried out a heavy aerial bombardment of Chechnya's many military targets and the capital Grozny. They were hoping that this show of force would eventually weaken the resolve of the Chechens to fight the mighty Russian army, but they were sadly mistaken. Pavel Grachev, the Russian Defence Minister had even boasted that he could with one airborne regiment topple Dudayev within a couple of hours if need be, but that was not to be. And though the Russian troops had entered Chechnya on 11th December to establish constitutional control over the area, but the worst was yet to come.

On that very day of 11th December, 1994 while the Russian troops were engaged in suppressing the secessionist movement in Chechnya, the Philippine Airlines Flight 434 from Manila to Tokyo via Cebu was targeted by Ramzi Yousef. He was an absconding and much wanted terrorist who had earlier master minded the bombing of the World Trade Centre in New York. Ramzi it seems had been experimenting with a deadly indigenous bomb and was planning to use them in a series of attacks on commercial passenger airliners of the United States of America in the near future. Ramzi Yousef had boarded the flight in Manila under the assumed name of Armaldo Forlani and it was during the flight to Cebu that he had assembled the bomb inside the aircraft's lavatory, and having placed it under seat 26K with a timer, he with some 25 other passengers deplaned at Cebu. At 11.43 AM, as the flight on its second leg of the journey from Cebu to Tokyo was cruising at 31,000 feet over the islands near Okinawa, the bomb exploded and ripped the body of Haruki Ikegami, a 24 year old Japanese businessman who had occupied that ill fated seat at Cebu. The explosion had blown off two square feet of the cabin floor, but luckily the fuselage of the aircraft had remained intact. The lower part of Haruki's body had fallen into the cargo hold below and though ten more passengers were injured, there was no panic as Captain Ed Reyes having put in a May Day call made an emergency landing at the Naha Airport on the island of Okinawa. Luckily the Boeing 747-283B was an older version and in which the seat 24K was two seats ahead and not directly above the centre wing fuel tank of the aircraft. Because had that been the case and the bomb had exploded in a horizontal manner and not vertically, then there probably would not have been any survivors at all to tell the tale. On an experimental basis and to avoid detection, Ramzi Yousef had only used one tenth of the explosive power. His deadly plan that later became known as 'The Bojinka Plot' was to use this same lethal weapon against 12 such United States aircrafts and that too on one particular day.

Meanwhile in India with rampant corruption in the Narasimha Rao's Congress government and with an eminent journalist like Kuldip Nayar openly declaring that though Indira Gandhi may have corrupted institutions but Rao had institutionalized them, the opposition parties were demanding the resignation of the Prime Minister and those ministers who were involved in the sugar and in the Bombay Stock Exchange scandals. On 14th December, following the adverse observations in the Gian Prakash report on the sugar scandal, Mr AK Anthony the Minister of Civil Supplies had resigned. When some leading Indian newspapers alleged that Narasimha Rao was scared to force the other concerned ministers to resign for fear that they may also drag his name and that of his family into the scandals, Monty decided to check back with his old journalist friend Unnikrishnan at the Press Club.

"Well if those ministers do not resign than I am afraid his own political survival will be threatened and I am sure Narasimha Rao will not like that at all. There is no doubt and as columnist Sunil Sethi had rightly pointed out that Rao's cabinet is crawling with get-rich-quick ministers, and I am sure with the backing of those close to the Prime Minister, these tainted ministers would eventually and ultimately will be compensated adequately both monetarily, politically and otherwise also in the near future. Therefore, I won't be the least surprised if all of them resign tomorrow," said Unni.

And rightly so on the very next day 22nd December, all three of them had put in their papers. With Kalpanath Rai, Rameshwar Thakur and B. Shankaranand now out of the cabinet, Narasimha Rao felt a bit relieved. But two days later, when Arjun Singh, the Minister for Human Resources also handed in his resignation letter citing that Rao had grossly failed to provide adequate leadership to the party, it took everyone by surprise. And later at a press conference after having praised the late Rajiv Gandhi, when Arjun Singh further suggested that the Congress will greatly benefit if his widow Sonia Gandhi decided to play an active role in the affairs of the party, it was now not only quite obvious that there was a rift within the party, but there were also strong rumours that Arjun Singh's move was primarily to stake his own claim to the hot seat in the near future. As it is in the recent assembly elections in Andhra Pradesh, Karnataka, Sikkim and Goa, the Congress party had suffered crushing defeats. And with the hill people of Uttar Pradesh and those from the tribal belts of South Bihar now asking for their own states of Uttarkhand and Jharkhand respectively, the further

Balkanization of the country it seems was also around the corner. For India unfortunately it would now be caste and communal based politics that would take centre stage as far as the assembly elections to the states were concerned and that would further weaken the hold of the centre.

Meanwhile as the United States and the Philippine police went on a massive hunt to trace the origin of Ramzi's deadly bomb and the bomber, in Russia on that 11th of December the mighty Russian army launched a three pronged ground attack towards Grozny. By that surgical strike Yeltsin thought that the Chechens would soon capitulate, but his troops and tanks soon got bogged down as the Chechens fought back gallantly using guerrilla tactics of hit and run. The raw Russian ground forces that comprised mostly of newly trained conscripts from the nearby military units and formations were in a quandary. Most of them were not even aware as to why they were fighting their own people. Their morale was literally in their boots and soon a large number of them started deserting. In spite of Russia's massive air and artillery power and as casualties in the Russian army kept mounting, it was a bad 'White Christmas' for Boris Yeltsin and his Generals, some of whom including Colonel General Boris Gromov, who commanded the Soviet army in Afghanistan now resigned in protest.

On that wintry and desolate Christmas Eve night of 1994, when Salim Rehman in Moscow boarded the flight back to Islamabad to take up his new appointment as the Additional Secretary-India desk, he wondered the source from where the Chechens were getting all those arms, ammunition and man power to fight the mighty Russians. With strong rumours that those veteran Muslim Mujahideens who had fought the Russians in Afghanistan and the Serbs in Bosnia and which also included a contingent of Pakistani militant radicals were now on their way to Chechnya, and that all this was was being done under the growing umbrella of the elusive Osama Bin Laden's Al-Qaida, Salim Rehman too was now worried about its fall out on Pakistan. The very fact that some radical Sunni Muslim Mullas of Pakistan were using the 'madrassas' the religious schools in his own home province of the North West Frontier as motivational halls to train young Jehadis to promote fundamentalism and spread hatred against those who were not Sunni Muslims was itself frightening enough. And if these people ever came to power politically, it would be disastrous for the country thought Salim Rehman while requesting the stewardess for an extra pillow. He was travelling first class and wanted to catch up with some much needed sleep after the spate of farewell parties in Moscow.

While Salim Rehman on Christmas Eve was heading home, Shiraz and his family were holidaying on the French Riviera. With the children having their Christmas holidays, and in order to celebrate his recent promotion to that of an Ambassador, Shiraz had decided to give the family a treat by showing them some of the more famous tourist spots of Southern France and those of the rich and the famous on the Cote D'Azur.

Shiraz's elevation as Pakistan's Ambassador to France had come about quite unexpectedly. It was partly because of the vacancies created by some of his seniors who had sought premature retirement from service, and also was due to the fact that his predecessor was a political appointee that was made by the previous Nawaz Sharif government. With the Benazir government now in power there was also a change of policy to post career diplomats at all such important sensitive world capitals and Shiraz was fully qualified for it. It was on the 24th December, 1994 late evening that they arrived at Cannes and stayed at the popular Martinez Hotel on Bouleward de la Croisette. This was the same very hotel where Maharaja Hari Singh of Kashmir's only issue and son Dr Karan Singh was born. Shiraz was made aware of this fact when he was commissioned into the Jammu and Kashmirs Rifles in 1965, when Dr Karan Singh was an honorary Colonel of the Regiment. On 25th December, Christmas day, the family took the train to St Tropez and they spent most of the time on the beautiful beaches that was made famous by the French bombshell of the early 1960's Brigitte Bardot. On 26th afternoon, they arrived at Marseilles. It was here during the summer of1915 that the Indian Corps under Lt General Wilcox had landed to take on the Germans at Flanders during the First World War and Shiraz remembered the heroic story of how Naik Khudadad Khan from the Baluch Regiment became the first Indian to receive the coveted Victoria Cross. However it was on the 24th December evening, when they arrived at Cannes that Shiraz had learnt about the hijacking of the Air France Flight 8969 by four armed Muslim terrorists who claimed that they were members of the Algerian GIA, (Groupe Islamique Arme). And by the time they arrived at St Tropez the next day, the hijackers had already killed an Algerian policemen who was also on board the aircraft. Led by the 25 year old Abdul Abdullah Yahia, the four armed terrorists from the Armed Islamic Group posing as Algerian policemen had boarded the aircraft at the Houari Boumedienne Airport at Algiers. The flight was scheduled to take off for Paris at 11.15 hours, but could not do so because the aircraft had been surrounded by the Algerian Army's Commando Force. The desperate hijackers in order to show that they meant business then threw the dead body of the Algerian policeman on the runaway and demanded that the staircase and the chocks on the aircraft's tyres be removed and the aircraft be allowed to take off, but the standoff had continued well into the night. By that time, and on the firm assurance given by the French Prime Minister that the aircraft would be allowed to take off for Paris, the hijackers had released the 63 women and children, but the Algerian Colonel from the Commamdo Force refused to remove the staircase and the chocks. The hijackers then executed a Vietnamese diplomat and followed it up at 2200 hours by killing an employee from the French Embassy. And when they reiterated that they would kill one every half an hour if the aircraft was not allowed to take off, the concerned authorities got jittery.In the meantime there were confirmed reports that besides being armed with AK-47 and Uzi submachine guns and grenades, the hijackers were also carrying more than 20 sticks of dynamite and that their plan as suicide bombers in the name of Allah was to blow up the Airbus 300 over Paris. According to the GIA, the hijacking was carried out in reprisal for French economic, political and military support to the Algerian government.

For the 230 odd passengers and crew on board the Airbus 300 who were looking forward to celebrate Christmas in Paris it was a deadly ordeal as they sat in fear and wondered who would be next on the hijackers list. In the meantime a crack commando hit team from the elite French GIGN, the crack counter terrorist force under Captain Denis Favier with the task to storm the plane and kill the hijackers with minimum loss of life to passengers had been dispatched in an identical Airbus 300. But in spite of circling for two hours over the airport, it was not allowed to land in Algiers and was ultimately diverted to Spain and where they were told to await for further instructions.

It was only at 2 AM on the morning of December 26th, and after 40 hours of intense negotiations and on the plea that the aircraft did not have the necessary fuel to fly directly to Paris, that flight 8969 was therefore allowed to take off for Marseilles and it landed there at the unearthly hour of 03.30 in the morning. Unaware to those on board, the French Special Forces from the GIGN had taken off from Spain and had also landed 20 minutes earlier and were waiting for orders to carry out their well rehearsed commando action. That very evening Shiraz and his family were also scheduled to catch their Air France flight from Marseilles to Paris and at around 4 PM when they arrived at the airport, it was swarming with French police, gendarmes, ambulances and fire tenders. Having learnt that the hijacked flight was now awaiting clearance to take off for Paris, and that all other flights had been either delayed or cancelled, Shiraz prayed for the lives of those who were being held hostage.

Tired and weary after two days of standoff, the hijackers it seemed needed some rest and they therefore during the day had maintained strict radio silence, but were now demanding an additional 27 tons of fuel which was three times more than what was required to fly to Paris. Meanwhile there were also intelligence reports that the hijackers were planning to crash the plane into the Eiffel Tower or blow it up over the city and therefore the only option that was now left was to storm the aircraft and kill the hijackers and even if it resulted in civilian casualties it had to be done.

It was around a little past five in the evening that Shiraz while standing near the visitors' gallery noticed the hijacked Airbus moving towards the Air Traffic Control tower and soon thereafter the rat-a-tat of machine gunfire was heard. The hijackers it seemed were losing their nerves and had demanded that the aircraft be moved nearer to the control tower and it was they who had opened up with their automatics at the airport installations and the control tower. Realizing that there was no more time to waste, Captain Favier gave the much awaited signal and the French commandos on board mobile staircases rushed towards the hijacked Airbus, while crack sniper teams with telescopic rifles from the control tower privided them cover. When the co-pilot jumped out from the cockpit window and ran for his life, it gave the snipers a more clear line of fire into the cockpit and minutes later after the commandos forced their way into the first class section of the aircraft, the real battle had now begun. While the passengers were being evacuated down the aircraft's emergency escape chutes, the commandos using their stun grenades entered the cockpit. The hijackers it seems were well trained and while the fight continued for a good 20 minutes inside the aircraft, both Shiraz and Saira in silence prayed for the safety of the crew and the gallant French commandos who had so daringly stormed the hijacked aircraft. Luckily only 13 passengers, 3 crew members and 11 from the GIGN had been injured and all the four hijackers had been killed.

Late on that night of 26th December 1994, when Shiraz with his family landed safely at the Charles De'Gaulle Airport in Paris, he wondered what a great tragedy would have befallen the historic city had the hijackers using the Airbus 300 as a flying bomb crashed into the Eiffel Tower or had exploded it over gay Paris. And as they drove to their apartment in a cab, the driver a French Algerian unaware of what would have been the fate of his city had the hijackers succeeded in their plot and thinking that his passengers were Indians simply said in his broken English, 'Indian women very very beautiful.'

"Yes, that is true, but in Pakistan they are even more beautiful," said an angry little Tojo who felt rather upset on being identified as an Indian. On reaching home, when Shiraz learnt that Pakistan on that very day had asked India to immediately close down its Consulate in Karachi and accused India of spreading terrorism in Kashmir, he knew that something was now afoot in internationalizing the Kashmir issue once again. For the subcontinent in particular and the world in general, the new year of 1995 too it seems was going to be a year of political uncertainties, communal riots, and more terrorist and militant activities by the so called Muslim fundamentalists.

CHAPTER-21

A World Gone Crazy

"But how is it that some small sections of Muslims in the subcontinent are diehard religious gun toting fanatics and they preach only death to the Kafirs, while the majority of them are very cultured, more pragmatic and are practical both in their outlook and in their religious beliefs. After all they too are devoted Muslims, but they don't make a hue and cry of being discriminated or being looked down upon by some stupid sections of the over populated Indians in this country," said Peevee as he presented his parents with the keys of a brand new silver coloured Maruti 1000 sedan. Peevee was celebrating his debut as a rock star singer and composer in a new film that was titled 'From Bollywood to Hollywood'. It was a story of an aspiring young Indian singing star who could sing both in English and in Hindi and whose ambition was to become a star like the late Elvis Presley.

"Well there is no dearth of talent in this country and if a 28 year old AR Rehman, a Muslim from South India who started his career as a keyboard player with local bands could achieve it, why not you," said a pregnant Dimpy who had come from Japan for her first delivery.

"Yes and I must say that the young man is a real genius as far as composing music is concerned,and his musical score on debut for the Mani Ratnam film 'Roja' has catapulted him right to the very top. And the very fact that more than two lakh audio cassettes of 'Roja' has been sold is proof enough of his immense talents," said Monty.

"Undoubtedly so but the credit should also be given to his late father RK Shekhar who was himself a talented music director in Malayalam films, and also to his loving mother who encouraged him into this line. It is a pity that he lost his father when Allah Rakha Rehman was only nine years old and the family had to get into renting out musical instruments to make a living," added Reeta as Monty switched on the TV to listen to the evening news on the CNN news channel and where the big news was regarding the successful storming of the Airbus at Marseilles.

"I also sometime wonder why these Muslim fanatics do such crazy things and what do they really achieve or gain by harassing and threatening the lives of innocent passengers while taking them as hostages. I think by carrying out such heinous acts by a handful of diehard crazy Islamist fundamentalists, they are only defaming the good name of the entire Muslim world," said Peevee.

"Yes it does sound crazy and I don't really understand as to why are they so anti American and anti western in their outlook," added Reeta as she proposed that the entire family go for a drive in the new car, followed by dinner at 'Karim's, which was Peevee's favourite restautrant for delicious Moghlai food.

Luckily for the United States and the world, a small slip up by the dreaded bomb maker Ramzi Youssef on the evening of 6th January,1995 had led to the timely detection of what could have been the mother of all terrorist bombing activities. On the 6th floor of the Dona Josefa apartments in Manila, Ramzi with his partner Abdul Hakim Murad while preparing the lethal liquid bombs that were subsequently to be used in another fortnight's time for launching 'Operation Bojinka', the careless duo while mixing the chemicals to make the explosives in the kitchen sink had accidently started a fire. When a neighbour reported the fire to the receptionist downstairs and the security guard was sent to check, Ramzi assured him that there was nothing to worry about. But when the stinking white smoke kept bellowing out of the window, the security guard first called up the police who did not respond. Then he called up the fire department and by the time the fire tenders arrived, Ramzi and Murad had left the building and were watching the proceedings from a nearby karaoke bar. And since there was no fire as such they were not unduly worried. But as soon as the firemen left, Ramzi very cleverly sent Murad back to retrieve his computer and other sensitive documents on bomb making that he had left behind in the apartment. And while Murad was busy packing the stuff, the police suddenly appeared and he was arrested. But once again Ramzi had managed to escape.

A few days later on examining the contents of the hard disc on the computer what the Americans found was a treasure trove of information not only of Ramzi's innovative method of bomb making, but also on how they were to be used in blowing up a dozen American commercial aircrafts over the Pacific Ocean. The bomber had already carried out his dress rehearsal, when on the 1st of December that year he detonated a similar low intensity device in the Greenbelt movie theatre in Manila and then followed it up by bombing the Phillipine Airlines Flight 434 on 11ᵗʰ December. Using nitroglycerine and other such liquid chemicals that would easily pass scrutiny through the metal detectors as contact lens solutions, Ramzi Yousef with his team of four other conspirators had planned to assemble the bombs on board the aircraft and after arming them with their Casio watch timers, they were required to hide them under their seats and elsewhere and then disembark enroute. Since most of these were long distance flights originating from Asian destinations and had a scheduled stopover in the Far East, there was therefore no problem for the bombers to do their job and get away. The bombs would so timed that they would all go off once the aircrafts took off on the last leg of their flight to Los Angeles and San Francisco and when they would be cruising over the vast Pacific Ocean. Ramzi and his conspirators were very confident that the plan would work, but thank God, fate willed otherwise. With the deadly information that Ramzi had left on his computer 'Operation Bojinka' which was also known as 'Project Bojinka' had to therefore be prematurely aborted by the deadly perpetrators.

But the downing of a dozen United States commercial airliners over the Pacific Ocean that was planned for the 20ᵗʰ and 21ˢᵗ of January, 1995 it seems was only part of the deadly 'Operation Bojinka' plot. The plot also included the assassination of Pope John Paul II during his visit to the Philipines during the World Youth Day on 15ᵗʰ January, 1995 and a suicide bombing of the CIA headquarters at Langley in the Fiarfax County of Virginia.There was also an earlier plot to assassinate President Bill Clinton during his visit to the Phillipines in November, 1994 but that was aborted because of the high security cordon around the U S President.For the assassination of the Pope, Ramzi had even selected the apartment at Dona Josefa. It was located in the Malete District of Manila and was just 200 meters away from the Embassy of the Holy See. According to the plan one of the suicide bombers would dress up as a Jesuit priest and detonate the deadly bomb while the Pope and his motorcade would be on their way to the San Carlos Seminary in Makati City. This was primarily meant to divert the attention of the intelligence sleuths from the next deadly phase of the most devastating Islamist terrorist attack, when 11 United States bound American airliners would be blown up in the sky and Ramzi's accomplice Abdul Hakim Murad a trained pilot in a small aircraft filled with explosives would in a grand finale on 21ˢᵗ January, 1995 crash headon into the CIA headquarters at Langley.

But with Murad's timely arrest and interrogation, together with the invaluable data that had been retrieved from Ramzi's computer and from the manual in Arabic on how to make a liquid bomb, the massive manhunt for Ramzi and his other accomplices had already begun and Ramzi's 'Operation Bojinka' therefore had to be shelved. Though 'Operation Bojinka' that was derived from the Serbian word meaning a 'loud bang' or 'explosion' had died with a whimper for the time being, but the possibility of radical Islamists like Ramzi, Osama Bin Laden and such like others unleashing a war of terror in the United States in particular and in the non Muslim world in general had now become a distinct reality. There were also reports that the operation master minded by Ramzi Yousef and Khalid Sheikh Mohammed had been funded by Osama Bin Laden, Wali Khan Amin Shah, an Afghan and a few other Muslim hard-line fanatics.

"My God what is this damn world coming to and it looks as if Pakistan is being used as the main terror base by these so called radical Islamists," said Shiraz to his wife Saira after Salim Rehman from Islamabad rang up on 19th January to inform him that the possibility of Ramzi Yousef and some others connected with the Bojinka plot seeking refuge in Pakistan was very much a possibility. According to Salim Rehman, a large number of them as part of Osama Bin Laden's Al-Qaida were now based in the North West Frontier and Baluchistan and since they had fought against the Russians in Afghanistan, the possibility of the ISI and other old friends giving them asylum therefore could not be ruled out. According to Salim Rehman, the main grudge of these fundamentalists was the support that the United States was giving to Israel in terms of economic and military aid and therefore they had now vowed in the name of Allah and the Holy Koran to teach the US a bloody lesson of their lives and they would continue to do so if the Americans kept supporting Israel.

Meanwhile in India in the state of Maharashtra and in the country's financial capital of Bombay there were hectic political activities that were directly connected with the forthcoming assembly elections, which were to be held shortly. For the Shiv Sena, the regional party led by their fiery Chief Pramukh, Balasaheb Thackeray and the BJP who had formed an alliance with their common cry for Hinduvta, it was a question of now or never. Riding on the fallout of the arrests and trial of the many Muslims in the state who had triggered of the infamous March 1993 Bombay bomb blasts, the Shiv Sainiks went all out to woo the large Hindu vote bank. For the Shiv Sena leader even the Pakistani cricket team was now his enemy and indications were that with a little bit of luck the saffron alliance could turn the tables on the fledging Congress Party that was being led by a corrupt Narasimha Rao in the Centre and by an equally corrupt Sharad Pawar, the Chief Minister of Maharashtra as was being alleged by the opposition. With the infighting and rebellion within the Congress in Maharashtra together with the lure of easy money and a ministerial berth to those who wanted to switch sides, the horse trading had already begun and the possibility of the Shiv Sena emerging as the dominating factor was now very much on the cards.

"With the Shiv Sena emerging as a force to reckon with in Maharashtra, I only hope that their so called spirit of Hindu nationalism and the 'Marathi Manoos' syndrome of Maharashtra for the Maharashtrians does not permeate into the everyday life of the Bombaites, since a large number of them are non Maharashtrians, and if Bollywood also comes under its spell then God help you, your film industry and the non Maharashtrian labour class in the city. As it is I believe the young budding stars and starlets are being dictated directly and indirectly not only by the big Dons with their black money power, but also by some unscrupulous rich businessmen, diamond merchants, and black marketeers who are masquerading as philanthropists and saviors of society and who in future with their big money and political connections can even make or break the government at the centre. like it did a few years ago with a handful of JMM members of parliament in order to save the Narasimha government from falling," said Monty to Peevee while signing on the dotted line to extend the lease of his flat at Maker Towers, Cuffe Parade by another 11 months with a ten percent increase payable in cash only.

"Well let us only hope that with Bombay being the financial capital of the country and a cosmopolitan city, Bal Thackeray and his Shiv Sainiks if they do come to power will change their attitude, or else like it happened with Jyoti Basu's CPM rule in Calcutta it will go the West Bengal way, and the big industrial houses will simply pack up and move their houses elsewhere," said Peevee.

During the month of February 1995, while the battle for the ballot to gain political control of Maharashtra in India between the BJP-Shiv Sena alliance on the one side and the Congress on the other gained momentum, the arrest of the dreaded terrorist and bomb maker Ramzi Yousef from the Su Casa Guest House in Islamabad on 7th February 1995 after a 23 day worldwide man hunt came as a surprise to many. Salim Rehman it seems had been proved right. Five hours after Abdul Hakim Murad was arrested by the Phillipine police at Manila, Yousef Ramzi on 6th January using a Pakistani passport in the name of 'Adam Qasim' had fled first to Singapore, but later surfaced in Islamabad. Only a day earlier on 6th February, he had checked in at the Su Casa Guest House with a Pakistani identity card that was in the name of Ali Muhammed Baluchi from the town of Pasni in Baluchistan. At around 9-30 PM, and on that very night he was joined by his old friend Ishtaique Parker, a South African Muslim whom Ramzi had recruited earlier. Parker was also instrumental in helping Ramzi in the making of those deadly bombs for 'Operation Bojinka." On the next day, when the guest house was raided by the Pakistan intelligence in conjunction with the United States Bureau of Diplomatic Security with their agents Bill Miller and Jeff Riner to the fore, the game for Ramzi was up. Ramzi was about to leave for Peshawar, when he was apprehended, arrested, handcuffed and taken for preliminary interrogation immediately.

Enticed by the 2 million dollar reward, Parker it seems had betrayed him. As the US army plane carrying the prized catch flew over Manhattan for landing in New York, Ramzi on seeing the Twin Towers of the World Trade Centre still standing, quipped and told the FBI agents on board that if he had a little more money, he would have brought the twin towers down and regretted that he could not complete the mission. However, Khalid Sheikh Mohammed the other mastermind who was also wanted for the World Trade Centre bombing and for the aborted 'Project Bojinka' was still on the loose. He was Ramzi's uncle and according to the FBI was now an active member of Osama Bin Laden's Al-Qaeda.

A few days later, when Salim Rehman sent a brief bio-data on Yousef Ramzi and his uncle Khalid Sheikh Muhammed to Shiraz in Paris, Shiraz was surprised to learn that both of them were highly educated and were qualified engineers by profession. Besides holding degrees in chemistry and in electrical engineering from the Swansea Institute in Wales, England, Ramzi was also fluent in seven languages including English, Arabic, Persian, Pashtu and Turkish. His uncle Khalid who like Ramzi was also born in Kuwait held a mechanical engineering degree from North Carolina's Agricultural and Technical State University and like Ramzi, he too had fought against the Russians in Afghanistan before moving to the United States in 1982.

With the arrest of Ramzi from the very capital of Pakistan and that to from a public guest house that was only a few blocks away from the Iraqi Ambassador's residence, Shiraz now wondered whether Ramzi was an Iraqi who wanted to take revenge on the United States. The bombing of the World Trade Centre in New York could well have been a fall out of the attack on Iraq by America and the coalition forces in 1991, and with the continuing economic blockade of Iraq there may well be others who with Pakistani and other passports and aliases have found a new haven inside Pakistan. After all these were the very men who were earlier given sanctuary by the ISI and the CIA when they volunteered as Mujaheedins to be trained, armed and to fight the Russians in neighbouring Afghanistan, thought Shiraz as he once again went through Ramzi's bio-data and did not rule out the possibility that though he was born in Kuwait, he could well be of Pakistani descent also.

Soon after Ramzi's deportation by a special US military aircraft to the United States that took place within just 8 hours of his arrest, and which was bitterly criticized by radical Muslim groups in Pakistan, Salim Rehman was now apprehensive that it could lead to retaliation by some of them against the Americans serving and working in Pakistan. The radicals even accused Benazir Bhutto and her government for overriding Pakistan's extradition laws in order to curry favour with Washington and it was probably because she was scheduled to officially visit the United States in April. As it is Karachi, the financial capital of the country was witnessing an unprecedented spate of lawlessness and violence not only between the Mohajirs and the Sindhis, but also between the supporters of the PPP and the MQM, and between the Sunni and Shia sects in the city. So much so that even the conduct of peaceful congregation for prayers in the mosques were being targeted by rival groups armed with automatic weapons. There were also rumours that Ramzi had strong links with the Sipah-e-Sahaba, a radical group of Muslims from the Deobandi School and most of whom were of Indian origin from erstwhile Punjab and Haryana and who had migrated to Pakistan at partition.In Karachi alone more than a 1000 had died in sectarian, ethnic and factional violence during the year 1994 and 1995 and it seems it was going to be even worse in the years to come. In a recent massacre at a mosque in Karachi when 13 Shite Muslim men and boys who had gone for prayers to celebrate the end of the holy month of Ramadan were lined up and shot dead in cold blood, it looked as if a civil war would soon engulf the port city. On that very day Arif Rehman and his wife Ruksana Begum now in their seventies happened to be in Karachi. They were on their way to spend a holiday with their son-in-law Shiraz and family in Paris and they wondered whether life in Karachi will ever be normal again.

And on the 8th of March, at around 8 o'clock in the morning and in broad daylight at a busy traffic signal when unidentified gunmen firing their automatic weapons killed two United States diplomats and wounded a third while they were on their way to the American Consulate in Karachi, Salim Rehman's worst fears were proved right. This was the first time that Americans and that too American diplomats on Pakistani soil had been targeted and he was of the firm view that these killings were in retaliation to the arrest and deportation of Yousef Ramzi. According to a press report the injured American had been identified as Michael Owen, the American Vice Consul and Salim was now worried that more such dastardly acts against foreigners and especially against Americans, Jews and Europeans could follow.

A few days later, when a Pakistani Foreign Ministry spokesman openly warned that if India carried out another aggression and a war broke out than it would no longer be a war of a thousand years or even a thousand hours, but one that would last only for a few minutes and that India should have no doubts about the potential devastation such a war may cause, Shiraz was indeed surprised by that statement of open belligerence by the Pakistan foreign office. He however was in no doubt that Pakistan's strategy vis-a—vis Kashmir was firstly to relentlessly pursue 'Operation Topac' and at the same time become a nuclear weapons power. And this particular open challenge at this stage to India only confirmed that either Pakistan already had a nuclear bomb or was on the threshold of testing one. Sitting in far away Paris it was difficult for Shiraz to verify if that was an empty threat or a real one, and he therefore got in touch with his brother-in-law Salim Rehman in Islamabad, who clarified that the warning was not by implication but was made in clear terms because the next war would only last a few seconds and it would be one that would cause inconceivable destruction and devastation. This further clearly indicated that Pakistan was capable of brazenly displaying its potential nuclear capability and it therefore had Shiraz very worried.

And while Pakistan was gearing up to become a future nuclear power, on 15th March, 1995 Murtaza Bhutto with a breakaway faction from the PPP and with his mother Nusrat's blessings and support launched his own political party the Shaheed Bhutto Group to challenge the authority of his own elder sister and Prime Minister. On hearing that, Ruksana Begum while having a dig at the Bhutto family very aptly remarked.

'Whereas in India both Meneka and Sonia, the two widowed 'Bahus' (daughters-in-law) from the Gandhi family with their vote catching Gandhi surnames are being used by the two main political rivals, the BJP and the Indira Congress respectively for political mileage, in Pakistan the fight for political supremacy within the PPP between the brother and the sister using the same Bhutto surname is no way different. This will not only further split the party, but it is bound to split the family too. A clever and calculative Benazir even after her marriage has very cleverly stuck to her surname Bhutto, because it is the Bhutto name in Pakistani politics that counts and as Benazir Zardari she would have been probably nobody. And I sincerely hope that Murtaza whose antipathy and hatred for her sister's husband, Asif Zardari is well known is not foolish enough to start a bloody family feud. As it is Karachi and Sind, the stronghold of the Bhutto clan has become like the Wild West and it would now become even worse if one challenges the other's authority by using strong arm tactics against each other. But I won't be the least surprised if in his quest for power the headstrong Murtaza who is also referred to by some as the 'Terrorist Prince' with the backing of his mother decides to take on his elder sister and her husband headon."

"Yes that will indeed be a real pity and I won't be surprised if Ammijaan's assessment of the internal feud within the Bhutto family and the PPP ends up with political murders and vendetta on both sides," said Saira as her daughter Sherry quoting from her knowledge of Moghul rule in India added.

"Well if Aurangzeb and his sister Roshanara could plot and kill their elder brother Dara Shikoh and blind their father the Emperor Shah Jehan and put him in jail just for the sake of usurping power, then our feudal lords like the Bhuttos and the Zardaris I am afraid are no exceptions either, After all as the saying goes all is fair in love and war and striving for power without the blessings of the masses only produces dictators like Hitler, Stalin and Mussolini."

During the month of March, while the two Bhutto siblings in Pakistan were getting ready to battle it out, the Shiv Sena and the BJP in India nominated their two stalwarts Manohar Joshi, and Gopinath Munde as the Chief Minister and Deputy Chief Minister of the state. And it was soon apparent that the men in saffron who had been waiting all these years to come to power in Maharashtra would also now challenge the Congress at the Centre. This was what Monty's friend Unni had also predicted a few days before the polls were held. And a few days later, when the poll results were declared, Unni in an in house debate at the Press Club spoke on the causes for the humiliating defeat that was suffered by the Congress in Maharashtra and he without mincing words had said very openly and categorically.

"'I am afraid that the Congress of today is no longer the Congress of bygone days where the country's interest came first and leaders and stalwarts like Nehru, Patel, Shyama Prasad Mukherjee, Rajendra Prasad, Abul Kalam Azad and such like great men guided the country's destiny and did their duties absolutely selflessly and without being corrupted. But the Congress of today I am afraid is now a party of self seekers, sycophants and stooges. It is undoubtedly the Congress (I) who have institutionalized corruption in the country and where the letter 'I' now is the most dominating factor when it comes to dishing out doles by their leaders to those who were willing to bend backwards. The party unfortunately has now become a party of pandering corrupt politicians and some of whom probably, and please pardon my saying so would even be willing to prostitute themselves in front of the leaders in order to be promoted up the ladder. Bereft of any worthwhile leadership qualities amongst their senior lot and with the growing infighting within the party, they are now hoping to rope in Sonia, the widow of the late Rajiv Gandhi and an Italian at that to resurrect the flagging fortunes of what was once the most dominant entity in Indian politics. After all the Gandhi surname still rings a bell among the millions of illiterate Indian masses and most of whom unfortunately are still under the impression that the Gandhis of Delhi today are directly related to the Father of the Nation. Therefore, when it comes to voting during elections and the so called achievements by the party are highlighted in the name and photos of the many Gandhi s with catchy slogans like 'Garibi Hatao' (Remove Poverty), and 'A government that works,' etc etc, it also does work in fooling the masses. But these gimmicks I am afraid may not work for them any longer. The illiterate masses that earlier used to fall for such publicity stunts have now become a lot wiser and they can no longer be taken for granted. The time has now come where even the villagers and the common man on the street have seen through the game, and the recent election results in Maharashtra have also amply proved that point conclusively. Therefore, the defeat of the Congress in Maharashtra that was lead by none other than a Congress heavyweight like Sharad Pawar and that to in India's most industrialized state and financial capital should serve as an eye opener to the political pundits in the Congress. And if they sincerely want India to remain really secular, then they must stop playing caste and communal based politics that has now become the order of the day," added Unni as Monty led the applause and invited the speakers for and against the motion for a drink at the bar.

Early next morning, when Monty and Reeta over a good English breakfast of smoked ham, sausages and eggs were discussing whether Mrs Sonia Gandhi should take up the challenge of leading the fledging Congress party, there was an urgent call from their daughter Dimpy in Tokyo. It was already well past midday in Japan and Dimpy was worried because her husband Paddy who had left for the embassy early that morning had not reached his office. There were all kinds of rumours flying about regarding some type of a gas attack by some terrorist organization on the busy Tokyo subway, and which Paddy also took daily to commute to office. But with her limited Japanese vocabulary, Dimpy did not know how to go about tracing her husband. Tokyo was a very big buzzing city and though she was in touch with the embassy, she was feeling helpless.

"Don't worry, just request the Japanese interpreter in the embassy to help you get someone from the tourism department or from any of the big five star hotels where there are many trained guides who are well versed both in English and in Japanese and they should be able to help you out. Try and communicate through them and pay them handsomely if required. Request the interpreter to get in touch with the police and particularly with those hospitals that are along that particular subway route. But don't panic, and pray to Wahe Guru that everything should be alright," said Monty as he tuned in to the BBC for the latest news.

Later that evening, when the telephone rang again and Dimpy conveyed the good news that Paddy was safe and out of danger, Reeta immediately took an auto rickshaw and went to the Bangla Sahib Gurudwara to thank Wahe Guru. Paddy was indeed lucky to have survived the deadly gas attack. On that 20th of March, 1995 some members from the 'Aum Shinrikyo', a Japanese religious cult that was led by Asahara Shoko who preached that it would soon be the end of the world had targeted the busy Japanese subway during the peak time office hours. Working in pairs the five handpicked teams without the knowledge of the other members of the cult while travelling on five different routes on the subway had carried out this attack at five different sections of the subway. While one released the deadly Sarin gas, his buddy and companion served as the getaway driver and surprisingly all of them were also very highly educated. The Tokyo subway system transports millions of passengers daily and people carrying umbrellas was something very common in that big sprawling city. That Monday morning as was his daily routine, Paddy as usual boarded the first car on train number A725K on the busy Chiyoda line. But when the train reached the Shin-Ochanomizu Station in the central business district of the capital, he noticed a Japanese gentleman wearing a surgical mask repeatedly puncturing a plastic bag with his pointed umbrella and then running out from the train at the next stop. Wearing such kind of masks during winter was quite common too, but to see a Japanese man puncturing a plastic bag in full view of the public was rather unusual. And by the time the train reached the next station there were people on board who had started complaining of nausea and quite a few had also started vomiting. Realizing that something toxic was in the air, Paddy luckily and in the nick of time had in cowboy style covered his face with his big handkerchief and started assisting the others who were suffering to detrain from the bogie. And it was only a little later, when he too complained that he was having difficulty in breathing, that he together with the others were rushed to the nearest hospital. But by the time he reached there he had momentarily lost consciousness. Luckily he had his official calling card in his purse and the hospital authorities had immediately got in touch with the Indian embassy. And it was only on the next day and thanks to timely medical help that Paddy survived to tell the tale.

On that morning of 20th March, the perpetrators carrying the liquid sarin in plastic bags that was neatly wrapped up in newspapers had boarded the earmarked subway trains at the appointed time, while their buddies in their getaway cars waited for them at the specified detraining stations. Sarin, a highly toxic nerve agent was developed by the Nazi scientists in the 1930's both in liquid and gas forms. The perpetrators had decided to use only the liquid form and each one of them were carrying a litre of that deadly poison, a single droplet of which was enough to kill an adult. It was later learnt that Hayashi Ikuo, the man who leaked the gas on the train that Paddy was travelling in was a senior medical doctor and a heart an artery specialist. In 1990, as the head of Circulatory Medicine at the National Sanatorium Hospital in Tokaimura he had resigned his job and had even left his family to join the cult. The cult it seems attracted people from all walks of life and they lived a secluded existence in communes. All of them had left their families and they stayed away from their near and dear ones. Though their leader Shoko combined elements of Buddhism, Hinduism and even Christianity in his teachings and the cult members regularly practiced yoga, meditation and breathing exercises, but why they feared that the apocalypse would soon destroy the world, and why they carried out such a deadly attack on unsuspecting and innocent people, which resulted in the deaths of 12, and injured more than 6000 others would however remain a mystery.

And as far as Paddy was concerned he was indeed very lucky to get away with only a chronic eye strain. On that morning of the 20th, when Dimpy rang up Aunty Shupriya in Havana and told her that Paddy was missing, Shupriya immediately caught a flight to Tokyo via New York and by the time she landed, thank God all was well. Throughout the long air journey Shupriya had kept praying to the Sai Baba of Shirdi and he it seems had answered her prayers Holding the big built nine month old chubby baby girl that Paddy and Dimpy had produced in her arms, Shupriya smothered her with kisses and presented her with a pair of pure gold earings that

Dimpy's grandmother had presented to her when she topped the Delhi University Bachelor of Arts examination. In memory of her grandmother and her favourite aunt the little girl had also been christened as Simran Kaur Padmanaban and Simi for short.

While the Sarin gas attack in Japan took everyone by complete surprise, in Pakistan and in India the cricket crazy public was appalled by allegations of match fixing that some Australian test players like Shane Warne, Steve Waugh and Tim May had recently made in public. According to them, Salim Malik the Pakistani cricket captain during the Aussies tour of Pakistan in the previous year had offered them hefty bribes to perform poorly.

'While I guess like in politics where there are no scruples and when it comes to showing numbers, horse trading becomes a national pastime, so I guess in cricket also where there is now so much money, everybody wants to be part of the winning side and I am sure some of our leading Indian cricketers must be in this big money game and league too," said Peevee as he paid a courtesy call on a well known Bombay bookie who was also a film financer and a friend. Peevee wanted to know if there was any truth to such allegations.

"Arre mere hero bhai, jua khelna tho hamara Hindustan aur Pakistan ka pesha hai, aur ye tho saadiyon se chali arahi hai. Is mein koi nahin baat tho hai hi nahin. Mahabharat main bhi tho jua khelte hue Draupadi ka chir haran hua tha, aur Diwali ke samay hum log sub lagatar, din raat jue mein dube rahte hain. Jeetna aur harna tho kismet ki baat hai, magar afsoos tho ye hai ki aaj kaal piase ke lalach mein log tho apna imaan ko bhi bechne lagen hain. Jahan bhi jao rishwat ke binna koi kam hi nahin hota, aur cricket tho sirf ek khel hai,' said the seasoned bookie as he poured Peevee a stiff peg of Blue Label whisky.

(Dear brother, gambling has been since ages a part of life in the subcontinent. Even in the great Hindu epic, Mahabharat, there is this famous story about Draupadi, the wife of the five Pandavas being put up as the last prized stake, And even during Diwali we gamble day in and day out and some win and some lose. But the saddest part is that today for the sake of quick money, people are also willing to sell even their honour and self respect, and one can get nothing done without paying a bribe, and cricket is only a game my friend)

With the bookie cleverly and diplomatically remaining non committal on the question of whether there were Salim Maliks in Indian cricket also, Peevee was convinced that the Indian cricket scene was not as holier than thou either as it was made out to be. But compared to what happened to

England's oldest investment banking firm, Barings Bank that only a month ago on 26th February lost 1.4 billion US dollars thanks to Nick Leeson's speculative gambling istinct, fixing cricket matches was chicken feed thought Peevee. Leeson who was the bank's securities broker had speculated wrongly on the Tokyo Stock Exchange, and as a result of which the bank completely collapsed added the cricket bookie as he proudly showed Peevee his latest gizmo. It was a Nokia mobile telephone. With the paging culture having already come to India, and while the big money businessmen tycoons in India's metropolitan cities waited eagerly for the mobile telephone era in the country to kick start in the near future, Peevee in anticipation and while on a visit to Dubai for a show by the big Bollywood stars and starlets had also bought for himself and for his father Monty two brand new Nokia mobile phones from the very well stocked duty free shop at the Dubai airport.

"'Such kind of stage shows by the Bollywood stars had now become a regular annual feature in some of the oil rich Gulf countries and these were mostly sponsored by the erstwhile'Dons' of Mumbai through third parties. Being a new comer and a starter in the Bollywood horizon and a shaven off Sikh at that, the mafia 'Dons' had already given him the Punjabi nickname of 'Chikina' meaning the young star with a little or no beard' That name Peevee felt was far more respectable than being called 'Hakla" the name that was given allegedly to Shahrukh Khan he had been told. This being Peevee's first show in Dubai, he not only kept a low profile, but also his distance from the senior stars and the Dons. There was no doubt in his mind that though the Dons blew away a fabulous amount of money entertaining the entire Bollywood troupe and showering the young good looking and upcoming female artists with expensive gifts, including cash for their shopping, but they with their big black money power in Bollywood productions also knew how to recover it fast. It was common knowledge that those who did not tow their line or did not live up to their demands both monetarily and otherwise were threatened by their goons and by their contract killers till they paid up either in cash or in kind, Therefore, it was always better not to mess with them and to try and be as accommodative as far as possible and on mutually acceptable terms, With that principle in mind Peevee alias Deepak Kumar on the day of the troupe's departure from Dubai presented the Don who really mattered in the Bombay film world with a return gift of a diamond studded bracelet that had the words 'la allah illah allah, Muhammed resul allah' neatly inscribed in Persian on it and which meant that there is no God but God and Prophet Mohammed is the messenger of God.

Right from his young days, Peevee's parents through the teachings of Guru Nanak and the Sai Baba of Shirdi had taught him that all religions were the same and that it should always be respected irrespective of a particular community's belief or customs. Peevee also knew that hardened criminals too when cornered think of God first and he hoped that the Don being a Muslim will therefore treat the expensive gift as a lucky talisman or a charm, and which in future could work as a bond of friendship between the two of them. That evening of 27th March, 1995 on his return from Dubai, when Peevee switched on the TV to watch the 67th Academy Awards presentation live from the Shrine Auditorium in Los Angeles and the film 'Braveheart' was given the Oscar for the best picture and also for the best director, his joy knew no bounds. Mel Gibson was his favourite actor and the film was also produced and directed by him. Set in 13th century England, it was a story of William Wallace, a commoner and a Scot who unites his clan to fight against the despotic English rule. Mel Gibson as William Wallace was simply superb and Peevee was a bit disappointed when he lost out on the best actor award to Nicholas Cage who bagged it for his performance in 'Leaving Las Vegas.' Though he was born in Peekskill, New York, USA on 3rd January, 1956, Mel learnt all his acting in Australia. A graduate from National Institute of Dramatic Art in Sydney, he first came into limelight as a stage artist. He was classically trained in the best British-theatre tradition and his first debut film was the 1977 Australian production titled 'Summer City', while his first Hollywood film was the 1984 drama 'The River' in which he played the role of a struggling Tennessee farmer and thereafter there was no looking back for him.

But a month later on 19th April, when two white Americans, Timothy McVeigh and his accomplice Terry Nicols carried out the bombing of a federal building that housed Federal Marshals and their families in Oklahoma City and killed 168 people including 8 Federal Marshals and 19 children and injured about 800 others, Shiraz who saw the rescue operations that was being telecast worldwide just could not believe it. Timothy was neither a Muslim radical nor a disgruntled black or a white criminal and yet he carried out this diabolical act against his own people. And since the bombing took place on the second anniversary of the Waco massacre, Shiraz wondered whether the two bombers were sympathizers of that movement and therefore had taken revenge. It was also on 19th April, **1993**, only two years ago that the terrible tragedy at Waco came to light. After a long 51 day siege that was punctuated with intermittent gun fights between a Christian sect who called themselves Davidians and the FBI, the ranch of the sect near Waco in Texas was finally subdued. The ranch ultimately was not only subjected to massive tear gas shelling by armoured combat engineering vehicles, but it was also assaulted by tanks. The idea was to flush out all the inmates from the building, but the Davidians it seems were not willing to give up so very easily and they fought back. Eventually the building caught fire and it resulted in the death of 76 people including 21 children who had been charred to death together with their Davidian leader Vernon Wayne Howell, better known as David Koresh. The inhuman manner in which the operation was conducted had angered many and McVeigh who had visited the place during the long standoff was one of them. However, McVeigh's luck ran out soon after he had successfully detonated the deadly handmade device that was equivalent to a 1,800 kg TNT bomb and as a result of which a third of that big nine-story federal building was destroyed and it created a massive crater that was 30 feet wide and 8 feet deep. Within 90 minutes of the explosion, an Oklahoma State Trooper on Interstate 35 by a chance of luck had stopped McVeigh's yellow coloured 1977 model Mercury Marquis car because it did not have a number plate and arrested him for having a concealed weapon. This was the getaway car that McVeigh thought would see him to safety and it probably would have had it not been for the alertness of the 26 year old Charlie Hanger the State Trooper who luckily was hanging around on the busy Interstate 35 at that crucial time. But it was the Ryder truck that McVeigh had used for the bombing that had given his game away. The vehicle identification number on the axle of the destroyed Ryder truck that had been rented under his alias name had been traced to the owner.

It all began on 15th April, 1995 when Timothy McVeigh rented that Ryder truck from Junction City, Kansas under the false name of Robert D. Kling and on the very next day he with his fellow conspirator Terry Nicols drove to Oklahoma City. Thereafter they stole a car and having removed the license plate, they parked it several blocks away from the Alfred P Murrah Federal Building. This car was to be used as the getaway car. Having done that, the duo with the bomb making material inside the Ryder truck drove to a lonely secluded spot to make the deadly device. On the 17th and on the 18th the duo prepared the devastating truck bomb near the Geary County State Lake, and once it was finally ready, McVeigh on the morning of 19th April drove the truck to Oklahoma City. Wearing a printed tee shirt with the motto of the Commonwealth of Virginia 'Sic Semper Tyrannis' (Thus Ever to Tyrants), which were the very words that John Wilkes Booth had shouted after assassinating Abraham Lincoln, McVeigh lit the long five minute fuze to the bomb, and having parked the truck in a drop-off zone that was situated under the building's day care centre, he locked the vehicle and then got into his getaway car and sped away from the scene. At exactly 9:02 in the morning the deadly explosion shook the city. It was the deadliest ever act of terrorism on American soil and Shiraz now wondered that if American citizens could turn against their own people with such deadly hand made bombs and could target their own very citizens who were the upholders of law and order in the country and carry it out so very easily, then what would be the fate of the common man on the street, and more so if terrorists and radical Muslims like Ramzi Yousef and others decide to take revenge on the Americans for their pro Jewish, anti-Muslim and pro Israeli foreign policy. The deadly bombing of the World Trade Centre in Manhattan was already a living example and with America being a nation of immigrants where people from all over the world still enter both legally and illegally, it must be a gigantic task for the FBI, the CIA and other such state vigilance bodies to keep a track of each one of them, thought Shiraz.

And when the bomber Mcveigh turned out to be a 27 year old ex-army man from the US army who had also earned a Bronze Star in 'Operation Desert Storm' and who later on being honourably discharged had worked for a while as a security guard in his hometown of Pendleton, New York, Shiraz was skeptical and wondered whether the United States was geared up to fight the war of terror that was now being unleashed in the name of religion by the various fundamentalist and radical Muslims of the world.

CHAPTER-22

The World Endangered Through Ethnic Conflicts

In early May 1995, with the passing of spring and as the pleasant summer breeze engulfed the picturesque Kashmir valley, 'Operation Topac,' the proxy war sponsored by Pakistan through their so called Mujahideen fighters from the Harkat-ul-Ansar group grew in its intensity. On the 9th of May 1995, when Monty landed in Srinagar for his export promotion business, the city was teeming with soldiers from regular army units, the police and the para-military forces. They were all guarding the vital areas and vital points inside the city. This was primarily a precautionary measure that had to be taken because the militants in large numbers under their leader Mast Gul had laid siege to the famous Charar-e-Sharif shrine. The siege began in the month of March and the militants were now bent upon torching it and reducing the holy shrine to ashes. The State government was also apprehensive that the capital city Srinagar too may be targeted and they were not taking any chances. The old historic shrine that was revered both by the Hindus and the Muslims was a place of pilgrimage for many and Sheikh Nooruddin after all was one of the greatest mystic saints of Kashmir and one who personified the Hindu-Muslim composite culture of the valley.

Born as Nand Rishi in 1377 AD, his ancestors had migrated from Khistwar and the Saint was an epitome of upholding moral values and he fervently preached against indulgence and against communal hatred. According to him, both the Hindus and the Muslims were brothers. The faith in him was judged, when more than nine lakh people including the then King of Kashmir, Sultan Zainul Abdin congregated at the shrine on his death in 1438.

But having failed to achieve their objective during the siege of Hazratbal earlier, the ISI's game plan this time it seems was to burn down the historic monument so that its destruction would ignite the flames of communal

528

passion and lead to an unprecedented upheaval in the valley. And as a result of which Pakistan would once again try and internationalize the burning Kashmir issue in various world forums. The well armed and well trained militants with sophisticated wireless sets in the cold winter of January 1995 had infiltrated in small groups into this area. A week later the group from their jungle hideouts in the nearby mountains that overlooked Yusmarg had sneaked into Charar-e-Sharif, and by February their numbers had swelled to well over two hundred. They it seems had reached an unwritten understanding with the locals that they would vacate the shrine and reoccupy their secret camps once winter was over. But by early March and after the Indian Army and the BSF threw a cordon around Charar, most of the villagers fearing a standoff kept migrating to other safe areas. After the Indian army intercepted many of the coded wireless messages that were being sent by the militants to their bosses in Pakistan, and it became apparent that Mast Gul and his Pak/Afghan outfit were preparing to blast the sacred shrine, the Indian authorities even offered a safe passage to the militants through the Suchetgarh border near Jammu. But very cleverly and in order not to show Pakistan's direct involvement in this operation, the offer was rejected by Mast Gul. And when the security forces started cutting off water and electric supply to the town, it only triggered off a mass exodus of the civilians from there. Thereafter the militants in a show of force and in order to defend themselves started planting IED's, improvised explosive devices at the entrance to the shrine and they even tested a few of them underground to see the effect. By April, from a total population of 25,000 only 1000 or so remained at Charar-e Sharif and they were mostly either the infirm or those who wanted desperately to guard their property.

For his own safety and in order to ensure that his work would be done, Monty after he landed at Srinagar was provided with an escort and transport by his old friend the Police DIG from the IB. And when the DIG over the police network invited him to drive up to Charar where he was camping and to witness what was happening there, Monty was thrilled. But by the time he arrived at the police camp near Charar, a major part of the town was already in flames. Mast Gul and his mercenaries it seems had already commenced with their nefarious plan of arson and destruction and by doing so also probably managed to ensure the escape of a large number of his militants who had taken shelter inside the sacred shrine. With strict orders not to fire at, or to attack the sacred shrine, the Indian army it seemed was helpless. Though there were some minor exchange of fire by both sides, but they were only sporadic in nature. Once again thanks to religious sentiments, the

Indian army was engaged in a task with their hands tied behind their backs and Monty felt rather sorry for them.

Finally on the night of the 11th of May 1995, when the fuse was lit and the massive explosion shook the ground under Monty's feet, he knew that it was all over. And while the sacred shrine, including the mausoleum of Sheikh Nooruddin was in the process of being reduced to ashes, and the town kept burning, Mast Gul managed to escape. His last communication 'Mission Khatam Kar Diya' (Mission accomplished) was intercepted in clear by the Indian forces, but it was already a bit too late. By then Mast Gul was already on his way to cross over into Pakistan occupied Kashmir, and Monty felt rather sad that the perpetrator of this shameless act could not be captured or shot dead, and could get away so very brazenly.

Next day morning, when Shiraz in Paris was conveyed the news by his superiors in Islamabad and was told to propagate the view that the burning of the town and the shrine was the handiwork of the Indian intelligence and the Indian security forces to break the morale of the brave pro Pakistani Kashmiri militant outfits that were fighting for the freedom of their motherland, Shiraz knew that it was all a cock and bull story. Because by then he had also heard from very reliable sources that Mast Gul no sooner had he stepped into Pakistan occupied Kashmir he had been lionized and feted as a hero.

And while India was still crying foul and their security forces were cursing themselves for not being able to capture Mast Gul, the handsome cricket icon of Pakistan was getting ready to tie the knot with his beautiful sweetheart. On the 16th of May, far away at the Islamic Centre in Paris, when the dashing Imran Khan in a two minute Islamic marriage ceremony married the gorgeous British heiress Jemima Goldsmith, it broke a lot of female hearts. Jemina was practically half his age and she had taken the Muslim name of Haiqa. It was an Arabic name that meant obedient of Allah. Commenting on the big age difference, when Saira remarked that love has no age barrier, her daughter Sherry who was now 16 and who also had a crush on that handsome Pathan promptly said.

'That is all very well Ammijaan, but I still wonder that with the conservative life style of the Muslims and the political instability in our country that is currently being riddled with sectarian violence, will the young Mrs Haiqa Khan be able to live happily and adjust in our country?'

"Well she did say that she would in spite of her many millions and try and follow our customs and traditions, and for all you know she may turn out to be a better Muslim than you and I are."

"Yes and why not. If the late Dr Khan Sahib, the elder brother of the Frontier Gandhi could marry a Scottish lady some seven decades ago and his daughter Mariam could marry a handsome young Sikh Piffer officer by the name of Kunwar Jaswant Singh and who was from the Princely house of Kapurthala in the early forties, then there is nothing wrong if Imran Khan a Muslim who incidently is also a Pathan takes Jemina who is a Protestant Christian as his legally wedded wife. This in fact is international integration and should be promoted. After all it is the Sai Baba of Shirdi who promulgated the slogan 'Sabka Malik Ek', meaning thereby that there is only one God and that God alone therefore is the almighty. And the so called colour of your skin and your faith in the religion of your birth is immaterial. So there is nothing wrong if Jemima and Imran, despite their vast age difference and their religion at the fag end of the 20th Century are now man and wife. And incidentally let me also tell you all that the ex Indian Piffer officer Kunwar Jaswant Singh later became a flying pilot and he finally retired as an Air Marshal in the Indian Air Force," said Shiraz.

"I must say you seem to be very well versed with pre—partition love affairs of all these oldies and with your love for the men in uniform, I sometimes feel that in your last life you too probably must have served in the erstwhile Indian army as a Piffer," said Saira somewhat seriously.

"Yes at times I too get that feeling and maybe I was in my previous life an integral part of that great regiment of brotherhood that still carries on even today and where the Pakistani, Indian and British officers of pre-partition days who had served in the Frontier Force Regiment still keep up with one another through their Piffer Association."

On the 24th of May, 1995 Shiraz with his family drove to London for a short holiday that was also combined with an official meeting on the 26th with Pakistan's Foreign Secretary and the Pakistan High Commissioner in London. On learning from the Pakistan Military Attache, Colonel Muktiar Ahmed that the old British officers with their wives from the erstwhile Piffers were hosting a reunion lunch at the Royal Overseas League on St James Street on 27th May, Shiraz immediately got in touch with Lt Colonel IAJ Edwards-Stuart, the Editor of 'Piffer'. The grand old man had been editing that magazine for the past 17 years and Shiraz had met Ivor and Elizabeth Edwards-Stuarts earlier also. It was kind courtesy the late Major General Gul Rehman Khan, and Shiraz had even visited their house in Dorset a couple of times when he was posted in London as the Third Secretary. The British couple and family were great friends of the Rehman family and Gul Rehman and Zubeida had even attended their marriage at the Lahore Cathedral in 1945.

The Reunion Lunch of the Piffers on the 27th of May 1995 was a grand affair for the veterans and their wives as they talked about their wonderful days in India and the regiment that they had served in. As they went in for their meals that was served in royal style inside 'The Hall of India and Pakistan,'some of them like old school boys kept patting each other on their backs, while some joked in Urdu and a few even in Pashtu as they recalled their days in the North West Frontier. A few of them who had attended the recent reunion of the regiment at Abbotabad were also full of praise in the splendid manner in which they had been looked after by the regiment. Lt General Mumtaz Gul had been appointed as the new Colonel Commandant and they even had the privilege of meeting the Prime Minister, Benazir Bhutto who was the Chief Guest at the luncheon on the 23rd of April.

When Shiraz was introduced to Brigadier Rakesh Dhir, India's Military Attache in London, and he saw the bonhomie and the camaraderie between the old Pakistani and the Indian officers, he wondered why the two countries could not be friends forever. That was also the day when Shiraz as Riaz Mohammed Khan passed his first test as an impersonator. He and the Indian Brigadier though junior to him had served together in a field area for quite a while, but with the passage of time, the erstwhile Indian hero and the Param Veer Chakra winner of the 1971 war it seems was now a forgotten idol as far as India was concerned. Next morning being a Sunday, Shiraz with his family went to see the Piffer Chapel and to attend the special church service for the veterans. The Piffer Association after India's Independence was given a side aisle in the St Luke's Church at Chelsea to house their memorials and mementos that they had brought back with them from India. When Shiraz noticed the colours of the 2nd Punjab Infantry that was carried by the unit from 1849 to 1867 and which was placed on the turret of the Officer's mess house during the relief of Lucknow in 1857 by Lt Bob Roberts, who later became Field Marshal and C-in-C India, he realized the kind of pride these veterans still have for the old Indian army. And when he was told that the broken staff was now a treasured possession of the officer's mess of Pakistan's 8th Frontier Force Rifles, Shiraz was reminded of the Mantalai Flag that was captured by the 4th Battalion of the Jammu and Kashmir Rifles during the Battle of Purang in a campaign that was led by General Zorawar Singh against the Chinese in Western Ladakh in August 1841, and which was now a prized war trophy of his old regiment.

After the solemn Church service, when the veterans debated the involvement of NATO in launching 'Operation Deliberate Force' in the war in erstwhile Yugoslavia that had now entered its third year and there were also confirmed reports of Slavic fighters from Russia and Greece siding with the Serbs, and Islamic groups from the Middle East and other Asian countries including Pakistan siding with the Bosnian Muslims, Shiraz was firmly of the opinion that as far as the United Nations Organization was concerned it had out lived its utility, and it was always the Americans with their allies who were now calling all the shots. And a few days later on 2nd June 1995, when the US Air Force pilot C Scott O'Grady's F-16 was shot down over Bosnia-Herzegovina while patrolling the NATO no fly zone, it seemed that history would once again repeat itself. After all both the World Wars had originated from this very heart of Europe, when Archduke Ferdinand was assassinated in 1914 and which was followed in 1938 by Hitler's forced occupation of neighbouring Austria. And whereas in the first case it was a Serb who killed the Archduke, in the second case under Hitler's Nazi regime, it had led to the extermination of the Jews and which subsequently gave birth to Israel. And with the present war in spite of NATO's intervention showing no signs of moving towards a just and peaceful solution, Shiraz was now worried that the ethnic war between the Christians and the Muslims in Bosnia-Herzegovina could well lead to a greater divide between the two largest communities in the world. As far as territory was concerned, it was the Muslims and Christians of various sects that dominated the world and with the oil glut in the predominantly Muslim region of the Persian Gulf becoming the most dominant factor in regulating the world economy and power play, Shiraz was apprehensive about the United States intentions in that region. As it is with the breaking up of the communist world, and with the shift in the balance of power, the erstwhile Balkan state of Yugoslavia had become a veritable powder keg and one that could explode into a holocaust at any moment. Moreover, with the rich reserves of the black gold in and around Iraq, Saudi Arabia, Iran, Libya, Nigeria and in the entire Gulf Region, which were predominantly Muslim countries and most of whom were being ruled by dictators, the fall out of the war in Bosnia could well lead to a larger conflict between the radical Muslim fundamentalists and the western powers. Even Saddam Hussein had started his non cooperation movement with UNSCOM and the IAEA, the International Atomic Energy Agency and the Iraqi dictator was now threatening to end all assistance if economic sanctions against his country were not lifted by 31st August, 1995.

With France and Russia now becoming more interested in making financial deals with Saddam, than in disarming the country, and the world wide call for an Islamic Caliphate by radical organizations like the Al-Qaida and others gaining momentum, it was now quite evident to Shiraz that it would be terrorism that would now take centre stage in settling various old scores. And with worldwide nuclear proliferation and technical knowhow being exported illegally by third world countries including Pakistan, North Korea and others, he shuddered at the very thought of an Islamic nuclear bomb falling into the hands of diehard terrorists who were being religiously motivated by the radical clerics to uphold the flag of Islam. And in the present scenario of the anti US and anti Israel stance taken by the radical Muslims, the use of a nuclear suitcase bomb and other weapons of mass destruction by them therefore could not be ruled out entirely, wrote Shiraz in his little red diary.

On 1st July, 1995 and in response to hard evidence that was unearthed by UNSCOM, when Iraq admitted for the first time the existence of an offensive biological weapons program, but denied its weaponry, Shiraz was not very wrong in his assessment and his contention was further substantiated when on 8th August, Saddam's own son-in-law Hussein Kamil who had supervised Iraq's unconventional weapons program defected to Jordan and spilled the beans. According to one report and following the invasion of Kuwait, Saddam had initiated a crash program to build a nuclear bomb and a specific one that could be delivered with a SCUD missile, but the plan was derailed as soon as the 1991 Gulf War began. And when Kamil further stated that Iraq had also developed and produced the deadly VX, a highly lethal chemical agent, and that Baghdad in response to the Security Council's vote on November 29, 1990, which authorized military action against Iraq had even armed twenty five SCUD missile warheads with biological agents anthrax and botulinum and that were only to be used as a last resort if Saddam Hussein's regime was ousted by the coalition partners, it sent shock waves around the world. It also proved to Shiraz how dangerous were these weapons of mass destruction in the hands of such despotic dictatorial rulers.

In the meantime there was also some very bad news for the Muslims of Bosnia and the world, when the Serbian war machine under the command of General Ratko Miladic and in complete defiance of the UN peacekeepers that were stationed in Srebrenica for protecting the Bosnian Muslim refugees in that besieged enclave started the ethnic cleansing of the area. The genocide was reminiscent of what Hitler had done to the Jews and in some cases it was even worse as Serbian forces killed, raped, burnt and looted at will, and by the time the mass scale massacre of the Bosnians ended, nearly 8000 Muslims mostly men and boys had lost their lives. Though by mid July, the Serbs were in total control of Srebrenica, but the war crimes that were committed by them was beyond anybody's imagination. When Shiraz read a few reports that were written by journalist David Rohde who had seen it all happening in what was supposed to be a 'safe haven' under the United Nations Dutch peace keeping force, he was convinced that such policing duties by the Blue Berets had no meaning in such ethnic conflicts. And while the dirty war between the Croats, Serbs and the Bosnians hogged the headlines in the European press, Shiraz in August with the launching of Windows 95 by Microsoft became even more computer savvy.

Now for Shiraz there was bad news from India too, when on the 4th of July, 1995 America's Independence Day, members from the Al-Faran terrorist organization kidnapped 6 foreign tourists and that to at the height of Kashmir's summer tourist season from the Liddarwat area of Pahalgam. The six foreigners, all young males included two British, two Americans, a German and a Norwegian. They had come for trekking in that popular tourist resort. The kidnappers were now holding them hostage, and for their safe return they were demanding the release of Maulana Masood Azhar and 20 other terrorists who were being held in jails by the Indian authorities. Born on 10th July 1968, Maulana Masood Azhar was the son of a school headmaster from Bhawalpur in Pakistan and who as a teenager was educated at the Jamia Islamia in Karachi. A follower of the Deobandhi School of Islamic teachings like his father, he became a diehard 'Jehadi' after the Russians occupied Afghanistan. In August 1989, and after the Soviets withdrew, he as an active member of HuM, 'Harkat-ul-Mujahideen' started publishing the 'Sada-e-Mujahid,' a propaganda magazine that was distributed free at public meetings and on Friday prayer meetings at the mosques to motivate the young Muslim blood to uphold the traditions of Islam and to take up arms against those who were anti Muslims. The young boys were not only given training in arms, but were also indoctrinated to fight for their Kashmiri Muslim brothers and sisters, who according to the young Maulana were being exploited and killed by the Hindus and the Indian government. This was the first time that a previously unheard of terrorist group had claimed responsibility for the kidnapping of foreigners in Kashmir and Shiraz concluded that the operation must have had the blessings of the Pakistan and the ISI so as to once again covertly internationalize the Kashmir issue.

In January 1993, the Maulana was tasked by the ISI to go to Kashmir and take command of the newly formed Harkat-ul-Ansar that had been formed by merging the elements from Harkat-ul-Jehad Islami (HuJI) and the Harkat-ul-Mujahideen.(HuM), but in February 1994, he was caught while travelling from Delhi to Srinagar. This was a prized catch by the Indians and Shiraz now wondered whether the Indian government will once again bow down to the demands of the terrorists like it did in the case of Mufti Mohammed's daughter, Rubaiya Saeed in 1989. However, his gut feeling was that this time the Indians will not compromise on the issue and he was dead right. Four days after the kidnapping, John Childs, an American had managed to escape and on 13th August, when the Norwegian Hans Christian Ostro's beheaded body was found near Pahalgam, Shiraz concluded that his execution could well have been in retaliation for Child's getting away. And with the Indian government not relenting to the demands of the terrorists, he now feared that the remaining four foreigners too may face the same dreadful fate.

CHAPTER-23

From Real Life to Reel Life

During that month of July 1995, while the search for the kidnapped foreigners and the hunt for the terrorists were intensified in the Kashmir valley, Monty with Reeta landed up in Srinagar to stay a few weeks with Peevee who was shooting for his new film. The story was based on the life of the late Major Shiraz Ismail Khan and his heroic deeds, both during the 1965 and 1971 conflict with Pakistan and was aptly titled 'Sherdil'. Monty had once narrated the story to one of the film producers and he was so fascinated by it that he took Monty as his advisor and Peevee as the hero of the film.

The fact that it was the son in real life playing the role of his own biological father in reel life was known only to Monty, Reeta and Shupriya, and they had decided that in the film Shiraz would live and die as a bachelor. But since the Hindi film must have a heroine, the script therefore included a Punjabi Sikh girl, Shiraz's first flame in NDA and the heroine therefore would play the role of his girlfriend on the screen. Since the film required the active involvement of the Indian army and for which necessary permission had been taken from the Army Headquarters in Delhi, Monty, Reeta, Peevee and the entire unit crew members were privileged to spend a whole month with the officers and jawans of the Indian army in an active field area. Staying in bunkers and eating 'langar'(common cook house for the soldiers) food they all enjoyed every minute of it. The Jawans from the Bravo Company of the Jammu and Kashmir Rifles, that Shiraz had commanded were simply thrilled because not only would they be taking part in the film, but they would also have the privilege to closely interact with Deepak Kumar, the handsome new budding Bollywood star.

On the final day and after the pack up was announced, a big camp fire with a 'Barakhana' was held and Monty who had come well prepared presented a big pure silver bust of his foster brother, Major Shiraz Ismail

Khan, PVC(posthumous) to the battalion. That evening seeing the moistness in the eyes of some of the veteran soldiers, when the presentation was being made, the crew of the film unit realized what comradeship and loyalty in the army was all about. They had no doubt that the infantry officers, JCO's and Jawans guarding the Line of Control in Kashmir were doing a commendable job. It was a 24 hour round the clock duty day in and day out and they could not afford to lower their guard even for a minute. Every day they risked their lives and limbs as they ceaselessly and actively patrolled the border to stop the infiltration from across by the terrorists and militants and which at times was literally a back breaking task. The Line of Control that ran for miles and miles along the high mountains, forests and valleys of what was once the Maharaja of Kashmir's kingdom was prone to infiltration and it was only through good intelligence network, which most of the time unfortunately was lacking that the Indian troops were at times able to ambush the infiltrators and capture a few of them alive.

Late that evening over a night cap in the officer's mess, Peevee after having entertained the officers with a few old popular Hindi and English songs on his guitar, he showed them on the VCR the 1995 national award winning film 'The Bandit Queen'. Based on the true life story of Phoolan Devi, the dreaded female dacoit that was brlliantly portrayed by Seema Biswas, the film was also equally brilliantly directed by Shekhar Kapoor. But it had faced a lot of flak and controversy initially because it portrayed not only brutal violence, but also some explicit sex scenes, and that unfortunately did not go down well with the Indian Film Censor Board. However, Peevee had somehow managed to get a pirated copy of the uncensored version and all the officers thoroughly enjoyed the movie.

Next day early afternoon, when Monty and Reeta were waiting at the Srinagar airport to catch the flight to Delhi and a news paper report said that Rajan Pillai, the fugitive tycoon at the age of 47 had died of cirrhosis of the liver in the casualty ward of the Deen Dayal Upadhaya hospital in Delhi, they just could not believe it. It was only the other day, when the biscuit tycoon looking hale and hearty had been picked up from a posh hotel in New Delhi by the Delhi police and now he was no more. The son of a cashew exporter from Kerala, Rajan was active in the hotel and food industries, but was presently going through bad times. He had been charged for defrauding the Singapore government of millions of dollars, but before he could be sentenced by the Singapore court he had escaped to India. Surprisingly the magistrate in Delhi before sending him to the Tihar Jail had rejected his appeal for medical treatment. There was no doubt that Rajan

Pillai loved his drinks and as a host entertained lavishly with only Blue Label for the whisky drinkers and Dom Perignon champagne for those who liked sparkling wine, but what Monty could not fathom was how a well known personality like the flamboyant Rajan Pillai who was internationally well known and who had featured on the covers of various business magazines could manage to escape from Singapore on an Singapore Airlines flight when his passport had already been impounded by the court.

"Well if that really be the case then I won't be surprised if he has been bumped off. After all he had a lot of political connections in India too and politics and money do go hand in hand," sarcastically said Reeta, as the Indian Airlines announced the departure of its flight to Delhi via Jammu.

During the last week of August 1995, Monty on the advice of his old school pal Charu drove down to Chandigarh. Charu had conveyed to him that since land in and around Chandigarh and Mohali was still going cheap, it was therefore well worth investing in the real estate there. Accordingly Monty decided to buy three big plots one each for himself, his wife Reeta and one for Peevee. Late on the evening of 31st August, after having concluded the deal for the three plots, Monty with Charu went to the Punjab government secretariat to call on and thank the secretary concerned. He was also was an ex Sanawarian and was the one who had helped Monty out with the deal. And while the three of them were enjoying a cup of tea in the secretary's office and talking about their wonderful days in school, suddenly there was a huge explosion that shook the entire building. As they rushed out they found that the Chief Minister of Punjab, Beant Singh had been targeted.

The Chief Minister was a Sikh from the Congress Party and though he had been provided with round the clock security by the elite NSG commandos, but the Sikh extremists it seems had managed to penetrate and kill him at his own office doorstep. The bizarre killing took place when the Chief Minister was about to get into his bullet proof car that was standing under the portico. And it was Dilawar Singh the suicide human bomber and a serving policeman who had triggered off the device. The powerful bomb not only killed the Chief Minister, but 11 others also who were responsible for his security.

"'My God, if the state cannot even protect its own Chief Minister in his own office, then I am afraid nobody is safe in this land," said Monty.

"'Yes I agree, but Beant Singh who was born in Bilaspur village near Ludhiana and who I believe had also served for a while in the Indian army as an Havildar in the Army Education Corps had been asking for it. His high handedness in seeking an easy solution by eliminating all and sundry who were even remotely connected with the Khalistan movement through fake encounters had only added more fuel to the fire and led to his own destruction," added Charu as he gave a few examples on how innocent young Sikh boys from villages were rounded up in the middle of the night, tortured and then eliminated.

And while the killings in Punjab on a tit for tat basis continued unabated, the search for the remaining four foreign trekkers who were abducted by the terrorist group loyal to Maulana Masood Azhar continued in an around the Kashmir valley. But the appeal by their near and dear ones to the Al-Faran militants to set them free fell on deaf years. Meanwhile inside Pakistan another coup by military officers led by a serving General Officer was in the offing.

Major General Zahirul Islam Abbassi, the man who had served in the ISI and who was deeply influenced by the program of Islamization in the Pakistan army by the late General Zia-ul-Haq had developed strong links with radical Islamic religious and political groups, and he was now preparing to topple the Benazir Bhutto government and proclaim an Islamic Caliphate in Pakistan. As a Brigadier and while serving as Pakistan's Defence Attache in New Delhi he was expelled from India and was declared persona non grata on charges of spying for his country. The same gentleman was now plotting a bizarre operation to assassinate not only the lady Prime Minister of the country, but also some cabinet ministers, the Army Chief and all the Corps Commanders also.

After the Siachen fiasco in 1991, when Abbassi as the Brigade Commander at Skardu without taking permission from his superiors launched an attack to capture an Indian post on the glacier and the attack failed miserably with heavy casualties to the Pakistanis, the then Army Chief, General Asif Nawaz Janjua had removed him from command. Abbassi was now the Director General Infantry at the GHQ in Rawalpindi and he knew that his future had been sealed. He and his co-conspirators, which included Brigadier Mustansar Billa, Colonel Mohammed Azad Minhas and some 40 other officers in the rank of Colonels, Lt Colonels and Majors had strong links with the hard-line Muslim groups such as the Jamaat-i-Islami and others inside the country. All of them together with the backing of these various fundamentalist religious leaders had planned the operation during the Corps Commanders conference that was scheduled to be held on the 30th of September 1995. The conspirators had planned to not only eliminate the Prime Minister who was scheduled to address the high powered meeting, but also all the top bigwigs of the army on that day and thereafter proclaim a radical Islamist state that would be akin to the Taliban regime in Afghanistan. But luck was not on Abbassi's side.

On 26th September 1995, when a truck carrying a cache of Kalashnikov rifles and rocket launchers escorted by a Brigadier and a Colonel in civil clothes in a staff car was on its way to Rawalpindi from the North West Frontier Province, it was stopped at the customs check point near Kohat. While the Brigadier and the Colonel got out of the car to urge the custom officials to let the truck pass, they were arrested by officers from the military intelligence directorate. Luckily Pakistan's military intelligence directorate under Major General Ali Quli Khan had got wind of the bizarre plot in time and he together with Lt General Jehangir Karamat, the Director General Military Operations at GHQ had timely foiled the dare devil design of the plotters.

A few days later, when Major General Aslam Rehman Khan gave a more detailed account of the plot to Shiraz on the telephone and told him that all of them including the kingpin Major General Abbassi had been arrested, Shiraz sitting in Paris wondered what would have happened if the plot had succeeded. He could never imagine that officers of Pakistan army could ever do such a thing by killing their own senior most serving officers. There was however no doubt in his mind that Pakistan's present policy of giving patronage to the Taliban in Afghanistan had only made matters worse and he dreaded the day when fundamentalists and Muslim religious leaders and organizations like the Tableeghi Jamaat, the Harkat-ul-Mujahideen and Harkat-ul-Jihad-al-Islami would start calling all the shots in Pakistan. It seemed that Major General Abbassi had forged strong links with these groups and had also actively worked with the Taliban Militia, and had he succeeded in establishing a radical Islamist state, the breakup of Pakistan would have been inevitable and that would been the end of Jinnah's great dream of having a secular and strong Pakistan, wrote Shiraz in his little red diary.

The very day Major General Abbassi and others were arrested in Rawalpindi, the orders for the promotion of Major General Aslam Rehman Khan to Lt General had been approved by the government and he was tipped to take over the prestigious Pakistan X Corps, the Corps that was responsible for the defence of POK, Pakistan Occupied Kashmir.

"That calls for celebrations Abbu", said his 13 year old daughter Nasreen who suggested that they should first go to see the new movie 'Jeeva' and follow it up with a sumptuous family dinner in one of the posh restaurants in the city. The film with its two very popular songs 'Janu Sun Zara' and 'Choo Kay Tere Man Ko Hawa' had a good story line and was making waves in Pakistan. The film ably directed by Syed Noor it seems had uplifted the fledging film industry of Lollywood as people from all walks of life went to see it in the movie halls.

"Alright and after the movie we will have dinner at your favourite restaurant 'The Golden Grill' on the Mall," said the loving father, as his wife Farzana and son Captain Samir Rehman Khan (Vovka) who was also ADC to his father presented him with his new pips.

"But do remember there is a always a slip between the cup and the lip and the 10 Corps vacancy can only be filled once the present incumbent retires on 30th November. And one never knows what can happen tomorrow if diehards like Major General Abbassi and others like him decide to Talibanize the Pakistan army, and which even today is recognized as one of the highly professional defense forces in the world," said Aslam Rehman very proudly.

For dinner that evening at the Golden Grill, Aslam Rehman also invited his brother—in—law Karim Malik and his family. Karim was married to his sister Mehmuda and had completed his tenure in war torn Kabul. He was now on his way to Khartoum as Pakistan's Ambassador to Sudan and he was eagerly looking forward to a comparative easier time with his family in that poor African country. For the safety of his family, he had not taken them to Kabul, except for a short holiday once, and since their married daughter Tarranum and her husband had taken up teaching jobs in an undergraduate school in the United States, his wife Mehmuda with her 18 year old son Javed had stayed most of the time in the Rehman's ancestral Haveli at Peshawar. Having been posted earlier in Egypt, Mehmuda who was now nearing 50 was also looking forward to her husband's new assignment. Her husband was indeed very lucky to get out of Kabul on the 5th of September, because on the very next day an angry mob had attacked the Pakistani Embassy and had burnt it down. These were the people from the other factions who were angry with Pakistan for supporting the Taliban in the civil war that was still raging in that country.

That evening during dinner, when Karim Malik in brief described the ugly situation in Afghanistan that had now engulfed the whole country and criticized Pakistan's ludicrous stance in supporting Mullah Mohammed Omar and his Taliban both overtly and covertly, Aslam Rehman was fully in agreement with him. Karim was of the opinion that the Taliban though they were Pashtuns, but it was a more autocratic militant fundamentalist organization and one that could not be trusted and which he felt would be detrimental to Pakistan's interest in the long run. According to Karim Malik it all started in early September 1994, when on the directions of the Benazir government and her Interior Minister, Major General Nasrullah Babar, the Pakistan army with its Frontier Corps artillery and the ISI supported the attack by the Taliban on Spin Boldak and which helped them to capture it. This was a strategic post on the Afghan-Pakistan border which had a big arms dump, and this covert support by Pakistan to the Taliban had angered the other war lords who were also vying to take control of the country.

After the withdrawal of the Soviets and the fall of the Najeebullah government, there was a power vaccum in Afghanistan, and even the efforts by the United Nations to bring political stability and peace to the region had yielded no results. And as a consequence of this, the civil war between the various factions continued unabated. For Pakistan the instability in neighbouring Afghanistan was seen as a boon for its own internal security and which they thought would give the country the much needed strategic depth and buffer against India. But when the Pashtun-Islamist group that was led by Gulbuddin Hekmatyar and supported by Pakistan failed to deliver the goods, the goverment decided to switch sides and was now fully backing the Taliban.

Formed in 1994, by the one eyed cleric Mullah Mohammed Omar with a handful of his followers, who were mostly young religious students, the Taliban with active support from Pakistan had grown from strength to strength. The students had all been schooled in Islamic seminaries that were locally known as' Madrassas' in Pakistan. These highly motivated Mujahideens had also fought against the Soviets in Afghanistan. The word Taliban meaning literarily students had now become a strong political militant faction not only in the Kandahar province, but also in Herat which they had captured only recently. Mulla Omar who was born in Nodeh, near Kandahar in 1959 had fought as a guerilla commander with the Harkat-i-Inquilab-i-Islami faction in the war with the Russians and had lost an eye when he was hit by shrapnel. The wound had also marred his cheek and forehead. Basically all his recruits initially came from the Quranic schools that had been set up in the many Afghan refugee camps in and around the North West Frontier Province of Pakistan and Karim Malik now feared that this highly motivated young lot with their strict Islamic Shariar laws and Kalashnikov culture would soon spawn the growth of more such radical Islamist militant organizations inside the Pakistan and that would further destabilize the nation. It was also widely rumoured that while fighting the

Russians in Afghanistan, Mullah Omar had also developed strong links with Osama Bin Laden who was now in Khartoum, Sudan and there was now every possibility of the Taliban being helped both economically and militarily by the Al-Qaida. Late that evening after the sumptuous dinner that was hosted by Aslam Rehman, Mehmuda in order to celebrate her favourite brother's promotion to that of a Lt General invited all of them for a nightcap and coffee at Karim Malik's ancestral house that had been recently renovated. Opening a chilled bottle of Dom Perignom champagne that her husband had brought from Kabul, Mehmuda raised a toast with the words. "To my dearest brother and may he look young forever and become the Army Chief one day."

"But let him first successfully command a Corps, and looking at the manner in which the officers, JCO's and soldiers are been constantly indoctrinated by the radical Mullahs and of which Major General Abbassi and his group are living examples, I would rather prefer that my husband is spared that unique honour," said Farzana somewhat sarcastically.

CHAPTER-24

Lollywood versus Bollywood and the Beginning of the Bomb Culture

During that month of October 1995, while the Pakistanis were still going gaga over their Lollywood hit movie 'Jeeva', in India the people were going crazy watching the newly released Bollywood blockbuster 'Dilwale Dulhaniya Le Jayenge.'The movie with Shah Rukh Khan and Kajol as the leading love birds and the versatile Amrish Puri as the heroine's old fashioned father was filmed mostly in Europe and that was released nationwide on 20th October, within the very first week itself had broken all existing records. Set to some delightful music by Jatin-Lalit, the family drama wonderfully directed by the debutant young director Aditya Chopra had even over taken last year's hit film 'Hum Aapke Hai Kaun' that had Salman Khan and Madhuri Dikshit in the lead roles and which was directed by the veteran Sooraj Barjatya.

Peevee who had seen both the films no less than three times each had jokingly written to his Mom Number 2 in Havana that at the rate the Khan trio of Salman, Aamir and Sharukh had started dominating Bollywood with their extraordinary histrionic talents, his chances of ever reaching the top would remain a distant dream and he was therefore seriously contemplating to change his screen name from that of Deepak Kumar to Sherdil Khan, which was the title of his new film that was to be released on 26th January, 1996 on India's Republic Day. But little did Peevee know that biologically he was actually a Khan and when Shupriya received his letter, she also wondered that if Shiraz had lived, what name they would have given to their loving son? Till today this thought had never struck her and when she noted the date for the premiere and the release of the film, she realized that she too was now getting fairly old. She had remained a silent suffering widow for the last 25 years and on the 26th January, 1996 it would be her 46th birthday.

Meanwhile in America, Bill Clinton and his government were not feeling too happy with the recent convictions of the ten accused that were directly and indirectly charged with the bombing of the World Trade Centre in New York in 1993. Shiraz too was also of the opinion that with Muslim fundamentalism on the rise all over the world, this was only the beginning and he felt that there was now an urgent and dire need for all members of the United Nations and also those in the Security Council to join hands, put their heads together and tackle this menace of terrorism on a worldwide global basis. According to him this was only the tip of the iceberg and if this hydra-headed monster was not beheaded soon, then the entire world would never be safe again. With the abduction of the foreigners from Pahalgam on 4th July who were all white skin people from the western world by the Al-Faran terrorist group, and with still no trace of them, though more than three months had passed, Shiraz wondered whether this was the handiwork of the Pakistani government who by training and using such proxy organizations were trying to once again focus world opinion in general, and the Muslim world opinion in particular on the ever burning issue of Kashmir. And while he was writing an official paper on the growth of world terrorism and the dire need for close cooperation between all races of mankind and irrespective of their colour, creed or religion to stem this growing menace, and which he wanted the Pakistan Prime Minister to present during the forthcoming UN General Assembly annual session, the headlines in an American magazine caught his eye.It read. 'The Million Man March in the nation's capital led by the leader of Muslims, Louis Farrakhan takes the White Americans by surprise.'

The mammoth march that was held on the 16th of October was basically to bring home to President Clinton and the whites of America that the great divide that still existed between the Blacks and the Whites must be removed once and for all. According to Farrahkhan there were still two Americas, one Black and one White and they were both separate and unequal in all respects. According to Mr Khan's logic, rebellion to tyrants was obedience to Allah and the basic reason why he had called for this mammoth march of the Blacks of America from every religion was to unite and fight for their rights as equal citizens and pledge as Thomas Jefferson had said years ago that America must work for a perfect union. The very fact that a large number of young Blacks in America had become Muslims and that they could be motivated by radical fundamentalist groups to even take up arms and fight for their rights was therefore now also a distinct possibility. While reading through Farrahkhan's long speech that was laced with history, facts and witticism, Shiraz was reminded of the late Martin Luther King's memorable speech that was titled 'I have a Dream' and which was delivered so very eloquently by the Christian leader nearly three decades ago. But he now seriously doubted whether the Whiteman would ever accept a Black as his equal in a sophisticated and developed country like the United States of America, the only super power and super policeman in the world that had now started blatantly dictating to the rest of the world of what was right and what was wrong economically, politically, socially and even morally.

And while some of the Whites in America including some Jews felt that Farrahkhan's outburst could well trigger off a racial backlash, in Tel Aviv a fortnight later on 4th, November, 1995 Yigal Amir a young orthodox Jew and a law student from Bar-Ilan University on the King of Israel Square in Tel Aviv pumped in three bullets from close range into his own Prime Minister, Yitzhak Rabin with his semi-automatic Beretta point 38 pistol and shot him dead. And though the reason given was that Yigal Amir was opposed to Rabin's peace initiative in signing the Oslo Accords, Shiraz however wondered whether it was a conspiracy and a plot by the hard-line Jews of Israel to derail the peace process in the trouble torn Middle East. At around 9.30 PM after Rabin had addressed the rally that was in support of the Oslo Accords and started walking down the City Hall steps towards his waiting car, Yigal Amir fired those three fatal shots. That day Rabin somehow chose not to wear his bullet proof vest though he had earlier been advised to do so and ironically he had in his blood drenched pocket the words 'Shir Lashalom' (Song to Peace). It was a popular Israeli song that conveyed the impossibility of bringing back to life a dead person and therefore the need for peace. And a few days later on 19th November 1995, when the Egyptian Islamic Jihad carried out an attack on the Egyptian Embassy in Islamabad, Pakistan and which killed 18 others including four diplomats and the two suicide bombers, and wounded nearly sixty others, Karim Malik and his wife Mehmuda were indeed very lucky to have escaped unhurt, and it was only providence that had saved the couple from that terrible disaster.

Having served in Egypt earlier and prior to their departure for Khartoum, Karim and Mehmuda at 10 AM that morning were scheduled to pay a courtesy call on Mr Mohammed Noman Galal, the Egyptian Ambassador to Pakistan. While on their way, they decided to stop by at the ANZ Grindlays Bank to collect their traveller's cheques. The bank was located right across the road near the embassy. At around 9.30 A.M and as soon as they entered the bank there was a deafening explosion outside. Had the car bomb exploded even a few seconds earlier, the couple would have eiher died or would have been badly wounded. According to one eye witness, the perpetrators had first attacked the embassy security detail that was guarding the premises with guns and grenades and seconds later a pickup truck with a 250 pound bomb had rammed into the embassy building. Most of those killed were innocent Pakistanis who were standing outside waiting to collect their visas or were in the process of applying for it.

"My God what is this wicked world coming to," said a badly shaken Mehmuda as she and Karim joined in the rescue operations. Seeing the carnage that included a few headless torsos, and the severed limbs of innocent men, women and children lying on the street, Mehmuda wondered which way Islam was heading. It was suppose to be a religion of tolerance and peace and she was therefore surprised when an Egyptian militant Muslim organization claimed responsibility for the blast. According to one reliable report this was in retaliation against the Egyptian diplomatic staffers who were reportedly gathering intelligence on the various Jehadi factions inside Pakistan and the attack according to one reliable source had been master minded by Al Qaida's number two man Ayman-al-Zawahiri. It seemed that Zawahiri's initial plan was to attack the American or some other western embassy, but since these were all very well guarded, the group was finally tasked to blow up the Egyptian embassy. Zawahiri who was Osama bin Laden's right hand man it seems was upset when reports of Egyptian diplomats using Pakistan as a base were found spying on the Arab Mujahideens and thereby helping the authorities concerned to throw them out of the country. This particular Egyptian group had earlier also attempted to assassinate the Egyptian President, Hosni Mubarak during his recent visit to Eithopia.

A week earlier, when another bomb in Riyadh, Saudi Arabia destroyed a three storied building that was being used by the United States military and civil personnel responsible for training the Saudi Arabian National Guard and it killed six people, including five Americans and injured sixty others, and a group that called itself as 'The Islamic Movement for Change' claimed full responsibility for it, Shiraz came to the conclusion that those Muslim countries that had close ties with the U.S. both militarily and economically were now under the scanner of such radical Muslim organizations and Pakistan was no exception either. Putting two and two together, Shiraz wondered whether Osama Bin Laden who was now in Khartoum together with his radical Egyptian partner Al-Zawahiri was behind this deadly explosion also. Having been expelled from his native Saudi Arabia and with his anti western outlook against an imperialistic America, Osama Bin

Laden was quite capable of expressing his displeasure through violent means against the Saudi royalty and according to him the King and others in his government had now become pawns in the hands of the Americans. And as the year came to a close, the only silver lining to a world that was now being driven by ethnic and sectarian conflicts was the signing of the Dayton peace accord. Brokered by the United States, the agreement that was reached on 21ˢᵗ November in Dayton, Ohio was finally signed by the three Balkan Presidents in Paris on 14ᵗʰ December, 1995.

That day with the galaxy of international leaders like Bill Clinton, John Major, Jacques Chirac, Helmut Kohl, Viktor Chernomyrdin and others attending the signing in ceremony, which was followed by a mandate given by the United Nations to NATO to implement the military aspects of the agreement, Shiraz wondered whether the 60,000 strong NATO led multinational force would be able to deliver the goods. The Bosnian conflict which was the bloodiest in European history since the end of World War II and which led to the ethnic cleansing of hundreds of thousands of innocent men, women and children and the majority of whom were Muslims could not be forgotten so very easily, unless the perpetrators of this dastardly crime were brought to justice, wrote Shiraz in his small red diary.

CHAPTER-25

Kalashnikovs from the Sky and Scams at the Drop of a Hat

While the world welcomed the Dayton Peace Accord, an old Russian made Antonov 26 cargo aircraft with a Latvian crew from Riga having landed in Burgas, Bulgaria got busy in picking up its precious cargo of 77 wooden crates.

Late on the night of 17th December, 1995 while Peevee was getting ready to dorn his make up in the role of an Indian Robin Hood for the shooting of his new film titled 'Bidrohi" (The Rebel) which was being shot outdoors near the village of Palamu in the Purulia district of West Bengal, he heard the loud drone of an aircraft. And as he came out of his caravan and looked upwards, he was surprised to see parachutes coming down from the sky. At first he thought that maybe the army and the Indian air force were carrying out a joint military exercise, but when a large wooden crate landed some 50 yards away from him and out came its contents, he got the shock of his life. It was literally raining Kalashnikovs from the sky that night. Suddenly on that cold winter December night with parachutes landing all over the place, the villagers of Palamu and those from the other nearby ones also came running outside to see what was happening. This certainly was not a part of the film script and with weapons and ammunition strewn all around the villages; soon the local police also arrived on the scene. With the commotion created all around, the film shooting had to be immediately stopped and the locale also had to be changed.

"I wonder what this is all about," said the harassed film Director as the unit packed up and drove towards the West Bengal-Bihar border to select a new site.

"Since these weapons were dropped clandestinely and in the dead of night, it could well be a consignment for some militant group like the Maoists who are fairly active in this region," said Peevee.

"Well let us only hope that they do not fall into the wrong hands and we are able to continue with our shooting schedule," added the Director while asking the driver to step on the accelerator.

Surprisingly, when Peevee returned to Bombay and he read in the papers that an Indian Air Force MIG-21 had intercepted an AN-26 and had forced it to land at Bombay's Sahar airport at around 1.40 AM on the morning of 22nd December and that the crew and others travelling in it had been arrested, the mystery of the Kalashnikovs that were dropped at Purulia was partially solved. The consignment of arms it seemed was for some militant activists from the Anand Marg organization. It was a socio-spiritual organization that was allegedly being targeted and eliminated by the Communist government of West Bengal and the Anand Margis had now decided to strike back with vengeance. According to a reliable intelligence source, the consignment of arms was brokered by Peter Bleach, a former Corporal in the British military intelligence for a Danish national who was an international smuggler and who went by the name of Kim Davey, but whose real name was Niels Christian Nielsen. Nielsen had been earlier arrested in May 1982 for two robberies and for money laundering by the Danish police, but had later escaped. He was now also wanted by the Interpol for drug and gold smuggling, as also for counterfeiting 100 dollar bills.

When the aircraft was forced to land at Bombay, and while all the others were taken into custody Kim Davey had quietly slipped away and disappeared before the police arrived. The Air Traffic Control at Sahar had no clue that this was the same aircraft that had dropped the arms at Purulia and it was under the impression that the aircraft had mistakenly strayed into Indian air space and while cruising on an unscheduled route it was forced to land at Sahar. But what was even more surprising was the fact that the intruding lumbering aircraft on 17th December evening had taken off from Karachi, it was refueled at Varanasi, and having dropped the arms over Purulia, it was again refueled at Calcutta before flying off to Phuket in Thialand. And when it finally landed there at Phuket on the morning of 18th December, nobody was any the wiser. Then on 21st December, from Phuket it again re-entered Indian air space and landed at Madras. After being refueled there it once again took off at 10.45 PM at night from Madras and was on its way to Karachi, when it was forced to land by the Indian MIG-21 at the Sahar airport in Bombay. After the crew and Peter Bleach had been thoroughly grilled by the Indian intelligence authorities and the cat was out of the bag, Monty in order to get a clearer picture called on his old friend Unni at the Press Club.

"But just tell me how on earth could a intruding aircraft of that big a size cooly fly across the length and breadth of the country and that to without being challenged. And if this is how we defend our skies, and if this is the deplorable state of our security at the airports, then I am afraid one day we will have to pay very dearly for it," said Monty as Unni ordered his third round of Old Monk rum and a beer for his guest

"However let me tell you very confidentially that there is more to it than meets the eye friend" replied Unni as they once again clinked glasses According to Unni, the Indian RAW had been tipped off and were expecting the aircraft to land with the consignment at an airstrip of a disused coalmine near Dhanbad that was known as Panshet Hill. But Davey it seemed thought that to be very dangerous and risky, and therefore had decided to have the consignment air dropped by parachutes instead. And what is still more surprising is that all the crates were marked 'Technical Equipment' and bore the name 'Central Ordnance Depot, Rajendrapur Cantonment, Bangladesh.' Unfortunately for Davey the consignment was dropped miles off target and it never reached the Anand Margis.

While the ineptness of India's intelligence agencies on the Purulia arms drop case in West Bengal hogged the headlines in the Indian Press, another big scandal of much greater magnitude in neighbouring Bihar involving top politicians of that state and the bureaucrats shook the nation from its very roots. The Animal Husbandry scam popularly known as the 'Chara Ghotala' and which involved financial irregularities amounting to a staggering amount of Rupees 1000 crores had become the biggest scam in India's history.

"Compared to this, the Bofors scam is chicken feed my friend and like all such scams, this too I reckon will be swept under the carpet," said Unni somewhat sarcastically as he cursed the system and the crop of corrupt politicians that were now ruling the state as their own fiefdom.

"Yes, and it is immaterial as to which political party they belong to. Whether it is Lalu Prasad Yadav or Jaganath Misra, all of them are birds of the same feather and in the present environment of 'Aaya Ram-Gaya Ram' political roulette and coalition politics that is being played out both by the centre and by the states; they will all one day I bet be exonerated most honourably. After all the CBI and other such investigating agencies in this country who are deputed to go deep into such cases and ferret out the truth are practically helpless. Unfortunately they are today being controlled and dictated by those who are in power and they dare not for their own future cross the line. The Quatrochhi episode in the Bofors case is one such living example where the CBI kept changing colours as and when governments changed in Delhi. And the recent 'Hawala Scam' involving payments allegedly received by top Indian politicians and bureaucrats through the Jain brothers, the big time hawala brokers is another one that has raised eyebrows. And though an enterprising journalist like Vineet Narayan has convincingly got to the bottom of that murky affair, but this too I can bet will never see the light of the day," concluded Unni as he gave a cynical smile and ordered the bar tender to serve him one more large rum with ice and soda.

"But why only blame India, because I think corruption and politics seem to go hand in glove all over the world. Look at the United States, where the Whitewater scandal involving President Clinton and his wife Hillary are hogging the limelight. Though it is strongly rumoured that it was a failed business venture in real estate dealings in the 1970's and the 1980's, but all the same the very fact that both the President of the country and the first lady have been summoned to testify before a grand jury, only goes to show that nobody is above the law in that country. But here in this country it is the other way round because the corrupt politicians are a law into themselves," said a worked up Monty while presenting Unni with a copy of Nani Palkhivala's book, 'We, the Nation' and a bottle of Old Monk Rum which was Unni's favourite.

"But what the hell for?" asked Unni as he called for another chilled beer for Monty,'

"To celebrate our 46 years of becoming a highly corrupted republic and tomorrow incidentally is 26th of January, 1996," added Monty in lighter vein as they once again in unison said cheers.

While India was celebrating their Republic Day with the usual impressive military parade on Rajpath, in Pakistan a handsome General Jehangir Karamat having recently taken over as the new Army Chief from General Wahid Kakkar watched the proceedings on the CNN television channel. Commissioned into the 13th Lancers, the officer from the 1961 batch of the PMA Long Course was the senior most General in the Pakistan army and for a change there was no supersession this time. A graduate of the Quetta Sttaff College and an alumnus from the prestigious US Army Command and General Staff College, Fort Leavenworth and the National Defence College of Pakistan, he had proved his competence at every level of command and staff and the Pakistan armed forces were indeed very happy with his appointment as the Army Chief. And with Karamat's promotion to a full general, Lt General Aslam Rehman Khan also took over the command of Pakistan X Corps from him. It was an active corps that was responsible for operations in Jammu and Kashmir and the Northern Areas including the Siachen Glacier. With his headquarters at Rawalpindi, and with the capital Islamabad next door, Aslam Rehman was also now privy to the high level of corruption that had permeated in each and every walk of life in the country. Led by the greedy politicians and their ever obliging bureaucratic sycophants, the cancer was now deep within the armed forces also. Leading the pack was none other than Asif Ali Zardari, the husband of the Prime Minister, Benazir Bhutto and who was now being openly referred to as 'Mr Ten Per Cent.'

Meanwhile in Havana, Shupriya on 26th January, 1996 while hosting an 'At Home' to celebrate India's 46th Republic Day was pleasantly surprised to see Lalima Sen there. Unknown to the world and to Lalima, they were actually related to one another. In fact they were first cousins. Lalima was the daughter of Shupriya's paternal uncle Samir Sen and his Russian wife Galina and she had recently been posted on deputation to the Havana University to do a research on the life of Che Guevara. With the ongoing talks to have the body of the legendary revolutionary and the hero of the decisive battle of Santa Clara returned to Cuba, Lalima had decided to write Che's biography that was to be published in Spanish, Russian, English and French simultaneously. The release of the book was planned on the day Che Guevera's body would be finally laid to rest in a specially built mausoleum in Santa Clara. Shupriya had first met Lalima and her mother Galina during the Olympic Games at Moscow in 1980 when she was posted there and that was nearly sixteen years ago. And since India's Republic Day coincided with her 46th birthday, Shupriya therefore after the 'At Home' at the Nacionale Hotel, invited Lalima home for some delicious Indian home cooked food which she knew Lalima always relished.

At 52, Lalima like her was also single and though she had never been to India, she was very knowledgeable about the country of her late father's birth. That evening over dinner, when Shupriya learnt that Aunty Galina was no more and that she had because of her heavy smoking died of lung cancer a year ago at the age of 72, she felt sorry for her cousin. While thinking about her own life and that of her cousin who too was now an orphan, she very much desired to disclose the close family link between the two of them and was about to do so by showing her an old family album, when luckily the telephone rang. It was Peevee on the line from Bombay conveying the good news that after the premiere of his latest film 'Sherdil' the press had hailed 'Deepak Kumar' as the rising star of Bollywood and that his portrayal as Major Shiraz Ismail Khan, PVC in the movie was being favourably compared to that of Dev Anand in the early 1950's film 'Hum Dono." Therefore on been reminded that she was now no longer Shupriya Sen but Yeshwant Kaur Bajwa, a senior Indian diplomat of Sikh origin, Shupriya held back the information in the nick of time from Lalima and having put the old album back into her safe, she locked it securely. That night as she got into bed she realized what a terrible blunder she would have committed had she in that weak moment of family bonding told Lalima about her tragic past.

Meanwhile as India, Pakistan and Sri Lanka were getting ready to co-host the cricket World Cup that was scheduled to begin from mid February, a terrorist bomb in Colombo brought down a huge section of the Central Bank building killing nearly a hundred people. And it further dampened the spirit of the island's cricket lovers, when Australia and the West Indies cricket boards for security reasons promptly declined to play any matches on Sri Lankan soil. This was no doubt the worst violence to hit the capital city and it could have been much worse had it not been a national holiday that day. Early morning at around 7 AM, a group of well armed terrorists from the Tamil Tigers exploded a massive truck bomb and then opened fire on innocent bystanders. The very fact that the attack took place in the key business district of the capital city and that too in broad daylight, only proved the point that the hand of terror was now everywhere and that the gun and bomb culture had come to stay.

Sitting in Paris, when Shiraz on television saw how the massive bomb had ripped through Central Colombo and how the three terrorists who were subsequently killed in a firefight were being eulogized and honoured as martyrs by the militant LTTE leader Prabhakaran, he wondered for how much longer would the 14 year old ethnic conflict linger on and take many more innocent lives in the bargain. And on the very next day, when Saddam Hussein's son-in-law, Hussein Kamel the leader of the Iraqi weapons program who had defected earlier returned home and soon thereafter was murdered along with his brother, father, sister and her children for having opened his big mouth, it only further deepened the ongoing Iraq disarmament crisis. A disgusted Saira on being told about the tragedy by Shiraz simply said.

"One always thought that rulers like Aurangzeb and Chengis Khan were demons, but Saddam Hussein seems to be the incarnation of the devil himself and mark my words one day both he and his family will also have to pay very dearly for this."

CHAPTER-26

Cricket Fever and Rimcollian Brotherhood

With the World Cup cricket fever gripping the subcontinent and both India and Pakistan having reached the knock out stage, Peevee decided to take a break from his busy film shooting schedule and he with his father Monty flew down to Bangalore to witness the first quarter-finals between the two arch rivals.

"Believe you me and though this is going to be the mother of all matches, but the pity is that either India or Pakistan will get eliminated. But all the same I am sure it will be a match to remember," said Monty as they drove down to the stadium in a big hired limousine. But no sooner had Peevee alighted from the car, there was pandemonium all around.

"Look, look that's Deepak Kumar, the handsome young Bollywood matinee idol,"shouted a young teenage girl as her group of young cricket enthusiasts mobbed the actor and kept asking for his autograph while others kept requesting for a photograph with him. And when one girl while giggling away boldly smacked and left her lipstick mark on Peevee's cheek an angry Monty holding his son's hand with the help of the police ran inside the jam packed stadium and took their seats inside the pavilion. With his journalist friend Unni's contacts with the top bosses of the BCCI, the Board of Control for Cricket in India and the press, and with cricket having become a big money spinner for the organizers, the presence of Deepak Kumar the actor only added to the glamour and popularity of the game. With his penchant for gambling, Peevee like many others had quietly wagered illegally a sizeable amount for an Indian win with the bookies, and with rumours of match fixing in the air, he hoped and prayed that both the teams winning or losing would play the game in a gentlemanly and fair manner.

"The very fact that Pakistan had won the world cup in 1992 was a factor that must not be ignored. But there is no Imran Khan this time and though he has retired, nevertheless the Pakistanis should not be underestimated, because when it comes to playing India it is like waging a Jihad a holy war," said Monty as India came into bat and thanks to a spirited 92 by Navjot Singh Sidhu reached a very respectable total of 287 for the loss of 8 wickets in their allotted 50 overs.

Peevee was feeling rather happy with the Indian score and more so because it was thanks to the valuable contribution that was made by the quick witted fellow Sardar from Punjab, and he was therefore confident that India would make it to the semi-finals. And if it did so, then he too would also make quite a packet with the concerned bookie.

"Come on Kumble, spin a web around the Pakistanis with your googlies and no dropping catches gentlemen because only catches win matches," shouted Peevee at the top of his voice as the Indian team took the field. In such a do or die match, tempers on the field was inevitable and Monty hoped that no untoward incident should take place. There was no doubt that it was a partisan crowd that strongly backed the Indians, and being the first day and night match, everybody was on tenterhooks from the very first ball.

With Pakistan off to a flying start with 84 runs in 10 overs, Peevee looked a little demoralized at first. But when on that very score the first Pakistani wicket fell and thereafter Pakistan kept losing wickets at regular intervals, Peevee gladly took on the cheer leader's roll. But when Pakistan's score card read 231 for the loss of 6 wickets and the match became a real cliff hanger, Peevee's morale was again down and wiith Javed Miandad still at the crease it was anybody's game. Then suddenly it all happened as Kumble keeping a good line and length snapped up two quick wickets. A little later, when Javed Miandad was run out with the score reading 239 for 8, a pall of gloom fell on the Pakistani bench. Having been already penalized for a slower over rate, they had only 49 overs to reach their target. So finally when Anil Kumble had Attaur Rehman plumb leg before wicket for a duck, it was curtains for Pakistan. India had won by an impressive 39 runs.

On reaching the hotel, Peevee immediately opened a bottle of champagne to celebrate the victory. He had made a cool 80,000 rupees from the bookie and now looked forward to India's semi final encounter with Sri Lanka at the Eden Gardens, Calcutta. With both the West Indies and the Australians refusing to play in Sri Lanka thanks to the bomb blast in Colombo on 31ˢᵗ January, Arjun Ranatunga's team therefore had an easy passage into the quarter finals and having beaten England by 5 wickets they were no longer the under dogs anymore. They had also convincingly beaten India in their league encounter by 6 wickets earlier on 2ⁿᵈ March at New

Delhi, and therefore Peevee this time decided to play safe and to keep away from the bookies.

"By God, only a city like Calcutta can produce such diehard cricket lovers," said Peevee as he with Monty managed to reach the Eden Garden stadium in the nick of time. With all roads leading to the ground they had been held up in a massive traffic jam not far from the huge stadium. And it all started right from the time they got out from their luxury suite at the Taj Bengal hotel and got into the waiting limousine when somebody near the car park shouted loudly in Bengali. "Aee shala dak, dak, ay to amader Deepak Kumar—film Sherdiler hero.' (Arre Look, look this is none other than our Deepak Kumar the hero of the film 'Sherdil') And as the other drivers including the taxi drivers nearby with the paparazzi converged towards the jet black Mercedes 250, actor 'Deepak Kumar' had no other option but to get out of the car and with folded hands request them to make way. Very obligingly they did, but it was all back to square one when the car reached near the Calcutta Race Course and the Red Road crossing. This time it was the paparazzi on motorcycles and scooters who kept demanding a few mug shots of the actor.

"I suggest that the next time you go out with me for cricket matches please keep your make up man handy, so as to give you a new identity," said a disgusted Monty as the Indian team led by Mohammed Azharuddin to the thunderous cheering of a lakh plus crowd took the field. With a disastrous start and the Sri Lankan scorecard reading a measly 35 for 3 and with Jayasurya back in the pavilion, it looked as if India would skittle the Lankans out. But that was not to be as the Sri Lankan middle order took control and fought back to post a respectable total of 251 for 8 in their allotted 50 overs.

"I think though it is quite a challenging total, but for the Indians playing before their home crowd it should not be difficult to win this match provided our openers do their job,"said Monty as Tendulkar and Sidhu walked in to open India's innings. India was cruising along at 98 for 2, till Tendulkar having scored a brisk 65 was brilliantly stumped by Kaluwitharana. However with Azharuddin now at the crease, and a fairly long batting line up to follow, Peevee was confident that India would wrap it up. And just when he was about to take a friendly bet with Monty, the debacle started as Indian wickets kept falling like nine pins.

"Bloody shit are they playing cricket or 'Gulli-Danda'? Even our school boys would have done better and I won't be the least surprised if some of them have been paid to throw away their wickets so very openly," said a highly agitated middle aged dhoti clad Bengali bhadralok. And when Jadeja was clean bowled by Jayasuriya for a duck and the scoreboard read India 115 for 6, the mammoth crowd became restless. Soon thereafter the anger of the spectators was vented on the players on the field as they bombarded them with bottles and half eaten fruits, while some others set fire to the stands. With India staggering at 120 for 8, the umpires briefly stopped the match. But after a few minutes, when it was again resumed and the spectators resorted to their usual hooliganism, the match referee Clive Lloyd had no other option but to call off the match and declare Sri Lanka the winner by default. Disgusted by the unsporting and childish behavior of the crowd, Peevee vowed that he would never ever again witness a cricket match at the Eden Gardens.

"I know the Bengalis are very sensitive people, but to lose under such humiliating circumstances a match that is being watched by millions across the globe on television, this is a bloody national shame and the BCCI should henceforth strike Calcutta off the Indian cricket map, "said a very agitated Peevee as Jagmohan Dalmiya, the President of the BCCI tried to cool ruffled feathers.

"No doubt the 13ᵗʰ of March proved unlucky for India, but the shameful manner in which India made her exit from the world cup was worse than losing the match honourably," said an equally upset Monty.

Meanwhile in Pakistan there was jubilation over India's dishonorable exit from the World Cup as Sri Lanka got ready to take on the mighty Australians in the finals that was to be played at the Gadaffi Stadium in Lahore on 17ᵗʰ March.

"Come what may I am going to root for the Sri Lankans,"said Ruksana Begum to her husband Arif Rehman as they took the flight from Peshawar and landed at Lahore on the 16ᵗʰ evening and where they were joined by Lt General Aslam Rehman and his family.

"I too wish the Aussies get a good drubbing because they think no end of themselves," said Aslam's son Samir Rehman who had recently been promoted as Captain.

"But irrespective of whoever wins, the match should not be a bore and as hosts we must not repeat the unruly behavior at Eden Gardens that we witnessed on TV the other day," said the father as he opened a bottle of champagne in honour of his son's promotion.

"But I am going to cheer the Aussies because my favourite Ricky Ponting will be playing and he is so very cute," said Aslam's 14 year old daughter Nasreen as her mother Farzana gave her a disapproving look and she quietly went to the next room and switched on the TV.

On the next day the Gaddafi Stadium was jam packed, as Aslam Rehman with his family took their seats next to the pavilion. "Come on Arjuna," shouted Samir Rehman loudly as Ranatunga the portly Sri Lankan captain leading his team walked on to the field, while Nasreen with her field glasses zoomed in on the Australian bench and spotted Ricky Ponting who was all padded up. While the Australians with their captain Mark Taylor leading from the front delighted the crowd with some remarkablel stroke play, Nasreen nearly fell of her chair when Ponting at one down and with the score reading at 36 for one at the fall of Mark Waugh's wicket walked in to join his captain. And as the second wicket pair with a century partnership kept the scoreboard ticking, Nasreen kept taunting her elder brother. But as soon as Taylor was dismissed for a brilliant 74, the Australian wickets too started to tumble. Nonetheless they had posted a respectable 241 runs in their allotted 50 overs. But for the Sri Lankans it was a disastrous start and with both the openers Jayasurya and Kaluwitharana back in the pavilion for a measly 23 runs on board it looked as if it would be a cake walk for the Kangaroos. But as the third wicket pair of Gurusinha and Desilva kept the scoreboard ticking with a delightful century partnership, Sri Lanka was back in the game. Thereafter it was Ranatunga with 47 and Desilva with a well made 107 who steered the islanders to a memorable victory. It was a resounding 7 wicket win and as Ranatunga held aloft the Will's trophy, a delighted Samir Rehman quietly surprised his dear sister Nasreen with an autographed photo of Ricky Ponting that was addressed personally to her.

'Arre Bhaiya.I must say you are not only a great sport, but also a very considerate and thoughtful brother,"said a delighted Nasreen as she discreetly kissed the photo of the Australian and then pecked her brother softly on his cheek. That evening after the finals, while the Rehman families with their friends were having dinner at the Punjab Club, Arif Rehman suddenly ran into some old Rimcollians, most of whom were retired service officers from the erstwhile British Indian army. They were part of the committee to welcome their Rimcollian colleagues from India who were scheduled to arrive on 24th March, 1996 on a goodwill visit to Pakistan.

"I sincerely hope now that since most of the Indian Rimcollians are also ex-faujis (ex service officers), we could therefore think off utilizing this forum to foster better friendly ties with India. Moreover, with retired Major General Nasrullah Babar as the Home Minister and also an ex Rimcollian from Robert House who is taking so much personal interest in this unique reunion, he should therefore sound Benazir and his other colleagues in the cabinet to initiate the process of starting a fresh dialogue with the Indian government so as to at least promote a sense of goodwill and trust between the peoples of both countries, which unfortunately is lacking so very badly these days. And with the Pakistani Rimcollians giving us the start, maybe the old boys from Government College Lahore on both sides of the border could also have a similar old boys get together to take the process even further,' said Arif Rehman as he too joined the group of ex-Rimcollians for a drink.

'That is indeed a very good and noble idea Sir and since you are probably one of the senior most Rimcollian's from the North West Frontier Province, we would therefore be delighted to have you and your Begum Sahiba with us at the get together which is being organized by Major General Nasrullah Babar at his residence in Peshawar sometime at the end of the month, and for which an invitation will follow," said the senior most organizer who was also responsible for reception and transport at the Wagah border.

"I must say friendship has no boundaries or borders," remarked Lt General Aslam Rehman to his Uncle Arif Rehman as he went through the detailed program and which also included a trip to Murree that was under his command. On arrival at the Wagah border, the back slapping, hugging and embracing not only by the men folk, but even by their lady wives who had not even met each other before took everybody by complete surprise, and most surprised were the smartly turned out Indian and the Pakistani border guards who had never witnessed anything like this ever before. And when one retired Indian officer told the waiting press that once a Rimcollian is always a Rimcollian and further added that 'Ye Dosti Hum Zindagi Bhar Nahin Todenge,'{This Friendship is Lifelong.) it drew loud cheers from everybody. And as some of them with total moistness in their eyes got into the fleet of Pajeros, Mercedes and Toyota cars that would take them to Lahore, it was nothing short of home coming for those Rimcollians from India whose ancestral homes were now in Pakistan. Though some of them had left Pakistan and India during partition as refugees and the senior Rimcollians from both sides had even fought wars against each other during the 1947-48 operations in Kashmir and again during the wars in 1965 and 1971, the very fact that some of them were meeting after nearly four decades was like brother meeting brother. The elders were so carried away with nostalgia of their good old cadet days at the PWRIMC and the IMA that a few even wept with joy. On that very evening, the fabulous dinner that was hosted by Major Nazir Fatehuddin who was from the 1941-1947 batch of the Rimcollians at the Punjab Club had set the benchmark for the next two weeks. The Pakistanis were hosts par excellence and they looked after their Indian guests as VVIP's. The meeting with 90 year old Mr Catchpole, the old legendary principal of that famous institution, the sumptuous lunch at Major Taj Mohammed Khanzada's ancestral house at Chak Shadi Khan on the banks of the River Indus where Alexander the Great had crossed the mighty river, followed by those delicious roasted quails at the high tea that was hosted by Major General and Mrs Nasrullah Babar at their palatial house in Peshawar only proved how very strong and deep the bond of the Rimcollians were and where caste, creed and religion had no place whatsoever.

On the 4th of April, while all the honoured guests were seen off at Wagah, it reminded the elders of that 14th of August, 1947 at Dehra Dun, when history forced them to part with each other's company. And some of them also remembered the first ever reunion that was held in the dining room of the Maidens Hotel in Delhi on the eve of partition. A few days later,when Shiraz received a letter from his father-in-law stating how happy the Indian Rimcollians were while visiting Pakistan, he wondered whether a few from his class at the NDA and IMA were in that group also. Some of his course mates of the IMA 1965 June batch were now in the run for becoming Lt Generals in the Indian army and he wondered whether he too would have ever made it to that coveted rank had he returned to India.

CHAPTER-27

The Return of the Prodigal

During that month of March 1996, while the veteran Rimcollians of India and Pakistan were trying to forge a Hindu-Muslim unity in the subcontinent, far away in Khartoum, Sudan Osama Bin Laden's Al-Qaida militants were gearing up for their next phase of operations. With the United Nations having imposed economic sanctions on Sudan for actively supporting international terrorism, there were now strong rumours that Osama Bin Laden, the Al Qaida leader who had taken refuge in that country ever since he left Saudi Arabia five years ago was now being forced with his henchmen to leave and seek refuge elsewhere. Sudan was already reeling under its own ethnic conflict between the Muslim north and the Christian south and since the government was dominated by the Sudanese Muslims led by their President Al-Bashir and the fundamentalist hardliner Dr Al-Turabi, the country was now faced with an imminent economic collapse. They therefore had no other option but to tell their friend Osama that the best bet for him would be to pack up and go back to Afghanistan where the Taliban were now calling all the shots.

Having got wind of it, Karim Malik casually informed both Shiraz in Paris and Salim Rehman in Islamabad about the likelihood of Osama Bin Laden returning back to his base in Afghanistan, unless the Sudanese government under pressure from the Americans deported him back to Jeddah, where he was unwanted by the Saudi Royalty. The Americans have been crying for Osama's blood ever since the day a bomb blast killed 5 American servicemen in Riyadh in early November, 1995 and the finger of suspicion had pointed towards the Al Qaida who under Osama's dynamic leadership was now a terrorist force to reckon with. While in Khartoum and though he was heavily protected both by Sudanese and his own personal bodyguards, there was at least one major attempt on Osama's life. And it happened while he was on his way to his office on McNimr Street and was lucky to escape unhurt. Two gunmen on a motorcycle had fired at him but they missed their mark. They were then chased by his bodyguards and both were shot dead and Osama put the blame squarely on the Saudis. According to one reliable source inside the Sudanese government, Osama with his closeness to Al Tarabi had through his construction business amassed a huge fortune and his ultimate goal now was to unite all Muslims of the world and to establish a Caliphate. With his devoted Al Qaida followers he was now getting ready to drive away the western influences that had corrupted the Muslim countries and of which there were now many in this world.

The ethnic cleansing of the Muslims in Bosnia and the hard stand of Moscow against the Muslims of Chechnya, together with the United States unstinting support to the Jews of Israel, both economically and militarily had angered the bearded leader. This had lead to the complete subjugation of the Palestinian Muslims in the Middle East and had therefore made Osama a very bitter man. There was no doubt that he had sent his Al Qaida fighters to fight in Bosnia and Chechnya, and on the 18th of April, 1996, when the Israeli artillery mercilessly shelled and massacred over a hundred Lebanese civilians and injured many more of the poor Muslim villagers who had taken refuge in the United Nations compound at Qana in Southern Lebanon, Shiraz was apprehensive that this would make Osama and his Al Qaida zealots to now seek revenge elsewhere, and the targets he feared would be the Americans and their close allies.

There was also new evidence that the long standing divide between the Shia and the Sunni Muslims was also now being bridged through the good offices of the 'Muslim Brotherhood,' an organization that was also being partially controlled by Osama Bin Laden and initial parleys with 'The Hezbollah International' for a United Muslim Front had already begun. The loose talk in many of the roadside cafes in Paris and amongst the many French Algerians who had made France their home also indicated a probable Al Qaida hand in the ongoing civil war in Algeria.

"My God if that multi-millionaire Saudi fanatic goes back to Afghanistan and his Al Qaida joins hands with the one eyed Mullah Omar's radical Taiban, then I am afraid the Muslim fundamentalist organizations in Pakistan and especially those in the North West Frontier and Baluchistan will become even more active. As it is there are now one too many of such fundamentalist fanatical organizations in Pakistan and it will become a big headache for the country in future since it would lead to further destabilization and erosion of democratic values," said Shiraz to Saira as he read out Karim Malik's informal but informative letter from Khartoum that had arrived by the weekly diplomatic mail bag.

"I really pity Mehmuda and Karim because after Kabul, Khartoum must be one hell of a place to be in," said Saira as their 17 year old daughter Sherry with her 13 year old brother Tojo in tow walked in with a piano shaped cake. Sherry had topped her class at the Ecole Normale De Musique and wanted her parents to share her joys with her.

"In that case how about playing for us Tchaikovsky's first piano concerto," said a delighted Shiraz as he kissed his daughter tenderly on her cheek and escorted her to the grand piano. And while Sherry's flawless notes on the piano had everybody spellbound, Shiraz was reminded of the day when he first heard that classical piece at the concert in Delhi and which was played by the Bombay Symphony Orchestra when he was courting Shupriya, and that was way back in 1970. Listening to that haunting tune, Shiraz was filled with old memories and discreetly kissed the photo of little Shupriya in his arms that was inside the old locket.

By the time the month of April was over, indications of Osama Bin Laden with his Al Qaida followers moving base to Afghanistan from Sudan were rife. It seemed that the three way deal between the governments of Sudan, Saudi Arabia and the CIA to hand over the much wanted Saudi of Yemeni origin to the Saudi government for trial had fizzled out. On the 10th of May, 1996 the veteran Jehadi and the hero of the Battle of Jaji flew into an airstrip near Jalalabad and from where he was whisked away in a helicopter to a secret place some 400 kilometers south of Kandahar. And there waiting for him was the one eyed Mullah Mohammed Omar, his new mentor and guru. The self styled 'Commander of the Faithful' was indebted to the man because he had funded much of the Taliban's campaign and would now continue to do so till such time the Taliban took total control over the entire country. Now nearing 40, Osama was an outcast in his own country. The barren desert land that on 23rd, September, 1932 was designated as the Kingdom of Saudi Arabia and from where in May 1939 the country's first tanker load of Saudi oil left the terminal at Ras Tanura did not want him back.

When King Faisal acceded to the throne in 1964, Osama was only 7 years old and at 10 he had lost his enterprising father who died in a helicopter crash. The father who started life working as a porter in Jeddah and who having befriended the King built palaces for the Saudi royalty had left his big family a massive fortune and Osama had also received a fair share from it. Sent to Beirut to study at the exclusive Broumanna High School, a school for the rich and the famous in what was then known as the Paris of the East, Osama was often seen at the famous nightclubs of the city. Soon the top nightclubs like 'The Crazy Horse, 'The Casbah' and 'Eves' became a regular haunt for the young man as he entertained his friends with nothing less than Dom Perignon champagne and Black Label whisky. Always nattily dressed in western clothes with matching ties, the handsome young Arab would be the connoisseur of all eyes as he raced through the streets of Beirut in his sporty Mercedes car. With his preference for European blondes, he would often be seen in their company at the nightclubs as he puffed away at his Cuban cigar and entertained them royally. But that entire luxurious playboy living suddenly came to an end, when on the 13th of April, 1975 an unknown gunman killed four Christian Philangists during an attempt on the life of Pierre Gemayal, the leader of the Philangist Party in Lebanon. And with that began the long drawn out civil war between the Christian Philangists and the Palestinian Muslims and soon Osama was back in Jeddah. A month earlier King Faisal, his late father's great friend had been assassinated by his nephew Faisal Ibn Musaid. The young nephew while studying in California's Berkeley University had been doing drugs and had fallen into wrong company and therefore had been recalled by the monarch. Angered by his Uncle's diktat to come back, he had shot and killed him from point blank range with his revolver

Two years later the 20 year old Osama was a completely transformed man. On his return to Jeddah he had joined the King Abdul Aziz University to get his degree in engineering and then one fine day, when he with his elder brother Salim whom he dearly loved and doted upon went to Mecca to pray at the site of the Prophet's revelation, he suddenly became a devout Muslim. It seems that his prayers to Allah at the very place where Angel Gabriel had conveyed to Prophet Mohammed the first revelation from the Holy Koran had made Osama realize that he must give up the good life and become a truly devoted Muslim. It was soon after the Soviet invasion of Afghanistan that the 23 year old Osama Bin Laden landed up in the North West Frontier town of Bannu in Pakistan and there in February, 1980 having conferred with his old teacher Sheikh Abdullah Yousuf Azzan, they jointly set up the MAK, (Maktab-al-Khidmat), the forerunner of what was now the formidable Al Qaida (The Base). After the Soviets left Afghanistan, Osama returned to Jeddah in 1989 as a hero and the rising star of the Islamic world. But soon his ideas of so called Jihad or just wars, his preaching's and sermons to rise against the corrupt Muslim states including that of his own

Saudi Arabia had made him an outcast in his own country. His belittling of the royal family led to his passport being impounded, and when his offer to the King to liberate Kuwait and fight the Iraqis with his own highly trained and motivated Al Qaida militants was rejected by the Saudi Monarch,and the King instead asked for American help, Osama only became even more belligerent. In April 1991, Osama quietly slipped out of Jeddah and after landing at Karachi made his way to Afghanistan via Peshawar where he was greeted with a volley of fire by his many Kalashnikov wielding comrades from his Al Qaida set up. But Afghanistan was now gripped in a dirty civil war as various warlords with their own private armies and for their own selfish political gains kept fighting with each other. And with reports of the Pakistan ISI in collusion with the CIA and Saudi Royalty was planning to capture him, Osama in December 1991 landed up in Khartoum.

On 30th June, 1989 a military coup led by General Omar Hassan-al-Bashir, a radical Islamist had taken over the country, and soon thereafter the General fell under the spell of Dr Hassan-al-Tarabi, the Sorbonne and London University educated spiritual leader. Dr Tarabi the enigmatic head of the Nationalist Islamist Front of Sudan was only too glad to have Osama join hands with him. As a father like figure, Dr Tarabi and Osama soon became good friends and during the period December 1991 and May 1996 besides giving sanctuary to the Al Qaida, fighters, the duo also became partners in big business. But now with the ongoing civil war in Sudan between the Muslim north and Christian south, together with the harsh economic sanctions that were imposed by the United Nations bleeding the country to death, Osama fearing that he was no longer safe in Khartoum had once again returned to Afghanistan.

Sitting in Paris while Shiraz with help from Karim Malik in Khartoum and his brother-in-law Salim Rehman in Islamabad and Fazal Rehman in Washington tried to keep track on the whereabouts and doings of Osama Bin Laden and his faithful deputies, the sudden appearance of Dr Mahdi Chamran Savehi in Afghanistan came as a shock to him. For the head of External Intelligence in the Iranian government and a Shia at that, his presence in war torn Afghanistan for a secret meeting with Osama Bin Laden seemed rather odd and somewhat sinister, thought Shiraz. He was afraid that if the Hizbollah, the Shia based terrorist group and the terrorist groups of the Sunni Muslim world like that of the Al Qaida and others joined hands, then as an international terrorist group they with their fanaticism to usher in a Muslim Caliphate could well become a real menace to the world. And when another intelligence report indicated that a high level top secret meeting of diehard Islamic fundamentalist leaders had been held on the outskirts of Teheran under the stewardship of Dr Savehi from 21st to 23rd June, and that it had the blessings of the Rafsanjani government of Iran, it was rather alarming. And with confirmed reports that they had unanimously formed a high level committee of three that also included Osama Bin Laden in the supreme council of Hizbollah International, Shiraz was now apprehensive that the fallout from this on the various Muslim terrorist organizations who have been armed and trained by the ISI in Pakistan to fight their dirty proxy war against the Indians in Jammu and Kashmir could be well exploited further by the government in Pakistan. And though there was a civilian government in Pakistan led by Benazir Bhutto, but the fact remained that Pakistan could never reconcile to Kashmir being part of India. For the Pakistani politicians and the military leaders, Kashmir had not only become an obsession, but also a prestige issue, and a regular excuse to blame all their short comings and failures on India. For all of them, Kashmir had become their favourite whipping boy.

Meanwhile in India too, the political fallout from the infighting between the various parties and their coalition partners had led to instability. The 13 day rule by the BJP, the Bharatiya Janata Party under the stewardship of Atal Bihari Vajpayee fell flat on 1st June, when it could not garner the required majority in parliament. This was followed by the United Front government led by Deve Gowda which though it had only 187 seats was being backed by the Congress (I) from the outside. With coalition politics becoming the order of the day, the fortunes of erstwhile Congress Party was now on the decline and it suffered another big blow on 2ndrd May, when Nemi Chand Jain commonly known as Chandraswami, the high flying wheeler dealer and a so called conman and faith healer was arrested by the police. The man who was also the spiritual advisor to Prime Minister Narasimha Rao was now charged for swindling money and for brazenly violating the foreign exchange currency regulations of the country. At 46, the so called 'Godman' who lived in his air-conditioned ashram fortress of pink granite and who drove only in luxury cars and jetted around the world with the high and the mighty and who with his political clout often showed two fingers too those in authority was now a total nervous wreck. On learning about the man's routine in the confines of the Tihar Jail during that hot month of June, Peevee who was shooting a commercial in Delhi for a men's underwear, simply told the press.

"Thank God for once the Indian police had the guts to put that man behind bars and take his bloody pants off, but it would have been even better if he had been stripped and paraded naked on the streets and then sent to jail. Such people not only take the innocent people for a ride and make fools of them, but they also with their contacts with the high and the mighty in the country are becoming a bloody menace and a nuisance to the society. And the very fact that the conman had close links to the highest in the country only goes to prove the level of decadence that has permeated and vitiated into our corrupt political system."

CHAPTER-28

The Bomb Culture and Izzy the Olympic Mascot

Shiraz's assessment of the Teheran terror summit was further vindicated, when on 25ᵗʰ June, 1996 the members from the Hezbollah group exploded a fuel truck in front of building number 131 at the Khobar Towers, a housing complex near the city of Dhahran in Saudi Arabia. The eight-story building housed the United States Air Force personnel and as a result of which 19 U.S. servicemen and one Saudi was killed and over 300 injured. My God and imagine all this happening soon after the terror summit, and with the car bombing at Riyadh earlier, and as a result of which the United States have raised the terrorist threat level to 'Threatcon C' this is indeed very alarming wrote Shiraz in his diary while watching the massive destruction that was being shown on TV. And had it not been for the alertness of Staff Sergeant Alfredo Guerrero, the casualties among the American servicemen would have been much higher. The alert sergeant who was stationed atop the building had noticed the petrol tanker truck being driven into a parking lot that was in front of the Khobar Towers. Subsequently, when he also spotted the presence of a few suspicious characters around it, he immediately on his walkie-talkie reported the matter to the security. And as a result of which the evacuation drill was automatically set in motion. But it was not fast enough. It was around 9:45 p.m. when the truck bomb was noticed and five minutes later the massive explosion rocked the building. The bomb was so very powerful that it left a massive crater, nearly 25 meters in width and more than 10 meters deep. It was much more powerful than what McVeigh' had detonated in Oklahoma City and the bomb was made of a mixture of gasoline and explosives.

Ten days earlier on 15ᵗʰ June, the Irish Republican Army had also carried out a similar vehicle bomb attack at the Manchester City Centre, but there they had at least sent a timely warning and as a result of which no lives were lost, but more than 200 were injured. That bombing was carried out on a Saturday morning at around 11:15 a.m. while shoppers were busy making their purchases on Market Street at the Arndale Centre.

"I wonder why this world is heading towards total anarchy, and one never knows where and when the next bomb will go off,"said Saira very seriously as she cautioned both her children to be alert while commuting in public transport, and not to touch any unidentified suspicious objects.

Meanwhile in Iraq, the disarmament crisis took a turn for the worse, when Saddam Hussein after having his son-in-law murdered refused the UNSCOM to inspect a number of sites. And as a result of which the United States in the United Nations Security Council once again called for military action. The United Nations however passed Resolution 1060 and demanded that Iraq grant not only immediate and unrestricted access to all those sites, but also to those that the UNSCOM team would desire to inspect in future also. Cornered by the threat of another U.S led U.N. force entering his country, Saddam Hussein meekly gave in. A month earlier the UNSCOM supervisors had destroyed Iraq's main biological warfare production facility at Al-Hakam and to Shiraz it seemed unlikely that Saddam had the capability of producing more weapons of mass destruction. And as far as the nuclear bomb was concerned it was rather farfetched to imagine that Saddam had a few of them in his so called secret arsenal. But the manner in which the United States and her other western allies were bullying Saddam with their so called oil for food program policy; it was rather humiliating for the Iraqis, thought Shiraz.

The economic sanctions imposed by the United Nations had totally ruined the country whose main export was oil. By the U.N resolution 712 of 19 September, 1991 it had allowed Iraq to sell its oil for food, but the sale of oil had to be restricted to 1.6 billion dollars six monthly only and it had to be paid to an escrow account and not directly to Iraq. Humiliated by that deal, a proud and defiant Saddam had initially outrightly rejected it, but with people now feeling the pinch, he had now signed a memorandum of understanding to implement that program also.

"But I wonder why the damn Yankees are always after Saddam Hussein's blood. I agree that Saddam's gamble to invade Kuwait had landed him in real shit, but that was nearly five years ago and if this kind of bullshitting, sabre rattling and brinkmanship by the Americans and their British allies continue, then I am afraid it would once again lead to another war. The Americans it seems are adamant in removing Saddam and his cohorts from their chairs, but with Saddam refusing to play ball, this will only lead to further confrontation between the Yankees and the Iraqis, and as a result of which many young Iraqis and others I am afraid will get drawn closer to Osama Bin Laden and his terrorist network, and which in turn will lead to more terrorist bombings of the Americans and the westerners, 'said Shiraz as he handed over the edition of Time magazine that had exhaustively covered the deadly Khobar Towers bombing to his wife Saira.

"Yes it is indeed rather sad that the Iraqi disarmament crisis is being handled by the powers that be in a most shoddy and disgraceful manner, and as a result of which it is the common poor people in Iraq who are being made to suffer. And what is even more ironical is the fact that the year 1996 has been declared as 'The International Year for the Eradication of Poverty' in this world," said Saira as her daughter Sherry reminded her parents that the year 1996 was also 'The Chinese New Year of the Fire Rat' and which traditionally brought worldwide disasters.

A couple of weeks later,when theTWA flight 800 that was scheduled to take off at 1900 hours on 17th July from the JFK terminal at New York got delayed by an hour due to some disabled piece of ground equipment and a mix up of a passenger's personal baggage, some of those who were heading for Paris and Rome were now getting a little impatient and bored. They had come fairly early and having checked in were now waiting for the final announcement to emplane. But little did they know then that the aircraft would crash soon after takeoff. Fazal Rehman with his family was also booked on the same flight. They were to go to Paris to spend a fortnight's holiday with Shiraz and his family, but a day earlier their 14 year old son Shafiq while playing soccer in school had fractured his shin bone and the trip perforce had to be cancelled at the last minute. Had they been on that ill fated flight they too would have met with certain death.

Soon after taking off at around 20.20 hours, the Boeing 747 with its 230 passengers including the crew climbed to an altitude of 15,000 feet, but suddenly at 20.30 hours it lost contact with the air traffic control centre at Boston. According to some eye witnesses there was a big explosion in the sky and soon thereafter a large fireball was seen plunging into the sea. The aircraft was being piloted by Captain Steven Snyder, an experienced pilot with more than 6000 flying hours and it sudden disappearance from the radar screen, and that too without sending an SOS or a May Day signal had got both the Americans and Shiraz worried.

"This may well be the handiwork of some terrorist organization, and the bomb could be a similar one that was manufactured for the aborted Bojinka project, or it could be even a missile strike. But keeping in view that no one has yet claimed responsibility, the possibility of some system failure like electrical short circuiting while doing fuel transfer from one tank to the other during the flight cannot be ruled out either. And though the rescue teams were quick to reach the disaster area, but the very fact that there were no survivors at all is what was bugging him,' said Shiraz while telling his wife Saira to immediately get in touch with her cousin Fazal Rehman in Washington and find out if all was well with him and his family.

"This reminds me of Zia's ill fated flight that had also within few minutes after takeoff from Bhawalpur plummeted nose down and there were no survivors either,"'said Shiraz while speaking to Fazal Rehman in Washington.

"'Yes, and it is now anybody's guess as to what actually happened. But I must say that Allah Talla has been very kind to us. Had it not been for that timely fracture of Shafiq's leg, we too would have probably met with a watery grave," said Fazal Rehman, while his wife Samina with her 21 year old daughter Sameera recited the 'Kalima' in the next room. It was a 'Kalima' that said that there is none worthy of worship than Allah. He is only one and there are no partners for him He gives both life and death. He is alive and will never ever die because he is the all powerful.'

With the trip to Paris now cancelled, Fazal Rehman in order to compensate the family who had been looking forward to a good holiday took them to Atlanta, Gerogia instead for the 26th Olympiad. With President Bill Clinton having opened the games on 19th July where a record 197 countries were taking part, Sameera was disappointed with the selection of the mascot. It was a mascot named 'Izzy', an abstract fantasy figure that had been created by a computer. The name 'Izzy' which was a short form of 'What is it?' was even more confusing because nobody knew what it was supposed to be, or what it signified.

"Well I guess the Americans are now so used to getting all their answers with the click of a mouse that they probably stopped using their own brains, and frankly to me it looks like a modern day Golliwog with Donald Duck's feet," said young Shafiq as they all got ready to witness the 100 meter men's finals. This was the premier event to choose the fastest man in the world and when Donavan Bailey of Canada set a new world record by winning the gold in a fantastic time of 9.84 seconds, the Jamaican born coloured West Indian who had emigrated to Canada at the tender age of 11, proved to the world in general and the Americans in particular that the Blacks of African origin if given the opportunity could prove themselves superior to the Whites in every possible discipline.

A month after the conclusion of the Atlanta Olympics, Fazal Rehman received the home posting that he had requested for. He had been promoted as Additional Secretary and was assigned the India, Pakistan and Nepal desk in the Bangladesh Foreign Ministry. He had completed nearly four years in Washington DC and as a senior diplomat had accredited himself well. Having celebrated their daughter Sameera's 21st birthday on 14th, August, Fazal Rehman with his wife Samina and daughter caught the PIA flight from Logan airport on the very the next day. To ensure that their only son Shafiq who was now 14 completed his schooling from the US, they had put him in the hostel.

CHAPTER-29

Marriage and Death—Both on the Rocks

Meanwhile in England, with the marriage of Prince Charles and Princess Diana on the rocks, and a divorce decree in the offing, there were strong rumours that the Princess was now being courted by a handsome Pakistani doctor who was based in London. When Monty and Reeta were told about this with some authority by their friend an Indian doctor and an ex Sanawarian who was also London based and who had to come to India to dispose of some of his ancestral property in Old Delhi, they just could not believe it.

'Come on you must be joking. It is just not possible, and that too in a place like London where the charming Princess and the most photographed person in the world is always being chased around by the paparazzi, and you mean to say that nobody knows about this affair?" said Reeta as she took out a copy of the book titled 'Diana-Her True Story' by Henry Morton and added that though she had heard about her affair with her riding instructor Captain James Hewitt, but she never heard of Dr Hasnat Khan and that to a Pathan from the city of Jhelum in Pakistan.

"Well in that case let me tell you a few more secrets of their hush-hush affair and the Princess I believe is now so much in love with him, that she I am told even keeps a copy of the Holy Koran near her bed. And the likelihood of the two getting married soon cannot be ruled out either. In fact dressed in a pure white salwar-kameez Pakistani outfit the beautiful Princess had even met his parents when she visited Pakistan in February for the fund raising dinner of Imran Khan's cancer hospital. The first time the couple had met was by chance, and it was only a year ago on 31st August, 1995 in the Royal Brompton Hospital in London where the handsome heart surgeon had performed an operation on one Mr Joe Toffolo and whose wife Oonagh was Diana's friend and acupuncturist," said the Indian doctor who like Dr Hasmat also had an apartment on Neville Street at Chelsea.

"Well I must admit that the Pathans are really manly and handsome, and if Jemina could fall for Imran, then the Princess falling for the 36 year old bachelor Hashmat Khan and who you say looks very much like Omar Sharif is no big deal either. In fact with her broken marriage, this could be an ideal match, but will Diana's two young sons who have gone through such a traumatic experience agree to it ? And will the Doctor's parents accept her as their 'Bahu?'(Daughter-in-law) asked Monty as he fixed a tall highball for his guest and helped himself to a chilled beer.

"'But just tell me with so much of security around the Princess, where and how do they meet?' asked Reeta who was now very fascinated with the Cindrella like love story of the charming Princess.

"Well I have been hearing all kinds of stories about the couple disguising themselves while going to pubs and to some other out of the way restaurants and it could well be true. I believe that one evening he even took her to a jazz club in Soho called 'Ronnie Scott's' and nobody recognized her because she was wearing a black wig. Once he also took her to a pub in Middlesex that was ironically called the 'Princess of Wales' and both were highly amused. After all she is a human being and she loves Hashmat's company because he is a thorough gentleman and treats her like a lady. And as against the shackles of royalty that had tied her down with mundane formalities and duties for so many youthful years, the Princess I am told now prefers to live like a commoner," added the Indian doctor while inviting Monty and Reeta to spend their next summer as the guest of his family in London.

"Well if what you have just stated about the romance between the Princess and the Pathan is true, and if you can promise me an introduction to them, then most certainly we will be there," said Monty jokingly as he raised a toast to their old school motto 'Never Give In'.

A month later on 28th August, 1996 when a certificate bearing Number 5029 of 1996 making the Decree Nisi final and absolute was announced, the fairy tale marriage that was witnessed by a billion television viewers on 29th July, 1981 was finally dissolved. As the news of the royal divorce became a subject of discussion at various ladies kitty parties in New Delhi and Diana relinquished her title of 'Her Royal Highness," Reeta wondered whether she would now become Mrs Hashmat Khan.

"The beautiful girl who would have one day become the Queen of England was now a free bird and her personal life was nobody's business, and I think she deserves her privacy," said Monty to his wife somewhat sternly while requesting her not to discuss the subject with her kitty party ladies.

In Pakistan too with rumours of the Diana-Hashmat affair doing the rounds among the few rich and the famous in the country, the happiest person was Begum Ruksana. She was of the view that if Jacqueline, the widow of John F Kennedy could marry the Greek tycoon Aristotle Onassis who was much older than her, and if King Edward VIII could give up his throne and tie the knot with Mrs Wallis Simpson, a twice divorced American socialite, then where was the harm in Hashmat Khan marrying the divorced Princess of Wales ?

"Yes, personally I am also not against this union, but will she be able to adjust to our way of life. One should not forget that till yesterday she was the Princess of Wales and moreover I doubt if the Doctor's parents will give their consent, because for all I know is that they too have been looking for a girl for Hashmat in Pakistan," said Arif Rehman.

"But one thing is for sure and that is they will make a very charming and handsome couple, and I believe the two of them have been seeing a lot of each other during weekends at Hashmat's uncle's palatial house on Stratford-on-Avon and which incidentally is also the birth place of William Shakespeare, the doyen of English literature who wrote Romeo and Juliet," said Salim Rehman.

"Quite.right and his Uncle with his English wife is also a renowned doctor, but I am afraid this love affair may well end up like the tragic story of Romeo and Juliet," said Salim Rehman's wife Aasma.

While the good Pakistani Doctor and the charming Princess Diana in England very discreetly continued with their secret love affair, in Pakistan a young hot headed politician from Sind was targeting his own elder sister who was also the Prime Minister of the country. Everyone now knew that there was now no love lost between Benazir Bhutto and her brother Murtaza whom some had dubbed as the 'Terrorist Prince of Larkana.' With his base in Karachi and having formed his own political party known as Pakistan Peoples Party (Shahid Bhutto), he had become a pain in the neck for the Benazir government as he kept accusing her, her party and her husband Asif Ali Zardari in particular for corrupt practices. However, to counter his gun toting brother Murtaza and his young party members, Benazir it is believed had requested him to mend his ways. She also in a private letter addressed to him had advised the brother not to go around Karachi with his security men openly displaying their weapons.

The matter however got further aggravated, when the head strong Murtaza with his cronies landed at Karachi from Islamabad on 16th September, 1996. On the same flight was his brother-in-law Asif Zardari, the man whom he hated and detested from the bottom of his heart. During the journey into the city from the airport, Murtaza and his cronies in the big four wheel drive Pajero kept following Zardari's car, and at once stage while overtaking it, they not only gave him a menacing look, but they even aimed their automatic weapons at him. A shaken Zardari instead of going home therefore decided to go to his father's house instead. And when Murtaza also turned and followed him, Zardari was petrified. And it was only when Zardari reached his destination and saw Murtaza driving away, did he feel safe. Zardari then immediately rang up the Chief Minister of Sind and it is believed gave him a big mouthful also.

Next day afternoon, when the Karachi police picked up Ali Mohammed Sonara, one of Murtaza's top lieutenants and Murtaza came to know about it, the battle lines were drawn. Fearing that Sonara may be eliminated in a fake encounter by the police, Murtaza with his gun toting cronies decided to rescue his friend from the clutches of the law enforcement agency. Taking the law into his own hands, Murtaza in broad daylight raided the police station. And when he found that Sonara was not there, a wily Murtaza threatened the cops that none of them would be alive if anything happened to his friend. Next morning and with news travelling fast, when Salim Rehman Khan rang up Shiraz in Paris and told him about the armed raid by Murtaza and his cohorts at a police station in Karachi, the only comment Shiraz made was. "I think the young hot headed Bhutto has now asked for trouble." And he was dead right. Because the very next day on 20th, September, which happened to be a Friday when at around 5.30 in the evening Murtaza left his residence at 70, Clifton to address a political meeting that was scheduled to be held in a suburb of Karachi, he was not at all surprised to see a contingent of policemen outside his house. In fact Murtaza it seems was expecting such a visit, but he was not the least bothered as he without permitting a check of his vehicle or making any enquiries from them, simply drove off with his motorcade. But around 8.45 p.m. that evening, when his motorcade made its way back to 70, Clifton little did Murtaza know that this would be his last ride in his favourite red Pajero. As the big car approached the main gate of the house, there was darkness all around. The street lights had been switched off and a hundred yards away from the main gate and on both sides of the road, the armed police had established road blocks. As the vehicle neared the road block, suddenly there was a burst of heavy gunfire and Murtaza with six of his cronies were soon all dead.

Subsequent to the raid on the police station earlier in the week by Murtaza, the Superintendent of police, Wajid Durrrani it seems had got his orders from the top to mount this very tricky and sensitive operation. After all Murtaza Bhutto was not just an ordinary person, he was the brother of the country's Prime Minister and the son of the late Zulfiqar Ali Bhutto and an upcoming young political leader of Sind. But with no policemen being seriously injured, during what the authorities called was a shootout, this operation it seemed was a well pre-planned stage managed operation by the police force to eliminate the young man and his close lieutenants. According to the version given by Haq Navaz Sial, the Station House Officer at Clifton Police Station, the police picket on seeing the red Pajero vehicle approaching the road block had ordered the vehicle to stop, but when those inside the vehicle pointed their guns at the police party and allegedly had even fired a few rounds that resulted in injuries to him, Shahid Hayat, the Assistant Superintendent of Police then ordered the police party to fire back in self defense. And it was as a result of the shootout that Murtaza and his accomplices were all killed. However, according to another police version the trouble started only after Murtaza and his supporters refused to allow their vehicles to be searched. It was part of the police drill that had been imposed following incidents of recent bombings and killings in Karachi. But looking at the manner in which all seven were gunned down in cold blood, and the type of serious wounds that were suffered by the victims in comparison to the two policemen who had received only superficial minor injuries, the version given by the police therefore looked like a cock and bull story. With all fingers pointing towards Asif Ali Zardari, it seemed more like a deep rooted conspiracy with those in power to eliminate Murtaza and his cronies once and for all and that too in a quick rapid fire action. According to the police all of them were rushed to various hospitals, but it seems they took their own sweet time to ensure that no one survived. And when a dead Murtaza's body was wheeled in at the nearby Mid East Hospital, already an hour had elapsed after the tragic event.

However, the news of Murtaza's death in a shootout with the police came as a rude shock to his two sisters and his mother. A heartbroken Benazir who arrived at the hospital some five hours later kept wailing and calling Murtaza to come back to life. She had seen it once before when her youngest brother Shahnawaz took his own life. But Murtaza's Palestinian widow Ghinwa with her little daughter Fatima on arrival at the hospital just could not believe the story that was given by the police to them. They were off the view that he had been murdered on the orders of Asif Ali Zardari.

Next day on learning about Murtaza's death, Shiraz wondered whether the Bhutto family like the Gandhi's in India for the sake of remaining in power perpetually would ultimately as time went by write their own death warrants. Because in this game of dirty politics nobody was a real friend and with terrorism on the rise both in India and Pakistan, together with sectarian and communal politics taking centre stage in both the countries anything could happen. According to Shiraz some Hindus were no less fanatical than the Muslims, and with the cries of Hinduvta gaining ground in India, and with Muslim fundamentalism on the rise in Pakistan and also in Bangladesh, the possibility of the ISI's hand in triggering off another round of Hindu—Muslim riots in India therefore could not be ruled out either.

CHAPTER-30

The Old Order Changeth

While the Bhuttos were mourning the death of Murtaza in Larkhana, in Afghanistan, Sheikh Abdullah Omar's Taliban with active support from the Pakistani ISI and Osama Bin Laden's Al Qaida were getting ready to capture Kabul, and which they did on 27th September, 1996. They not only drove out President Burhanuddin Rabbani from the capital, but they also executed in public Mohammed Najibullah who had earlier taken refuge inside the U.N sanctuary In Kabul. The dreaded ex chief of the Afghanistan secret police KHAD and his brother were taken out of the UN compound, beaten mercilessly to death, castrated and their blood soaked dead bodies were hung from a traffic light post on the street for public display. When Shiraz saw the photograph of that bizarre hanging that was sent by one of his junior colleagues who was posted in the Pakistani Embassy in Kabul, he was reminded of how Benito Mussolini of Italy had met the same fate. Bur it was not as brutal as what the Taliban had done to Najibullah. The junior colleague was also a good friend of his, and they had served together earlier in Moscow But what surprised Shiraz was the information on Pakistan's involvement in promoting the Taliban and the manner in which it was being done. This confidential report that was sent for his information by his friend from Kabul also highlighted the fact that the Pakistani Ambassador in Kabul was also of the view that the current Pakistan-Taliban friendship in the long run would be detrimental to Pakistan. According to him, the Ambassador Qazi Humayun had way back in October 1995 felt that a Taliban government in Kabul with its ultra-conservative religious and radical outlook would be even worse than that of Rabbani which was then in power, and now by arming and training the Taliban clandestinely with more sophisticated weapons, and by providing them with fuel for their amoured tanks, there was every possibility of the same weapons backfiring on Pakistan someday. And though the Taliban government after taking over the country had closed the militant training camps that were closely associated with Hikmatyar and Pakistan's Jamaat-i-Islami, but they had not closed those of Osama Bin Laden's Al-Qaida, Pakistan's Jamait-Ulema-i-Islam and that of the Harkat-ul-Ansar's. The main training camps of these militant groups were at Khost and they were located close to the Pakistan-Afghanistan border. Shiraz was also aware that the HUA, the Harkat-ul-Ansar was the main terrorist organization that Pakistan had been actively supporting in its proxy war against India in Kashmir and he was therefore apprehensive that the recent three way tie up between the Taliban, the Al Qaida and the HUA may well turn out to be a monster in the making and one that would be very difficult for Pakistan to control. Besides Pakistan, only Saudi Arabia and the U.A.E had officially recognized the Taliban government of Afghanistan and with the recent 'Fatwas' of anti American hatred being churned out regularly by Bin Laden, America also now feared that the three headed monster in that land of large opium growers with their strict 'Shariat' laws may soon become the biggest terror hub of the world. A few days later, when Shiraz came to know confidentially through his brother-in-law Salim Rehman Khan in Islamabad that one retired Captain Shafqat Cheema who was posted in the Pakistani mission in North Korea as the ISI's liaison man with North Korea's nuclear and missile establishments had been selling nuclear secrets to Iran and Iraq for monetary gains and that the gentleman on his return had now been arrested, Shiraz's earlier apprehension that one day such a deadly weapon could fall into the hands of some fanatical terrorist group was not very farfetched, and he dreaded the day when such a weapon would be used by them.

Meanwhile in Bangladesh, with the Awami League that was led by Shaikh Hasina, the daughter of the late Mujibur Rehman having won the elections in June, the party in order to avenge the death of the Bongobodhu and his family who were brutally killed by a group of army officers in August 1975, decided to lodge an FIR and bring all the culprits to book. On 2nd October, 1996, after the FIR was lodged at the Dhanmondi Police Station in Dhaka against the 23 accused for conspiring and killing Mujib and his family, Fazal Rehman who with his wife and daughter were now back in Dhaka, however wondered whether the culprits would ever be physically tried in a court of law in the country, since most of them had disappeared and had settled in various parts of the world.

"But I think that it is high time that these officers were tried and hanged, and if such a thing occurred in a country like Israel then the Mossad I am sure would have got them nice and proper by now," said his wife Samina while visiting their old house at Dhanmondi where she had met Fazal Rehman for the first time and where their daughter Sameera was also born.

"Well 21 years is a fairly long time, but all the same I agree with you that such crimes should not go unpunished," added Fazal Rehman as he narrated to his daughter Sameera and his 14 year old son Shafiq on how the massacre of the entire Mujib family was carried out by Major Faroukh, Major Rashid, Major Dalim and others.

"But then why has the government woken up so very late, because by now some of them may be fairly old and a few may have even died or changed their names and identity like Adolf Eichmann had done," said Sameera who had recently seen the video film 'The House on Garibaldi Street' and which depicted in detail as to how the Mossad eventually captured the much wanted S.S. man who had killed thousands of Jews during the holocaust.

"Well as far as the delay in bringing the culprits to justice is concerned, that's unfortunately another sad story of our country's short and bloody history, because Khondakar Mushtaq Ahmed who was elected President after Mujib's death by these very officers who had staged the coup had very conveniently enacted an indemnity ordinance that barred any legal action against all those who had committed that ghastly crime. And later, when General Ziaur Rehman turned that ordinance into an act and incorporated it into the constitution, the same group of officers they were not only let off scot-free, but they were also handsomely rewarded with plum postings to diplomatic missions abroad. But the new government of Sheikh Hasina has now taken a firm stand to scrap that act and have them all tried in court," said Fazal Rehman as they continued with the tour of the capital city and of those very places that he with Samina had frequented as young lovers.

While Bangladeshi sleuths were on the hunt of Mujib's killers, in Pakistan the cricket poster boy Imran Khan who had in the month of May launched the Tehrik-e-Insaff, his own political party was now going full steam ahead to nail Benazir, her husband and her party with some serious allegations. Besides calling them highly corrupt, he also kept accusing Benazir and her husband for master minding the brutal assassination of Murtaza Bhutto. And when the media too started its own disinformation campaign blaming her and Asif Ali Zardari for the murder, Faroukh Leghari the President of Pakistan decided to blow the final whistle. On 5th November, 1996 having charged the Benazir government with extra-judicial killings,corruption and mismanagement of the economy, and for the complete breakdown of law and order in the country, the President using his powers under the 8th Amendment and having taking the judiciary and the armed forces into full confidence dismissed her government.And on that night of 4th November and 5th morning, when Salim Rehman Khan and his wife Aasma were returning home late from a party and they noticed armed troops in jackboots were on the move in the capital city, it seemed to them that the army was probably once again getting to ready to stage another military coup. But early next morning, when it was announced that Malik Meraj Khalid had been appointed as the caretaker Prime Minister and that fresh elections were to be held on 3rd February, 1997 it was generally welcomed by the people of Pakistan.

Meraj Khalid a lawyer by profession had joined politics and had got elected to the Punjab Provincial Assembly in 1965. He had also served in Mr Bhutto's government as a cabinet minister. And during his political career was also appointed the Speaker of the National Assembly. But after he lost the 1993 elections, he generally kept away from politics. And though he was now 80 years old and was the Rector of the International Islamic University, the President however nominated him as the Interim Prime Minister of the country. Commenting on the sudden dismissal of the Benazir government and the President's choice of appointing the elderly Khalid as the new interim Prime Minister of the country, Ruksana Begum who with her husband Arif Rehman had come to Islamabad to spend a few days with their son Salim Rehman, said rather candidly.

"But I wonder why the Radcliffe and Oxford educated Benazir and her husband Zardari who is also well educated had to get into all this. They both have so much of ancestral property and money of their own and there was therefore no need for them to indulge in such shameless ways of making more and more money, and that to at the cost of the poor starving millions of Pakistanis who had voted for her and for a better future".

"But what is even more shocking Ammijaan are the rumours that most of this ill gotten money has been siphoned off as commissions from fat defense related deals by the clever Mr Ten Percent and his wife, and the money has been safely deposited in their many secret Swiss bank accounts," said Aasma rather authoritatively.

Listening to the two ladies, Salim Rehman too was not the least surprised. But when his mother cursed Nehru and Jinnah for having divided India and added that the British Raj as far as corruption was concerned was far cleaner, he did not disagree entirely with her either. However, when Salim did say that such like big defense deals are big money spinners for making a fast buck not only for the blood sucking politicians and their political parties, but also for their 'Chamchas'(ass lickers and flunkies), the bureaucrats and the senior officers of the armed forces and India was no exception, nobody disputed that either. But when he further added that the never ending Bofors scandal even after Rajiv Gandhi's death in 1991 was still raging in India, and that and it must be still haunting him in his grave, Ammijaan checked her watch and requested him to switch on the TV for the news in Urdu. There were rumours that some senior bureaucrats had also been arrested and she wanted to find out if that was true. Therefore, when the Urdu newsreader on PTV announced that Rehman Malik, the Chief of the FIA, the Federal Investigation Agency and his deputy Ghulam Ashgar both of whom were appointed by Benazir had been arrested on non specified corruption charges, Ruksana Begum openly castigated Benazir and her husband Zardari for introducing corruption at the highest level in the government.

'Just imagine the big bosses from the very agency that is suppose to investigate corruption charges against others are themselves now in the lock up and I won't be the least surprised if they too are linked to Mr Ten percent and his many nefarious deals to make a quick buck at the cost of the country's exchequer.". And no sooner had the old lady finished her diatribe against the sleazy Benazir government, the blaring siren of a pilot jeep heralded the arrival of Lt General Aslam Rehman Khan.

"May be you can enlighten us a little more with all those million dollar costly defence deals from which Mr 10 percent I believe has made a real killing," said Salim Rehman as he warmly hugged his cousin brother and instructed his old cook to ensure that the military escort with the Corps Commander was also well looked after.

"Janab in fauji aur khaki vardi military walon ke liye toh hum apna jaan bhi qurban kardenge, lekin woh beiman police aur unke audedaro ko to juthe mar mar ke khatam kardena chahiye.(Sir for the military in khaki I will even sacrifice my life, but as far those two senior police officers and their cohorts are concerned they should be thrashed and killed by raining shoes on them.) There was no doubt that Hasan Miya the old faithful cook had been listening to the PTV news also and the anger clearly showed on his face.

"Needless to say that the army has been keeping a tag on Mr 10 percent ever since he started blatantly interfering in government affairs and in its day to day functioning. And now that he had shamelessly and brazenly started putting his fingesr in all major government defence deals, General Karamat the army chief and our own senior general officers are of the firm view that it was high time he was given the boot. That bloody bastard soon after Benazir took her oath of office and even before he was made a member of her cabinet had tried to cream off between 10 to 30 percent in three major defence deals and these included the French Mirage aircrafts, the Agosta submarines and the Ukranian T80 main battle tanks. And in most of these deals Zardari was the main negotiator and he must have skimmed of millions," said Aslam Rehman while adding that soon after the Constitutional coup, not only the boss of the FIA, but also Masood Sharif whom Benazir had appointed as the Intelligence Bureau Chief had also been arrested and their offices sealed and serving Major General Rafiullah Niazi had been appointed as the new IB chief.

"But is it also true that both the IB chief and the FIA boss with blessings from Benazir had been hobnobbing with the Israeli secret service, the Mossad to help them in cracking down on Islamist terrorists who had found haven in Pakistan and especially so after the dastardly bombing of the Egyptian embassy in Islamabad last year,' asked Arif Rehman.

"Yes very much so and the CIA's hand I believe in this was also very much in evidence. Her idea was to eventually root out the importance of the ISI and make it defunct, but we are no fools and having seen through Benazir's game plan, which was no different from what her father tried to do when he set up the infamous FSF, a private army whose main job was to eliminate those who dared to challenge Bhutto's authority, we heartily welcomed the dismissal of her government,"' added Aslam Rehman.

"But what about arresting Mr 10 per cent and putting him behind bars?" asked Ruksana Begum with a sly smile.

"Well Ammijaan I guess his turn will also come and I am sure he too will be sorted out nice and proper," said Salim Rehman very confidently as Aasma his wife announced that dinner was on the table.

While the people of Pakistan looked forward to fresh elections and a clean government, in India the six month old United Front coalition government headed by Mr Deve Gowda kept limping along. The 66 year old from the village of Haradanahalli in Hassan District of Karnataka with a diploma in civil engineering was originally from the Congress Party, but he later joined the Janata Dal and was instrumental in forging the Third Front that took office on 1st June, 1996. It was however, on the morning of 13th November, 1996 that Monty by chance and under very tragic circumstances came face to face with the new Prime Minister of the country. On the previous evening, Monty was at Palam airport to see off an old friend who was on his way to Dahran in Saudi Arabia to take up a new lucrative job with an international oil cartel. But ten minutes after takeoff the Saudi Arabian Airlines flight SV 763 with 289 passengers and a crew of 23 met with a massive mid air collision over Charki Dadri with the Air Kazakastan Flight 1907 that was descending to land at Delhi. At 9 PM, when he heard the news about the terrible accident, Monty immediately with Reeta and the wife of his dear friend rushed to the accident spot. And though they with the help from the villagers kept searching the whole night through the debris that was spread for miles, there was not a single survivor. This was the first headon collision in the history of civil aviation and 349 people on both the flights simply perished. The Saudi Arabian Boeing 747 and the Kazakh Illyushin 76 on impact had created a mighty ball of fire and the time was 6.40 in the evening. As the grim faced Prime Minister of India walked through the charred wreckage of the Saudi plane that was carrying 215 Indians and 40 Nepalis, most of whom were heading for jobs as drivers, cooks and housemaids, Monty who unlike his wife Reeta never believed in horoscopes wondered whether all those who had perished were born under the same planet and around the same time. It was simply not possible and what was destined to happen will always happen thought Monty.

Meanwhile in India with the United Front coalition government of Deve Gowda trudging along with a simple majority, and with the Bofors scandal once again belching intermittent fire, thanks to the induction of Joginder Singh, a police officer from the Karnataka cadre as the new CBI chief, the tremors were once again being felt by the Congress party head honchos and by the Gandhi family at 10, Janpath.

Deve Gowda prior to becoming India's eleventh Prime Minister on 1st June. 1996 was the Chief Minister of Karnataka and he had personally handpicked the Sikh officer from the IPS 1961 batch to take charge of the country's principal investigating agency and that was on 31st July, when the investigation into the massive hawala scandal was at its peak. On that very day, when Joginder Singh, the policeman who was always in a hurry first sat on that coveted seat, he vowed that he would not leave any stone unturned till he got to the bottom of all the murky scandals that had badly tarnished the image of the nation. Sitting on that powerful chair, he had decided that come what may he would make sure that all financial scandals from the Hawala racket to the Chara Ghothala, to Bofors and such like others must be fully exposed and the culprits brought to book. Most of these scandals involved high level politicians who had betrayed the trust of the people and therefore irrespective of their party affiliations, the new CBI boss was determined to expose and punish them.

In 1990 and 1991, though the VP Singh government was obsessed with the Bofors scandal that had brought the Rajiv Gandhi government down, but the letters rogatory that had been sent by the Indian government to the Swiss authorities from time to time only made a big noise at home and nothing came of it. When the Congress returned to power under Narasimha Rao, the CBI was ordered to go slow and it reached its climax, when India's Foreign Minister, Madhav Sinh Solanki made a solid goof up in public by handing over a note to the Swiss authorities with a request to halt all investigations on the Bofors deal.In 1993, a bold investigative story in the Indian Express had forced Quatrochhi and his family to flee from India like a theif and now it was the Deve Gowda government who had triggered off the latest salvo and as a result of which the highest court in Switzerland in December decided to hand over to the Indian government the relevant documents concerning the various pay offs that Bofors had made to the various beneficiaries who had brokered the deal.

"But do remember that the CBI is a government agency my friend and one that frequently blows hot and cold depending upon which party is in power and therefore looking at the batting line up of the political bigwigs from all parties who are involved in all these various scams, Joginder Singh like all his previous predecessors I am afraid will not last long in this coveted chair, and neither will his mentor Deve Gowda," said Unni to Monty while ordering his fourth large Old Monk rum with water for the day.

"The fact is that these corrupt politicians and no matter to which party they belong to are all birds of the same feather and they will go to any lengths to scuttle all such probes. For them in times like these it is a question of you scratch my back and I will scratch yours and they will do everything possible to ensure that the real truth never ever comes out. Corruption is their bread and butter and they would like to keep it that way. So the DG's in the C.B.I. may come and DG's may go, but the politicians will go on making money forever, and that unfortunately is the truth and we will all have to live with it till the cows from the fodder scam come home," said Unni in good humour as he got into Monty's car to take a lift home.

And while on the way, when they were discussing about the grim economic situation in Iraq, and Unni told him that some unscrupulous elements from various countries including India were bypassing the laid down United Nations economic sanctions that were imposed on Iraq and were indulging in underhand business in the oil for food campaign to make a fast buck and that it also included the son of a senior Indian politician from the Congress(I), Monty too decided to try his luck.

CHAPTER-31

For a Fistful of Dollars More

Having got a little more information on the subject from a well to do Indian businessman who had earlier been doing some export business of carpets and rugs with Iraq, Monty on 10th December, 1996 landed in Baghdad with a letter of introduction from that gentleman to his contact in the Iraqi capital. And when the Iraqi contact who was a Shite Muslim frankly told him that Monty would have to first grease the palms of those who were authorized to issue import permits, and that too grease them fairly heavily in American dollars, Monty was not very surprised either. According to the Iraqi's contact, all the players in such deals were influential Sunnis who were close to Saddam and his family. But, when he further added that none of them would be willing to give any guarantee in writing on the proposed deal, Monty realized that he was barking up the wrong tree and the risk was therefore not worth taking. But now that he was in the ancient land of the Babylonians, the friendly Iraqi persuaded Monty to spend at least a few days more and see some of the ancient sites in and around the historical capital city.

On 12th December 1996, after visiting the National Musuem of Iraq and a few other important landmarks inside the city, their last stop before sunset was the splendid tomb of Zumurrud Khatun on the west side of the capital.

"Come now let me show you the lighter side of life in Baghdad and the pretty girls who often on a night before the Muslim weekend that begins tomorrow, on a Friday, can be seen walking and shopping in the sophisticated Mansour area of the city. And for all you know we might even bump into Uday Hussein, the lecherous sadist son of Saddam. Because every Thursday evening like a weekly ritual, he with his bodyguards in tow stalk and scout for good looking females in that area and he then abducts them to his palace in order to have a good time," added the middle aged Iraqi as they made their way to this up market part of the city.

"I think we are just in time," said Monty's guide as the Prince of Baghdad's golden Porsche came slowly cruising along the main avenue. As usual Uday Hussein was driving slowly while scouting along the main street looking for his prey. The time was nearing 7P.M. and it was getting fairly dark. A little later and while they were enjoying their ice cream on the sidewalk outside a popular ice cream parlour, the 32 year old much married Uday cruising along merrily passed them by. Then a few minutes later the sound of automatic gun fire was heard.

"My God I think they have got him," exclaimed the guide as the small sports car with its wind screen and passenger shield shattered came to a halt and the limp body of Uday slumped to the right.

"There is no time to waste and I suggest you get back to your hotel and try and take a flight back to India tomorrow," said the Iraqi as he quickly vanished into a side street. That evening, when Monty got back to his hotel, the only topic of discussion was who could have done it. Strangely that day Uday Saddam was without his regular bodyguards, but he was not dead. Though struck by eight bullets, he had only been badly injured. Known as a terror and a big bully, the well educated eldest son of Saddam in a fit of rage had even brutally murdered Kamal Gegeo his father's personal valet and food taster. The man's only crime it seems was to introduce his master to a young woman by the name of Samira Shahbandar and who ultimately became Saddam's second wife. So bloody whimsical was Uday that he took sadistic pleasure in torturing people and in one particular case he even shot and killed an army officer because the man did not salute him.

And It was much later and after the hunt for the killers began that Monty through a letter and a season's greeting card from the Shite Iraqi bussinesman came to know the real truth as to who had carried out that daredevil but unsuccessful assassination that unfortunately only crippled the man for the rest of his life and probably made him impotent too. It was a four man hit squad led by a certain Salman Sharif who had carried out that dare devil attack. The 27 year old Salman was a God fearing young man and as a religious Shite Muslim he hated the Sunni government of President Saddam who were hell bent in prosecuting and repressing the Shites. As the atrocities kept mounting, Salman joined a resistance group that called itself the '15 Shaaban Movement'. They chose this name, because it was on this day in the Muslim calendar that the Shite uprising had begun. In a recent conclave, the group had decided that henceforth instead of killing the low level Baath party officials, they would now train their guns on the party bigwigs and Uday Saddam was chosen as the number one target because of his weekly night sojourns into the city looking for good looking young females. From their main base around the marshes near Basra, the hit team had come well prepared to Bagdad and they had carried out a thorough reconnaissance of the area for nearly a whole month. And prior to the shooting they had very discreetly also stalked their prey, and they got their chance on 12th December. Surprisingly Uday that evening in his sporty Porsche was cruising along merrily and that too without any of his regular bodyguards even following him. Not very far from the ice cream parlour where Monty had bought the ice cream that day, Salman and his party was waiting in the shadows to kill the man whom everybody hated. While the driver in the nearby getaway car kept his engine running, the two sharp shooters got into position. And as soon as the Porshe came within close range, they opened up with full fury with their AK-47's. After having rapidly fired nearly 50 rounds into the car and which took only a minute or so, they successfully sped away and made their escape to the safe house. Early next morning they took the first available bus to Nasariya and to safety. It was originally planned as a suicide mission against Uday and his bodyguards and Salman and his boys had gone well prepared to die if need be, but lady luck on that day was on their side and they got away scot free. And when Monty narrated the incident to some of his close friends, they simply would'nt believe that he was actually there standing next door enjoying his cream when it all happened.

A few days earlier, Peevee too was witness to a high drama, but which was of a completely different kind of course and It took place in the early hours of 7th December,1996 when Peevee after a late night shooting schedule was returning to his hotel room in Madras. At around 4-30 A.M. early that morning, when his car neared Poes Garden he found a road block that had been established by the police. The Poes Garden residential area in the heart of the city was prime property and where all the rich and the famous including the controversial former Chief Minister of the state Jayalalitha Jayaram lived. Her political party the AIADMK having been badly routed in the recent state elections, her arch rivals the DMK was after her blood and she was now being hounded by her main adversary, Mr. Karunaniddhi for her many alleged misdoings while holding office.

When Peevee enquired from the police Havildar at the road block as to what was happening and he was curtly told to mind his own business, Peevee knew something concerning Amma was afoot. And when the Havildar rudely told him that the road was closed to all traffic and that he should take the long detour, Peevee who was already very tired got into a heated argument with him and would have probably landed up in the lock up, but luckily a police sub-inspector who had timely arrived at the scene recognized him and let him go.

At seven o'clock in the morning with rumours floating that 'Amma' was soon to be arrested, Peevee for the sake of sheer curiosity drove down to Poes Garden. Besides a huge contingent of police personnel and the media, there were a lot of Amma's supporters too shouting pro Amma slogans. At 8 A.M. having finished her 'puja' (prayers) when the police took her into custody, it did not surprise her one bit. Dressed in a sari she looked very elegant thought Peevee as he took a close up picture of her being escorted by the police with his zoom camera lens. However, a few hours later after interrogation, when she was remanded into judicial custody till 21st December, and the producer of the film telephoned Peevee to say that in view of the tense situation in the city the shooting schedule for the day had been cancelled, Peevee immediately rang up his father Monty in Delhi and informed him about the arrest of the lady and that they were mainly on charges of corruption.

Monty, fearing that there may be more trouble therefore conveyed to Peevee in chaste Hindi to be careful. 'Arre ye toh sub political vindictiveness ka khel hai aur kuch din jail mein rehne ke baad jub Amma bail par chut jaegi toh uski popularity aur bhi badh jaegi. Phir jub who dobara kursi mein baitegi toh who apna revenge zaroor legi. Yehi toh hai Hindustan ki rajniti ka dustoor, aur samay ke sath sath ye kissa ko bhi sub bhool jaenge. Aaj tak kabhi dekha koi bhi political leader ko corruption charges pur jail jate huye. Ye toh unka subse badha roj ka dhandha hai.Lekin tum beta koi risk nahin lena aur hotel ke andar hi rahena aur press walon se door rehna. Yaad rakna ke tum bhi ek popular film personality ho.'(This is all a game of political vindictiveness and after a few days in jail when she is freed on bail, her popularity will soar even further. And when she comes back to the chair and to power again, she will definitely take her revenge. This is what politics in India is all about and as time passes by it will all be forgotten. Till today have you seen any political leader in India being jailed for corruption although that is their main and only occupation and pastime these days? But you take care and don't move out of the hotel and do also remember that 'you too are a popular film star now.) advised Monty.

Born in Mysore on 24th February 1948, Jayalaitha as a young girl had seen very hard times. She lost her father when she was only two years old, but thanks to her mother Sandhya who was connected with the South Indian film world, she soon became a very popular film star and with her close relationship with M G Ramchandran, she jumped on to his political bandwagon in 1981. Having studied in Bishop Cotton School Bangalore and the Presentation Convent in Madras, she had a good command over the English language and thanks to her immense popularity as a film star, she like her mentor MGR capitalized fully from it. Popularly known as 'Amma' meaning mother and 'Puratchi Thalaivi' the revolutionary leader, the 48 year old buxom lady it seems had allegedly amassed so much of ill gotten wealth during her tenure as Chief Minister that a host of charges of corruption including criminal charges were now being slapped on her.

And while the once heart throb of the South Indian cinema was languishing in a cell that was meant for common criminals and with no special facilities whatsoever, Peevee having completed his shooting schedule decided at the invitation of a producer friend to celebrate the Christmas week on the emerald island. Having heard so much of the virgin beaches and the exotic flora and fauna of Sri Lanka from his Mom number two, that besides surveying the beauty of what was once Ravan's kingdom, Peevee was also keen to visit some of the hideouts of the LTTE in the north of the island and if possible also to meet Prabhakaran and to see how the dare devil young Tamil Tigers operated. The Tamil film producer it seems had good contacts with the LTTE and he was also keen to make a feature film on the life of the ever illusive LTTE leader and he wanted Peevee to play the lead role in it and for which he was even willing to pay him in American dollars.

"Don't worry or be afraid because Prabhakaran is not a bad man. He is only a fighting for the rights of the Tamil people who though since ages having settled in Sri Lanka are even today considered second class citizens in their own country," said the producer as the two of them having spent the first four days in Kandy and Colombo made their way up north to Jaffna by road in a Pajero land rover. Very cleverly the producer who also had good contacts in the Sri Lankan government had managed to secure the required permit to shoot a documentary on the flora and fauna of the island and this was only going to be a preliminary visit to select the various locales. It was already four in the evening, when they crossed the famous Elephant Pass and at the given milestone met their guide, a teenage boy who was dressed only in an olive green lungi and a black vest. The strategically located pass was not only an important gateway to the Tamil dominated Jaffna Peninsula, but it was also the heartland of the LTTE. As the young lad got into the vehicle, he quickly pulled out a small unsigned chit from under his lungi that read. 'Drive another approximately five kilometers and look out for a mound of stones on the left of the road. 50 meters ahead of the mound turn left on to the forest track and drive for another 100 meters and where you will be received by our representative and the armed escorts. Thereafter without asking any questions please do as you are told.'

Having read the note Peevee on the wheel having ensured that no other vehicle was following from behind or was approaching from the front, he on the indication given by the young lad quickly swerved left and got onto the forest track. A few minutes later and in the midst of the jungle track when the young lad ordered him to stop, Peevee was surprised when the armed escort party who had been hiding well camouflaged deep inside that jungle suddenly appeared from nowhere.

"No vehicle beyond this point and we are sorry but we will have to blindfold both of you till we get to the camp, which is another kilometer inside. And while we all walk there will be no talking or smoking", said the young LTTE escort commander and guide as the lookout party camouflaged the big Pajero with branches of tree branches and took position around it.

"Don't worry this is our territory and your vehicle will remain hundred percent safe till we return," added the guide as the two young armed scouts zigzagged their way through the dense narrow jungle track.

When they reached the camp and the blindfolds were removed, what Peevee saw was really something amazing. It was an underground camp that had been painstakingly tunneled and it had a cook house, a dining room, a recreation room and quite a few dormitories for its large number of inmates and most of whom surprisingly were very young too. It also had a harvested rain water reservoir, a mini canteen and also a medical inspection room with a small operation theatre.

"My God I think they have even beaten the North Vietnamese as far as tunneling and improvisations are concerned, and no wonder the Indian army was given a tough time. And the Sri Lankan armed forces must be finding it even tougher to tackle these diehard highly motivated Tamil Tigers,"said an excited Peevee to the Camp Commander who apologized for all the inconvenience and for the absence of their leader and hero Prabhakaran.

"Unfortunately something very important has cropped up suddenly in Vavuniya and he had to go there immediately," said the leader somewhat apologetically while he showed them around the camp, but prohibited all photography. Finally after a good cup of freshly brewed Sinhalese tea and a few glucose biscuits as they walked back from the camp and Peevee got into the Pajero for the long drive back to Colombo, he was dead tired. As a film star he was not used to walking so much and certainly not in such dense jungles.

"It's a pity that we could not meet the LTTE Supremo and I believe he normally does not like publicity and rightly so because that could lead to jeopardizing his own security. Nevertheless, he does deserve to be complimented for his resilience to fight for his people and to take on the Sri Lankan armed forces single handedly," said Peevee as the film producer at the wheel stepped on the accelerator.

CHAPTER-32

Wishful Thinking and the Big Money Game

During that month of December, 1996 while Peevee was visiting Sri Lanka, Shiraz was visiting the French Military Academy of Saint-Cyr in Brittany. And while they were on their way, when the Pakistani Military Attaché casually mentioned to Shiraz that his uncle who was from the First Regular Course of the 1946 batch had recently with his wife visited the Indian Military Academy at Dehradun as an honoured guest to attend the Golden Jubilee Reunion and that they were simply delighted in the manner in which they were looked after as VVIP's, Shiraz wondered whether he would ever get to see Dehra Dun again. Ever since he passed out from the IMA in June 1965, he never had a chance to go there again. And when he suddenly realized that had he stuck on with the Indian army he too would have had 31 years commissioned service and may have become at least a major general if not a lieutenant general by now, he had goose pimples on his body.

"Well let us hope that there are more such reunions of such likeminded people from both sides of the border in future too, because it is high time that both the countries stopped their senseless saber-rattling and sat across the table to peacefully resolve all issues including the mother of all the core issues and which for both the countries is that of Kashmir, "said Shiraz as he read the short brief about the academy. The French Military Academy was the brain child of the great Napoleon Bonaparte and was founded in 1802. Though it was considered to be as one of the foremost military academies of the world, but Shiraz after being briefed on the curriculum and the extracurricular activities of the institution felt that his old alma mater the National Defence Academy at Kharakvasla in India was far superior and much better organized. Though the St Cyr motto was 'Study to Vanquish' but in both the World Wars and during the Indo-China war and at Dien Bien Phu in particular the overall generalship of the officers from St Cyr was nothing much to write home about, thought Shiraz as he listened to the briefing that was being given by the conducting officer. However, their colourful ceremonial uniform was far more attractive than the IMA Blue Patrols, and the Academy Museum with its many artifacts was like a veritable treasure house of France's military history.

With the year 1996 gradually coming to a close, Shiraz on 17th December, while sitting late at night to carefully go through the new year's greeting card list and which included both official as well as those that were to be sent to friends and to the near and dear ones, was shocked to hear on the BBC news channel that members from the Tupac Amaru Revolutionary Movement led by their leader Nestor Cerpa had taken hundreds of high ranking diplomats, government and military officials and even some well known businessmen as hostages. And it took place while all of them were attending a gala dinner party that was being hosted by the Japanese Ambassador at his official residence in the Peruvian capital of Lima. The Japanese Ambassador Morihisha Aoki was hosting the party to celebrate Emperor Akihito's 63rd birthday and he too was also on Shiraz's mailing list. According to the news report the heavily armed guerrilla group had entered the well guarded residence of the Ambassador and which according to some was like a fortress. They had succeeded by blasting a large hole in the garden wall of the ambassador's residence, while the party was in full swing. Once the guerrillas were in full control, they demanded not only the immediate release of 465 of their comrades who were in Peruvian jails, but also a revision of President Fujimori's neo-liberal free market reforms. The leader also criticized Japan's foreign assistance program which they felt benefited only the privileged few and not the common man on the street.

"My God this kind of mass hostage taking of VIP's by terrorists and that to inside the residence of an ambassador of a foreign country is rather shocking indeed, and it is something unheard of in the annals of diplomacy. But I only hope that there will be no bloodshed," said Saira after Shiraz had conveyed the terrible news to her.

"Yes and I have all through been advocating that if the world is to remain safe, then all countries irrespective of their religious beliefs must join hands to eliminate this growing menace of terrorism. This has become an international phenomena now, and no country how powerful it may be is safe from such terrorist attacks," added Shiraz while remembering that 'Operation Tupac' that was launched by the late President Zia ul Haq in Kashmir way back in the early 1980's and which was still being pursued relentlessly by the ISI in waging a proxy war against India. And he feared that this may one day snowball into an ugly fourth round, and one that could be disastrous for both the countries.

Moreover, in early 1996, Shiraz was privy to some disturbing news that had surfaced from the Pakistan Embassy at Beijing. According to one reliable source, the A Q Khan Laboratories at Kahuta had received 5000 ring magnets from the China Nation Nuclear Corporation and which Shiraz feared could well be used to substantially increase Pakistan's capacity to enrich weapon grade uranium. And though the Pakistan government had been constantly maintaining that they have no desire to produce HEU, the highly enriched uranium, and the government to that effect had also given a written assurance to the United States government in 1993, but the fact remained that they were secretly on the job to become a nuclear power in the near future. As he made a note of all this in his little red diary in a code that had been evolved by him for his own consumption, he dreaded the day if ever India and Pakistan triggered off a nuclear war in the subcontinent.

Consequent to Pakistan's flirting with the radical Taliban regime and providing the one eyed Omar Abdullah and his government both with food and military supplies, the recent 'fatwa' that was announced by Osama Bin Laden to kill Americans anywhere and everywhere were factors which were not conducive to good US-Pak relations thought Shiraz. The very presence of Osama and his Al Qaida militant network working hand in glove with the Taliban inside neighbouring Afghanistan were all very disturbing factors that were detrimental to Pakistan's relations with the United States. Moreover with Bin Laden and his band of Al Qaida fighters sitting next door, at Khost, the matter could not and should not be taken lightly either thought Shiraz, as he glanced through some confidential correspondence that had emanated from the American Embassy in Islamabad and made additional notes of this ominous development in his secret diary.

In a confidential cable to Washington D.C. on 12th November, 1996, Thomas V Simons Jr, the U S Ambassador to Pakistan after his meeting with Taliban's acting Foreign Minister Mullah Ghaus had reported that though Mullah Ghaus had vehemently denied the presence of Osama Bin Laden in Afghanistan and he also reiterated that there were no training camps of the Al Qaida and that of the Harkat-ul-Ansar, the Kashmir based anti Indian militant organization at Khost near the Pakistan-Afghanistan border, but the Ambassador however expressed strong concern to his government that the Taliban were developing policies to shelter Muslim terrorists inside their country.And a fortnight later, when an unnamed British lady journalist informed the US Embassy in Islamabad that she had personally visited two such terrorist camps in Paktia province on the Pakistan-Afghanistan border on 14th November, 1996 and that besides the Pakistanis belonging to the Harkat-ul-Ansar who were being trained in the first camp, there were also Chechens, Bosnian Muslims, Sudanese and many others from the Arab world who were also being trained in a second camp, it came as a shock to Shiraz. With that critical input from the British journalist, Shiraz was now convinced that a Talibanised. Afghanistan with Osama Bin Laden's support and with the Pakistan ISI and other sponsors of international terrorism providing both financial and arms aid to the militant Harkat-ul-Ansar in Kashmir, there was now every possibility of Pakistan now taking the war of proxy against India to a much higher level. The very fact that the Pakistan's Pashtun based Frontier Corps elements were being actively utilized to command, control and train the Taliban, and if necessary even to fight alongside them was no longer a well kept secret. And it all started ever since Major General Nasrullah Babar, Benazir's Interior Minister with the help of the Pakistan IB and the CIA took charge of supporting and creating the Taliban and helped them in capturing Kabul.

Though America's interest in supporting the Taliban was basically political in nature so as to bring about a stable government in war torn Afghanistan, but Pakistan's involvement was in its totality, as they kept arming them to the teeth There was no doubt that a friendly Pashtun led Taliban government on Pakistan's western borders would be to the country's advantage both militarily, politically and strategically. But now with the presence of Osama Bin Laden and his Al Qaida fighters being given asylum in that country, both Afghanistan and the North West Frontier Region of Pakistan could well become the world's number one terrorist centre, thought Shiraz as he looked for Khost on the map.

A few days later in order to usher in the new year, Shiraz with his family held a party for all the embassy staff at a resort on the outskirts of Paris, and that night before going to bed he prayed that the year 1997 should be one of total peace and prosperity in the subcontinent. But unfortunately for Pakistan the year 1997 started off with a spate of sectarian killings and it climaxed on 18th of January with a massive bomb blast within the premises of the heavily guarded sessions court complex at Lahore that killed 30 including 12 policemen on duty. It seemed that the bitter rivalry between the Sunnis and the Shias had led to a revenge killing of Ziaur Rehman Farooqi; the leader of the Sunni backed Sipah-i-Sahaba.

It was nearing noon, when the police van with a heavy escort that was bringing Farooqi and his right hand man Maulana Azam Tariq from the Kot

Lakhpat jail for the court hearing arrived in front of Judge Khalid Mian's court. But no sooner had they alighted, when a massive explosion ripped apart the entire area. Luckily for Judge Khalid Mian, he at that time was in a meeting with the District and Sessions Judge at the Aiwan-i-Adil that was located well away from the scene of the blast, but the news of the tragedy had stunned the city. And it just so happened that on that fateful Saturday afternoon, Salim Rehman with his wife Aasma and some other family members were also present there at that time at the court house. There was to be a hearing at 12.30 that afternoon on a property litigation case that was being contested by Aasma's many cousins, and though Aasma was least interested in that disputed ancestral property, but all the same her physical presence in the court to sign certain documents was required. The property once belonged to her paternal grandparents and was located in the heart of the old congested city. Luckily they were also near the Aiwan-i-Adil, when the bomb exploded and therefore escaped unharmed. Seeing the terrible mayhem that was caused by the dreadful blast, all of them immediately joined in the relief and rescue work. With scores of blood soaked bodies littering the area that was around Khalid Mian's courtroom, it was imperative to first ascertain the dead from the living, and thereafter arrange for their immediate evacuation to the nearby hospitals. Besides the 30 dead, there were about a hundred injured and some of them very critically too. Since the police were expecting trouble, the DSP Gulberg with a platoon of commandos and a large contingent from the police mobile force had accompanied the police vans that were bringing Farooqi and other prisoners to the court. Prior to the arrival of the prisoners from Kot Lakhpat jail, the policemen who were stationed at the two entrance gates to the courts with their metal detectors had even carried out random checks of those seeking entry that day, and yet somebody had managed to plant the bomb at the required place in order to ensure that Farooqi and his henchmen would never live to tell the tale. As the Sipah-i-Sahaba leader and his deputy alighted, many of Farooqi's followers who had been waiting since early morning started shouting slogans and kept showering rose petals at him. And while they were busy shouting, a big loud bang accompanied by a bright flash of light devastated the area. And even before the smoke and dust could settle, the cries of pain and agony could be heard from those who were in the near vicinity of the court room.

"My God what is this country coming too,'said an exasperated Aasma to Salman Siddique, the Lahore Divisional Commissioner who with other senior police officers had reached the spot.

"Yes it is rather sad, but don't you worry we will catch the bastard,' said Tariq Parvez, the DIG Lahore very confidently. And he was damn well right because soon thereafter a man sporting a wig in order to hide his real identity was picked up by the police for questioning. He looked a suspicious character as he tried to get away from the scene of the crime. Mehram Ali, a Shia with a police record had at 7am on that Saturday morning quietly parked the explosive laden motorcycle outside the window of the Additional Sessions Judge Khalid Mian and had triggered the blast with his remote control.

"But what is the bloody use of catching the perpetrator after the bloody deed has been done," said a visibly agitated Salim Rehman to his wife as they got into their car to make their journey back to Islamabad.

Meanwhile in Dhaka with the FIR against the killers of Mujibur Rehman and his family having been launched by the leader of the by the Awami League, the eminent criminal lawyer Serajul Haq was appointed as the special Public Prosecuter. On 15th January 1997, Mr Haq with his high profile array of eminent lawyers that included Barrister Mosharaf Hussein and others submitted the charge sheet against the 23 accused including the 3 dead in the court of the District Sessions Judge, Kazi Gulam Rasool. And as soon as the prosecution started presenting their case in the court room, the group of army officers who perpetrated that ghastly crime and who were now mostly settled abroad also started getting the jitters. There were also strong rumours that a few amongst them were also clandestinely hatching a plot to kill the Awami leader and the country's lady Prime Minister Shaikh Haseena.

Not to be left behind, in India also, the New Year brought in some very bad news for the Congress. With the Bofors scandal having been resurrected by the Deve Gowda coalition government, it not only had the stalwarts from the grand old party and the residents of 10, Janpath in a tizzy, but it also had some of the bigwigs from the Bhartiya Janata Party jumping with joy. Based on their cries of Hinduvta, the party was now poised to take on the Congress at the polls and with Bofors once again in the limelight, it was time for them to cash in on it by accusing the Congress of blatant corruption and for hoodwinking the nation.

On 21st January, 1997 after nearly seven years since the CBI, the Central Bureau of Investigation had filed a charge sheet in the case, and while the Congress Party made all efforts to scuttle the process, the Swiss Justice Ministry finally agreed to hand over the first set of relevant documents to the CBI Director Joginder Singh and his team. An at 1000 hours on that day inside the Swiss parliament building, when the Chief of the Cantonal Police at Berne handed over the big set of documents to the Indian Ambassador, there was a big smile on Joginder Singh's face. He was now confident that he with his sleuths would now be able to identify the real culprits who had cheated the nation by accepting large kickbacks on the murky howitzer deal. The coded Swiss bank secret accounts like that of the Tulip, Lotus, Mont Blanc and others, which had the CBI in a spin for so long would now not only be traced to those who had taken the graft, but it would also help the investigating agency to trace out as to where these large amounts had been spirited and stacked away. Chitra Subramanium was in Switzerland when the scandal broke out in 1987, and it was she who first opened the can of worms for Rajiv Gandhi and his government and all this was now testimony to her brilliant, brave and truthful investigative journalism.

The arrival of Joginder Singh and his team at Berne was a well kept secret by the government, but the cat was out of the back as soon as the CBI chief landed back in Delhi. When Monty learnt about the arrival of those highly volatile and politically sensitive papers and came to know that they had all been whisked away to the CBI headquarters in Delhi, he immediately made a beeline for the Press Club to find out from his journalist friend Unni about his reaction to the CBI's having finally hit the jackpot on the ever elusive and politically sensitive Bofors deal.

"So what is your gut feeling about Rajiv Gandhi's involvement and his getting a cut of that big largesse through his old Italian friend who conveniently with his family scooted from the scene on 30th July, 1993 by surreptitiously boarding a late night Lufthansa flight to Milan," said Monty as Unni ordered the usual chilled Golden Eagle beer for his guest.

"Well those papers and secret accounts will definitely not have Rajiv's name or that of his family on it and that's for sure. But it will definitely have the Quattrocchis, the Hindujas, and the Win Chaddhas and their so called front companies, together with some in the Congress Party running for cover again. And if the 3 percent cut for Quattrocchi's A.E. Services was meant for the Congress party and he was only being used like a pimp and which to my mind sounds fairly logical, but still it will be very difficult to prove that charge in a court of law. It is also quite possible that Sonia Gandhi only came to know about Quattarocchi's involvement in the deal much later, when the clever Italian like the Hindujas tried to put all kinds of spokes into the wheel in order to scuttle the investigation. It should also be remembered that it was the Narasimha Rao Congress government that was in power in 1993 and which conveniently closed its eyes and may have even helped the

Quattrocchi family to quietly getaway like a thief and run away from this country. I may be wrong, but I have a strong hunch that the bulk of the money was actually meant for the Congress coffers, but when things started getting really hot during VP Singh's short reign, Quattarocchi was probably told to hang on to it. Therefore my reading is that it is only Sonia Gandhi and a few top people in the Congress who are probably aware of this. But it will be suicidal for her and the party if this ever comes out into the open. And the Congress Party knowing the magic of the Gandhi surname and to uphold it will now perforce try and get rid of Sitaram Kesri, the current President of the party and give Sonia the coveted chair and she would have to accept it I guess as a quid pro quo. And if the Deve Gowda government that is being supported by the Congress from outside is pressurized to play ball, then I am afraid either Joginder Singh will have to go or the government will fall. And the cloak and dagger game that is being played for the past decade to keep the Bofors papers under wraps will carry on and on and on," said Unni as he merrily tossed a rupee coin and said. 'Heads I win, tails you lose.'

While the Congress In India on the Bofors issue was once again getting the jitters, and the politicians of Pakistan were busy canvassing for the forthcoming elections, Fazal Rehman in Washington D.C. was bracing up to promote Bangladesh's economic problems with Bill Clinton's new Secretary of State. Having been sworn in for a second term as President of the United States, Clinton had selected a lady for the first time in US history to guide the country's foreign policy, while he would lead the country into the 21st century and the new millennium. In his inaugural speech Clinton had said. 'What a century it has been! America became the world's mightiest industrial power; saved the world from tyranny in two world wars and a long cold war; and time and again reached across the globe to millions who longed for the blessings of liberty.'

As he remembered those famous words, Fazal Rehman wondered whether America would be able to contain and eradicate the growth of Muslim fanaticism and terrorism that was being fanned by radical Muslim fundamentalists and which was slowly gaining ground all over the world and Bangladesh was no exception. On 23rd January 1997, when Fazal Rehman told his wife Samina that the Senate had approved Albright's appointment as the new Secretary of State, and Samina simply smiled and commented that the lady was not only Albright,but she is also very bright, Fazal knew that Clinton had made the right choice. Born in Prague, Czechoslovakia as Marie-Jana Korbelova on 15th May, 1937, the family in order to avoid

603

persecution from the Nazis had converted from Judaism and had become Roman Catholics. The daughter of a Czech diplomat, she with the family had fled to London in 1939, when the Jews were being rounded up, and they fled once again in 1948, but this time to America, when the Communists took over the country. She adopted the new name Madeleine when she attended a Swiss boarding school as a young girl. Later she finished her schooling from Denver and majored in political science from Wellesly College, Massachusetts. In 1957, she became a US citizen and two years later married Joseph Albright, a Chicago newspaper journalist whom she had met while she was working on a summer job with the Denver Post. The happy couple soon produced three daughters Alice, Anne and Katherine, but the marriage did not work out and they divorced in 1982. The multilingual lady who was also fluent in Russian had earlier served as Chief Legislative Assistant to Senator Edmund Muskie, and later was also a staff member from1978 to 1981 of the White House and the National Security Council. She also served as a Research Professor of International Affairs at the George Washington University's School of Foreign Service and during Clinton's first term was US Ambassador to the United Nations.

On 3rd February, while Madeline Albright was being briefed about the recent elections in Pakistan, the news arrived that Nawaz Sharif's Pakistan Muslim League and its allies had handsomely swept the polls both in the National and Provincial Assemblies. On hearing that, Ruksana Begum wittily commented to her husband. "It seems that the Sharif's and the Bhuttos have taken the monopoly to rule over this country, and I only hope and pray that Nawaz Sharif keeps his election promises of rooting out corruption and lawlessness, and of giving Pakistan a honest and stable government."

"Well with the kind of brute majority of 134 seats in the National Assembly, I hope he doesn't go the Zulfiqar Ali Bhutto way by becoming too dictatorial in his method of governance, because he it seems is adamant in scrapping Article 58 from the Zia era's 8th amendment that gave power to the President to dissolve parliament without taking the Prime Minister recommendations on the subject. And there is also a strong rumour that he also wants the prerogative to appoint the three service chiefs, which hitherto was that of the President of the country," said her husband Arif Rehman while ticking the names of those winners whom he thought were less corrupt.

"But don't you think that it is rather a pity that Imran Khan's party drew a complete blank, and the PPP have been reduced to a measly 18 seats and as result of which there will be no worthwhile opposition," said the Begum Sahiba as she tuned in to listen to the latest world news from the BBC.

Hardly had Nawaz Sharif been sworn in and won the vote of confidence in the National Assembly, when fresh sectarian violence at Multan on 19th January and another car bomb attack near the Lahore railway station a week later made the new elected members and the newly appointed ministers to sit up and take stock of the ever deteriorating law and order situation in the country. Whereas earlier Sindh was being targeted, it was now the turn of Punjab to bear the brunt of such like terrorist activities. At Multan the Lashkar-e-Jhangvi claimed responsibility for the gunning down of Mr Rahimi, the Director of the Iranian Cultural Centre and three others who were Shias, whereas at Lahore the car bomb killed three and injured 13, some very critically. And in another incident on the same day at Lahore, two traders who were said to be financiers of the Sunni outfit Sipah-i-Sahaba were gunned down near the Masjid-i-Shuhada by some unknown assailants.

"'I think its high time that these Lashkar, Sabaha and other such like militant organizations were banned, and if we don't do it now, then more such destructive groups will emerge and we will become one big terrorist state," said Aasma as Salim Rehman showed her the gruesome pictures of the Lahore bomb blast.

"What do you mean we will become, we already are one, and I am afraid the way things are moving and with the Taliban next door, the Baluchis and the Pathans will not lag behind either in destroying Mr Mohammed Ali Jinnah's dream of a secular Pakistan," said Salim Rehman as their 16 year old daughter Nadia returned home with the good news that she had topped her class in the school finals.

"Well in that case it calls for a celebration and we will all go out for dinner to any restaurant of your choice my love," said the proud father as he lovingly pecked Nadia on the cheek and presented her with a ladies Omega wrist watch.

While the strong man from the Pakistan Muslim League and Prime Minister of the country got his team together, in India following the Swiss Court order, the special court of Judge Ajit Bharihoke on 6th February 1997 issued an arrest warrant against Quattrocchi. Not to be left behind the CBI too followed it up with an international red-corner alert against the elusive Italian. Following that Sten Lindstrom, the top Swedish investigator who had headed the Bofors investigation also broke his silence. And on 8th February when Lindstrom openly declared that if the Indian government probed the Quattrocchi link a little deeper then it would reveal the connection between the gun deal and the political payoffs, it had the Congress party bigwigs in a huddle. It seems that Lindstrom also had very authentic information that Quattrocchi had transferred part of the bribes to an account in the Channel Islands. With the documents received from the Swiss authorities, there was no doubt about Qattarocchi's link in the murky deal, but the fugitive unfortunately was now well ensconced in Malaysia and there was nothing that India could do about it right now. The arrest warrant against the Italian and Lindstrom's disclosures had badly shaken the Congress and those staying at 10, Janpath. It had come as a bombshell to them and it was therefore time again to ensure that the CBI probe under Joginder Singh's stewardship did not proceed in the manner that the CBI Chief wanted it to.

"I am afraid that in today's politics in India only money talks, and with their money power, and on the pretext that they have no confidence in the Deve Gowda government, the Congress today can topple any minority government at the centre and install a new one of their choice, while maintaining that the so called democratic values and principles were in no way being violated. And I think with all the heat now again being generated by the Bofors issue, the Deve Gowda government will also soon be on its way out. Moreover, there are also very strong rumours that the Italian lady and the widow of the ex Prime Minister is being roped in by the Congress not only to officially join the party, but to also take over the mantle of the Congress President from the incompetent Sitaram Kesri. With the Bofors stink again in the air and looking at the speed in which things are moving in the higher echelons of the Congress party there are now strong indications that she may well now be willing to do so. And since the Bofors topic is no longer just a Gandhi household matter, but a serious Congress issue, the party will have to now doubly ensure that the trail does not come anywhere near 10 Janpath. For if it does, then the party I am afraid will have no other option but to defend the erstwhile first family, and usher in a more pliable Prime Minister at the centre who would be willing to rein in the present CBI Chief and have him substituted by someone of their own choice and who will then ensure that the matter is once again swept under the carpet," said Unni as he and Monty under the winter sun enjoyed their gin and bitters at the Delhi Gymkhana lawns.

"Yes I guess when the chips are down anything and everything is possible and the top cops in the CBI are not saints either, "added Monty as Peevee and Reeta joined them for the sumptuous buffet lunch.

"But Dad, all said and done one must give full credit to Mrs Sonia Gandhi for the resilience shown by her. Any other foreigner by now would have probably packed her bags and gone home to her own country, but she has doggedly stuck on through thick and thin,' said Peewee as he helped himself to some more of the delicious lobster thermidor.

"But my dear filmi hero, running away from the scene now would have only added more fuel to the fire, and as far as she is concerned she at this stage just cannot afford to let her late husband whom she loved so dearly and his party down. Maybe the payoffs were meant for the party and she had been kept in the dark and the family did not get even a penny from it, but the fact still remains that it was her husband, the once Mr Clean who in a ham handed manner while trying to cover up the issue had messed the whole thing up. And I am afraid the senior bureaucrats who were then serving in the Prime Minister's Office are equally to be blamed. They too probably for the sake of their own career had wrongly advised and guided the late Prime Minister,"said Unni as Reeta very diplomatically changed the topic to the yet to be released Hindi film titled 'Border'.

The film based on the 1971 Battle of Longewala was shot in the Thar Desert of Rajasthan with Sunny Deol in the role of Major Kuldip Singh Chandpuri, the intrepid Sikh officer and company commander. It was a true story and a saga of raw grit and courage of the brave Indian officer and his soldiers who while facing a deadly enemy in the face of overwhelming odds had routed the Pakistanis. The gallant officer and his men from the Punjab Regiment of the Indian Army had with the timely help from the valiant pilots of the Indian Air Force had not only repulsed many attacks on this isolated post by a Pakistani armoured brigade, but they also by the time the Sun came up next morning had made Longewala a graveyard of Pakistani tanks and vehicles. There was no doubt that the director of the film, JP Dutta had done a very thorough study of the operation, and Peevee having seen the early rushes of the film was firmly of the view that the brilliantly made war film deserved not only the Filmfare award but also the National Award for the best Hindi feature film for the year 1997.

"It may seem a little ironic, but maybe the same Bofors gun with its shoot and scoot capabilities, both in the mountains and in the plains and which today is haunting 10, Janpath and the Congress Party, could someday in the near future be a weapon to reckon with," said Monty who after his recent visit to Srinagar, Baramulla and Kupwara for his carpet export business was disillusioned in the manner in which the Kashmiri Pundits and Hindus in the valley were systematically being eliminated. Monty was also very surprised to see and learn about the massive induction of more formations of the Indian army and other para-military forces into the valley. And though in mid February, Deve Gowda, the Prime Minister of India visited Srinagar, Jammu, Udhampur and the volatile Uri border to see the ground reality, there was however no let up in the killings of the Kashmiri Hindus by the ISI aided militant Muslim Kashmiri groups in the valley.

A week after the Indian Prime Minister's visit to Kashmir, the U.S.Ambassador to India, Frank Wisner also visited the area and he too was overwhelmed by the plight of the homeless Kashmiri Pundits who were now living like refugees in their own country. It seemed that the Nawaz Sharif government having restored back the vast powers to the ISI that Benazir had curtailed earlier had once again put 'Operation Tupac' in top gear, while at the same time cleverly initiating talks on Kashmir between the new Pakistan Foreign Secretary, Shamshad Ahmed and his Indian counterpart Salman Haider.

While the situation in Kashmir was getting from bad to worse, thanks to the ISI sponsored proxy war against their arch enemy India, the state of affairs in Afghanistan with the Taliban getting the upper hand was now becoming a cause of worry even to the Americans. There was no doubt that Pakistan acting as the Taliban's Godfather were constantly, overtly and covertly supplying them with all the wherewithal that was required to take full control of the country, but the involvement of the Russians and the Iranians to arm and support Ahmed Shah Masood, the warlord in the north of that country was also a very disturbing factor for Pakistan.

Surprisingly in that very month of March, while Pakistan intensified their terror war in Kashmir, at Dehra Dun in India on the 13th of March, 1997, the Rimcollians from India, Pakistan, Bangladesh and England who had initially lived as comrades during the British Raj and who subsequently had fought against each other in many wars ever since partition, were now celebrating the platinum jubilee of what was once their alma mater. Known earlier as the PWRIMC, it was now known as the RIMC, the Rashtriya Indian Military College, The three long days of festivities and merry making that commenced from the 11th of March climaxed with an address by the President of India, Shanker Dayal Sharma on the 13th morning and was followed by a gala dinner and dance that carried on till very late at night. Some of the lady wives from Pakistan, who had never been to India before, were literally overwhelmed with the magnanimous hospitality that was shown to them by their Indian hosts.

"I wish we had remained as one country," said a visbly moved Ruksana Begum, as she with her husband Arif Rehman took the floor to do the waltz. As the military brass band played the age old favourite 'The Blue Danube' and the many old couples gracefully glided on the heavily powdered dance floor, Arif Rehman narrated to his wife the many stories of brotherhood and camaraderie that existed between the cadets, irrespective of their class creed or religion in that great institution. Present at the gala dance that evening were Generals, Air Marshalls and Admirals galore from both the countries and it included stalwarts like Noor Mohammed Khan, Ashgar Khan, Gul Hassan Khan, Sahibzada Yakub Khan, Nasrullah Babar, Taj Mohammed Khansada, MA Latif from Pakistan and veterans like Atal, VN Sharma, Candeth, Zaki, Padmanabhan, Virendra Singh, Vinod Patney from India. Besides them, there were also many more highly decorated officers who had brought laurels to their respective countries. On the morning of 14th March, when it was time to finally disperse, some were virtually in tears and it was the old Pakistanis and their Indian counterparts who were laughing and crying the most. It was no doubt a nostalgic reunion for those who were now in their eighties and who were also aware that this was probably going to be their last and final get together. And when the military band in honour of the departing Pakistanis played the haunting 'Auld Lang Syne' some of them literally broke down. Later that evening, when Arif and Ruksana reached Peshawar, they immediately rang up Riaz (Shiraz) and Saira in Paris to tell them about the wonderful time that they had during their short stay in India.

"Why not go as Pakistan's Ambassador to India next," said Saira rather seriously to her husband while reminding him of his great love for Hindi films and music.

"Inshallah that will be the day, and when we visit the Taj Mahal and Akbar's Fatehpur Sikri near Agra, I will sing to you one of KL Saigal's old favourite song 'Diya Jalao" (Light the Earthen Lamp) from the film 'Tansen' and Tansen as we all know was a great artist who sang in Emperor Akbar's court," added Shiraz somewhat coyly when the telephone rang again. This time it was from their daughter Sherry who was on the line from Washington D.C. to give the good news that she had been selected with a scholarship as an undergraduate student to study journalism at the George Washington University that was to commence the following semester.

"So from music it is now journalism for your ladli beti (spoilt daughter), but I hope she takes it seriously this time," said Saira as she handed over the cordless telephone to her husband. After congratulating his daughter, when

Shiraz put the phone down and told Saira quite seriously that Sherry would never give up her love for the piano,but he would be very happy if Sherry after her graduation returned to Pakistan and like Chitra Subramanium who literally took the pants off the Congresswallas in India by her investigative reporting on the Bofors scandal, Sherry too should take Zardari's pants off and let the people of Pakistan know the dubious manner in which the man has made his millions." Hearing that from her husband, Saira gave him an impish smile and called out to her 14 year old son Tojo to stop playing golf games on the computer and to start studying seriously.

"But Ammijaan I seriously want to become a professional golfer when I grow up. Because that's where the money is and I will be travelling all around the world seeing more foreign countries than what the Pakistan Foreign Service has to offer," replied Tojo somewhat bluntly. Thanks to the encouragement from his father, Tojo was already a steady 12 handicap player.

"That's all very fine but if you want to become a Jack Nicklaus or an Arnold Palmer then playing golf on the computer is not the answer and you will have to devote at least four to six hours if not more everyday on the golf course practicing very hard and that too without cutting school," said Shiraz who had also taken up the game as a social pastime and more so because the golf course and the 19th hole in particular was one place where diplomatic brownie points could be scored and valuable information gained over a drink or two' and that too without being officially formal.

While Joginder Singh in New Delhi like an Indian Sherlock Holmes got busy in finding out as to who all got how much on the dirty Bofors deal, Shiraz in Paris like Dr Watson was also unofficially trying to find out a little more as to how Zardari and Benazir could suddenly amass so much of wealth and that to in such a short time during her second stint as Prime Minister Though the Nawaz Sharif government was now also after their blood, and the new Prime Minister was determined it seems to unearth the scandal, but it was not going to be all that easy. And with the press also playing it up, the people of Pakistan too were taken by surprise in the manner in which the Zardaris had looted the nation. Some people however felt that it was nothing but political vendetta to finish off the PPP leader and the party once and for all.

Shiraz however got a wind of it by chance on the golf course, when a senior ex Citibank executive who was partnering him in a four ball playoff during an Amateur Golf tournament that was being played at the International Golf Club Du Lys in Chantilly, Paris, inadvertently blurted out that if somebody was keen to get quick money on sleazy business deals in Pakistan then the right man to contact would be Zardari, but the ex banker was not probably aware that Zardari and his wife were no longer in power in Pakistan. The senior Citibank official had earlier served in Dubai and till recently was also in Geneva. It seems he had quit his well paid job because he did not like the manner in which certain big deals were being conducted and handled by his superiors. According to his information, Benazir Bhutto and her husband during her second tenure as Prime Minister had received huge cut backs in connection with the pre-shipment inspection of goods contract that the Government of Pakistan had signed with SGS and Cotecna sometime during March and June 1994. Both SGS and Cotecna were inspecting firms that dealt with the various Pakistani import contracts. The ex banker had also casually mentioned that the Benazir government had also awarded an exclusive gold import license to one Mr Abdul Razzak Yakub, a gold bullion trader living in Dubai to import five hundred million dollars worth of gold, and from that deal also they had made quite a packet and the big kickback from this shady deal was initially deposited into a Citibank account in Dubai that was in the name of MS Capricorn Trading. That account was opened in early October, 1994 by Mr Schiegelmilch, a Swiss laywer who was not only the family attorney of the Bhuttos for the past two decades, but also a close personal friend of the couple. Two very large deposits amounting to 10 million US dollars were credited almost immediately, and the third deposit of 8 million US dollars was made sometime during end February, 1995. Thereafter the entire money during the spring of 1995 was transferred from Dubai to various Swiss Bank accounts and all these were routed through Citibank's New York office," added the gentleman as they got ready to tee off for the 18th and final hole.

"Then there must be many more such illegal deposits in their Swiss bank accounts, because Benazir was ousted from power only a few months ago," said Shiraz as he inspected his new golf driver and got ready to play his final tee shot.

"Yes I guess so, and the husband and wife duo during these past few years while in power I am sure must have amassed a huge fortune. And compared to what they received as kickbacks, the political payoffs in the Bofors scandal in India I must say was just peanuts," added the golfing partneras Shiraz registered a rare birdie on the difficult par four eighteenth hole.

"Well I hope all these are facts are true and not simply hearsay, because they could sue you for slander," said Shiraz as he shook hands with his opponents and walked to the 19th hole, the elegant Club House for some chilled beer and lunch.Later on that afternoon of 31st March, during lunch at the Golf Club, when Shiraz narrated to Saira the colossal amount of money that was made by the Benazir—Zardari duo in the various underhand deals, she simply refused to believe it.

"But I knew Benazir when she was in school with me in Murree and how could she ever do such a stupid thing like that. And in any case why did she require so much money. As it is she has inherited the major chunk of the Bhutto property and there was no need for her to steal more from the country's coffers. But as far as Zardari is concerned, I am not in the least surprised. After all and till recently he held the tag of Mr Ten Percent, didn't he?" said Saira as she helped herself to some more of the delicious French cuisine from the well laid out buffet table.

While Shiraz kept trying to figure out as to how a mind boggling sum of over a billion dollars that many in Pakistan including the government and the press were now alleging that Zardari and his wife had siphoned off, in Delhi during end March, the first official level talks between Pakistan and India at the Foreign Secretary's level got off to a fairly healthy start. Needless to say that though Shamshad Ahmed, the new Pakistan Foreign Secretary kept insisting that Kashmir was the core issue, his Indian counterpart Salman Haider maintained that all issues were equally relevant and important for a durable and lasting peace in the subcontinent, and all these therefore must be discussed diligently and truthfully. With the four day meeting having ended in a cordial and purposeful manner, Monty hoped that Pakistan would at least now see reason and stop the nearly decade old proxy war in Kashmir. However, it was only a week earlier on 22nd March, when 7 Kashmiri Pundits were brutally killed by terrorists in Sangrampura village near Budgam and Monty was apprehensive that more such brutal killings of non Muslims in the valley could follow.

Unluckily for Salim Rehman, he could not make to Delhi for the secretary level talks since he was on long leave and he with his family were in Paris enjoying his brother—in—law's magnanimous hospitality.

"'But do you think Zardari and Benazir will be able to wangle their way out on the many serious charges of corruption that is now being leveled against them," asked Saira somewhat seriously.

"Maybe and maybe not, and it all depends on how thoroughly the investigation is carried out and by whom, and mind you it won't be all that easy. The fact is that most of that ill gotten money has been safely stacked away in various Swiss banks, and the Swiss authorities as we all know maintain a very strict code of conduct as far as the secrecy of such accounts are concerned. And with Benazir having once again found refuge abroad while her husband is being grilled in Pakistan, my own gut feeling is that by now quite a bit of that money may have already been siphoned out from Switzerland to some of the other private investment companies in the British Virgin Islands that Zardari allegedly controls," said Salim Rehman.

"'Well if the recipients from the Bofors kickbacks could have such attractive names of their accounts like 'Mont Blanc', 'Pitco', 'Lotus' and 'Tulip', the Zardari-Benazir accounts must be also having their share of code names too but the only person who can open the Pandora's box is none other than Mr Shelegelmilch, the old faithful who has been Bhutto's man Friday for donkeys years," said Shiraz somewhat jokingly.

"Yes and looking at the way the Bofors deal in India was struck and the manner in which the SGS and Cotecna deals were made in Pakistan, there is also a lot of similarity between the two. Whereas in the Bofors case it was the Italian Quattrochi and Martin Ardbo the big Swede and both of whom still hold the keys to that mystery, in the case of Pakistan, it is the half German and half Swiss Shelegelmilch who had brokered those deals and ensured that Zardari and Benazir kept holding on to that golden key. But all said and done since all the players have made their respective killings, they definitely would not like to talk about it now at this stage at least," said Salim Rehman.

"But with Mr Zardari now behind bars, who will now stay in that palatial Tudor Mansion with its 365 acres of land in Rockwood Estates in Surrey County that Mr Ten Per Cent had bought allegedly for a whopping 8 million dollars in 1995, or for that matter in the 4 million dollar luxury resort that the Prince Consort of Pakistan acquired not so very long ago in Palm Beach County, Florida," said Sherry somewhat naughtily.Sherry too had just recently returned to Paris from Washington and where the current favourite topic in the Pakistani Embassy in the US was Zardari and his millions.

"But.what will he now do with his many millions if he is going to remain in jail," said young Tojo as he with his new expensive Ping putter in hand thanked his dad for it.

"Well one never can say, and like all such like corrupt rich people and politicians, he too with his immense money power may one day buy his own freedom back," said Aasma somewhat sarcastically.

"Yes anything and everything is possible in this dirty game that the politicians play all across the globe to fill their own coffers, and one never knows how much the next man will make while sitting on that same damn chair," said Ruksana Begum who with her husband Arif Rehman gave everybody a pleasant surprise when they landed in Paris that very morning unannounced.

CHAPTER-33

Bofors Back in Action Again

On the 1ˢᵗ of April 1997, a day that is widely known all over the world as April Fool's Day, when a beaming Nawaz Sharif announced the 13ᵗʰ Amendment that abrogated and repealed the infamous 8ᵗʰ amendment, Ruksana Begum only hoped and prayed that the power should not go to the man's head. There was no doubt that not only the new amendment would give the Prime Minister immense powers, but it would also ensure that the President who earlier had discretionary powers to either dismiss the government and appoint the three service chiefs and the Governors, he would now only remain as a ceremonial figure head. Therefore having got what he wanted, Nawaz Sharif was now all set to usher in a new era of democratic freedom and political stability to the country. And while the poor people of Pakistan looked forward to a better and prosperous life in the coming future, In India the Congress (I) was once again getting ready to destabilize the country.

"It seems that Mr Joginder Singh the Sardar chief of the CBI is moving a bit too fast for comfort. And in his efforts to bring all the Bofors culprits to book, and together with the Congress and 10 Janpath already feeling the heat, I think Mr Deve Gowda's days are numbered," said Unni as Monty drove him to the airport.Every year in early April, Unni as a ritual went and prayed at the famous temple of Balaji at Tirupati and then went to his old village near Kottayam to spend a few days with his nephews, nieces and old childhood friends.

"But how soon do you think the government will fall and will there be another mid—term election?"said Monty.

"Well as per the strong rumours and indications that are emanating from the Congress high command, it could be very soon. And according to my source of information, the Congress in order to get the Bofors heat of their backs may support another United Front government and that too with a new Prime Minister who would be able to either derail or will be told or rather directed to adopt a go slow attitude on the ongoing Bofors investigation," said Unni.

"Well if that be so then Mrs Sonia Gandhi I am sure will also soon join the Congress bandwagon," said Monty as he bid goodbye to his mentor and friend.

"Yes I guess so because there will be no where else for her and her family to go,"said Unni

While Unni was enjoying his short sojourn with old friends and relatives in his village, the news arrived that one of his old childhood Muslim friend with his entire family who had gone to perform Haj in Mecca had perished in an accidental fire. According to the press reports, the fire was caused by an explosion of a gas cylinder at midday on 14th April, and it had swept through the vast tented city and killed nearly 300 people and injured many more. The nearly 2 million Muslims who had gathered at the Plains of Mina for the traditional old sacred ritual were about to begin their journey to Mount Arafat, where Prohpet Mohammed had delivered his last sermon, when the tragedy struck the camp. Strangely most of the victims were Indians, Pakistanis or Bangladeshis, and the day also happened to be the Bengali New Year's Eve. Late on that mournful evening, when all the villagers irrespective of their religion, caste and creed gathered together to pray to the Almighty for the souls of Wajid Mohammed and his family to rest in peace, Unni realized that the small village of his was really the secular India that Gandhi had truly desired and which the politicians of today with their caste and communal based regional politics and their greed for power and money were determined to destroy.

Two weeks later on 21st April, 1997, when the Deve Gowda government was given the boot, Unni's prediction had come true. So once again with outside support being given by the Congress, and in order to avoid another mid—term election, a new United Front government was sworn in. And this time it was led by Mr Inder Gujral, an ex Congress minister who was now with the Janata Dal. To ensure that the new government and its leader towed the desired Congress line, the outside support therefore was with the proviso that the new leader will have to consult the Congress party before taking any important major policy decisions. The new Prime Minister with the goatee beard who hailed from Jhelum, Pakistan knew very well right from the start that he was on a sticky wicket. As a young man he took active part in India's freedom struggle and he was also the Minister for Information and Broadcasting in Mrs Gandhi's cabinet during the emergency till he was shown the door by her son Sanjay Gandhi and it was simply because the man stood up to him. But he was now also vary of the fact that with Sonia Gandhi's entry into the Congress, which was imminent, the party may once again put spokes into the ongoing Bofors investigations.

The recent submission to the CBI by Mr Oza who was India's Ambassador to Sweden at that time and who was the man on the spot when the balloon went up in April 1987 had badly shaken the Congress and 10, Janpath. Oza it seems in his statement had categorically told the CBI that it was the PMO's office under directions from Rajiv Gandhi that was responsible to ensure that the true facts of the Bofors deal, and who took how much in the payoffs did not surface at all. According to him, all this undoubtedly was a well orchestrated conspiracy to save the ex Prime Minister's skin and those of his close friends, and the senior bureaucrats who were also his advisors. And with such like statements coming from a seasoned diplomat, and with the relevant papers having arrived from Switzerland, Joginder Singh and his team were now going full throttle to name those who were responsible for the millions of dollars of loss that was caused to the state exchequer.

"But do you think the CBI will also question Sonia Gandhi?"asked Monty somewhat seriously.

"Well it may, but I don't think they will, because there is no reference to Rajiv or to Sonia as far as the payments from Bofors directly to them are concerned. Neither are there any payments by cheque from Bofors in their personal names. But the possibility of Quattrocchi sharing some of that loot with them and maybe with the Congress party cannot be ruled out. But such like allegations I am afraid will be very difficult to prove in a court of law. And it all now depends on how Gujral and his government in order to stick to their chairs will approach the matter," added Unni while presenting Monty with a sandalwood statue of Balaji, and Reeta with a beautiful Kanjeeveram saree.

"Well let me tell you a little more about the famous Balaji temple at Tirupati, which is also known as the Tirumala Venkateshwara Temple. Located amongst the many hills in the Indian state of Andhra Pradesh, it is the most sacred place of the Hindus and the second most visited holy place in the world after the Vatican. And those who pray to the self manifested idol of Lord Vishnu with reverence and with their heart, the merciful deity always grants them their wishes," said Unni to Peevee as they while on their way to the Delhi Gymkhana Club for lunch drove past Number 1,

Safdarjung Road which was now a museum and a memorial to the late Mrs Gandhi.

"Well if what you just said about Balaji is true, then I think the Congress should advice Mrs Sonia Gandhi to also pay a visit to the temple soon and maybe the diety will take the terrible load on the Bofors affair off her chest and give her some much needed peace of mind. The damn thing has been haunting the poor widow for a whole damn decade and I think it is time that the press and the opposition stopped their never ending charade of castigating her and her family on this issue, just because they were friendly with the Quattrrochis," said Peevee as Unni gave him a few tips on how to get to Tirupati and to seek Balaji's blessings without standing in the long queue and without getting mobbed.

"Therefore you mean to say that to get inside that inner sanctotum of that holy temple and to get an exclusive darshan of Balaji and to seek his blessings once has to donate a large sum of money. And if that is really the case then even our poor Gods and Godesses are also being forced to get corrupted, "said Peevee as popped one big blessed laddoo into his mouth.

While the Prime Minister of India was in two minds on how to handle the delicate Bofors issue and the Fodder Scam that the CBI was now insisting upon to bring it to its logical conclusion, the arrest of Squadron Leader Farook Ahmed of the Pakistan Air Force in New York by the N.Y.P.D., the New York Police Department on charges of selling drugs and the dismissal of Admiral Mansural Haq, the Pakistan Naval Chief on charges of corruption and misappropriation of funds shocked the people of Pakistan. For the common man in Pakistan, the men and officers from the armed forces in uniform were generally held in high esteem, but it seems that the lure of making easy money had also seeped into both the junior and the senior officers in all the three services.

And as both the governments of India and in Pakistan in their respective parliaments tried desperately to play down all such cases of corruption and scams that was giving a bad name to their countries, far away in Peru, President Fujimori announced to his people late on the evening of 22nd April that in a daring commando operation, the Peruvian armed forces had freed the remaining dignitaries who had been held hostage for a record 126 days inside the Japanese Ambassador's residence at Lima. The operation code named 'Chavin De Huantar' was in reference to a Peruvian archeological site, which was famous for its underground passages. At around 15.23 hours that afternoon the Peruvian army commandos having tunneled their way into the building from the adjacent houses detonated three explosive charges in three different rooms on the first floor where most of the hostage takers were enjoying a game of indoor soccer. Their leader Crepa had also unwittingly helped with the plan, when on hearing noises and suspecting that a tunnel was being dug, he moved all the hostages to the second floor. As the Commandos stormed into the building from all sides, it took Crepa and his men with complete surprise and in the ensuing gun battle all the 14 MRTA guerrillas were killed, together with one member of the Supreme Court and two Peruvian army officers, a Lieutenant Colonel and young Lieutenant who had led the assault.

During the last week of April, when the Indian government received a detailed confidential report from its embassy in Peru on how the hostage rescue operation in Lima was carried out, it was simply filed away because firstly no Indians were involved and secondly because it was not considered all that important. But Shupriya who happened to be in Delhi for some official consultations felt that since such like situations may well arise in New Delhi where there are so many big important missions, the home and the defense ministry could have atleast been briefed, and a joint case study should have been carried out and some useful lessons learnt from it. However, on her return to Moscow, she decided to at least review all the security arrangements within the embassy premises and carryout a mock evacuation and fire drill for the entire staff. With the Russian mafia gangs inside the capital city ruling the roost, and with Muslims from Chechniya wanting to take revenge, she did not want to take any chances.

Meanwhile in India, when the CBI Chief, Joginder Singh made a genuine request to the Cabinet Secretariat asking the Gujral government to declassify 15 highly classified files in the PMO's office and some 20 odd files that were lying in the Ministry of Defense, it created a virtual storm in the corridors of power. This would have enabled the intelligence agency to use the same as evidence. But the catch was that these could not be used as evidence in courts without the same being declassified first. And as luck would have it, the second set of documents, which was the key to the third secret Swiss Bank accounts were yet to arrive from Switzerland. But it seems that Joginder Singh was in such a tearing hurry to complete the probe that he without waiting for the declassification of those secret and top-secret files, dispatched the proposed charge sheets for immediate action by the government. The list of those accused included the late Prime Minister Mr Rajiv Gandhi, MadhavSinh Solanki the former Union Minister, Gopi Arora, former Special Secretary to the Prime Minister, former Defence Secretary SK Bhatnagar, the Italian businessman Ottavio Quattrochhi and his wife Maria,

Win Chaddha, his wife Kanta and son Harsh Chaddha. Moreover, to prove to the politicians and the press that he as the CBI boss meant business, and that nobody was above the law, when Joginder Singh also decided to indict Lallu Prasad Yadav in the fodder scam case, the chips were now down. And when the Governor of Bihar, AR Kidwai gave his consent to prosecute Lalu Prasad Yadav, and the man simply refused to step down, the ball was back in Mr Gujral's court.

"Unfortunately Joginder Singh does not realize that politicians in India are above the law and they in order to stick to their chairs will go to any length to ensure that they survive. After all the present United Front government is in the hot seat because of the Congress and the Janata Dal, which has 45 Members of Parliament, and Lalu happens to be one of the main stalwarts of that Dal and he is also the Chief Minister of Bihar," said Unni while giving a brief resume of the man who had made Bihar his own personal fiefdom.

Lalu Yadav was born in a poor peasant family in the village of Phulwaria in the Gopalganj District of Bihar on 11th June, 1948. In the early 1970's inspired by the socialist leader Jai Prakash Narayan, he as a student leader in Patna University with his command over the Bihari language and a wacky sense of humour had led the student movement, and at the young age of 29 on a Janata Party ticket became a Member of Parliament. In 1990, he became the Chief Minister of Bihar and with his secular approach to forge unity between the many Muslims and the majority Hindus in the state; he had won the hearts and minds of his people with his non communal approach to all Bihar's problems. And with the very large number of the Janata Dal seats in the Lok Sabha, he was now a political leader to reckon with.

And while Prime Minister Inder Gujral in order to keep his chair kept humouring both the Congress and Lalu's faction in the Janata Dal, Pakistan on 25th May. 1997 officially recognized Mullah Omar's Taliban government in Afghanistan. That very day, when Salim Rehman conveyed the news on telephone to his father Arif Rehman, he was visibly very upset.

"Well son I think this is one big policy blunder that Pakistan will have to regret for a very long time to come. And where was the damn major hurry. Afghanistan is still in a state of civil war and the best course of action would have been to wait and see. I feel sorry to say that though the majority of them are Pashtuns like us, but the Taliban simply cannot be trusted. And with a maverick leader like Mullah Omar who is a religious fanatic and a fundamentalist to the core, this so called move I am afraid will greatly annoy the Americans. We must realize that the U.S.today is the only super power in this world and whose support is vital for our own existence, both economically and militarily. And I believe only two other countries, Saudi Arabia and the UAE in this whole wide world have followed suit by giving recognition to the Taliban and I really wonder why," said Arif Rehman as he called out to his wife Ruksana who was in the garden pruning the roses to come and speak to her son on the telephone.

The news about Pakistan having recognized the Taliban had also upset Ruksana Begum and she too felt that it was rather premature and hasty. But she was now more worried about the emergence of the Lashkar-e-Jangvi, a radical Sunni militant organization who were regularly targeting the Shia community and whose dreaded leader Riaz Basra with a two million rupee reward on his head was still at large. Born in the village of Chak Thandiwala in the Sargodha District, the 30 year old Basra who had studied at madrassas in Lahore and Sargodha was now the undisputed leader of this terrorist group. As a young Mujahideen he had also fought against the Russians in Afghanistan and became a member of the Sipah-e-Sahaba in 1985. But only last year in 1996, he broke away from the Sipah-e-Sahaba to form his own Lashkar-e-Jangvi, and which he had named after his mentor Haq Nawaz Jhangvi who was killed in a retaliatory bomb attack by Shia militants that took place on 23rd February, 1990.

"I wonder how many more such Laskar, Harakat, Hizbul and Sipah-e-Sabaha militant organizations will mushroom in this country, and if it carries on like this then I am afraid Pakistan is doomed," said Ruksana Begum while reading aloud to her husband a news item in a local news paper that stated that the same Riaz Basra with vengeance and in the name of Allah has vowed to get rid of all Shias in Pakistan.

"Well in the earlier days it was the Ahmediyas, then came the turn of the Mohajirs irrespective of the fact whether they were Shias or Sunnis, followed by the Christians and now it is the turn of the Shias, and God alone knows who will be next. The fact is that these so called militants are nothing but a bunch of illiterate young men who are unfortunately led by radical leaders and who in the name of so called religious beliefs and dogmas are slowly and steadily for the sake of power ruining this nation. And the pity is that the present government of Nawaz Sharif is doing nothing at all to check this growing menace. And my biggest fear is that with the advent of the Taliban in neighbouring Afghanistan, the people who will be the most affected will be those from the frontier regions of the North West frontier and Baluchistan. So far the only good thing that the new Prime Minister has done is to revert the weekly holiday back to Sunday," said Arif Rehman somewhat mockingly.

CHAPTER-34

God's Own Country

In the month of May 1997, while the Bofors payoff case was hotting up, Mrs Sonia Gandhi's entry into politics was hailed by the Congress party. And needless to say it also indirectly served a warning to the Gujral government to tread softly on the Bofors issue. To the Congress party members the very name Gandhi always spelt magic and to them though she was an Italian it mattered little. After all she was now an Indian citizen and the widow of their late Prime Minister Rajiv Gandhi. But ever since the 'Rath Yatra' by LK Advani, the BJP had also been slowly gaining ground, and with their cry for Hinduvta becoming louder, it too now had an all India reckoning. Though the party under the leadership of Atal Behari Vajpayee had earlier tasted power only for just 13 days, they were now confident that they could on their own take on the fledging Congress party at the hustings. And when Joginder Singh and his CBI team decided to name the former Prime Minister Rajiv Gandhi as one of the accused in hatching a conspiracy to cause willful loss to the national exchequer on the Bofors deal by allowing middlemen like Qatrocchi, Win Chaddha and others to make a killing, the BJP decided to once again rake up the Bofors issue.

"But only God and God alone can save this blessed country, and if people like Lalu and other such like political leaders can swipe off millions and yet hold the country to ransom, then one can imagine what will be our future," remarked Peevee to his makeup man as he switched on to his favourite TV sports channel only to learn that Saeed Anwar, the Pakistani opening batsman while playing against India at Chennai in a one day match had established a world record by scoring 194 runs.

"Jee Ha Janab, the 6th September 1968 Karachi born attacking cricketer and an engineer by profession who had earlier planned to go to the United States to do his masters, but gave it up for his love for the game had also during the 1993-1994 Champions Trophy that was played at Sharjah notched up three successive hundreds. And the man was not only a favourite with the crowd, but he was also a very religious person too," said the young makeup artiste who was a devout Muslim and like Peevee was also mad about cricket.

Peewee was shooting for his new film that had a story line based on one day international cricket and its connection with a match rigging and betting syndicate. He was playing the role of an investigative journalist who with the heroine was required to carry out a sting operation to expose the nexus between a few top ranking international cricketers, the cricket board and a Mafia don of Bombay who was now controlling the show. The opening scene was the mysterious death of India's number one batsman in a road accident on the night prior to the crucial semi-final day and night match between India and Pakistan. And on that very night the three rogue cricketers were also being lavishly entertained with booze and girls by the don in one of his own exclusive private dance bars in the city. The dead cricketer's famous last words to his driver who luckily survived were "Lagta Hai ke Ye saala Don sirf paise ke lalach mein humme kabhi jeetne nahin denge.'(This bloody Don with his penchant for making a quick buck will never let us win) And with the mad passion for cricket in the subcontinent, the film producer was certain that the film with its catchy title 'Sirf Chauka ya Chakka'(OnlyFours and Sixes) and with its four deadly hot and sexy item numbers the film would definitely be a box office hit, and Peevee felt the same way too.

While the final climax scene of the film was being shot at the jampacked Wankhede Stadium in what was now Mumbai and not Bombay, thanks to the new Shiv Sena government's diktat; Peevee was pleasantly surprised to see Mom Number 2 with Mom Number 1 and Monty there for the grand finale. Shupriya with Monty and Reeta had arrived from Havana via New York early that morning and they all wanted to give Peevee a big surprise.

"My God I just cannot believe it that you have come all the way from Castro's Cuba to see me at work," said Peevee as he touched Shupriya's feet and introduced all of them to the film unit.

"Well now that you are a famous film personality, I hope you will at least give me an autographed photo of yours too,"said Shupriya jokingly as she hugged Peevee and presented him with a box of Romeo y Julieta Churchill cigars. That particular brand of Cuban cigar was one of the most expensive in the world. And with that beautifully decorated cigar box was an emerald studded cigar lighter that had the words 'From Mom Number 2 With

Love.' And below that on a small silver plate was Yeshwant Kaur's signature beautifully engraved in running hand.

"That definitely calls for a grand party at my new pad on Pali Hills, Bandra," said an excited Peevee as he got ready for the next shot. That evening after a few drinks at home, when Peevee took them out to dinner to his favourite restaurant 'Olives' at Khar, which was also a meeting point of all the top film stars of Bollywood, Shupriya who kept observing her son's way of talking and laughing was reminded of her late husband Shiraz. That evening as she went to bed she wondered whether Peevee would ever come to know about his real father and mother.

On the next day there was still more good news for the family, when Monty's daughter Dimpy rang up to say that her husband Paddy had received his transfer orders. Having done more than three years in Tokyo, Paddy was now going on promotion as First Secretary to the Indian High Commission in Islamabad and they were looking forward to it. Not only was Tokyo a very expensive station, but with the low pay and allowances it was practically a hand to mouth existence for them.

In that month of May, while the Bofors scandal was once again playing havoc in India, and Benazir and Zardari were being targeted for corruption in Pakistan, Tony Blair the young 44 year old new Prime Minister of England was getting ready to usher in his brand of socialism into the country. Anthony Charles Lynton Blair was born on 6th May, 1953 and was popularly known as Tony Blair. His Labour Party had won a landslide victory in the recently held general elections and the party had finally managed to oust the Conservatives who had held power for a record number of 18 years. The Edinburgh born Tony who as a college student played the guitar and sang for a rock band called 'Ugly Rumours' had joined the Labour Party after graduating from Oxford in 1975. In his maiden speech in the House of Commons on 6th July, 1983, the young Member of Parliament had created a minor sensation when he declared that he was a socialist not through reading a textbook that had caught his intellectual fancy, nor through unthinking tradition, but because he firmly believed that at its best, socialism corresponded most closely to an existence that was both rational and moral and that it stood for cooperation and not confrontation and it also stood for fellowship, and above all it also stood for equality. The man who as a boarder at Fettes College, Edinburgh was once arrested after wrongly being accused for attempted burglary was now also the Number one politician of the United Kingdom. That arrest took place when Tony as a student after a late night binge tried to sneak in to his college dormitory by using a ladder and was caught red handed. But that apart, he was now all set to take England into the next millennium also. And while he with his wife Cherie who was the daughter of actor Tony Booth and their three children moved into 10 Downing Street, the rumours were that the first couple was now all set to produce their fourth one soon. And if they did so then that too would then create some sort of a record and history. Because not only was Tony at 43 the youngest person to attain this coveted office after Lord Liverpool in 1812 became Prime Minister at 42, but he would also be the first British Prime Minister in over 150 years to produce a legitimate child ever since Francis Russel was born to Lord John Russel on 11th July, 1849.

In that very month of May, while Tony Blair was still finding his feet, some well to do Indians who had settled in Britain and who were once part of the pseudo Godman Chandraswami's inner circle were shocked when they got the news from India that the so called 'Godman' was not only a damn cheat, but also a bloody schemer and a conman. It seems that when the CBI told a Delhi court that there was enough evidence on record to frame charges of criminal conspiracy and forgery not only against the 'Godman', but also against the former Congress Prime Minister Rajiv Gandhi and Foreign Minister Narasirmha Rao and his erstwhile deputy KK Tewary in the controversial St Kitts affair that had been orchestrated by Rajiv Gandhi to malign VP Singh, it not only sent shock waves throughout the country, but it also had the Congress party desperately looking for cover. And as a result of this, the party therefore immediately took a holier than thou stand and vowed that it would make all efforts to uphold the good name of their beloved and departed leader. But when Mr Rao's learned Counsel RK Anand told the Special Judge Ajit Bharihoke that whatever his client had done was entirely at the instance of the late Prime Minister Rajiv Gandhi, it automatically spelt the death knell of Narasimha Rao's political career.

"I think with this sensational new admission in court by Narasimha Rao's counsel, his political career as a Congress party bigwig is now finally over I guess," said Monty as Unni chronologically brought out the facts of the case. In August 1989, when the Bofors scandal kept tarnishing Rajiv Gandhi's image, a report in the Kuwait based Arab Times alleged that VP Singh was the main beneficiary of a secret bank account that had deposits amounting to 21 million US dollars in the small Caribbean Island of St Kitts. This was of course a planted report in order to fix VP Singh who had resigned from Rajiv Gandhi's government earlier and who had been rather vocal about the government's involvement in the Bofors and other such dubious defence deals. And based on this news report, the Enforcement

Directorate was immediately ordered by the PMO's office to probe the matter. Mr KL Verma the Director in the Enforcement Directorate therefore promptly deputed Deputy Director Mr A P Nandy to proceed to St Kitts and get those documents pertaining to the accounts that were allegedly held by VP Singh and his son Ajeya. While Nandy was on his way to St Kitts via New York, the Indian Foreign Secretary Mr S K Singh was told by Rajiv Gandhi on telephone to get in touch with the Indian Consulate in New York and to tell them to help out the Enforcement official in procuring those documents from St Kitts. On procurement of these documents, the Indian Consul General in New York was also directed to have them attested by him and he dutifully obliged. But all these documents were all actually forgeries. But since they had been attested by none other than the Consul General of India in New York, they were therefore considered to be authentic and genuine by the Rajiv Gandhi government. The whole game plan was not only meant to defame VP Singh and his family, but to also tell the general public that the man was no saint either. So on his return to Delhi, when Mr Nandy's with the attested documents submitted his report while knowing fully well that these were not genuine, it hardly mattered. It was a question of his own career and he simply towed the line. And when that report on October 1989 was presented to the Indian Parliament, it did create a big furore no doubt, but it was not big enough to let Rajiv and his government off the hook on the raging Bofors issue.

With the ardent hope that the allegations against VP Singh would tarnish the man's image and that the people would again vote for the Congress, Rajiv Gandhi therefore in November 1989 decided to call for fresh elections. The gamble however backfired on him and the Congress eventually lost. And soon after VP Singh became the new Prime Minister the St Kitts files were reopened and in May 1990 the CBI registered criminal charges against the Enforcement Director KL Verma, 'Godman' Chandraswami, his man Friday, Aggarwal alias Mamaji, Larry J Kobb the son-in-law of the notorious arms dealer Adnan Kashoggi and George Mclean the Managing Director of the First Trust Corporation Bank at St Kitts. Unfortunately the entire conspiracy to defame VP Singh was done in a most amateurish and unprofessional manner and which only further lowered Rajiv's credibility and prestige. Mr Anand as the Defence Counsel had also submitted to the court that Narsimha Rao who was then India's Foreign Minister had also been instructed by RK Dhawan an officer on special duty at the PMO to help in having these documents duly attested, and Rao only obeyed orders. Rao it seems had only instructed the Indian Consul General in New York to have the signature of the Managing Director of the FTCL, the First Trust Corporation Limited in St Kitts Island where the alleged account was opened duly attested and it was duly carried out. And mind you this was the time when the Bofors scandal in India was at its peak and VP Singh was in the opposition and he was now looked upon as a future leader and Prime Minister. He had fallen out with Rajiv and the Congress Party and had been accusing them of corruption not only in defense deals, but also of colluding with big Indian business houses and granting them licenses for cash during the so called infamous 'License Raj," added Unni who was now planning to write a book on such like sensational scandals that shook the nation ever since the country got its independence. Starting from the jeep scandal during Krishna Menon's tenure as High Commissioner to the United Kingdom, the book also focused on the Mundra scandal, the TTK affair, the Chara Ghotala and a host of others.

"And may I know what will be the title of this sensational book, of yours, "asked Monty as he presented Unni with a laptop on his 75th birthday.

"Well I have not thought about that as yet, but I think the title 'India's Greatest Scamsters' or 'Sensations India' or even 'Nothing But!" could be quite apt I guess," said Unni as he called for his final round of Old Monk rum.

"But you jolly well have all your facts and figures correct or else you will be asking for trouble. And going by the criminalization of politics in India today, some one on directions from the very top may even try to bump you off." asserted Monty in a lighter vein.

"Well in any case I think it is already time for me to go and if they do that then I will be all the more grateful, because that will certainly make my book an all time best seller," said a happy Unni as he with his new cell phone that was presented by Peevee rang up for a taxi to go home. And as he got into the cab, he in his imitable style said. "These so called court tamashas concerning our politicians and scams no doubt add to the circulation of our newspapers and periodicals, and also for the many news channels on the television screen, but the end result is always the same. Everybody gets honourably acquitted and nobody ever gets convicted. And it is like in our many Hindi movies where the honourable judge always and invariably ends up with the words.' Witness ke bayan aur kanoon ko madhe nazar rakhte huye, accused ko honourably bury kar diya jata hai.' (Keeping in view the evidence given by the witness and the laws of justice prevailing in the country, the court therefore honourably accquits the accused.) And that is why my friend I always maintain that India is God's own country.'

CHAPTER-35

The Two Million Dollar Prized
Catch and the Pot of Gold

Early on the morning of 16th June 1997, when Salim Rehman woke up Shiraz in Paris and gave him the sensational news over the telephone that the four and a half year manhunt by the Americans for Mir Aimal Kansi was now finally over, and that he had been picked up from a hotel in Dera Gazi Khan and flown to the United States, Shiraz wondered who could have got those 2 million dollars rich reward. Mir Aimal was a well educated Pathan and the son of a wealthy building contractor of Quetta. An ethnic Pashtun from the Kasi tribe, he had entered the United States in 1991 with fake papers that he had bought in Karachi. While in America he stayed with his Kashmiri friend Zahed Mir in his apartment in Virginia, and having invested some money that he had brought along with him in Excel Courier Services, he also took up the job as a courier driver for the company.On the morning of 25th January, 1993, Aimal Kansi as usual got into his brown Datsun station wagon car and with a loaded AK-47 that he had bought from a gun dealer in Chantilly, he drove along route 123 and stopped at the major intersection from where one road led to the CIA headquarters at Langley. Normally at that particular crossing during the peak office hours it was always quite a long wait for all the motorists and Aimal it seems had made a good study of it. At around 8 that morning he stopped his station wagon behind a number of vehicles that were waiting at the traffic red light on the eastbound side of Route 123, near the Dolly Madison Boulevard in Fairfax County, Virjinia. Then having identified his victims, he simply walked up and shot dead the two CIA officers, Lansing Bennet and Frank Darling and wounded three others. Surprised by the lack of armed response from those around, he climbed into his vehicle and drove to a nearby park. After waiting there for nearly 90 minutes, he drove back to his apartment, and hid the weapon in a green plastic bag under the sofa. Thereafter a cool Aimal went to a nearby McDonald's for a bite. And having enjoyed the meal, he went and bought an airlines ticket to Pakistan from a convenience store and booked himself for the night at the Days Inn Hotel. Watching the CNN news reports in his hotel room, Aimal knew that the police had misidentified his vehicle, and what was even more surprising was that they did not have even have his license plate number. Early next morning Aimal took the flight to Pakistan and having spent a few days in Quetta with his family, he without telling anybody just disappeared across the border into Afghanistan.

Soon thereafter an investigative task force code named 'Langmur' for the Langley murders was set up by the CIA and the hunt for the elusive killer began. Going through the recent sales of AK-47 assault guns in the States of Virginia and Maryland, the FBI came across the name Mir Aimal Kasi who had exchanged another gun for the AK-47 from a gun store in Chantilly. On his arrival in the United States, his faked papers and passport had the surname Kasi and not Kansi on them Two days after the broad daylight shooting of the two CIA officers, Aimal's friend and roommate Zahed Mir also reported him missing to the police. Soon thereafter a police search of Kasi's apartment resulted in the murder weapon being found, and a worldwide manhunt for the fugitive with a 2 million dollar reward began. Finally it was sometime in May 1997, that an informant walked into the US Consulate at Karachi and claimed that he could lead them to Kasi. As proof he also showed the copy of the driver's license application that Kansi had submitted under a false name, but it had his photograph on it. According to the informant, Kansi was in the Afghan border region and with the offer of that fantastic award of 2 million dollars; the whistle blower was now willing to turn him in. The informant then tempted Kansi with a lucrative business offer of smuggling Russian electronic goods into Pakistan and Kansi it seems fell for it.

On the evening of 14rh June, 1997, Kasi arrived at Dera Ghazi Khan and checked into the Shalimar Hotel. On the next day and early morning at 4 o'clock, an armed team of FBI agents working in close cooperation with the Pakistan ISI raided his hotel room. And after an on the spot finger print was taken and it marched with that of America's most ten wanted men, the thirty three year old Kansi was whisked away to a secret place for interrogation. And on 17th June an American C-141 transport aircraft with the prized catch was on its way to Fairfax County, Virginia.

"But why did Kansi kill the two CIA officers,?' asked Sherry after Shiraz narrated the incident to all his family members at the breakfast table.

"Well according to one report, though Kansi during the Soviet occupation of Afghanistan had worked with Mujahideen groups to transport US supplied weapons to the Muslim freedom fighters, he was also upset and angry in the manner in which the Americans kept supporting the Jews of Israel and kept meddling with Muslim countries like Iran, Iraq and even Pakistan for that matter" added Shiraz while insisting that oats at breakfast was very good for health and Tojo must have his full share.

"Or maybe while in Afghanistan, he too had become an ardent disciple of Mullah Omar and Osama Bin Laden, because both of them were now propagating an anti American hate campaign, and with their recent fatwa to eliminate Americans wherever they may be, Kansi probably decided to kill them at their very doorstep. After all it is the CIA factor that often guides the American foreign policy makers, doesn't it?" said Saira as she sternly warned everybody that henceforth there will be no such discussions on the dining table.

When the early morning arrest of Kansi at Dera Gazi Khan by the Americans, and his sudden deportation to the United States was leaked out by the press, the Nawaz Sharif government was in a fix. While some felt that the government was hand in glove with the Americans in having the Pathan arrested and deported, there were others who blatantly accused the government of being a stooge of the Clinton led U.S. administration. According to them 'Operation Kansi' simply could not have been executed without the active support, assistance and connivance of the Pakistan Foreign Office and the ISI; and as a result of which the Nawaz Sharif was now being branded as the biggest American 'Chamcha'. (Slave)

"Whatever one may say, but I think that it is utterly shameful to allow a foreign power no matter how powerful it may be to abduct a citizen of our own country from our very own soil and whisk him back in their own military aircraft to stand trial in their own country," said an angry Ruksana Begum to her husband as she cleared the breakfast table.

"Yes I fully agree with you, but beggars cannot be choosers," said Arif Rehman as he with full facts and figures enumerated the colossal amount of money that successive heads of governments in Pakistan and their families had made, and it was irrespective of the fact whether they were in military uniform or in civvies. And mind you it was all done in the garb of getting aid for the poor people of this land of the so called pure." added Arif Rehman sarcastically.

On 15th June, 1997 the day Kansi was captured, Paddy with his family arrived in Islamabad. On their way from Tokyo they had managed to spend a few days with their respective parents in Delhi. To felicitate Paddy on his well deserved promotion to that of a First Secretary, Monty through a lavish party at the Delhi Gymkhana. Peevee also took a few days off from his busy shooting schedule and landed up in the city to be with his sister and family. This was the first time in nearly four years that the entire family was together.

"Do be very careful and do not take any undue risks because Pakistan is not a safe country any more. Having recognized the Taliban and with the Sunnis and the Shias having created their own militant groups, there is trouble every day. Though the Pakistanis generally are a very friendly people, but some elements unfortunately are very anti Indian too," cautioned Reeta.

"Yes and I think your mother is very right and with the kind of Kalashnikov culture that they have inherited after the Russians occupied Afghanistan, and the atrocities that are being committed by the police on their own people, nobody in that part of the world is safe any longer," added Unni.

During that month of June, while the sleuths of both India and Pakistan in their respective countries got busy preparing charge sheets against those politicians who were responsible for forgeries and for making ill gotten money through dubious means, Shiraz was summoned by Pakistan's Foreign Secretary for a meeting in London. The meeting was of all Pakistani Ambassadors in Western Europe and they were to be briefed on the recently concluded Indo-Pak Secretary level talks. Knowing his love for books, Shiraz immediately on arrival at his hotel in London, went to the bookstall. After browsing through the section on the latest best sellers in the market, he picked up 'Chicken Soup for the Soul' and "Tuesdays with Morrie' for himself and a children's book for his son Tojo. The books that he chose for himself were both non-fiction, while the one for Tojo was based on fantasy.

'The book 'Chicken Soup for the Soul' by Jack Canfield and Mark Victor Hansen was a collection of inspirational stories and motivational essays, while "Tuesdays with Morrie' was a true story of Morrie Schwartz, a professor who was on his death bed and his close relationship with his student Mitch Albom. And the book that he chose for Tojo was by some new author and of whom he had never even heard off, but it was the title of the book that had caught his fancy.

"Abbu, thank you for the book, and I think the author J.K. Rowling is a genius and it is a pity that such schools of wizardry do not exist anymore," said a happy Tojo as he briefly narrated to his father the fascinating story of the 11 year old Harry Potter, an orphan who had suddenly discovered that he was a wizard. Shiraz too never realized that overnight the book would become such a rage. As a young man Shiraz had seen a Satyajit Ray film in Bengali that was titled 'Parosh Pathor' (The Philospher's Stone). It was a story of a poor man who had found a stone that could turn anything and everything into gold. And when in the children's section of that London book-store he read the title of the book, he simply bought it out of curiosity. At the same time, he also wanted his 14 year old son who was least interested in books to develop the habit of reading. In most homes the idiot box had become more of a damn nuisance and the habit of reading books not only by children, but by adults too was slowly dying away.

Born on 31st July, 1965, the 32 year old young lady author, a divorcee with one daughter had with her very first book hit the jackpot. The same very book for children that had been rejected by 12 publishers earlier had suddenly become a best seller overnight and had made Joane Rowling a celebrated author.Joane as a child always enjoyed writing fantasy stories and it was only sometime in 1990, when she was travelling from Manchester to London by train that the idea of writing a story of a young boy attending a school of wizardry got embedded in her mind. And by the time the train which was running fours late reached London, she had the synopsis of her first book with all the relevant characters fully worked out. Unemployed and living on state benefits, the young lady had put her heart and soul into the book as she sat day in and day out with an old typewriter in various little cafes to type out the manuscript. And in end June, when Bloomsbury initially published only a thousand copies of 'Harry Potter and the Philosopher's Stone' the publisher was still not very sure whether the book would sell at all. Because with the advent of exclusive TV channels for kids, such like children's stories were now passé and the publisher even advised the author to look for a day job so that she with her four year old daughter Jessica could live a little more in comfort. Jo Rowling as she was known to her close friends also had never dreamt that Harry Potter would eventually present her with her first pot of gold.

SYNOPSIS

"NOTHING BUT!" is a saga of the 20th Century history of India and the Indian Subcontinent in particular and the world in general covering the period 1890-2002 It is a story of eight Indian families and one British family and their five generations. Though they were from different religions they were all once very close friends and comrades and how circumstances beyond their control separated them and some even became each other's sworn enemy

The complete book is in 6 parts and its main focus is on the disputed Indian Territory of Jammu and Kashmir—a volatile region that has been in the eye of the storm ever since the Great Game began in the late 19th century and remains the main bone of contention between India and Pakistan ever since the two countries became independent in 1947.

Book One—'The Awakening' covers the period 1890-1919 and tells the story of the advent and rise of Indian nationalism through the eyes of these fictional characters and how the Great Game was played and how and the Great War (1914-1918) effected the lives of these people.

Book-2—'The Long Road to Freedom' covers the period 1920-1947 and tells the story about the sacrifices made to attain freedom and how partition came about.

Book-3—"What Price Freedom' covers the period 1947-1971 and tells the story of the horrors of partition and the 3 major wars that took place between India and Pakistan and which also gave birth to a new nation called Bangladesh.

Book-4—'Love has no Religion' covers the period 1971-1984. It is a tragic love story of two couples from the fourth generation with different religious and cultural backgrounds and how it affected their lives and those of their countrymen.

Book-5 'All is Fair In Love and War' covers the period 1984-1994 and tells us about the rise of communal, religious and regional politics in the subcontinent and corruption in politics together with the rise of fanatical religious organizations throughout the world in general and the subcontinent in particular.

Book-6 "Farewell My Love" covers the period 1994-2002 tells the story of the people from the 4th and 5th generation of these families and how the rise of militancy, terrorism and selfish coalition politics affected their lives and those of the people on the streets.